THE HEARTLESS LIGHT

GERALD
GREEN

THE
HEARTLESS
LIGHT

NEW YORK

CHARLES SCRIBNER'S SONS

c. 5

CHIEF CHARACTERS

THE ANDRUS FAMILY
LAURA ANDRUS, 35, *a housewife*
FRANCIS M. (FRITZIE) ANDRUS, 34, *her husband, a television director*
Their children:
　　AMY, 4
　　KAREN, 7 *months*

THE SANTA LUISA POLICE
CASPAR RHEINHOLDT, *Chief*
LIEUTENANT JOSEPH V. McFEELEY, *Chief of Detectives, Precinct A*
SERGEANT IRVIN MOLL, *Precinct A*
JAMES RAFFALOVITCH, *Director of the Police Laboratory*
PATROLMAN CLYDE HERTMANN, *Rheinholdt's secretary*
SERGEANT W. E. (FARMER) BAINES, *Rheinholdt's chauffeur*

WITH THE *LOS ANGELES TRUTH*
THEODORE T. HANSEL, *Editor & Publisher*
HERBERT HOOD, *General Manager*
ED KALAIDJIAN, *Managing Editor*
BILL TRIGG, *Acting City Editor*
MONA MEARS, *syndicated columnist*
HARVEY SWINNERTON, *a reporter assigned to Santa Luisa*
CONNIE POTENZA, *Herbert Hood's secretary*
WERNER SCHLOSSMANN,* *an overnight editor for the World News Association, affiliated with the "Truth"*

WITH UNITED BROADCASTING CORPORATION, LOS ANGELES
MATTHEW M. HINRICHSEN, *Vice-President*

* Deceased before the story begins.

vii

Tom Ballstead, *News Director*
George Brack, *a newscaster*
Eliot Sparling, *a news writer, formerly with the "Los Angeles Truth"*
Jim Farrell, *news editor*

OTHER MEMBERS OF THE LOS ANGELES PRESS CORPS
Victor DeGroot, *Associated Press*
Dave Arnspeiger, *"Los Angeles Argus"*
Martin Ringel, *Television Station KYOT*
Duane Bosch, *"Santa Luisa Register"*

RESIDENTS OF SANTA LUISA
Mayor Palmer Speed
Dr. Walter L. Todd, *a dentist, distant relative of Laura Andrus*
Maurice Krebs, *a shipping clerk*
Rosemary (Roz) McFeeley, *wife of Lieutenant McFeeley*
Harry *and* Babe Emerson, *neighbors of the Andrus family*
Timmy Emerson, *their son*

RESIDENTS OF LOS ANGELES
A. M. Feldman, *President of Kay-Bee Printers*
Francis Culligan, *President of Four State Shippers and Consigners*
Roy Brand, *a state's attorney*

THE HEARTLESS LIGHT

MONDAY

THE child awakened abruptly, disdaining any ritual yawning or stretching. She made the transition as if turning a coin from its reverse side, *sleep,* to the obverse, *awake.* In the dry heat of her pink bedroom, the desert sun piercing the blinds with golden spears, she remained motionless on the mussed blanket, savoring the delicious notion: *her father was coming home that day.* She knew he was, because Cally Horner had told her so and Cally was her best friend—a friend who didn't tease her or steal her crayons or squeeze the glue on the floor. And her father would bring her Scotch tape and a new scissors and rubber bands (these she loved better than toys), and then he would imitate Mighty Joe Young (*Mighty Joe Young* was the best movie she had ever seen).

She bounced purposefully from the bed and dressed swiftly, with a deftness remarkable in a four-year-old. In one quick motion, she discarded seersucker pajamas and thrust her meager brown body into cotton underpants, a scarlet sun suit, red canvas sneakers. Then she squinted at her brown double in the midget vanity, brushing her short chestnut hair with angry strokes and proclaiming in a harsh, loud voice: "I don't like my face. Everyone likes blondes better. When I grow up, I'll be a blonde and change my face."

In the carpeted corridor, she glanced at the closed door of her mother's bedroom, then crossed to the nursery, peeking into its muted yellow interior. A wet diaper, airfield to two sluggish flies, decorated the rubber-tile floor; in the crib, Karen sucked at an empty plastic bottle. She felt less annoyed with Karen that morning. With her father due to come home, her seven-month-old sister seemed less of an enemy.

Delighted with her generous feelings, joyous over her father's imminent return, she was impelled to share her happiness with her mother. Gently, she eased open the bedroom door: she would not

1

really wake her mother up, just whisper in her ear a little. In the master bedroom, also, the sun oozed heat through blind and curtain. The child blinked her dark eyes as she advanced to the vast double bed.

"Mommy, I have something to tell you."

The woman, vengefully seeking sleep beneath one twisted sheet, did not stir.

"Daddy's coming home."

The sleeper snapped her head away from the whispered voice. "Amy, please let me sleep a little longer. Karen had me up half the night."

"I just wanted to tell you about Daddy."

The woman's head, shoulders and nude arms jerked upward from the bed as if propelled by a spring. She seized a man's wrist watch from a night table. "Good God. It's 7:20. Amy, *darling*. Please try to amuse yourself just a little while. Do a project. Eat some cornflakes. But you must, *must* let Mommy sleep a little longer."

The child stayed. She whispered again—the breathy sounds more tormenting to the woman than her daughter's customary loudness.

"It must be true about Daddy, because Cally Horner told me."

Wrenching her head away from the unnatural small voice, her mother said: "It's not true, Amy. Your father won't be here today. There isn't any Cally Horner. Now, sweetheart, you must let me alone for half an hour."

"When will that be?"

"When the little hand is on the eight and the big hand straight up."

Amy departed in brisk, quick steps—not the sullen shuffle of a rebuffed child. In the enormous kitchen, she collected a box of dry cereal, a bottle of skim milk, a sugar bowl, a soup plate and a tablespoon. With the precise movements of a child accustomed to doing things for herself, she prepared a brimming plate of dry cereal and milk, crowning the mixture with three heaping spoons of sugar. Then, perched on a red leather stool at the red formica bar, she ate noisily and greedily. When she had finished the cornflakes, she lifted the bowl and slurped the sweet milk. For a few moments she stared at the kitchen clock, hoping she could make the big hand go faster.

Amy slid off the high stool and walked from the kitchen

to the den. The northern two-thirds of the house was one large arena comprising kitchen, den, dining room and living room. There were no true divisions or doors, and the effect was one of a carpeted stadium enclosed in glass, yellow-stone, grass-clothed walls. The child walked about the arena with a proprietary air— a swiveling of her tiny butt and skinny legs that suggested a teenage cheerleader. She was as brown as topsoil. Unlike most California children, whose flesh exudes a creamy-tan luster, hers had a muddy quality—mottled and shaded, but not without charm.

In the den, she turned on the mammoth television set, clicked past a few test patterns and halted at an animated cartoon. A goat and a parrot were having lunch; the goat was serving the parrot old phonograph records and a victrola. She watched it for a few minutes, then, sighing, turned it off. "I saw it already," she complained. "Then they dance." She remained seated in her father's massive brown leather lounging seat, surrounded by autographed pictures of actors and actresses, framed citations and awards. Then she hopped out of the chair and crossed the living room to the glass panels that were the rear wall of the house. Outside, she could see their swimming pool, a pale turquoise glare, the tepid rectangle imprisoned in a four-foot cyclone fence.

Amy turned the aluminum handle. The glass panels slid noiselessly on greased runners. She walked around the pool, passing the wooden shed for the filter, her mother's shabby cactus garden, the sandbox glinting in the morning sun. Then she entered the log cabin, sat on a tiny rustic chair and talked to a mangy panda. "I don't have so many friends here. I had more friends in Great Neck. Mommy sent me to Sunny Sky Nursery School here, but I quit because they had messy lunches. Cally Horner also quit school."

She halted the soliloquy. Her mother's warnings had taken some of the joy out of her fantasy. Abandoning Cally, she wondered if they would have company today. Maybe it was Selena's day to come and clean and cook. Or maybe Carlos, the gardener, would come. He never talked to anyone, but he let her climb into his truck. When her father was living in the house, before he went to Hollywood to stay because he and her mother used to fight so much, they always had a lot of company.

Leaving the log cabin, she sampled the back-yard treasure— the Jungle Jim she could climb better than most five-year-old boys, the lean English tricycle, the quoits game—each plastic hoop hot as a frying pan's underside. She hopped onto the tricycle and pedaled lazily down the cement driveway leading from the garage to the sidewalk. Across the palm-shaded street, she could see Mr. Skopas get into his white Cadillac and start the engine. Amy could never understand why her parents called it a *vulgar* car, when Timmy Emerson from next door said it was a Cadillac. As blown-up as the car was, Mr. Skopas seemed to be stuck in tight, with hardly any room for his fat body. Amy was a little bit afraid of the Skopas family—all very big and dark and never talking to anyone. But she waved at Mr. Skopas anyway. He didn't wave back, and the great wheeled yacht, as white as Antarctica, rushed toward the freeway.

Amy left the tricycle in the driveway and walked across the wide front lawn. She saw Timmy Emerson wheeling his bike down Nespoli Drive, tossing rolled-up copies of the *Santa Luisa Register* onto lawns and walks. Halting on the flagstone path that bisected the frontage of her home, she called: "Hi, Timmy!"

"Hiya, Amy," Timmy answered. "Why you out so early?"

"My daddy's coming home today."

"Hey, that's neat. I saw his name on the TV Friday night. Did you?"

"I can't stay up late. I went to the studio once with him."

Timmy, operating on a meticulous schedule of breakfast-delivery-school bus, pedaled off, whistling his matitutinal, hurling fresh *Registers*. Amy watched him leave, resting against the scabby trunk of one of the six squat palm trees that fronted the plot. For a moment she wondered what time it was; at 8:00 she could wake her mother up. Then she decided against it—her mother would shatter the joyful fantasy. It was better just to waste time and think about all the Scotch tape her father would bring, the crayons and the glue, and the way he would imitate Mighty Joe Young holding the girl and the piano on his head.

At the northern end of the long, rectangular house, a patio had been enclosed in glass jalousies to form a studio, which her mother used for sculpturing. Amy squinted through the cracks between the louvers, studying the long wooden table flecked with clay and bits of plaster; the gray, deformed body growing on a wire tree; the litter of dust and plaster chunks. The room always scared Amy a little when her mother wasn't in it. When she was, it was fine—her mother let her make things with clay, and paint on old pieces of plaster.

She turned away from the studio and saw a car stop in front

of the house, right near the flagstone path. It was a plain brown car, not fancy like Mr. Skopas' or low and sporty like her father's. The man who got out of the car was just a plain man.

"Good morning, honey," he said. "Want to go for a ride?" She walked away from the studio, stopping on the path. The man was about twenty feet away, standing on the sidewalk. He had on a white shirt and brown pants and there were three or four pens and pencils in his shirt pocket.

"I'm not allowed to take rides or money or candy," she said.

"Well, you could come with me. I'm your mommy's friend and your daddy's friend."

"Do you know my daddy?"

"Sure. He's a television director, isn't he?"

"He's coming to see me today. Cally Horner said so."

The man waited a moment before speaking again. Then he walked several feet up the curving path. When he was quite close, he bent over, his head a few feet from hers. "Honey, suppose I take you to see your daddy."

"How could you?"

"I know where he works. We'll drive off right now."

Amy scratched a constellation of mosquito bites on one brown ankle. "I have to tell my mommy." She kept scratching; a ruby head bloomed on one bite. The man took a slip of paper from his pocket—the one with all the pens and pencils.

"See what I'll do? I'll leave a note for Mommy so she'll know where you went. Okay?" He picked up a stone and placed the note under it in the middle of the path. Then he took Amy's hand. "Come on, honey, we'll go see your father."

Inside, the car smelled clean and new. The engine was running. "There. We're all set." He drove off, glancing at the dark child beside him.

Amy picked at the insect bites. Her brown eyes watched the houses on Nespoli Drive speed by—the Emersons, the Kaplans, the Tozzis. Then the man turned a corner and they were riding past Buena Terra Park.

"I knew Cally Horner was right," she said. "I'm seeing my daddy anyway."

"You betcha you will," the man said.

Migraine was like racial hatred, Laura Andrus maintained. No Jew, she would say (with remarkable perspicacity for a nonpracticing New England Congregationalist), can ever articulate fully

to a Gentile his sentiments about anti-Semitism. And no migrain-
eur—and she was a veteran of a thousand blinding headaches—
can convey the irrational pain to a nonsufferer. The pain was one
thing, brutal and blinding, but bearable. It was the cursed sense
of disorientation, of distortion, a weighting of the head and a
heaviness of limbs that were the ultimate horror. It had come
on that morning—a few minutes after Amy had awakened her—
with a palpable click, as if an invisible hand had turned a switch
in her right temple. Fighting the onset, she dressed quickly in gray
shorts and a white sleeveless shirt. Her yellow squaw boots she
abandoned when she had difficulty tying the laces. There was
another facet of migraine that defied definition: *the magnification
of petty annoyances.* Once, in its tyrant's grip, she had almost
been driven insane by the distant, wispy sound of Timmy Emerson's
radio, a hundred feet away. *Strike one, ball two, bases loaded, two
out* had crashed and slammed about her fevered head louder than
summer thunder.

She swallowed three ergamine tablets, offering a silent prayer
that they would blunt the pain, knowing that she stood less than
an even chance of relief. Her mirrored face was haggard, the clean
beauty filmed with worry. She had no pride of the flesh, but her
distrait appearance irked her—less because she did not look
attractive than as a cruel reminder of a hundred failures and shortcomings, a hundred things done badly, mishandled. Through the
veil of pain, she thought of a pet lizard strangled through her
carelessness, a worshipful girl friend in prep school she had insulted, her career as a sculptress, unfulfilled and halfhearted—
and, now, the wreckage of her marriage.

She gulped down a tranquilizer and a vitamin pill, whispering,
"There's a nice mess for the gastric juices," and left the hot bed-
chamber for Karen's nursery. The heat reminded her of the endless
arguments she and her husband had engaged in over the air conditioning. He had wanted it; she was opposed, arguing that the
natural temperatures of the desert were better than artificially controlled air. She had won; he had sulked; now she wondered if
perhaps he had been right. Changing Karen's diaper (the infant
was as placid as a spayed cat), she began searching for a rationale,
a substantive basis for the endless arguing in which she and
Fritzie had indulged—Amy's upbringing, the mortgage terms, their
friends. It was like attempting to untangle the backlash of a
fishing line; eventually one got disgusted and snipped away the
impossibly snarled knots with a knife.

Karen's slothfulness pleased her: they were a family with too many sharp edges—the vigorous, verbalizing father; the unyielding mother; and Amy—yeasty, precocious, a child who had never been a baby, walking at nine months, talking sentences at eighteen.

Karen was blonde and pink and given to long, motionless naps. Once, on one of their rare visits to Fritzie's family in Greensboro, North Carolina, her mother-in-law had shown her a photograph album—faded memorabilia of the proud Andruses (any number of whom had worn the gray, one of whom had been a brevet colonel under Longstreet). Now, observing her baby's rosiness, she recalled dozens of similar faces in the ancestral Andrus gallery. They ran to roundness—stocky, smug people, tinted rose and gold.

She took the empty plastic bottle into the kitchen. As she fetched a frosty new bottle from the cavernous refrigerator, she saw the soup plate on the breakfast bar, the opened cereal box, the half-filled bottle of skim milk. She ducked her head: she owed Amy more than this. Perhaps Fritzie had been right in insisting on sleep-in help. A maid in the house might have organized the mornings better—the time of day Laura was at her lowest. But she had argued that maids made her miserable; she spent the day feeling sorry for them and preferred a four-days-a-week cleaning woman, one with whom she had no emotional ties.

As she heated the bottle she glanced at the kitchen clock. It was 8:42. She had been abed too long. Retiring early was no solution: she was one of those unfortunates doomed to seek sleep after long hours of wasting wakefulness. She hurried to the nursery and gave the bottle to Karen. The little dummy barely seemed interested. Laura managed a wry smile, recalling the way Amy would grab at it feverishly and drain it with an alcoholic's greed.

She looked for Amy in the den. When she saw the television mute, she called her name. She was not upset. Amy was a wanderer, a neighborhood character who showed up in back yards and kitchens. Laura saw the opened glass panels and assumed she had taken a morning stroll. She had warned Amy many times not to leave the house before she was awake, but Amy was not a notably obedient child. Laura glanced quickly at the menacing pool, then strode to the rear of the house, calling her name. When she saw the log cabin empty, she experienced her first pinprick of anxiety. She turned down the driveway, noting the tricycle, then walked to her right across the front lawn. In her hurried search, she did not notice the folded paper beneath the stone. She told herself that Amy, contrary to orders, had wandered off to a neighbor's kitchen and was probably munching a second breakfast, while a critical maid muttered *sotto voce* comments about that Andrus woman who didn't watch the kid. The notion of ringing doorbells on that insular street of rich homes, each protected by hedges and palms, high iron fences and lush lawns, appalled her. She had lived on Nespoli Drive for six months but, aside from the Emersons, scarcely knew her neighbors. She walked toward the Emersons' orange stucco castle—a relic of prewar Santa Luisa—telling herself that Amy was probably gorging herself with waffles in Babe Emerson's slovenly kitchen.

Red-eyed, her nose alive with beauty cream, Babe answered the door. She wore a wretched cotton wrapper and brandished a coffeepot. "Laura!" Babe cried. "Come in—Harry's cooking kippers!"

The smoky aroma all but made her swoon. The migraine's power of magnification overwhelmed her with the stench of a fish-processing plant. "No thanks, Babe. I'm looking for Amy. Is she in your house? Have you seen her?"

"Nope. I haven't seen the peanut. Harry! You seen Amy?"

Harry Emerson's rude negative traveled through high-ceilinged rooms littered with old art magazines, unframed Picassos, an antipasto of dirty socks, odd shoes, underwear. The Emerson children shed clothing like molting pigeons.

"I thought she might have invited herself in for pancakes," Laura said.

"Oh, you laid the law down to her, but good," Babe said. "She didn't come back."

"I'll try the Kahlers." Laura hesitated. "I hate ringing their bell. If Amy walked on their lawn, they'd probably eat her."

She left the flaking orange ruin and crossed her lawn again. The sun-seared street, baking in desert heat, was as soulless as the moon. The residents seemed to go to work, do their shopping, dispatch their young to school via a system of underground tunnels.

A gardener's truck, crammed with lawnmowers, rakes and luminous, coiled green hoses, rumbled by. When it had concluded its noisy passage, the hot silence unsettled Laura. The prospect of intruding on people she did not like; the child's bothersome truancy; the insidious headache—all these rendered her weak and faintly dizzy.

Crossing the flagstone path, she saw the folded paper and picked it up. She opened it. Someone had clipped words from a newspaper to form a message. She wore no sunglasses and she had to hold it a distance from her eyes, shading it from the invasive sun. The printed words, neatly assembled in eight straight lines of almost identical length, had a cranky perfection about them, and her immediate reaction, as she read them, was that it was a practical joke—something dreamed up by one of Fritzie's nuttier friends.

CHILD SAFE UNLESS YOU CALL POLICE OR NOTIFY PAPERS LEAVE FOUR THOUSAND TWO HUNDRED DOL- LARS IN FIFTIES PACKAGE RIGHT SIDE KOHLMEYER ENTRANCE BUENA TERRA PARK TONIGHT EIGHT FIF- TEEN AND CHILD RETURNS HOUR LATER SAFE MEAN BUSINESS DON'T SCREAM MAKE TROUBLE TELL ANY- ONE THIS DEAL JUST YOU AND ME NOBODY ELSE AND CHILD ALL RIGHT OTHERWISE TROUBLE

Her heart was suddenly engorged, hyperactive. It pounded insanely, frantic to tear itself from her breast. Involuntarily, her mouth opened to form the shriek of recognition: she suffocated it with a fist. Then she stumbled backward, skinning a bare heel against a step. Now her lower limbs—knees, calves, feet—seemed to vaporize, to leave her without anchorage. Vision blurring, she saw the street with its livid greens and carnal reds undersea. She walked into the house, sitting stiffly on the endless sectional sofa in the carpeted stadium. The walls—glass, stone, grasscloth—had a tomb- like quality, and despite the heat, she shivered. Soon she was trem- bling. With an effort, she locked her eyes and subdued the shaking. In a few minutes she was prepared to think.

Her mind scanned the possibilities. First, she could abide by the instructions: keep the dark secret, leave the money and wait. It was 9:05. Eleven hours of torment. Again, she advised herself: it's a prank, one of those long-running, insane tricks that people like Cy Mailman, the writer, was always playing on his friends. Abruptly she banished such nonsense: *it was real*. It demanded a course of action. She thought of calling Fritzie. He was probably still at his suite in the Duval Château, a crumbling monument to old Hollywood, where he had taken up bachelor diggings when they had separated. She had spoken to him only two days ago, when he had phoned to plead that she let him take Amy to Disney- land. She had refused. *You had no time for her before,* Laura had said, *why should I let you see her now?* Moreover, Fritzie, with his compulsion to verbalize, would be broadcasting the tragedy to the world in minutes. Her meditations halted: she realized how dreadfully isolated she was. In six months in California, she had made no close friends; she had no relatives in the area, except for a man named Todd, a dentist who was a second cousin of her mother. She barely knew him, having met him once at a City Council meeting, when they discovered their relationship by accident.

And so it would be the police. In spite of the warning in the note, Laura understood that the police were inevitable. They were impersonal, detached, professional—they would understand the need for secrecy. It occurred to her she knew them only as uniformed custodians in gray-white Fords, leisurely cruising the palm-lined streets of Santa Luisa, nodding amiable greetings. Once, when she and Fritzie had gone to Arrowhead for a weekend, she tipped two of them five dollars each for looking after the house. They were both polite, unexceptional men of middle age.

Walking to the kitchen phone, she tried to buoy herself with an assurance that all that was needed would be secrecy, some guidance from the police, an enactment of the ritual—and Amy would return. She did not know the number of the police, and as she dialed operator, she was shocked by her palsied hand.

His wife's morning ministrations to the four children inevitably filled Joseph McFeeley with a sense of injustice. His eyes concentrated on Humbert's *Organic Chemistry*, McFeeley, between sips of coffee, would glance upward from time to time to watch Roz's prods, pats and invocations of authority. The baby, Dale, was slung over her narrow hips like a football. Jeanie, three, was clutching one of her mother's legs, bunching the cotton house dress. The adhesive small fry barely impeded her attentions to Joey, nine (she was adjusting his eyeglasses), and Mary Grace, six, who wanted to "bring" rather than "buy" lunch at St. Brigid's. "Since when is Monday a bringing day?" Roz asked impatiently. "I thought you loved macaroni and cheese."

The sight of his wife tyrannized by the eroding demands of the children made McFeeley frown. It seemed to him that his off-hour studies in quest of a college education were a pitiful contribution to the teeming household.

The yellow bus from St. Brigid's stopped across the street in front of one of the 123 near-identical homes in Santa Luisa Garden

Vale. Joey and Mary Grace waved good-bys and raced for it. Roz returned to the kitchen from the foyer, still bootlegging Dale on one hip, trying to disengage Jeanie from her skirt.

"Vatican roulette," she said acidly. "Why didn't we give it up sooner? You think Father Boyle knows?"

"He knows," McFeeley said. "They have ways of knowing." An uneven smile germinated on his crooked mouth. All of the man's slender features had a lopsided quality. One gray eye seemed fractionally higher than its mate (or was it McFeeley's vaguely amused frown that made it rise?). His nose, the odd beak of certain Irishmen, took a leftward detour one-half inch from the tip. His ears, too, were out of whack—one tight against his narrow head, the other off on its own. His hair was brown and wavy; the off-center part completed the effect of asymmetry.

Roz refilled his coffee cup and kissed the top of his head. "Joseph Vincent McFeeley, student, aged thirty-three," she said. "You got *Organic Chemistry* licked?"

He studied his wife warmly, wishing he could lift her above the household labors, the budget that didn't stretch, the sense of lost glory. Rosemary O'Keefe had been voted most beautiful girl in Valley View High School fifteen years ago. At eighteen, a man from Paramount wanted to give her a screen test and she was being invited to parties at USC fraternity houses. The son of a rich liquor distributor in Beverly Hills had proposed marriage. Instead, she had married Joe, who had been a year ahead of her in high school, captain of Valley View's District II basketball champions, and had settled for a mortgaged tract house, four children and a slow wasting of her lucent beauty. The glorious teen-ager of the white skin and black hair was now a weary woman of thirty-one, a veteran of six pregnancies—a miscarriage, a child dead of leukemia, and four demanding youngsters, all fiercely competitive for her love. Withal, Roz McFeeley did not spend lost hours mooning over vanished beauty, thumbing through yellowing dance programs and basketball clippings.

The baby, with the infant's unseen speed, had touched the coffeepot and was now shattering the morning air with wails.

"Dale!" his mother shouted. "Hot, hot, hot!" She scooped butter from the plastic dish and smeared it on his offended fingers. Jeanie, aggravated by the dividend Dale had just gained, began to cry.

"I didn't have enough French toast," Jeanie whined.

"Sorry, pal," Roz said. "The kitchen is closed. The help has to make beds." She hefted the wailing infant to a hip and left. McFeeley returned to his textbook. He was a slow reader, and he had few illusions about his capacities. The decision to study for a college degree, nights and weekends, after five years of military service and five more on the job, had been a difficult one. But he was, by and large, a calm and uncomplicated Irishman who accepted life's problems with wry patience. Perhaps the college degree would mean little in the way of promotion. In his line of work salaries were fixed, advancement was slow. But the goal had value in and of itself. When you started something, McFeeley believed, it was generally a good idea to finish it.

He rose from the table, a slim, round-shouldered man, his arms and shoulders well muscled and delicately white, in contrast to his sun-reddened face, neck and hands. The Christopher medal around his neck dangled as he stole a last fragment of *Organic Chemistry*. Then he inspected a white shirt, decided the collar was clean, and put it on. A dark gray tie and the lighter gray jacket of his suit transformed him into an exemplar of lower middle-class drabness. In the hall closet, on a high shelf, he located the police .38, reached in his pocket for the bullets and inserted them, then thrust the gun into a small black holster set back on his belt.

Glancing at his watch, he saw it was almost 9:30. He had been up past 2:00 in the morning, wringing, with crafty patience, a confession from two kids who had held up a liquor store, and he had arranged with his subordinate to cover for him until 11:00. But the fact was, he loved his work; if he were awake, he would report.

"I'm off and running, Roz," McFeeley called. "Want anything from the supermarket tonight?"

She appeared on the landing, her arms laden with enough clean linen for a hospital ward. "So early, Joe? You getting overtime? You didn't sleep at all and you're not due in till eleven. Catch the rest of your buddies giving the city extra time."

"I like it there. I found a home on the force."

"Joe, if you'd only realize the way that old boob takes advantage of you——"

The telephone halted their *pro forma* arguing. Both were relieved, knowing that the disputes solved nothing. Joe took the call, hearing Irvin Moll's thick voice, hung-over and apologetic.

"I wake you, Joe? Chief's got something he wants you to look at."

"I was on my way in. What's up? Someone put sugar in his gas tank again?"

"Not *that* bad," Moll said. "Just a squeal, but he wants you to go. A dame out on Nespoli Drive. The high-rent district. She called headquarters and wanted the chief but wouldn't tell us anything. She kept saying a life was at stake and it had to be secret, and could one person in plain clothes come out to talk to her."

"Give me the name and address."

"Yeah. Here it is."

Joe waited. He could see Sergeant Irvin Moll, his deputy, fumbling with one blunt paw for his scrawled notes. "Mrs. Andrus, 4217 Nespoli. Didn't give a phone number."

"All she said was it had to be secret? And someone's life was at stake?"

"Yeah. The chief thinks she's a crank, especially with that address. Where they're always throwing broads in the pools and eating sleeping pills."

"I'll check it on my way in," McFeeley said.

Roz turned from a soaring pyramid of dirty dishes. Could a single breakfast so burden a sink with bowls, plates, cups, cutlery? "What was that all about?" she asked. "Rheinholdt pass the buck again? Why doesn't he send Moll or Case to run his errands? Why only you?"

"It's no sweat, honey. Probably some actress with a snootful of seconal." He picked up his textbook. When she bent to the sink he kissed her neck. "So long, sport," he said, "and don't worry what Father Boyle thinks. I straightened him out."

"I'll *bet.*" She eyed him with amused wariness. For a moment her fine features revived and she was the adolescent cheerleader— so young, so fair—who had spurned the screen test and the liquor millionaire's son.

"He was kidding me—how come you weren't with child," Joe said. "So I told him we finally figured out what was causing it and we quit."

McFeeley hurried through the patched screen door into the garage; the floor was littered and he made a mental note to get after Joey to clean it for him.

A few minutes before Lieutenant Joseph McFeeley left his home, Francis M. (Fritzie) Andrus had arrived at a lawyer's office on downtown Wilshire Boulevard. Andrus was early for his

9:30 appointment and the attorney was several minutes late. Delay was normally painful to Andrus, but on this hot September morning he was able to ease his attendance with the airmail edition of the *New York Times*. The newspaper's television critic had given a scathing review to one of Andrus' colleagues, an agonizingly successful youth whose dramatic triumphs rendered him suspect, envied—yes, hated—by second-rank directors like Fritzie. The critic's opinions affected Andrus like a tingly massage. He felt energized, ready for a bustling, fruitful day. He read the column for the third time . . . *in this instance, Whitehead Sales, one of television's bright young directors, seems to be in over his head. Instead of the drama emerging as an exercise in ideas and social comment, which is surely what the playwright intended, we have a series of leaps and turns, arbitrary violence (so beloved on TV) and meaningless emotional peaks. Chalk up a loss for Mr. Sales. . . .*

Andrus grinned at the printed words. His heavy square head, set firmly atop his heavy square—almost stout—torso, bloomed with joy. The naturally high color intensified; a ruddiness blossomed on his well-fleshed cheeks and infused his bold features—blunt, hard nose; wide, mobile mouth; manly gray eyes. It occurred to Fritzie that, in many ways, a rival's bad notice was better than one's own good review. Andrus was a connoisseur of bad reviews, an authority on other people's hard luck. Indeed, he had a talent for interpreting even a *good* notice (in recidivistic Southern accents) in such a way as to make it emerge a knock. "Y'all see what Crosby did to the NBC *Macbeth?*" he would drawl. "Shoot, he couldn't say anything nice, so he praised the *credits!*" (The fact of the matter was, the critic had given the drama an excellent notice.)

The lawyer to whom Fritzie had been directed by his agent arrived at about 9:35. A depressingly small man in a blue suit a size too large, he greeted Andrus dolefully in the anteroom. "I'm sorry I'm late, Mr. Andrus, but I had to help Mrs. Salter with her charity luncheon. These *women.*"

Inside Mr. Salter's office, Fritzie slumped into a maroon chair while the attorney fussed with some papers. Then he turned to the director. "I believe Mr. Wettlaufer, the agent, recommended you. Is that right, Mr. Andrus?" Words dripped from his rudimentary mouth, identical in emphasis, evenly spaced. "Oh, before we get to the business at hand, Mr. Andrus, my wife and I both have seen your plays on the television and we admire your integrity."

"Why, thank you kindly, Mist' Salter."

"You are entirely welcome. We don't get too many of you show-business folks as clients down here in the business section. Our work runs to rather dull corporate affairs, and so forth, so I was looking forward to this meeting."

"I reckon we're about like other folks."

"No," said the lawyer slowly, "no, I don't think so. Creative people have to be different." The gnomish man allowed himself a second's admiration of the ruddy, blond client opposite him—talented, native American, vigorous. Mr. Salter knew that he himself was small and homely and he was glad to be of help to Francis M. Andrus. "When we spoke on the telephone," Salter resumed, "you said you and Mrs. Andrus had separated and you were not being permitted to see your children."

Fritzie lurched forward. "That's right. I want to see my children."

"I understand." Salter reached for yellow pad and a pencil. "You'd better review the circumstances of your breakup for me, and please try to be objective, Mr. Andrus. As I said, we don't get too many of you show business folks here and I—"

"Fine, fine," Fritzie interrupted. "I know what you want. Play the reality, not the off-stage circumstance."

Mr. Salter's contracted face inflated slightly, as if sighting the Higher Truth. "Exactly. How well you phrase it. You'd make a splendid trial lawyer."

Andrus' verbal locutions invariably had this effect on professionals. Doctors informed him he would have made a wonderful diagnostician; clergymen that he had missed a grand career in the service of faith; engineers that he might have built suspension bridges. That much of what he said was nonsense never seemed to dilute their conviction that he could do anything—anything at all.

"Laura and I reached an impasse last month," Andrus said. "No point in detailing it heah. We been married seven years and it's been rugged. I made it the hard way—sweepin' floors in off-Broadway theaters and paintin' flats in summer stock. Then hack work in New York TV—floor manager, script editor—and now I'm kinda proud of what I've achieved. My work is everything. I teach. I'm doing a book on theory of directing. I feel I'm involved and relevant for the first time in my life."

"I understand exactly, Mr. Andrus. In my own case, I worked my way through——"

"Now, Laura, she's somethin' else again. She's always *wanted* a career. Sculptress. I guess she has talent. But she's never made it.

I feel she resents my success. Now, instead of my wife boostin' me and rootin' for me, I find she's criticizin' and takin' pot shots at me and my friends. Worse, she's turnin' the children against me. Lord knows why. I loved her. We loved each other. At least we did once. That house in Sanlu set me back fifty grand I could ill afford. Two cars. Help. I built her a studio for sculpturin'. What else can a man do?"

Mr. Salter made a tepee out of his finger tips and lifted the peak to his tiny mouth. "But in what way, Mr. Andrus, has she criticized you?"

"A million ways. Why, just before we broke up, I had a little class of young actors at the house and I made a speech discussin' directors' prerogatives and actors' instincts in relation to the dramatic *Gestalt*."

"Fascinating," murmured the lawyer.

Andrus dusted him away as if he were a fruit fly hovering over an apricot. "You know what my wife said? And she is *not* a professional, has no theater training at all. She said, 'What about the playwright?' I like to died. The *playwright*! What has he got to do with anything? Where does he come in? But she got the whole discussion sidetracked and confused." Fritzie halted. "This may all sound like gunk to you, Mist' Salter, but I assure you it's my *life*."

"No, no. I see what you're driving at."

"I've been wrong a little, too. My hours are irregular. Maybe I'm not as attentive to the kids as I used to be. But a woman must understand these things. Laura won't. She's jealous. She never made it with her statues, that's why."

Attorney Salter nodded compassionately. "What are your plans now, Mr. Andrus?"

"We got none. I'm livin' in Hollywood and she's at the house in Sanlu with the children. Oh, I guess we'll talk divorce soon. I don't know. We ain't neither of us much good at decisions."

"And your immediate problem—you want to see the children?"

"She won't let me!" cried Andrus. "Amy—my little Amy—can you imagine being kept from your own children?"

"You have two children, don't you, Mr. Andrus?"

"Yes. Of course, I want to see Karen also. But, heck, she's just seven months and I don't reach her yet. But Amy! Mr. Salter, that child is as smart as a raccoon. She talks better than most ten-year-old brats and she can outrun any boy on the block. And you know what her mother did? Hung up on me when I asked to see her!

'You gave her no time before,' Laura said, 'I'll give you none now!' "
The ruddy head dropped to Andrus' chest, the blond mane
flopping lushly. He wore it not cropped, like most practitioners
of his art, but lank and long, suggestive of a *Luftwaffe* officer, a
Tyrolean ski master.

"That's it," Andrus said hoarsely. "Y'all got to force Laura to let
me see Amy."

The lawyer rose from his chair, walked around to Fritzie and
patted his shoulder. "Don't be so downhearted, Mr. Andrus. Pine,
Dublin and Salter will get you to see the children. I think a single
phone call from me to your wife will suffice. Don't fret about it.
I'll be in touch with you by late afternoon."

Fritzie got up, engulfed the lawyer's hand and pumped it. "Why,
thank you kindly, Mr. Salter. It will be easy, you think?"

"Easy as pie."

As Andrus turned to leave, the lawyer stopped him. "May I say,
Mr. Andrus, I fully appreciate your grief. I happen to be a father
myself and I know that if anything separated me from my beloved
children, I would be beside myself."

The television director frowned. "I'm sure that's so. Good-by,
Mist——"

The attorney gripped his sleeve. With the other hand he lifted
from his desk a giant photograph, turning it around and displaying
it pridefully. It was hideous—a green-velvet frame, three inches
wide, and, within, a color photograph of four children, three boys
and a girl, squatting balefully in a garden swing. They were over-
fed and drowsy-looking.

"Now these happen to be my four children," the lawyer said.
"Fortunately my dear wife Carol and myself agree wholeheartedly
on their upbringing and we could never envision harming their
happiness because of our own selfish errors. I can well imagine the
pain it would cause me to be separated from them. Mr. Andrus,
for that reason alone, I promise you I will see to it personally that
you are granted access to your darling daughters."

There was a moment of hypnotic silence—the lawyer displaying
his issue in the manner of a kindergarten artist exhibiting first
prize; Andrus immobilized by the man's effrontery. Then, in a
swift, angry motion, Fritzie tore the photograph from Salter's hand,
glared at it and tossed the treasure to the lawyer's desk.

"How dare you!" Andrus screamed. "How dare you show me that
picture of your four brats! Four fat kids in a sandbox, that's what

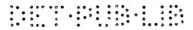

you got! *Get rid of 'em! Those kids must go! Lose 'em!* What earthly right do you have to show me those children and brag about them? How do you have the gall to compare them to my Amy? Why, my Amy is a lady! She knows more words than *you* do! She's fine and delicate and, dammit, her mother and her father are *creative* people—artists! And you dare to show me those smilin', fat, contented kids of yours——"

His high voice liquefied; he was sobbing. Lost in unreasoning tears, he fled through the reception room, into the corridor and down the stairs. Mr. Salter, shaken, still compassionate, sped after him on midget legs. The attorney caught a flashing glimpse of Andrus' olive jacket and black knitted tie—spinning, spinning, ever downward.

"*Mr. Andrus!*" he shouted. "Please, Mr. Andrus! You're overwrought!" He bore no ill will toward the man who had abused him; rather, he saw him as a tormented creative fellow who needed help. Salter cupped his hands and shouted: "Mr. Andrus! Come back! I had no right to intrude my personal life!" But Fritzie heard nothing. His blockish figure vanished, seeking the neutralizing sunlight.

"You have to understand!" Salter yelled. "We aren't too familiar with you show business people——"

In less than ten minutes, McFeeley was at the Andrus house. Sanlu, except for the old mission section, was a simple gridiron, the streets wide and free of traffic. (Chief Caspar Rheinholdt's traffic division regularly won awards for efficiency and courtesy.) The detective approached Nespoli by way of Kohlmeyer Street, which paralleled Buena Terra Park. Inside the park, he caught a hedge-blurred glimpse of two older men playing stylish, vigorous tennis. Their darting white forms gave him a moment of envy. He had not played tennis since high school; he had even given up basketball when the church league games got too fast for him.

As he turned left on Nespoli, he saw one of the department's gray and white Fords coming toward him. McFeeley pulled up alongside it and greeted the two uniformed patrolmen, Charlie Ullman and George Lopez. Ullman was about to raise headquarters on the two-way when he saw Joe. "You after the squeal at 4217?" the patrolman asked. "The chief asked us to look in also." He indicated a yellow-stone ranch house halfway down the street.

"Andrus?" Joe asked.

"Yeah. We rang the bell and she took one look at us and chased us. I asked if she was the one called headquarters and she wouldn't say a word, just for us to go away."

McFeeley was silent. His boss, Chief of Police Caspar Rheinholdt, had acted with typical vagueness. He had asked Joe, Chief of Detectives at Precinct A, to look in on the squeal. Then, worried that Joe would not move fast enough, had dispatched two uniformed patrolmen, in spite of the caller's plea for secrecy.

"I'll take a look," Joe said. "Tell Moll I'll be in in half an hour."

Ullman winked. "Watch your step, Lieutenant. She had that wild look in her eyes."

McFeeley drove the extra hundred feet and parked next to a soaring white colonial, noting the sign depicting a black silhouette of a coach-and-four and the name SKOPAS.

The detective crossed the street, surveying 4217 swiftly: a long, yellow-stone ranch home with a glass-enclosed patio at the north end. He took in the two-car garage with the red station wagon; the child's tricycle stopped halfway down the driveway; the thick palm trees. The house seemed newer and less lavish than its neighbors: the stone work, the green tile roof had a fresh appearance. McFeeley pressed the buzzer. Immediately the aperture opened and a woman's blue eyes looked at him.

"Mrs. Andrus?"

"Yes."

"I'm Lieutenant McFeeley. I'm Chief of Detectives at Precinct A. I believe you called this morning."

She drew in her breath. "Are you alone? No one in uniform with you?"

"Yes. I brought my own car, not a prowl car. There was a mix-up at headquarters; that's why those patrolmen called."

She opened the door. McFeeley saw at once she was agitated. She was a good-looking, tall woman, pale and uncosmeticized, with a broad, clear forehead, large features, lank brown hair. She sounded eastern, and her casual shirt and shorts were eastern: not theatrical east, but suggestive of universities and social work. She was, the detective understood, no Hollywood broad, no producer's doll, hardly the sleeping-pill type or the kind you'd shove into a swimming pool. In the enormous living area—four rooms bleeding into one another—she asked him to sit on the sofa. He had the sense of a house barely used. Aside from the massive sofa and a few patio chairs, the rooms were sparsely furnished; there was no dining-room set.

"What's the trouble, Mrs. Andrus?" he asked.

"My little girl is missing."

McFeeley afforded himself a secret sign of the cross. Missing children were no problem in Sanlu; any loose child was suspect and was immediately reported to the police.

"I wouldn't look so upset. We haven't ever failed to find a lost child. Why don't you tell me where——"

He stopped. She had shut her eyes. Her bloodless fists were pressing at her throat. Then McFeeley, cursing his own dumbness, recalled she had said someone's life was at stake. He had wanted to believe the easy solution. "What is it, Mrs. Andrus? Do you feel sick?"

She pointed to a half sheet of white paper on the mosaic coffee table in front of the sofa. "Read it," she said.

McFeeley picked up the note and began to read. Halfway through, he set it down, not wishing to mar any prints.

CHILD SAFE UNLESS YOU CALL POLICE OR NOTIFY PAPERS LEAVE FOUR THOUSAND TWO HUNDRED DOLLARS IN FIFTIES PACKAGE RIGHT SIDE KOHLMEYER ENTRANCE BUENA TERRA PARK TONIGHT EIGHT FIFTEEN AND CHILD RETURNS HOUR LATER SAFE MEAN BUSINESS DON'T SCREAM MAKE TROUBLE TELL ANYONE THIS DEAL JUST YOU AND ME NOBODY ELSE AND CHILD ALL RIGHT OTHERWISE TROUBLE

"Where did you find this?" he asked.

"It was on the path, under a stone."

"Mrs. Andrus, I won't try to minimize this. Your daughter is in danger. But if you want a cop's opinion, she's safe and we'll get her back before long."

Laura studied his narrow, awry face. He seemed to her singularly ineffectual, a minor man unfit for big tasks. He had a thin, unconvincing voice and he had mispronounced several words. It was a kind of low effrontery on his part, she thought, to be so sure that Amy was safe. He suggested to her the kind of indifferent civil servant one associated with City Hall crowds. Even the Irish name —McFeeley—bothered her.

He took a steno pad from the inner pocket of his gray jacket and she caught a glimpse of the black holster. It gave her no confidence. "Why don't you tell me what happened this morning? Then I'll call Chief Rheinholdt and you can call Mr. Andrus and we'll work something out."

"Didn't I read somewhere that the FBI is supposed to handle this?" They were both, Laura noticed, walking decorously around the word *kidnaping*.

"They're allowed in after seven days. But a local police official can request them sooner."

"Do you think they should be requested?"

McFeeley scanned the note again—the white half sheet with its meticulous lines of cannibalized newsprint. "My guess is we're better off following this guy's instructions. Keep everyone ignorant for a while. Newspapers, FBI, even the Sanlu police—except for maybe three or four of us."

Laura looked at him challengingly: the detective had a sense of having seen her before—a meeting, a rally. The sharp, pretty face evoked a blurred memory. "Why do you assume my daughter is safe?"

He frowned. "The ransom money. So little—four thousand two hundred. Whoever did this wouldn't be *hard* enough, enough of a pro, to harm a child. I think he'll realize what he's done and release her, try to get out of it. Maybe before the day is over." He got up from the couch and gazed through the picture window at the uninhabited street. "Have you told anyone about this?" he asked.

"I mentioned it to a neighbor—Mrs. Emerson next door. Not about the note, but just that Amy was missing—that I couldn't find her."

"You'll have to lie to her. We've got to keep people stupid for the next twelve hours. Do you expect any help today—maid or gardener?"

"No. I have a maid who comes in four times a week, but she's off today."

"Good. Now tell me just what happened this morning—what time you got up, what time the little girl got up, when you found her missing."

Laura began her narration, speaking calmly and slowly, trying to suffocate the notion that her salvation lay in the hands of this drab man in a cheap gray suit. He took notes in a slanted scrawl.

"So the last time you heard or saw her was in your bedroom?"

"Yes. I was up most of the night with the baby. I was a little impatient with Amy." The migraine tightened its belt of pain around her temples and she winced.

"You sure you don't want a doctor?" McFeeley said. "Are you well enough for me to bother you like this?"

"It's all right. I have a migraine headache. What did you ask?"

"The time you last saw her."

"About 7:30." She cut ten minutes from what she conceived to be her hour of negligence.

"When did you first notice she was missing?"

"I'm not sure. Maybe an hour later. I guess I let her roam around and sort of be on her own for an hour." McFeeley kept writing, his narrow face bland with the law's diffidence. He cocked his head.

"Look, Mrs. Andrus, don't start blaming yourself. This is California. Kids live out of doors more than indoors. Mine roam the streets all the time. No one's expected to watch children every second."

She had not sought his assurances and did not seem to welcome them.

"When did you find the note?" he resumed.

"Oh—I can't be certain. Maybe 8:35. Or a little later."

"Then you waited about twenty minutes before you called us."

"If you say so. I'm not sure I had any idea how much time passed."

McFeeley tapped at the pad. He tugged his projecting right ear and got up. "Could you show me around the house? We'll make a systematic search later, but I'd like to get an idea where she might have been picked up."

They toured the house—the den, where Laura seemed to recall hearing the noise of television for a few minutes that morning; the kitchen, with the child's breakfast bowl still on the red bar; and the living room. The opened glass panels, leading to the pool, hinted at the path that the vanished child had taken. No doors or windows had been forced; there were no signs of struggle; she had heard nothing.

In Amy's bedroom, the drawn blinds englooming the rumpled blanket and the litter of toys, she began to tremble. Her daughter's pajamas were a yellow seersucker puddle on the floor. She sat, somewhat ludicrously, in the child's maple rocker and cried freely.

The detective stood silently in the doorway, pretending to study the room.

"I'm sorry," Laura sobbed. "I wish I could control myself."

"You've been trying too hard. Cry it out."

She dabbed at her eyes with a handkerchief. "I wish I could do something. If I could race up and down the street, shriek for her, offer everything we own for her. Promise anything to have her back——"

McFeeley was touring the bedroom, noting the screens, the window fastenings. "Mrs. Andrus," he said, "you better get your husband here. Would you like me to call him?"

"I will."

"In these deals, it's often good to get a third party in on the operation. Not a cop. But a friend or a business associate. Someone to make contact. Parents are too close."

Laura thought a moment. "It sounds silly—we've been in Santa Luisa six months and we have hardly any close friends." She thought of Babe and Harry Emerson. They were too nosy, too emotional. She dismissed Fritzie's television friends—those bright, creative talkers. Cy Mailman, in his two-hundred-fifty-dollar suit and antelope shoes, meeting a kidnaper on a shaded street, was outside the realm of human experience.

"I have a distant relative here, a second cousin of my mother's. Dr. Todd. Walter Todd. He used to be on the City Council."

McFeeley nodded. "The dentist. Ask him to get over here at once. Do you have forty-two hundred dollars in the bank?"

"I doubt it." They were in the vast northern end of the house, and she appeared to hint, with a morose sweep of her eyes, that the burdensome overpriced house, even with its marginal furnishings, had left them bereft of cash.

"When you talk to Todd, tell him to contact his bank and have the bank president stand by."

She walked to the kitchen phone. "Don't tell your husband what happened either. Just get him to come home at once."

Her tears she had diked. Her eyes were clear. McFeeley marveled at her.

"I'll use my car radio," he said. "We'll get the chief out here and arrange a setup for tonight."

She walked to the phone, the freezing fear in her breast making a mockery of his casual confidence, his *deals* and *operations* and *setups*.

A slow reader, one who chewed each hard word before digesting it into a dyspeptic sentence and then into a cramp-producing idea, Chief Caspar Rheinholdt suffered pitifully from the recurrent newspaper attacks on him. The chief was old and tough and stupid. Like many such men, poorly educated, proud of accidental attainment, he was as thin-skinned as a supermarket sausage. Stubborn, honest, fearful of exposure, convinced *they* were out to nail his hide to the Sanlu station house, he ran his force of 189 men (more than ample for a city of 97,520) with an uncertain, fussy hand. He changed orders, he confused lines of authority so that precinct chiefs were perpetually at war with division heads, and he observed consistency in but one area—his hatred of newspapers, radio and television.

On the morning of Amy Andrus' disappearance, Rheinholdt was gnawing his way through an editorial assault upon his ministry in the *Los Angeles Truth*. It was a brief editorial, a kind of funny-guy thing, but it goaded him, reinforcing his conviction that they were *all* a bunch of bastards, all out to hang him. That was fine with him. They'd get less and less from the Sanlu cops, and he'd make it tougher and tougher for them. As he clipped the offending words from the *Truth's* editorial page (Rheinholdt saved his bad notices, turning to them for sustenance in those moments when he began to entertain milder sentiments toward newspapers), he read it again, his wooden face impassive, barely betraying his black thoughts.

WHAT NEXT, CASPAR?

We don't like to preach to our neighbors, especially wonderful little communities like Santa Luisa. But, really, isn't it high time something was done about Police Chief Rheinholdt? His latest move—abolishing the press parking section at Sanlu headquarters—is just the latest of Clever Caspar's guerrilla moves against the newspapers. The *Truth* and its fellow papers don't mind the shoving around. We'll survive long after Caspar has been retired. But his freeze on police information; his highhanded refusal to talk to reporters; his one-man tyranny—all these merit serious study by our friends in Santa Luisa. That the crime rate in Sanlu is low and that Rheinholdt is presumably an honest fellow are beside the point. . . .

The words scalded him. No one could understand the horror of being insulted in print. There it was—insult after insult, lie after lie—for thousands to read, for his wife to see, for his force to gossip about. How he detested them, all those glib, bow-tied liars he knew at the courthouse back in the days he was Lieutenant Rheinholdt, head of traffic division, before a wartime gambling scandal had propelled him to high authority. He had come (his feet flattened and his soul scarred by accidents, lying motorists, a thousand evasions and falsehoods) to be Number One—because they knew he was incorruptible and thickskulled. And he intended to stay put—*Number One*—weathering the glib wise guys, the smart-aleck reporters, the new crusading gang on the City Council who were after him.

Rage froze his blockish head: the features immobilized. At best, he was distressingly homely. The square face, the bristly white hair growing vertically on the crown and laterally at the sides, the blunt features, the hidden eyes—all these suggested Velázquez' Aesop, without the slave's wisdom. He had a habit of peering fretfully over rimless bifocals, as if studying a lapsed driver's license.

Rheinholdt buzzed the intercom and spoke to his secretary, a young patrolman named Clyde Hertmann. "Send that guy in," he said hoarsely.

Hertmann opened the door. A slight, middle-aged man in a rumpled tweed suit, nervously stroking an outlandish tan guard's mustache, entered apologetically.

"Siddown," Hertmann said, indicating a hard-oak chair. The man complied.

Rheinholdt held up the clipping. "You write this, Swinnerton?"

The man shook his head. "No. I didn't even know about it, Chief. I'm just a district man for the *Truth*—you know that, sir."

"You bitched about the parking lot, didn't you?"

"Well, I felt it my duty to tell the paper that we weren't allowed to use it any more." Swinnerton had a soft, polite manner of speech, faintly tinged with Britishisms. "I gather that one of the executives at the paper decided it was worth an editorial."

Rheinholdt's muscled hulk leaned over the desk. His massive hands formed fists. "Goddam rats," he said. "All of them. They're after me. But they won't get me. You tell those people in LA they can't scare me. We're clean. We got the lowest crime rate in California. We're a hundred times better than LA."

"We're all aware of that, Chief," Swinnerton said. He smiled indulgently and his tongue flicked at the mustache. "It's just that ——"

"It's just that they hate my guts!" Rheinholdt brought his fists down on the desk top and Swinnerton started. "Ever since Mc-Cabe! And before that! I was a hero all right to the papers back in forty-three when they found out the force was on the take with the gamblers! Sure, old Rheinholdt, the honest cop, got called in from traffic division to clean up. Well, I cleaned up all right, and that went for all the reporters who were after me. Then that guy McCabe"—he leveled a bloated finger at Swinnerton's mild face— "that guy McCabe from your lousy paper, the *Truth,* bribed his way past a turnkey and talked to a prisoner!"

He was roaring, inflamed with memories of that harrowing event that had turned the newspapers against him forever. Swinnerton had heard the story a hundred times. It was part of press legend in Sanlu.

"Know what I did to him? I belted him. He went down like a rotten fence post. Sure, I hit a reporter. It served him right. I'd hit one again, if Mayor Speed would let me. But I got to be nice to you people, he says. Nice to you rats, printing filth about me so my wife can read it. You think I'm sorry I belted McCabe eight years ago? The hell I am!"

Swinnerton managed a polite smile. He did not mean to be offensive. "I'd say Bill McCabe has survived rather well. He got a big public relations job at Lockheed just after you hit him."

Rheinholdt turned sideways, peering at him with one eye over the top of his bifocals. "You making fun of me, Swinnerton? Get out."

The reporter for the *Truth*—district man in Sanlu—got up smartly. "I'm deucedly sorry about that editorial, sir. But I assure you I hadn't a thing to do with it."

"Beat it. Tell the rest of those cheap reporters you hang out with there won't be any centralization of the Santa Luisa Police Department. We're keeping the precinct system because I want it that way. We won't revive the job of chief of detectives because I don't want one. Mayor Speed'll back me up, no matter how much the papers yell about it."

The chief's sudden introduction of the centralization squabble did not surprise Harvey Swinnerton: it was the old man's *bête noire.* He had deliberately muddled the department's organization, restored the outmoded and wasteful precinct system (unnecessary in a city of less than 100,000), and abolished the post of chief of detectives—moves aimed at maintaining his own total grasp of police matters.

In the anteroom, Swinnerton looked innocently at Patrolman Clyde Hertmann. "I'm afraid to ask if there's anything doing today, Clyde," he said softly. "After that session."

Hertmann, a slender, bright young cop—he had a year at Santa Luisa Junior College—smiled noncommittally. It did seem a shame that Harvey Swinnerton, the mildest of reporters, had to catch it from Rheinholdt. But Hertmann said nothing, taking an incoming call from Joe McFeeley and switching it to the chief.

Inside, Rheinholdt, ruddy with rage, took a few seconds to make the connection when McFeeley mentioned 4217 Nespoli. "I sent a car to take care of her," he said dumbly.

"She chased them, Chief. Didn't want any uniformed police around. Chief, I need you out here. I think it's a kidnaping."

Rheinholdt's hand fussed with a sheaf of "Consolidated Weekly Reports" he had failed to read, a stack of personnel recommendations. Paper work was forever inundating him.

"Kidnaping? Here? In Sanlu?"

"It looks that way. Chief, the less people know, the better. We'd better talk about it here."

Rheinholdt said he would hurry out. He buzzed Hertmann to summon his car and his chauffeur, jammed a floppy white panama over his Aesopian skull, and left, darting a poignant look at the soaring bookcases of law and criminology and penology that the City Council had purchased for him. For a tender moment, he appeared to be regretting his stupidity.

Fritzie Andrus had gone from Mr. Salter's office to his own, there to interview a young actress sent to him by his producer's sister-in-law. Andrus was an emotional chameleon. His frenzied tears in the attorney's office soon gave way to a fatherly largesse in the presence of the young woman, so long of leg, so high of breast. They discussed her ambitions—where she "studied," who her "teachers" were, what she had read on dramatic "technique." They invested their mimicry with an academic aura that suggested the graduate faculties of Columbia University combined.

It developed she had attended Pembroke, a women's college in Providence, Rhode Island. This intelligence caused Andrus to fold his hands on the rise of his young-man's paunch and intone: "I have been spared Providence." The effect was devastating. Andrus' ignorance of this major New England center reduced the city to rubble; one saw Brown University going up in smoke, the state capital in ashes, lumber mills and textile factories crumbling. A judgment by Fritzie—even a *vaguely* critical one—had fearsome strength. Once, he had informed a professor of English literature at UCLA, an authority on Smollett, that he, Andrus, viewed all novels as "unstimulatin'." The miserable man spent a week wondering if his life's work had not been a waste.

His caller then advised him she had read his article in *Living Theatre* and agreed that the dramatic epiphany *was plastic and visceral* not *intellectual.* How grand! She spoke his language—that delectable, self-perpetuating theology! It was resolved that while he could not honestly give her a walk-on in his current TV drama (*this li'l mess of Brunswick stew we are cookin' up*), he would look kindly upon her for future "work." Then he invited her to dine with him that night, enjoying a view of heavy thigh, pleased with her slanted green eyes. She departed, leaving Andrus in better frame of mind than an hour prior, when Attorney Salter had shaken him.

When his secretary advised him that his wife was calling, he assumed Laura was coming around; he would be able to take Amy to Disneyland that week.

"Fritzie, something's happened to Amy." The taut, modulated voice irritated him.

"Whut? Whut happened? The hell you say, Laura. Is she hurt?"

"She wandered off this morning. She's missing. I think you'd better come home right away."

"*Damn!*" he exploded. "Damn! That all you can say? Didn't I tell you to hire sleep-in help? Get people to watch the children?"

"Fritzie, this isn't any time to argue. Are you coming out?"

"What are you doin' about it? Who have you called?"

"The police are here."

"When—how—what do you mean lettin' her get lost? I'll have a few things to tell you, Laura."

"Are you coming out?"

"You damn said it."

He seemed unaffected by the gravity of the situation—only wroth with his wife for some delinquency. Living so comfortably in his world of fiction, devoted to his own windy metaphysics, he inevitably had difficulty recognizing reality. It was only after he had streaked away from the network parking lot and was weaving his red sports car recklessly along the freeway to Sanlu that it dawned on him that his daughter was endangered, that his wife had been concealing something.

Rheinholdt arrived at 10:35. To McFeeley's distress, he drove up in his gray official car with its huge black insignia, S.L.P.D. CHIEF. Sergeant Baines, his chauffeur—an old farmer whom Rheinholdt had elevated from traffic—sat stiffly at the wheel in uniform. Peering from the picture window, McFeeley wanted to kick himself: he should have suggested that the chief come out in an unmarked car without the chauffeur. Behind the chief plodded Sergeant Irvin Moll, Joe's second-in-command at Precinct A.

Both men walked with the slow, heavy tread of big eaters. McFeeley ushered them in and introduced them to Mrs. Andrus. They both read the note. Moll whistled, and the schoolboyish noise made Laura shudder. The chief said nothing. The message, hideous in its neatness, had been inserted by McFeeley in a transparent plastic envelope from one of Andrus' scrapbooks. All awaited some word from the highest enforcement authority in Santa Luisa, but Rheinholdt seemed to be rereading the note for the fourth time. At length, he sat lumpily on a canvas chair and addressed Joe. "It could be a phony," he said.

"I don't think so," McFeeley said.

"Forty-two hundred bucks? Guy take a chance on the gas chamber for that?"

"Why'd anyone fake something like this?" McFeeley asked.

The color spread upward on Rheinholdt's face, reds and purples rising from his choking white collar. "A nut. A psycho. One of those LA psychos." His outraged eyes sought the paper again, secure in its protective envelope. "It's no kidnaping," he said. "It's no kidnaping."

Moll mopped his neck. He had a vague, small head, out of sorts with the weight-lifter's body below. In the summer he favored loud sports shirts, reminders of the time he had worn them to entrap homosexuals in the public parks, armed with guitar and perfume. "The chief could be right," Moll added. "A nut. A thrill seeker. Like that kid setting the fires last month."

Laura looked from one to the other desperately—three untalented men, her unlikely saviors. "Does that make it easier for me?" she asked. "Are you saying some pervert—some maniac—has my child?"

"It's not a kidnaping," the chief rumbled. "But don't you worry, Mrs. Andrus, we'll catch the person. You give us your hundred-per-cent co-operation and we'll catch him. And bring your child back safe. I don't allow this in my city."

McFeeley glanced at his watch: 10:45. They could expect Dr. Todd any minute. The husband was also due to arrive. McFeeley had to rouse Rheinholdt from his stupor.

"I don't want to hear the word kidnap!" Rheinholdt shouted. *"Not in my city!"*

Laura exchanged a startled look with McFeeley. He seemed her only ally in the stifling room—a poor one, but at least someone with whom she could communicate.

"However you want to look at it, Chief," McFeeley said, "we've got to agree about that drop tonight. We've got to keep it a secret. Just between us."

Rheinholdt was squinting through his bifocals at the note. He was not reading it but appeared to be seeking portents in the newsprint—a wizard divining from chicken entrails.

"No," he said.

"What do you mean?" Joe asked.

"No. No deals with that maniac."

"Chief, we've got to try it. At least to get the child back."

"What makes you think that psycho is going to keep his word? You'll leave that money and he'll never show. I'm going to find *him*. I'll give the terms. I won't do what he wants. I'll teach him a few things." He rubbed one giant palm over a fist, peering at Laura with bemused eyes. "Your child is safe, Mrs. Andrus, I'll promise you that! But I don't take orders from crooks. I never have. I'll get this rat on my own terms."

Lieutenant McFeeley paced the living room, hands thrust in rear pants pockets, his face aslant and uncomplicated. When he spoke again, Laura noticed the odd political quality in his voice.

"Now, Chief, there isn't any reason we can't do *both*," he pleaded. "Let's figure on making the drop, but let's start a little investigating right here—nothing that'll make people suspicious and nothing that'll bring the newspapers out—but enough to get us going. We can search the house and grounds, start checking records, interrogate some people. And also get ready for 8:15."

Rheinholdt's eyes were opaque, haunted. He had absorbed McFeeley's outline only in part.

Joe continued. "I'd like to interrogate Mrs. Andrus if she's up to it, then the neighbors, servants, gardeners—anyone who might have been up and about this morning. I want to find out anyone who might have a grudge against the family—anyone who's been nosing around lately—check hospitals for women who have lost babies recently. But meanwhile"—and here he slowed his discourse and spoke with almost pedantic precision—"we'd better get the drop ready. Dr. Todd should be here soon and he can get the money for us. Then we better look that location in the park over and think about a stake-out."

The chief rotated his bristly head, as if blending and liquefying the mass of duties McFeeley had hurled at him. He appeared ready to veto everything the detective had suggested, but when he spoke, all he said was: "Anyone tell Mayor Speed about this?"

His query seemed the ultimate nonsense, but McFeeley understood that Rheinholdt, in his numbed state, would naturally turn to his patron. Joe, observing the chief's purpling face, realized that he was scared silly—scared as only the stupid and incompetent in high authority can be. McFeeley understood the freakish rarity of kidnaping, a crime following no predictable rules, one in which a fragile balance among police, family, criminal and victim must be maintained. Moreover, it was a crime destined—more than any murder, any rape—to become public property, an arena for press, cranks, a rubbernecking public. He knew how kidnapings are transformed overnight into public spectacles—the shivering suspense of search, of imminent harm to a child—bringing on all the agents of air and talk, crippling investigation, harassing the family, making the most efficient police force appear inept and cold-blooded. He did not wonder at Rheinholdt's terror.

McFeeley saw Laura Andrus' white face—she was pressing a palm to her left temple, propitiating the headache—and he knew he could not let the chief's stupefaction infect them. Rheinholdt appeared to view the crime as an affront against his clean city. The criminal had dared to mar Sanlu's enviable statistical reports, and Rheinholdt would settle that with *him*. The child's safety seemed secondary; his refusal to hear the word "kidnaping" was indicative of his refusal to comprehend.

"The mayor ought to know," Rheinholdt insisted.

"Look, Chief," McFeeley said, "if we strike out tonight, we'll probably have to blow the whole thing. Everyone'll know. Meanwhile, we've got to keep this guy thinking he's got a private deal between himself and Mrs. Andrus. He tells her not once but twice not to make any noise—not even to scream. That's why I think it might be someone like a hopped-up kid, some rock who wants to buy a car and is willing to take a wild chance. No police, nothing in the papers, just a little exchange."

Mrs. Andrus had thrust her head back on the sofa. McFeeley cautioned himself. He must stop talking too much in front of her. He sensed that she did not care for him particularly.

"Mrs. Andrus," Joe said, "while we're waiting for your husband, can I ask you a few questions? I need a list of all domestic help you've ever had here—even a girl who may have cleaned or baby-sat for one day. Then, delivery boys, repairmen, unusual phone calls, unusual people in the neighborhood. We'll take our time, and whenever you want to quit, let me know."

"Yes. Whatever you want."

He sat opposite her, the coffee table between them, and began asking questions. She mentioned the part-time maid, Selena; Carlos, the gardener; a half-dozen delivery boys; and was trying to think of any strange telephone calls when the redwood door burst open and Fritzie, a blaze of flashing blond hair and agitated rosy flesh, charged into the room. He had removed his jacket and his black tie; his white shirt was soaked.

"What's the meanin' of this?" he shouted. "You found Amy yet? Laura—I warned you time and again about havin' help in the house to watch my children! Oh yes, they're mine, too, though you'd like to deny that!"

Andrus had hurled their intimate conflicts into the group, oblivious of the three strange men. In ignoring them, he obliterated them, just as he had razed Providence, Rhode Island, a half hour earlier.

"Where is she?" he howled. "Laura, I know you. Lettin' her roam the streets. Sleepin' late. Up all night with your damn clay an' plaster! And refusin' to let a colored woman sleep in the house because of those guilt feelings you entertain about Nigras!"

McFeeley picked up the note, snug in its plastic folder, and walked over to him. "Mr. Andrus, you better sit down. No point in yelling at your wife."

"Who you?"

"Lieutenant McFeeley." He introduced Moll and Rheinholdt. Andrus snubbed them impartially, as only a man of lower middle-class origins can snub members of his old level.

"Well, that's dandy," Andrus mocked. "The gang's all here. Why aren't you out lookin' for my daughter? Whirlybirds. Bloodhounds. Boy scouts. I tell you this. Wheah I hail from, in Tarheel country, the sheriff would have the dogs out by now. And you three arms of the law sit here as if——"

McFeeley gave him the note. "Sit down and read this, Mr. Andrus. Your daughter has been kidnaped."

Andrus lowered himself in painful stages into a canvas chair, his eyes, rimmed with delicate globules of sweat, hypnotized by the message. His mouth opened, jaw slack, thick red lips trembling. Then, plaintively, he appealed to all of them—his wife, the three officers. "Why me?" he asked shakily. He sounded like a boy singled out for birching. "Why me?" he repeated. "What have I ever done? Why should anyone single us out? We ain't rich. We got no enemies. We have troubles enough just bein' married. We ain't even lived here six months!" Unexpectedly, he switched from self-pity to a brash, accusative manner, turning on the police. "Dammit, do somethin'! What do you mean permittin' my child to be kidnaped?" Chaotically, he shouted at Laura: "And you— what a mother! Sayin' *I* was the one who neglected the kids!" He leaped from his seat and hurled himself, in clumsy lunges, against the yellow-stone fireplace which filled the northeast corner of the room. Andrus pressed his head against the projecting stones and began to sob.

"My fault. Blame me. I know I wasn't much of a father. Not meant for it. I admit it. Yes." He turned a damp, flushed face toward the four witnesses. "Say somethin'. I'm not afraid to accept blame for this horror." His voice gurgled away in gasps.

"Stop, Fritzie," Laura said. "Control yourself. I'm trying to help the police. Why don't you? They think Amy might be back with us tonight."

He appeared temporarily shamed by her serenity. Wiping his eyes on his sleeve, he sat on the sofa.

"I was asking your wife," McFeeley said, "about any suspicious phone calls, any strange visitors or people hanging around the neighborhood. I know you're upset by this, Mr. Andrus, but if we can get as much information as possible——"

"Why ask me?" Fritzie said wanly. "I ain't lived here for a month."

McFeeley looked puzzled. Rheinholdt turned his head sideways, as if the disclosure offered him a new aspect of the case.

"Mr. Andrus and I are separated," Laura said flatly.

"Excuse me. I didn't know." McFeeley glanced at his notes again. "Ah, the last thing was the TV repairman who——" Fritzie suddenly bounded from the sofa. He pointed a finger at Rheinholdt. "Where is the FBI?" he asked.

Rheinholdt's glazed eyes blinked. "They're not allowed in for seven days and I'm not calling them. I'm wise to the FBI. Feeding stuff to the newspapers and taking all the credit for what's good and blaming the local cops for what's bad. And no state cops or LA police in my city. This is my job, my department."

Andrus circled the old traffic expert warily—a gladiator sizing up a water buffalo. Center stage, he addressed Rheinholdt with murderous calm. "Why, you Keystone Kop. I happen to be good friends with the FBI agent in charge of this district and I'm very big with the LA police. I use them as consultants. I intend to phone them and kick you and these two underlings of yours out. They'll find Amy for me. They'll bring her back. Not the likes of you!"

The policemen watched him with silent, uninvolved faces. Laura moaned and covered her eyes.

"You can call them all you want," McFeeley said dryly, "but we've got jurisdiction here. It's our case, unless we ask for assistance."

"We won't," Rheinholdt said.

"We will see about *that!*" yelled Andrus.

Much of Harry Emerson's day—he was a successful commercial photographer who spent a lot of time at home—was devoted to preventing his wife from nosing into the affairs of neighbors and friends. Babe was goodhearted—too goodhearted, Harry felt—and she craved intimacy . . . with anyone. Postmen told her of their marital troubles; delivery boys about their gambling debts; Harry's clients invariably found themselves disclosing more than they cared to about their sex problems.

On the morning of Amy Andrus' disappearance, Harry and Babe, after lingering in the kitchen long after the children had been dispatched to school, heard Fritzie Andrus shouting.

"What's he doing back?" Babe asked. "Laura said she'd never let him in the house again."

Emerson helped himself to an onion roll, thickly smeared it with two varieties of cheese, crowned it with a slice of raw onion, and cautioned her. "Butt out," he said. "No sneaking under their windows to hear the fights, either."

"I beg your pardon," Babe said haughtily. "I never eavesdrop."

"Yeah, but you always got to inspect the cracks in the driveway whenever they start in over there." Emerson was a stout, hairy man, the kind of emphatic Semitic type who could have served as an illustration in a textbook of physical anthropology (*Armenoid facial type common to certain Bedouin tribes, Ashkenazim, and other Levantines*). There was a dark coarseness about him that belied his delicate skills as a photographer.

Fritzie's voice soared. Babe Emerson pressed an ear against the kitchen's screen door. "Oh, I'm *dying*. I'm dying," she said. "I'll drop dead if I don't find out what's happening. Harry—it's serious. He's been away all this time; then he's back one day and they're battling like crazy."

"He's a southern corn-pone *schlepp*," Emerson announced. "She —I can stand. She minds her business, not like other women I know. Him, he's got hominy grits in his ears. A professional ridgerunner."

Fritzie's voice diminished, then grew loud again. Babe imagined she heard the voices of other men. *Men*. Who?

"Remember when Laura came around and asked about Amy being lost this morning?" Babe asked. "How about that? Doesn't the whole thing sound fishy? The kid is missing. Then, out of the blue, Fritzie shows up, yelling his head off."

"Butt out," her husband muttered. "Did I ever tell you what my old grandfather Avram Yosele Immerman used to say—the fellah who took me to the Hebrew Educational Society, where I learned to take pictures?"

Her ear was tangent to the copper screen. "I'm not interested."

"My grandfather used to say we should not *unterfere* in the arguments of *goyim*. We got enough trouble being Jews."

Babe walked purposefully out the door, holding the cotton wrapper around her chunky legs. "Timmy left his bike on the lawn again. I'll bring it in."

"Since when did you get so neat?" Emerson called after her. He abandoned his efforts to stay her curiosity, diverting himself by studying the broken hinges on the door of their new refrigerator. Why *his* refrigerator? Wasn't it bad enough that he and Babe were natural-born slobs? Did the world have to fall apart for them perpetually? *Their* Siamese cat got enteritis and died. *Their* new color television caught on fire and burned merrily for ten minutes. *Their* driveway cracked and crumbled. Emerson sighed and waddled off to his cool, private darkroom.

Babe, managing to make the retrieving of Timmy's English racer a five-minute project, saw at once the police car at the curb. A uniformed policeman lolled against one fender, and on one door was the legend, S.L.P.D. CHIEF. The thrill of discovery, the excitement of secret knowledge—these were what Babe lived for. She was a connoisseur of gossip, an expert in the field of bad tidings. The three bits of evidence convinced her of some anguish in the Andrus house—the child missing, the husband returned, the police chief's car. She started back to her home, and then, propelled by her obsession with other people's troubles, walked to Laura's front door and rang the bell.

A heavy man in a green, floral sports shirt answered the door, and Babe stepped back, surprised.

"Yeah?" Moll asked.

"I'm Mrs. Emerson from next door. Is Mrs. Andrus at home?" She delivered her response with a swift survey of the interior—noticing two other strange men, Laura, sitting stonily on the sofa, and Fritzie, standing at the fireplace, his back to her.

"Laura! It's me—Babe! Can I come in?"

Laura looked at one of the men—a thin, young fellow—and then got up and walked to the door. She looked awful, Babe thought—too lean, too pale.

"I thought I'd ask about Amy. You find her?"

Laura hesitated. "Yes. She—she was down the street."

"Oh. I mean—everything's all right?"

"Yes; thanks, Babe."

"Is she here? Could I take her off your hands for a minute?"

"No. No thanks." Babe made no motion to leave: her greedy black eyes swept about the inner rooms.

"Babe, maybe we can have a drink tonight. Fritzie and I have a little private business to resolve. If you'd excuse us."

"Sure! Sure! You need any help, holler! Like shopping or such-like." She felt idiotic on the hot steps, the three strange men staring at her.

"Hi, Fritzie!" she yelled. "Welcome home, stranger!"

Andrus waved. "Hello, Babe. How you?"

"Swell! Everything's great!" To her shock, Laura was gently easing her out the door.

"Babe, we'll have a chat later. We're in the middle of a—a rather involved discussion." The redwood door clicked and she was alone on the cooking flagstone, frustrated.

Back in her deplorable kitchen, Babe sipped her fifth cup of coffee. She was miserable. She could not keep a secret. She could not bear to have anything kept from her. As a child, she invariably discovered hidden presents and opened them beforehand. She had a nose for tragedy, a positive sense of exhilaration when confronted by sorrows and strains and rifts. *She had to know.* More-over, Laura's rudeness disturbed her. Was she not Laura's best—and only—friend in Sanlu? Had not Laura said so? Now she wondered how close Laura was to her. Laura was lovely, refined, Gentile, poised—and so, so snobbish (about the right things, of course). And she, poor Babe (she detested her given name, Bea-trice) was none of these. She was as bright and as well educated as Laura, yes, but not in the same league with her when it came to those maddening externals that made for status. She wondered: was Laura *really* her friend? Did Laura have any use for her, as anything more than a sounding board to reinforce her own harsh sentiments about Sanlu, about California, about Fritzie's work?

She had to know what was going on in there. Amy missing. Fritzie turning up suddenly and carrying on like crazy. And the chief of police—she guessed he was the white-haired man with glasses. But how did one find out these things? Babe's mind swarmed with notions, with suspicions, like a bread crust covered with ants. The police would surely know what was happening at 4217 Nespoli—certainly with the chief there. But calling them was out of the question. Even Babe understood that. Who else? Who? Who could call a police station and find things out? Harry's early career as a free-lance photographer in New York gave her the answer: *newspapermen.* They had access. They were allowed to call police stations and ask questions. She racked her brain trying to think of some reporter she had once met, someone of whom she could ask a favor.

They no longer knew any newspaper people. Harry had long graduated from journalism and the American Newspaper Guild. Now he commanded high prices for his work, had an agent, and turned down jobs. And then a fruitful recollection roused her; she got up from the kitchen chair and located the Los Angeles directory, deep in a clutter of pots, pans and percolators, below the sink. About two months ago, she recalled, a young man had come to Harry for "contacts." He was a Bronx boy, and his father—a pharmacist—knew Harry's older brother, also a pharmacist. The young man—his name was Spengler, or Spinrad, or Sperling—had just been fired from a newspaper and needed a job very badly. Harry had sent him to several movie publicity departments. They had lost track of him, but Babe knew he was working, because every now and then, on a news show, she would hear news edited by . . . what was his name? *Sparling.* That was his name. Erwin

Sparling. *The 7:45 news edited by Erwin Sparling.* She made another rapid connection: the 7:45 morning news was channel eight. Channel eight was United Broadcasting. She riffled the pages in the directory, ripping a few.

Tom Ballstead, news director for United Broadcasting, spent most of the day on the sagging couch in his minuscule office. He was not a lazy man; it was simply that, supine, his ravaged chest (he had chronic bronchitis) and his aching stomach (he had a duodenal ulcer) hurt less. Ballstead was agonizingly thin. His bony skull and limbs looked like the remains of an eminent Italian cardinal, dead some four-hundred years and encased, for the faithful to ogle, in a glass coffin.

Ballstead was reading the morning log—the news broadcasts that had gone out since midnight, plus important phone calls, bulletins, breaks in the routine. He scanned them swiftly; Ballstead had been in the news business since he was fourteen. A ruined fifty-two, he performed his editorial chores with casual speed. He lived in sour expectation of the rare big story. Few things made Tom Ballstead laugh any longer (laughter was painful, summoning up coughs and gasps from his corroded innards), but on the morning of Amy Andrus' disappearance, he was enjoying a hoarse chuckle over an item in the 7:45 morning news. As he read, he wolfed his breakfast —the same breakfast he had eaten for thirty years—a fried-egg sandwich on soggy white bread and black coffee.

The item that amused him was a "kicker"—a light afterpiece to the newscast proper. On the 7:45 TV news—"Newstime with George Brack"—the kicker was termed Brack's "Brightspot," a title Ballstead detested, but one which the California audience apparently found palatable.

> . . . And now for Brack's "Brightspot" . . .
> One of our favorite columnists, Miss Mona Mears of the *Los Angeles Truth,* has a problem. Like most of us in the news business, Miss Mears gets invited to a lot of cocktail parties. In this morning's column she tells us of two she's been invited to and why she selected one over the other. I quote: "Seems as how the California Association of Paleo-zoologists wants me to heist a few brews with them so's they can tell me about a new, thrilling fossil fish they've dug up outside Palmdale. Sorry, mates, I'm spoken for today. Much as I'd like to trade fossils with you egghead

types, I'm obliged to drink Nehi and Moxie with the California Newspaper Publishers' Association. So give my regards to any hot rocks that turn up, and I'll think of you when the caviar is passed around." End quote. Miss Mears, you've made a bad choice. As between fossils and fossils, I will take a dead fish over a publisher any day. After all—what can the newspaper publishers tell you aside from the fact that the cost of newsprint is too high? At least the paleozoologists, while unlikely to serve caviar, might disclose a smidgen of new facts about our world and its creatures. As a journalist, Miss Mears, I'm sure you prefer one small fact—even a fossilized fact—to a seminar on what's wrong with the Newspaper Guild. And that's George Brack's "Brightspot" for today.

Ballstead smiled crookedly. The news director was a city-room man from way back, a battler for overtime, a defender of working stiffs—underpaid reporters, cranky photographers, weary deskmen. His antagonism to publishers was wide and deep. And he had no patience with the editorial person—a Mona Mears—who ran their errands. The Brack piece was a little too much for the trade, but it pleased him, and he sat up jerkily, confronted by its author, a tall, young man, who was standing in the doorway. A comforting hum of teleprinters and typewriters rose behind the caller.

"Can I come in, Tom?" the young man asked.

"Yeah, Sparling. Nice piece on Mears. Nobody'll get the joke except newspapermen, but that's all right."

"I hope you don't think I was taking revenge on my alma mater —the good old *LA Truth*."

Ballstead got up from the couch and eased himself, sectionally and arthritically, into his abraded swivel chair. The writer's large frame slouched against the doorway. "Everything okay in the overnight report, Tom?" he asked. His voice was loud and invasive; it reached resonant, brassy levels, and he seemed to have no control over it.

"Yeah, fine, Sparling. Why don't you go home? You been here since 1:00 A.M. It's after 10:00. When do you sleep? I'm an old overnight man myself—I know what it's like."

"It's too hot in my apartment. I grab a few hours before coming in—after it gets dark." He bellowed as if addressing a mob. Ballstead did not seem to mind his loudness. The news director tolerated all writers—particularly fast, bright ones like Sparling.

He had hired the young man, for reasons he himself could not articulate, when Sparling had come to him a month ago—fired from the *Truth,* rank with self-pity. And the twenty-eight-year-old goof had been a gold mine. He wrote faster and better than any overnight man United Broadcasting, LA, had ever had. He listened; he took orders; he showed initiative.

"Any chance of my getting off the overnight—not right away— but like in a few months?" Sparling laughed self-consciously. The noise trembled the window at Ballstead's back. "I had three and a half years of it at the *Truth* and, boy, I haven't learned to sleep or eat or live a normal life yet."

Ballstead's sick face studied Eliot Sparling casually. The writer was a beauty, all right, a huge man with a disturbing fraudulence about his heft. Observed hastily, Sparling appeared rather attractive—a tall, strong body; a long, fair head, crowned with a crew cut. On closer examination the fraud was exposed. Sparling's body was merely big: it was shapeless and soft, as unmuscular as a baby's. His head was a disaster—the eyes spaced too far, the long nose terminating in a glowing bulb, the lips blunt. Somewhat vain, Sparling had tried manfully to alter his homeliness; everything had failed. A burning salve, once employed to divest his cheeks of acne, had left them delicately pitted; his crew haircut grew raggedly and was thinning at the temples; a pair of financed contact lenses had induced pinkeye, and he had abandoned them in favor of a myopic squint. *But his feet!* These pedestals for his thick, long legs he had inserted in scientifically fashioned, gum-soled, side-laced "health" shoes, in which he clopped along clumsily in the manner of an illtrained bear.

"I can't pull you off overnight, Sparling," Ballstead said. "You're valuable there. Go on home."

"I'll knock off a few letters, if that's okay." How could he ever explain to the news director how he truly felt about United Broadcasting? Could he say, simply and honestly, to Ballstead: *I don't like to go back to my hot, tiny room in North Hollywood because I love it here . . . because I love everything about UBC . . . because I love you, Mr. Thomas Ballstead, for saving me from defeat and misery and from the dreaded* Los Angeles Truth? He loved everything at UBC. His desk. His typewriter. George Brack, the blond newscaster for whom he wrote every morning. The men's rooms— clean and spacious and restful. The banks of teleprinters, the icy-cold radio booths and the antiseptic television studios. They were the be-all and end-all of his life, and he was not ashamed of his infatuation. Only people who have worked for bad companies, Sparling knew, could appreciate a good one.

Plodding back to the city room, its yellow walls alive with bulletin boards, work schedules, rows of spikes sprouting piles of copy, Sparling slumped at his desk. He sat opposite the dayside deskman, Jim Farrell. Farrell was gray and solemn. He was a pipe-and-vest man, an old friend of Ballstead's, dating back to Tom's newspaper work in Indiana.

"Mind if I bang out a few letters?" Sparling tried to keep his thunderous voice down.

"No, no. Go right ahead." Farrell bent to his ritual reading of the AP report. "I got a laugh out of that Mears piece."

Sparling's elongated head glowed. He inserted onionskin and began a letter to his father in the Bronx. *Dear Pop, my job continues to delight me. Boy, am I glad I never went to med school as you wanted. Everything, everyone is terrific here.* As he typed, accurately and swiftly with two index fingers, he reflected that half the joy of his new post with United Broadcasting was the omnipresent thought that he was no longer in the clutches of the *Truth.* He had difficulty shaking off his old terror of the newspaper, nursing, long after the event, a poignant outrage over the way he had been fired. He, Eliot Sparling, twenty-eight, had been the best overnight man they had ever had. And for fifty-eight dollars a week (Guild scale)! They had rewarded him in typical *Truth* fashion—fired by Herbert Hood, the general manager, at the request of T. T. Hansel, Editor & Publisher. And for so picayune a reason—his public pronouncements about the Schlossmann suicide!

Eliot sighed noisily. It had all turned out rather well. Now he could look back and laugh at the *Truth*—that sweatshop of journalism, where it was assumed that people worked best when abused. What a bat's nest it had been! Old Herbie Hood prowled the city room like a dyspeptic turtle, looking for miscreants, warning everyone to hold costs down. Upstairs in his eyrie, T. T. Hansel, Editor & Publisher, a burning man, hot with glorious plans for the sickly newspaper, spent as much time dreaming up ways of punishing employees as he did pondering the *Truth's* dwindling circulation. Their Dickensian antics had never really frightened Eliot. On the overnight, a principality of its own, peopled with the wreckage of journalism, the young, the old, the alcoholic, the unlucky, Sparling had become the office jester. Once he had written a parody of Tennyson's "Bugle":

The splendor falls
On Hansel's balls
And Herbie Hood, so old and whorey.
The day side quakes
When Hansel wakes;
Kalaidjian shivers in the glory.
Blow, Hansel, blow;
Set the newsroom flying.
Answer, Herbie, answer,
Dying, dying, dying.

He had the feeling that some company fink—maybe Bill Trigg —had told Hood who had written the masterpiece. Then there had been the business of the fire in the trash bins, one hot July night, when the sprinkling system refused to work and the overnight staff set up a bucket brigade before the smoke chased them into the street. The next morning Sparling had tacked on the city-room door the legend:

TRIANGLE SHIRTWAIST FACTORY

Herbie Hood did not get the joke. T. T. Hansel did, and was furious. Did he know that Sparling was the author of that impertinence? Eliot suspected he did. The Editor & Publisher knew everything.

Farrell was talking to the network's New York headquarters on the phone. The overnight man in New York wanted a fast one-minute on the California housing scandal for the eight o'clock news. "Glad he called *me,*" Farrell said softly. "I hate to make a long-distance phone call, the way New York is on Ballstead's back to keep costs down."

Unified in their concern over Ballstead, both men looked into the news director's office. He was hidden by an opened airmail edition of the Sunday *Times,* that tower of excellence to which all newsmen turn for sustenance. Farrell, an old-timer, and Sparling, the new boy, both knew that Tom Ballstead had been kicked out of the New York news operation. Ballstead had brought it on himself, many said. Tom was stubborn. He had made his mind up that he hated television; he had refused to learn. Memoranda slid from Ballstead's desk to wastebaskets, assignments were fumbled, meetings with sponsors ignored. The West Coast brass accepted him reluctantly after his fall from grace. A new vice-president had been

assigned to the Los Angeles office, with a mandate to clean house—
cut costs, chop away deadwood, *get the show on the road.* The men
in the newsroom suspected Ballstead was on the executive's list.
At all costs, they were united in wanting to protect the ravaged
man who, for so many years, had been a good shepherd to newsmen.

Farrell picked up a phone. "For you, Sparling," he said. Eliot
took it from him, yawning endlessly.

"Sparling, UBC," he said.

"Oh. Mr. Sparling, is it? I thought it was Sperling." A woman
was speaking rapidly and nervously in the familiar accents of New
York City—Bronx or Brooklyn, Eliot surmised.

"It's Sparling. Eliot Sparling. Who's this?"

"I'm not sure I have the right person. Is your father a druggist
on Tremont Avenue?"

"Yeah, Abe Sparling. You know him?"

"Well—we've met—you and I, that is. I'm Beatrice Emerson—
Harry Emerson's wife. It's very involved. My husband's brother is
also a druggist in the Bronx, and your father wrote to my Harry to
help you get a job at the movie studios, in publicity."

"Oh—sure I know you. Of course, Mrs. Emerson!"

"Babe."

"Hah?"

"Babe. Everyone calls me that."

"Well, it was swell of Mr. Emerson to get me those appointments. I didn't get a job, but I made some good contacts." Eliot's
voice was a roar. Farrell turned his head and covered an ear. "As
it is, I got a position with United Broadcasting. I was very lucky.
But, thanks anyway."

"It was our pleasure. Anything for an old Bronx boy. Listen,
Eliot, here's why I called. Now this may sound nutty to you, but
I think one of my neighbors is having some real trouble—police
and so forth. I'm dying to help her, but she's a funny sort of a
woman who won't *let* anyone help her. If I could find out what it is
—why the chief of police, of all people, is with her—I might be
able to help."

Dumbly, Eliot asked: "Why'd you call me?"

"You being a reporter, I figured you could ask the police and let
me know. They'd know why the chief was there and other suspicious things around here."

Eliot tried to raise a mental image of his caller. He barely knew
the woman. He had called on Emerson in his days of disaster, after

the *Truth* had fired him, and he remembered the slovenly home, the good-natured photographer (receiving Eliot in his underwear) who had gotten him the studio interviews.

"I don't know what I can do, Mrs. Emerson," Sparling said. "I'm a deskman and I don't know any cops. But I might make a routine call if you'd give me some information."

She complied, relating the events of the morning on Nespoli Drive: the child missing, the return of the irate husband, the appearance of the chief, the mother's odd behavior. Then she added shrewdly: "You know, this might have some interest for you, too. After all, the father's a big TV director, so if anything is wrong——"

"What do you mean?"

"This is just my own *hunch*, Eliot, but I think the husband is hiding the child because they're separated and she won't let him see her. A custody fight. That's what he was yelling about, I'm sure."

Eliot nodded. He had written down the address, the name of the family, a few other facts on a yellow sheet. "O.K., Mrs. Emerson, I'll check the police, although, as I said, don't expect me to learn much."

"Thanks, thanks," the woman said quickly. "And look—Eliot—don't let on I told you this. Never. Don't even act as if you know me."

"O.K. It's probably nothing at all."

Sparling started to assemble his weary bones—he had slept only three hours in the wasting heat the day before—and convey the tip to Ballstead. Then he heard the news director coughing painfully and he decided not to bother him. Instead, he told Jim Farrell, the deskman.

Farrell was an old hand—cautious, unexcitable, as bland as a state-wide weather roundup. "You'll never learn anything from the Santa Luisa cops," he said. "That's Rheinholdt's barony. He never even talks to the police-beat guys."

"What if it's really something?" Eliot asked. "Heck, I don't mind telling this dame I didn't learn anything. But I'd hate to blow a story."

Farrell yanked a thumb over his shoulder. "Tell Tom about it." They both looked solicitously into the news director's office. Ballstead had smothered the awful noises and was studying the *Times* again. Eliot walked in. "Tom?" he asked. "Can I bother you a minute?"

"Jesus, Sparling, go to sleep," Ballstead said. "I know you love it here, but we're short on desk space."

Sparling apologized. Then he told Ballstead about the call he had received—a missing child, a family argument, a chief of police at the house. Ballstead jerked his body away from the desk and locked his hands behind his neck. It was always prudent, he had learned in years of city-room sweat, to anticipate the worst. *A child missing.* It could be nothing—nothing at all. Sparling's informant might have had it cockeyed. It could be a simple case of a brat wandering off, turning up later at the police station, where she would be given an ice-cream cone. Or perhaps a custody case— reasonably good copy—the father grabbing the kid from the mother—page-four stuff. And it could be (Ballstead inhaled deeply as the idea quivered his body) it could be the grandest prize of all, the most horrible, most suspenseful, most readable, most hideous prize in the journalistic grab bag. You waited a decade to cover one; you waited a lifetime to get the *beat* on one.

"Santa Luisa?" Ballstead rasped. "Isn't that where they have that traffic cop running the department? The guy who smacked Bill McCabe around?"

"That's him," Farrell said. "Caspar Rheinholdt."

"Good Christ," Ballstead muttered. "If it really did happen. With *him* in charge."

"If what happened, Tom?" asked Eliot.

Ballstead bent his shoulders forward. His cadaverous hands vanished in his lap. "If it's a kidnaping."

"You think it might be?" Eliot asked.

"I don't know. I'd like us to get on it right away. Don't call the Sanlu cops. Let's just get out there." He spoke to Farrell. "Got any Indians around?"

The deskman scratched his gray hair. "We're short again, Tom. I sent George Brack to the housing hearing. Robinson's sick and we've still got a man on vacation."

"What about me?" roared Eliot. "I'll go! Please, Tom, you got to——"

"Go home and go to sleep," Ballstead said.

"Tom—I got the tip!" cried Eliot. "I'm very big with the neighbor, that Mrs. Emerson. Let me go out! If it's nothing, I'll call in; if it's big, you'll need a full crew there—cameraman, lights, sound —I'll do all the contact work——"

"Jesus, shut up," Ballstead said. "Stop running the department."
He looked at Farrell again.

"You got a crew available?"

"I could scare one up," Farrell said. "Billik's off—he's painting his garage. It'll be double time if we call him in. We're over budget as it is, Tom, and I hate to see us go deeper on a story we can't even check."

He wanted to protect Ballstead—from the accountants, the efficiency experts, the vice-presidents, all the well-groomed men in dark suits.

"Get the crew," Tom said. "Have 'em stand by on aircall, about a block from Sanlu police headquarters. Don't send them to the house—yet."

He spun about, eying a vista of Sunset Boulevard below him— sun-bright, smoggy, as devoid of character as a supermarket sandwich loaf. The back of his starved head was covered with wispy gray strands growing irregularly behind his waxen ears.

"A kidnaping," Ballstead said quietly. "Ours, maybe. Not a Washington story about a rivers and harbors bill, or some junk from Rome or London that nobody understands, or a dirty Hollywood divorce or a dirtier wedding, with the boobs gawking at the mummies. To hell with all of them. But the big one." He turned around. "The most horrible story in the world. You can't stop hearing about it or reading about it. It's everybody's bad luck. It kicks everyone in the groin. It's so personal you can't stand it, but you sure want to know all about it. And this might be it. Ours. Ahead of everyone."

"Can I go? Can I go now, Tom?" shouted Sparling. "It's my story!"

"It's your ass, too," Ballstead said. He drummed on the desk— attempting to summon up some stratagem that would keep the story theirs, away from the competition, yet enable them to ferret information from the police, the family, the neighbors.

"I guess I'm not good enough to cover a big one," Sparling whined. "Sure, send George Brack with the golden tonsils and the golden curls. He's no newsman. And it's my tip. My contact. O.K., send him. I'll do leg work, anything. Besides, it probably isn't much of a story anyway. They probably found the kid by now——"

The room rattled with Sparling's appeal. Ballstead, overwhelmed by the noise, surrendered.

"Got your car here?" Ballstead asked.

"Sure."

"Grab a tape recorder and go out to that house. Talk to your friend next door. Nose around. I'll try to get something out of the Sanlu cops. Soon's you learn anything, call in. The crew will be standing by to film if it's a story."

"Oh, thanks, Tom. Thanks. I'm off."

"One thing, Eliot." Ballstead's scratchy voice sounded almost solicitous. "Be careful of Rheinholdt. He's an old hardhead and he hates newsmen. He'll hate you most of all because you're young, big, loud, ugly and smart. Now beat it."

Sparling, his feet impeding one another, galumphed through the newsroom, stopping at the engineering office for his tape recorder. They heard him talking to the chief engineer, and then, in a minute or so, he was back. "Tom, I was wondering," Eliot said, "what is the best approach? I mean—should I threaten them? Pretend I'm someone else? Or come right out and say I'm from UBC?"

Ballstead locked his eyes. "Go on, Sparling, get out there. Just mind the place long enough so we can get George Brack on the way."

"Oh, I'm as nervy as they come," Eliot said lightly. "It's just I've done desk work so long, I'm a little rusty."

Farrell returned to the slot, to round up a camera crew. Ballstead, with a sense of purification, returned to his Sunday *Times*.

The arrival of Dr. Walter L. Todd engendered a good deal of tranquillity in the Andrus home. Less than ten minutes after the dentist had bounced in, the tortured parents found themselves remarkably calmer. Even the three officers now viewed the crime as far from insoluble—a malfeasance that would soon be resolved to everyone's happiness. Dr. Todd always had that effect on people. He was a born placater, a man whose mastery of life's problems, whose sure-footedness infused listeners with the same brand of courage. Moreover, if sometimes this valorous view of life was short-lived, his imitators always attributed it to their own shortcomings—not to Dr. Todd's inspirational example. He himself remained inviolate. As soon as he learned of the crime, he had thoughtful words of assurance for Laura and Fritzie. He went into a profession tête-à-tête with the police, supported McFeeley's plan, and even succeeded in rousing Chief Rheinholdt from his stupor by advising him that his handling of the case thus far was impeccable and that he, Todd, would see to it that Mayor Palmer Speed was so informed.

Laura knew Todd only slightly, having met him at a City Council meeting in the spring, at which time they discovered their relationship. Todd was a second cousin of Laura's mother—a member of the California branch of the Connecticut Todds. The narrow New England hardness Laura knew to be a Todd trademark (her mother's family ran to leanness and pessimism) seemed to have been softened and warmed by the southern sun. The dentist reminded her of one of those sectarian California preachers with pulpits in converted theaters—friendly, optimistic men with a good word for everything, liking everybody, reducing the world's sorrows to a few affirmative bobs of the head, a pain-dispersing grin, a hearty handshake. Todd never sat still. He gyrated jauntily from Rheinholdt, frozen in a deck chair (you're right, Chief, you've hit the nail on the head), to Fritzie, pouring himself a tumbler of bourbon in the kitchen (catch hold of yourself, son, these things seem worse than they really are), to a professional chat with Lieutenant McFeeley at the window (we've got to touch all the bases, Joe); and, after a while, Laura began to wonder if his soothing syrup might prove indigestible. Like the California preachers, there was no negativism in him, no capacity to comprehend evil, since his own blameless life was so free of it.

"There'll be no problem on the money," the dentist was telling McFeeley crisply. "I have a custodial account at Valley View Savings and Loan and I'll make the arrangements with Mr. Deckler pronto. He's a golf partner of mine and he'll be glad to accommodate me. Don't anyone worry about reimbursing me—that's the last thing any of us should think about."

"That's very kind of you," Laura said. "It's good of you to help us."

The dentist waggled a pink hand. "Now, Laura! I'm a Todd, like your dear mother, and if we can't help our kin, what good are we? I'm amazed you and Francis didn't contact me earlier."

"We called you as soon as we spoke to the police," Laura said.

"Oh, not about this awful business. Just in general. I was very sorry to hear about your breaking up. I—ah—might have been helpful. I'm an old bird, you know, seventy-one, and I've seen a lot."

Fritzie turned away when Todd mentioned their separation. The police officers pretended not to hear. Laura, taken aback by his snooping, said nothing. In any case, Todd expected no comment. He had pivoted away and had joined McFeeley and Sergeant Moll, who were comparing lists of subjects for interrogation.

"In the matter of tracing the currency," Todd asked with a crisp, professional tone, "do you want the bank to mark the bills in any way? Keep a record of serial numbers?"

McFeeley looked startled, Moll offended. The dentist had intruded as if just having completed a year's study at the FBI school. "No, Dr. Todd," McFeeley said. "We'll keep our own record of serial numbers. We don't want the bank to get suspicious. And no marking at all—there are easier ways of tracing."

"Really?" Todd jiggled his pince-nez. In defiance of California heat and informality, he wore a navy-blue suit, black pumps and black silk socks, a stiff white shirt and a carnelian-and-white tie advertising his eastern origins (he was a Cornell man). Todd's head was so hairless as to suggest he shaved it once a week with a child's plastic razor. No furrows—physical or spiritual—marred the pristine perfection of the outer man; he was a peeled, hard-boiled egg.

"What we'll probably do is dust the bills with a staining powder," McFeeley said.

"I'll be darned," the dentist said. His eyes blossomed.

"You can't see the powder, or feel it, but it rubs off on the hand and it fluoresces under ultraviolet light. We use it in robberies a lot. We caught two kids who had been robbing liquor stores by smearing some on doorknobs."

"Fascinating. What sort of powder?"

McFeeley seemed impatient with his probing. "Oh—uranyl nitrate, uranyl phosphate. There's a dozen of them."

Laura had overheard their conversation. "Lieutenant," she said, "didn't we agree not to do anything that would scare him away?"

Fritzie, sipping his bourbon, moved out of the kitchen. "Yeah. I don't appreciate these Dick Tracy stunts."

"It can't hurt," McFeeley said. "The powder's invisible. He'd never know—until we caught him and stuck his hand under an ultraviolet lamp."

"I'll veto *that*," Fritzie said. He moved heavily across the carpeting, carrying his glass. "I have some rights in this affair. I'm the child's father, even though her mother would like to deny that."

"Fritzie, Fritzie," Laura pleaded, "don't burden everyone with our problems. What we've done has no bearing on what's happened to Amy."

"It's all tied together," said Andrus. "Yes, ma'am. It is. You know there's a relationship."

Todd pivoted away from the two detectives and hopped across the room to Andrus. "Now, Francis, we'll make believe we didn't hear any of the foregoing. We're all under strain here and we appreciate that you and Laura, above all, are suffering." Center room, he did a full turn. "I feel we're all acting with admirable courage. And that's half the battle."

"Mr. Andrus, you can take my word that using tracing dye on the bills won't tip anything," said McFeeley. "We realize your child's safety comes first. Chief Rheinholdt—me—all of us—we want your child back before anything else."

The doorbell's bleat made all of them start—even the chief roused from his torpor with a twitching of his bristly head.

McFeeley walked to the redwood door, opened it and stepped outside into the midmorning glare. He closed the door behind him. A tall, fleshy young man in a yellow shirt, shading his eyes, was smiling at him. McFeeley spoke politely to him.

"Can I help you?"

"I'm not sure," Eliot Sparling said.

"You want to see someone here?"

"Ah, yes. I do. Chief Rheinholdt, I guess."

"What about?" McFeeley asked.

"Well, are you a detective? You see, I'm not too familiar with Sanlu because——" Eliot laughed stupidly. "I—ah—I'm a newsman with United Broadcasting. We don't staff Santa Luisa regularly and I——"

"A reporter? You have any identification?" Joe cursed silently; he had a feeling that Rheinholdt's official car with its blatant initials, the presence of Sergeant Baines in uniform had something to do with the leakage. He would have to get the car off the street, chase Rheinholdt, enforce a tight secrecy.

Sparling fussed through a wallet and found his working-press card. "There it is. Approved by *Good Housekeeping.*"

Joe read it. "You're Eliot Sparling?"

"That's me. UBC. Channel Eight, Always Great. Officer, we got a tip this morning that a child was missing and that Chief Rheinholdt was handling the investigation, and my boss sent me out to check on it."

McFeeley's slanted face betrayed nothing. "So?"

"It occurred to my boss, Mr. Ballstead—that's Tom Ballstead, the UBC news director—that we would like to aid in finding the child, if the story is true. We'd like to make the nationwide facilities of UBC available—television and radio—to the Santa Luisa police and to the parents. We mean it!"

"That's generous of you, Eliot," McFeeley said. "But there's no story here."

"Why's the chief here?" He pointed to the parked car. Farmer Baines dozed at the wheel.

"Only because he's a friend of the family. There's no mystery, no story. A small family problem. There isn't anything worth a line."

Eliot rubbed a sweaty forearm against his forehead.

"May I quote you? What's your name?"

"There's nothing to quote."

"Your name?"

"Joe McFeeley."

"Ah—Mr. Rheinholdt's assistant?" Sparling was scribbling on a sheaf of yellow copy paper.

"I'm Chief of Detectives at Precinct A."

Eliot's primitive feet remained rooted to the flagstone walk. In the fractional moment in which McFeeley had left the house, the reporter had seen a woman and three men. "All those people in there—are they cops, too? You sure Rheinholdt won't say a few words? Or maybe the parents——"

"No. Not a chance."

"But UBC wants to help, Joe. If a child is lost or in danger——"

"No one's lost. You can go back to LA. If you want, you can phone headquarters this afternoon." McFeeley turned to leave. "Where'd you get that phony tip from?"

"Oh—around."

"Someone at Sanlu police?"

"No. I just got it. You know, you can't keep a good story quiet. Or a good reporter away from it." He winked oafishly at the detective.

"Listen, Eliot, the smartest thing you can do is to keep quiet about this. There's nothing worth talking about." Joe had his hand on the door. "Why are you staying?"

"Maybe someone in there'll change their mind—like the chief, or Mrs. Andrus, or Mr. Andrus. Mind if I wait?"

"I can't stop you. But stay some distance from the house, will you? The family is upset—they shouldn't be, because there's nothing to be upset about—and you might make it worse for them."

"Oh. Then the Andrus child, little Amy, that is, is still missing?"

Joe took his hand from the wrought-iron door fixture. "I didn't say that. Where'd you hear that nonsense?"

"I guess you didn't say it. See, that's what I mean. If you'd level with me, tell me what's going on, I could help."

"No. Nothing doing."

Eliot blew warm breath through his blunt lips. "Hot. It's tough just getting up, let alone putting in a day's work. I been up since yesterday afternoon—overnight man."

"Go home and get some sleep. Eliot, I don't like to be a book cop, especially with reporters. I asked you nicely to beat it. Don't push me." McFeeley entered the house. Once again, Eliot caught the interior—a huge, sparsely furnished room; a pretty, slender woman; several men.

From inside, McFeeley peeked through the kitchen blinds. He saw Eliot cross the lawn and walk toward the orange Emerson home.

Sparling was by no means discouraged. At the age of twenty-eight, he was convinced that the only good thing that had ever happened in his life was his job at United Broadcasting. Everything up to then had been rather miserable: an impoverished Bronx boyhood; the torments of being oversized, clumsy, cowardly and intelligent; two grinding years at the City College of New York; listening evenings to his father's whining complaints about the chain pharmacies' stealing his customers; four years of drudgery in Army Ordnance; a government-paid resumption of his education at the University of California in Los Angeles; a half year of feverish unemployment; and then three years of the overnight on the *Los Angeles Truth*. Then had come UBC and Ballstead. He could not fail them. He would die, be brave, fight back (something he had never done), before he would let United down. If there were a story at the Andrus house, 4217 Nespoli Drive, he would nose it down. UBC deserved nothing less.

He rang the Emerson bell. Hearing no sound, Eliot assumed correctly that it was out of order. He rapped the peeling frame of the rusted screen door. In a few seconds Mrs. Emerson appeared. She opened the door halfway, glancing nervously toward the Andrus house.

"Hiya, Mrs. Emerson—Babe. It's me—Eliot Sparling. You know, from UBC."

Curiosity and guilt fought for control of her haggard face. "I told you not to let on you knew me. What did you find out?"

"I wouldn't tell a soul you tipped me."

"What is it? What's happening?" Babe was whispering—anxious to dissociate herself from the caller, but not before learning something from him.

"The detective wouldn't tell me anything. There's at least three cops there, maybe four."

"One's Mr. Andrus. Fritzie. They're separated. Did I tell you that?"

"Yes. Listen—you can give me some more dope." Eliot whipped out his copy paper. "How about the little girl—how old is she? What does she look like? Maybe you've got a photo—something you took with your own kids?"

"I can't tell you anything." She pressed a hand to the side of her head. "God, why did I start with you?"

Dr. Todd joined McFeeley at the window. They could see Sparling lingering at the Emerson door, the woman acting as if she wanted to get rid of him. Joe turned to Laura. "Mrs. Andrus, I wish you'd go out and talk to that guy."

"Why?" she asked. "I don't think Babe knows anything. I've lied to her once already—about Amy being found. I don't think she believed me. Why must I compound it?"

"He won't quit," McFeeley said. "An appeal from you might move him." He spoke to Rheinholdt. "That sound all right, Chief?"

"Huh?" Rheinholdt raised his head.

"To stall that reporter. He got a tip somewhere. I want Mrs. Andrus to con him. Say the child's at the beach. Then I think we'd better set up a newspaper policy. They're going to be on our neck soon."

"No. Nothing to the newspapers. They don't get a word."

Fritzie, leaning against the stove, agitating his bourbon in small circular motions, spoke with disgust. "We are in the hands of the Keystone Kops, Laura. That's the sad fact."

For a moment, all appeared frozen, divested of will and purpose. The baby's polite whimper, emanating from the nursery, came as a relief—a soft noise that brought them back to easier problems.

"She must be wet again," Laura said. "Poor thing's been stuck in the crib all morning."

McFeeley walked from the window. "I'll do it. You go out and tell that reporter a few lies."

"Really, Lieutenant."

Joe was moving toward the nursery. "It's no sweat, Mrs. Andrus. I have four of my own. I know the procedure. Go on. Go outside and talk to him. His name's Sparling."

The mission, in Laura's eyes, appeared pointless. Then, hearing Karen's wails terminate after the detective had entered the nursery, she realized, without resentment, that McFeeley had tricked her. Yes, he was a City Hall schemer, a dealer in trades and favors: *you talk to the guy, I'll change the diaper.*

She walked out of the house, toward Babe and the young man, hearing her neighbor's embarrassed *sotto voce* advisory: "There she is." The reporter, pivoting, smiled flabbily at her.

"Mrs. Andrus? I'm Eliot Sparling, UBC. Channel Eight. Always Great."

"What do you want?"

"We want to help. Our office got a tip that your child was lost, and we thought we'd offer our network facil——"

"That's not so. My daughter was found." She paused, then resumed rapidly, knowing that she could never lie well. "She's at the beach. With my maid."

"Am I glad to hear that!" Sparling bellowed. "That's just marvelous, Mrs. Andrus! What beach?"

"Santa Monica. Will you leave now?"

Sparling did not budge. He remained on the Emerson walk, feet glued to the cement. Laura found herself hating him—gross, loud, masking his triviality with protestations of public service. She darted an angry look at Babe, as if associating her with the caller.

"I haven't told him a single solitary thing, Laura. I've been trying to get *rid* of him." Babe sounded faintly hysterical.

"I hate to keep pestering you, Mrs. Andrus," the young man persisted, "but may I inquire why Chief Rheinholdt and those other officers are at your house?"

Laura turned her back on him. "It doesn't concern you." She started walking away. Eliot followed.

"Nothing to do with Amy?"

"How did you learn my daughter's name?"

"I asked around."

Babe Emerson, her homely face contorted, cried after Laura: "I didn't tell him anything, Laura!"

Laura bit her words off. "Get away from here. My daughter's at the beach. There's nothing mysterious going on."

"She be home soon?"

"That's none of your business! Go away!"

The young man halted. He found the revulsion in the woman's hard eyes. Momentarily it shamed him, overcoming his dedication. "Whatever you say, Mrs. Andrus. I'm just doing my job as a newsman. As I said, our network wants to help."

"I don't want your help. I don't want you loitering here."

Sparling plodded away, his feet raising cloudlets of dust on the parched frontage. The woman watched him go, knowing that he had believed nothing, that she had not discouraged him.

"Laura!" Babe called. "Believe me, Laura, I didn't say a word!"

"It's all right, Babe," she said. She walked quickly to the door. The hot morning was an iron strait jacket, each minute hard, suffocating, impersonal.

Rheinholdt was leaving. McFeeley had persuaded him that his continued presence might harm their efforts at secrecy. It was 12:15. With luck, they might yet keep the press ignorant, or better yet secure an agreement from them.

"We can do this two ways," McFeeley explained. "We can start calling the papers, the radio stations, and level with them, ask them to lay off. I think they'll agree. Or we can play it by ear and hope they won't learn anything."

Rheinholdt clamped his floppy panama over his head. Under the uneven yellow brim, his broad face pouted. "I wouldn't tell those lice anything They'll print it, Broadcast it. Spit in my eye. Nobody knows what's happened here."

"That kid from United does," Joe said.

"We got rid of him, didn't we?"

Laura joined them. "I don't think he believed me."

"I'm worried, Chief," McFeeley said. "That guy won't drop it. It'll spread. If we start calling them, tell them it's a kidnaping, that there's a drop tonight—they'll agree to withhold it. Otherwise, they'll be on our backs."

Rheinholdt blinked. "No."

"Why?" Joe asked.

"Because no lousy newspaper will run my department," Rheinholdt said.

"That's not what I want, Chief," the detective said earnestly. "We don't have to tell them much—just that it is a snatch and they have to honor our request. It's been done before."

The chief tugged at the brim. "Listen, McFeeley, I can see those slobs jump all over it. They been waiting to hang me for years. They'd print it just to make me look bad. Sure, if I was the kind of chief who had picnics for the reporters, who made speeches on the television and who kissed their feet and fed them stories, they'd do me a favor. But they know me. And I know *them*. Nothing on this goes out."

McFeeley looked appealingly at Todd. The dentist's sure grasp of events had cast him as a kind of mediator, an advisor to the party. His round, hairless face was as assuring as a mutual fund.

"What do you think, Dr. Todd?" McFeeley asked.

The dentist danced across the room. "Lieutenant, you have a good point. On the other hand, I can understand the chief's hesitancy. I'd suggest this." He folded his arms and his small hands fluttered against his elbows. "Let's wait an hour. If there are no further indications that the press knows of our secret, let's assume we've been successful in keeping it secret. On the other hand, if the papers begin to call—let's follow Lieutenant McFeeley's plan. We'll tell them the truth and request withholding."

McFeeley shook his head very slowly. "We're looking for trouble. That Sparling knows too much already. I know how those reporters work. He'll keep asking until the word spreads, and then we'll have the whole LA press club out here."

"One hour can't hurt," Todd said.

Rheinholdt made no further comment. He left the matter of informing the newspaper unsettled and walked outside with McFeeley.

"Chief, I want to set up a tape recorder here, with a tap on the phone. We also have to run a special line into the house—in case the kid isn't returned tonight." McFeeley indicated the plastic envelope in Rheinholdt's pocket. "Crime lab ought to give us a run-down on that note."

Across the street, Eliot Sparling came clopping back to his car. He had just returned from the telephone booth at the corner, where he had reported to an irate Ballstead. The news director was emphatic: *stay with it; don't leave.*

"Look who's back," McFeeley said.

Rheinholdt beheld the ancient enemy—the glib adversary of his old traffic days. The enemy had come back, intruding on his ordeal. The chief's eyes were nailed to Sparling's unwieldy figure. McFeeley realized his superior had heard nothing he had said; he would have to call headquarters and relay everything to the lab chief, the communications desk. His mind swarmed with things to be done, precautions to be taken. *Thirteen-state alarm* popped into his head. Looking at Rheinholdt's bemused face, more concerned with the newsman than with the investigation, McFeeley experienced a draining sense of inadequacy. Perhaps the FBI should have been called—the state police. But he knew Rheinholdt would never—unless everything caved in, unless Mayor Speed demanded it—countenance their intrusion.

Rheinholdt moved off. At the curb, Sergeant Baines hopped out of the car and held the door open. Then, to Joe's horror, the reporter, who had stopped at his own parked car and opened the trunk rack, started across the street to intercept Rheinholdt. The young man lugged a portable tape recorder and was brandishing a pencil microphone.

"Good afternoon, Chief!" he cried exuberantly. "How are you today?"

Rheinholdt stopped a yard from Eliot, staring at him as if he were a diseased dog, then continued toward his car. Sparling flopped alongside, pointing the mike at him, shivering the desert air with his huge voice.

"Now about this Andrus case, Chief, do you have any comment? Anything at all, sir? There's a rumor around that Amy Andrus is missing, and my boss, Mr. Ballstead at UBC, asked if we could help. He just won't take no for an answer, and I'm under strict orders to stay here until someone talks to us. Mr. Ballstead feels that unless the police talk, it'll be worse for everyone concerned. Now, sir, might I have the Santa Luisa Police Department's official view of this case?"

Sparling's mad oration had come at Rheinholdt like a flight of hornets—painful, hateful, senselessly torturing him.

"How about it?" Eliot shouted. "Any comment at all?"

"Beat it, pimp," Rheinholdt said.

"I can understand your displeasure with me, sir," Eliot said. "But our personal sentiments about each other have no bearing on this case. You're suppressing a news story."

"Get away from the car," said Rheinholdt. The newsman had moved his body between the door and the chief's oncoming figure.

"Now just what is happening here?" yelled Sparling. "What gives, Chief? You'll have to tell us. The sooner, the better."

The chauffeur shoved Eliot gently. "The chief said beat it. Now don't get me sore. Go on in, Chief." The Farmer's creased face was emotionless: Eliot was one more pest.

Sparling's eyebrows arched; his nose incandesced. Groggy with fatigue, fearful that he was in over his head, eager to help UBC, he essayed one last assault. "Very well, Mr. Rheinholdt, if that's how you feel. Mr. Ballstead said it would be *your* funeral if you don't inform us. He said he'd see to it personally that you were made to blame for withholding facts to which the American public is entitled. He'll do it, too. Mr. Ballstead said——"

Rheinholdt had not struck a man since that awful day when he had dropped McCabe for interrogating the arsonist. Now—as then —the action was a reflex, swift, savage, direct. He slapped Eliot across one cheek, then, with the reverse of his hand, knuckles and fingers, slapped him again on the recovery. McFeeley, standing in front of the Andrus house, heard the *crack-crack*—delivered with a beat intervening.

And what of Eliot? The newsman was of that breed of oversized, unathletic men who are instinctive physical cowards. He could not fight; he hated violence. Sparling had spent his youth as a target of younger, wiry, stronger boys who gave him his lumps with a malice and savagery he had never forgotten. (Once his adversary was a skinny Negro who pummeled him around the schoolyard while his dark confederates cheered him on: *yah, yah, yah, kick him in deh haid! He jes' a big sheeeet!*) Fortified behind his heft, he spent his young manhood in dread of any recurrence of those old humiliations. In a vague way, Eliot blamed his father for the drubbings he took. The elder Sparling, a pharmacist with access to free samples, had stuffed his only son with vitamins and health-builders since infancy. Cod-liver oil drops, poly-vi-sols, theptines, riboflavins, niacins, thiamine chlorides, and a dozen other alphabetical health-givers had been crammed down Eliot's maw from his first bottle of formula well into his City College days. As a result, the younger Sparling contended, his frail frame and musculature (both parents were little people) had been arbitrarily enlarged. There simply wasn't enough muscle and bone to support all that flesh, Eliot argued, and he had emerged, tallowy and outsized, like a cortisone-fed hog. The bigger he got, the more cuffs and insults he took. *The horrors of the schoolyard! The old fears!* These, not the substantive present, were what agitated the newsman when Chief Rheinholdt slapped him.

"What was that for?" Sparling stammered. He touched his ruby cheeks. Hot salty tears brimmed in his eyes. Sergeant Baines hustled Rheinholdt toward the car. "Come on, Chief, to hell with him," he said.

"For being a lousy reporter pimp," Rheinholdt said.

The incident assumed its proper perspective in Eliot's mind. Sparling viewed it in terms of the *block,* the candy store, the poolroom. Eliot, heir to the gutter tradition of the Bronx, would make the old rube understand *that.* He stepped back, a mound of false dignity.

"You don't own the street," Sparling said. "I'll stay here all I want."

"Huh?" Rheinholdt gasped. "What'll you do?"

"You heard me. I'm gonna stay here all day. And all night. I'll hang around until I learn what's going on in that house." His calmness delighted him. The tears had retreated. "And don't lay a hand on me again, Rheinholdt. It'll be your ass."

The chief tugged at his panama. Second thoughts agitated his mind. Was he living it all over? Dropping McCabe to the floor with one stiff right? "Go on. Get outa here," the chief muttered.

"I will not. Not till I find out what you're hiding. I don't mind you belting me. You'll find out what it means to strike a working newspaperman. But what really burns me is that you're withholding information which the American public is entitled to. You're being un-American."

The sun burned a hole through Rheinholdt's hat, addling his anguished brain. With one wooden arm, he shoved Eliot into the car. The young man hit the seat like a sack of cabbages.

"What's the idea?" cried Sparling. "I can stay here."

"You're under arrest," said the chief.

"What for?" Eliot sought for the edge of steel in his voice, but all that came forth was a wail. "What did I do?"

Rheinholdt lifted himself into the rear seat and pushed Eliot into the opposite corner. He ordered Baines to drive off.

"I have a right to know why I'm being arrested!" shouted Eliot. "You're covering something up! Don't think you can get away with it! The American press has a right——"

Rheinholdt was not listening. He hawked an oyster out the window and settled back. Frightened and confused a few minutes earlier, he now was admirably calm. The kidnaping of Amy Andrus no longer strangled him; he had responded to the crisis by arresting a busybody. All of McFeeley's warnings about the maintenance of secrecy, all of the detective's plans had vanished from his clouded head.

Sparling, in turn, was rather pleased with himself. He had stood up manfully to the old bum, and now he would be a hero— a reporter manhandled, threatened, punched by the police! The desert heat rushed through the window and, thus lulled, Eliot half dozed.

McFeeley, witnessing the incident, realized there would be no stopping them now. Sparling's superiors would start asking about him. Other reporters at Sanlu headquarters would get wind of the arrest. As soon as word got out that the chief had been driven to hit a reporter, they would assume he was sitting on something big. McFeeley felt impelled to start calling the newspapers himself. *They would have to be told. A life was at stake, a child's life— please don't print or broadcast anything.* Secrecy would only make them hungrier, more relentless in their probing, more adamant that they be informed. But Joe knew he dared not cross Rheinholdt. He had pushed him all morning, and while the chief appreciated McFeeley's skills, he did not tolerate insubordination. Suddenly it occurred to McFeeley—who would do the calling, if Rheinholdt gave the green light? Rheinholdt did not have a press secretary. Whoever was on the desk filled the job. Sometimes Farmer Baines was enlisted to issue statements, sometimes Patrolman Clyde Hertmann. He halted his musings, beset with a sense of too-much-to-do-in-too-little-time, hiding the turmoil inside him with a bland, half-sad expression. Dr. Todd was on the telephone, talking to his banker friend.

"That is right, George," Todd was saying, "from my custodial account, the cash balance. Forty-two hundred in fifties. Doesn't matter whether they're old or new bills. Mix 'em, I suppose. Now you'll have to take my word, George; there is nothing untoward about this. A personal, a highly personal, matter. Right. And George, as an old golf partner, may I ask that you handle this yourself and talk to no one? I'll explain it to you—later. I'll see you at 3:45 at the bank."

The dentist spun from the phone. "Done."

"You'll go pick up the cash yourself?" McFeeley asked.

"Yes. Mr. Deckler wanted to send it over with a bonded messenger, but I felt the less people involved, the better."

McFeeley walked over to Irvin Moll, seated at the desk in the den, his steno book open. Irv seemed helpless, as inadequate as Rheinholdt, more pathetic. The chief had confronted the crime with ignorant fortitude. Refusing to admit its existence, he retreated into a film of stupidity. Moll wanted desperately to help— perhaps to make amends for all the loot he had taken, all the twenty-dollar bills in matchbooks, all the free gasoline, the cases of booze, the frozen steaks.

"Irv, get Raffalovitch at the lab," Joe said. "Tell him we want to dust some bills. Any reagent that'll last a long time. I think we can get going on an interior crime search. Prints, dust, traces—all inside stuff, so no one'll get curious. Tell Raffalovitch to park a few houses away—and to come in his own car." He turned to Laura. "Any objection if we do a little work in the house, Mrs. Andrus?"

"No. Whatever you think is right."

"It'll throw things out of whack, but we'd better start right away. There'll be no one in uniform around. No one walking around the grounds." He went back to Moll. "Ask the lab to rush that note through. Any latent prints, whatever they can give us on the paper, the words he clipped out of the papers. You make a copy of the text for us?"

Moll waved it at him. He had pecked it out on Fritzie's upright. McFeeley continued. "Get the tape recorder out here. We'll rig it to the phone and record everything. We ought to set up in a different room—this is sort of in the middle of everything. Mrs. Andrus, where can we set up a headquarters?"

"We have only three bedrooms. Amy's room, I guess."

"I'd rather not disturb anything there. We still aren't certain where she was picked up. There's a chance there might be some prints."

"I could move Karen into my bedroom. You could use the nursery."

"That's better. I want to run an extra phone in."

"In case Amy isn't returned tonight?"

McFeeley nodded. "There's no guarantee of anything on a deal like this. You may leave the ransom, it may be picked up, and he may decide he wants to wait—return her at a different time or place. And I have to warn you—it'll be that much tougher if any word gets out that the police are on it, that the papers know. If that happens, and he's scared off, we'll have to give him every chance in the world to reach *us*."

"I understand."

"If it'll make you feel any better, you'll never be alone. We'll assign two men to stick with you all the time—if you leave the house, they go with you."

"You mean—I might have to go out and meet him?"

"It's possible. The main thing is, if we miss tonight, we've got to give him every opportunity."

McFeeley wandered off to the vanished child's bedroom. He stood in the hall light of the corridor, surveying the interior. The blinds were still drawn, the bed unmade. A giant Pinocchio doll, with loops on its hands and feet, so that a child could dance with it, sprawled on the floor. There was a complete set of child-sized maple furniture—a dresser with mirror, a table, two chairs. On a long desk, built into the window wall, rested a bright clutter of coloring books, crayons, colored pencils, pots of glue, rolls of cellophane tape. A child's vivid painting of a blue swimming pool swarming with misshapen children was tacked to a cork bulletin board on one wall. In a white bookcase, a parliament of dolls, rabbits, bears and ducks gazed across the room to the maple dresser, littered with beauty-parlor junk—perfumes, lipsticks, rouges, hair curlers.

McFeeley entered, lifting the blind gently and studying the copper screens. They were stout, permanently locked from the inside. Any attempt to force them from without would have been extremely difficult—especially for an amateur. He was convinced that the intruder had simply plucked Amy from the grounds—someone who had cased the street, knew of her habit of wandering about. He had opened his car door, offered some bribe, some promise, and driven off without a trace—not a fingerprint, not a footprint, no sign of struggle—just the note. He returned to the living room, hearing the woman say: "I'd better make some lunch for us."

"You don't have to feed us," Moll protested. "I'll go out for sandwiches. Right, Joe?"

"Sure. The department'll spring for lunch." Saying it, he regretted it. The notion invested the ordeal with a picnic quality. Mrs. Andrus was putting on a blue apron and opening the refrigerator.

"I don't mind," she said. "I have to do something. I feel useless."

She removed a carton of eggs from the refrigerator. An intense recollection of her father's death made her shiver. After three days of agony, he had died of coronary occulsion in their shabby summer cottage in Wellfleet, on the Cape. He had been a professor of sociology, a disciple of Francis Ward, a soft-voiced, good-tempered man, the kind one never associated with heart trouble. She could recall his final gasping moments in the sea-misted room— and then her mother's thin voice, some minutes later, announcing calmly: *The table is all set. We might as well have dinner.* The trivia of life, she kept telling herself, the infinite details—all these aided in the maintenance of sanity.

Laura began to break eggs in the mixing bowl. *Amy would be playing in the back or coming in to steal a cracker.* McFeeley sat on a leather stool and opened his pad on the red breakfast bar.

"Can I pump you a little more?" he asked.

"Yes. Go ahead." She looked up. "Officer—would you mind asking Mr. Andrus if he'd like to help me? He enjoys fooling around the kitchen. I think he wandered outside a few minutes ago."

McFeeley slipped off the stool. He did not mind running errands. He sensed he did not have her confidence yet.

The detective walked out the sliding doors. The rear of the plot had been devoured by the swimming pool and its attendant fence, cement walks and patios, the huge shedded filter. No grass remained in the pool area—not a tree to offer protection from the sun. The detective knew it was typical of the neighborhood—yards of useless frontage (decreed by the Sanlu zoning laws) adorned with palms and cacti, and not a blade of grass in the rear. He walked parallel to the pool, passing the rock garden, the empty log cabin, the scuffed panda stuck in the hot sand. As he turned the southeast corner of the house, he saw Andrus. For a moment, the detective thought that the man was practicing golf shots, and he halted—as if reluctant to witness the mad indifference. Fritzie had a number two iron in his right hand and was striking it against the low hedges bordering the house.

"She has *not* been kidnaped," Andrus announced. His voice was calm; he was dry-eyed. "She is playin' some joke on us. She's here. In the neighborhood, around. I'll find her without you Keystone Kops. I'll find her." He resumed poking at the ilex and ailanthus, swinging his chunky arms.

"You may be right at that," McFeeley said. "I hope so. Would you mind joining us inside? I'd like to talk to you some more."

Andrus turned his back to him. With his golf club, he began poking in crates piled outside the garage. "When I'm good and ready, officer," he said. "Not before."

He wandered into the garage. He opened the door of the red station wagon, peering inside, moving as if propelled by some off-stage hypnotist. McFeeley had seen him drinking—but surely not enough to intoxicate him, to plunge him into a trance. Watching him meander about the garage, peeking into trash bins, running the club along paint shelves, the detective understood that Andrus was acting out what all of them *felt*. His capacity for shock had been violated; he refused to believe. Like Rheinholdt, he would deny the crime, spin his own web of fantasy, avoid the horrid facts. Disbelief was the common enemy; McFeeley knew that the web of fiction would get thicker and more confusing when the press descended. The crime had to be invested with reality; it could not become a three-act play produced, directed and written by reporters and radio and TV people. Burdened, fretful, wondering whether he was man enough to handle the job, he left Andrus (now on hands and knees and looking beneath the automobile) and returned to the house.

In the course of the morning, several reporters had dropped by Santa Luisa headquarters but were told nothing about the Andrus affair. They were given the usual summation of arrests, drunks, traffic accidents, but nothing was said about the missing child. Nor did anyone mention Rheinholdt's prolonged absence. The reporters were mostly district men, assigned to cover Santa Luisa for Los Angeles papers, and they were aware of Sanlu's aridness as a source of crime stories. Moreover, they saw the chief so rarely that his absence was not noticed.

One newsman had seen Rheinholdt rush from his office that morning, but he suspected nothing, assuming that the chief was off on an inspection of traffic control—the one department he understood.

The reporter was Harvey Swinnerton, the Santa Luisa correspondent for the *Los Angeles Truth,* who, earlier that morning, had weathered the chief's insults because of the newspaper editorial. Now, shortly before 12:30 P.M., Swinnerton, having made some routine calls around town—the sewer commission, the Chamber of Commerce, the high school—had returned to the area of the police station for lunch. He was seated on a stool in the adjacent Jumbo-burger Drive-in, sipping hot tea and nibbling a cheese sandwich. His post afforded him a view of the rear entrance to the station and the parking area that Chief Rheinholdt had declared off limits to the press. Swinnerton planned to finish his lunch, call at the police desk, then phone the *Truth* with a few pieces.

He was a rare bird among California newsmen, Swinnerton. Nursing his tea, conversing politely with the high-rumped waitress, he seemed anything but a journalist. Indifferent to the withering heat, he wore a suit of rumpled brown tweeds. The gum soles on his scuffed bluchers were an inch thick. Swinnerton was short, spare and very fair. His concave, refined face suggested Albrecht Dürer's heroic bronze of King Arthur in the Innsbruck Hofkirche—a decent Anglo-Saxon gentleman surrounded by monstrous Hapsburgs and their hideous women. The reporter's eyes were a Siamese-cat blue, but without feline cupidity. His dented nose, his thin lips—all sought retreat in the nicely shaped skull. His fulvous hair was parted in the middle, and the total effect was one of inconsequence —except for a thick guard's mustache hinting at good breeding.

Swinnerton was one of those impoverished drifters on the fringes of American journalism, about whom there arises legend. It was rumored in city rooms that he was the scion of old San Francisco money, the beneficiary of a Harvard education. Swinnerton himself was uncommunicative about his background. He had little capacity for small talk, no friends, did not drink, and was neuter sexually. Like a spinal cat or a decorticated dog, he went through the motions of living, content with the pittance the *Truth* paid him as their Sanlu district man, some earnings from the Santa Luisa radio outlet for a weekly feature roundup, and occasional alms for publicity handouts for local industries. He was well liked and respected. Most Los Angeles newsmen regarded him with not a little pity—a good man fallen on bad days. Were it not, they imagined, for some scandal, Harvey would probably be sitting in a suite of rooms on Nob Hill sipping tea from Rosenthal china.

"The tea hot enough, Mr. Swinnerton?" the waitress at the Jumboburger asked. "I could getcha some more hot water."

"You're too kind, Margaret," the reporter said. His voice was almost inaudible. It had trouble working its way through the hayrick mustache. "But I've really had quite enough."

He paid his check and started across the asphalt no man's land that separated the drive-in from the police station. In accord with Rheinholdt's order, he had parked his battered Austin at the curb. Swinnerton paused at the car to get his notebook and a pack of tissues (he had chronic sniffles, complete with postnasal drip and rheumy eyes); then he saw Rheinholdt's car careen down the street and screech into the parking lot, Farmer Baines slamming it into the yellow-bordered slot labeled "Chief."

Swinnerton, curious, walked toward the lot. The doors of Rheinholdt's car flew open. Baines got out first, ushering his superior. To Swinnerton's surprise, the chief was handcuffed to a prisoner— a circumstance so outlandish that the reporter quickened his pace. Rheinholdt was dragging the man up the stairs to the door of the county jail. He poked a huge finger in the buzzer and awaited a response. As Swinnerton drew closer, the prisoner, a young man with a crew cut, turned his head. At once, the two newsmen recognized each other. Eliot, a recent alumnus of the *Truth,* had met Swinnerton at least half a dozen times. To Sparling, the sight of Swinnerton's tweedy figure was as inspirational as any sighting of the godhead.

"Swinnerton!" he shouted. "It's me! Eliot Sparling! I'm under arrest!"

"Shut up!" Rheinholdt growled. He yanked the chain; Eliot landed on him. The door unopened, Rheinholdt fetched a ring of keys from his coat pocket and jammed one into the lock.

"Swinnerton!" Sparling yelled. "Call Tom Ballstead at UBC— tell him I'm in jail! Rheinholdt's covering something—there's a kid missing——"

The gates of hell had opened; Sparling, his voice shattering the air, was shoved in. The steel door slammed shut. Swinnerton, twenty feet from the incredible tableau, remained immobile for a moment. In twenty years of fringe work in journalism, a good deal of enterprise had been leached out of Harvey Swinnerton. His rewards had been marginal, his career trivial. Yet he was not unintelligent, and he was not without the curiosity of a good reporter. And the circumstances were intriguing—a reporter jailed, a child missing. Softly, on gum-soled bluchers, he strolled to the chief's automobile. He guessed that Rheinholdt, a slave to paper work, would never have left his castle without a trip ticket. The district man leaned through the front right-hand window and opened the glove compartment. From it, he extracted a yellow slip of paper and quickly read the entry, "10:22—4217 Nespoli Drive." Casually, he flipped the compartment closed and walked to the Jumboburger's telephone booth. He stroked his mustache, ruminating. He would phone the *Truth* at once, seek guidance. As for Sparling's appeal to call Tom Ballstead—he was not certain.

Dr. Todd, shading his eyes, perched on the edge of Fritzie's desk, surveyed Nespoli Drive. "So far so good," he said cheerfully. "Perhaps the chief did the right thing arresting that chap. Of course, I didn't like the idea of his getting slapped."

McFeeley said nothing. A half hour had elapsed since Sparling had been hustled off to jail. The detective was finding it harder to blame Rheinholdt. The only issue was the child's safety, her survival. Everything else—the press, the police, the public—was secondary. McFeeley would settle for a hundred Eliot Sparlings belted across the face, a thousand rights of the press canceled, a million newspaper readers left ignorant—if Amy Andrus were returned that night.

Joe was reading a nursery school application for the child. The mother had given it to him when he had asked for a description. The child was scheduled to re-enter Sunny Sky Nursery School (she had quit that summer, complaining of "messy" lunches) in a week, and the information had been entered on a large yellow card. There was even a passport-size photograph. Amy squinted at him—a wary elf, her dark hair growing in an uneven diagonal across her brow.

McFeeley copied the information into his steno book. *Height . . . 39 inches; weight . . . 34 pounds; hair . . . dark brown; eyes . . . dark brown; childhood diseases . . . measles, chicken pox, mumps; inoculations . . . polio, smallpox, three-in-one; marks . . . scar on left knee. . . .*

The vanished child took shape and form as he copied the entries. A moral man, who believed that marriage was a sacrament as well as a stable social institution, he sensed an impatience with the unbending proud woman, the outrageously conceited man. He halted his musings: that was none of his Irish business.

In the nursery—the baby's crib had been moved into the master bedroom—he could hear the department's communications chief, Harris, and a man from the phone company at work. The tape recorder was going in; a private number was being installed. Joe had decided on getting the gear in at once. Andrus had protested that it would attract attention, but McFeeley had insisted. It was interior work. More importantly, if the drop did not come off, if the exchange, *money for child,* did not materialize, they would be at the kidnaper's mercy.

The brief check of the house and grounds that he and Moll had made had revealed nothing. There were no footprints, no signs of disturbance, no forcing. Amy had been taken, or enticed, outside. For all they knew, the kidnaper had not even gotten out of his car. *Car*. They would have to search for tire marks, and they would have to do it quickly, before the day's traffic obscured traces. Moll, completing his fourth aimless tour of the house, loomed in the hallway. "Nothing, Joe. Nothing in or out. On the driveway, the path. The guy was like a ghost."

"Better get some camera gear," McFeeley said. "We ought to look for tire marks—then check 'em against neighborhood cars."

Andrus was stretched out on the sofa. "Place'll be swarmin' with cops. I thought you were going to keep everyone away until after tonight."

"I was, but I changed my mind."

Laura had set a pot of coffee and cups on the mosaic table. She invited McFeeley to join them.

Harris, the communications chief, and the man from the phone company came into the room. "All set, Joe," Harris said. "The two phones are on the table. Both are rigged to the recorder. Soon's you lift the receiver, the tape rolls. If you don't want to record, just throw the switch. I left you three rolls of tape on the table."

When they had gone, Fritzie sat upright. "Great. Just great. Now the whole General Telephone Company of Southern California will know. We sure got lots of secrecy." A lot of his belligerency had evaporated. His voice sounded frailer and his Tarheel accents were minimal. "Why you had to run to the police," he whined; "Laura, you and me—just the two of us—we should have gone through with it."

"Mrs. Andrus did the right thing," McFeeley said.

Todd walked over from the window and helped himself to coffee. "Laura did the *only* thing. The police must be notified in these cases. Why, in England and Canada, it's illegal to even *pay* a ransom. Once there's a kidnaping, all bank funds and assets are impounded. Result—no kidnapings in those countries."

"We don't need no geography lesson," Andrus muttered. Then, noting Todd's innocent face, he tried to apologize. "Forgive me. All of you." He held his head in his hands. "I suppose I'm not quite equal to this sort of thing. Really, I'm trying to be helpful."

Almost imperceptibly, Laura seemed to move toward him. They were sitting opposite each other at the coffee table, and McFeeley caught the forward motion of her head, the straining of her shoulders.

"Mrs. Andrus, is Amy a healthy child—normal?" Joe asked.

"Yes. She gets a lot of colds, but she's supposed to have her tonsils out when the weather turns cooler."

The detective searched his limited vocabulary for diplomatic words. "Is she of—of average intelligence?"

"What—what are you talkin' about?" Andrus cried. "Average? She's brilliant. She's smarter than most of you cops!"

"I mean, she has no physical or mental ailments that might help us locate her?"

Laura frowned. "I'm not sure I know what you mean."

"If she needed a special kind of medicine, for example, or certain care. We could get word to the kidnaper about it, and it might help in tracking him down. He might go to a drugstore to buy the medicine, and we'd alert pharmacists. It's been done before—with babies who need a certain formula, or drops, or vitamins. The information is printed in the paper."

"I thought we were leaving the papers out," Laura said.

McFeeley leaned back. "We may need them later."

Andrus was circling the room, swinging his arms in short arcs. "I believe I see what he's after, Laura. He's a shrewd one, that McFeeley. Physical or *mental* ailments. Note the word mental."

"What are you getting at, Fritzie?" Laura asked. Andrus halted. They all awaited some judgment from him—McFeeley, Dr. Todd, Moll.

"Yes. *Mental* deficiencies. A quiet hint, officer, that perhaps the parents had something to do with the child's disappearance? Correct, officer? Isn't that a line of police theorizing in kidnapings?"

Laura gasped. "Fritzie—how can you speak about anything so dreadful?"

"I didn't bring it up," Andrus said. "*He* did."

An ashamed silence settled over the group. The rock of truth beneath Andrus' accusation disturbed them. There had been a previous case in California, some years ago—a child vanished, a presumed kidnaping, and a lingering suspicion when it was learned the child was an epileptic. It had been marked unsolved.

McFeeley's face lengthened, the crooked nose drooped. "I don't care what you think or what you feel about me. Or what Mr. Andrus reads into my questions. If your daughter isn't returned tonight, you'll have no privacy any more. Not just the newspapers, but cranks, tipsters, madmen. Yes—and us. We'll have to know everything about you, even if it hurts. I'm not paid to worry about hurting people's feelings."

"Even to the extent that we may be suspected of killing our child?" Fritzie cried.

"Good heavens, Francis!" Todd shouted. "You must stop that!"

Laura shook her head. He was dramatizing again, adding a twist of plot, a change in characterization, experimenting for an obligatory scene—and yet there seemed some basis to his histrionics. Laura rested her forehead on one hand. The migraine's torture had lightened; now she suffered the sickening aftermath—a persistent low throb, an aching of limbs, a dryness in her mouth.

"There's nothing wrong with Amy," Laura said impatiently. "She's invented an imaginary girl friend she calls Cally Horner, but that's normal in children. I think she has it all mixed up with California."

"That ain't what he was after," Fritzie said. "Probably dyin' to hear she couldn't talk, or was low I.Q. Damned insinuations."

Dr. Todd strolled back to the den window, glancing at the desk clock: it was 1:15. In two and a half hours he was scheduled to meet his banker friend and pick up the ransom money. He studied the street, pleased with its silence, the absence of curious people, of police, of reporters. Like McFeeley, he was beginning to think better of Rheinholdt's severe action. Then, to his surprise, a green station wagon, its door bearing the gold legend "UBC," roared into the driveway and came to a shuddering halt in back of Todd's black Buick. The intrusive noise brought Andrus and McFeeley to the window. There were three men in the car, two in front, one sitting in the rear, surrounded by a pile of camera gear—cases, tripods, cartons.

The man at the wheel got out. He was stumpy and hairy and wore a striped T shirt. Under a bushy gray crop, his face was bunched around a cigar the size of a souvenir baseball bat. Around his neck dangled an exposure meter; he cradled in his hands a 16-millimeter movie camera. He directed his meter at the house, then adjusted a lens, pointed the camera at the Andrus' front door and began taking motion pictures. A faint buzzing noise filtered through the open window; to the observers it sounded like a fissure opening in the earth.

Laura and Moll joined the others. All five looked gravely at the callers in the green car. The other two men, middle-aged fellows

with the bored mien of technicians, began unloading equipment—
a tripod, three battered cases, a coil of cable.

"Hah!" Fritzie mocked. "Y'all gonna arrest *them* also?"

The cameraman flipped a lens, rewound rapidly, and, shifting his
stance, directed his lens at the white address sign on the lawn
and its wrought-iron numbers: 4217. He resumed shooting.

McFeeley frowned, trying to put his vexed mind in order. Andrus
had posed a good question. He wished he had an answer for him.

The United Broadcasting cameraman who had been assigned to
the Andrus case was named Steve Billik. He was a sour, wealthy
hang-over from Theatre Newsreels, union-protected, longing for
the lost glories of his youth—*the elephant on water skis, the At-
lantic City baby parade, the waiters' race.* He did not know Eliot
Sparling, and, when, after an hour of waiting one block from the
Santa Luisa police station, he heard nothing on his air call, he
telephoned Jim Farrell. Billik assumed there was no story; he
wanted to go home and paint his garage. The deskman switched
the cameraman to Ballstead.

"Mr. Ballstead? Steve Billik. That kid hasn't got in touch with
me. No one has."

Ballstead waited a moment, reviewing in his mind Sparling's
call of more than an hour ago—the detective's conduct, the neighbor's fearful behavior, the woman's story about the beach. All of
Ballstead's gloomy instincts told him that something enormous was
being hidden.

"Stick around another half hour, Billik," Ballstead said. "Sparling's still trying to learn something."

The cameraman grumbled. "O.K., but I'm warning you, Mr.
Ballstead. After two o'clock, I'm on triple time."

The UBC news director moved his bony head irritably from
side to side, waiting for the cameraman to conclude. He saw Jim
Farrell leaning over the desk. "Tom—there's a guy named Swinnerton on the other phone. You know him?"

Ballstead handed one telephone to Farrell and picked up its
mate. "Keep Billik on," he said. "Jesus, I'm losing my mind." He
spoke into the other phone. "Swinnerton? Harvey Swinnerton?"

There was a muffled laugh at the other end. "Tom? I say, you
do remember me. I did a little nightside work for you a few years
ago. Wartime shortage, I guess. At UBC, New York."

"Sure, sure. Mustache and tweeds."

"Well said," Swinnerton laughed. The reporter shared a common experience with a hundred other newspapermen—he owed Tom Ballstead something. He was of the army of semidrunks, loners, drifters, who once in their career had found a job with Ballstead— a few weeks of sustenance, of self-respect, relief from a bad marriage, or booze, or analysis. Swinnerton's old loyalty, nothing more, had prompted the call.

"Tom—what I have to tell you is in confidence. Please don't let on I told you."

"For Christ's sweet sake, Swinnerton."

"I'm sorry. I'm a bit of an old maid. You know, I'm the *LA Truth's* district man in Santa Luisa. Have been for over a year."

"Great."

"I was having lunch at the drive-in in back of police headquarters when I was witness to an odd sight. Rheinholdt drove up, hustling one of your men into the city jail. Chap named Sparling. I knew him when he was overnight man at the *Truth.* Sparling recognized me and shouted at me to call you. He said Rheinholdt was suppressing something."

Ballstead's shriveled arms pressed against his torso. "Yeah, that's my guy. He say anything else?"

Swinnerton paused. "Something about a child missing."

"And you being the conscientious newsman you are, Harvey, you've told the *Truth,* and Hood and Hansel are after it. Right?"

"Naturally, Tom. I wasn't going to call you at all. If Hood or Hansel find out, I'll be in for it."

"Okay, Swinnerton. Thanks." Ballstead hung up, then took the other phone from Farrell. Billik was waiting for him.

"Mr. Ballstead, this kind of operation doesn't help anyone," the cameraman whined. "I was talkin' yesterday to the business agent of the union and he said——"

"Shut up. Get over to 4217 Nespoli Drive in Santa Luisa. Pull your car into the driveway and start shooting movies. Anything— the house, any people, the street. See what happens."

He dropped the phone to the cradle. Farrell, standing by, raised his eyebrows. "Eliot's in jail?"

"Rheinholdt pulled him in. It's a kidnaping. I know it is. It's got that chief of police so scared he doesn't know what to do. You better alert New York. We might have a big hunk for the network later. Got anybody to take over for Sparling?"

"George Brack's in."

"Send George out there and have him work with the camera crew. Nobody would arrest Brack. He's too nice."

Farrell lingered. "What are you going to do about Sparling?"

Ballstead got up from his swivel—in sections, it seemed, like a toy assembled from prefabricated plastic parts. "Let him sit a while. Be a better story if he stays in a few hours. Big dope. We could have had this all alone. So he gets himself arrested, opens his big trap so another reporter gets the tip. And the *Truth*—of all things."

"Tom, you better get him out. New York'll scream."

"Yeah, I know." He paced the office, his buzzard's frame wobbling. "Get me Rheinholdt. No. Get me that mayor out there. What's his name? The guy we interviewed during the housing scandal?"

"Speed. Palmer Speed."

"That's the bird. We'll shake him up a little."

McFeeley walked out of the house. Immediately, Billik filmed him. The bushy-haired man, chewing the mammoth cigar, then moved toward the detective for a close-up (not having the faintest idea who he was, but following Ballstead's orders).

"What's the idea?" Joe asked. "Where are you guys from?"

Billik pointed a thumb at the insignia on the station wagon. "Don't you give me a hard time. I got enough troubles with my boss."

"Why are you taking pictures?"

"I wish I knew. Look—just lemme get a few more." He aimed his camera at Amy's tricycle, resting on the driveway.

"That's enough. Pack up. I'm ordering you off." Joe flashed his badge. Billik, happy to be chased from the assignment (Where was the bear that rides the roller coaster? What happened to the middle-aged mothers' beauty contest?), shouldered his camera and got into the car. The detective waited until all the cases had been loaded into the station wagon.

Billik started the engine. "What's so secret?" he asked.

"Nothing. Go on, move."

"How far away can I stay? I'm supposed to hang around until something happens."

"Far enough to stay out of trouble."

"A block, a half a block? Officer, I got a job, too. I'm on assignment."

"A block away," Joe said. It did not seem a good response: Rheinholdt appeared a lot smarter than he was.

"Block away, the man says," Billik chanted. He blasted the station wagon off the driveway. About a hundred feet down the street he recognized Sparling's Ford—not the car, but the UBC sticker on the sun visor. While it was not quite a block away, it seemed as good place as any to park. He swung the station wagon around and halted in back of Eliot's car.

McFeeley made no move to chase Billik again. Something more elaborate, a plan more encompassing, was demanded. As he stood in the early-afternoon glare, tormented by a thousand doubts, two more cars came down the street. One was Harvey Swinnerton's Austin. The second was a red coupé, with the insignia, "L. A. TRUTH RADIO PHOTO CAR." Both cars parked behind the UBC station wagon. McFeeley walked back to the house, heavy with ineptitude, wishing Rheinholdt would move on calling the newspapers.

In the house, he resumed interrogating the parents about neighbors, servicemen, any recent caller who had acted curiously. Andrus was of little help. He seemed to regard his four-week absence as evidence of his blamelessness.

"Why are you botherin' me with all that?" he cried. "I haven't been associated with this house for a long time. My wife has seen to that!"

She ignored him. McFeeley marveled at her self-discipline—a discipline that made her apologize for crying, rebuff his efforts to console her.

"We've checked servants, haven't we?" Joe asked.

"Yes. Selena, cleaning woman. Carlos, gardener. I think his name is Valdez. I haven't any idea where he lives. He just shows up every Friday."

"You don't remember anyone hanging around? Sort of snooping? Or any crazy phone calls?"

"No. Nothing like that. It's so quiet here, I'm sure I would have noticed."

McFeeley's page of scrawled notations stared at him. The prospects for investigation seemed dismally barren.

"Mrs. Andrus, who might be up and around at 8:30 or so? Like delivery boys—newsboys? Someone who might have seen Amy."

Laura touched her forehead; a nudge of guilt bothered her—*she* should have been up then. "The Emersons' oldest boy—Timmy—

he delivers the *Register*. Some of the neighbors might have been leaving for work then."

He asked her to identify the residents of the surrounding houses. The Emersons lived to their right as they faced the street; the Skopases across the street; the Kahlers to their left. Behind was a vacant lot. She indicated again how little she knew about any of them except Harry and Babe Emerson.

"Yeah," Andrus interrupted. "We didn't mingle much. They're a bunch of car-washers and lawn-worshipers. Lieutenant, you wash your own car dutifully?"

McFeeley tried to ignore the rudeness. "No. My oldest boy does it for me."

Embarrassment colored Laura's face. "Forgive us, officer. I wonder how we manage to be as awful as we are. Maybe we deserve what's happening to us."

Moll entered the room. "Joe? Can I talk to you in here?" Mc-Feeley followed him into the nursery. The baby's crib and dresser had been removed. A folding aluminum table had been set up for the phones and the tape recorder.

"I think Rheinholdt's flipping," Moll whispered. "I had to plead for ten minutes to get more men out here. He gave me an argument about a twenty-four-hour shift, about the lab, about everything." Moll mopped his face. "He kept yelling about that reporter he arrested—thinks it's solved everything. I swear, he'd forgotten there was a snatch."

"I'll call him," McFeeley said. "He's got to talk to the newspapers. There's a half-dozen people out there already."

Moll flexed a wrestler's arm. "I'll chase 'em."

"It won't help. They'll beat it around the corner or a block away. They'll stay away only if their bosses tell them to." He dialed headquarters.

Soon a fifth press car was at the encampment across the street from the Andrus house. It was a low-slung MG, the property of newscaster George Brack. On Brack's arrival, a brief meeting was held by Swinnerton, his photographer, Brack, and the UBC crew. It was decided they would take turns calling Sanlu head-quarters every fifteen minutes and that they would share (*pool* was the technical word) any information. Whatever facts they pried out of the yellow-stone house on their own initiative would be theirs alone. The house appeared to be vacant, absolutely quiet, shuttered. Once, a car bearing James Raffalovitch, the Santa Luisa lab chief, pulled up. Both Brack and Swinnerton tried to question him. He did not even greet them. After a while, Swinnerton napped in his Austin and Brack took a tour of the grounds around the house. He saw nothing to excite him, and he returned to run a few voice tests on the 16-millimeter sound camera.

Jim Farrell tracked down Mayor Palmer Speed at a luncheon for the Santa Luisa Hoosier Club at the Valley View Inn. The mayor willingly left his peach Melba to talk with Tom Ballstead, taking the call in the Valley View Inn's redwood bar. Ballstead identified himself, and although the mayor had never met him, he inquired if Tom were not the same Ballstead from Fort Wayne, Indiana, who worked for the *Sentinel* in the twenties. When the news director acknowledged that he was, the mayor was overjoyed. "Well, for goodness' sake, Tom! You've got to come down to the Hoosier Club luncheons! I'll bet there are dozens of fellows who know you!" Mayor Speed saw good in all men, got along with everyone, and had served nine successive terms in office. His backers, the nonpartisan Citizens Committee, called him "Old Inevitable."

"Mayor, I'm calling about a serious matter concerning your chief of police." Ballstead stifled a few gasps.

"Chief Rheinholdt? About that parking lot? Don't worry, Tom, I'm talking to him——"

"Not the parking lot," choked Ballstead. "He's arrested one of my men." He went on to tell of Eliot's misadventures and demanded the reporter's release. Mayor Speed hesitated. He detested controversy. He wanted everyone to *like* everyone else, and he had succeeded remarkably as a mediator—whether it was an argument over the use of prayers in schools, garbage disposal, or parking meters.

"I'm puzzled, Tom," the mayor said. (He was a dogged first-namer. After five minutes, Charles Evans Hughes would have been Chuck.) "I'm not clear on what your man was doing that got the chief so mad."

"Listen, Palmer," Ballstead said, accepting the invitation to familiarity, "Rheinholdt was trying to suppress something, and my man got wind of it. If he wants to sit on stories, we're allowed to try to find out. That's the fun."

"What in the world would he want to suppress? There's nothing in Santa Luisa worth suppressing. My goodness, Tom, you people learned that during the housing mess. We were the cleanest community in the southland."

"I guess he hasn't told *you* either." An edge of nastiness crept into Ballstead's voice.

"What? What hasn't he told me?"

"We think there's a kidnaping in Santa Luisa. We know there's a child missing."

"Kidnaping." Speed's inflection was not interrogatory; he uttered the word flatly and breathily.

"That's why Rheinholdt better open up. If not, every paper and every radio and TV outlet in LA'll be on his back. And yours. And the family. We know the name and address."

Mayor Speed rested his eyes on his reflection in the bar mirror. He was framed by a comforting row of liquor bottles; he sought assurance in his long, tanned face, his thick white hair. "What do you suggest, Tom?"

They had come full circle. Ballstead had come to him a supplicant; in five minutes he had the mayor asking his advice.

"First, you've got to let Sparling go. He did nothing out of line. Any reporter would have done the same." Ballstead had not the faintest idea what Eliot had done—the important thing was to keep his grand design in motion. "What's Rheinholdt going to do? Arrest everyone? Fifty newsmen? A hundred? This goes against my newsmen's instincts, since I might still have the story exclusive, but he's got to talk—he's got to tell everyone. No secrets."

"I don't know, Tom. The chief may give me an argument."

"Want a little advice, Mayor? Win the argument. I'll expect Sparling free in fifteen minutes. You need any professional help, Palmer, you call me."

"I will. Thank you very much, Tom."

Immediately, the mayor located Rheinholdt at his house, summoning him from pot roast and hashed browns. Rheinholdt was polite, attentive, almost servile.

"This fellow Ballstead claims there's a kidnaping in Santa Luisa, Caspar," Speedy said. "Why haven't I been notified?"

"Well, sir, we aren't sure."

"I don't understand. Is a child missing? Is there a ransom note?"

"No. Yes." Rheinholdt had answered negatively, as a child will deny an obvious misdeed, fully aware that he has lied, knowing he will fool no one. Then, sensing his guilt, he admitted the truth.

"Good God, Caspar. Why did this have to happen in Santa Luisa? I'm sure you're doing everything that can be done."

"Yes, sir. We're on it one hundred per cent."

"About this reporter you arrested. I think you'd best release him."

"Mr. Mayor, I can't."

"Why? One reporter?"

"He knows. It's got to be secret. We got a drop tonight. If it gets out—the papers, the radio—the kidnaper won't show."

"Well, that brings me to the second part of my call. I think we must tell the newspapers—immediately—and request that they keep our secret."

Rheinholdt gulped down a final cheekful of potatoes. He had stored them, chipmunklike, out of politeness, but Speed's request gave him pause, and he used it to digestive advantage. The mayor continued: "Caspar, you know I give you a free hand. You're your own man. But you also know how the papers are. The rumor will get around. I must tell you it simply isn't good policy to offend the press. Certainly it's intemperate to arrest a reporter doing his job. He wasn't roughed up or anything?"

"No. He isn't hurt."

"You'd best release him. Caspar, you might hint that we'd like him to forget the incident. His boss, Mr. Ballstead, is an old Hoosier chum of mine, and we might be able to smooth it over."

Rheinholdt's wife, a pyramidal, homely woman with a head of gray Brillo, watched her husband fretfully. "Okay, sir. Whatever the mayor wishes. We'll start calling the newspapers."

"I think that's wise."

"If they don't play ball, that child might be harmed—killed maybe."

"They will. They must. It'll be put to them on that basis." The mayor's voice rose. "I pride myself on my relations with the press. I am not afraid to give information. I'm always available."

Rheinholdt, a checkered napkin spotted with brown gravy tucked in his stiff white collar, heard only scattered words from his superior.

"Caspar, I want to be advised of every development on this thing. Do you think I should run out to the house?"

"Oh no, sir," Rheinholdt said. "It's pretty hectic there. That's why I left."

"Yes, that sounds sensible to me."

For a long time after the mayor had hung up, Rheinholdt squatted morosely in the kitchen chair. There were no marks on his head, but his attitude was one of a man who has just absorbed a beating with a truncheon. His wife begged him to finish his pot roast; there was baked apple for dessert. The self-pity of stupidity choked him, wrecked his appetite. Palmer Speed was his best friend, his protector; he had elevated him from traffic division to the top job. The chief respected Mayor Speed, never argued with him. But underneath this subservience there smoldered a dimly understood resentment against the man who had raised him so high— too high for an old traffic man with no education. There were moments when Rheinholdt would think back with blissful nostalgia to his traffic days—his high percentage of traffic convictions, his insistence on the drunkometer tests, the awards he had won for traffic control. When he did so, he nurtured a small, edgy dislike for Palmer Speed, who had removed him from the work he loved best.

Rheinholdt undid the napkin. If that's what Speed wanted him to do, he would do it. If he wanted that young snot freed, he would free him. If he wanted the newspapers informed, he would do that also. He would tell the whole world about the Andrus case, blab it out to everyone, and then beg them like a little puppy to please be nice and withhold the story and not print or broadcast a word. The kitchen clock, a yellow teakettle, told him it was 2:30. In less than six hours the drop would be made, the criminal given his chance to get the money, return the child. For a moment Rheinholdt was tempted to disobey. He would keep Sparling locked up, take his chances on secrecy being maintained, clear the area of any reporters—yes, jug them also. *Six hours. Five hours and forty-five minutes.* Then a comforting notion occurred to him—something so gratifying as to make the old chief feel a little underhanded. *If he told the papers—at Speed's order—and if they violated the confidence, and if any harm befell the child, he would be in the clear. They could never blame him. He had followed orders from upstairs. What was he supposed to do? Disobey Mr. Mayor?*

Fifteen minutes later, Eliot Sparling was released, emerging into the dry, sucking sunlight of the parking lot. He had rather enjoyed his sojourn. He had spent an hour and fifty-two minutes in jail, and he made a note of the time. It would add authenticity to the special program he would do later on his role as martyr to the truth. His cell companion had been a decrepit old dandy, with pencil mustache and slicked-down hair, who had been arrested that morning on the complaint of a woman passenger on the Green Bus lines. She had complained of his manual attentions, and he had been taken into custody, he told Eliot, for what was technically known as *frottage*. Sparling, who counted all experience fruitful, jotted down the word. It had a nice, foreign, dirty sound. Wishing the old fellow a fair trial, he made for the telephone booth at the Jumboburger Drive-in and called Ballstead.

"Hey, Tom!" Eliot shouted. "They sprung me. I guess Rheinholdt got scared when I warned him the wrath of the press would hit him!"

"You damn dope. I got you out. I had the mayor put the screws to Rheinholdt. Go home and get some sleep. I might want to stick you on the news tonight."

"Me? On the television?"

"Yeah. Hero reporter, working newsman upholding the tradition of John Peter Zenger and Elijah Lovejoy. You might win a Peabody. You get socked?"

"He slapped me twice. It didn't hurt."

"Too bad. Any marks?"

"No. My face was red for a while, that's all."

Ballstead chuckled. "Oh, Jesus, this is fun. Maybe I'll let the make-up department paint you up."

"Hey, Tom, I don't want to sleep. Let me go back to the Andrus place." Eliot, sleepless, foodless, sounded exhilarated. Jail had invigorated him.

"No. Go home."

"I have to go back anyway and get my car."

"Get it and leave. You've loused us up enough. Getting jugged, blowing your foghorn so Swinnerton got the story. The *Truth* is all over the place, thanks to you."

"I couldn't help it. Swinnerton was the only guy I saw to yell at."

"George Brack's covering. You can go back on the overnight tonight."

Eliot's enormous voice soared, then sagged and broke. "George *Brack?* The voice? Hey, Tom—he's a *reader.* He reads what I write for him. Please, please, Tom, let me go back. I'll do leg work for Brack; I'll take orders. I got to make it up to you, please."

"When'd you last sleep?"

"That's beside the point. I can go forever without sleeping."

Sparling had come to work at 1:00 that morning. Because of the insufferable heat in his one-room flat, he had awakened at noon the previous day. He had been without sleep for almost twenty-seven hours. But he was an overnight man, a lobster-trick veteran who had learned to dispense with sleep, the way he had learned to dismiss food and ignore women.

"Tom—I know the cop, McFeeley. I have a terrific in with the dame next door. You have to let me go out!"

"Jesus, shut up," Ballstead muttered. "Go, go, report to Brack. Stay out of trouble."

"Thanks, thanks, Tom. You better get someone to take my overnight for a few days. This may be a long haul."

His gleefulness made Ballstead squirm.

As improbable as it might seem, Eliot Sparling had a girl friend. Her name was Connie Potenza, and she was an employee of his alma mater, the *Los Angeles Truth*. Connie, a slim, bouncy, third-generation Italian with wide eyes the color of black coffee, was secretary to the newspaper's general manager, Herbert Hood. Eliot had begun dating her toward the end of his tenure at the *Truth*. Now that he had arrived and was a television newsman, earning almost one-hundred dollars a week, he saw her with more frequency. He was the kind of self-denigrating young man who needed status—*any* kind of status—to ensure his relationships with women. At the *Truth* he had been almost celibate. As a proud UBC man, he took Connie to dinner once a week. Sometimes they went to the beach at Santa Monica.

After getting Ballstead's permission to return to the Andrus house, he telephoned Connie at the *Truth*.

"You hear about me?" Eliot asked.

"What did you do now? Get married to Mr. Ballstead?"

"Don't be so smart. I was in jail." Proudly, Eliot related his high adventure of the morning; *danger is my business,* he seemed to be saying.

"I bet it's all tied in with what's going on here," Connie said carefully. She looked over her shoulder. Within Mr. Hood's englassed office, an assemblage of the *Truth's* top brass—Hood, general manager; Ed Kalaidjian, managing editor; Bill Trigg, the acting city editor. The door was closed and she could hear nothing. "It's all about Swinnerton's call—ever since he phoned, they've been running around like crazy. Bill Trigg spent a half hour arguing with police headquarters in Sanlu and couldn't learn anything. What is it, Eliot? Is it a kidnaping?"

"That's what Ballstead thinks. Boy, I wish I hadn't tipped Swinnerton—me and my big mouth. What else is the *Truth* doing?"

"Eliot!" she whispered. "What am I—a spy? Swinnerton and a photographer and the radio car are there." She looked up and saw the purposeful figure of Theodore T. Hansel, Editor & Publisher of the *Truth,* burst through the city-room's swinging doors. He was on one of his rare forays from the fifteenth floor. The glint of great deeds imminent fired his predaceous eyes. Swinnerton's report had reached him, and he was planning to direct strategy personally.

"Eliot! I've got to hang up. Mr. Hansel's on his way—they're all waiting for him in Hood's office!"

"T.T. himself?" Eliot cried. "He'll be eatin' ass like it was steak. Tell Mr. Hood to stick the bulldog edition in his pants."

"Oh, you slob. Good-by."

"Good-by, ol' Connie. Hey, catch me on the TV news tonight. I'm getting interviewed about my imprisonment."

"Hero."

Over a jelly doughnut and a coke at the drive-in, prior to taking a cab back to the Andrus house, Sparling found himself entertaining a delicious notion. The race for primacy, for exclusivity on the Andrus case was now strictly between himself, representing UBC, and the hated *Truth.* He envisioned himself, bold Sparling, a latter-day Richard Harding Davis, taking on the newspaper, that vestige of a vanished era of dingy journalism, with its abusive policies. He would show them. He ate his sugary lunch like a dog, mouthing huge chunks of doughnut, gulping the coke in icy swallows, tasting nothing. Then he flagged a taxi and rode off to drink delight of battle with his peers.

The first thing T. T. Hansel did after hurling his handsome presence into Hood's glass cage was to call New York, the headquarters of the *Organization*—that congeries of newspapers, and syndicated services, of which the *Truth* was a lesser member. He spoke briefly to some executive of the Organization, secured permission to spend money on the Andrus mystery, and then turned his flushed face on his subordinates. T. T. Hansel was not quite fifty. He had glistening black hair, parted in the middle. His flesh possessed a preternatural redness, which he utilized for dramatic lighting—to terrify, to charm, to confuse. Hansel was almost twenty years Herbert Hood's junior. Both had been candidates for the top post immediately after the war. Hood was then general manager and Hansel was his subordinate—managing editor. Actually, it had been no contest. Herbie Hood was a Neanderthaler, a hard-nosed journalist brawler. Hansel was of the new breed—a confidante of senators and governors, a lecturer at journalism schools, a friend to deposed kings. He was handsome, articulate, fearless—and, above all, he had command presence. T. T. Hansel had made the great leap forward—to the combined post of Editor & Publisher; old Herbie had stayed in his glass vivarium, dreaming of a Chicago newsroom and a Sigma Delta Chi award he had once won for exposing loan sharks in Cicero, Illinois.

"Why haven't we heard from Swinnerton again?" Hansel asked. His questions were always peremptory, accusative. He would never merely ask *if* Swinnerton had called; he would assume that someone was delinquent, that some knavery was afoot in Swinnerton's *not* having called.

"Ah, he's at the house now, Ted," Kalaidjian said softly. Kalaidjian was neuter: his lavish Armenian features were perpetually morbid. He had been in the Organization twenty-three years—Chicago, Pittsburgh, New Orleans, New York. His mind was a dollop of ionized jelly reacting electronically to stimuli from the Hoods and the Hansels. He never made a decision. He rarely spoke. He never initiated action. Best of all, he was never blamed for anything.

"I didn't ask that," Hansel said. "I asked had we heard from him again."

"We have, haven't we?" Hood asked. "Trigg, didn't you talk with him?"

Bill Trigg, the acting city editor, moved toward the desk. He was twenty-four years old, a redheaded, anemic youth. There was a note of innocence about him that was utterly false. Trigg was sharp, smart and professional. He and Eliot Sparling, at one time, had been regarded as a team of brilliant young men at the *Truth*. Sparling—loud, insulting, involving himself needlessly in the Schlossmann matter—had won only the overnight and eventual discharge. Trigg was now a regular day-side man with a future in the Organization.

"I spoke to Swinnerton, Mr. Hansel," Bill Trigg said. "The police aren't saying a thing. The family won't talk. We're not on it alone any more. United Broadcasting has a crew standing by."

The blood-coloring in Hansel's face fluttered. "Why wasn't I told that? Why was I led to believe we were on it alone?"

Hood's bald head wobbled. "That's my fault, Ted. I thought I mentioned that Swinnerton got the tip from this kid Sparling, when he was being jugged. You remember Sparling, Ted? He used to work overnight here."

Hansel sat on the edge of Hood's scarred desk; the executive behind pressed against the general manager's pending file. He folded his navy-blue arms. His square face was intense.

T.T.'s fierce thoughtfulness shuddered each of them with little fears. The Organization had been built on fear, and its members had been conditioned to feed on fear, to expect it, to feel cheated if their efforts were not motivated by fear. They *needed* the sense of imminent disaster, of inevitable accusations, of anticipated wrongness, to function. It was all they had. Hansel had always understood this, and this understanding had rocketed him to the seat of authority. Hood, who had once been his superior, Kalaidjian, who had worked the ETO with him as a war correspondent, and Trigg, who had once been his nightside copy boy, all deferred to him willingly, fearfully. They realized that his mastery over them was honestly earned. The bald truth was that the Organization was shaky, in a state of financial disrepair. The *Truth* was one of its more ragged members, and Hansel had been charged by the men in New York to restore it to its vanished eminence. Mergers, financial convulsions, wholesale firings, economy waves—all these were part of the rhythm of existence in the Organization. It was a tribute to Hansel's vigor that his coruscating presence dispelled the odor of decay.

"I have gotten a green light from New York," Hansel said crisply. "No one in New York appears to know anything. None of the wire services, the networks. We may still be ahead."

"Ah, except for that Sparling fellow," Hood mumbled. "He——"

"Do you know what you're talking about?" T.T. asked. "You don't know what you're talking about." The rhetorical question, self-answering, was part of Hansel's arsenal. "I want Swinnerton to get the confirmation before anyone else does."

"We'll certainly keep after him," Hood said quickly. "I've advised Harvey that——"

"He isn't strong enough," Hansel interrupted. "He's only a district man, isn't he?"

"Why, yes, Ted," Hood said. "But he knows Sanlu better than ——"

"He isn't strong enough. Where's Mona?"

"She's in San Francisco."

Hansel cogitated. "Get her back here at once. I want her on this story."

Kalaidjian started for the door. "Shall I call her?" He inevitably ended up phoning, arranging, making schedules, busying himself with operational trivia, duties that precluded his being blamed for anything.

Herbert Hood rotated his shiny head. "I don't know, Ted. We aren't sure it *is* a kidnaping. We'd spend all that money flying Mona in, and have nothing to show. I mean, we can't be sure, and I'm thinking of the budget."

Hansel got up swiftly from Hood's desk. "Get Mona out there at once. We'll worry about the budget later. New York will overlook any expenditures on this. Is the radio car there? Is a photographer with Swinnerton?" He had been so informed ten minutes earlier; indeed, his queries were instigated by his *remembrance* of the information. "Herbert, why must I think of these things?" So saying, Hansel felt a little sorry. From time to time he wished he were still one of the city-room gang. Yet they refused to meet him halfway; at his merriest, they slunk in fear before him, stammered excuses, maintained formality.

"We'll move fast on this," Hood said. "Don't you worry about us, Ted."

Hansel was not listening. He took a dramatic stance at the door—one which would have made lesser men appear ludicrous. "I'd like to remind you that this kind of story—the big crime, the kidnaping, the murder—is what has made the Organization. I'm not ashamed of it. I never have been. We must feel this story is ours and ours alone, that the others are there at our sufferance. The day the *Truth* started downhill was when it lost this image of itself, when it became chummy and conversationally informative. I want to recapture some of the old smell of blood. We must get the family's confidence. We must anticipate the police. We must aid in apprehending the criminal, offer our facilities as a meeting place, call in psychologists, handwriting experts, mystery-story writers. We must, if you will, dominate and *control* the case. Am I making myself understood?"

"You bet you are, Ted," Hood said. He darted querulous glances at Kalaidjian and Trigg. "We're with Ted on this, aren't we?" They nodded.

"I'll be quite brutal about this," Hansel continued. "You've all heard rumors about the *Truth* being in trouble. That's one of the reasons I'm here—to get us *out* of trouble. To raise circulation and linage and make us the powerful voice we once were. I intend to make this Andrus affair an opening wedge in this newspaper's revival. If any of you don't understand me, you don't belong here."

After he had gone, Hood shouted through the door to Connie Potenza to call Mona Mears at the Mark Hopkins in San Francisco. He did not call her *Connie,* or *Miss Potenza,* or even *hey you.* Hood had dispensed with salutations a long time ago, except in addressing superiors. Trigg and Kalaidjian lingered. They seemed uncertain of what to do, where to go. Hansel's mandate was enormous, but their powers to execute his program were feeble. Rheinholdt would not talk. Swinnerton, a lightweight, had no entree with the family or the police. Hood paced the office, smacking fist against palm.

Trigg excused himself. "I better tip WNA," he said. "They'll scream their heads off if I don't. They're still mad we forgot them on the last landslide."

WNA—the World News Association—was a syndicated press service, a pauper's Associated Press, a small brother to UP and INS. The Organization kept it going largely out of sentiment. The arrangement was for WNA to occupy a cubbyhole in the office of the Organization daily. A reporter or two, a teleprinter operator were the usual staff.

Trigg walked swiftly through the city room to WNA's tiny, partitioned room. An elderly, stout man in green eyeshade, sleeve garters, and a soiled blue vest was punching tape for the WNA state wire. To one side, the national teleprinter was sending out copy from the East.

"Where's Brady?" Trigg asked.

The operator did not look up; his fingers played a minuet on the keys. "He's at the luncheon for the Dominican Republic Consul. Malamud's at lunch."

Trigg paused. "We have a tip on a kidnaping. I think you should alert New York." Trigg sat at an ancient upright. On a yellow half sheet, he typed:

TIPT POSBL KIDNPNG SANLU. AWAITING POLICE CONFIRMATION.

He yanked it from the typewriter and gave it to the operator. "Better get it out fast." Trigg, his duty to WNA, the weak sister, concluded, left for his desk. The name *Andrus* sparked a memory, and he tried to recall where he had seen it in the papers.

The operator set the yellow paper under the clamp on the rack and awaited the end of the incoming piece. When it had finished, with two rings of the bell, he broke the wire by signaling with five bells. An answering two bells told him to go ahead. He typed briskly, adding a greeting and a signature, per custom.

ER

  TIPT POSBL KIDNPNG SANLU. AWAITING POLICE
  CONFIRMATION.

SN

The seven words thus transmitted made it inevitable that the Andrus kidnaping would become public property. The national curiosity was aroused, the public eye and ear titillated, the secret disclosed. Trigg's brief message, sent out by an old man in sleeve garters, was read in the offices of 242 clients of World News Association—newspapers, radio and television stations, journalism schools. It was sent out at 3:16 in the afternoon, Pacific Standard Time (6:16 P.M. in New York), and within five minutes the switchboard at WNA, New York, was jammed with calls. Eager clients demanded more—names, addresses, details—so that they could staff the event themselves or, at least, call the Associated Press, whom they were more prone to believe. The New York office forgot the economy wave and telephoned Los Angeles. With the bureau unmanned, the operator referred the call to Bill Trigg of the *Truth*—who had nothing to tell anyone. By now, 3:35 (Coast time), the pack was in full cry. They smelled blood; they wanted more. An alert radio news editor in New York saw the message and phoned a friend in Los Angeles at television station KYOT. KYOT at once dispatched an eager young reporter named Martin Ringel to Santa Luisa. Nosing about, he located the Andrus house. A Chicago newspaper read the message and notified the Associated Press man, Victor DeGroot, who set four reporters to cruising the streets until they found the encampment of automobiles on Nespoli Drive. Even the *Santa Luisa Register,* usually the last to be aware of events in the community, followed the WNA lead. Its editor rounded up a dozen newsboys, dispatched them on bicycles, and located the Andrus home. A vacation replacement on the *Register,* an eighteen-year-old boy named Duane Bosch, a sophomore at

Sanlu State, was sent out to cover the story. Bosch, who four years earlier had been trading bubble-gum cards, was now in the big time.

At 3:35 P.M., Walter Todd jumped from a red-leather stool at the breakfast bar and advised McFeeley he was due at the bank to get the ransom money.

"Handle the stuff as little as possible," Joe said. "And don't tell the bank people what it's for." As he uttered the cautionary advice, he realized how ineffectual their attempts at secrecy had become. There were three more cars parked outside.

The dentist realized this also. He nodded thoughtfully, tried to find a word of consolation for Andrus, then departed.

As soon as he issued from the redwood door, they were at him. Harvey Swinnerton recognized Todd and called his name. Steve Billik and the UBC crew raced across the lawn with the soundgear. George Brack, Eliot's "voice," carried the microphone. The photographer from the *Truth* took a picture of Todd, having no idea who he was. Todd behaved admirably: he said not a word, brushed aside questions and made for his Buick. As he entered the car, he noticed Swinnerton. The two men had met about a year ago as fellow members of the Santa Luisa Library Committee. Todd had been intrigued with Swinnerton's fine manners, his evident high breeding, his interest in books and music. The reporter had been invited to the dentist's club for lunch, and over the martinis Todd had admitted to certain literary ambitions. He wanted to write his life story. He was convinced that the career of Walter L. Todd, D.D.S., was of enormous interest. As a man who had mastered the lateral incision for impacted wisdom teeth (while still in Cornell Dental School), he felt he had something to say. However, he had no literary bent. He needed a young chap who could write to assist him in getting his voluminous notes, recordings, pictures—the memorabilia of a man of consequence—in order. Swinnerton almost choked on his fried sandab. He begged off, but he encouraged Todd. Perhaps later, perhaps after he had finished his magazine piece, perhaps after the radio work let up. Then Swinnerton had stroked his tawny mustache and added: "But you've got a perfectly wizard book there, Walter. A smasher."

The memory of that luncheon meeting came back vividly to Dr. Todd. He not only recognized Swinnerton, he was downright glad to see his gentlemanly face.

"I say, Walter," Swinnerton said, pushing his way past Steve Billik and George Brack, "I didn't know you were in the house of mystery. I'd have presumed on our old friendship to buzz you."

Todd winked. "Wouldn't have helped, Harvey." He started the engine. "Don't know why you fellows are taking my picture. I'm not that pretty, and nothing's happening here."

George Brack invoked his pulpit tones. He was a striking, blond man, without guile or meanness. "George Brack, sir. How about a statement for UBC? Is it a kidnaping? Is it a custody fight?"

Todd started backing away, shaking his head negatively. At the edge of the driveway, he halted to look for traffic. Swinnerton, trotting alongside, poked his inoffensive head in the window. "Walter—would you mind running me into town?" he asked. "I might as well get to my office if there's nothing doing here."

Todd paused. In view of the circumstances, the answer should have been an unequivocal no. But Swinnerton, after all, was an old friend. Moreover, he was a man of taste and refinement who would not ask questions. "Ah—I don't see why not," said Todd. "But remember, Harvey—no questions."

"Word of honor."

To the fascinated horror of the others, Swinnerton hopped into the front seat. The Buick drove off.

"How did Swinnerton pull that off?" George Brack cried. "It's not fair!" Brack yearned to be a newsman: a professional voice who had never worked for a newspaper, he would have traded part of his annual earnings of $70,000 to be accepted as a working journalist. Brack was too nice to be a reporter. He could not be pushy; he could not ask embarrassing questions. Subterfuge and sneaky tricks were alien to him. He was mulling over these short-comings, standing amid the hot, disgusted group of newsmen at the edge of the Andrus driveway, when Eliot's trumpeting roused him.

"Hey, George!" Sparling yelled. "Georgie boy!"

"Oh, hello there, El. I heard you were in jail."

"Nah. That was way back when. A half hour ago. What plays here?"

Brack filled him in. "It's a case of watchful waiting, I'd say," the newscaster said seriously.

"A good phrase, Georgie," Eliot shouted. "Remind me to write it for you. Ballstead wants us to do a bit—two heroes outside the house."

"That's a swell idea," Brack agreed. "You mean I'll interview you—about jail—and how Rheinholdt slugged you?"

"That's us. Like when there's no news and the two big wheels talk it up with each other. Joseph C. Harsch and Irving R. Levine. We better get middle initials." Then Sparling halted, recalling Ballstead's edict—he was working *for* Brack. He reminded himself again: stop talking so much. *Keep mouth shut. Soften voice. Smoke pipe.*

But George Brack was the least insultable of men. He ran a pocket comb through his billowing yellow waves. "That's really a neat idea," he said. "We'd better set it up with Billik right now." The camera crew shifted gear. Eliot and George stood stupidly on the sidewalk watching the silent house. Blinds drawn, doors closed, it might have been a tomb.

As soon as Todd had gone, McFeeley called Rheinholdt again, asking whether he had begun to call the newspapers. Rheinholdt said he had, prefacing his response with an invocation of the mayor's authority. "His Honor said it should be done, so I'm doing it. I got Baines working on it." McFeeley shuddered. Sergeant Baines, the old farmer, seemed the least apt man in the world for the job.

McFeeley pushed the kitchen blind aside and saw the growing mob—seven or eight cars, ten or eleven men. Perhaps with all the breaks, with Baines completing his calls, they would be pulled off, the secret would be kept, the child returned.

". . . and no damn thirteen-state alarm till I say so," Rheinholdt was growling. Joe had merely asked about it. The chief's reaction surprised him. "Just get more people curious," he explained. Then he laughed. "Except the reporters. The mayor says I got to be nice to them. Tell 'em everything. Release that young punk." He went on to denounce the FBI and the state police.

When McFeeley had concluded an aimless ten minutes with him, he sat quietly in the kitchen trying to formulate their next step. Andrus and his wife were in the studio. He heard no voices and he assumed they were resting. The woman baffled him. The detective had been witness to a hundred human disasters. He had observed, with an uncomfortable sense of eavesdropping, hysterical women, weeping men, people ravaged and beaten and stripped of defense. Now he could only marvel at the cruel bondage in which Laura

Andrus held herself. What wrenchings went on inside her, he could not imagine.

In the nursery, Moll was calling Records, asking them to pull anything they had on sex offenders, extortionists, anyone who might in the remotest manner be associated with the crime. Anyone they could lay their hands on would have to be tracked down, interrogated. Even as McFeeley heard Irvin's heavy voice repeating his request, Joe realized the futility of their labors. There remained LA—three million people—where the criminal might just as well have come from.

Three million people—a city so huge that it swallowed up other communities, like a whale gulping plankton, encompassing beaches, oceans, deserts, lakes and rivers. They could look forever in tiny Sanlu (pop. 97,520) and delude themselves for as long as they looked.

He tried to create a mental image of the criminal—some amoral boob, risking the gas chamber for forty-two hundred dollars. Possibly a man desperately short of cash, envisioning the theft of a child as a temporary lapse, not a terribly bad thing, since no one would get hurt, a sort of trade (child for money), and the cash coming from people who obviously could afford it. McFeeley smiled wryly. He thought of the woman's admission that they did not have that much cash on hand, the sparsely furnished living room.

Joe roused himself. He could not think of everything. At least the reporters were being handled. He drifted into Amy's room, where Raffalovitch, the lab man, was dusting the pink dresser for prints. He had little hope of finding anything—the room was probably covered with them—the kid's, the mother's, the maid's. McFeeley watched him working methodically in the late-afternoon light, whistling tunelessly, and got the feeling they were engaged in some pointless game. But he said nothing.

The enclosed patio, shaded with translucent jalousies, occupied the north end of the house. The flagstone floor, the exterior house wall, which served as the long side of its trapezoidal shape, the northern exposure, rendered it cooler than the rest of the squat home. In the center of the floor stood Laura's worktable—a set of two-by-sixes resting on sawhorses. A wire skeleton, clay-daubed, grew from its center. Spatulas and probes were spread on the table's surface. The floor was a litter of plaster chunks and lumps of clay.

A fine patina of white dust covered everything—the meager furniture, the drawn louvers, the yellow stucco wall.

Laura rested on the day bed. Fritzie, uninvited, had followed her into the studio. Now he sat lumpishly in a canvas deck chair, from which he would bounce up every few minutes and circle the patio.

He seemed agitated by an inner eccentric wheel. His movements were swift and jerky as he walked around the wooden table, peeked through the louvers at the encamped reporters, or skirted the bed on which his wife rested, immobile and wide-eyed.

"Fritzie, stop moving around," she said.

"Sorry." He paused in mid-tour of the table. "I'm not blessed with your staggering capacity for control. Why don't you cry? Shriek. Scream. Roll on the floor—the way any other woman would."

She turned her head toward the yellow wall.

"Ah, hell, I'm sorry. Sorry as can be. Don't seem to be able to say anythin' right." He plumped into the deck chair, his body divested of bones. "I'm no he'p. You're the strength around here, Laura. I guess that's what really galls me. You've been a hill of granite. I'm about as brave as a sick possum."

"Maybe you're better off, Fritzie."

Andrus closed his eyes. "Could be—could be you are right." He suddenly doubled over. His blond wheat field of a head was almost at the level of his belt buckle. "Why us?" he wheezed. "Good Christ in heaven, Laura, why us? Of all the people in the world. As if you and I haven't brought enough misery on ourselves. Now this. You think maybe we're bein' punished?"

"Fritzie, you've got to stop these dramatics. You'll infect me. I don't believe in divine retribution."

"That's right. You wouldn't. New England Unitarian stock." He laughed self-mockingly. "But me. I am a beauty. In times of stress I smell the hell-fire of my old Baptist daddy and his daddy before him. I sniff brimstone. Yes, we're bein' punished, they would say."

"Fritzie, if that kind of illogic will make you bear this better, go on and believe it."

He lifted up his head; the blond mop flapped about the temples. "I don't really believe it. You must indulge me, Laura. I'm the world's worst man to be afflicted with suffering—the poorest victim that ever lived. I'm good only when I'm front-running."

"Fritzie, can't you accept things as they are? Must everything be in extremes? This morning you were blaming everyone in the world for this—me, the police. Now you're after yourself. You have to find culprits."

Andrus sighed, resting his head against the cool shutters. "How well you know me, Laura."

"I haven't any insights into you. I've never had any. Let's say I'm cursed with clear vision. Particularly where people like you and your friends are concerned." She paused, reluctant to open up old surgical stitching. A suspicion that the infection still festered nagged at her.

"We've been round and round on this one," Andrus said. "I know your speech. Inability to contend with reality because we're all fictionalized. We create ourselves. You know something, Laura? About a month ago, when we called this quits, I began to believe you. I do believe you. That's why I had to move out. I can't change now. If I do, that's the end of my career, my life. I may be fictionalized, but that's all I got."

"I should be more tolerant."

"Toleration isn't your strong suit, Laura. It never became you to participate in my work. Know somethin'? You were right about us. We don't have any—what'd you call it?—substantive existence. Helluva word."

For a while they sat silently. The clay-daubed, deformed torso on the table rose between them like some arbiter, observer and judge to their self-examinations. Andrus got up and paced the stone floor. "That's the biggest joke of all," he said thickly. "What a joke."

"What is?"

"Havin' this ghastly thing happen to *me*. To my child, my family. Me, who's made a career out of fictions, out of language that doesn't say anythin', phony tragedies that don't mean a hoot and comedies that ain't really funny. Yeah, I guess you called the turn on me long ago—even those arguments we used to have back in Greenwich Village. A metaphysician, you said I was. Suffocating in my own nonsense."

"You're making me feel dreadful. I shouldn't have begrudged you your work."

"*Work.* I love the way we invest our gaseous behavior with the language of the shop. Oh, you were wise to me." He ducked his head as if trying to roll with a blow. "Why Amy?" he gasped. "Why my Amy?"

She was too exhausted to contest his meandering analyses. "I don't know, Fritzie. Maybe you're right. Maybe there's some unseen hand moving and shaking us—and we get what we deserve."

"I kicked her once."

Laura barely heard him; he had buried his voice.

"That is correct. I kicked her. Right smack in the back. Oh, I'm a good deal more disgustin' than you know, Laura. I was workin' one night, editin' a script—there's no doors in this damn house, so I could never lock her out of the den—and she kept comin' at me. You know how Amy is when she's got her mind set. That child never played alone for two minutes. Borrowin' and breakin' my pencils, stealin' paper, crawlin' in my lap, tuggin' my hand, twistin' my fingers—Laura, she was like that——" He seemed ready to weep again but, with a wrenching of his shoulders and neck, held back the tears. "And me tryin' to concentrate on my work. I simply could not get rid of her. So I kicked her. Pretty hard, too. With the side of my foot, right in the holler of her back. How does that appeal to you? Are you horrified?"

"Don't tell me about it. I don't want to hear."

"You won't even permit me the luxury of despisin' myself, will you? Yes, I kicked her. You know somethin' about that child? She didn't cry. Didn't whimper. Looked at me, the way she can, all squinty and dark—and danced off."

"She never told me about it. I think you've made the story up." She looked at his swollen face and knew he was not lying.

"Yeah," Andrus sighed. "What a fine daddy I turned out to be." Imploringly, he cried out to his wife: "Laura, how could a man love his children as much as I did and be such a son-of-a-bitch toward them? How could a man adore his little girls, dream about them at work and brag about them to his friends—and then have no patience with them, no time for them, no capacity to sacrifice for them? How, Laura? You know all the answers."

She sat up on the day bed, resting on one elbow, turning toward him. "Amy loves you very much."

"In spite of me. A tribute to the child's persistence."

"No. She worships you. Fritzie, you weren't a bad father. It's just—just—oh, I don't want to talk about it any more. Especially now."

"You've said it before. Say it again. You always did my confessin' rather well for me."

"This isn't the time to go into it."

"Go on, go on," Andrus said vigorously. "We need the catharsis. Let's you and I assume Amy's unharmed . . . she'll be back here tonight. And let's pass the time figurin' out how to do better by her."

"Fritzie, there isn't any connection between what happened today and any parental failings on our part. You make everything worse by harping on it."

Andrus sat beside her on the day bed. His blockish body seemed to suspire, to give off air, like a hydraulic system adjusting itself. He placed a hand on her bare knee. "No, don't move away," he said. "I know how much you dislike me. I know I deserve a lot of it —not all of it—but a lot of it. Maybe if I touch you, stay close to you, I'll catch some of that bloodless self-control. Laura, you once said I'd been hanging around actors so long that I no longer had any personality, any character of my own. I want you to know that hurt me, Laura. It's one of the reasons I moved out, one of the reasons I gave up tryin' to reach you, to mean anythin' to you or the children."

"I shouldn't have said it."

"But you told the truth." Andrus sounded plaintive, injured— a child agreeing he had turned in a bad arithmetic paper. "Still an' all—that wasn't a good reason for rubbing my nose in it. I got to have my illusions, Laura."

"Fritzie, can't we discuss this—later?"

He got up from the bed and strode to the jalousies, peeking through an aperture. "Those bloody vultures," he said. "Why are they still heah? Where's our esteemed relative, Dr. Todd?"

"He's only been gone a few minutes. Let me rest, Fritzie, please."

He did not hear her. Eyes fixed on the sun-bright line of cars, the torpid reporters, he said: "Amy'll be back. I know it. This is all a damn hoax, a fraud. She's safe. We'll give that bastard his money and wish him well and take our child and let the cops worry about it afterwards. I am confident we'll see her tonight. I promise you, Laura, I'll never kick her again. You hear me? Do you?"

"Yes, yes, Fritzie." His conversations, as usual, were one-way streets. He expected that all of his circumlocutions, his theorizing (laced with hillbilly accents and the syntax of the southern polit- ical orator) would flow freely, uninterrupted, to his listener. On the other hand, he was required to hear only bits and pieces of his partner's words. His wife, white as the plaster chunks on the heavy table, aching with the departing grip of the migraine, was unable

to discredit him. In his desperate, immature manner, he was coping
with his agony, summoning a counterfeit courage which would
serve him as well as her own metallic self-control.

Dr. Todd drove swiftly through Sanlu, passing from the wealthy
Buena Terra district, where the Andruses lived, to the modest
homes in Colchester, then, via side streets, into the bright business
section—each store shiny with new chrome and glass, each bulging
window attesting to the community's high per capita income. The
motifs were rustic desert-cum-Old English; hitching posts and
heraldry were effectively mingled.

The dentist handled the car deftly. Swinnerton, silent beside
him, admired his co-ordination—it was that of a man twenty years
younger. The reporter could envision Todd pirouetting about the
dentist's chair with the grace of a ballet dancer.

"We've missed you at the Library Committee," Todd said. He
was a friendly man and it seemed unfair to keep poor Swinnerton
in chancery. The committee was good neutral ground. "We still use
that crackajack fiction survey you did for us."

"It was my pleasure, Walter," said Swinnerton. "I'm a bit hung
up these days. I've gotten a few magazine assignments, and what
with my radio stint and the *Truth,* I'm at sixes and sevens."

Todd cocked his hairless head. "How I envy you your talent,
Harvey. If I had one-tenth of it, I'd have my book under way. All
my notes are in apple-pie order—my recordings, my scrapbooks.
Just last Thursday a chap at the club, a stockholder in a New York
publishing house, told me my book was sure-fire, that he could
interest his friends back east in it."

An edge of light shimmered in front of the Siamese-cat eyes of
the reporter. Swinnerton was guileless, yet he understood Herbert
Hood's mandate, and he was not a bad newsman.

"Walter—this is hardly the time to discuss it—but I'd like to
have another look at your material. Perhaps when this magazine
stint is over, I could have a go with you."

"Could you? Really?" Todd was elated. "That would be marvelous, Harvey. I bet you'd find it intriguing."

"I might at that. *Fifty Years of Dentistry.* I don't believe there's
ever been a good book written about a dentist. Doctors, yes, too
many."

Todd patted Swinnerton's prickly knee. "You have a date,
Harvey. Dinner at the club." *The club* (he belonged to several)
kept dropping into the dentist's conversations the way a nervous

housewife will toss a favored spice (rosemary, sage, oregano) into all dishes as insurance.

The car pulled abreast of the Valley View Savings and Loan Association. Todd braked the Buick and turned off the ignition. "Far as I go, Harvey," he said. The reporter did not move.

"Walter—I say, Walter," he began cautiously, "just what is going on at the Andrus place? What are you doing there anyway?"

Todd waggled a stout finger. "Now, now, Harvey. I've got someone waiting for me inside."

"The bank's been closed for an hour."

"They're always open for me. I'm on the board."

Both men got out. The dentist walked briskly toward the bank. Swinnerton followed. "Look here, Walter," the reporter persisted. "Suppose you tell me what's afoot, and suppose I promise to keep my mouth shut. Not to say a word. That is to say—it'll be *off the record*."

"Off the record?" asked the dentist. He liked the sound of the words. They paused at the entrance to a shaded alley that led to the rear of the bank. The heat was insufferable, yet neither man—one in wintry tweeds, the other in severe blue—seemed to mind.

"That's a bit of journalistic lingo, Walter. It means we get the information—for future use or as background—but aren't permitted to print it. The President, the Secretary of State—all those public blokes—they often brief us off the record."

The dentist was impressed. He patted his pink crown, spread his dancer's feet. "I'm of two minds on this matter, Harvey. I respect you and I know you well enough to know you'd keep a promise. On the other hand——"

"All I'm asking for is a fill-in, Walter," Swinnerton pleaded. "I promise I'll use not a word, so long as you say I can't. On the other hand, should the story be released, I'd have a nice advantage over my competition, and I'd regard whatever you'd given me as *unprivileged*. You see, you'd be doing me a marvelous turn—a much-needed boost to my laggard career, one might say. I say again, I would not divulge a word about this affair until the police gave us the green light."

It was a remarkably long and a remarkably shrewd speech for Swinnerton.

"I'll tell you this, Harvey. The chief *is* planning on giving the information out. Perhaps he's doing it right now. Not to you fellows hanging around Nespoli Drive, but to your editors."

"Is that a fact?"

"But that won't help you any. He's asking everyone to lay off. Not to print or broadcast anything, because of certain arrangements with the kidnaper."

Swinnerton suppressed a gasp. "The kidnaper."

"Now that was stupid of me, wasn't it? I had no business telling you that. However, it really doesn't matter, because all you chaps are being requested to observe secrecy. We're sure there'll be agreement. After all, Amy Andrus' life is at stake." He halted. "Goodness, I'm a regular blabbermouth."

"Please, please don't be in a flap over it, Walter. We agreed this was all off the record, didn't we? I made a promise—not to use a word until the police say all right. May I ask what your role is—Walter—how you figure in this? You see—all this would be of inestimable help to me, give me a leg up, as it were."

The dentist, aware that he was on the verge of becoming a national monument, disarmed by Swinnerton's assurances, elaborated. He spoke quickly, describing his relationship to Laura Andrus, the summons that morning, the meetings with McFeeley, his role in arranging for the ransom money. He did not, however, disclose the details of the note or mention the time or circumstances of the rendezvous. Through it all, Swinnerton, unblinking, sweatless, his neat head bobbing, said nothing.

"Ah—there is a note, is that correct, Walter?" he asked.

"Yes. But don't press me on it. I've said too much already. If it weren't that we're old friends, Harvey, and that I felt you were a notch or two above the average newspaperman, I'd not have uttered a syllable. You must promise me—nothing in print."

"What if the embargo is lifted?"

"Beg pardon? What embargo?"

"The ban on using the story."

"Embargo. You fellows have a language all your own, don't you?" Todd was delighted with the manner in which the reporter had welcomed him into his esoteric fraternity. He glanced at his watch: 3:42. "I've got to go, Harvey. Please, not a word, not a single word to anyone. For heaven's sake, even if the story is released by the police, don't quote me, don't attribute a word to me. Perhaps later on. I'd be severely compromised otherwise." He stepped into the alley, then spun about. "Whole thing seems a bit odd, doesn't it?"

"The kidnaping? It is a terribly rare crime. I guess it takes a while for people to accept the reality." Swinnerton's heart pranced; if he could not reach a telephone, he would faint.

"Yes, the kidnaping—and what it's done to all of us." The dentist bit his lower lip. "Do you have, as I do, a sensation of *strangeness?* Of things not being what they seem? Here we are, for example— you and I—two rather average men—and we're up to our hip boots in what may well be the crime of the decade. Lindbergh. Urschel. And now the Andrus case. And here we are standing in an alley in Santa Luisa talking about it. I have the feeling I'm somebody else."

"Walter, it's a good thing you're the man you *are*. Were I those parents, I'd want no one other than you to handle the details for me. Are you going to make the rendezvous with the kidnaper? Is it tonight?" His voice fluttered.

"No more, Harvey. I've told you everything in confidence. Please respect that confidence." He pivoted and vanished. Swinnerton remained in the alley until he heard the cold click of the electrically operated door. Then the reporter ran into the breathless street and raced to his left to a drug-department store. He flew from the desert heat into its frigid interior and hurled himself into the nearest phone booth.

Rheinholdt was capable of only one job at a time. Having ordered Eliot Sparling released, he waited until the jailer advised him that the reporter was free before turning to the onerous task of contacting the newspapers. Mayor Speed's admonitions rattled about his large head. *Be nice, be helpful, tell them about it.* He would tell them. And let the mayor squirm and scream when they shot their mouths off. He, Rheinholdt, would be in the clear if the kid was hurt. It was long past the hour's delay that he, Todd, and McFeeley had agreed upon as deadline for calling the papers. The wall clock registered 3:22. Rheinholdt buzzed for his secretary, Patrolman Clyde Hertmann. "You and Baines come in," he said.

"Want the car, Chief?" Farmer Baines asked. He had a clotted voice, muffled by the dust of a dozen farms parching in prairie sun. The creases in his veal-colored neck appeared embedded with yellow earth.

"No. I got a job for you. Call the newspapers and the radio stations. The mayor wants it that way. Tell them there's been a kidnaping in Santa Luisa, but they can't print anything. A child's life is at stake and they will be to blame if anything happens."

Baines was stupefied. "Why me? I'm no good at that."

The chief pointed to Clyde Hertmann. "You help him. You look up the newspapers and radio and television—the phone numbers. Baines, you do the calling."

Hertmann nodded his slender, intelligent head. "What exactly would you like us to say?" he asked.

"I'll dictate it," Rheinholdt said. Hertmann picked up his steno pad. The chief turned away, covering the bristly top of his head with his laced hands. "You're calling for Chief Caspar Rheinholdt of the City of Santa Luisa. A kidnaping has taken place in Santa Luisa. Because of arrangements with the kidnaper for the return of the victim, we ask you to print or broadcast nothing at all until we advise you that you can. Please disregard any rumors, anything from sources other than the police. Remember that a child's life is at stake."

Baines' dried face developed webs around the eyes, the mouth. "I ain't sure I can handle it," he protested.

"Yes, you can. Take your time. I want you to do the talking. Hertmann, make the list. Don't answer any questions." He cracked his knuckles. "They print anything, it's *their* fault. Not ours. That kid gets murdered, or we never see her again, it's on *them*. Not us."

In the outer room, Hertmann thumbed through a Los Angeles red book, found the listing *Newspapers,* and with a red pencil checked off all the Los Angeles dailies and several other community papers. He did the same in the Santa Luisa red book. Then he shoved both books across the desk to Sergeant Baines and started transcribing, swiftly and accurately, Rheinholdt's statement. At 3:31 P.M., seven hours after the crime had been committed, the police were attempting to keep it out of print.

Bill Trigg, the *Truth's* city editor, took Swinnerton's call from the drugstore. He heard Swinnerton's first three words—*it's a kidnaping*—and stopped him. "Hold it, Harve," he said, "let's make it a conference call." Trigg flashed the operator and asked her to put Mr. Hood and Mr. Hansel on. Ed Kalaidjian, the managing editor, circling Trigg's desk warily, was not included.

"Swinnerton?" Hansel asked. "This is Mr. Hansel. I want you to talk fully. Leave nothing out. Nobody interrupt. Trigg? Are you ready to take notes?"

Trigg already had a sheaf of papers in his typewriter, already had clamped a headset over his frizzy red hair. But he knew better than to anticipate T.T. "Yes, sir," Trigg said. "I'll do it right now."

"It's a kidnaping," Swinnerton said. "I'm sure I'm the only one who has it. They all suspect it, but I *know* it is. I got it from a Dr. Todd, Walter L. Todd, a dentist in Santa Luisa. He is a distant relative of the woman, Mrs. Laura Andrus. He's acting as a go-between. He's at Valley View Savings and Loan this very minute, and he wouldn't say so, but I'm positive he's getting the ransom money. He wouldn't tell me how much." Swinnerton halted. "Ah —let me look at what I've scrawled here. When he spoke to me, I didn't dare take notes."

They awaited him, the man who was paid ninety-one dollars a week for covering P.T.A. meetings and high school basketball. For Hansel, the enforced silence was a rare circumstance. But he understood the enormity of the secret knowledge and he dared not break the thread of narrative. In a moment, Swinnerton resumed. He spoke softly and clearly, recounting, as accurately as he could, Todd's information: *it was a kidnaping; there was a note; the child was Amy Andrus; she had vanished that morning; a rendezvous with the kidnaper was planned—where or when, Todd would not say.* Swinnerton speculated it was imminent—or else why should the dentist be hurrying to the bank after hours? As Harvey spoke, Bill Trigg glanced at a morgue clipping—a paragraph from a local gossip column—that he had located earlier.

> . . . friends of TV director Fritzie Andrus and his sculptress wife Laura are upset by their sudden breakup. Fritzie, brilliant young talent from New York, has taken up bachelor quarters at the Duval in Hollywood. Laura remains with the children at their Santa Luisa home. No reasons given, but people close to both hope. . . .

"Is that everything?" asked Hansel.

"Well, not quite," Swinnerton said. "I'm giving you all these details in the hope that the story will be released."

"Released?" shouted Hansel. "What are you talking about? Do you know what you're talking about? No, of course you don't!"

Swinnerton swallowed. "Mr. Hansel, you can't print any of these facts I just gave you. I promised Dr. Todd it was off the record. That's the only way he'd tell me. Not a word can be used, because it might frighten the kidnaper. I phoned them in so we could build up a backlog—get a leg up on the story, if and when the police say we can print it."

"Have they said we *can't?*" roared Hansel.

"Ah—not yet. But I'm told the Santa Luisa police are calling everyone to confirm it's a kidnaping, but asking people not to use it."

Hansel's voice invaded his tortured ear, like a painful injection. "Let me get this straight, Swinnerton. You say you have this exclusively?"

"Yes, sir. I'm the only one. Dr. Todd said——"

"Just a minute. This dentist who told you these facts then demanded you keep them secret?" Hansel might have been in the phone booth with him, screaming at him.

"Not exactly, Mr. Hansel. Before he'd tell me anything, he made me *promise* it was off the record. Or, rather, that's the only way I could get him to talk—by promising beforehand."

They awaited T. T. Hansel—Bill Trigg hunched over the typewriter, his fingers alert; Herbert Hood immobile within his glass cage, his hard gut jammed against his desk; Ed Kalaidjian fingering his line-up of automatic pencils. In the phone booth, Swinnerton had a recollection of a day when the brakes in his Austin burned out and he careened down Malibu Canyon Drive— terrorized, helpless, at the mercy of a mechanism that had failed.

By 4:00 P.M., there were, by Eliot Sparling's count, eighteen newsmen assembled across the street from the Andrus house. Many of them Eliot recognized. The Associated Press had sent two men and a photographer. The senior AP reporter was Victor DeGroot, a gray, professorial man—a sort of dean among Southern California correspondents. There was a boy from the United Press, dressed in narrow eastern clothing, flashing alarming white teeth in a tennis-tanned face. The *Santa Luisa Register* had dispatched Duane Bosch, eighteen. Also among the newer arrivals was a frenzied young man named Martin Ringel, a newscaster-reporter for an independent television station, KYOT. He was a blond, squat lad, twenty-three, who had made a lavish reputation for himself, first by revealing Communist infiltration at UCLA (he had been, he admitted, a courier for the Reds), and then by parlaying his confessional into a job. Now he was well known for nasty interviews in which he provoked his betters into making public asses of themselves. Ringel was much feared and envied, and when Eliot saw his pugnacious white face poking around the Andrus home, the UBC reporter knew that here was an enemy.

"Look at that fink Ringel," Eliot confided to George Brack. "He's here five minutes and he thinks he owns the story."

Martin Ringel waddled by, making notes in a pad. "Hey, Ringel, what's the inside dope?" Sparling mocked. "The Commies kidnap the kid? The mother an agent of the MVD?"

Ringel paid no attention to him. Eliot was not even a regular member of the press corps. The snub was painful to Sparling. "I'll show *him*," he said to Brack. "He couldn't get to see Mrs. Emerson, but I will." Presuming on his friendship with the woman who had tipped him, Eliot galumphed across Nespoli Drive and started up the Emersons' lawn. Halfway toward the door, between a shedding palm and a pool afloat with old newspapers, Joe McFeeley intercepted him.

"Beat it, Sparling," Joe said.

"Can't I pay a visit? I wanna see Mrs. Emerson."

McFeeley shaded his eyes. "They should have kept you in the pokey. All of you belong there." The detective looked at the waiting troupe. Bordering the long line of vehicles was a litter of coffee and Coke containers, cardboard boxes, wax-paper wrappings. A convention of slobs appeared to have held an afternoon picnic.

"Joe, your boss isn't helping," Eliot said. "Until someone talks, we'll hang around."

"Stay away. You guys belong across the street."

"Why can't I see Mrs. Emerson?"

"Because I am."

McFeeley left him on the lawn and rang the bell. Babe Emerson, still in soiled wrapper, her hair kerchiefed, her face glowing with cream, ushered the detective into a high, musty living room. He introduced himself, and Babe invited him to sit in a high-backed, fuzzy chair, which, like the rest of the room, had the quality of a museum gone to seed. The ceiling was cracked, the fireplace coated with cold ashes.

McFeeley did not say that Amy had been kidnaped. He did not mention the note. But he told her that the child was missing, that a search was under way.

"She's kidnaped," Babe sobbed. "I know it. I knew it. Oh, God, poor Laura. As if she doesn't have enough to worry her. No wonder all those reporters are hanging around. Harry was right. I blab too much."

The detective had no reason to suspect she had talked to Eliot Sparling, and his mind, occupied with a thousand problems, did not linger on her weepy utterances. He explained that he wanted to speak to her son Timmy, the boy with the morning newspaper route. Before she could call for him, Timmy slouched into the living room. He was a thin, dark boy of fourteen, wolfing a peanut butter sandwich.

"I hear my name?" he asked. Darkly mustached, sideburned, he had a shrewd, sharp look. "You say Amy was kidnaped, Ma? What a jolt." A basso's throaty rumble intruded on his boyish pitch. He slumped into a brocaded armchair.

"We're not sure," McFeeley said cautiously. Babe introduced them. She advised the detective pridefully that he was an honor student in science at Sanlu High.

"What a jolt," he repeated. "Boy, right here in Buena Terra. Got any leads?"

McFeeley smiled. "Your mother said it was a kidnaping. I didn't. I understand you have a newspaper route in the morning."

"Yeah. The *Register*. I oughta have the whole north Buena Terra district, but the circulation manager took Kohlmeyer away from me 'cause some big shot's kid wanted it."

"I used to deliver the *Register* myself. You still call the non-tippers deadheads? And the big tippers sports?"

"Sure. All I got are deadheads. One of the richest routes in Sanlu and some of the cheapest people."

The detective laughed. He had a fleeting wish to be back in the simple rhythms of high school—*the route, basketball practice, homework.* "What time do you go out in the morning? Give me a schedule when you start, when you finish, what streets you pass."

Timmy obliged him. He left the house about 7:30, rode north to Kohlmeyer Street and Buena Terra Park, then turned east and then south. His route took about forty minutes and he was back just in time for the 8:20 school bus, which stopped at the end of Nespoli.

"Did you see Amy this morning?"

"I talked to her."

The detective inched forward. "Where was she?"

"On her bike. On the driveway. She got off and walked down the path and we talked."

"That was about ten after eight?"

"Yeah. I know, because I was almost through and Fatso Skopas across the street was blasting off in his Cadillac."

"Timmy!" his mother reprimanded. She explained to Joe.

"That's Mr. Skopas—the wholesale fruit family. That's his house across the way."

"Go on, Timmy. What did Amy say to you?"

The boy frowned. "I don't remember. She talks all the time—to dogs, flowers, herself."

"How about this morning? Remember what she said?"

"Something about her father coming home."

Babe intervened again. "Lieutenant, you know the Andruses are separated, don't you? It's tragic—the way that little girl worships her father. Now *this*. Honestly, I don't know how much Laura can take. If only I could help her!"

McFeeley listened patiently, then returned to the boy. "That was all? You didn't see her again or talk to her again?"

"Nope. I said something about how I saw her father's name on the TV. Just to cheer her up."

A picture was forming in McFeeley's mind—not necessarily a useful one, but something that at least gave the crime dimension, specificity, an existence in time and space. None of Timmy's information led anywhere, but it invoked helpful disciplines. The facts had a ritual value, like the way he used to cross himself before a basketball game.

"You up on cars, Timmy?" Joe asked. "Models and years?"

"I used to be, when I was a kid. I'm kind of rusty now. Solid propellants interest me."

The detective smiled. "Timmy, in the past few days—particularly this morning—have you noticed anyone in the neighborhood who doesn't belong here, cruising around or walking around? Any car that didn't seem familiar and kept turning up?"

The boy closed one sepia eye and stroked his long nose. "Nope. I see so many. I don't notice any more. Any creep who was casing a house here would get noticed. You could get arrested just for taking a walk here."

"Concentrate on this morning. Did you see anyone walking around who looked strange to you? Like he didn't belong here and was snooping? Acting as if he didn't *want* to be noticed?"

"Nope."

Joe sighed. The basketball game was under way. The benediction was fine, but it couldn't shoot fouls. He tried again. "How about a car? Any car at all that you'd never seen before?"

The boy shut both eyes. "Nope."

"Let's try to test your memory," McFeeley said. "Let's see if you can name every automobile on the block—the family it belongs to, make and year. Maybe that way you'll remember the odd one."

"That's easy," Timmy said. He rattled them off—their own two cars, the Andrus station wagon and sports car, Skopas' three autos (Cadillac, MG, Dodge) and so on down the street. He missed neither a household nor a car.

"Now what about any that *don't* belong to your neighbors. See any this morning—a car you couldn't associate with someone on this street?"

"A Ford."

"What year?"

"A '49 Ford, maybe a '50. I saw it on Casagrande, going opposite me. Then I saw it behind me when I came back."

"About when you passed Amy on the way home?"

"Yeah. I think so."

"Coming from Kohlmeyer Street?"

"No. If he was behind me, he couldn't be. He was coming from Meridian."

"You're sure it was a Ford? And you saw it twice?"

"Yep. You pulled that trick making me think of cars, and it greased my memory."

McFeeley glanced at the mother as if seeking credentials for the boy. She obliged him. "He doesn't make up stories, officer. He has a memory like crazy—too good, if you ask me."

Turning to Timmy again, he asked: "What color was it?"

"Ah—light brown. Tan."

"Two-tone?"

"No. All tan."

"Dirty, banged up?"

"No. Clean."

"Did you see the driver?"

Timmy finished the last of the sandwich and licked peanut butter from his fingers. "Nope. I didn't notice."

"You notice the license plates?"

"Nope. I could even be wrong on the year—'49, '50, maybe even this year's."

"What model? Tudor? Hardtop?"

"I'm not sure. Just a sedan."

The detective, jotting notes in his pad, halted, tapping his pencil against the page. The boy had started marvelously—sure of himself, precise. Now he was hedging. McFeeley reviewed the information.

On the major points Timmy stood his ground. A light-brown or tan Ford—a '49, '50 (maybe '51) —cruising the streets, seen in two directions just prior to Amy's disappearance. The detective was convinced the boy was not inventing a story for self-aggrandizement, as adult witnesses tend to do. By and large, Joe knew, teenagers were excellent witnesses—sharp of memory, accurate on details.

He remained in the disorderly living room (a woman's shoe rested on the fireplace; an unexplained loaf of French bread decorated an ottoman) another few minutes. Gently, persistently, he tried to elicit more information from them—something, anything —about the Andrus family, their habits, their friends, conversations overheard, odd visitors. It became evident that Mrs. Emerson was less of a confidante of Laura Andrus than she had indicated. Actually, she knew her marginally; Mrs. Andrus did not invite friendships. The best that could be said for their relationship was that Laura did not treat her with the indifference she reserved for people like the Skopases and the Kahlers.

McFeeley declined a glass of iced tea (the pitcher was flecked with bits of dried sugar and lemon pulp) and left. As he crossed the driveway, he saw the reporters—some lolling on lawns, others resting in their cars, a few fiddling with newsreel gear—and he afforded himself a humorless smile. His assignment, as they used to say in his basketball days, was a hanger. All he had to do was find a tan Ford—'49, '50 or '51—and he'd have it solved. Of course, Timmy Emerson could have gotten it all wrong. And in the event he were right, what guarantee was there that the early-morning cruiser was nothing more than an ambitious real-estate agent scouting a few listings?

Rheinholdt's secretary, Patrolman Clyde Hertmann, found it nothing short of miraculous. Their luck was holding out. As incredible as it seemed to him, Sergeant Baines was getting the job done. The Farmer had started calling the newspapers at 3:36. Now, twenty minutes later, he had all but finished the first list Hertmann had made. Most encouraging, he had secured the grumbling co-operation of everyone he had telephoned. Somehow, his arid, nasal tone, recalling dusty village squares, fields of alfalfa glinting in the Iowa sun, proved more effective with the editors than any glib spiel by a paid press agent. A few argued with him. Some insulted him. Others demanded more information. Many asked to speak to Rheinholdt personally. But Baines, firm, dedicated, un-complicated, stuck to his litany, always ending with the crucial warning—a child's life is at stake.

When Dr. Walter L. Todd returned from the bank, carrying a thick manila envelope, the reporters milled about him, shoving microphones at his hairless head, shouting questions. They noted that Swinnerton was not with him, and they were suspicious and annoyed.

Young Martin Ringel, the television gadfly, slithered at the dentist around another man's hip, through a cameraman's legs. He maneuvered his blocky figure with the artful skill of a feverish three-year-old boy adept at pushing a slow older brother away from toys.

"What'd you tell Swinnerton?" Ringel yelled. "Is that the ransom dough? How much?"

The swarm clotted around the dentist, but he sashayed and pirouetted, working his way through the mob. There were at least twenty of them, he estimated, and he wondered what was delaying Rheinholdt. Polite, evasive, he made his way to the redwood door. "Really, you fellows should leave. I suspect you'll get official word soon."

"But Swinnerton!" Eliot roared. "What'd you tell him?"

"Not a thing," the dentist said airily.

From the motor pool across the street, one of the reporters came charging up to the mass around Todd. He was an older man, white-haired and pudgy, with the look of a dependable police-beat man. Eliot knew him slightly—Dave Arnspeiger from the *Los Angeles Argus*. Arnspeiger was waving his hands and trying to tell them something, but his shortness of breath made his words unintelligible until he was on top of the group.

"It's a kidnaping!" Arnspeiger gasped. "A kidnaping! The cops just confirmed it! I got it on the car phone from downtown!"

Todd took advantage of their diverted attention and slipped into the house. The reporters gathered around Arnspeiger.

"Here's the deal," the white-haired man said, "near as I could write it down." He read from a pad. "Some cop who was calling for Rheinholdt said there was a kidnaping in Sanlu; that's all—no name, no place, nothing. Because of arrangements with the kid-naper, newspapers and radio and TV were asked not to print or broadcast anything. That's it."

"Good old Rheinholdt," Sparling said. "Bighearted Caspar."

"What's the pitch, Dave?" DeGroot, the senior AP man, asked. "What's the *Argus* doing?"

Arnspeiger replied: "Not printing. Nobody is, according to my desk."

"Nobody?" asked the UP's young eastern type.

"That's what the cops said," Arnspeiger replied.

The group ebbed and flowed around Arnspeiger; he had little else to tell them. A few ran to phone their own offices and confirm his gloomy message. DeGroot emerged as spokesman, an *éminence grise*. "I don't get it, Dave," the AP man asked. "Are we yanked off? What did your desk say?"

Arnspeiger shaded his eyes from the descending sun. "Hell, no. The way I got it, Rheinholdt didn't say *anything* about pulling us off. Nothing about not being allowed to *cover*. The only thing he asked was that nobody *print*." He hesitated. "I don't know about you guys, but I'm hanging around until I get run off."

"Me, too!" bellowed Eliot. "They can't keep us from the story!"

No one paid attention to him. DeGroot rubbed his chin. The AP man had a tolerant, weathered face. He was intelligent and honest and had won several awards. "I can't figure it. They want secrecy, and yet nothing was said about our leaving."

"I'm staying," piped Duane Bosch. At eighteen, he was already a crusader.

Others similarly announced their intentions: they would stay until ordered off.

"And I almost had it *alone*," Eliot said sadly to George Brack as they walked back to the UBC car. "Me and my big yap."

"Had what, Eliot?" Brack asked.

"The Andrus kidnaping. *I had the tip*. I blew the whole thing. Don't you see, Georgie? I blew it?" His larded figure drooped in the heat—head on neck, neck on chest, chest on paunch. "Ballstead oughta fire me. I deserve it."

"Oh, for goodness' sake, El," the newscaster said, "you couldn't help it. Getting jailed made a good story. Come on, we'd better do that interview for the TV news."

Sparling stretched out his unmuscled arms. "What's the use? You heard what they said. The whole story's on ice. We can't talk about it. I'm sure Ballstead went along."

Brack frowned. "You're right. It does seem kind of aimless."

Steve Billik had set up the 16-millimeter camera. The soundman was fiddling with knobs. "Ya doin' it or aincha doin' it?" Billik called.

"We might as well, El. They might lift the ban. Besides, Tom asked for it. Let's follow orders." Brack took the microphone and placed himself with the Andrus home in the background. He cleared his throat and invoked the holy tones. "I'm standing here on the lawn of the home of Mr. and Mrs. Francis Andrus in Santa Luisa. With me is the UBC reporter who first learned of the kidnaping of Amy Andrus and who. . . ."

After an appropriate introduction, Eliot moved into the frame.

"Tell us about your run-in with the chief this morning, Eliot." Brack asked.

"Well, George——" The soundman waved his hands. "Hold that voice down, willya, kid? You almost broke the needle. Take it all over and don't yell so loud."

The money lay on Fritzie's desk in the den. There were two stacks. One contained fifty new fifty-dollar bills and was bound with a brown wrapper. The remainder of the ransom, seventeen hundred dollars in old fifties, was held together by a thick rubber band.

"Now that is something," Andrus murmured. "A child's life dependent on that sum." He was slumped in his swivel chair. McFeeley and Todd stood to one side. Laura sat alongside the desk.

"And such new bills," Andrus went on. "Isn't that a mistake, officer?"

"He didn't specify," McFeeley said. "He knows he can't keep us from keeping a record of the serial numbers—whether they're new or old. That's what caught Hauptmann. Some fellow at a filling station checked a number."

Andrus spun about in the swivel. "Yes. They got him. And I recall what happened to the child."

"One thing had nothing to do with the other," the detective said defensively.

"Fritzie, you've got to stop," Laura pleaded.

"It's the truth. I can't help it if I have total recall. I been going over in my mind all the kidnapings I can remember. Laura, the odds are against us. I know it. We better stop deludin' ourselves."

Dr. Todd placed a firm hand on Andrus' shoulder. "Now, Francis. That won't help. We have every reason to be hopeful. I have some good news. As I came in, one of the reporters had just gotten word that the chief has phoned the newspapers. I guess they'll be leaving any minute."

McFeeley's lopsided face camouflaged its confusion. Rheinholdt hadn't told him. He glanced out the window, disturbed again by the row of cars, some double-parked; the litter of dozens of lunches and snacks; the milling, gossiping men. Someone was shooting a soundfilm interview on the lawn.

"Y'all mean," Andrus asked, "that that chief *told* the papers?"

"It should have been done four hours ago," Joe said. "We'll be lucky if we can stop them now. Look—let's get on with the bills. The bank didn't take down numbers, did they, Dr. Todd?"

"No. Per your instructions."

"O.K. How's your typing, Mrs. Andrus?"

"Fast hunt and peck."

Andrus appeared chagrined at not having been invited. He made a flapping gesture with one hand. "Heck. I'll he'p out. I'll dig out the Olivetti and Laura can use the upright."

"Good," McFeeley said. "Double-space the list. Three carbons and an original. Each of you take a pile of bills, then cross-check each other's list. Can you type with gloves on? I don't want any more prints on them."

"I can use a pair of my own gloves," Laura said. "Fritzie can wear those rubber kitchen gloves."

A few minutes later they were seated at typewriters in the den. Laura took the new bills after McFeeley slipped off the brown wrapper; Fritzie took the old ones. Joe cautioned them on accuracy and left to phone Rheinholdt again. The uneven clacking of the two machines was time come to life—a muted, insistent passage of seconds, as irregular as a fibrillating heart, as lulling as the summer buzz of winged insects.

Her husband was squinting at his stack of currency. Fritzie refused to wear eyeglasses; contact lenses annoyed him. "Damn," he muttered, "my list's gonna be full of mistakes. Yours'll be perfect. Never could type good."

He was the implacable foe of the practical, Laura realized. For all his alleged communion with the written word—all the books, plays, short stories he claimed to read—the simple mechanics of writing, the elementary disciplines, would elude him forever. He rarely kept notes on his scripts, never wrote anything down, did not indulge in that precise, microscopic examination of text, the marginalia and mnemonic devices that most directors employed. His technique was one of *Gestalt;* visceral, instinctive, overwhelming and—in his opinion—superior. He had no ear for subleties, no patience with nuances, was blind to social reality.

Seeing him now, hunched over the portable, battling the recalcitrant keys and numbers (he could not fathom them; they had limits, size, specificity), she had a vivid recollection of their first meeting. Six years ago—the summer of 1945—she had come to Greenwich Village to study sculpturing. She shared a cold-water walk-up with two other late-comers to Bohemia—three daughters of the Protestant Ethic, seeking lost gods and forgotten rites in a stew of predatory Sicilian galoots, feverish NYU students, winos, sailors and *invertiti*. What encouragement Laura received from her instructor at the Art Students League, a frank and capable man who assured her she possessed a genuine, if cautious, talent, was diluted each hot night when she returned to Horatio Street. An incurable realist, Laura had a clear view of the Village; she saw it not as a spawning ground for the talented young, but rather as a retreat for the aimless and rootless—a place where people better suited to stenography and lathe work deceived themselves and bought forged tickets to the grand arena of art. So thinking, she would become depressed, sullen, weary. Her work in clay, wood and bronze showed no growth, and her teacher, once convinced she was an artist of promise, revised his estimate of her. She sensed his changed attitude, accepted it as closer to the truth than his early enthusiasms, and made plans to leave the Village after her course at the League ended.

At a point where she was ready to abandon New York and slink back to her parents in Connecticut (there to marry a pining associate professor of Romance languages), Fritzie burst into her life. One of Laura's roommates was an actress of sorts and had just gotten a part in an off-Broadway production. The girl invited Laura to a rehearsal—in a stifling loft on West Tenth Street. There, Laura sat quietly at the rear of the hall as the company of players went through the first reading. They were quite wretched—querulous, overeager young people, battling their way through bloodstained magnolias. (The play was an original by a dank young man from Georgia.) And yet, for all their sad ineptness, Laura found herself flushed with admiration for them.

They had nerve; they were not afraid to subject themselves to public immolations. Laura, not a notably sentimental young woman, wanted to weep for them. *I am like you,* she thought, *but without your courage. I have quit without even a small effort.*

When the first act had been concluded, the director delivered his critique. Andrus was twenty-seven at that time, a florid, chunky young man, newly arrived from North Carolina. During the reading, he had prowled about the dingy confines, coatless and tieless, grimacing, grunting, staring out of a cracked casement window at a stickball game below. Now he was ready to talk. In minutes, they were hypnotized—the actors, willingly; Laura, a stranger to their eccentric world, much against her volition. Insulting, bombastic, encouraging, he invested their threadbare lives with sureness, confidence, a capacity to grapple with problems. In a magic tongue that mingled the worst southern political oratory and glib show-biz jargon, he won them over—and made better actors of them.

"Ain't none of you playin' the reality!" Andrus howled. "Ain't none of you actually in this girl's college! *You*, there—you girl readin' Emma Sue! You sound like you tryin' to win the spellin' bee at New Bern High School, 'stead of defendin' yourself against a charge of homosexuality! Don't read—*talk!* Live! Get *involved!*"

He would halt abruptly, disgusted with all of them (and yet, curiously, still their loving leader), do a quick turn, then stop in their adoring midst and resume. This time, Laura noticed, he used his artful flapping hands, elevating them like two soaring doves, leading the way to a heavenly throne. "None of you have integrated," Andrus began—and the elegant hands went from his knees to his groin. "None of you are relatin' "—groin to chest. "I beg of you—talk to each other"—chest to head. "Look at each other"— hands, pointed and arched, over head. "*Love* each other!"—hands and arms outstretched, full length, over head.

The actors resumed their reading. At once, Laura was astounded by the change in them. They now appeared quasi-professional. Something in his windy, insulting, irrational discourse had touched them. The wild gestures, the fruity voice, the wizard's tongue— even his thick-blooded face, the lank mop of yellow hair—all these had infused them with courage, with purpose. "Have I captured it?" Laura's roommate asked him once. And the director, pressing chubby fists to his forehead, eyes locked, replied, "Play along, my dear—you are in communion with the *essence*."

Later, Laura, her roommate (a shy, shivering girl from Midland, Michigan) and Fritzie sat in a chrome-and-plastic bar on Sixth Avenue. After a few wary probings, Laura tried to bait him, to make him explain some of his more esoteric announcements. The young director scented the enemy but took no offense. Airily, he told her: "My dear young sculptress, the technique I use is like jazz. If it has to be explained to you, you'll never understand it."

His explanation explained nothing, but it established him as a

True Believer. Perhaps he was a confidence man, a dealer in an absurd palaver that defied parsing. Yet there was still a power in him, a strength that brought understanding to his pupils. She, reared in a hard academic household where words were used sparingly and precisely, found him intriguing and novel—a gaudy tropic butterfly, one that could not be pinned and spread on her entomological board.

"But do you really believe what you tell your actors?" she persisted. The roommate blushed at such blasphemy.

Andrus afforded her a mobile, mocking smile. He was delighted with her aloof, pretty face, her apparent good breeding and fine education (Bennington? Sarah Lawrence?). "Y'all believe in your sculpture?" he asked.

"I'm not sure," Laura said. "I haven't had a chance to learn if I really have any ability." She hesitated. "It's not a matter of believing. I can believe I'm a genius for a year—and still turn out a lot of junk."

"And so we part company," Andrus said. "I ain't got time to have doubts. I can't let my actors have doubts. By God, they better *believe* in my talent, and I better believe in it, else there won't be any play!"

"Suppose you're deceiving yourself?"

Andrus shook his wide, ruddy head. "Not a chance. I got the confidence of a coon catchin' crayfish in a millpond. Looks to me like you could use some. You really any good at what you do?"

The roommate, timidly, spoke up. "Oh, she's terrific, Fritzie, really. You know—modern but not crazy. Her teacher says she's great. Honest."

"That's so?" Andrus asked.

"Not quite," Laura said.

"Know somethin'?" Andrus asked airily. "I know your problem already, Miss Laura Todd. You lack any capacity—any desire, let me say—to dramatize yourself. Oh, I'm a lot sharper than my cornpone accents indicate. I'm willin' to assume you have a lot of talent. There's intelligence there, an original mind, and so forth. But what you lack is that crucial element that any artist needs— the skill at self-exploitation. Hell, art ain't enough no more. It's your public image. You can't be considered a serious writer if you're just a colorless clod. You can't write a poem in a split-level house. You can't paint masterpieces with a middle-class myopic view of life—and yourself."

"But that's fraud," Laura protested.

"Mebbe it is. But me an' you can't help that. If it makes me a better director to sound off like a ridge-runnin', possum-eatin', piney-woods political candidate, that's fine." He eyed her carefully. "I don't believe I'm gettin' to you."

"I'm afraid you're not. Public images are largely lies. I don't give a damn what mine is, so long as I'm left alone. If my art suffers for it, I can't be too concerned."

"You'll never make it then," he said—not cruelly.

"I prefer it that way. I'll let your actors be dazzled by your communions and essences and realities. I don't begrudge you your humpty-dumpty language as a tool to bend and shape them—but I wish you'd admit it's nonsense."

"*That* will be a cold, cold day in August," said Andrus.

And on that tenuous, wary basis, they had come first to find stimulation in one another, then a deep and pleasurable interest, then love. Laura remained the scoffer, the taunter, Fritzie the high priest of the temple. And, inevitably, their friendship—fragile, faintly mocking, edged with rivalry—turned on their artistic efforts. Laura stayed on at school, Fritzie wandered through bleak lofts and firetrap theaters, shouting, cajoling, insulting, and exalting his wretched actors. As he progressed, she stood still—in spite of his entreaties to dramatize herself, to create an image in keeping with a career in art. Deaf to his pleas, she realized he was righter than she would admit. There was no argument that in a swarm of small talents—her class at school, for example—any group of Fritzie's actors—success would touch those few who worked as hard at creating a new, exciting self as they did at their professional skills. Yet this was repugnant to her. In rejecting it, she found herself rejecting a good deal more—the world of performers, critics, dabblers, hangers-on; the congeries of initiates and novitiates; the whole apparatus of Recognition. Her talent—unquestionably a real and viable one—diminished as his soared. Through the years of courtship, marriage, and eventual breakup, she willingly (she assured herself) watched him expand, inflate, and rise on the warm wind of success, while she, alone in her studio, chipped and molded and worked, keeping her skills private and restricted. It could not have been otherwise, she knew. Fritzie, for all his shouts of encouragement, would not have tolerated another success in the house. Other people's triumphs depressed him. Tipped in advance that a colleague's television drama was superb, he would find an excuse for missing it—perhaps an urgent nocturnal visit to the PTA, an organization he normally avoided and mocked.

Laura glanced up from her typing. Fritzie was far behind her. She would end up finishing his work, pitying him. Compassion aroused, she became annoyed with him. He had no right claiming her pity—only Amy merited it. Yet it was impossible to hate him for the artless manner in which he aroused sympathy. Was it because she had always been shrewdly aware of his deceits—and sensed a grudging respect in him? In the furnace-hot den, surrounded by plaques attesting to his excellence, she was confounded by the way he had made her love him. Their six years of proximity had an outrageous, outlandish quality. Watching him struggle with the typewriter keys, squinting at the bills, she wondered if he still loved her—if he still had some awareness of that fragile web that had once united them.

He looked up abruptly. "Stop starin' at me. I know I ain't much."

"I wasn't thinking that." She was alarmed by the hidden terror in his voice; a world he had known only in *pastiche* had grown hair and teeth and was threatening to annihilate him.

"I reckon this might be viewed as a sort of therapy for us," he said. "Isn't that Irish cop somethin'?" With chagrin, he stared at Laura's stack of bills. "How come you're about finished and I'm still scratchin' along like an old hen?"

"I worked for four years in offices—when I got tired of sculpture."

"No, that ain't why. You're just smarter than I am. I expect Amy is also." He typed a serial number, one painful digit at a time, copying it from bill to yellow paper. "Maybe that's why I didn't get along so good with her. I always figured if she'd put her mind to it, she could direct better than me. I used to think—some day she'll try it and make me look silly." The memory of his daughter shivered his thick body. Laura reached across the desk and placed her gloved hand on his fist.

"Don't torment yourself—not now. You'll get a chance to change it. I don't know, Fritzie, I'm always the pessimist around here. I can't help feeling we'll be all right tonight."

"That's the name of a play I directed once in YMCA camp," he said dreamily. "One of my first successes." Memories of piney woods and a mountain lake in the Great Smokies brought a film to his eyes. "It will be all right on the night," he said. " 'Bout a rehearsal. Only this isn't no rehearsal."

McFeeley, coatless and tieless, his .38 nesting in his belt, returned. "I think we're in good shape with the newspapers," he said. "I just spoke to Rheinholdt. Everyone's agreeing to lay off."

Fritzie peeked through the den window. In the late afternoon glare he could see the newspapermen across the street, the file of parked cars. "What about them goin'?" he asked. "It's one thing not to print, but what good's that gonna do if they don't move? There ain't no criminal in his right senses gonna show up in the middle of that mob."

"I'll take care of that," Joe said. "They'll be gone long before 8:15."

"You gonna arrest 'em all?" Andrus asked.

McFeeley scratched his neck. He was delaying, awaiting orders from Rheinholdt—orders that might never come. An uncomfortable feeling that the task was too much for him, that he would drown in details weighed on him. He needed at least ten more men in plain clothes; he needed the laboratory report; he wanted someone to begin calling hospitals, mental institutions, parole boards. Yet he was a good dissembler. He nodded at Andrus. "That's right. If it means I have to back a trailer up and cram them in. They'll go."

"That," Fritzie said, bending to his stack of bills again, "I should like to record on film."

By 5:00 P.M., the reporters, photographers, motion-picture cameramen and assorted technicians assembled across the street from the Andrus house had grown irritable, hot, and frustrated in the extreme. By now, their respective editors and supervisors had been called by the Santa Luisa police and asked to observe secrecy in the Andrus matter. No editor, no radio or television news director had seen fit to remove his man at the scene. Rheinholdt's brief message, relayed by Sergeant Baines, had said nothing about removing reporters; all stayed.

Repeated calls at the yellow-stone house had produced nothing but rebuffs from McFeeley and Moll; endless Cokes were consumed, endless speculation indulged in. A poker game was begun on the tail gate of the UBC station wagon. Kibitzers and players lolled in the dry desert heat. *Hit me light. All pink. I got a small pair and a busted straight.* Eliot Sparling, a rank outsider, and George Brack, a church elder who disdained gaming, rested against the cooking green flank of the camera car. It was not quite 5:15. Eliot, shading his eyes, glanced down Nespoli Drive. There were close to twenty automobiles parked on the quiet street, perhaps thirty people in the waiting group. Padding on gum-soled shoes, his neat head and neuter face greeting none of his colleagues, Harvey Swinnerton came walking down the street from the direction of Buena Terra Park.

"Look who's back," Eliot said to Brack. "Lucky Pierre." The overnight writer eased his heft from the car. "Hey, Harvey boy! What'd Todd tell you? He give you the story?"

Swinnerton stopped. He patted his guard's mustache.

Eliot shouted again. "How about it Harvey baby? You wanna pool whatever he told you?"

Victor DeGroot, the AP man, darting an annoyed look at Sparling, walked over to Swinnerton. "You look like you've been through a wringer, kid," DeGroot said. "You get anything from him?"

"Hmmmm?" Swinnerton asked. "Who?" In subtler men, his puzzlement might have been guile. But Swinnerton was an innocent; it appeared that he honestly did not understand the AP man's question.

Sparling, Brack, Arnspeiger (the *Argus* reporter) and several others gathered around Swinnerton. He seemed oddly enchanted—his Siamese-cat's eyes were glazed and his skin was sweatless and sickly pale.

"Where you been all this time?" Eliot demanded. "Don't tell me—I can guess. You been down at the LA *Truth,* spilling everything Todd gave you to Herbie Hood and T. T. Hansel. Right?"

"I haven't left Sanlu," Swinnerton said thinly.

"What good would it do 'em anyway?" DeGroot asked the group. "Everyone's abiding by the embargo. Rheinholdt's luckier than he knows—catching 'em all at the last minute."

Swinnerton seemed to lose his bearings. He closed his eyes as if weary of all of them, swayed slightly.

"Hey, are you all right?" George Brack asked solicitously. "Too much sun, maybe—and that heavy suit. You'd better sit down—in the shade."

Like the good shepherd he was, Brack led Swinnerton to the front seat of the UBC station wagon. On the tail gate, the poker game continued. *Dead-man's hand. Three whores. Beats.*

Arnspeiger confided to DeGroot: "He looks awful. I bet he blew it—didn't get a word out of Todd—and Hansel canned him."

DeGroot shrugged. "It could be. On the other hand—he may

have gotten a potful. Once the cops give us a free hand, they'll be way ahead."

Inside the station wagon, the radio played softly. A ridge-runner's nasalities violated the air.

> In my old duffle bag
> There's a piece of the flag
> And it cheers me and carries me along. . . .

Swinnerton rested his head against the plastic seat. The others stood outside, apprehensive, annoyed, aware that the awesome secrets inside the house would probably be denied them for many hours. Moreover, they suspected that Swinnerton had gained some special knowledge; they envied him and distrusted him for it.

Abruptly, the hillbilly chant ended. An announcer's oily voice, faintly edged with excitement, read:

> Here is a bulletin from the KYOM newsroom:
> The Los Angeles Truth has reported that a child has been kidnaped and held for ransom in Santa Luisa. The newspaper, in a special edition, identified the child as Amy Andrus, four, the daughter of Mr. and Mrs. Francis Andrus of 4217 Nespoli Drive, Santa Luisa. The paper further reported that an attempt to contact the kidnaper will be made later tonight. Santa Luisa police had requested no publication or broadcast of the story, but apparently some misunderstanding. . . .

The men gathered about the station wagon remained mute for several seconds. Sparling's mouth opened but, miraculously, his foghorn voice did not issue; he levelled an outraged arm toward Swinnerton, and the latter opened the opposite door of the car and walked away unsteadily, embracing his chest in tweedy arms, as if avoiding a cold wind.

"What the hell, Swinnerton?" Dave Arnspeiger cried.

DeGroot was incredulous. "It's out," the AP man said. "That damned fool Rheinholdt—waiting all day to call."

"Rheinholdt?" shouted Eliot. "What about the *Truth?* Hey— Swinnerton—don't run off like that! What happened? You got it from Todd, hey—and Hansel ran it anyway, right? To hell with the cops—the family—the kid——"

Harvey Swinnerton turned around. Two dozen of his peers stood in judgment; the poker game stopped.

"Don't blame me," he said tearfully. "I—I begged them not to—I have no idea what happened at the office. I'm just paid to report what I know. You all know that—none of you would have done anything different——"

The UP's young tennis player burst out of the Skopas house, where he had been phoning. "What a mess!" he cried. "The *Truth* hit the street at 5:07 with an extra—no explanation why they printed! Rheinholdt still won't talk! Everyone's going with it now." He did not break stride, walking swiftly across the street toward the Andrus house. "They got to talk to us now," the UP man said. "No more secrets—now that it's out."

In frantic processional, they followed him. Sparling, bearing the microphone for George Brack, galumphed along in the rear rank. His clouded eyes blinked; he looked pained and puzzled. "Oh, boy, did they ever run true to form," he said to Brack. "Leave it to old Hansel to pull a trick like that. He spit right in that dumb police chief's eye."

"I wouldn't be too sure, El," Brack said. "I can't imagine anyone in the world—anyone—running that story—when the child was still missing. You know what I think? I think the police never got to the *Truth*—or there was some misunderstanding."

"Yeah," said Eliot gloomily. "Some misunderstanding. Like, we really didn't think it would matter—the kid was only four years old, so what's one kid less?"

"El, that's awful," protested Brack.

The agitated, angered mob swarmed around the flagstone steps beneath the chubby palm trees. By now, the television networks, several local TV stations—including KYOT and its persistent news hawk, Martin Ringel—together with two of the theater newsreels, were represented. With alarming speed, a semicircle of cameras, tripods, cables, batteries, portable lights, and microphones were set up on the parched lawn. In the driveway, a yellow station wagon belonging to a theater newsreel had backed in. On its roof, a monstrous 35-millimeter soundfilm camera pointed its thick snout menacingly at the redwood door.

DeGroot knocked at the door several times. After a few minutes, Dr. Todd and Joe McFeeley emerged. The dentist, the first target of the aggrieved newsmen, crisply defended himself.

"I've no comment," Todd said. "This breach of secrecy is shocking. I'm assured that Chief Rheinholdt telephoned everyone —including that newspaper."

"What did you tell Swinnerton?" shouted Eliot.

"Nothing. Nothing at all," the dentist said. "Nothing that had anything to do with the publication of the story. I'll say no more."

Martin Ringel shoved his microphone at McFeeley. "Come on, Joe," he said. "When's the drop? How much ransom?"

"Can we have the text of the note?" asked Arnspeiger.

"Where's the mother?" Eliot boomed. "Let her talk to us!" Others took up the cry.

"What the hell is this, Joe? Give us something—you aren't Rheinholdt!"

"The father! Is he in there? Let him talk!"

"A photograph of the kid?" a photographer pleaded. "You could at least let us have a photo of the kid!"

McFeeley could barely make himself heard over the babble. "Nothing. You're all going to get out of here. You've done enough harm."

"Not us, not us!" Eliot howled. "Them!" He pointed to the *Truth* car.

"You're all in on it," Joe said. He folded his arms across his white shirt. "Nothing else tonight. You might as well start moving. Rheinholdt says to call tomorrow morning."

A conglomerate roar of derision greeted his reference to the chief. They would not be moved; they demanded information.

McFeeley was adamant. "If you'll all be quiet a minute, I'll lay it out for you."

"How can we believe you?" Sparling shouted. "You didn't level with me this morning! You and that Mrs. Andrus!" He rotated his head looking for support from his colleagues, but they ignored him.

"It's 5:25 now," McFeeley said. "This area must be cleared of cars and people no later than 7:15. I mean cleared. Understood?"

"Hah!" Martin Ringel cried. "That must be ransom time. Right, Joe? An hour later maybe? Nine o'clock? Where?"

"I'll repeat what I said—7:15. Everybody out."

"How far away?" asked DeGroot.

"How far?" McFeeley asked. He hesitated—as if he had not thought the problem through. "Five blocks in each direction, including the north end of Buena Terra Park."

"Five blocks?" DeGroot asked. "But, Joe, that'll just about put us out of Sanlu."

"That's the idea," the detective said. He turned to go.

"What if we don't move?" Eliot asked.

"You'll be jugged. Second time around for you, Sparling. That'll be a new record for a reporter. I'll put all of you under arrest for hindering police officers. It's a California law and it covers everything." McFeeley had not raised his voice. His calm, slanted face was veiled with a weary sadness.

"Oh stop, Joe," said DeGroot. "You can't arrest forty men."

"I don't want to. But don't test me."

Arnspeiger snorted. "Sounds like one of Rheinholdt's bright ideas."

"No," Joe said. "It's mine. I repeat, 7:15, five blocks each direction. I'll have men cruising to pick up prowlers or loiterers."

They believed him. Most of them had known Joe McFeeley since his days as a patrolman after the war—an honest, ambitious cop. He was no Irvin Moll, always on the take; no Rheinholdt, wallowing in stupidity.

Of all the news executives now impelled to follow the *Truth's* lead, none choked on wormwood and gall more than Tom Ballstead. Turgid with rage, he read the AP's story over and over, rubbing his hands over his starved face, furious with himself, with the *Truth,* with Rheinholdt, and, most of all, with Eliot Sparling.

BULLETIN FIRST LEAD

SANTA LUISA, CALIF., SEPT. 17—(AP)—THE FOUR-YEAR-OLD DAUGHTER OF A PROMINENT TELEVISION DIRECTOR WAS KIDNAPED AND HELD FOR RANSOM TODAY IN THE LOS ANGELES SUBURB OF SANTA LUISA.

THE CHILD, AMY ANDRUS, WAS SEIZED NEAR HER PARENTS' LAVISH $40,000 HOME IN THE LUXURIOUS BUENA TERRA DISTRICT AT ABOUT 9 A.M. (PDST). A RANSOM NOTE WAS LEFT. POLICE INDICATED AN ATTEMPT TO CONTACT THE KIDNAPER AND SECURE THE LITTLE GIRL'S RELEASE WAS IMMINENT.

THE CHILD IS THE DAUGHTER OF FRANCIS M. ANDRUS, 34, A TV DIRECTOR, AND LAURA ANDRUS, 35. THE COUPLE HAS BEEN SEPARATED FOR ABOUT A MONTH. THEY CAME TO CALIFORNIA LAST APRIL.

SANTA LUISA POLICE CHIEF CASPAR RHEINHOLDT

ATTEMPTED TO SUPPRESS NEWS OF THE CRIME AND
LATER ASKED THAT NOTHING BE PRINTED OR BROAD-
CAST ABOUT IT.

   HOWEVER, AN AFTERNOON LOS ANGELES NEWSPA-
PER PUBLISHED THE STORY, APPARENTLY THROUGH
SOME MISUNDERSTANDING. AS A RESULT, THE SE-
CRECY REQUEST WAS WITHDRAWN, AND ALL MEDIA
WERE PERMITTED TO PRINT OR BROADCAST NEWS
OF THE SHOCKING CRIME.

                                             MORE

"Goddam dumb dope," Ballstead choked out.
"Rheinholdt?" Jim Farrell asked.
"No. Sparling. My fault also. Letting that idiot wander around
out there. My hunch was right. It was a kidnaping. I should have
pulled that dope off." He covered his face. "We had it, Jimmy.
Had it all by ourselves, hours before anyone. And that dirty name,
the *Truth*, gets the beat. Swinnerton heard Sparling yell about a
kid, the guy went out and dug, and he got it. That extra in the
Truth had a lot more than the cops gave out. I'd like to know
how Swinnerton learned so much."
   Farrell clucked consolingly. "Well, we're on it heavy now. We
were a minute ahead of CBS with the bulletin and two ahead of
NBC." It was pitiful balm for Ballstead. "Brack is sending in three
hundred feet of film, some of it sound. Interviewing Sparling,
neighbors."
   Ballstead was inconsolable. He had sniffed triumph. Now, bereft
of the one circumstance that could bring joy to his dyspeptic life,
he had no stomach for trivia.
   A slender, immaculately tailored man entered his office. His
name was Matthew M. Hinrichsen, and he was the vice-president of
UBC's West Coast operation—Ballstead's boss. He was as thin as
the news director, but it was a meagerness of physique both grace-
ful and intentional—not brought on by the inner rot that was
shrinking Ballstead.
   "Hello there, Tom," Hinrichsen said pleasantly. "Thought I'd
check you on this kidnaping."
   "We look pretty good," Ballstead said. "What was it, Jim?
Minute ahead of CBS and two ahead of NBC?"
   "Very good. What's this about one of our men being jailed?"

Hinrichsen had an almost inaudible voice. At labor negotiations it became a strangled whisper; people were forced to crane necks and cup ears to catch his words. "Is it anyone I know?"

"Don't think so," Ballstead said quickly. "A kid on the overnight. Sparling."

The vice-president tapped manicured fingers against Ballstead's desk top. The gesture irritated Tom, but he dared not show resentment. Hinrichsen was a comer, a man to be watched. At thirty-five he was a vice-president—married to an heiress related to a moneyed family that carried much weight in network hierarchy. He was, Ballstead understood, a professional in-law, a discreet young man who yearned to be part of the news operation. It was this yearning that Ballstead feared. Hinrichsen's fascination with news (he had been business manager of his college paper at Amherst) might mean Ballstead's eventual displacement. Beyond the West Coast newsroom, the company had little else to offer Ballstead.

"Sparling? No, I don't know him."

And you never will, if I can help it, Ballstead thought. *In the old radio days no blue-suited fruits of nepotism, direct or collateral, nosed around my newsroom.* . . . But he did not bait his superior; he had long stopped talking back to brass. Instead, with Farrell's aid, he described Eliot's adventure. He concluded by saying: "We're on it good now, Matt. Lots of film, sound, interviews."

Hinrichsen, with that air of certainty which rises out of wifely wealth and permits ignorance to masquerade as knowledge, asked, "Close-ups?"

"Huh?" Ballstead muttered.

"Are there close-ups on the film?" Hinrichsen asked.

Take a close-up of this. I've got your close-up. Ballstead strangled the insolence. Ten years ago he would have chased fifteen Hinrichsens out of *his* newsroom. But television had changed everything—and he had changed with it. Everyone was a swell guy today. The newsroom was a public meeting hall for any executive who nurtured dreams of journalistic glory. They were issuing working-press cards to disc jockeys and advertising salesmen.

"Well, Jesus, I assume he's shot close-ups, Matt," he choked out. "Billik's been shooting newsreel since the Spanish-American War."

"That's just the point," Hinrichsen said. "You fellows from newsreel and newspapers and radio haven't learned how intimate television is. It's personal, intensely so. That's why I asked if there were close-ups." The vice-president turned on one black shoe.

At the door, he paused. "A shame we couldn't have scooped the others. Too bad that man of yours ended up in jail. I hope we'll fight back."

A spasm fought its way up Ballstead's trachea. "He didn't—have it—confirmed—Matt. The *Truth* had some source of its own. We think it was a relative of the woman."

Hinrichsen's eyes were sea green—the eyes of a man who took golf and bridge seriously. "We can still recoup," he said. "Why don't we offer our network facilities to the woman? Does that make sense?"

"That's the first thing Sparling did this morning, Matt. She didn't take him up." It pleased him that Hinrichsen was a step behind his oafish newsman in ingenuity.

"In any case, Tom, give it some thought and let me know *your* thinking. This is the kind of intimate reportage that television must develop. It's what I was stressing in my speech to the Advertising Council. We've got to take the lead in upgrading people. I'm not ashamed to invest our brand of journalism with morality. Why can't human conduct be improved through the mass media? Where newspapers and radio failed, maybe we'll succeed. This is a grand opportunity. The person who took that child might choose UBC as the proper agency for his surrender."

"He might at that," Ballstead wheezed. "He could get upgraded in between the used car pitchman and Popeye."

The words were barely out of Ballstead's mouth when Hinrichsen departed, slender as a water moccasin, discreet as a nun. *Another nail in my coffin,* Ballstead thought. *I'm helping him bury me.*

Farrell returned with a stack of afternoon newspapers. The violent letters shouted the agony:

BABY GIRL KIDNAPED!

TV DIRECTOR'S CHILD
KIDNAPED IN SANLU!!

The *Truth's* decision had made it a free-for-all. Ballstead's fear of Hinrichsen gave way to his misery over Sparling's incompetence.

"Brack's on the phone," Farrell said. "All hell's breaking loose out there. Everyone's screaming for more—the cops say everybody has to clear out by 7:15. Want to talk to Brack?"

"No," Ballstead said. "Just tell him to start *recouping*. You heard what Hinrichsen said."

Farrell smiled wryly; a note of exhaustion, of surrender in Ballstead's cracked voice disturbed him. When he had left, Ballstead, still standing, studied the *Truth's* front page. He tugged a shriveled ear and muttered: "Oh, you shrewd bastard, Hansel. You got it all. You'll eat it all up, won't you?"

What had drawn his comments was not the *Truth's* lead story under the savage black headline. Obviously, the newspaper had unearthed some private source for the detailed information—a bribed cop, a gabby relative, a nosey neighbor. Tom Ballstead knew the routine; the bland journalese, telling so much, compromising so much, was not what had stirred him. He was even less stirred, at that moment, by any moral judgments that might be made of the newspaper; like most of his peers, he assumed some act of omission by the stupid police. What intrigued him, and what had elicited his grudging praise of T. T. Hansel, was a black-bordered box to the left of the main story.

TRUTH OFFERS $10,000 REWARD!

The *Los Angeles Truth* is offering a reward of $10,000 for any information leading to the arrest of Amy Andrus' kidnaper or to her safe return. Please telephone any information you think is valuable to CAstle 7-8800, Extension 405. In addition, this newspaper hereby offers its facilities, its news columns, its offices, all of its staff members to Amy's parents, to the police, to the kidnaper, as a means of making contact.

T. T. Hansel
Editor & Publisher

Ballstead collapsed into his swivel chair. "I'd hate your guts, Hansel," he said, "if I wasn't so goddam jealous of you."

When the radio bulletin informed the Andrus household that their private agony had been publicized, Fritzie appeared ready to collapse again. He lurched about the living room, clutching his abdomen, grimacing, cursing. "Damn their miserable, corrupt souls," he gasped. "Damn them all."

His wife barely heard him. She sat at the desk, transfixed, staring at the sheets of typed digits. The money had been placed in a cigar box.

"That miserable relative of yours, that Todd," Andrus said. "Laura, he spilled it. Didn't you see those reporters badgering him? One got inta his car."

"I didn't notice."

"He spilled it. I'll kill him. I'll kill *all of them!*" His voice rose in a womanish shriek. He slammed his clenched fists against his thighs.

She covered her face. "I guess it was bound to happen. We had to become public property, I suppose. That stupid man, Rheinholdt. He was smarter than any of us. He should have arrested every one of them."

"Would not have helped," choked Andrus. "We're cursed, Laura. The curse is on us. No good can happen to this family, and it's my fault. Amy's gone. You think we'll see her?" He was jerking and bobbing, as if something had become dislocated in his nervous system. "I don't. Not any more. Those leeches out there. That paper. Tell the world! *Tell everyone!*"

His wife's incredible control humiliated Andrus and plunged him into new spasms. When news had reached them that the story was out, she had permitted herself a single wail, locked hands over her mouth, and, with an effort more strenuous than any of the men in the room would ever comprehend, had crushed hysteria with three shuddering inhalations. Andrus, his mind bright with images, shrieked and fell to the sofa. To Irvin Moll and Joe McFeeley and the four plain clothes men now in the house, his performance was more understandable than the woman's chilling discipline.

Fritzie hurled himself across the room and leaned over the desk. "Laura," he gasped, "there's still time. You go out there. Both of us. Let's you and me make an appeal—say it's all a mistake—theirs, not ours. There won't be any reporters here tonight. No cops. Just how he wanted it. We promise. We'll see to it."

"I don't know," she said. "That mob——"

Moll lumbered over. "That won't be true, Mr. Andrus. The lieutenant is going to make a pinch if the guy shows."

"*The hell you say!*" roared Fritzie. "You and that smart mick and all the others! You've fouled our nest enough! We'll call the shots. Come on, Laura, Let's tell 'em. They still got time to get it on the radio!"

She got up. It occurred to her how he had hit on the notion of an appeal: he had thought of their tragedy in terms of script. He had acted as if he were editing a play, criticizing plot, deploring characterization, seeking the gimmick. Now he had discovered what he described to his students as the *obligatory scene.* With a boy's gumption, he hitched his belt and guided his wife to the door.

Patrolman Clyde Hertmann had been a minor actor in the events of that Monday afternoon. His role had been restricted to looking up telephone numbers, advising Sergeant Baines, helping answer occasional queries. And yet—when word came to them that the story was out, that the dark secret had been exposed, that a child's life had been endangered—he could not suppress a pang of personal guilt, a feeling that he had been neglectful, careless, incompetent. He and Baines had touched all bases, he was convinced. And now their efforts to protect Amy Andrus had failed. Hertmann's narrow, shrewd face betrayed nothing to Baines—the latter silent, creased and immobile across the back-to-back desks. When one of the uniformed men had come racing in breathlessly at 5:20 with the news—*It's out! Somebody pulled the cork!*—the two officers had stared at each other stupidly, and then Baines, his voice hoarse and faint, had said: "They done it. We did what we could, didn't we?" And Hertmann, sorry for the old farmer, sorry for poor Rheinholdt—still stewing in his locked office, ignorant that the story was out—sensing some awful argument imminent over who said what, who called who, who was guilty, shrugged and replied: "You bet, Farmer. We did what we could."

At length, they decided to tell Rheinholdt. They were admitted to his locked office. The chief, in dark solitude, was studying some crackpot criminologist's charts of the human body portioned off like a butcher's beef map. Hertmann disclosed that the *Los Angeles Truth* had printed the news of the kidnaping and that other papers, radio and TV stations were following suit. Oddly, there was no wild, screaming outburst from the chief. Behind his distorting lenses his eyes grew opaque and began to close. One hairy fist tapped the desk rhythmically, and he said in a choked whisper: "I knew it. I knew the lice would do it to me."

Shortly before 6:00 that evening, Rheinholdt clamped his panama on his bristling head and, without a word, walked into the reception room. Rheinholdt was hungry: the wife was barbecuing chicken. He would down a few cold beers, then maybe ride out to the Andrus place for a check—for all the good it would do now. He had a hunch the FBI would be nosing around, and he wanted to make sure they were made unwelcome.

Hertmann looked at him pityingly. "Chief," he said, "maybe you ought to call that paper and bawl them out."

"Why?" asked Rheinholdt. "What good would that do—now?"

"Just to get it on the record," Hertmann said. "To let them know how sore we are."

Rheinholdt mulled the idea. "Okay, get them for me. Who's the guy there?"

"Hood," Hertmann said, dialing. "Fellow named Herbert Hood. I think he's the general manager."

The Andrus home faced almost due west. Fritzie and Laura emerged, staring into a burning sliver of the sun, descending behind the high dormer windows of the Skopas house across Nespoli Drive. Both shaded their eyes, as much, it seemed to the nonplused McFeeley, from the fiery slants as from the wild mob that surged around them, thrusting microphones, taking photos and movies, hurling questions. McFeeley held his hands up. "Stay back," he said. "Don't crowd us."

The milling ceased for a few minutes. There was some more intestine-shoving and setting of equipment, an exchange of snarls between Eliot Sparling and Martin Ringel, entangling microphone cables a few feet from the woman's head.

"You sure you want to do this?" McFeeley asked Laura. "You don't have to. I'm chasing them in an hour."

"Mr. Andrus and I have decided it's the best way." The cameras hummed.

"What time did Amy get lost? Where were you when it happened?" someone shouted.

"Can we have a photograph?" another cried.

"How much ransom you paying?"

"You calling the FBI? Are you satisfied with the local police?"

"When are you leaving the money? Where?"

Eliot's trumpeting blared over them. "Why did Todd spill the story, Mrs. Andrus? You could at least get us even with the *Truth!*"

Sparling and Martin Ringel were engaged in a wrestling match on the lowest step. Each was attempting to force his microphone closer to the mother yet avoid McFeeley's guardian figure. A half-dozen other microphones bloomed around her, forming an electronic necklace. Ringel's almost stabbed her in the breast, as Eliot shoved him. There seemed a calculated insanity about the scene, an invasive, poking, rubbernecking madness. They had been frustrated all day by Rheinholdt; they had been humiliated by the *Truth;* and now they were under orders to stand by, to hang on, to get *something.*

"I'd go back in, Mrs. Andrus," Joe said.

"Butt out, McFeeley!" Ringel called. "Let her talk!"

"Yeah, we're on your side, Mrs. Andrus!" a voice cried. "Tell us—we'll help!"

"I need your help," Laura said falteringly. "I—I'd like you to broadcast a message from Mr. Andrus and myself." Their relationship suddenly shocked her. They had harassed, badgered and tortured her. One of their fraternity had been guilty of a lapse that might destroy her child—and she was appealing to them.

"You bet!" roared Eliot. "You name it, Mrs. Andrus! Just what I suggested this morning!" Several of the others tugged at his soaked shirt; he was told to shut up.

"I want to ask whoever it is who took our child to accept our assurance that we tried to keep it secret. If the person will return our daughter tonight, we will live up to his terms. There will be no police interference. No attempt at an arrest will be made. No one will witness what he does. We aren't after revenge or punishment. Just give us our child. Take our money. Mr. Andrus and I promise this. Please believe us."

When she had concluded, her voice low and controlled, breaking only on the last few words, the reporters were silent for a few seconds. Perhaps the enormity of what was at stake, perhaps their own peculiar involvement stayed the flood of inquiries. Cameras were rewound. A crouching soundman barked, "Watch it, willya?" —and shoved aside the legs of a photographer.

"Is that all, Mrs. Andrus?" DeGroot asked. He sounded solicitous, faintly ashamed of their ferocity.

"Yes. That's all."

Eliot elbowed out a forward niche for George Brack and slipped the pencil mike to the commentator. Brack, like DeGroot, had a certain dignity. He leaned forward. "Mr. Andrus, sir, would you like to add anything?"

Fritzie shook his head. He had kept his eyes downcast during Laura's speech. "I got nothin' to add," he said. "We just want our child. Y'all go home now. You've done enough harm."

There was a murmuration in the throng, the shuffling of a group of students caught cheating on exams. Again, Victor DeGroot was impelled to plead for all of them.

"I wish you and Mrs. Andrus wouldn't feel that way," the AP man said. "The police should have told us the truth hours ago. We want your child returned as much as you do. There isn't a man here who wouldn't give up the biggest story in the world to see your daughter back safely. We have kids of our own. We want to help."

He spoke the truth. The somewhat abashed faces of the reporters supported him. Yet something had gone wrong; some mechanism was inoperative; somehow, good sense and decency had died. It was impossible at that fragile moment to diagnose precisely what had happened, what complex of circumstances had cast the reporters as heartless villains, as knaves whose cruel acts might lead to the destruction of a life. DeGroot did not dissemble. He and the others wanted the child unharmed, prayed for her safety. But what impelled them to linger? Was it the mandate all had gotten from their desks to stand by? Their frustration over the *Truth's* beat? Or was some idiot's engine at work, some jerry-built tower of eccentric wheels and camshafts that, once in motion, could not halt until someone was destroyed?

"Sure," said Fritzie as his wife walked past McFeeley into the house. "Y'all want to he'p. Like that newspaper. I'd like to see the face of *that* reporter." He stepped forward, outrage drying the damp film over his eyes, seeking Swinnerton.

"Remember what I said," McFeeley advised them. "By 7:15 I want the street cleared." Victor DeGroot led the retreat from the steps. His gray hair, his polite voice attested to his decency. It appeared that if he had any influence, all would leave before the deadline. "You don't have to lecture us, Joe. We'll go."

The detective opened the door. "That was my last lecture," he said, and entered the house.

Connie Potenza drove home, bolted a few mouthfuls of her mother's ingenious eggplant Parmigian', while listening to the radio broadcasts about the Andrus case (in which both her employer and her boyfriend were deeply involved), and then drove to Nespoli Drive. The Potenzas lived in Droitwich Spa, a stretch of tract housing adjacent to Santa Luisa, and she was at the site of the crime in fifteen minutes. The crush of automobiles and reporters and gawkers confounded her, and it was several minutes before she located Eliot's Ford. He was doubled up on the rear seat, his figure jackknifed in misery, but he was not asleep. It was almost 7:00 P.M.

and Sparling had been awake for twenty-eight hours. He had reached the stage where he was getting stubborn and surly about the whole thing. *No sleep? O.K., no sleep,* was his attitude. Even with the skies darkened and a chill threading the air, he remained awake, his fatigued mind crammed with guilt, with second-guessing, with abrasive might-have-beens.

Connie gave him an eggplant sandwich on white bread. He offered no thanks, but munched it gratefully (his intake that day had consisted of two jelly doughnuts and three Cokes).

"Why'd your old lady ruin this with *goy* white bread?" Eliot complained. "You can only eat this with Italian bread."

"You can't get it in Santa Luisa," Connie said sadly. She was not insulted. Allowances had to be made for Eliot, who was, by his own admission, brilliant. "Mom has to go all the way to Venice to get Italian hot sausage. She bawled out the man at the A&P last week because he doesn't carry good macaroni."

Eliot wolfed the pungent sandwich. "It figures." The subject— the generalizing effect that southern California exercised on ethnic groups—was one he had discussed at length with her. "It's the sun, mostly," Sparling contended, "the heat, the movies, the used car business; the whole thing together makes everyone come out kinda bland and blond and good-natured. You can't buy hot sausage. The pastrami is phony. The kids don't even look like little Jews or Italians or Irish any more—just kind of fuzzy, yellow-haired, healthy *Amurricans.* I suppose it's O.K. In fifty years, the Negroes on Central Avenue'll all be blond, and that'll solve *that* problem once and for all."

Gratified with his mastery of physical and cultural anthropology, he would go on to explain that back east, in his own Bronx, or in Haverhill, the Boston suburb Connie had last seen when she was five, everyone was pleasantly aware of Yom Kipper, made jokes about Columbus Day, shared the alcoholic zest of Saint Patrick's day. There was a spice and a fun to the rites of subgroups. "But here? In LA?" Eliot would ask, horror rising in his voice, "Passover could be Arbor Day! Elijah the Prophet's makin' Westerns! I haven't felt at home with a matzoth since I left Bruckner Boulevard. Ever hear of a Paddy's Day parade out here? I miss it. Here, the Irishmen are all watering their avocados and the Italians are playing golf. All the fun's been boiled outa people."

The exegesis wore him out. He finished the last of the sandwich, licked tomato sauce from his fingers and turned challengingly to the pretty girl. "Hey, what happened at the *Truth?* Why'd they print the story?"

She arched her eyebrows. "I can't make any sense out of it. Mr. Hood says they were never called. The only call from the police was at 6:04 from Rheinholdt—your pal."

"That late? 6:04? Boy, did they goof. How could they miss the *Truth?*"

"It's all mixed up. I know this much—*I* didn't get any calls from the police before."

Eliot shook his head. "They'll murder Rheinholdt," he said. "Not that I should care."

"Mr. Hood was furious. They started blaming each other, and Rheinholdt called him a cheap, lousy bum." She giggled.

"Go it, husband; go it, bear," Eliot yawned. "They should eat each other up." In his mind's eye he saw his two enemies— Neanderthaler Hood and Cro-Magnon Rheinholdt—circling each other with spiked clubs in some mossy arena. "And Swinnerton. I bet he got it all from that dentist, right?"

"I don't know. It was all hush-hush. Mr. Hansel took over personally."

Eliot, ever suspicious of the *Truth,* tried to find some flaw in their bold act. A tremor of doubt agitated him, but he could not quite find the area of softness.

"When'd Swinnerton call in?"

"Oh—the first few times it was early—I guess when he learned about it from you. You know—1:00, 1:30, again at 2:00."

"Hurrah for me. I mean, when he had the dope—the stuff Todd gave him."

"A little after 4:00, I guess. Everyone locked themselves in Hood's office and Hansel took over."

Sparling tried to line up a timetable in his mind: Swinnerton getting the story from Todd a little after 4:00, the paper out at 5:07, Rheinholdt not calling them until 6:04. At that moment he was too enmeshed in gloom, in self-hatred, to pursue it. His ancient enemies were having the laugh on him. He, Sparling, had stumbled on the story of the year and had lost it to the despised *Truth,* to Hood and Hansel. Through dumb luck (Swinnerton's), through boldness (Hansel's), and then more dumb luck (Rheinholdt's omission), they had won the grand journalistic prize and left him disgraced. And there was poor Tom Ballstead to consider—Ballstead, who had helped him raise his tortured head. It seemed to

Eliot in these self-examinations that he had done nothing right, betrayed Ballstead and UBC, handed the bloody honors to the *Truth*.

> *The splendor falls*
> *On Hansel's balls*
> *And Herbie Hood, so old and whorey.* . . .

Well, he had made his jokes at their expense; now they could laugh at him (if he were worth the effort). They were tougher and smarter than Eliot Sparling, twenty-eight, and perhaps they deserved the victory.

"Why don't you try to nap?" Connie asked. "How long can you stay awake like this?"

"Forever. I got my pride." A yawn stretched his long face. "I'm off the overnight for a few days. Ballstead's letting me stay on this. I don't know why, after the way I loused him up."

George Brack came by. "Hey, El," the commentator said, "you missed yourself on the TV news. We were great."

"You?" Connie asked. "You were on television?"

"Yeah. Me and George did a Murrow and Sevareid. Oh, George, you know Connie Potenza? Connie—George Brack. The man with the golden tonsils."

They exchanged greetings. Brack approved of Eliot's having such a pretty and well-mannered girl friend. He would have officiated at their wedding if they had wanted to get married. There was nothing like married life, George believed.

"Mrs. Andrus' appeal's been on everywhere," Brack said. "We got it on just a few minutes ago—some kind of record for the hot developer. I wonder if that guy'll show up tonight."

"Only if he wants to audition for a television job," Eliot said. "He better wear a blue shirt and have his make-up on."

Brack laughed lightly. "How about that Mrs. Andrus? Isn't she a cool one? Ice water in her veins. Never batted an eye. You think everything's on the up-and-up? Ringel's been dropping hints he's got something on her. On both of them."

"Don't believe Ringel, George," Eliot said. "He thinks the newsboys' soapbox derby is fixed."

George ran a comb through his moonlit, golden waves. "Swinnerton's clammed up. He won't say a word."

"He's smarter than me," Sparling said gloomily.

Brack drifted off to help the crew. He had bought dinner for the technicians and would now surprise them with chewing gum.

Connie took his hand. "Why are you so miserable? You did the best you could."

"Yeah. It's never good enough." He lurched forward, resting his head on the front seat. "What good am I? When you get right down to it, what good am I really? Have I ever finished anything in my entire life? I got beat out for managing editor of the *Daily Bruin* because I insulted a professor. I got fired from the *Truth* even though I was the best overnight editor they ever had. And now I louse up Ballstead. It's like my swimming. I'm a fraud, a flop."

"Your swimming?" she asked. "What has that got to do with anything?"

"Ever notice how I swim? No, no kidding, ever notice? People admire me in the water. My arm strokes and my breathing are perfect. Perfect form. Like this." He started rotating his arms, raising and lowering his head, mouth sucking air, in approved Australian crawl fashion. "Beautiful, hah? But what no one notices are my flabby legs! I'm not doing a scissors kick. I'm doing a frog kick because it's easier. There I am—gorgeous form on top, no form below. Know why I do the frog kick? Because I can't learn a scissors kick. Since I was eight years old at the Castle Hill Pool, I've been trying to learn it. Everytime I do a scissors kick, I sink. *Sink.* Fall to the bottom of the pool. *I cannot learn it.* I don't care what the books say about it—relaxed from the hips. *I sink.* So I frog-kick, with my beautiful arm and head motions, and I deceive the world. They think I'm a great swimmer."

"I think you're crazy. You've been awake too long."

"I'm sane, all right. That swimming deal—it's symptomatic of my essential inferiority. Look at UBC. What they mean to me. I love United Broadcasting. I am proud to announce to the world that I am from United. I want to help them. It's not the hundred and two bucks a week, although that's part of it, considering the fifty-eight dollars a week I got from the *Truth*. I am for UBC one hundred per cent because it isn't mean, like the *Truth*. That's what's killing the *Truth*. Meanness. But United is different. It has a character."

"Oh, it's got a character, all right. You."

Eliot sighed. "You wouldn't understand."

"I understand, Eliot. You won't ever get over Hood and Hansel firing you, will you? You just refused to believe it could happen to a genius like yourself. Eliot, the pressure is on *them,* too, all the time. You know why you were fired."

"Schlossmann," he said sadly. "He deserved a better memorial than me getting canned." Across the street, the Andrus house was illuminated. Within, it was jammed with detectives and plain-clothes men. The reporters had watched them troop in since dusk. There was speculation that the rendezvous arrangements were being changed.

"Eliot, you went around telling people you knew why Werner Schlossmann killed himself," Connie said softly.

"It was the truth. He told me—well, he almost told me—the day before he did it, with me sitting fifteen feet away."

"You couldn't prove it. Then you went and talked about it in the greasy spoon, and someone snitched to Hansel, and they fired you. You shouldn't have blabbed so much! What good did it do anyone?"

Sparling opened the car and stretched his legs. He could see the reporters and cameramen gathering around Victor DeGroot's car. McFeeley's deadline was approaching.

"Ah, that makes it worse," Eliot said wearily. "I knew why Werner committed suicide. I could have made it public—gone to some columnist, another paper. I owed it to Schlossmann. But I was yellow, gutless. I've always been. The big goof the little kids used to beat up. I was scared stiff of Hansel and Herbie Hood. So I got what I deserved."

George Brack, in the group around DeGroot, was calling Eliot. Sparling stood up. "You better beat it," he said to Connie. "The cops are clearing everyone out in a couple of minutes."

She got out of the car. "Stop worrying. What a pessimist you are. Schlossmann, the *Truth*—that's all behind you. Just do a good job and cheer up." They kissed lightly and she hurried away. Eliot afforded himself an unashamed stare at her bouncy figure, the black, glistening hair. Then, lifting each foot as if plodding through a swamp, he joined the other reporters.

There were more than forty people around DeGroot. The AP man was standing on the tailgate of a station wagon, and Eliot, observing the tableau under the lamplight, had a vivid memory of Communist street meetings in the Bronx in the thirties. They were always denouncing Roosevelt, he remembered, a circumstance he could never understand in his later years, when, as a newspaper addict, he learned that FDR was a Red himself.

"Are we agreed?" DeGroot asked. "We start leaving now, and wait at the—what's that place, Dave?" He looked down at Arnspeiger, the *Argus* man.

"Patio Diner. It's on Coronado, six blocks away, so McFeeley has no kick. They got the best coffee in Sanlu."

"Right," DeGroot continued. "Same deal for everyone. We all leave at once; we all stay in the same place."

There was no rising shout of approval. There were murmurs, whispers, some shuffling of feet, a few curses. Then Martin Ringel's brash tones rose above the muttering. "Not me, DeGroot. You newspaper guys do what you want. I'm under orders to stay put." He started moving off cockily with his crew.

"Son, don't turn your back on me," DeGroot said. "I'm under the same orders as you, and I've covered a lot more stories than you. Sometimes you do what the police ask." He looked about him. "Anyone else? It has to be one hundred per cent. If you hang around, you'll get arrested. I believe McFeeley."

"I'm staying," Eliot trumpeted. "Not that I want to. But if Ringel stays, I stay."

DeGroot wrinkled his nose. "Television people," he said. "Who else?"

A man from an LA morning paper raised his hand. "I won't move if they stay," he said apologetically.

Duane Bosch, eighteen, the *Santa Luisa Register* man, indicated his intrepidness. "Me, too, Mr. DeGroot. I think we all oughta stay. Let's call that cop's bluff. This is a big story."

Victor DeGroot appeared puzzled, hesitant. "I'll try again. I think I know what's right. I say let's get out of here. Let's give that child a break."

Another tremor agitated the crowd. There were groans, meditations and reflections. Nothing had been settled. In the incandescent yellow glow, they seemed like the first detachment to reach the moon—unsure of anything, unconfident in their leaders or themselves.

A large map of the area had been spread on the beige carpeting in the Andrus living room. Creased and coffee-stained, it rested on the floor, bearing the legend, SANTA LUISA 3rd TAX DISTRICT (BUENA TERRA). With a red pencil, Joe had marked off the boundaries of the area to be patrolled by plain-clothes men in civilian cars.

Eight men, working in four cars, were to cruise the neighborhood. Irvin Moll would remain at the house with Joe. Moll had been manning the telephones, and already calls were flooding in—cranks, informants, sympathizers. An hysterical woman claimed she had seen two Negroes dragging Amy into a house in Pasadena (describing the child as blonde); the minister of a California cult had offered his church (Temple of the Risen God) as a sanctuary for the kidnaper.

"Here's Kohlmeyer," Joe said, pointing with the pencil. "Here's where it meets with Nespoli. The entrance is a few feet west of the intersection with Nespoli. The package will be placed at the foot of the stone pillar on the right as you face it—the one nearest Nespoli. There won't be anyone planted in the street. No phony couples necking in cars, no Good Humor salesman with a .38 stuck in his change machine. But we *will* have a stake-out. There's a thick hedge fifty feet west, toward McKinley, just after the tennis courts. Matthews, you and LaBarre can hide there." He pointed to the map again. "This house on the corner—the garage almost faces the park entrance. It's owned by a Mr. Boland, and we've arranged to use his garage and his Continental convertible. The top will be down, and Ed Case and Milt Bannon can settle down in the rear seat. You should be able to climb over the trunk rack and make it to the park in about four seconds. That's it. Nobody else. The others, cruising. Reporters will be chased. Arrest them if they give you an argument. Rubbernecks have to move also, but any normal traffic, kids on bikes, pedestrians, O.K."

One of the detectives leaned forward. "That's all we got to go on? A tan Ford?"

"That's it. A '49, '50 or '51—a tan Ford. Don't count on it. Look everything over. You've all had a chance to study the photographs of Amy. Remember, her mother says she has a loud voice. She may start yelling when she recognizes the neighborhood."

Laura and Fritzie were waiting in the den. Todd, subdued, much of the bounce gone from him, was sipping coffee at the fireplace. The bills had been dusted with uranyl nitrate, their appearance in no way altered. Anyone handling them would have traces of telltale powder on his hands; fluorescence would emerge under ultraviolet. The money was snug in a cigar box sealed with Scotch tape. The box, in turn, had been placed in a large manila envelope.

"We gave our word there'd be no interference," Andrus said plaintively. "Lieutenant, I hate that person more than anyone in

the world. I don't care what you do with him. But if he learns y'all
waitin' to pounce on him like a duck on a June bug, he may not
——"

"He won't find out," McFeeley said. "*You* made the deal with
him. Not me. The police haven't been party to any agreements."

Andrus waved back his golden mop and looked appealingly at
his wife. "You think we did the right thing, Laura? Makin' that
statement? Lettin' our voices go out like that?"

"I don't know what to think any more," she said. Her voice
was dispirited, diluted, as if, at last, her power was crumbling.
"Maybe I shouldn't have called the police. Maybe I should have
followed his orders."

McFeeley worked his tie knot up to the collar button, put on
his gray jacket. He did so with a clerkish prissiness, not the de-
termination of a man about to arrest a good part of the Los
Angeles press corps. "I hate to say this, Mrs. Andrus," Joe said,
"but we're long past that. You did the right thing. But the minute that newspaper let the story out, all bets were off." The
plain-clothes men and detectives rose from around the map.

"O.K.," McFeeley said. "Let's clean up outside."

Not a man had moved. They were still in a ragged huddle,
some holding cameras, others lolling in cars. McFeeley and his aides
crossed the street and confronted them.

"You've overstayed," Joe said. "It's 7:16. Everybody start moving
or you're all under arrest."

DeGroot's gray head appeared singularly tormented under the
light. "Joe, give us a break. I know our problems don't concern
you or Mrs. Andrus. But we *are* responsible to our editors, our
papers. Every man here's been ordered to stick it out."

They voiced their agreement. At some time in the evening,
they had all had similar conversations with their respective editors,
deskmen, news directors. *You don't budge until they all go. Let 'em
try to arrest you. It's bad enough the* Truth *getting this, but now,
etc . . . etc. . . .*

"You're right, Vic. It doesn't concern me," McFeeley said. He
noticed that the mob of gawkers had grown. There were more old
women, a mob of kids on bikes, people with the eager faces of
voyeurs—the kind who scream *jump!* at ledge-sitters. "You five
guys around Vic—move off with Ed Case. He'll drive you to jail.
The next five, you go with Bannon——"

They refused to believe him "Oh, for Chrissake, Joe," Arnspeiger said, "stop that nonsense. We've known you since you ran the softball league."

DeGroot pleaded again. "Joe, we were all in favor of going. That is, almost all. Three or four people refused to leave. You know what that meant—*nobody* would go. So we decided we'd set up a pool."

"Pool? You mean a few guys to cover for all? Nothing doing. Nobody stays."

"Joe, be reasonable. After the way Rheinholdt botched this, you can't blame the guys for refusing to go. The miracle was, almost all of us agreed to quit. Anyway, three men picked the short straws, to cover for everyone—a reporter, a still photographer, a newsreel man. No pictures, we agreed, unless there's a pinch. The rest of us will beat it. There's a diner on Coronado where we can wait. Does that sound all right?"

"Where do these three men stay?" McFeeley asked.

"We figured we'd stick a car in there"—he indicated the Skopas garage—"and, that way, they'd be out of sight. They wouldn't leave the car till you said O.K. That is, when the child was released or you'd made an arrest."

The detective hooked a finger over the bent tip of his nose. "No. No deals. We're wasting time. It's 7:20. Let's move off."

"Joe, Joe, listen to reason," DeGroot pleaded. "You'll wreck your career, kid."

McFeeley prodded him. "Move, Vic. This isn't personal. I can't fool around any more."

The astonished group—reporters, police, the curious citizenry—were suddenly illuminated in the yellow floodlight of Rheinholdt's car. Sergeant Baines had driven the automobile to the edge of the group. Rheinholdt bustled officiously out of the car. To McFeeley's surprise, he was followed by Mayor Palmer Speed.

"What's up, Joe?" Rheinholdt asked. "I thought it would be a good idea to bring His Honor along to see how things are going." He glared at the reporters.

Speed honored the journalists with a wide grin. "Say, everyone's out here tonight! Hi, there, Mr. DeGroot! Dave! Charlie!" He knew at least half a dozen of them by name.

"Hey, Mayor!" someone shouted. "You think after this mess the City Council will reorganize the police?"

Rheinholdt gulped. His eyes swept the mob, trying to find the miscreant. Mayor Speed was unperturbed. "Now, boys, that isn't called for. You may quote me that the chief and Lieutenant Mc-

Feeley and all the police force are doing a marvelous job. I know Amy Andrus'll be returned."

"Why hasn't the thirteen-state alarm gone out?" Arnspeiger shouted.

"None of your goddamned business!" exploded Rheinholdt.

Martin Ringel had snaked his way forward and was jamming a microphone into Rheinholdt's face.

"Hey, Chief, where's the FBI?" Ringel cried.

"Shut up!" roared the chief. "McFeeley, why ain't they cleared out yet?"

Joe took Rheinholdt and Speed aside and explained. He did so quickly, consulting his watch. It was 7:25. He had to start arresting them at once. When the mayor heard the word *arrest*—not just one man, but some forty reporters—he tugged at his collar. "Arrest *them?*" he asked plaintively. "You can't. You just can't. *It isn't done.*"

DeGroot moved toward them. "We offered Joe a deal, Mayor." He explained the pool arrangement—three men to cover for everyone, hidden in a garage. "Look, Mayor, we have no dope on that ransom pickup. We don't know when, or where, or anything about it," DeGroot said. "What harm can there be in three men hiding in a car and promising not to move out? For all we know, someone'll have to drive to Long Beach to leave the money."

McFeeley sucked in his breath. "I'm against it. All we need is for one guy to violate it. Unless we arrest everyone, we're taking a big risk. Mayor, it's getting late."

Speed hesitated. In two months he would be up for re-election, his ninth successive term in office. He loved the job. He was a good administrator. The money—a token fifteen hundred dollars per annum—meant nothing to him. He owned Santa Luisa's most prosperous sporting goods store. Being mayor, he felt, was a public trust. It bothered him that since the war there had been rumblings of discontent with his genial administration. In the new tract housing areas, all kinds of odd people with strange names and harsh eastern accents were sniping at him, organizing "nonpartisan" groups to fight his Citizens Committee. They were going to run some wiseacre college professor against him. He'd let the new people hold their meetings and make noise and circulate leaflets; he always had the newspapers on his side. The papers would back him. They always backed him. His ninth term would be his finest. He would push through his beautification plan for the shopping center.

"I propose," Mayor Speed said firmly, "that we agree to this—what did you call it? Pool. Chief, what do you feel?"

"Whatever His Honor wants," Rheinholdt said.

McFeeley did not move. "You're sure, Mayor?"

"That's right, Joe. It sounds fair. It won't compromise your work. The boys will keep their word."

McFeeley and DeGroot walked back to the reporters. The men were advised that the pool was acceptable. In a few minutes, the cars started driving away. The three pool men went to make arrangements with the Skopas family for use of the garage. Dave Arnspeiger, the LA *Argus* man, would cover for newspapers and wire services. Steve Billik of UBC had drawn the newsreel assignment. A man from Acme Wirephoto had won the photographer's spot. Soon, only DeGroot, lingering like a sheep dog, was left. He shook hands with McFeeley, then drove off to the diner.

The detectives, bunched around Joe and Rheinholdt, appeared relieved. "How about the patrols?" one man asked. "If any of those guys try to sneak back, should we stop them?"

"I don't think they will," McFeeley answered. "They'll keep their word now."

Rheinholdt tugged the panama tighter on his head. "Don't arrest any reporters. You heard His Honor."

The forward thrust of the chief's head, his rooted stance—neither of these camouflaged a vague hysteria. Palmer Speed, his patron, had forced him to kneel to the hated press—not once, not twice, but three times. First there had been Sparling's release; second, the informing of the papers; third, the agreement to partial coverage. He was like a boy who hates eggs being forced to clean the chicken coop.

At 7:40 the street was empty, save for a few teen-age boys circling on bicycles. McFeeley, in clearing the street of rubberneckers, had decided to let the boys stay. They were local kids, including Timmy Emerson. Moreover, a barren street might be as suspect as one jammed with people. With a final look at Nespoli Drive, the detective walked up the flagstone path with Rheinholdt.

The newspapermen crowded into the Patio Diner, overflowing the blue plastic booths, lining up two-deep at the counter, congregating around the cashier's stand. Calls were made to editors, to deskmen; notes exchanged; the pool arrangement analyzed. On learning of the pool (at best, a limited way of covering a story), most of the editors grumbled but accepted the reporters' assurance that they had no choice. It was pool or jail.

Sparling was jammed into a booth with George Brack, a UBC soundman, and an electrician, and a tape engineer whom Tom Ballstead had sent from radio-side. Brack's frank, manly face was unmarred by the abrasive events at the Andrus house. Not a hair of his golden crown was misplaced. His soothing presence always served to buoy Eliot.

"Ballstead still sore at me?" Sparling asked. Brack had made the last telephone call after the pool had been established.

"You know how Tom is," Brack said. "He's mad at the whole world. The radio mobile unit will be out later. They want a cut-in from us at 11:00 and a spot on the morning news tomorrow. I guess it's an all-night vigil for us."

Sparling sipped his black, burning coffee. It barely stimulated him. During his labors as an overnight man at the *Truth*, he had consumed gallons of the acidulous stuff. He had come from night-work inured to it, like a pernicious variety of mosquito, impervious to DDT.

"We have to make it up to Tom," Eliot said gloomily. "I got a few leads I wanna pursue." He thought of Mrs. Emerson—*call me Babe*—and made a note to try her the next day.

"Eliot, stop looking so glum," Brack said. "Tom isn't sore. Well, not as sore as he was. Everyone liked the 6:15 bit we did. You keep it up, you'll be talent." George disliked seeing anyone unhappy. His own life was such a comforting cycle of job, family, barbecue, boat that he deplored misery in others. In the morning, when he came to work, he always brought Eliot fresh coffee and a jelly doughnut.

The technicians, silent, counting overtime, uninvolved with the drama, ordered a second round of coffee. When Brack volunteered to treat, they also ordered pie. Abruptly, Sparling, who had been making an informal count of noses, stood up in the booth. His tones rose loud and clear above the general hum. "Where's Ringel?"

Brack turned in the booth. "He must be here. Didn't everyone come here together?"

"Where's Marty Ringel?" Eliot shouted. "The little punk. I bet he stayed. I bet he's hiding somewhere."

"Oh, El, come on," George said. "He's probably in his car. Or making a call."

Unhearing, Sparling hauled his body out of the booth. He shoved his way through the crowd and found Victor DeGroot in a corner booth. The AP man was sitting with a quiet, older group of newsmen. They appeared to be an *ad hoc* committee, a council of tribal elders. Eliot recognized a white-haired AP photographer, a man from a Los Angeles morning paper, and Harvey Swinnerton, the *Truth* stringer. The latter was sipping tea.

"Hey, Mr. DeGroot," whined Eliot, "I don't mind a pool, but I won't stand for dirty pool."

"What's bothering *you?*" asked DeGroot.

"Martin Ringel's bothering me. He isn't around. I bet he stayed. Aren't we gonna do anything about it?"

DeGroot rubbed the bridge of his nose. "Sparling, I can't keep tabs on everyone. I haven't any idea where Ringel is. This is strictly a voluntary agreement. We're all on the honor system, as strange as that may seem to you television people."

Eliot darted what he imagined to be a chilling glance (he succeeded in looking half-witted) at Swinnerton. "Honor system? That's great. Ask your buddy Harvey over there about the honor system. How about it Swinnerton? Who pulled the cork at the *Truth?*"

"Oh, get away from us," DeGroot said.

Sparling needed no prod. He had already fled through the diner's revolving door.

The telephone had become troublesome. It rang continually. The Andrus number was listed in the Santa Luisa book and it was not difficult for the curious, the morbid, the helpful to locate it and contact the scene of the tragedy. Moll, manning the phone, realized that a red blinker would have to be installed and the bell silenced if they were to sleep.

Meanwhile, he kept a meticulous log. McFeeley, standing in the doorway, could hear him saying politely: "That's right; I have your name. You're Mr. Powers, scoutmaster of Valley View Troop 72, and if there's any searching, you'll organize the boys. Thank you. Thank you."

McFeeley walked to the makeshift office and examined Moll's log —a steno pad, the top page held in place with a rubber band. He read the last entries.

7:42—Father Menardi, Church of Blessed Sacr. Offering prayers for Amy; Kidnaper can hv sanctry in church. Told him O.K.

7:44—Mr. Oldham, San Francisco Examiner. Told him no press statements at all. Wait tomorrow.

7:47—Woman Van Nuys refused give name claims saw Mexicans carrying child, well dressed, Anglo-Saxon, into car. Referred VN police.

7:52—Man calling from bar downtown LA, said worked as stoolie LA police, willing make deal with us underworld connections. Referred him Rheinholdt tomorrow.

8:01—Mr. Mailman, personal frnd Mr. Andrus, offering sympathies, help, raise money ransom. Thnks. Call tomorrow when calmer.

He left Moll in his office of Mother Goose cutouts and baby furniture and walked into the living room.

"8:10," McFeeley announced. "Let's do it."

The thick envelope, containing the box, lay on Fritzie's desk. Andrus rose from the sofa, weaving fingers through his blond mane. "I'll take it," he said softly. "I can manage a short walk." They watched him—his wife, Dr. Todd, McFeeley, the other detectives. He seemed in control of himself, but when he picked up the package, his hand shook. Andrus set it down again, studying it with swollen eyes. "I'll be O.K. in a minute," he said.

McFeeley looked at Laura. She was sitting in her husband's swivel chair. A few minutes ago they had crowded into the den to watch the motion pictures of her appeal on television. The film, streaky and murky, had been rushed to the screen, interrupting a half-hour adventure story about the South Seas. It had seemed to Laura, staring at the bloodless copy of herself, hearing her faltering voice, seeing again the pitiless mob, that the cheap fiction (*Back again, O'Brien? I warned you to stay away from these pearling grounds!*) was more alive than her own flickering image.

"We better get moving," McFeeley said.

Andrus was immobile. "That box," he whispered; "it's all wrong. That ain't a fair trade—that box for my child. I can't touch it."

"It's almost ten after," Joe said.

"I'll be fine in a minute, officer," Fritzie said. Still he did not take the package.

Laura got up. "I'll go, Fritzie—doesn't matter which one of us goes."

McFeeley hooked his hands in his belt. "One or the other."

She picked up the envelope, cradling it on her right forearm, the way a schoolgirl ports her burden of loose-leaf notebooks, texts, lunch, gym uniform.

Andrus looked up mournfully at his wife. "Yes. Of course, Laura. You do it. Might be better if you did. You're the one he figures he's doin' business with."

Joe held the door open for her and she walked into the cool street, heavy with the scent of blossoms and greenery, that reassuring, perfumed odor of California-by-night, when the smog has cleared and the air is thin and sweet. She started down the flagstone path. The street appeared deserted, except for Timmy Emerson and another teen-ager, circling each other on bicycles about fifty feet to the south.

She walked past the palms, through the high iron gate. At the sidewalk, she paused. A station wagon, one not belonging to the Skopas family, was parked in their driveway. There were several people sitting in it. Under the street light's diffused glow, she saw them staring at her. McFeeley had told her that the reporters had agreed to leave, but he had said nothing about the pool. She was puzzled. Then she turned right and started walking north toward Buena Terra Park. It was too late to protest, to turn back to the house and complain to the police. She had not advanced a dozen steps toward Kohlmeyer Street when a lavender sports car, shivering the night with flatulent bursts, scudding so low as to suggest it moved on a cable, parked alongside her house. The noise made Laura halt and turn.

Out of the car stepped a slender, well-dressed woman. Like the car, she was all lavender. The new arrival looked swiftly at the Andrus house, the quiet street, stared for a moment at the woman carrying the thick package, and then ran towards her, *clack-clacking* on noisy heels.

"Laura Andrus? Laura, darling?" she called.

"Go away. Go away," Laura said. "You aren't supposed to be here."

"Laura, darling. It *is* you." At closer range, Laura saw the face —aged, cruel and lapstreaked—giving the lie to the elegant young body. "I'm Mona Mears. I'm from the *Truth*. Oh, my dear brave woman—let me help you——"

"Stay away from me," Laura said. "Do you want me to call the police?"

As she spoke, one of the men in the station wagon got out and studied them. It was the pool photographer, cradling his camera as if it were some loot of which he was ashamed. "Hey, Miss Mears!" he called. "This is pool coverage! No one but us three are supposed to be here!"

"Pool?" Mona called back. "I've never agreed to one in my life."

Laura walked away from them. The woman in lavender followed her. The miraculous circumstances of timing, of sheer good luck that had brought the columnist to the Andrus home at the precise moment at which the child's mother was about to deposit the ransom did not seem unusual to Mona Mears. Like most great reporters, she had come to believe in herself. She was omniscient, omnipresent. She *assumed* that the breaks would be hers. Some she fashioned herself—through hard intelligence, excellent contacts with people in seats of power, a not inconsiderable charm. But she was also fantastically lucky, a queen of serendipity. Mona had come to believe that no story was *official* without her presence, no public event had truly gotten underway until she arrived. Indeed, she had reached that stage of journalistic eminence where *she herself* was as newsworthy as the stories she covered. Her name got into headlines as often as it appeared in by-line. The *Truth* often bannered her on the front page.

MONA MEARS THRILLED BY
FIRST TURBOJET RIDE!

In the chill night, Mona knew she had stumbled on something grand. But the prospect of another monumental coup did not cause her to tremble or render her lightheaded. She accepted the gift as no less than her due. With a few swift steps, she was abreast of the Andrus woman, her immaculate coiffure bobbing as she *clack-clacked* alongside her. Miss Mears' figure was a marvelous fraud— supple, lean, rounded at bosom and hip. It was of such linear perfection, so free of bulge and slouch, that it suggested she had been sheathed in one long corset, extending from neck to toe. From the rear, she might have been Laura's younger sister, dolled up for a hospital league luncheon.

"Why don't you let me carry it, Laura?" Mona asked. "You've been through so much. It is the money—isn't it?"

Laura stared ahead. The park entrance, at the intersection of

Nespoli and Kohlmeyer, was less than a hundred yards from her house. She could see the stone pillars that flanked the entrance.

"I flew in the minute I heard about it," Mears said, "this horrid, horrid thing. Did you pray? What were your first thoughts? I mean—how can you be so brave? That's all everyone is talking about. Your courage."

Laura stopped. Across the street, the three men in the station wagon had emerged and were strolling down the street. They remained on the opposite side, perhaps ten yards behind the two women, but they had given up all pretense at hiding. They moved at a laggard's pace. The photographer and Steve Billik carried their gear as if they were burdens of guilt; the pool reporter, Dave Arnspeiger, shuffled behind them. Laura heard one say: "For Chrissake, give her a break; let's go back to the car." And then a mumbled response: "What about Mears? She can't get away with this. She's breaking the pool."

Laura looked sharply at the desiccated face. "Why don't you go?" she pleaded. "Don't you realize my child may not live if this madness continues? If you'd leave—*they* would."

A lavender glove touched Laura's arm. Some arcane scent, evocative of Paris, roiled the night air. "My darling!" Mona Mears said. "I want to help. I *can* help. Don't you know that criminals always surrender to the police *through me*? I've made no agreements with these rube cops here. *They're* to blame." She fixed two popping eyes on Laura—wet black grapes on a plate of dough.

"Damn you," Laura gasped. "Damn all of you. Get away."

When she resumed walking, the three men did not follow her immediately. But Mona Mears did. She sniffed the grand prize. She trailed Laura, a few discreet paces to the rear, tiptoeing ludicrously to eliminate the tattoo of her heels.

Eliot Sparling, careening insanely down Nespoli, saw the lunatic tableau halfway down the street and slammed on his brakes. He could see Mrs. Andrus, straight-backed, walking toward Kohlmeyer Street; Mona Mears, whom he knew of old from the *Truth* and whose lavender Corvette he recognized immediately, trailing her like a pointing dog; then the pool men—Billik, Arnspeiger and the photographer—resuming their embarrassed pilgrimage. Behind all of them, two boys on bikes wheeled and circled like buzzards.

Eliot pulled abreast of the reporters. "Where's Ringel?" he asked. "You guys seen Marty Ringel?" His fragmented brain could find no other point of reference. The idiot processional on the sweet-smelling street; the unexpected vision of Mona Mears; the sight of Mrs. Andrus in the act of making rendezvous, possibly embracing the child—none of these made impact on his stupefied mind. He was intent only on Ringel, that fink, that goad, that shover of microphones and insulter of public figures.

"Ringel?" Arnspeiger asked. "He ain't here. Sparling, get out of here. You're violating the pool."

"That's right," the photographer said. "You have no right to be here. Get lost."

Eliot gestured at Mears. "What about *her?*"

"She has no right either," Arnspeiger said. "But at least she wasn't told—I guess." His rationale settled nothing; the parade, once begun, could not be halted. Eliot started rolling again in low gear, just ahead of the youths on bicycles. *I follow the elephants,* he thought. His eyes swiveled, seeking Ringel. He had to find him, if only to excuse his own contemptible presence.

Ed Case and Milt Bannon, the detectives whom McFeeley had posted in the garage near the park entrance, saw the parade and debated a plan of action. It was not quite 8:15. The interlopers could still be chased off. Theoretically, the criminal might yet make an appearance. Case, the younger man, whispered to Bannon, "They should have sold tickets," then vaulted the rear of the convertible in which they were hiding and waved his arms at the promenaders.

"Off the street," Case said. "All of you, except Mrs. Andrus. Come on, you guys, back to the car. You—lady—get moving."

They were beyond threats. The massive engines that propelled them, that lubricated mechanism, built on curiosity, nosiness, the morbid delight in the misery of *others,* was in motion. They halted —not because of the detective's halfhearted protests, but because the woman was kneeling at the base of a stone pillar and placing the package on the grass. She seemed—to Eliot Sparling, anyway— to be participating in a religious rite, a nocturnal propitiation of the gods. Rising, Laura surveyed them: the girlish figure of the lavender woman, the puzzled detective, the three men across the street, the halted Ford, the bicycles. She started walking quickly back to her house. *There must be a reason why they have acted this way,* she thought. *They cannot consciously want my child dead.*

"Dammit, move!" Case said. "It's 8:15. You people never take no."

The journalists walked quickly to the Skopas house; Miss Mears hurried to her Corvette; the boys on bicycles vanished down a driveway. Eliot, inside his idling Ford, saw the detective striding toward him and made a right turn on Kohlmeyer Street. As he did, his motor stalled.

In the silence he heard a persistent, intense voice issuing from—where? The street was deserted; his car radio was turned off. The voice buzzed on—low, hurried, in the cadence of a radio newscast. It dawned on Eliot: *it was Martin Ringel's voice.*

He leaped from the car. His ogrish head soared, gyrated, seeking the taunting sounds. "Ringel!" he whispered. "Where are you? I'm wise to you, you punk! Where are you hiding?"

An answer was hissed at him—from above. "Get lost, Sparling. Scram."

Sparling looked up. Above him, nesting in the crotch of a sycamore, was Martin Ringel. His pudgy figure was crammed into the branches. Moonlit leaves provided effective camouflage. He had a portable tape recorder slung about his neck and he was speaking in the low, breathy tones of a golf announcer.

"I'm standing by at the ransom rendezvous spot at the junction of Nespoli Drive and Kohlmeyer Street in the luxurious Buena Terra Park section of the city of Santa Luisa, California, a city praying and hoping tonight for the safety of Amy Andrus. This is RR time—ransom rendezvous—and I have just seen Laura Andrus, a brave and lonely woman, mother of the kidnaped child, place a package which——"

"Oh!" Eliot groaned. "Oh—you louse! You cheat! How'd you—why'd you——"

Ringel sealed the microphone with his hand. "Sparling, get out of here. It's my business how I got here and how I found out. At least I'm hidden. But you—you big jerk. You're right in the open. You better beat it, I'm warning you."

The admonition from Ringel was unnecessary. Sparling was stunned, heartsick, beaten. Back he had come, snorting and braying —and had gained nothing. Mona Mears of the *Truth,* with that maddening good luck that clung to her like cologne, had walked the dark street with Laura Andrus. Ringel, his television competitor, had outsmarted him. The pool man would match—legally and honorably—anything he would have. And all of them had excuses. He alone, Sparling the foul-up, had violated the agreement, with his usual blatant stupidity. How dumb could he get?

Ringel's voice hummed in Eliot's ears like a flight of stinging gnats. "I can see the package clearly. It is a thick yellow, or, more properly, tan, envelope, probably containing a box. It's resting on a patch of grass at the base of a stone column and. . . ."

At 10:00, Joe McFeeley walked out of the house and duplicated the journey Laura Andrus had made two hours earlier. As he passed through the wrought-iron gate he saw the teen-age kids on bikes studying him from the Emerson driveway. One was Timmy, his informant regarding the car.

"Some reporter pay you kids to hang around?" Joe asked.

They hesitated. "Ah—not exactly," Timmy said. When the detective continued walking, they followed him on their bikes. Dave Arnspeiger ran out of the Skopas house: he had just telephoned the diner. "Joe!" he called. "O.K. if we come? Nobody's showed. You gonna take the money back?"

McFeeley halted. "You better stay here." The other two pool men joined Arnspeiger in the gutter. "Ah, what the hell," McFeeley said wearily, "the damage is done."

They followed him. It occurred to McFeeley, with a sickening impact, that the stretch of street where the press had encamped was filthy with coffee containers, wax wrappings, soft drink bottles. In the confusion, no one—neither reporters nor police—had remembered to clean up the mess. The most imbecilic of criminals would have reared with fright at that vista of litter—the unmistakable leavings of a waiting group. With a shiver, it dawned on McFeeley why they had overlooked a garbage detail: *they had never believed for one minute that the money would be taken, the child returned.* He had tried to protect Amy Andrus, devising makeshift stratagems, lying, delaying, plotting, with a calmness he hoped would buoy the parents—and it had been a fraud, at least from the moment the newspaper had published the story. As he continued down the silent street, he thought of the stiff-backed woman, the weepy man, the vanished child—people as alien to him as Eskimos. He had attempted not only to solve a crime but to strengthen and sustain them. Now, staring at the ketchup-smeared wrappings, the white cardboard containers, he realized he had been deceiving himself—and them. Secretly, he knew that *nothing* would have helped—not after the crime had become public knowledge.

"What now?" Arnspeiger asked. "What's next?"

"We'll think of something," Joe answered.

At the park entrance, McFeeley picked up the package. It was wet with night moisture. Case and Bannon came out of the garage. The two men hiding in the hedges also emerged. They stood in the selenial glow—five police officers and three reporters—eight men each nurturing some personal guilt.

"See anything at all?" Joe asked.

The detectives shook their heads. Ed Case looked sorrowfully at the pool men. "You guys might have given that kid a break. Jesus, why you all didn't just go——"

"Lay off," Dave Arnspeiger said. "Almost everyone said they'd go. But a few wouldn't. So we rigged the pool. We would've stayed in the garage if Mona Mears hadn't busted in. We couldn't let her get away with it."

The boys on the bikes raced back to the Emerson house. They were getting two dollars each from the World News Association man to work as eyewitness informants.

McFeeley started back to the Andrus house. The others trailed him. For some reason, the men did not take the sidewalk, but promenaded along the deserted roadway, treading an invisible central path. They trooped in silence, McFeeley bearing the spurned ransom—eight men awaiting judgment because of some dimly understood collective sin.

When they had gone, Martin Ringel jumped down from his perch in the tree and whistled. A motorcycle popped out of a driveway a few houses east on Kohlmeyer. Ringel gave the courier a reel of magnetic tape on a plastic reel. The motorcycle belched off, its blast violating the tranquil night, the exhaust lingering in the sweet air like the bad breath of hell.

Chief Rheinholdt studied the damp package. He looked at Laura. "Don't you worry, Mrs. Andrus. We'll find your child. Those newspapers stopped us today, but tomorrow it'll be different. No more interference. I'll take care of *them* in the morning." He appeared more intent on evening scores with the press than solving the crime. Laura barely heard him. After a few words with McFeeley, Rheinholdt left, asking that he be called if something developed, cautioning Joe to keep Mayor Speed informed.

"I suppose we shouldn't have expected anything," Laura said weakly. "We all kept making believe it would happen, going through the routine—as if anything could have helped. I knew I wouldn't see her."

Fritzie was in his swivel chair, staring at the package. He got up and walked across the living room and sat down next to his wife.

"We'll see her again," Andrus said. Laura could not tell whether the decisive note in his voice was sincere—or whether he was calling on some dramatic technique. She had long despaired of gauging his moods, the roles he assumed so swiftly.

"I think you will, Mr. Andrus," Joe said.

"You don't have to deceive me," Laura said to both of them. "What do you really believe, Lieutenant? Don't you suspect my daughter has been murdered? Isn't that what the note said would happen?"

Her shoulders jerked upward, and she was convulsed with dry, racking gasps. In her stubborn pride, she would dike her tears at the expense of everything else. She would surrender to convulsions, a thousand migraines, before she would cry again. Fritzie saw her agony. He helped her to her feet and guided her toward the bedroom. Andrus was not ashamed to weep for his daughter.

McFeeley moved toward them. The other detectives turned away; some joined Moll in the nursery. "Maybe you'd want me to send for your family doctor?" Joe asked. "Mrs. Andrus might want a sedative or something."

Laura was wearing a tan sweater and skirt, and the clonic seizures wrinkled and stretched the clothing rhythmically and made her lank brown hair rise and fall on her shoulders.

"No, we'll manage, officer," Andrus wept. "We got pills we haven't used. Miz Andrus and me, we'll be all right. You might call our maid, Selena—her name's in the book on my desk—Selena Masters—and ask her to come out early tomorrow to he'p."

His words were uttered clearly through a thick curtain of tears. Undistorted, they had the effect of a man passing under a waterfall's trajectory, undampened. There seemed a poignant bravery about him at that moment that McFeeley had to admire.

When the parents had closed the bedroom door, Dr. Todd wandered into the nursery. Irvin Moll and McFeeley were both on the telephones and ignored him for a few minutes. Moll was calling the photography lab, asking that a picture of Amy Andrus, sent over earlier in the evening, be circulated to newspapers and TV stations, accompanied by a physical description. Then he talked to communications: the same material was to be held in readiness for the thirteen-state alarm, for release as soon as Rheinholdt gave the word. McFeeley was talking to Records. He wanted the mug file yanked; the parents, the servants would have to start going through them tomorrow. He asked the Records division to contact the Los Angeles police for access to their files.

They remained on the phones for almost ten minutes, starting in motion the interminable routine work that represented the bulk of investigatory procedure. Todd waited until they had concluded. "I guess I'll run along," the dentist said. "Sorry I couldn't be of more help." He indicated the package. "Shall I take that?"

Joe waited a moment. "Well—it's your money, Dr. Todd."

"Oh no, no, I didn't mean that. Goodness, I didn't mean that. I meant just for safekeeping—I'd return it to the bank or keep it in my vault."

"If you have no objection," Joe said, "maybe we'd better keep it handy. We might get a call from this bird and have to race out with it. That all right?"

"Yes! Yes! Whatever you say, Lieutenant!" His bounciness was diminished. "I—ah—feel rather badly about this affair," Todd said slowly.

"How come?" Joe asked. "We all tried."

"Well, as you've probably guessed, I told Harvey Swinnerton a few things."

"It's past worrying about," McFeeley said.

"I don't think it is," the dentist said. He removed his pince-nez and tugged at the bridge of his nose. "I don't understand it at all. Swinnerton promised that everything I told him was off the record."

"You didn't mean any harm," Moll said vacantly. "I don't think any of us were ready for this. We were all kind of stunned. Jesus, kidnapings are rare as hell. No one knows what to do at first."

"I guess you're right, Sergeant." Todd was immersed in doubt. The tiniest twinge of guilt would inevitably act upon him with enormous effect—he lived a sublime life, free of culpability. "Still —maybe I shouldn't have said anything to Swinnerton."

"We'll know tomorrow," McFeeley yawned. "Rheinholdt's not through with them, and they'll have some hot ones for him to handle. Nobody better get in between them."

Todd left. The authoritative snap in his voice had vanished. When he had gone, the telephone rang. Moll answered it. It was a woman with a shrill voice advising him that Amy Andrus had not been kidnaped at all. It was a plot to get publicity for her father's TV programs.

Herbert Hood, per his custom when a big story was breaking, had stayed late at the *Truth* office. A widower, childless, shy of friends, he often had his dinner sent up to his glass cage. He would eat quickly in his shabby vivarium, staring out at a near-empty city room—a cleaning woman, a sports writer finishing a boxing story, a night deskman, a night cable man.

Swinnerton had already phoned him with the pooled story of the fruitless ransom drop—the basic facts that all the papers would have available. During their conversation, Swinnerton kept mumbling that Mona Mears had been there, had broken the pool agreement, and had vanished. Swinnerton had gotten this secondhand from Arnspeiger. Hood wondered why Mona had not yet phoned in her *I-was-there* piece.

In any case, Hood would wait until the overnight editor arrived and then give him some guidance on coverage, photos, layout. The bulldog edition would have to be overwhelming, a vigorous carry-over of the first-day's beat, something that would make people anxious to stay with the *Truth* through the case and long after.

Hood gulped a cup of cold coffee from the tray on his desk. Then he waddled out of his enclosure for a leisurely tour of the city room. He exchanged baseball talk with a sports writer (Hood was a loyal White Sox fan), glanced at the wire service machines, all of them loaded with copy on the Andrus case. He admired the way they kept running off at the mouth, with so little to go by—there were background pieces, interpretations, legal angles, summations of past kidnapings, but very few hard facts—and most of these swiped from the *Truth's* beat. He was gratified to notice little censuring on the part of the press associations. They assumed that the full story on the *Truth's* breakage was not yet known, that it would be wrong to condemn anyone—newspaper or police. To no one in particular, he suddenly uttered the numbers "5:07 and 6:04."

The Andrus case had crowded everything else—foreign affairs, Washington news—off the machines. Abruptly his thoughts turned to the vanished child. A bothersome choice rattled around Hood's head—the life of a four-year-old girl against the survival of a newspaper, an increase in circulation. Was he phrasing it too coarsely? Was that what Hansel had meant by "the public's right to know?" The musings did Hood no good; he was too much of a hard-nosed old cynic to accept that high-blown crap of Ted Hansel's. Let the publisher save that for the journalism schools. He and Hansel both knew damned well what sold newspapers. Herb Hood had known it since he covered Chicago fifty years ago for the World News Association. Looking out of the city room windows at the smog-hazed lights of downtown Los Angeles, an exaggerated error built on the used car business, he longed for

Chicago. A bred-in-the-bone midwesterner, born in Quincy, Illinois, near the bend of the Mississippi below Hannibal, he missed Chicago —rough and dirty and thick with the smells and sounds of real industry, real wealth: cattle, steel, corn, hogs, rails. In his reverie, the night deskman summoned him.

"Mr. Hood—Mr. Hansel's on."

Hood took the call in his office, evincing a palpable gloom as Hansel's spirited voice came to him. In the background, Hood fancied he heard the high babble of a party. The Hansels were very social. Mrs. H. was California oil money, a tenacious woman, older than her journalistic husband, zealous of her own status as a force in state politics. Hood found himself begrudging Hansel everything—his job, his power, his rich wife.

"I have marvelous news," Hansel said. "Mona got to the house just as the Andrus woman was going to leave the money. *She walked the street with her.*"

"She did? Well, that's a break. Swinnerton mumbled something about it, but I couldn't believe him. How'd Mona swing that? I thought the reporters had set up a pool——"

"Who cares?" T.T. said rudely. "She's a great reporter. She made her own break. Now listen to me, Herbert. I want a red banner tomorrow—seventy-two point type—MONA MEARS AIDS MRS. ANDRUS: TWO WOMEN MAKE VAIN TRIP TO KIDNAPER."

"Ah, it sounds a little long, Ted. I'll work something out with the overnight. We're gathering stuff for a big——"

"Overnight? What are you talking about?" Hansel asked the questions as if there had never been an overnight at the *Truth,* as if this aspect of his newspaper's operation had eluded him. "Herbert, no high school boys on this story. Mona will come in to write the eyewitnesser and the news lead. Two by-lines. We're past the Swinnertons."

"He got us the beat. We could give him a——"

"Herbert, don't you see what Mona's done for us? She's made it *our* story. We own it."

"It sounds marvelous, Ted." He did not smile, although his voice was buoyant. "Can Mona call me?" Mears rarely called him. She went directly to Hansel, circling Hood as if he were an old floating wreck. A secretive chuckle issued from Hansel's throat. "She's right here with me. She'll be in the office in twenty minutes. Give her everything she needs, Herbert."

Hood's reptilian eyes darted about, trying to add something helpful to the soaring pyramid of good luck, of frantic drive, of sensationalism that Hansel was erecting. "Ah—maybe I'd better bring in Kalaidjian and Trigg. A few extra hands never hurt."

Hansel weighed the suggestion. "Kalaidjian, yes. Trigg, no. Trigg gets overtime. Mona's leaving now. Call me when she's finished the lead and the eyewitnesser."

"I sure will, Ted." Hood heard the voices in Hansel's home grow louder, more joyous. "Ted? Are you still on? Kind of rough on that family, isn't it?"

"What family?"

"The Andrus family. Losing that child like that. And that ransom deal blowing up tonight."

"Of course. It's tragic. Why do you mention it?"

"Well, the kid just might have been returned tonight. That bastard might have come for the money and left the little girl."

There was no response from Hansel, and for a moment the party noises ceased. Hood guessed that Hansel (he did such things) had hung up. But T.T. had merely placed his hand over the phone while wishing Mona Mears Godspeed.

"You still with me, Ted?"

"Herbert? I guess that's all. Mona's left."

"A shame that child wasn't returned. God knows what that dirty son-of-a-bitch will do to her now. You know how these kidnapings generally go." It occurred to Herbert Hood, with pungent clarity, that his employment of epithets to describe the criminal—*bastard, son-of-a-bitch*—were ways of striking back at Hansel. The cuss words, Hood realized, were aimed at the Editor & Publisher's ruddy head.

"I don't know what we can do about that now," Hansel said crisply.

"Don't misunderstand me, Ted. We're clean. Rheinholdt didn't call us until 6:04—almost an hour after we were out. It's just that there may be a fuss raised tomorrow. You know, some of our competition. As if they wouldn't have given a million bucks to have had the story. And those radio and television people might pop off— the dirty whores." He spat the words out—aiming them not at some miserable Eliot Sparling, but at Hansel's face.

"That's exactly what I'm counting on *you* for," Hansel said firmly. "I realize we may be attacked. Start building a file. Statements from everyone—Swinnerton, Trigg, Kalaidjian, our telephone operators. We must be foolproof. Of course, I'm not worried.

Not only are we clean, we acted in the best tradition of journalism. Any time a newspaper battles censorship, it's performing a service. That's axiomatic. I can't imagine that half-witted policeman daring to take us on. Let's not waste any time discussing it."

"I hope you're right, Ted. I suppose we shouldn't worry about it. God knows we've got our work cut out for us—no matter what happens to that child."

"What the devil are you muttering about now? What in the world has one thing to do with another?"

Hood paused: the wonderful blindness of the man! The expedient deafness! Ted Hansel could summon up a thousand names and places out of his past; he never forgot the fine print in a contract. But when it served him, he could be a castle of opacity.

"Nothing at all, Ted. As I said, we're in good shape. I just have a feeling that that cop may sound off. Maybe the woman——"

"It doesn't concern us. The police are to blame. Why weren't we called?"

For a long time after Hansel had hung up, Hood sat silently in his dingy office. Outside the high casement windows, the *Truth's* neon sign splashed the general manager's hairless head with toxic greens. More than ever he appeared a ponderous frog, malevolent in appearance, but venomless and weak. He had a longing (silly, he realized, in a man of seventy-one) to be back in Chicago, holding down a job as night man for a bureau, listening to the wind whistling in from the cold lake.

Headset clamped to his head, his eyes half shut, Eliot Sparling heard the engineer in the UBC newsroom in Los Angeles whisper, "Cue Brack," then jabbed a finger into George's thigh. The two men were crammed into the rear of the network's mobile radio unit. Brack began reading the lead story for the 11:00 P.M. local news. Eliot's prose glittered.

> . . . and so a night of watchful waiting, a night of prayer and hope and torment for two grieving parents descends on quiet Nespoli Drive. Here in front of the yellow ranch house—4217—where our UBC truck is parked, only a corporal's guard of newsmen, in comparison to the fifty or so here earlier, is in attendance. Far into the night there will be speculation, second-guessing, argument about the fate of little Amy Andrus. If a newspaper had not printed the story of her kidnaping, would Amy be back in her little

bed this very minute—safe, unharmed? At the moment, no one can say who is to blame for the unfortunate printing of the story. But, somewhere along the line, a grave error was committed. Police sources in Santa Luisa have hinted that their best hope for getting the child back now lies in making immediate contact with the kidnaper. Meanwhile, inside the yellow house, the stricken parents. . . .

Sparling, listening attentively, savoring each word he had pecked out for Brack on his portable, was offended by them. The copy originally had been much tougher on the *Truth*. When he had read it to Tom Ballstead on the phone, the news director had made him delete specific references to the newspaper, to tone down the accusative tone. Ballstead, coughing and groaning, was concerned only with the fact that UBC had been scooped, not that the *Truth* had been guilty of an ethical lapse. "Ethics, my ass," Ballstead retched; "they were lucky. If they say the cops missed them, I believe them. That jerk Rheinholdt—waiting six hours to request secrecy on a story the whole city knew . . ."

Brack was concluding: "UBC is standing by outside the Andrus home through the night to bring you any late-breaking developments in the kidnaping of Amy Andrus. George Brack reporting from Santa Luisa. Now back to the UBC newsroom in Los Angeles."

They remained in the truck with the engineer, listening to the rest of the newscast, with the silent dedication of professionals. They heard the familiar *meanwhiles* and *so much fors* and *now a look ats* with the sensitized ears of music lovers lulled into euphoria by pure sound. Eliot adored newscasts, all newscasts. At night, he often listened to four in a row on different networks, making pertinent mental (and sometimes written) notes about emphasis, order of stories, use of humour, background material. He wished newscasts were twice as long. A half hour would be fine. An hour of news. The pleasant, artful usage of voice and inflection by the reader; the headlong parade of related facts; the outpouring of real events; the inevitable ball scores and weather; all these, to Eliot, were signposts of immortality, of a grand continuum. Long after he was dead and consigned to some atheist's limbo, long after George Brack was steering his forty-foot cabin cruiser across a heavenly lake in a Protestant paradise, a man with a soothing voice in an air-conditioned, soundproofed, englassed room would be saying: *And now a look at tomorrow's weather for the Los Angeles area. . . .*

"Why don't you catch some shut-eye, Eliot?" Brack asked solicitously. "Nothing more'll happen tonight."

"Oh, I'm not tired, Georgie. I think I'll take a stroll."

"Suit yourself, El. I'll hang around to see if the desk has any last minute requests. New York might want an early-morning spot —that'll be 5:00 A.M. our time, or earlier."

"They can't scare us, can they Georgie? We're too rich."

As he piled out of the rear of the mobile radio unit, he was sorry he had insulted Brack. George was a kind man; he had no reason to be subjected to Eliot's boorish onslaughts. Hating himself, disgusted with his own failings, he let the desert air chill him as penitence. He had been without sleep for thirty hours. But the weariness that inundated him, that turned his body to a sack of stones had its origin less in fatigue than in self-repugnance. He was about to creep into his Ford when he saw a group of reporters gathered around Victor DeGroot. Duane Bosch, the boy from the Sanlu *Register,* had just arrived from a diner with hot coffee for all. The men stood about quietly, five or six of the night watch, sipping the scalding brew. Wisps of steam arose from the containers.

Sparling rested his form against DeGroot's car. "What's the betting, men?" he asked rudely.

"What do you mean?" The UP boy asked. In the darkness, his teeth glittered like panther's eyes. He was too well dressed, too eastern, to stay with a wire service long. Eliot envisioned him graduating to a news magazine in a year or so.

"I mean, what odds you guys giving? Is the kid dead or alive?"

DeGroot's sedate face appeared to resent Sparling's question. Then it dawned on him that it was a legitimate question—if badly phrased.

"I don't know," the AP man said slowly. "I'd hate to be those parents. That child was old enough to remember things. Old enough to be a witness, to identify a man."

"That doesn't follow," the UP boy said. "If he's an amateur, he might be scared stiff—not have the guts to go through with it. He might just be waiting for a chance to sneak the kid back and run—ransom or not."

DeGroot shifted his pipe. "You've got a point there. If he's got any brains at all, he must know what he's liable for. If he does, God help that kid."

"What do you mean, Vic?" asked Eliot.

"I know what he means," the UP boy said, flashing his teeth. "Kidnaping's a capital offense in California if the victim suffers any harm. The law is explicit—death in the gas chamber or life without chance of parole."

"You mean he wouldn't have anything to lose by murdering the kid?" Eliot asked.

"That's the idea," DeGroot said quietly. "He might want to make sure they don't get him—that's all. And that kid is evidence, witness, victim, habeas corpus, the works."

They sipped their coffee silently. The lights in the Andrus house appeared to have gone out, except for some dim illumination from a rear room. Every few minutes a car with two of McFeeley's men in it rolled down the street. The air was desert-cold, the sky frantic with stars.

"It's not a pleasant thought," Duane Bosch piped.

"No, it isn't," Eliot said. "Where does that leave the LA *Truth?* What's Swinnerton been saying for publication?"

"Oh, lay off him," DeGroot said. "He isn't saying anything, because he can't. The poor guy didn't make any high-level decisions."

The AP man's evaluation seemed to terminate discussion; it was 11:30. Eliot slouched off, numb and miserable, to his car. He crammed his clumsy form into the rear seat and prayed for sleep.

The last thing he saw before his eyes locked was Harvey Swinnerton, the lapels of his tweed jacket turned up against the chill, pacing the street, his apologetic stride and his downcast face suggesting a man searching for a lost wallet—one that held every essential document to prove his existence.

It was not until shortly after midnight that Joe McFeeley was able to call his wife. He and Moll had been on the phone without a break. Until a duty roster could be set up, he and Irvin would take turns staying awake through the night—four hours on, four hours asleep. A folding cot had been moved into the nursery. Moll's long, thick body was partially covered by a blanket; he was dozing off.

McFeeley had spent a good part of the last few hours talking to newspaper and radio stations (no comment, call tomorrow), assorted tipsters, cranks, teen-age brats looking for a thrill, a few honestly helpful people, consolers, some known to the family, others strangers. The sound of Roz's voice—weary, weighted with the day's trivia—pleased him as a reminder of simpler, less troublesome things.

"Joe? You all right?"

"I'm fine, Roz. I guess you've heard all about this deal. You can imagine why I didn't call sooner."

"Your Irish kisser was all over the TV tonight. My mother saw the morning paper. You're page one, kid, standing in back of Mrs. Andrus." It was natural for her to be excited. Cops in Sanlu rarely got their pictures taken—even for the *Register,* let alone for television and the LA dailies. She halted. "I suppose it's terrible my acting so excited over your picture. Considering what that poor woman has to go through. Is there any hope, Joe?"

He heard nothing from the master bedroom. Moll was punctuating the air with delicate snores. "I don't know, Roz. Don't talk to anyone about this. I'm worried. This guy is no ordinary hood, so who knows which way he'll jump? He wanted forty-two hundred bucks. Imagine risking your neck for that?"

"Is that all he wants?"

"I thought it was printed. I wasn't supposed to tell you. I can't remember anything any more."

"Too late for secrets, pal. Not the way the papers jumped on it. I'll bet your esteemed chief booted that one."

Joe was exhausted, his mind unresponsive. "I don't know how it happened. The paper says they weren't called in time."

His wife asked: "Joe, what do *you* think that little girl's chances are?"

The detective rubbed his eyes. His mind followed the same line of reasoning that DeGroot had pursued earlier. "I wish I knew. I just hope he doesn't get too scared or doesn't know the law on kidnaping. If he does, he may try to get rid of her. She's a smart kid. She'd remember places and faces. The longer he has her, the shorter the odds get. I don't even want to think about it."

"Well—are you hopeful? You think you'll find her?"

He thought of the vacuum in which they were operating: no clues, no hints, no suspects, nothing but the ransom note.

"Oh, I'm always hopeful. They call me the Hopeful Harp. How are my four Horrible Harps?"

"Don't make me cry, Joe. I had my fill today. Dale's got a bug again. Doesn't he ever stop getting sick? He threw up the baby aspirin and wouldn't let me give him a suppository. Maybe Dr. Matzkin should examine him again."

"Take him."

"It'll have to wait till you're home. I won't pay a dollar an hour for a baby sitter."

"That's one Harp. What about the other three?"

"Jeanie's fine. Silent Sam. Never gives me any trouble. She's so quiet I'm suspicious. Mary Grace—that character. They were discussing the annual pageant of saints at school, and Sister Priscilla asked our daughter which one she wanted to be. You'll die. She wanted to be Saint Agnes, because they stood her naked in the arena, and her hair grew miraculously to cover her body. Can you beat that?"

"You better hide those religious books. What about Joey?"

"Talk about miracles. He swept the garage. I gave him a good lecture about how lazy he is, with his father working such long hours and studying nights, and how little he does for you. I almost had him in tears."

"Go easy on the kid, Roz. He isn't that bad." McFeeley had an image of his nine-year-old son—the pinched, lopsided face; the eyes mangled by glasses—dutifully raising puffs of dust in the garage with an old push broom.

"When do we get to see you, Joe?" she asked.

"I'll drop by tomorrow. Maybe for lunch. I want to spend the night here."

A gossipy curiosity crept into his wife's voice. "That woman, Joe, what's she like?"

"Mrs. Andrus? How do I know?"

"Don't kid me. I know you can size people up in a second. She sure came across the television like a cold one. No tears, nothing, hardly a crack in her voice."

"That's her business. You take my word for it, she's suffering. Maybe worse than people who scream when they're hurt."

"I think we ran into her once," Roz said. "You remember the Council meeting about using the Lord's Prayer in the schools? She was with the *opposition*. I'm sure it was her. She made some nutty speech—you know, wise-guy stuff about why we didn't include the Koran and the Hindu religion. Don't you remember? You fell asleep at the meeting. Midge Callahan made us go."

That was where he had seen her. He barely remembered the ill-tempered meeting. He had gone only because Roz had insisted and didn't want to offend the Callahans, who were active in that sort of thing. He recalled the Andrus woman—thin, pretty, eastern, sharply dressed in a gray suit, making the ladies from the Lord's Prayer Committee look like a delegation of laundresses. No one applauded when she sat down. Nobody—not even her own side—

had gotten the joke. McFeeley reflected that she must have been new in the community then. It had taken a lot of nerve, he thought, for her to plunge into a controversy that had left scars all over the place.

"I guess that was Mrs. Andrus," he said. "She did look familiar to me."

"It's terrible what's happened to her, just terrible. But I had a creepy feeling—I don't know—that she didn't *care*. Oh, I'm a gossipy, Irish broad. Why can't I shut up?"

"She cares, Roz. She's just—hit hard."

"I'm sorry I said what I did. I'm sure I'm wrong. It's just—well, women like that seem to have it all figured out. Clothes, brains, what to do, what to say. I sort of resent it."

McFeeley smiled. "She isn't like that at all. She's no more sure of herself than anyone else."

"I suppose so. Well, night-night, Lieutenant. I miss you."

"I miss you, honey."

"I'm some bargain. With my hair in curlers and grease on my face. Not to mention big dark rings under my eyes."

"Good night, kid."

McFeeley rested his narrow head against the pink nursery wall. Red clowns, blue lions, purple seals danced around him. He wished his wife had not refreshed his memory about the woman or delivered a critique on her behavior. He wanted no value judgments to interfere with his search for her child.

Andrus had forced his wife to down a giant sleeping pill—a football-shaped brown capsule, currently in favor with his TV friends. Then he took one himself and collapsed on the bed, fully clothed, and kicked off his suède boots. In a few minutes he was sleeping as stonily as if he had been clubbed into unconsciousness. He lay spread-eagled on the outsized double bed from which he had been absent four weeks, not stirring, breathing lightly. The drug had no immediate effect on Laura. She was a bad subject for sedatives, narcotics, stimulants. All of them created harsh discords in her metabolism, leaving her weak, unsettled, taut with aches. She remained wakeful (how long she could not tell), her eyes teased by the play of passing auto lights on the wall and ceiling, her ears sensitized to each insect hum, each muffled whisper from the nursery, where the detectives were spending the night. Once she went into Amy's room, where Karen was sleeping, and covered the infant.

The baby slept dopily, her lips sealed around the empty bottle. She was perpetually placid, as inert as mashed potatoes. Laura had always been thankful for the infant's lassitude. She had said, with a twinge of guilt, after Karen was born, that another Amy would have finished her. Motherhood had always been a conscious effort; Amy was a test for any mother.

Now, resting on the bed, her senses dulling, she detested herself for her past criticisms of Amy, the bad temper she had displayed at the whining child, her impatience, her reprimands, and, most of all, the perpetual invidious comparisons with dumb, innocent Karen. She thought to herself: *I am sorry, Amy. I am sorry for not having been better to you, for trying so hard and giving so little.* She recalled something her father had once said, something about people's being no more and no less than what their children judge them to be.

The threat that overhung her child forced vivid memories on her and made her cry out softly—a soughing, lost sound. They were living on East Fifty-second Street in a drafty, rat-ridden brownstone (a good address, Fritzie said), and Amy, always a wretched sleeper, given to nightmares and nocturnal soliloquies, would often stay up late with them, watching television. Fritzie would invariably deliver his nasty running commentary of his rivals' work whenever they watched TV drama. He would have some annihilating comment for everything—performances, sets, commercials. Leaping from the studio couch, he would wave his arms at the innocent screen and shout: *Project, damn you, project!*

Amy, worshiping her handsome father, would imitate him, in the belief that *this was what you were supposed to do* when you watched television—it was part of the fun. She would jump from her miniature rocker, a brown peanut in a shaggy trundle-bundle, and wave her arms at the screen, crying with characteristic loudness, *Perjeck! Perjeck!* It didn't matter what was being shown—a baseball game, a musical number, a soap commercial. Laura and Fritzie would weep with laughter at her antics, and Fritzie would tell the story to his friends at the network with much embellishment. "The kid's two years old and she's a TV critic already. Know somethin'? She makes more sense than most of them police reporters."

Thus stimulated, Amy would refuse to go to bed: she had an audience, she had something to divert her. More often than not, her assault on the television set would end in hysterics. It seemed to

Laura that the child's years on earth had been a series of peaks and valleys, of unbearable, thrilling joys alternating with abandoned hysteria. She was a child too much a part of her environment, too eager to grow and learn and experience. Once, they were at Easthampton for the summer (again, Fritzie said, a good place, even though they were being robbed). One soft evening—that marvelous sea-blessed time when the sun's departing warmth lingers and a smell of spume and wrack haunts everything—Amy had picked herself off the floor and begun to walk. Fritzie was on the couch reading; Laura was sitting in an easy chair about eight feet away. The infant, in white terry-cloth bathrobe, her face intense and purposeful, had essayed a few wobbly steps toward her father. "Y'all wanna walk—walk," he said. Then, gently, he shoved her behind toward Laura. Amy walked—making it halfway across the cottage floor. She lost not a second, picking herself up and continuing her pilgrimage to Laura. Then Laura took her gently and shoved her off again, toward Fritzie: Amy did not laugh—this was work, concentration, achievement. In a few minutes she was making the ten-foot hike unaided; soon she was parading around the house, flaunting her new skill.

Some liar's logic, a wisp of optimism as fragile as the scent of tropical blossoms that came through the window (a euphoria perhaps engendered by the pill Fritzie had given her), consoled her for a moment. Amy *had* to be safe, *had* to come back to them—if only to reap that share of life's experiences that were her due, if only to give her parents another chance to do better by her. Through the swathings of terror, she jabbed deceit's sharp point —Amy would be reborn, a new child, with new parents, living under new circumstances. The comfort was short-lived, yet she found herself returning to the assurance whenever her imagination forced images on her too awful to contemplate without the prop of illusion. Gazing at her husband's drugged body, his chest rising and falling in mindless rhythms, she saw the grandeur of his fictional world, that lush garden from which he plucked flowers and herbs. She envied him. She admired him.

In the darkness, she saw him stirring. He seemed to be muttering, his voice surprisingly clear. "Y'all should have let me take that money out," Andrus said. " 'Nother minute I'd have been fine. Y'all should have let me do it."

Laura touched his hand. "Yes, I know, Fritzie. I should have."

TUESDAY

THE heat intensified on Tuesday. Southern California gasped and blinked under an autumn hot spell, drier, more enervating, more laden with man's contrived impurities than the worst days of the summer past. It could continue this way, hitting 106 and more in the Valley, Joe McFeeley knew, into October. He and Irvin Moll were sipping coffee at the breakfast bar. Both had been up since 7:00—Irv on the early-morning watch, McFeeley unable to sleep during his four-hour relief. The night before, they had telephoned the Andrus maid, Selena Masters, and she had arrived early, bursting her vigorous presence into the silent house with an assurance that amused McFeeley and confounded Moll. The latter, thanking her for the coffee, had winked and muttered, "Sure 'nuff, honey." Selena was the wrong woman for these crudities. With a hard eye, she informed Moll: "Don't *sure 'nuff* me, officer. I'm *honey* only to my husband, understand?" Sergeant Moll understood. The maid was very black and very energetic, trim in a yellow piqué uniform. Her speech was barren of southernisms; she was one of Eliot Sparling's neutralized minorities, adopting the rolling *R's* and constricted vowels of Los Angeles. Not seeing her dark intelligent face, one would have gauged the voice as that of a Westwood Village matron, ten years out of Iowa. After she had served the detectives coffee and toast (they politely declined eggs, uncomfortable about their tenancy), she settled down with a morning newspaper and began reading the stock market quotations. While she was thus engaged, McFeeley questioned her about her whereabouts the previous day, any recollections she had of people hanging around, of overcurious delivery boys or repairmen, of strange cars cruising the neighborhood. She answered him precisely, missing not a beat in her scrutiny of the financial reports. Selena Masters, Joe realized, was her own woman. She was the only kind of Negro Laura Andrus would want around: independent, unservile, probably charging

167

double what ordinary maids did for housework—and doubly efficient.

When the parents emerged from the bedroom a few minutes later, the maid greeted them quietly. "I'm awful sorry about what's happened," Selena said. "Maybe today'll be a good-news day." She charged off to the bedrooms.

Moll took his coffee into the nursery. During the night, a phone company technician had deadened the bells and installed red blinkers on the phones. Someone would have to remain in the office continually. McFeeley greeted the parents, then studied his notebook. He wanted to take the mother to headquarters at once and start her on the mug file.

"Sleep well?" he asked.

Andrus did not answer him. His face was bloated with drugging, redder than normal. The woman had the glassy look of an invalid, as if she had not slept at all. "Oh—we managed," she said. "I'm a little groggy. Did anything happen during the night?"

"Few crank calls," McFeeley said. "A couple of tips we're running down—nothing promising. We can expect more of the same. Too bad your number is in the directory."

"Didn't occur to me my child would be kidnaped when I had it listed," Andrus muttered. He settled on the sofa with his coffee, warming his hands on the cup, although the room was heavy with heat.

The three had little to say to each other. The previous night's horror—the absolute failure, overcast with the intrusions of the press, had left them all with a wan sense of uselessness, of playacting. Sipping their coffee, discussing the weather, the day's shopping, Fritzie's commitments at the network (all of which he would cancel), they avoided the radio, the morning TV news show, even the front page of the *Santa Luisa Register*, resting on the kitchen bar. KIDNAPER SPURNS RANSOM; AMY STILL MISSING. Once, Andrus walked by it, hastily scanned the bold black headline and the five-column lead of the article (by Duane Bosch, staff correspondent—age not given), and muttered: "We a buncha national celebrities."

McFeeley told the parents he would escort them to police headquarters in a half hour. Before that, he wanted to talk to the neighbors. He did not want to bring the Andruses to the station house too early—Rheinholdt had summoned a press conference, and he didn't want them subjected to the reporters again. He could think of nothing else to tell them: no assurances, no hopeful hints at great discoveries that day. When the detective left, Andrus phoned his secretary to cancel his work and to advise the network to get a substitute director for his current project. Mrs. Andrus was talking to the maid, arranging for her to come in every day, instead of the four days she now worked.

Outside, only a handful of reporters remained. The bulk of the press corps was covering Rheinholdt's conference. In contrast to the caravan of the previous night, there were only four cars parked across the street. Two men he did not recognize were sipping coffee and munching sweet rolls. He did not see Sparling, or DeGroot, or Ringel, or any of the feverish crew that had so harassed him twelve hours ago. However, the litter remained, augmented by several dozen lunchroom suppers. The street cleaner had not yet been around.

One of the reporters called to him: "Anything new, Lieutenant?" And he ignored him, skirting the parked cars and walking up the path to the Skopas house. When McFeeley was halfway to the door, the proprietor emerged—a mountainous, dark man, his head thick with resiny black hair, his eyes like two of the black olives he imported in boatloads. McFeeley identified himself. The master of the house, his nourished face unrevealing, consented to postpone his departure a few minutes to talk to the detective.

Inside, as soon as Mr. Skopas had disclosed—in a hoarse whisper —the detective's errand, his family gathered in a huddle, forming a mass of dark flesh on and around a brocaded sofa which stood at one side of a baroque fireplace. Flanked by marble urns and alabaster lamps, they seemed to be posing for a tribal portrait.

It was amazing how they had herded together for protection: an enormous matriarch in a quilted silk wrapper, rising from the breakfast table; a gross boy in his teens, shuffling in from the kitchen with a sandwich in his hands; a girl in her twenties, fat and sullen, descending the marble staircase; then all four gathering on the sofa to face the inquisitor.

They answered him in monosyllables, nods, occasionally muttering in Greek to one another, awaiting the word from Papa, who restlessly cracked his knuckles, anxious to stuff himself into his white Cadillac and burst off to the freeway. No, they hadn't seen anyone around; no, they didn't know the Andrus family; yes, they had read about the case; yes, they had let some reporters use their phone, but they would no longer. They offered no opinions, volunteered nothing, betrayed no emotions. Studying them, McFeeley could not help make comparison with the Andrus couple. The

Skopas people seemed to him of that breed of human beings whose insularity frees them from tragedy. He imagined they were the kind whose tax returns were never examined (if they were, they were never penalized), whose children had no unhappy romances, whose names never knew scandal. The equation was simple: wealth brought them happiness, and their united front to the world was their warning that they meant to keep everything they had, let no one in on the secrets. By comparison, Fritzie and Laura Andrus were quivering fledglings. They possessed no outer fortifications, no hard shells of confidence; they had enough difficulty getting from day to day, let alone having an awful crime thrust upon them. Skopas expressed no curiosity over the case, offered no expression of sympathy, made no move to escort McFeeley to the door. All four remained impacted on the sofa until he had left.

He had spoken to Mrs. Emerson the previous day. There remained a family named Kahler, owners of a two-story Tudor-style house on the south side of the Andrus home. Their names had not come up in any discussions with Laura, and he had no idea what they would be like. McFeeley noted the immaculate lawn and gardens: each blade of grass cropped, bright and firm; each shrub glazed with good health.

The door was answered by a slender man in his sixties—straight-backed, somewhat clerical in manner, wearing rimless glasses. When Joe identified himself, he nodded, unsmiling, and ushered him into a sedate living room. Mrs. Kahler joined them. She had a dried-out quality—a gray, lean woman, not unattractive. Both were dressed rather formally. The man wore a vest and a tie, the woman had on a dark green dress and three strands of pearls.

"Funny thing," Mr. Kahler said, when they were seated, "when I heard you ringing, I figured it was that guy down the block, Hausman." McFeeley looked puzzled. Kahler continued: "I fixed his dog the other day and I guess he's sore, so I expected him to come barging in." Mr. Kahler went on to explain how Hausman's fox terrier had been "making" in his flower beds. The dog refused to be scared off, so Kahler had purchased some small firecrackers. He would lay in wait in the garage, and when the terrier came scratching around, he'd let fly with a cherry bomb. "Scared the hell out of him," Kahler grinned. "I hit him in the ass once." Both grinned at the detective. "Finally, all I needed was to throw a little piece of red wood that looked like a firecracker and that dumb dog would run ki-yi-ing for his life."

McFeeley imagined some comment was called for. But he merely indicated the reason for his visit. Kahler would not be dissuaded from what was his most cherished subject of conversation—the protection of property. "You see that big fence I had to put up on both sides?" he asked. "To keep that low element away. You don't watch 'em, they'll have their kids and dogs all over your place. You know how much that lawn cost me?"

Joe commiserated with him; he realized Mr. Kahler had legitimate complaints. He was about to ask them if they had seen Amy wandering around, if they had seen any strange people in the locality—but both of them were inspired by the captive audience.

"Like that Emerson guy," Kahler went on, "giving me lip when I chased his kids out of my driveway. Of course, I'd expect it from his type." He looked narrowly at McFeeley, his eyes shrewd behind the rimless spectacles, and added, having reached a conclusion regarding McFeeley's heritage, "You know what I mean."

It occurred to Joe that his interrogation of them could proceed only if he took advantage of their dedication to property. He began by asking them if Amy had been in the habit of poaching on their preserve. She had. She was one of the worst brats in the neighborhood.

"Couldn't keep her away," Kahler said loudly. "Of course, I'd never hit a kid, but I yelled at her plenty. I told that woman fifteen times if I told her once. The guy was never home, else I'd have had it out with him."

But they had not seen her yesterday morning, both agreed. Nor had they seen anyone unfamiliar in the neighborhood. "My husband and I mind our business," Mrs. Kahler said. "We've been on this block thirty years and everyone *knows* we want to be left alone." What was Mr. Kahler's business? Joe inquired. He was a *naturotherapist:* he was retired some six years, having done rather well administering port-wine enemas and filbert cutlets to California invalids.

They talked some more about the Andrus family, the vanished child. She was, Kahler said, a kid who wouldn't take no for an answer—hang around, talk to everyone, get in your hair. "I was putting in seedlings one day," Mrs. Kahler said, "when she came and stood watching me—her feet smack-dab on our lawn. I must have warned her three times to beat it, but she stayed. You know what? That afternoon I caught her in the flower beds, sticking a pencil in to make the holes—you know—how you plant seedlings— making believe she was doing what she saw me do. All I could think was, that mother sure doesn't give her child any attention, to have her wandering around bothering people."

"I go broke on fertilizer alone," Kahler said irrelevantly. "We fired the Jap gardener last year. Me and the wife do a better job than he does anyway."

He was a true nature lover, Joe realized, in love so much with his shrubs and trees that he hated people. He had made a fortune in banana-oil rubdowns and spinach compresses, had stuffed nuts, fruits and roots into human beings until he had come to adore vegetables and detest their eaters.

McFeeley got up to leave. He had learned as little from them as he had from the Skopases. At the door, the woman asked her husband: "Is it all right to tell him what I heard her say?" Kahler shrugged.

"Something Mrs. Andrus said?" asked McFeeley.

The woman folded her arms and spoke. When the Andruses had first moved in (leaving all that junk—crates and excelsior and lumber—outside, so that a lot of it ended up on *their* lawn), Mrs. Kahler had made an attempt to be friendly. Well—not really friendly—but just to let them know the kind of people they were, that they liked privacy. She had told Mrs. Andrus, cordially, to be sure, that their grounds were not a playground; they had no children and simply weren't used to the noise and dirt. Mrs. Andrus had agreed to keep her children away—an agreement she had never honored.

Mrs. Kahler remembered the scene very well. The woman was giving the infant a bottle and the little girl was racing around the house, leaping from one piece of furniture to another. The child's behavior embarrassed her, and she had apologized. "I don't know where she gets the energy," Mrs. Andrus had said; "it's all I can do to handle her. I don't know how I can manage, now that the baby takes all my time." Mrs. Kahler remembered her exact words.

McFeeley waited some further intelligence. "That what you wanted to tell me?" he asked.

"Yes," she said. "Her *exact* words. Didn't know how she could manage the girl, now that she had the baby."

"But—am I stupid or something?" Joe asked. "My wife says that six times a day—about all our kids."

"*Your* wife is not *that* kind of a woman," Mrs. Kahler enunciated. "I don't believe in gossiping, but I thought of only one thing when I heard the child was gone."

"Me, too," Kahler said. He fussed with a giant philodendron, plucking a few brown leaves, frowning at the roots. "The maid left this thing outside too long," he said.

McFeeley cocked his head. "Are both of you saying you think *she* might have harmed the child?" He succeeded in suppressing the revulsion. "Do you have any reason to suspect that?"

Kahler adjusted his specs. "The wife and I aren't hinting at anything. You asked us what we knew; we told you. Me, I don't believe it's a kidnaping. Those people there—arguing all the time, leaving their kid trample other people's lawns."

"I wouldn't put anything past *her*," the woman said with a savage finality.

Outside, in the morning heat, McFeeley tried to lick the bitter aftertaste of morning coffee from his mouth. *Love Thy Neighbor.* Could people become so enamored of grass and shrubs that it drowned human understanding? He shook his head. Distracted, he started across the Kahler lawn when he heard the old man's brittle voice. "Officer, you're on my grass." Kahler was on his front steps, wagging a finger. "Have to give the grass every break in this heat." Joe blinked and took the long route, via the path.

Should he have thought of it? Were there not cases on record— purported kidnaping, unexplained disappearances—in which unbalanced mothers were suspected? The notion made him shiver. Yet he knew that if nothing turned up in the next few days, if no contact were made, if all avenues of search proved fruitless, he would have to face up to that sickening possibility.

Eliot Sparling and George Brack were among the early arrivals for Rheinholdt's press conference. The chief, through Baines, had notified all the papers, radio and television stations, and wire services shortly after midnight that he would have something to say. Tom Ballstead then decided to break down the radio mobile unit at the Andrus house and send it to Sanlu headquarters. It seemed unlikely that anything would develop at Nespoli Drive. In any case, they would remain covered with a tape setup. Rheinholdt's meeting with the press, an occurrence singular in itself, took top priority. The meeting had been called for 8:30 A.M. By 8:45, with the corridor outside Rheinholdt's office jammed with reporters, technicians and cameramen, no summons from the chief was forthcoming. The door to the reception room, where Clyde Hertmann and Farmer Baines had their desks, remained locked; and despite efforts by several newsmen, notably Martin Ringel, to break in, Baines kept it locked. Finally, upset by the clamor, the Farmer phoned the desk downstairs and had two uniformed officers assigned to keep order in the hallway. The arrival of the policemen touched off considerable hooting.

"Hah!" Eliot Sparling shouted. "Hallway monitors!" On three hours' sleep, he was distressingly loud and energetic. But his pale eyes were half shut and his skin was glazed with sweat.

The officers made them line up. Resentfully, Eliot noticed that Mona Mears was being spared the press conference. She had no doubt been up through the night writing her eyewitnesser, her syndicated column—and Hansel was rewarding her with slumber.

At 8:50 Baines unlocked the door. His cracked face surveyed them with less emotion than if they had been a herd of Poland China hogs. "Walk in one at a time and take places around the chief's desk. Don't push, or shout, or get too close. No pictures until the chief says so."

"Do we get short-arm later?" bellowed Eliot. George Brack blushed. "El, that wasn't necessary," the commentator said.

Rheinholdt had backed his chair against a window. His desk had also been moved back to afford several extra yards of space. Hertmann had hidden the idiotic charts, guides to a criminal subdivision of the human body. Behind his distorting lenses, the chief seemed no grumpier than usual. When the last man—a syndicate photographer—had been ushered in by the policemen, the door was locked. Eliot squatted in the front row, waiting to thrust his microphone.

"This won't take long," Rheinholdt said. "No questions. I just gotta statement to read. Then you can all beat it."

"We have to set up, Chief," Ringel said. "Can you give us ten minutes to get our mikes set? Get a voice level?"

The cameramen began focusing. Men bearing microphones hovered about the protective desk. Rheinholdt looked at all of them hatefully. "Awright. No more than five minutes."

The setups arranged (amid much grumbling by the newspapermen, who resented television's waste of time), Rheinholdt took a typewritten sheet from a manila folder on his desk, adjusted his glasses and began to read.

"This is for immediate release," the chief said. "A statement by Caspar Rheinholdt, chief of police, City of Santa Luisa." He glared over his spectacles once, cleared an oyster from his throat into a pocket handkerchief, and resumed. "The kidnaping of Amy Andrus has shocked all residents of Santa Luisa, all right-thinking people everywhere. The police of Santa Luisa are doing everything in their power to insure her safe return and have reason to think she will be returned safely. However, if any harm should befall the child, the blame lies squarely on the head of one newspaper. You all know which newspaper I mean. I will not dignify it by mentioning it. This newspaper deliberately and willfully disobeyed a request by the Santa Luisa police to withhold the story until after a rendezvous with the kidnaper. Everyone else honored the request. Had this newspaper also honored the request, there is every reason to believe Amy Andrus would be safely in her home at this very minute. Now, it is impossible to know what the outcome of the case will be, although we are making every effort to find her and bring her home safely. I repeat, if one newspaper had not ignored our request, this case might have been solved by now. I hope the people at this newspaper who made the decision will think about what they have done to that child and her parents. Meanwhile, we request your co-operation in future matters."

He took off his glasses and wiped them on a tissue. The cameras stopped. DeGroot was the first to speak. "Is that all, Chief?" the AP man asked.

"Yeah. You can all go. Sergeant Baines has copies outside."

They did not move. Dave Arnspeiger edged forward. He had covered too many police stories to be frightened off by Rheinholdt. "You mean the *Truth,* don't you, Chief?" he asked.

"I said no questions." The bristling head retreated toward the suit's lapels.

"But you do mean the *Truth,* don't you?" Arnspeiger insisted. "After all, the *Truth* reporter, Mr. Swinnerton, is in the room, and you ought to say outright which paper you mean."

A few men turned to look at Harvey Swinnerton. The *Truth* reporter was in the rear rank—as if eager to make his escape.

"Okay, it's the *Truth.* Baines—let 'em go. I'm through."

"Just a minute, Chief," DeGroot said politely; "you can't leave an accusation like that hanging. There's a report going around that your men never got to the *Truth*—not till after it was on the street at 5:07 yesterday afternoon."

"No!" Rheinholdt shouted. "They were called! They know it! Clear out!"

Ringel, slithering, leaned over the desk. "You're right, Chief, let's forget the whole deal. There's more important things we have a right to know."

"You don't have to know anything," he said. Others, emboldened by Ringel, edged closer.

"Now about that ransom package. How come it was filled with straw instead of money? Was that a good idea?"

Rheinholdt slammed a fist on the desk. The microphones leaped, but Ringel was unimpressed. "It was not! I seen the money myself!"

A man at the edge of the crowd called out: "When's the FBI coming in?"

DeGroot asked: "That's right, Chief—we have a right to that information. Will you call the FBI? What's Mayor Speed's feelings on that?"

Eliot's thunder rose above the swarm. "What about the ransom note? You gonna let us see the ransom note?"

Rheinholdt jumped from his swivel chair. His arms flapped. "Out! Out! No more questions! You heard me! Not another word!" He shouted for help. "Baines! Hertmann! Clear the place—I don't want a single goddam reporter in the building in five minutes!"

Cursing, they retreated. The technicians removed the microphones, undid cables; the others edged reluctantly toward the door. Baines, Hertmann and the two "hallway monitors" started shoving the mob out. Eliot was a prime target. His size, his clumsiness, the absence of dignity or ferocity in him drew the officers to him automatically. Baines and another patrolman were giving him the bum's rush, maneuvering his lumpish figure through the group like an icebreaker.

"Hands off, willya?" Eliot cried. "Why pick on me?" No answer was needed. There was a quality in Sparling that demanded persecution. As a boy in elementary school in the Bronx, whenever generalized misbehavior aroused the teacher, Eliot was invariably singled out for chastisement—a note to his father, a session on the thinking chair, a reprimand from the principal, Dr. Shapiro. He oozed guilt; that foghorn voice, that long, doughy body invited retribution.

George Brack, in his tolerant heart, understood this. (No one ever picked on George.) "You needn't be so rough," Brack said politely. "He didn't do anything that the others didn't do."

In the corridor, released by Baines, Eliot sneaked into the men's room, motioning Brack to join him. "Listen," he whispered, amid the ammoniated stench, "I wanna ask a few questions. Wait for me downstairs. You call Ballstead."

"Who are you going to talk to?" Brack asked. "El, you'll get in trouble again. You've been in jail once."

Sparling winked. "Baines. I think Rheinholdt's telling the truth, but he's so dumb, he ruined his case. The *Truth'll* murder him. No times—no evidence—nothing. Baines did the phoning. He oughta know."

Brack left. Eliot hid in a toilet booth, and after a few minutes, while the building emptied of reporters, he emerged. The door to the chief's anteroom was open, and he paused.

"Sergeant Baines?" he called.

The dirt farmer looked up. "What do you want? Dint you hear the chief?" He got up. "I'll throw you out on your ass." Baines moved toward him. Eliot retreated to the corridor.

"Move," Baines said. "You wanna get hit?"

"Listen, *listen.* I'm on your side. I think Rheinholdt told the truth."

"Whaddya mean, you *think?* Of course he did."

"Sure, sure. But he loused up his own case. Look—you did the calling. Did you keep a log or anything? A list of times when you called the papers? I can't understand how you missed the *Truth.* If you got a log, let me see it, and I'll——"

There was no log. Baines, unfamiliar with the task, had merely followed the numbers Hertmann had listed. It had not occurred to either of them to note the time the calls were made.

"None of your business," Baines said.

"Well, just tell me this—when did you call the *Truth?*"

Clyde Hertmann's shrewd face, incongruous with the gray uniform, appeared in the doorway. "Sarge," Hertmann said, "better not tell him anything."

"Why?" Eliot cried. "What are you hiding? I'm trying to *help.* How many times do I hafta say it? I'm on your side. Just tell me— did you guys call the *Truth* when you called the others?"

Baines and Hertmann exchanged grieving looks. It seemed to both of them, Baines via his simplicity, Hertmann through his intelligence, that silence was indicated. Rheinholdt had made his statement. They would stand on that.

"We can't say nothing," Baines said.

"That's right. You'll have to believe the chief. The *Truth* knew." Hertmann indicated the chief's locked door. "Sparling, you better get out of sight. He'll murder you. I heard about you coming back and trailing Mrs. Andrus. What's the matter with you people? Don't you have any decency?"

It was a fair question, and Eliot could not answer it. The only response seemed to be: *Right. We have no decency. Not where our God-given rights to sell newspapers are concerned.* He raised his arms helplessly and lumbered away.

Brack was waiting for him in the parking lot. Billik and the film crew had been sent back to the Andrus house. There was a rumor the mother would make another appeal.

"What'd you learn, El?" Brack asked.

"Nothing. Rheinholdt's dead now. He'll be crucified."

"Why should you care?"

"I shouldn't. It's a tossup who I hate more—him or the *Truth.* But one of 'em's lying and I'd hate to think it was Rheinholdt. What'd Ballstead say?"

"He wasn't terribly excited about Rheinholdt's statement," Brack said. He started the engine and drove off. Around them, the desert heat rose. It rushed through the car windows, searing and choking them.

"He wasn't excited?" Eliot asked.

"No. He said it's a sidebar. Said the public doesn't care. Tom said the story would have been released by *someone* yesterday, and he's just jealous of the *Truth.*"

"Tom said *that?*" Eliot asked.

"Yes. He said this is the worst police mishandling of a crime he's ever seen. He wants us to concentrate on the neighbors and try to get in with the cops."

Eliot slumped in the seat. Ballstead, his hero, was indifferent. Perhaps Tom was right. Eliot wondered: am I so ready to believe the worst about the *Truth* that I am acting as I am? Is it not possible they were merely lucky, enterprising—and blameless?

He made a note to call Connie. Perhaps she could do some spying for him.

About a half hour after the reporters had left headquarters, McFeeley escorted Laura and Fritzie in, via the rear door at the parking lot.

He took them upstairs to Records. The mug file was ready for them. Fritzie and Laura sat at a long table, each facing a thick file of cards. The room was spacious, airy and light—the Sanlu police plant was one of the most modern in the state.

"There's a double photo on each card—profile and full face— and under it there's a *portrait parle,*" McFeeley explained.

"What'd you call these—portrait what?" Fritzie asked.

"Portrait parle. It's a word description of the individual—physical traits, voice characteristics, manner of dress, language facility, social position. Also, marks, deformities, habits, occupations."

Laura nodded. The project seemed less hopeless in these terms. McFeeley's thin voice, the scientific amassing of information gave her a moment's hope. Her optimism was like that of a cancer victim—buoyed by a tour of the Sloan-Kettering Institute.

"Y'all want us to read all that stuff?" asked Fritzie.

"No," the detective said, "just look at the faces. If any one of them rings a bell, read the descriptive data, then put it to one side. Then I'll discuss them with you. I have to talk to the chief."

He left. They began turning the cards. They studied the faces of murderers, rapists, conmen, auto thieves, perverts, burglars—all to no purpose. Once, Fritzie laughed bitterly: "It's like goin' through the television casting directory—except there's more originality in these birds."

After an hour, McFeeley returned from a bleak conference with Rheinholdt. At long last the chief was considering roadblocks; beyond that, he seemed embedded in a gelatinous mold that impeded his movements, blurred his limited capacities for thought, his small talents as an administrator. As McFeeley had sensed the previous night, the chief was most concerned with evening scores with the newspapers.

McFeeley sat with the Andrus couple another hour. By 11:30 A.M. they had finished turning cards, studying photographs, scanning *portrait parles.* None had evoked any associations, and McFeeley decided to drive them back to the house. Two or three reporters were waiting at the police parking lot when they emerged into the noon sun. They asked a few questions; no one answered them. When McFeeley and the couple drove off in the detective's Dodge, the newspapermen followed.

Following Rheinholdt's inept press conference, the reporters and cameramen returned en masse to the Andrus house. Under the burning sun, they watched, waited, speculated. They saw the parents come back with Joe McFeeley; observed Walter L. Todd's frisky entry; stared at the Emersons as they entered the house and left minutes later, the woman wallowing in tears. Attempts were made to question all, but nothing was revealed to the anxious journalists.

Back among his peers was Sparling, similarly trying to draw information from the participants in the enormous event. It distressed the young man that there was almost a total absence of discussion on the subject of the dispute between Rheinholdt and the *Truth*. "Who cares?" Dave Arnspeiger said to Eliot. "Rheinholdt's probably got it all wrong anyway—wait till the *Truth* gives its side. Besides, it's a can of worms nobody's interested in. Not with the kid under the gun."

But Sparling felt some old challenge stirring. His natural curiosity was piqued by the bitter quarrel between his two tormentors—the chief who had struck and jailed him, and the newspaper that had degraded and fired him. He felt rather like a Christian martyr on his day off, privileged to witness a struggle to the death between two lions. Taking advantage of the tranquillity outside 4217 Nespoli, he telephoned Connie Potenza from the public booth near Buena Terra Park. His remarkable talent for intruding at the wrong time was unfailing: at the instant Connie answered the call T. T. Hansel was marshaling his legions in Herbert Hood's office to plot a counterattack on the police. Connie attempted to explain her precarious position: she simply could not talk to him now about the Andrus case.

Insensible, Eliot boomed away. "Fraud! Fraud! Rheinholdt's telling the truth, but he's too dumb to defend himself! What did they say when Rheinholdt accused them?"

"Eliot, if you stay on this phone another minute, I'll get fired."

"Keep your big Italian eyes open, Con. Learn something. I swear there's a missing part. I don't believe they weren't called."

"No one called Mr. Hood—until way too late."

"That doesn't mean anything. Someone might've called Hansel upstairs." He sang insanely: *"Oh, have you talked—with the man upstairs?"*

"Oh, shut up."

Eliot blasted away. "I can see it now! *Truth* defends right of people to know! Free press must be kept free! Rheinholdt attacking last bastion of Americans' right to information! Lower the price of newsprint! Guild demands make publication impossible!"

"Are you through? Are you through with your jokes? Eliot, my other phone is buzzing."

"Yeah. Probably the American Society of Newspaper Editors with a citation for Hansel."

"You're horrible." Seated sideways, she could see the group in

Hood's glass box: Hansel, pre-empting the general manager's desk; Hood at the window; Bill Trigg and Ed Kalaidjian at a respectful distance.

"Let's have dinner tonight," Eliot said. "Unless I call you, come out and meet me at the Andrus house. Try to learn what happened."

"Why should it interest you so much?"

Sparling did not have an answer for her. No other reporter seemed concerned with the vendetta between the ignorant police chief and the newspaper. The kidnaping was their meat—the child, her fate, the criminal, the search, the incomparable suspense story with its overtones of depravity, the horrifying manner in which an innocent family had been chosen for disaster. This was infinitely more newsworthy than an argument about telephone calls.

Sparling himself was puzzled by his own fixity of purpose. Was it simply a scheme to avenge himself on the newspaper that had treated him so rudely? Certainly, he had no urge to be Caspar Rheinholdt's champion. Rheinholdt had cuffed and jailed him, kept him from getting the beat. On the other hand, there was the mother. She was imprinted in Eliot's scheme of things—that straight-backed, aloof, good-looking product of an eastern education who had lied to him the first day and who might have blamed him for the whole sordid mess. He had gotten the tip from Mrs. Emerson (there was a beauty!) and he had blabbed to Swinnerton—and, after that, it was all aboard. In some dim way, he imagined he owed Laura Andrus something. There remained a third, deeper, more painful reason for his persistence in the matter, one that Sparling understood imperfectly and which occurred to him only in odd moments of relaxation, of release from his work. It had to do with his father, that crushed, unhappy druggist, sitting at the rear of his dingy pharmacy in the East Bronx and reading Francis Ward (The Father of American Sociology) and William Graham Sumner. Once, when Eliot was in high school, he had come into the store and found his father half asleep in the dark room, while a customer waited unhappily at the sagging counter, at the bower of rubber pants, nipples, razor blades and cheap fountain pens. "Hey, Pop," Eliot had whined, "why are you sleepin'? There's a customer in front—first one today, I bet." Abe Sparling had looked up dazedly and replied: "I'm awaiting the primacy of the intellect." Eliot, despairing, brimming with that oceanic pity of son for father that must be suppressed lest it ruin both, mumbled, "Well, I guess that's O.K., but Mrs. Parenti is awaiting some cascara pills," and he had run off to the apartment to do his homework.

"It just interests me," Eliot said flatly. "Not only that deal with the *Truth,* but the whole picture—why everyone was allowed to hang around, why the cops didn't get tough. If I had been in charge, everyone woulda been jugged—not just me."

"Fine talk for a newspaperman."

"It's the truth. What's more important? That kid or circulation?"

They agreed to meet that night. When she hung up, she wondered if anyone had overheard her, whether the telephone operator was to be trusted. It was no secret that Herbie Hood had his spy system. On a matter as touchy as the Andrus affair, he might be moved to stern punishments. Connie turned to her typing—the daily run of critical notes to miscreant employees.

Hansel accepted Rheinholdt's challenge. It would be too easy. The Editor & Publisher displayed impatience with Hood's hand-wringing, with Trigg's grave, freckled face. Kalaidjian offered no opinions; he remained neutral.

"The old bastard said some rough things about us," Herbert Hood said. The general manager had been up most of the night. When his labors at the office had concluded at about 2:00 in the morning, he had repaired to a saloon where he was well known and where a cot was kept for him in a rear room. Hood was an awesome drinker. He never showed the effects, except for a reddening of his face. After a night's intemperance, he could put in a full day. His iron entrails never suffered the corrosive effects of alcohol. Whisky made him strong and healthy.

"That stupid policeman is scared stiff," T. T. Hansel said. "Do you notice one thing about this statement? Not a word about *times.* He ignored that completely. That proves he's wrong."

"I wouldn't be too sure," Hood said. "It just proves he's dumb."

"Can he be *that* dumb?" Hansel asked fiercely. "Not to defend himself?"

Herb Hood waddled around the dingy room. A worn space on the carpeting attracted him and he planted two splay feet on it. In Eliot Sparling's heroic day, the bare spot was known as "the firing line"—the place where wretches about to be sacked were required to stand when sentence was pronounced. "He's so upset he can't think straight. He should have, if he had any brains, mentioned them. He'll mention it sooner or later."

Hansel threw back his blazing head. Last night's victories still burned in him. He had sent Mona Mears back to the Andrus house, to worm her way in, to get next to the mother. "Herbert, you shouldn't sound so happy."

Hood would have enjoyed slapping that blooded face. Fear had done him no good the previous night; perhaps a little insolence would help—if there was anything that could be salvaged out of the awful mess. Rheinholdt's statement was doing to him what no amount of bad whisky could—making him sick to his stomach.

I hope the people at this newspaper who made the decision will think about what they have done to that child and her parents. . . .

Bill Trigg spoke up. "Mr. Hansel, we're keeping a hole on page one for our answer. What'll I tell the composing room?"

T. T. Hansel moved Hood's typewriter into position and took a few onionskins from the desk. "I'll write it myself. I'm not worried, and I want none of you to be. Just keep your mouths shut. I'll set a policy and we'll follow it. Herbert—when Swinnerton calls, I want to speak to him. I assume someone's warned him about discussing this?"

"Oh, sure," Hood said. "Harvey's got the message."

Hansel began typing. Once he had been a superb reporter, a brilliant deskman. The old skills had not left him. When he paused, Trigg moved forward. "Mr. Hansel, I had an hour free this morning and I started calling police chiefs around the state, to ask them how they'd handle a kidnaping."

Hansel looked up. "Yes?"

"Rheinholdt did everything wrong he could possibly do wrong. The chiefs don't feel there's a chance of that child being saved—because of his goofs. You know—no alarms, no roadblocks, no leveling with the reporters, refusing to call the FBI."

"You have all that?" Hansel asked.

"That sounds great, Bill," Kalaidjian offered.

"Right here," Trigg said. He waved a sheaf of papers. "I could do a piece on it."

"Do it," Hansel said.

Trigg walked out quickly. Kalaidjian followed.

"Smart lad, Trigg," Hood said. "You want to squeeze that piece into the next edition?"

Hansel resumed typing. "No. I'll use it elsewhere."

"I may be old and thick, Ted," said Hood, "but where are you going to print a hot piece like that? Give it to WNA so they can scoop us?"

"Don't concern yourself, Herbert," Hansel said slyly. "You'll be amazed where it turns up."

Hood turned his back on him and stared hostilely at the formless mélange of stores, factories, office buildings, the poisonous air covering them impartially. Even the pleasant taste of last night's booze failed to shore him up; he'd sneak a few belts as soon as Hansel departed.

At 11:45 A.M., at the moment when Ed Case and Milt Bannon were arriving to relieve McFeeley and Moll, the telephone glared red and the latter picked it up. McFeeley was not present. He had been summoned back to headquarters by James Raffalovitch, the head of the Santa Luisa police laboratory.

As the light flickered red, Moll threw the switch to put the tape recorder in operation. The plastic discs spun noiselessly and he asked politely: "Yes?"

There was a pause, and then someone whispered: "Is Mrs. Andrus there?"

The whispering took Moll by surprise, and he found himself answering: "Yeah. Wait a minute." McFeeley had ordered that neither of the parents be allowed to speak to callers, unless they stated flatly that they had the child; otherwise, they would be exposed to a parade of cranks. But Moll, who had spent the morning and the previous night fending off a distressing assortment of loonies, was caught off balance by the whisper. As soon as he left the phone and walked into the kitchen, where the woman was forcing strained spinach into the baby's mouth, he wondered if he had done the right thing.

"You feel like talking to someone?" Moll asked.

"Do you think I should?" She set down the infant's spoon. "Didn't the lieutenant say not to—unless——"

"Maybe you're right. You know anyone who whispers?"

"No. Our friends are shouting types."

Moll shrugged. "You might as well try it once. First let me call headquarters and get a trace started. Remember, it takes at least fifteen minutes to trace a call, so you got to keep him talking."

Andrus, in the den, heard them conversing and joined them. Moll explained. "Hell, can't do any harm," Fritzie said. "We might as well get used to these. I don't know why McFeeley said we couldn't talk in the first place."

They walked into the nursery. Moll cautioned Laura to wait. He picked up the private line, dialed the communications room at headquarters and said softly: "Put a trace on the incoming call at Andrus. Get the prowl cars on a red alert. Then have Mc-Feeley call me." He pointed to the other phone and nodded to Laura.

"This is Mrs. Andrus," she said. "What do you want?"

The whispering unnerved her. "Mrs. Andrus? The mother?"

"Yes. Who are you?"

There was a pause. "Never mind. You alone?"

"I can only answer certain questions. If you have any information about my child, tell me. I'll co-operate."

"No cops? Who answered the phone before?"

She hesitated. "My husband."

"O.K. I can't stay on too long. I know how the cops trace calls."

"They won't. I've told them not to." Her hand began to shake; she shut her eyes. Fritzie moved toward her, as if to take the phone. She shook her head.

"O.K. I know where your child is."

"Tell me what you want me to do."

"No police?"

"I promise you. Is she all right? Is she well?"

Fritzie and Moll edged closer, as if by the presence and weight of their large bodies they might succor her.

"She's all right. But I won't say for how long."

"Do you have her? Is she with you? How do I know you're telling the truth?"

Again, the whisperer waited before speaking. "You have to take my word. She's all right."

"When can I meet you? Do you want me to leave the money somewhere?"

"I don't have her myself."

"You said——"

"I know who does. I'm working with him. He's with your daughter and she'll be okay if you do what I say."

"I'll write it down." She reached for Moll's pen and the steno pad. Her hand was trembling so badly she could not grasp the pen. Fritzie took it and put his head close to the receiver.

"Leave the money in an envelope under the overpass at Patio Road. Where it crosses New Toledo. Right-hand side as you go east. I'll leave a message in a folded-up copy of the Sanlu *Register*. You leave the money, but don't open the paper to read the message till you're a block away. And no cops. Just you—alone."

"Yes. The same ransom as yesterday?"

The speaker hesitated. Then she heard the aggravating whisper again. "Add two thousand bucks. For double-crossing us yesterday."

"When will you return Amy?"

"Tonight. There'll be instructions in the note."

"What time should I leave the money at the overpass?"

"Between 4:30 and 5:00 this afternoon. I've been on too long. Just do what I said and the kid'll be okay." He hung up. Laura held the phone for a moment, looking at Moll for instructions. He looked sadly at his watch. "Six minutes. Not a chance to find him. Well, you did your best. You can hang up."

For a moment they sat transfixed. Andrus, sweat streaming from his florid head as if he had been drenched with water, studied his scrawled notes. Moll switched off the tape recorder.

"Let's play it back," he said. "How's he sound to you, Mrs. Andrus? Like he was leveling? You know, you're a sitting duck for any spook, any nut who has the price of a phone call."

"I can't tell," Laura said. Her voice was strangled. "I suppose we'll go through with it."

"We'll have to," the detective said. "I'll get McFeeley back here."

The plastic reels reversed, Moll set them in forward motion and turned up the volume. The whispering—remote, disembodied— hissed into the hot room: *Mrs. Andrus? The mother?*

McFeeley was in the laboratory when he received word of the call. He advised Rheinholdt about it, and the two men planned a stake-out for the new point of rendezvous. Both felt that it was pointless to make any further deals with the criminal, to observe any rules. Seven men, either in disguise or hidden, would be planted around the Patio-New Toledo overpass—two in a delivery truck, another picking up trash on the grass islands on the freeway, the others secreted in office buildings and garages. All uniformed personnel and prowl cars would be ordered away from the area. Mrs. Andrus would ride out alone, leave the money, take the newspaper.

Joe had his suspicions about the whisperer. He had toyed with the idea of having all callers identify words in the ransom note. But even that was no guarantee. A caller could always claim, as this one had, that he was not the actual kidnaper and had not seen the note but was a go-between. It added up to an impossible situation—harder for the mother than for any of them. She would suffer ordeal by telephone: the summons to the Patio overpass loomed as the first of many such missions for her, McFeeley feared.

When Joe had concluded his discussion of the new drop with Rheinholdt, he went to the police laboratory to confer with Raffalovitch. The lab chief was a stoop-shouldered, sour man, an excellent technician carried on the personnel records with the equivalent salary rating of a full division captain. Scholarly, embittered, he was singularly out of place in the locker-room atmosphere of headquarters. James Raffalovitch was a trained chemist, a man who had missed his Ph.D. in chemical engineering by a half-year's work—and he considered Sanlu lucky to have his services. Though respected by the men, Raff was never one of the boys. His insularity dated back to an outbreak of goosing some months after his engagement as lab chief. One of the department jokers—probably Irvin Moll, Joe McFeeley seemed to recall—had discovered that Raffalovitch had an abnormally sensitive buttocks. The lab chief would flap his arm and hoot in terror if someone as much as made a gesture toward his behind or even whistled in back of him. He was the world's most goosey man. The high school humor of Sanlu headquarters gave him no peace. Once, the men hid a 16-millimeter camera and made films, first of Raffalovitch being goosed by Milt Bannon—rising vertically, cackling, eyes agoggle— and then *not* being goosed by Bannon, who sneaked up behind him, whistled, and sent the tormented man soaring almost as high. In time it became evident that Raff's health was suffering, that his painstaking work with microscope and centrifuge, infra-red camera and Backstrom filter was being destroyed by these indignities. Raffalovitch produced a note from his doctor.

To Whom It May Concern——

Mr. James Raffalovitch is suffering from anxiety, insomnia and loss of weight incurred by certain offenses against his person. Unless these are halted at once, he will be in serious physical condition and may need hospital care.

M. H. Hershkowitz, M.D.

Chief Rheinholdt was advised of the lab chief's fragile health and an edict was issued, tacked on the bulletin board next to Dr. Hershkowitz's medical opinion. The goosing ended forever. Once a year, at the police smoker, the movies were screened of Raffalovitch being goosed and Raffalovitch *not* being goosed, and everyone reminisced about the good old days before Raff got neurotic and ended the best laughs they had ever had.

The lab director tolerated McFeeley more than the others. Joe had never been party to the assaults on his rear. However, Raffalovitch did not leave his seat at the microscope; nor did he offer any greeting. A typewritten report on the crime search, completed that morning, lay alongside him, and he shoved it toward Joe with acid-stained fingers. Dyes and inks smudged his white smock. A yellow powder was smeared on his long, hooked nose, and his rimless eyeglasses were eternally fogged. Working, he smoked cheap cigars; it was a miracle that his analyses of trace materials did not always contain tobacco ash.

"Lousy crime search," Raffalovitch said. "Nothing."

"Don't blame it on the men," Joe said. "We figured the kid was enticed into the car. The guy never went into the house or on the grounds, for all we know."

"It was still lousy." He squinted balefully into the microscope. "What'd they use, strip method? Spiral?"

"Double strip. Did you get the soil samples from Moll?"

"Los Angeles desert. Nothing. No tire marks worth a damn, no prints on the bike. It's a good thing more people don't know how easy it is to steal a kid. Easier than breaking and entering."

McFeeley nodded. "Except it goes harder if they find you."

"You'll never find this one. Not on what we have to work with."

"I wouldn't be too sure." He would not accept Raffalovitch's pessimism. Hope was cheap and comforting.

"I'm still on that note," the lab chief said. "I'll give you what I got so far." He left his stool and walked to his desk, returning with the ransom note, still in the plastic folder. McFeeley noted that the first few words of cannibalized newsprint had been removed.

"I took 'em off so's I could get a reading on the mucilage. It's dime-store glue, the kind you can get anywhere in the United States. We took photostats of the note, so don't look so worried if it has to be evidence. I'm putting the words back on later."

"What else?" McFeeley asked. He wished Raffalovitch would deliver his reports sitting at his desk. It was uncomfortable looking over his shoulder at the lab table. Perhaps this was Raff's revenge. *You will all stand like bad boys at my desk. . . .*

"Well, first, the words. They were clipped from the *Los Angeles Argus*. The guy must have been saving copies. I tried to see if they came from any one day, but they don't. Take the street instruction—Buena Terra Park. Last time that appeared was four days ago. The other words he could have cut out of almost any edition last week. Nothing there."

"Everything from the *Argus?*"

"All theirs. Can't tell anything by the inks. It's standard printer's black, and what would it tell us anyway?"

"Nothing. You mentioned it."

Raffalovitch peered sourly over his glasses. "Did I? Well, I'm thorough. The city pays me so good, I might as well give them their money's worth. I don't get any chance to pick up small change from storekeepers."

"Come on, Raff. I'm Joe McFeeley. Did I ever take advantage of you?"

"O.K., the paper. That's even less help. It's sixteen-pound white bond. Usually comes in 8½ by 8 or 8½ by 11. Sixteen-pound means that a thousand sheets weigh sixteen pounds—not the small sizes I mentioned, but the master sheets, 17 by 22, that they cut the smaller ones out of."

"Are there any watermarks on it? Anything we can trace?"

"Wouldn't you love that?" Raffalovitch asked. "No. Not a thing. It's sixteen-pound white bond. Every office in the United States uses it. Every paper manufacturer makes it. Every jobber makes forms out of it. Every printer works on it. It's one of the most common kinds of paper in the world. You'd never trace it, not if you checked every paper firm in the country."

"Great." McFeeley pulled up another stool and sat down. "What else?"

Raffalovitch took the ransom note out of its transparent folder with a tweezers and held it up to the light. "See what I mean? No pattern—no watermarks—no defects in composition—just paper."

"Prints?"

"A couple of smeared ones. The woman's, I guess. Is she the only one who handled it?"

"And me. But I didn't leave any. We printed her this morning, so if you want, you can check them."

"If it'll keep you happy. Now, take a look at the edges." He held the paper in front of them. The evenly spaced, neatly lined words stared at them insolently. "The left-hand edge and the top—they're machine-cut. The way the paper was made. Right?"

"Right. And the others are sloppy."

"Cut with a steel-edged ruler. I ran some tests on white bond, and I got that kind of jagged edge. The guy trimmed off part of the original paper with a steel-edged ruler. With me?"

"Sure." McFeeley leaned forward.

"The sheet is five and a half inches wide. If you ask me to guess, I'd say he tore it right down the middle of the long side. How much is five and a half doubled?"

"Eleven," Joe said.

"That's it. The long side of an 8½-by-11 white bond sheet. You'd figure he'd use the full eight and a half inches of the short side, which is now the long side. Follow me? He'd have a half sheet, 5½ by 8½."

McFeeley studied the ransom note. "But this is shorter than eight and a half inches. And there's a rough edge at the bottom. So I suppose he tore a piece off the bottom with the ruler."

Raffalovitch nodded. His beakish nose twitched. "Six and thirteen-sixteenths inches. He sliced the rest off. I figured he did it to make a smaller note. But it didn't seem logical. Usually you cut a paper in half—that's all. So what if there was extra white space at the bottom?"

"You mean he shortened the sheet to get rid of something?"

"Maybe." Raffalovitch held the rough bottom edge of the note to the light. "See anything?" the chemist asked.

"No. Nothing."

"You wouldn't. I dissolved it off."

"What was it?"

"Little red traces. I found a row of them on the bottom. They began about a quarter inch from the left-hand edge, the machine-cut edge, and ran all the way to the end of the paper."

"Red marks?"

"Bright red. There was some red printing on the paper, and the guy thought he was ripping it off clean with the ruler. The only trouble is, on this kind of paper, with cheap ink, it runs a little into the fabric. It looked clean to him, but the red traces were there."

McFeeley frowned. "You find out what they are?"

Raffalovitch lowered his voice, as if fearful to find Rheinholdt eavesdropping. "There wasn't enough for chemical analysis—just traces. So I dissolved them and sneaked them over to the LA lab this morning. I asked them to run the stuff through a spectrochemical analysis." He rubbed his nose. "Don't tell Rheinholdt I was there."

"What did you learn?" McFeeley asked. There was a faint pounding in his chest.

"You know how spectrochemical analysis works? They burn the material in front of a narrow slit of light. When it becomes gas, it gives off light waves. No two are alike. They got charts for each element—spectrum charts. When the light from the stuff you're burning goes through the slit, it's broken up by a prism into component colors."

"How does that work for a compound—like an ink or a dye?"

Raffalovitch wagged a yellow finger at Joe. "They don't teach you much in those night courses, do they? Every element is detected *separately*—you get a different spectrum for each."

"What did you get for the red traces?"

"It's printer's ink. The tip-off was mercuric sulfide—red pigment."

"Anything else?"

"We have a full analysis of the ink, which might be useful later if we can match it. It's a standard printing ink with a resin and linseed oil base. What they call Very Bright Red. Most of these inks are the same composition. I don't think we'll be able to trace it back to one manufacturer. I'm asking LA lab to check their files."

McFeeley stared at the note. "Let me get it straight, Raff. There was some kind of red printing on this. Probably a straight line in red ink. And you think it ran along the eleven-inch side and began about a quarter inch from the left-hand margin." He turned the sheet on its side. "Of course, that's an assumption. Suppose our guy isn't like anyone else—someone who'd slice a sheet down the middle, then trim off the printed area. Suppose he tore it vertically first, measured five and a half inches over on the eight-and-a-half-inch side?"

"He could. But it's unlikely. Five and a half is half of eleven. That figures."

"But suppose he did. Then this red line, or red printing, would have been about seven inches down on the eleven-inch side. Right?"

Raffalovitch shrugged. "It could be. I asked the LA boys to pull every office form they have with red ink on it. We can look at them later. If we strike out there, we'll have to message the FBI for help. Then New York. An awful lot of office forms are manufactured and printed there."

"When will we hear from LA?" Joe asked.

"Any minute. I don't think we have to go look at the forms. All we want is a sheet with a red line about six and three quarter inches down the short side. Then you can start looking for someone who manufactures it and someone else who uses it."

"And someone else," McFeeley said, "who stole a piece and cut it up for a ransom note." He started to leave. "Are we kidding ourselves, Raff? Suppose it isn't an office form at all? Suppose the red marks got on by accident?"

The lab chief returned the note to the transparent envelope, using the tweezers. "It's printer's ink. You don't have that kind of stuff around the house. You *print* with it. And when you print in a fairly straight line on sixteen-pound white bond, you're printing an office form. Or some kind of special, marked paper."

"How good is that LA document file?" Joe asked.

"One of the best, they tell me." He turned to his crucible, communing with a white paste, lit a Bunsen burner, and tickled the bottom of the small pot with the blue flame. "They can't keep it a hundred per cent up to date. There's new forms out every day. But it's a start."

"What if they can't match it?"

Raffalovitch looked up owlishly. "Start ringing doorbells. You'll have to visit every paper manufacturer, jobber and printer in Los Angeles, and there's lots of them. Then you can start on New York, Chicago and all the others."

As he drove back to Nespoli Drive—to help set up a *modus operandi* for the new rendezvous—McFeeley sensed a twinge of excitement, the first expectation of discovery. Perhaps Raffalovitch's theorizing about the white paper and the red traces was conjecture. Nevertheless, the bits of Very Bright Red ink were a beginning. It occurred to the detective that there was perhaps a certain consistency in the preparation of the note that neither he nor the lab chief had commented on.

It was an observation more subjective, more speculative than any of Raffalovitch's deductions, and McFeeley had hesitated to mention it to the lab man. With the self-effacing shrewdness of a City Hall doorkeeper, McFeeley had always possessed a sharp capacity to categorize people. And now it seemed to him that the man they sought was characterized by a certain determined neatness. The perfectly spaced, immaculately scissored words, the methodical trimming of the white sheet of paper—down the middle on one side, then above the red marking—all these pointed to an old-maidish fussiness. A phrase from a psychology text Joe had labored through in one of his night courses came to mind: *an anal person.* The detective thought of Timmy Emerson's recollection of a light-brown Ford, clean and neat. Was that part of the man? A compulsive car-washer? A clipper of newspaper words and trimmer of sixteen-pound white bond? Driving back to Nespoli, he abandoned his speculations. Too much analysis of that kind would lead only to frustration. He would await word from the Los Angeles lab. Then they could start looking for anybody in southern California who was neat. *Neatness counts,* he thought.

Moll played the phone call back a third time. *Mrs. Andrus? The mother? . . . Never mind. You alone?*

"It's no use," Laura said. "I don't recognize it."

"I don't," Fritzie added. "The son-of-a-bitch. I'd tear his damn whisperin' tongue out of his head."

"He sounds young," Moll said. "Like maybe a guy in his twenties? Joe's better at this than me. He oughta be back soon."

The doorbell made them start, as if they were eager to be drawn from the whispers on the recording tape. Selena opened the door, and as the three emerged from the nursery, they saw it was Babe and Harry Emerson calling.

The neighbors stood hesitantly at the threshold. "O.K. if we come in?" Harry asked. He waggled a chocolaty cigar.

"Yes," Laura said. "It's all right."

Babe Emerson's face was chalky and swollen, malformed by prolonged weeping. Her eyes lurked behind smoked glasses; she was unable to look at Laura.

"Thought we'd see if we could help. I'm home mosta the time this week, so anything you'd like, I could manage." Emerson scratched his blue-black stubble. He was of that race of men who, three minutes after shaving, appear in need of another shave. "Like shopping, or running errands, or whatever you need."

"That's sweet of you, Harry," Fritzie said. "But I reckon we're managin'."

The Emersons remained standing uneasily. Laura tried to ease their embarrassment. "Sit down, please. Harry, I'm sure we could use a little buoying up."

Still, they did not sit. Emerson waved his blunt hands. "A terrible thing—who could imagine it would happen here? We feel so helpless, Babe and me. Anything, anything we could do—money, help."

Babe's pale face turned to water. Her mouth curved at the edges and gouts of tears blurred her eyes. "Laura! Laura!" she wailed. "I have to talk to you! I have to tell you something!"

"Jesus, honey, don't carry on like that," her husband said. He moved to hold her and she shoved his arms away. "Come on, Babe, Laura and Fritzie got enough to worry about without you making a *geshrei.*"

"What do you know what I'm crying about?" howled Babe. "What do any of you know? Oh—if only you knew——" She hurled herself across the carpeting and plunged into Laura's arms. "Laura, can I talk to you somewhere? Without anyone? Oh, my God—how awful it is—Amy—Amy——"

Laura took her to the studio. The damned illogic of the situation was irrelevant—she, the afflicted, comforting Babe for reasons not apparent. The husbands looked at each other miserably.

"I wish she wouldn't carry on like that," Emerson said. "I told her to butt out, to leave you two alone. You got enough to worry about."

Andrus watched his wife close the studio door. "I suppose she's shook up a little." He invited Emerson to have a drink with him. Harry declined. In the den, the men sat quietly, listening to Babe's muffled crying. "I guess what happened to us is kind of like a public horror," Andrus said. "It's sort of everyone's property, and maybe 'cause Babe feels close to Laura, she feels it stronger."

"It could be," Emerson said. "But, what the hell—she shouldn't *nudge* Laura like that."

In a few seconds, Babe's spasms ended. Only an occasional salty trickle escaped her eyes. She removed her sunglasses and breathed deeply a few times before speaking. "Laura, I have a confession to make," she said.

"What is it, Babe?" She was losing patience with the sniffling woman. "Babe—I have a lot of things to do. You won't help by inundating me in tears. What is it?"

"Oh, if you knew. If you really knew how—how *despicable* I am. How rotten and miserable." A fresh gush of tears distorted her features. The mouth, disarranged by wailing, seemed incapable of forming words. "If anything happened to Amy—you can blame me. Me. *Me.* I'm the monster who did it. I have to tell you."

"What in the world have you done?" Laura left her canvas chair and walked to the day bed. Babe was hunched over, her hands thrust between her knees. "For God's sake, Babe, tell me, if it will make you feel better."

"It won't. I should kill myself. I should be killed. It'll be worse if I tell you, but I deserve anything you want to think about me."

Skepticism muddled Laura's compassion; was it possible that the woman was *enjoying* her performance, wallowing in some kind of false guilt she had contrived, something to make her a more active participant? "I'll think what I want to think, Babe," she said. "I always do."

Dabbing at her eyes, the neighbor studied Laura. "Yes. You do. That's what I envy in you, Laura. That's why I've always watched you with a kind of dumb wonder. You think what you want to, and do what you want to, and you cut through all the garbage we're buried in, and then you tell the truth, or if you know it, you don't say anything to slobs like me, which is worse."

Laura made an impatient motion with her head. "If you don't tell me what you're driving at, Babe, I'll ask you to leave."

"Laura," Babe gasped. "I was the one who told the newspapers."

"What are you talking about? You didn't even know——"

"I told them! *I told them!*" Her head jerked backward. "Laura, I couldn't help it. I'm nosy. I have to stick my miserable two cents into other people's lives. And when you—you—rebuffed me yesterday morning, when you were so short with me, I just had to find out more. Will you forgive me? Can you ever forgive me? Oh, God, how do I dare to ask you that? When if it wasn't for my big mouth, maybe nobody would have known! Maybe it wouldn't have gotten into the newspapers; maybe Amy would be here——"

She was inventing, thought Laura. Her need for *involvement* in the lives of others, for exits and entrances in places where she was not wanted, had possibly affected her reason. The nearness of the tragedy—the fact of physical proximity had impelled her to *invent* an association.

"Don't shake your head, Laura; don't act as if I'm crazy and you don't believe me. I started the whole thing." She gulped air. "You remember that first reporter who came out here? Eliot Sparling? The one that the chief of police put in jail?"

"Yes. That idiotic young man."

"I called him. I told him there was something funny going on here, and that's what got him out."

For the first time, a glitter of truth illuminated her recital. "You did, Babe? Why?"

"If I could have known, Laura!" she wailed. "If I had really known what had happened. But I never suspected Amy was kidnaped. I heard you arguing with Fritzie and I saw the police car and the strange men in the house, *and I had to know*. I had to! I would die if I didn't know. Can I explain to you how I felt?"

"And you called this man to tell him about us? Babe, how could you?"

"Because I'm horrible. Because I'm vile and nosy and because— I admit it Laura—I'm so jealous of you. Maybe I hate you a little." She closed her eyes. "I had to say it."

"But—but—what was this reporter supposed to do? How could he possibly mean anything to you?"

"I had to call *someone*. I didn't care a damn about him—I had met him casually. I had to tell somebody who could call the police and find out for me what was going on. I thought it was a custody fight—when you told me Amy was missing and when I heard Fritzie yelling, I figured he had hidden her somewhere. I had to know. That's all—I had to." She appealed to Laura with bovine eyes. "So blame me. I'm the one responsible if anything happens to Amy. First Sparling came, the others found out, and then that newspaper printed it, and then——"

Laura touched her arm. "Babe! Don't cry, please. What am I supposed to say to you? They would have learned anyway. Lieutenant McFeeley says it was a miracle we kept it from the papers as long as we did. There aren't any secrets any more. Nothing's private. Not the worst of our tragedies, the deepest misery. We're all public property, Babe. You just made it happen a little faster."

Babe rose painfully from the day bed. "I did it because I know I hate you, deep inside, Laura. It's taking me a lot of courage to admit it, but I do. You're the kind of woman I've always wanted to be—aloof, and smart, and poised, and not *involved*. You take the world on your own terms and you discard what doesn't suit you. Me, I let the world make demands on me. I do what I'm told. I do what I think is expected of me because I'm scared and lonely."

Babe walked to the door. Her garish red cotton was rumpled, and a fringe of slip protruded from the hem. "I tried so hard to be your best friend, to imitate you, to please you, to help you. But you just tolerated me. I was a little better than those awful Kahlers." She looked up. "That's a good one. A little better. I'm the most vile creature in the world. *I* told the reporter. *I* ruined you. You and Fritzie and Amy."

"I'm sorry, Babe. I never knew I was hurting you."

"Don't be sorry. I deserved it." She wiped a handkerchief across her eyes and replaced the sunglasses. "I've made my confession. I guess the Catholics have something there, all that soul-baring. But I don't feel better."

Laura took her limp hand. "I could say I forgive you, but I'd be lying. Let's say—I understand why you called."

"See what I mean about you, Laura? You take us only on your own terms. Why can't I be like that?"

"It's not the virtue you think. I can't get angry with you. I'm past anger."

Babe threw herself at Laura and hugged her. "Oh, God, let's know soon! If I could change places with Amy—I'd do it—now—what good am I—I wouldn't be afraid to die, to make up for what I've done."

Again, the question formed in Laura Andrus' mind—how much of Babe's confessional was true and how much was self-indulgence, which, for all its protestations of remorse, was not a little motivated by her compulsive need for membership—with anyone, in anything?

As the two women emerged from the studio, McFeeley, who had returned during their confrontation, came out of the nursery. The relief detectives had arrived, and Irvin Moll, yawning mightily, was departing. McFeeley spoke briefly to him about the plans for meeting the whisperer, then turned to Laura. "When you have a minute, Mrs. Andrus," he said. "Couple of things we should go over. I have some information from the lab." He glanced with bland authoritative eyes at Harry and Babe. They accepted his unspoken censure and left.

Laura, awaiting McFeeley's advices, found his monotonous voice comforting after the emotionality to which she had just been subjected. His political impartiality, his colorless manner were welcome. Unlike Babe Emerson, he was *uninvolved*. Whether this made him a good investigator, she had no idea.

Eliot inveigled Tom Ballstead into having lunch with him. Nothing seemed to be happening at the Andrus house. Rheinholdt's cops were as closemouthed as ever. No more press conferences had been scheduled. The rumor about the Andrus woman's issuing another statement proved to be only some nonsense circulated by Martin Ringel. The poker game was resumed in the back of the UBC station wagon and the familiar clichés hung listlessly in the noonday stillness. *Hit me light. All pink. Three whores. Who paid twice?* When Victor DeGroot, the senior AP man, was pulled off the story temporarily, and when Mona Mears made no appearance, it became evident that the papers were reducing coverage until something concrete developed. It was felt in most editorial offices that the only way of prying information loose would be through personal contacts—friends of the family, police officers who might talk for money, other secret sources. They remembered bitterly Swinnerton's dumb luck of the previous day, with the result that Dr. Walter L. Todd's telephone rang continually. But by now the dentist was uncommunicative. He had been hurt by the fuss his innocent remarks to Harvey had caused. Now he would say nothing. In fact, he explained to Martin Ringel, who camped at his office door (posing as a man with an impacted wisdom tooth), the aspersions being cast upon him as the person who divulged the secret were prompting him to prepare a detailed statement of his activities of the previous day, which he would release at the proper time and which would absolve him of complicity.

A curiosity of another variety nibbled at Eliot Sparling. He realized that little information would be forthcoming from police or family or friends concerning the crime. Therefore, he would claim as his arena the dispute over the broken secret, particularly since none of his colleagues, apart from a few curses the night before, seemed terribly aroused by the Rheinholdt-*Truth* argument. In Sparling's eyes, however, the issue loomed larger than a quarrel between a decaying newspaper and a stupid police official. "But above all things," he had said grandly to Ballstead, when making the lunch date with him, "truth beareth away the victory." "Who the hell said that?" the news director asked. "I don't know. But it's on the front of the New York Public Library," responded Eliot.

Armed with afternoon editions of the *Truth* and the *Argus,* Sparling met Ballstead at the Quickee luncheonette.

A dazzling cross section of what Eliot called "southland wogs and gooks" was jammed into the yellow-and-blue booths. There were show-biz broads in tight, tapered slacks; fagots in frilled shirts and odd haircuts; stout, tanned men in white-on-white shirts (agents? hoods?).

Ballstead was sitting in a corner booth, bent over a cup of steaming tea. He appeared to be inhaling the vapor. Jim Farrell was sitting opposite him, pecking at a salad. The sight of his two superiors surrounded by the mongrel leavings of the theater, the sexually malformed and the financially shadowy, filled Sparling with a mild inspirational thrill. Farrell and Ballstead, after all, were dedicated to small pieces of truth. They were diligent, dependable men, and while, unlike T. T. Hansel, they delivered no speeches about the public's right to know and the sacred mission of the newspaper, they were devoted to a dim principle: to tell the truth—and to do it as best they could. Eliot was glad to be of their company. His clumsy arm brushed the green-sheathed behind of a television blonde. No joy accrued to Sparling; he was fatigued beyond such pleasures.

"Hiya," Eliot said. "Sorry I'm late. Nothing's happening at the house. Georgie's holdin' the fort and he never looked greater."

Farrell smiled gently. "We'll make a reporter out of Brack yet. The poor guy was reading *Fundamentals of Journalism* last week. He'll never live down those beer commercials."

Eliot sighed as he settled against the plastic booth. A waitress, clearly a gorgeous refugee from some moribund studio, took his yawned order: a peanut butter sandwich on white toast and a large Coke. Ballstead looked up sourly from his tea. "You try to get that guy Todd today? After the way he blabbed to the *Truth*, he might want to even things up and talk to us."

Sparling blinked his weary eyes. "He's on my list. He's part of my secret plan."

"Jesus, you never quit," Ballstead rasped.

"Ah, come on, Tom," Sparling pleaded. "You know, I'm a little surprised you don't see the value in following up that *Truth* angle." Neither of the older men commented.

Turning sideways, so that his elephantine legs protruded into the aisle, menaces to navigation, Eliot unfolded the two-star *Truth*. There was, of course, an eight-column banner on the Andrus case with a Mona Mears by-line. It was typical early-afternoon newspaper fraud. There was not a solitary new item of fact in the story, but it had been so rewritten and rearranged (by Bill Trigg, Eliot guessed) as to give the impression of startling freshness. *The grieving parents of little Amy Andrus today awaited some contact from their child's kidnaper, snatched from the lawn of her plush Santa Luisa home.* . . . No one had told the newspaper that contact was awaited; anyone could assume the fact (not just a newspaperman, but a plumber, a chiropractor, a millwright) and publicize it and be reasonably sure of being accurate. Yet this was assumed to be *information*.

Beneath the lead article, under a one-column head, appeared a brief, unsigned story headed:

SANLU POLICE CHIEF
ATTACKS NEWSPAPER

There followed a factual account of Rheinholdt's press conference, including the text of his statement. The article made no connection between Rheinholdt's singling out of "one newspaper" and the *Truth*. The story emphasized the chief's refusal to comment on other aspects of the case, the attempt by police to cover up the kidnaping the previous day, and Rheinholdt's loss of temper that morning.

A third item on the *Truth's* front page concerning the Andrus kidnaping provided Hansel's rebuttal. It was a two-column box, bordered in black and headed simply: AN EDITORIAL. It was not signed.

Sparling arched his eyebrows. He glanced across the formica table, challenging Ballstead. "How about this, hey, Tom?" he asked. "You say it's trade stuff? Hansel doesn't think so. He's stuck his answer on page one." He read with mock histrionics. " 'Chief Caspar Rheinholdt of Santa Luisa has leveled serious accusations at what he chooses to call "one newspaper." We will assist the chief in making himself clear: he means the *Los Angeles Truth*. Mr. Rheinholdt contends that the *Truth* ignored a police request to withhold publication of the Andrus kidnaping yesterday, and that, as a result, an effort to make contact with the kidnaper failed. Further, he contends that this newspaper will be held responsible for any harm that befalls Amy Andrus. These are serious accusations, particularly if they are true. Unfortunately for Mr. Rheinholdt, this newspaper has evidence that he at best is misinformed and, at worst, lying. The facts of the case are these: the *Truth,* through old-fashioned journalistic enterprise, learned of the kidnaping while the Santa Luisa police were still denying there was one and were circulating makeshift lies. Several efforts were made to get the police to confirm or deny the *Truth's* exclusive information. These failed. In the finest of journalistic traditions, a decision was then made to force the hand of the Santa Luisa police—

by printing the story. The edition carrying the story of the Andrus case was on the street yesterday at 5:07 P.M. At no time prior to this was any official request made by Chief Rheinholdt that the story be withheld. At 6:04 P.M. yesterday, Mr. Rheinholdt at last called the *Truth* with his secrecy request—more than nine hours after the crime had been committed. It seems to the editors of this newspaper, which has long prided itself on community service, that Caspar Rheinholdt might best occupy himself with the solution of this awful crime. Thus far, he and his men have shown little skill and less tact in handling the case. Is it possible that Rheinholdt's attack on the *Truth* is merely an inept diversionary tactic aimed at drawing attention from his tragic mishandling of the Andrus kidnaping?' "

Eliot ended on a high note of triumph. "Boy, you ever hear anything like that in your life? Tom, in your whole career as newspaperman, did you ever dare put out any *shlock* like that?"

"It's pretty good," Farrell said.

"Except it leaves out a lot," Eliot protested. "Why didn't they mention that every single other paper laid off? Every radio and TV outfit, and even a dirty fink like Marty Ringel? Only the *Truth*——"

"Because they *had* it," Ballstead rasped. "How dumb can you be? No one sits on a story like that. They *had* it."

"Suppose they did? And suppose they were asked to lay off? Who's right?"

"For Chrissake, Sparling, read it again. They weren't called until 6:04." Ballstead suppressed a belch.

"Rheinholdt says they knew before. Someone's lying. That kid may have been murdered——"

Ballstead waved his hand at Eliot, as if to silence him. The young man's larynx was going full steam; diners in adjacent booths, waitresses, countermen were staring at the source of the deafening blasts. "You're all wound up over nothing," Ballstead said, not cruelly. "All you have are suspicions because you hate Ted Hansel and Herbie Hood. You haven't got a bit of evidence against them except that chief's word. If you did have, what would it prove?"

Eliot leaned back. He polished off his peanut butter sandwich in one gulp, then sipped his Coke. "I won't quit," he said firmly.

"You'll do it on your own time," grumbled Ballstead. "You're going back on the overnight."

Eliot looked from Tom to Farrell, sorrow clouding his eyes. "Why? What did I do wrong?"

"Nothing, Eliot," Farrell said. "The fellow we put on in your place isn't any good. The morning newscasts need you."

"I get it. Pushing me out of the way, so I can't cover the Andrus case. Suppose I did get jailed? Suppose I blew it? I'm entitled to another chance."

Ballstead waved a bony hand for a check.

Sparling would not be dissuaded. "Tom, let me ask you this. Suppose you had an exclusive on the Andrus story yesterday. Let's say I—or George Brack—had gotten it out of Todd. Then you were asked to lay off. You knew you had it exclusive—but you were asked. What would you do?"

Ballstead's features were halted in mid-scowl. Sparling had scored—a dirty tactic perhaps, but a palpable hit. "I'd use it," Ballstead muttered.

"You really would? With a child's life at stake? With a police request to lay off?"

Ballstead hesitated. He ran his hand across his hawkish face, beginning at the high forehead, pressing the palm against the deep-socketed eyes, the skeletal nose. "I would."

"Think real hard, Tom. Would you?"

"You're so honorable, you disgust me," Ballstead said. "Who knows what I'd do? I'd run like a thief with it. If I was asked to withhold, I'd invent every excuse in the book to get it on the air, I'd want something in writing—I'd fuss around and procrastinate and make conditions—and by then I'd go with it. I'm jealous as hell of Hansel. So's everyone else in this town."

Farrell added an amen. "It sounds rough, Eliot, but that's the business. It's O.K. to be noble when you don't have the story, when you're left out. But when you have it the way the *Truth* had it——"

"I thought better of you two guys," Sparling mumbled.

"Oh, you did?" Ballstead asked. "Well, aren't you a beauty! Aren't you an authority on the ethics of journalism! You, flying back to the place and busting the pool agreement so I had to apologize to Victor DeGroot this morning. Where did you get so ethical, Sparling, on the *Daily Bruin?*"

"Never mind," Eliot whined. "There was more integrity on the *Daily Bruin* than there is around here."

Ballstead groaned. "Integrity, my ass. What has that got to do with newspapers? You want to know what keeps newspapers in business? Why people read 'em?"

This sudden passion startled Eliot. The news director appeared irritated beyond even his own capacity for self-torment.

"I'll tell you a little story," Ballstead said. "When I was a kid in Fort Wayne, the big event in our lives was the Sunday drive to Ohio. Don't ask me why, but it was considered mandatory to pile into the jalopy and cross from Indiana to Ohio. You can't tell one state from the other, but it was pretty hot stuff to go to Ohio. I remember one day we were on a dirt road and my old man saw a bunch of cars pulled off the road. There must have been twenty-five cars, lined up on the grass, up a little incline. So he pulled over and we got out. About halfway up the hill there was an old shack, and people kept straggling in and out of it. My old man and my mother and myself, we climbed the hill also. When we got to the front of the shack—there was no door, just a kind of gap in the boards—we saw a sign. The sign said: DIRTIEST MAN IN THE WORLD ADMISSION TWO CENTS. We followed a couple of farmers in, and inside the shack there sure as hell was a dirty man. He was one of these half-witted hermits you used to find all over the Middle West before Roosevelt, a guy who hadn't bathed or shaved or changed his rags in twenty years, squatting on the dirt floor, mumbling to himself. There was a cat snoozing in one corner and the place stank like all the cesspools in Ohio. The floor was full of moldy magazines, some rusty pots, old tin cans and— I remember it to this day—an old toilet seat. Next to him there was a dirty milk bottle, and the farmers would drop their two cents into it, look him over a little, try to get him to talk, and then walk out, properly horrified, the women cackling how dirty he was and feeling proud they were so clean, the kids a little scared. What I remember most was, he hardly had a face. What with the dirt and the whiskers, it seemed as if he only had a pair of spooky eyes. We walked back to the car and my old man said proudly, 'Well, son, now you've seen the dirtiest man in the world,' and my mother kind of simpered and said, 'Yes, and let that be a lesson to you, Tommy—see what happens if you don't wash your ears?' And then they laughed. It was a lesson to me all right, but it had nothing to do with my ears."

Sparling and Farrell were silent. There was an undercurrent of native horror in the news director's narrative, a revelation of sordidness that stunned them. Eliot in his mind's eye saw the sunny green hillock, the old cars—Hupmobiles, Chandlers, Essexes—assembled on the roadside, the parade of scrawny farmers and their stout wives hiking up to the weather-beaten shack to pay their two cents for a look at the lunatic.

"I tell you what I learned," Ballstead went on. "I learned what interests people. Why they'll cross the state line, go out on some dirt road and climb a hill. You think it's a Washington date line? The UN story or the foreign affairs interpretive? Like hell it is. *It's the dirtiest man in the world.* Something so awful it makes you feel good, because it isn't you. So don't talk to me about integrity or ethics of journalism, Sparling. I once saw the dirtiest man in the world and I've been seeing him ever since. I owe that old half-wit more than he knows, and someday, in that great big newsroom in the sky, I'll stake him to his first bath."

Ballstead paid the check and nodded gloomily at Farrell. "Let's go." He looked at Eliot. "Don't look so sad. Sure there's room for good honest journalism. But it's that old bum in the shack who pays the freight. Yes, and a kidnaped child who might be murdered."

Farrell eased himself past Eliot. "Sorry about the overnight, kid. You can sleep tonight, but tomorrow—Thursday morning, 1:00 A.M. —you're on again."

"You want me to lay off the Andrus thing?" Eliot asked plaintively.

"Brack'll cover the house. We're sending a man to stay at police headquarters." Farrell seemed apologetic. Ballstead was threading his way through the mob of varicolored behinds, white-on-white shirts, fey men in narrow pants.

"Jim—suppose I nose around on my own? I think I can find something out. On my own time, of course."

Farrell shrugged. "Your time's your own, Eliot. Just don't compromise Tom. He's got enough troubles."

"I'll be very discreet," Sparling exploded. "No hard feelings about the overnight, Jim. I can take it."

Farrell left him. Eliot ordered a second Coke, then opened the other newspaper he had brought to the luncheonette, the *Argus*.

The second-day coverage of the kidnaping was roughly the same as the *Truth's*. A more conservative paper, its headline was less garish (only six columns) and it had incorporated the story of Rheinholdt's attack on the *Truth* in the body of the lead piece.

Eliot scanned the material quickly. It was under David Arnspeiger's by-line, an honor more honestly earned than Mona Mears'. Then he noticed a small box in italics reading: *See editorial page 26, Section III, "A Disgraceful Episode."* Eliot turned the pages.

> The kidnaping of Amy Andrus is a tragedy that stirs the hearts of every southland citizen. The *Argus* joins its readers in prayer for Amy's safety, in hopes that she will soon be back with her dolls and coloring books. Nonetheless, the threat overhanging the missing child is real and grave. In this connection, the *Argus* is impelled to point out certain incredible mistakes committed by the Santa Luisa police. The dreadful mishandling of the case, from its inception yesterday morning, must be placed at the door of Chief Caspar Rheinholdt and his willing, but incompetent, force. We enumerate these lapses only to set the record straight.
>
> 1. Why did Rheinholdt's men at the scene deliberately and repeatedly lie to reporters? Indeed—why was the child's mother induced to lie? Having thus aroused newspaper curiosity, was it not natural for the reporters to refuse to leave?

At this point, Sparling halted and held the editorial at arm's length. "Unclean, unclean," he said aloud, causing several diners to regard him momentarily, then dismiss him as a harmless nut. Aware of the stares he was drawing, Sparling then answered each rhetorical question, speaking softly. "First question—to save a child's life. Second—ditto. Third—who the hell are reporters to set conditions by which people live or die, hah?"

He then resumed reading the editorial. It went on to list other instances of police malfeasance. *Why were not roadblocks set up? Why was not the FBI summoned? Why no thirteen-state alarm? Why was the chief's car parked outside the house to call attention to the scene of the crime? What right had Rheinholdt to seclude himself in his office and refuse to see reporters?*

Then came a concluding paragraph that, for Sparling, was the strangest touch of all.

> Chief Rheinholdt's lame attempt to blame a newspaper for his botching of the investigation will fool no one. Far be it from the *Argus* to go to bat for a competitor. In most matters, we're delighted to see them squirm. But in this

instance, we are obliged to point out that Rheinholdt's attack on the *Los Angeles Truth* is nothing more than a clumsy diversionary tactic to draw attention away from his own bungling.

The *Truth's* editors are big boys. We'll let them defend themselves. We're sure they have a fair explanation as to why they printed the Andrus story yesterday.

Beyond that, once the charges and countercharges have subsided, we can only pray that the Sanlu police do not lose sight of their prime objective: solving the crime.

The editorial astounded Sparling. If ever there had been a made-to-order opportunity for one newspaper to embarrass, insult, attack and possibly annihilate a competitor, this had been it. The *Argus* detested the *Truth*. A sedate, old-fashioned paper with narrow headlines, a widely read pet department and frequent features on gay nonagenarians, it tended to ignore the lurid bleatings of the *Truth*. Both newspapers were notably conservative in their policies, but the *Argus,* in a cranky, crusty way, maintained a good deal of fairness in both editorials and news coverage.

Moreover, after a long circulation war, the *Argus,* an independent paper stressing local affairs (its favorite headline, Eliot Sparling remarked, was LA DOG CHASES LA CAT OVER LA FENCE), had at last overtaken the faltering *Truth*. It appeared to Sparling that here had been a grand opportunity for the *Argus* to crush the competition forever. But nothing of the sort had happened. The *Argus* editorial, correct in its accusation that Rheinholdt had botched the investigation, was strangely solicitous of its rival's good name. No attempt had been made to ascertain whether the chief had told the truth or not; it was assumed that the *Truth* was right.

A sick, weak sensation overcame Sparling: as if he had just observed his mother drunk or his father adulterating a prescription. Enough of his infatuation with journalism remained to make him shiver at a vision of high corruption.

Being of a meticulous nature, he took a notebook from his breast pocket, selected an automatic pencil from his arsenal, and jotted down a list of names. He had the day to himself, since he was officially relieved of the Andrus coverage, and was not due to work until Wednesday night.

DR. TODD
SGT. BAINES & OTHER GUY
SWINNERTON
HOOD (ASK CONNIE?)
RHEINHOLDT

Then he plodded out of the luncheonette. His first stop would be the dentist.

A Western Union messenger called at the Andrus house a little before 1:30 P.M. Detective Ed Case, answering the door, was surprised to see the boy bearing an enormous box of candy. The detective tipped the boy and brought the gift into the living room. It seemed an unwelcome intrusion—redolent of festive occasions. Laura, coming out of the bedroom, where she had been resting after diapering and giving Karen her midday bottle, was surprised to hear it was for her. An envelope was attached to the box. She opened it.

> *My dear, brave Mrs. Andrus——*
>
> *First, my apologies for last night. You must believe I acted in good faith; no one told me of any arrangements. Secondly, I believe I have certain private information and contacts in LA that can help you reach the criminal. But I must talk to you—personally and alone. I'll drop by later. I am praying.*
>
> *Mona Mears*

She showed it to Fritzie. "Old bitch," he said. "As if she didn't make enough trouble last night. How'd she have the nerve to send you this? She comes here, I'm throwin' her out on her corseted can."

McFeeley read it. "I know what she means about contacts," Joe said. "I had a hunch she'd drag that out before long."

"What can she possibly know about this?" asked Laura.

"Underworld," McFeeley said. "She works with them a lot. Hoods are as bad as anyone else today. They all want to be in the newspapers. A couple of years ago some safecracker surrendered to her in her office. Ever since, she's been a clearinghouse for criminals. They pass information through her, tip her on stories—when it won't hurt them—try to stay on her good side. Sounds crazy, but it's true."

Andrus nodded. "Yeah, I've heard of that. Fellah gave us a script about it last month."

"What should I do when she comes?" asked Laura. "I can't stand the sight of the woman. What do you suggest, Lieutenant?"

Joe massaged the back of his scrawny neck; fatigue was devouring him. He wished Raffalovitch would call back with some word from the Los Angeles police documents file. He wondered if the thirteen-state alarm—at long, long last—had gone out. (Did it matter any more? Any police department in the country could now know what Amy looked like, what her physical description was, by buying the local newspaper, by watching the local TV news program. The child's pinched face was as well known as a movie star's by now.) He wondered, too, about the rendezvous they were to make in three hours. In the emptiness that surrounded them, the wide plain of ignorance on which they were isolated, it was conceivable that Mona Mears might be of use.

"I'll let you decide, Mrs. Andrus," Joe said carefully. "I know you have no use for her, but she does have pipelines to the hoods. The only thing is—I think Amy was taken by some amateur, the kind of guy who won't particularly care about surrendering to Mona Mears, not even if she guarantees him a two-page spread."

"Y'all might as well talk to the biddy," Fritzie said. Andrus understood her value: she was of the *word*, as he was, and the word accomplished things. Often it accomplished more than did deeds, facts, reality. All of McFeeley's lab work and tape recordings and crime searches might produce nothing; one cunning Mona Mears dealing in gas might be more to the point.

Case was at the door again. Miss Mears had arrived, fresh in a lavender shirtwaist dress and lavender suede shoes. The skirt billowed around her elegant legs; the hag's face was cosmeticized with pale powder and purple lipstick. Her arrival had stirred the handful of stand-by reporters, and these indignant males gathered at the door.

"If she gets in, we all get in!" Duane Bosch cried. He had received a commending note from the editor of the Sanlu *Register*.

"It ain't fair, Joe," Dave Arnspeiger said. "What right's she got to bust in?"

Harvey Swinnerton remained silent. Mona was his co-worker. Moreover, he was happy to minimize his involvement. His incredible good luck of the previous day, his great coup with Dr. Todd, had turned to ashes in his mouth.

"I don't like to stand here like a fool, Lieutenant," Mona Mears said. A smile displayed her meticulous, capped teeth—a seven-thousand-dollar job, fashioned by a man in Beverly Hills who turned down applicants whom he deemed insufficiently celebrated. McFeeley glanced at Laura. She nodded affirmatively. Mona Mears, with not even a sneer of victory, crossed the threshold. The other reporters protested. McFeeley ignored them and closed the door.

"Goddam that broad," Arnspeiger said angrily. "I spend thirty years on the police beat, I nursemaid kids like Joe McFeeley, and then a witch like that, with her syndicated column and her political connections, gets the nod."

Inside, the columnist made known her conditions: she would talk only to Laura and Fritzie. No police were to be present. McFeeley glanced at Laura, leaving the decision to her. Andrus waved his hand. "Y'all don't need me. I'd be in the way."

"You're welcome to hear what I have to say," Mona Mears said. "It concerns both of you. I hope you understand why I don't want the police in on it—as much as I respect Lieutenant McFeeley. But the way his boss is acting, particularly regarding my newspaper, I can't run the risk of him denouncing us again. Is that unreasonable?"

No one responded. Laura took her into the studio and closed the door. Miss Mears' grapey eyes surveyed the worktable, the plaster casts, the clay figures, the array of crusted, flecked tools. "Oh—I didn't know you were *creative*. What lovely work." She smiled—with so little sincerity that Laura winced.

"I'm an amateur," she said.

"Have you shown? Do you sell? I just love that torso. I'm good friends with Mark Del Balso—you know, the Del Balso Gallery. He'd give you a showing like that"—she snapped a lavender finger and a lavender thumb—"if I asked him."

The columnist fixed her eyes on Laura. "Poor dear. Poor suffering dear. Am I forgiven about last night? I didn't want to intrude like that. But I swear it to you, I never *knew*——"

"Yes, yes, I'm past all that. You were all guilty. Every one of you." She found her voice firm, cold. "Now what is it you want to tell me?"

The question evoked no response. Instead, what seemed the

ultimate in nonsense issued from the newspaperwoman's varnished lips: "Who is your analyst?"

"What's that got to do with anything?" Laura asked. She was irate with McFeeley for advising her to see the columnist. What was the compelling power that they held over everyone? Why had they been allowed to torment her the previous day, to camp on her doorstep, to *demand* as their rights and privileges her last secret, access to every shred of misery?

"You're so calm. I wonder what kind of treatment you're getting. Your analyst must be marvelous."

"I've never been analyzed. Will you please get on with what brought you here?"

The caller crossed her unmarked legs. She rested her temple in one hand. "You're an odd one," she said. "So original. Don't you ever crack? Break down? Bawl?"

Laura got up. "You'd better go."

"I have to talk like this to loosen you up. How did it feel last night when you learned? Were you as brave as you are now?" She hesitated craftily. "Or is it possible you *don't* care?"

"Damn you," Laura whispered. "Get out of my house."

The woman in lavender did not move. "Sweetheart, you'll have to *throw* me out. Don't take anything I say too seriously. It's just an old news hen's tactics—trying to get you to unbend a little. Really, I can help you. I wouldn't come here to waste your time, or mine."

"I don't want your help. Go."

Laura walked to the door and opened it. Miss Mears shifted her legs; there was a secret rustle of hidden silk.

"You're an original, Laura. You make it hard for people to sympathize with you. To *love* you. Yes, I think that's your difficulty —you have trouble *loving*. Marriage broken up—children neglected —no close friends or family. I wish I could help you. I don't mean just about Amy. But all the things that have gone wrong for you. You must learn to *love,* Laura darling."

"You wretched old woman," Laura said. She turned her back and walked out of the studio, past McFeeley and her husband, and opened the redwood door. The sight of four of the reporters, waiting, forever waiting, in the brutal sunlight, filled her with a momentary nausea. "I don't want to see you again or speak to you again," she called to Mona Mears, who, unperturbed, was mincing through the living room. At the foyer, the reporter halted.

"I want to put you in touch with some people I know," the

columnist said. "Some people who can get things done, who have contacts. You know, criminals love publicity. I think I could make better arrangements for this man's surrender than the police could."

"Y'all gonna let her get away with that, McFeeley?" Fritzie asked. "Come on, stick up for your gang."

Joe said nothing. He knew when to keep his mouth shut. Laura noted his reticence. She took it to be fear—the fear of an insecure middle-class man, awed by the high power Mona Mears symbolized, the gift of fame and love she could endow, or the revenge she could take.

"But you must come with me yourself, Laura darling," the woman said. "No police. Not your husband. No dentists. Just you and me—and I guarantee you my contacts will do you more good than a roomful of FBI agents."

Still, she did not leave. McFeeley, standing casually in the corridor, seemed unequal to her, just as the previous night he had tolerated, cajoled, and negotiated with the mob—instead of enforcing the law.

Andrus, who, no less than the detective, understood the woman's power to destroy, and who stood to suffer considerably by affronting her, moved swiftly across the carpeting. He grasped one elbow firmly and, as if escorting an inept actress through her movements, guided her to the opened door. "Old woman," Fritzie said, "y'all gettin' on our nerves. Git yo' ass outa heah, 'fore I take a sycamore branch to it."

Mears was out the door, blinking in the burning daylight, surrounded by her amused colleagues. She tugged at her girdle, touched her dazzling hair a few times, and then clack-clacked off to her convertible. None of the men said anything; but the grins, the winks, the nudges (Duane Bosch whistled at her waggling rear) cut her. At the sidewalk, she started to enter her car, and then, with that unerring instinct that had served her so well in her career, changed directions and walked toward the Kahler house.

McFeeley allowed himself a discreet laugh. "I wish I had the guts to do that," he admitted. "We're on the spot now. You know—with Rheinholdt fighting the papers."

Andrus was invigorated by his own daring. "Your problems ain't mine, McFeeley," he said. "That bitch will skewer me alive next time I show my face in public. But, man, I couldn't care less. I been nice to people like that too long. Too long, oh, Lord."

Laura managed a faint smile. Her husband's outlandish assault on the invader revived in her memories of a younger, more innocent Fritzie—the starving director of amateur groups who rehearsed over garages in the Village. Andrus noted her approval, but he made no comment. Instead, he followed McFeeley into the nursery, saying as he did: "There ain't nothin' like that Tarheel accent when you wanna eat someone out. You see that ole possum scat?"

Dr. Walter L. Todd's office occupied the top floor of the Santa Luisa Professional Building, a five-story edifice of native yellow stone, with one entire wall constructed of glass brick. It was functional, prosperous-looking, and frigidly air-conditioned, and the moment Eliot Sparling entered the antiseptic self-service elevator, inhaling fragrances of iodoform and pine deodorant, he began to cough. The dazzling décor—there were mosaics throughout—made him a little ashamed of his unshaven jaw, his rumpled yellow shirt, his shapeless tan slacks. He looked like a slob, and felt like one, in the grand surroundings.

However, the magnificence of the dentist's pine-paneled waiting room did not surprise him. A starched nurse, a raven-haired temptress, bade him await Dr. Todd's imminent return from lunch. When Eliot confessed he had no appointment, she conceded that perhaps the doctor could "squeeze him in," and the newsman dozed in a Danish modern chair. The reason Sparling was not unprepared for the luxury was that, for some time, he had been a student of the *Cult of the Dentist* and had formulated a thesis concerning the high status of dentistry in southern California. It was the young man's contention that, in the curious ethos of the southland, dentists were exalted far beyond their tiresome chores of unimpacting wisdom teeth or capping molars. They became confidants, advisers, counselors, gray eminences. One's dentist, if a good dentist, combined the services of minister, psychiatrist, tax consultant and market analyst. In the higher income brackets, notably in show biz, this was particularly noticeable. You went to your dentist for love—comfort—courage—advice—good tidings. In time, Sparling claimed, an intense affection developed between patient and tooth puller, something cryptosexual, deeply rooted in both psyches. Why was this so? Eliot sensed it had a lot to do with "all that *futzing* around the oral cavity." There was something about the painful probing of the opened mouth—the yanking, polishing and scraping—that inevitably led to a relationship deeper and finer than bridgework. Often, Sparling had heard TV directors and producers, "starlets," motion picture executives discuss their dentists in these intimate terms. "I felt lousy all morning, so I ran over to Dr. Glattner to have him look at my incisors," he once heard a network rajah say. "He really straightened me out. The guy's a genius. He made it clear to me why I hated my wife. Then he told me to sell those Public Authority Sewer Bonds for the City of Seattle. And then he called a guy who can get me a Vespa wholesale for my oldest boy. And he only charged me two thousand bucks for the works." In his mind's eye, Eliot envisioned the vignette: the dentist, a hairy, muscular type from Brooklyn—possibly with a thick, graying mustache—leaning his handball-hardened bulk into the TV chap's blue-serged, slenderized form, whispering practical wisdom into his scrubbed ear, all the time groping with two stubby paws in the man's opened maw.

He gathered, sitting in Todd's handsome waiting room (walled in Japanese grass cloth, bright with framed hunting scenes) that Laura Andrus' relative was of this breed of dentist. He counseled patients on the disciplining of arson-prone children and supplied dependable tips on over-the-counter securities.

At about 2.15, Todd, who had bypassed the waiting room and returned to his office via a rear entrance, buzzed his nurse on the intercom. She mentioned the prospective patient by name. Todd made no response, but in less than a minute he was in the waiting room, his roseate face as smugly self-sufficient as ever, his figure boxed in a finger-length white coat.

"Mr. Sparling?" he asked. "You're not here as a patient, are you? You're the reporter."

"Ah—yes." Eliot gathered up his failing bones. "I'd like to chat with you, Dr. Todd. I—ah—I'm doing a story for UBC on yesterday's events—because, as you know, there's quite a fuss over the *Truth* disclosing the story—and I was sure you'd have something to add. Considering the part you played in yesterday's events."

"Oh no. Oh no. I've talked quite enough."

"Well, what I wanted was to set the record straight. You know—just what you said to Swinnerton, what time it was, what he told you."

The dentist's head wagged horizontally. "No. I've had my lesson. The fact is, I'm preparing a statement of my activities yesterday. That'll explain everything to my satisfaction, and, I trust, to everyone else's."

"A statement?"

"Yes. I'm working on it right now."

"Maybe I could help," Eliot boomed out. "I know how you should word these things. I can tell you what people are saying about you and what you did yesterday. How can you explain everything if you're not sure what you're being accused of?"

"Accused? Why in the world should anyone accuse me? I was the first person to volunteer my help! I supplied the ransom money. I offered to meet the kidnaper."

"Oh, *I'm* not," Sparling said quickly. "But you know how reporters are. How gossip spreads." He searched for a piece of live bait. "That rumor that there was only straw in the ransom package —they're saying *you* started it."

"That's a lie," Todd said. "A damnable lie." He darted a look at the staring secretary and she turned her gorgeous face to her typing. "Come inside, Mr. Sparling," Todd said.

In the inner office—maroons and deep browns were favored— Eliot plopped into an armchair. Todd closed a door. Eliot was just as happy—through the opening he had seen the hateful drill, chair and fountain. Like all cowards with carious teeth, he lived in perpetual dread of the apparatus.

"Let me read you what I've written," Todd said. "Then you tell me what I've left out, what other accusations, as you say, I should answer."

"My pleasure, sir."

Todd cleared his throat. "I've titled this 'Remarks by Walter L. Todd, D.D.S., Concerning His Role in the Kidnaping of Amy Andrus.' How does that strike you?"

"Perfect." Sparling held up a circled thumb and index finger. "Gets right to the point."

"Yes. I thought so, too." He adjusted his glasses. "On the morning of September 17, 1951, a Monday, I rose, as is my custom, at 7:00 A.M., showered, shaved, and prepared my own breakfast. I ate lightly in deference to the heat—just some unbuttered whole-wheat toast and black coffee—and then read the *Santa Luisa Register,* noting with some consternation an editorial criticizing Chief Rheinholdt for refusing to allow press cars the use of the parking lot. Since I feel that both our fine police and our hard-working reporters are integral parts of our community, I made a mental note to try to offer my good offices in the matter and effect some understanding. I note here that I have always felt public service an obligation of the intelligent citizen. My work with the Santa Luisa

Library Committee, the United Church Appeal, the Beautification and Cleanliness League is well known. As a bachelor, I have a good deal of free time, and I give it unselfishly to the fellow residents of our splendid little town." He looked up from the typewritten sheets. "Read all right to you, Eliot?" the dentist asked. "It's not overwritten?"

"Oh no, doctor. It's terrific. You have a helluva style."

The dentist resumed. "On that particular morning, I drove to my office in the Professional Building at about 8:05, arriving at 8:17, a time I can verify, since I have retained the stub from the adjacent parking lot where I leave my Buick. At my office I changed from my suit coat to a white coat, read some routine mail, and adjusted the air conditioning. My nurse, Miss Thelma Schreiner, arrived at 8:29, and we discussed the list of appointments. No one was due until 9:00, so I busied myself studying some new scented plastic molds that a supply house had sent me on approval, while Miss Schreiner typed some bills. At exactly 9:02, the first . . ."

He read on, his voice vigorous, accenting each phrase with the perfection of a commercial announcer. Eliot listened, transfixed. The man was clearly insane. It was a lunatic's recital of trivia, the confessional of someone convinced that every act of his life, every rising and going to bed, every meal eaten, friend greeted, purchase made was of enormous moment, was of lasting value, and had to be preserved for history.

Sparling's eyes wandered—to the framed diplomas and citations, the bookcase laden with expensive texts, the machines for recording and rendering words permanent: a dictaphone, an electric typewriter. He was dozing off, staring at his own feet, when Todd got to the heart of the matter—his conversations with Harvey Swinnerton. Here, the reporter listened attentively. The dentist did not cheat. He related his discussion with Swinnerton fully, stressing the reporter's promise to keep it *off the record*, to use the material only if the police gave the go-ahead. He gave specific times: it was exactly 3:42 when he spoke to Swinnerton. He remembered glancing at his watch and then hurrying off to the bank. Eliot etched the time in his weary brain: *3:42*. Once Todd had concluded with his account of Swinnerton (which, in his egocentric way he imagined neither more nor less important than what he ate for lunch), the report again became a jumble of self-testimonials. "I advised Lieutenant McFeeley that I stood ready and willing to carry out any mission he might devise for me. I add here that I have never been afraid of anyone or anything, and I had no qualms about encountering the kidnaper of little Amy singlehanded, unarmed except for a belief in my own inner strength."

At last he concluded, set the sheaf of papers down, and looked at Sparling. "Does it read all right? I'm not worried about my facts. I'm a stickler for facts. But I'm interested in your comments on my *style*."

"It's the greatest, Dr. Todd. It's pure prose. You gonna give this out soon?" Eliot leaned forward. The chair was of extremely soft leather, and his thighs had sunk too low. When he tried to move, he became further entrapped.

"I'm hanging on to it until the storm breaks. I want to add something about the package containing paper. Not only was it real money, it was *my* money."

Eliot lurched upright. "That time is correct—3:42—when you talked to Swinnerton?"

"Absolutely. With his promise not to tell a soul. It was in confidence."

"You don't know what he did then?"

"I had other things on my mind. I left him in the alley. I assume he went back on his word."

"He's never spoken to you since?"

"No. I rather like Harvey. It would be embarrassing for both of us. He's—excusing your presence, Mr. Sparling—more of a gent than some of your confreres."

"Oh, you can't hurt my feelings." Eliot got up. He had confirmed the first of his suspicions: Swinnerton had been told a potful, enough for a beat, enough to make Hood and Hansel slobber.

"You've been very helpful, young man," the dentist said. "You do any outside literary work? I mean, aside from your chores at the network?"

"A little magazine free lancing," Eliot lied.

"Interesting. Perhaps someday you and I can get together on a project of mine." He chuckled secretively. Then he rose from his chair and lifted a heavy copper ash tray from his desk. A wire ran from its base, hidden under the desk blotter. "I've recorded every word we've said." Still chuckling, he opened a mahogany cabinet at his rear. Inside, a tape recorder spun merrily.

"That certainly is a hot one on me," Eliot said mirthlessly. "The biter bit."

"Beg pardon?" Todd was studying his tape machine lovingly.

"The biter bit. I'm the newsman, and I come here to interview you, sir, and maybe *I* should have made the tape, and here you are recording *me*."

The dentist beamed. "Don't feel badly, Eliot. I record everyone who sits in my office—if they're of particular interest, unusual professions." With that, he spun in his seat and opened a companion mahogany cabinet. Inside were stacked hundreds of reels of magnetic tape. "You see, Mr. Sparling, I'm saving these for my biography."

"You sure have lots of material."

"Yes. At the moment my nurse and a part-time stenographer are busy transcribing them. I've got miles of stuff. Patients—friends—colleagues—and very often just my own intimate thoughts as they occur to me. I simply switch this on and ad-lib."

"Mighty interesting, Dr. Todd. Well, I'd better be going now, so——"

"No, no. Let's talk about this." Todd bounced around the desk —he seemed to move in prearranged little dance sequences—*step-step-ship-come together*. "I know I have a marvelous book in my life story. Particularly now with the key role I'm playing in the Andrus affair. I thought when you have some free time we could talk about a collaboration."

It took a good deal to turn Sparling's stomach, but the dentist had succeeded.

"Dentistry is a way of life with me," Todd said. "But that doesn't obscure other interests." He fished around on his desk and thrust a brochure at Eliot. "I lecture. I write. I teach. I *serve*."

Sparling read the heading on the brochure. Above a picture of Walter L. Todd, D.D.S., appeared the title:

YOUR TEETH ARE YOUR BEST FRIENDS
A SERIES OF HUMOROUS, INFORMATIVE LECTURES
BY SOUTHERN CALIFORNIA'S BEST-LOVED,
MOST FASCINATING DENTIST!

"I run a little color film with the lecture," Todd said. "Would you like to see it?" He hopped away to a furled motion picture screen standing in one corner and began to unroll it.

"No, no thanks, doctor. I really don't have the time today. Maybe when we discuss this little project of yours."

"Right!" agreed Todd. "That's the time for it! Oh, I have files, records, stories, notebooks laden with fascinating material. You won't have any trouble finding a book in them—you'll worry about what to discard!"

Nothing would do but that Todd see him to the elevator. The dentist laced an iron forearm in one of Eliot's flabby arms, and they strolled through the waiting room to the mosaicized hallway. As they waited for the elevator, Todd asked him: "Now about a title. What do you think of *Forty Years a Dentist?* Or *Wider, Please?* Or *Cavities and Caveats?*"

Eliot thought he would faint. People had no right to be that sure of themselves, that successful, that happy in their own stupidity! Todd's indifference to everything in the world except his own self nauseated the young newsman, filled him with a revulsion, the first symptom of which was a desire to urinate on the dentist's glistening black feet. Sparling, overworked, frustrated, eaten alive by a million worms of inferiority, miserable for his father in the East Bronx, his own ludicrous front to the world, gasped for air like a beached fish, and, as the elevator door opened, said: "How about this? *Memoirs of a Self-Centered Man?* Or, maybe, *I'm All That Matters?*"

Todd's visage was unclouded. Either he was so cocooned in self-love, in his own words, that his conversations were one-directional and anything addressed to him was immediately interpreted as a compliment—or else he did not understand Eliot's gross humor. In any case, he smiled and shook the newsman's hand. "Excellent!" he cried. "You're full of good ideas! Remember—call me and we'll work something out!"

The horror! The horror! Eliot rested his graceless shape against the aluminum wall of the elevator. He could only shiver at the dreadful mischance, the misshapen sequence of events that had plummeted Walter L. Todd's overflowing ego into Laura Andrus' tragedy, into the fate of the missing child.

McFeeley sent the recording of the whisperer to headquarters. Then, after phoning Rheinholdt, he sat down with Laura again and reviewed their plan for the 4:30 ransom drop at the overpass. She would leave the house alone in the station wagon. No one would follow her, but, at the site, detectives would be on the alert for any appearance by the whispering man. It was agreed that the package would be left at the designated location for an hour, then retrieved, if no one came for it. The detective resumed interrogating her. It had occurred to him that the newspaper stories about her breakup with her husband might have been the impulse for the crime. Conceivably, Joe reasoned, the account of their personal troubles, the news of a fatherless house, a "rich" family, the casual freedom of the neighborhood—all these might have induced some warped mind to single them out. The notion was farfetched, but Joe explained that nothing could be overlooked, that the remotest possibilities had to be explored. He was asking her to recall the circumstances of their separation, anything that appeared in the newspapers. She had difficulty remembering; the events were unpleasant. His request that she try to remember any strangers in her house, on the phone, during those days, evoked no response in her. Abruptly, Laura realized she was not thinking clearly. Her mind was befuzzed, vagrant. She, who had always prided herself on clarity of mind, on fixity of purpose, was distressed by it. "You'll have to excuse me, Lieutenant," Laura pleaded. "I don't seem to be able to focus. I think those drugs my husband gave me last night are wearing off. I can't handle them—particularly the aftereffects." McFeeley nodded sympathetically. "Sure. I shouldn't be bothering you so much. In an hour and a half you'll have to make another trip." She suddenly appeared concerned about him: when would he sleep? When would he see his family? The detective explained he had "snoozed" the night before; his wife and kids were inured to long absences. Their house, McFeeley told her, was so full of people—four children, his wife's mother and sister as frequent visitors, Midge Callahan, their neighbor—that his absence would hardly be noticed, except for a little less noise. She smiled. His recital of his bland domestic life seemed to cheer her momentarily, but McFeeley did not pursue the subject. His home was his business; hers was hers. When he left her—stooped, his neutral face now showing lines of fatigue—she felt lonely.

His unexciting presence was a diluent to her misery, and when he walked into the nursery, to telephone headquarters for his half-hourly report, she missed him. Fritzie was in the den, speaking to his office. She could hear his hoarse voice. *"Yeah. We just hopin'. No, I can't tell you nothing at all. I hope Bates likes that script better'n I do—not that I can do much for him now. . . .*

How lucky they all were! Laura thought miserably. How lucky to be with the quick, the living, the breathing, the viewers of daylight and the listeners to music and human voices! She knew now that her surge of terror, after talking to the whispering man, was nothing less than a foreknowledge of her daughter's death. She tried stifling it; but she had no armory of illusions, of daydreams, as did her husband; nor could she be detached and analytical like McFeeley. She was the mother.

She was the earth and water that had produced the child; and the child, quite possibly, no longer lived. *I will never fear death for myself,* Laura thought. *I have seen the pit, the final horror.*

With that iron will that had allowed her to remain poised, she tried to suffocate the vision. It did no good. If her appearance seemed normal—pale and haggard, but normal—the torment within her was a bleak, freezing void that could not be minimized. Half aloud, her voice escaped her, her lips formed words: "I hope he didn't hurt her."

Andrus, not hearing the words, but catching the broken voice, turned in his swivel chair and called: "Y'all say somethin' to me, Laura?"

She shook her head and gripped the rough fabric of the cushions. *Do not hurt her, do not hurt her.*

Raffalovitch called back at 3:30. He was not encouraging.

"There's nothing in their document file like what we're looking for," the lab man said. "Lots of forms that use red ink, but not ours. The nearest was an interoffice memo some oil company has, with a red border running all the way around. Ours was just on one side. Also, it was watermarked. Ours is plain white bond."

"What did LA think?" Joe asked.

"Well, they admitted their file isn't one hundred per cent. They try to keep it up to date, but that's impossible. Each guy with a little business thinks he can invent a better one."

Joe sighed. The promise of the red particles—verified as printer's ink by the spectroscope—seemed to be vaporizing. He was too anxious for leads, too ready to pin his hopes on any fleeting connection with the criminal. And yet, the spectroscope did not lie: there was red printer's ink on the paper, and printer's ink was not an ordinary household item. It was a special substance used for special purposes.

"What should we do now?" McFeeley asked.

"I'm getting a wire out to the FBI documents section and one to New York. The Los Angeles people told me that New York printers manufacture and job more than half of the printing forms in the country. They might have something like it—and if we could find a West Coast outfit using it, we might have a lead."

Again, the enormity of the search staggered the detective. Those tiny flecks of red—so small he did not even see them when he had the note—were supposed to light the way to the child, the criminal, to restore happiness to the stricken house, to enforce the law, to impose punishment.

"I suppose we've got to start phoning now," Joe said. "How many printing firms are there in LA?"

"Enough to keep a few guys busy the rest of the day," Raffalovitch said. "Then you better call the surrounding cities—Santa Monica, Santa Luisa—how far you want to go? It might've been printed in San Francisco."

"Or Seattle. Or Vancouver, B. C. Don't cheer me up, Raff. It sounded so good a few hours ago. I'll have Rheinholdt send a couple of men up. Get them started. Do me a favor, buddy. If any printing outfit has something that sounds even remotely like what we want, get on the phone."

"O.K. When you speak to Rheinholdt, don't say anything about the LA lab or the New York lab or the FBI. Last year, when I sent those glass samples to LA for diffraction, he almost canned me."

"Your secret is safe with me, Raff."

McFeeley immediately called Rheinholdt. Two men were assigned to the lab chief to begin phoning printers in the Los Angeles area. It would be slow, painful work, Joe knew—and work poorly done on the telephone. The job of describing the form was not an easy one. A team of men should have been assigned to call personally on each company. But this was a luxury they could not afford; each minute gained might be a minute gained toward saving the child.

The parents awaited him in the living room. The sight of their expectant, dependent faces depressed him; he wished he had better news.

Following his unnerving audience with Dr. Walter L. Todd, Eliot drove to the Andrus house in search of Harvey Swinnerton. The district man was the next logical participant in the chain of events that led to the publication of the story. Swinnerton's Austin was among the cars parked opposite the house, but the *Truth* reporter himself was not present. Eliot talked briefly to George Brack, who expressed his sorrow that he had been taken off the story. "Gee, El, it won't seem the same without you. You were always good for a few laughs." And Sparling, flicking away the commentator's compliment, responded: "Whaddya need me for, Georgie? The new guy can hold the mike for you just as good as me." Sparling then spoke briefly with Victor DeGroot. The AP man, relieved that Eliot's offensive person had been removed from coverage, was more friendly toward him.

A few more men drifted over—Arnspeiger, Duane Bosch, some new reporters—and Eliot directed the conversation toward the *Truth's* breaking the story. None of the men seemed concerned. They were under no orders to pursue an investigation of the matter. Like Tom Ballstead, and their editors, they regarded this as a "trade" matter. "Let *Editor & Publisher* worry about it," Arnspeiger said. "With that kid missing—maybe dead—and the whole country waiting to see what happened, who cares whether Hansel is lying or Rheinholdt's dumb? Can you think of anything duller, when maybe the girl is in a lime pit somewhere?"

Thus advised that his poking was of little interest, Eliot drove to the Santa Luisa headquarters to make another effort at questioning Sergeant Baines or Patrolman Hertmann. He realized Rheinholdt would not speak to him. But he also reasoned, with a certain keenness, that the double attack on the chief—the *Truth's* sharp editorial response and the rival *Argus'* denunciation—might force some explanation from the cops. It was highly possible that the *Truth* was right—that a lapse by the police had caused the story to be printed. In that case, neither Hertmann nor Baines would say anything. Or, Eliot mused, as he parked at the Jumboburger Drive-in, they might *invent* a story. There were wheels within wheels, the fatigued young man realized. He was almost happy that he had allotted his investigation only two days. By the following night—Wednesday—more properly, 1:00 A.M. Thursday—he would be on the overnight, yawning his way through newscasts, catching driblets of sleep on Ballstead's couch, awaiting the fierce hot dawn and another day of misery in his apartment. "Nuts to this hero business," Sparling muttered. "I'm not the type." Yet he was not quite ready to give up. He telephoned Patrolman Clyde Hertmann from the phone booth, gauging that he was more intelligent, more communicative than Farmer Baines.

"Come on down, Clyde," Eliot said. "I'll buy you a Coke."

"No. You guys want to make us look bad." Hertmann was talking in a guarded voice, as if shielding his words—probably from Baines, possibly from Rheinholdt himself.

"Me? UBC? We haven't attacked you—yet. Look, Clyde, I'm after a run-down on the phoning yesterday. You and Baines did it, didn't you? The *Truth* says you didn't call until 6:04. You better have an explanation."

Hertmann paused. After Eliot's clumsy attempt to quiz Baines that morning, Hertmann had hastily jotted down a chronology of telephone calls, as best as he remembered. The list was his own secret, and he would utilize it only for self-protection.

Eliot resumed. "You see the *Argus?* You see the case they're building up against you people? You better answer. Look—I won't quote you. I just want the straight stuff—*who called who when.*"

"I'll be down in five minutes," Hertmann said.

They sat in Eliot's car. Hertmann looked about cautiously.

"I can only stay a minute," he said. Then he gave Eliot his hand-written list of times and names. Sparling saw at once what it was. "Can I have this?"

"No. It's the only one I have."

"Can I copy it?"

"I guess so."

Eliot got out his pad and pencil. "You do this yesterday? While you and Baines were calling?"

"Baines did the calling. I looked up phone numbers."

"That ain't what I asked. You do this yesterday?"

Clyde Hertmann frowned. "I wonder why I'm showing this to you. What are you going to do with it?"

"A special report," Eliot said quickly. He was too exhausted to worry about lying.

"What kind? What are you talking about?" Hertmann still had one hand on the sheet of yellow paper.

"On the TV, Clyde. On United Broadcasting. You see, we're competitive with newspapers. It looks like they all got an agreement to hang Rheinholdt—and the rest of you cops. You won't find any one of them attacking the *Truth.* But *we* can do it."

Hertmann did not seem won over. "*You're* no bargain. Weren't you one of the people who followed the woman down the street? How'd you get so innocent?"

Eliot blinked. "A misunderstanding. I'm sorry for what I did. I was wrong. I'd admit I was wrong publicly. Catch Mona Mears admitting that. You show her this list?"

"I haven't shown it to anyone."

"And you did it yesterday—while Baines was calling?"

"I did it this morning. After the reporters left."

Sparling smiled. "Pretty bright guy you are, Clyde. A little prevention worth a pound of cure, hey?"

Hertmann released his hand. "It's accurate. I just don't want to be quoted. Rheinholdt'll guess where this came from. I have my own neck to think of." He looked sharply at the reporter. "I don't care whether you believe me or not—but I don't want to be responsible for what's happened to that kid. I got kids of my own."

"Sure, Clyde, sure." The relentless sun, low at 4:00 P.M., turned the yellow sheet a fiery gold. Eliot began copying the entries.

The first notation read: *3:36: Argus.* Eliot scanned the other listings. The other newspapers were listed, evidently in alphabetical order. Then there appeared the entry: *4:10: Swinnerton, LA Truth.* This was followed by a series of entries for radio and television. He wondered why only Swinnerton's name was listed; the others merely indicated the name of the newspaper or station. There was an entry for UBC at 4:23, then a few more broadcast organizations. And then, puzzlingly, appeared this listing:

4:30: Hood, LA Truth, called back

This was followed by entries for the AP, UP, INS and WNA, all made between 4:30 and 4:45. Finally there appeared a notation:

6:04: Rheinholdt called Hood

Eliot allowed himself a few minutes to digest the entries. The three listings for the *Truth* were the heart of the problem, but he had trouble making any sense out of them. He went back to the first listing: *4:10: Swinnerton, LA Truth.*

"How come you wrote only his name down? And how come you called a district man, instead of the desk, like with everyone else?"

"What's the difference?"

"I have to know. Is this why Rheinholdt's statement was so vague? Why he left everything out? Big Jerk. He shoulda leveled. And you better, Hertmann."

The young patrolman flushed. "Baines didn't call Swinnerton."

"He didn't?" Eliot's eyebrows met in a pointed arch.

"Swinnerton called us—just about when we were getting ready to call his office. He wanted Rheinholdt, but Rheinholdt wasn't talking to anyone. Can you blame him? So we—Baines and me—we figured, why waste a call? We told Swinnerton about the kidnaping, to give the word to his people. That is, Baines did. I never got on the phone to talk."

"How come you know all this, then?"

"I monitored the calls on an extension. Swinnerton kept blabbering that they had a lot more dope than we gave them and that he had to talk to Rheinholdt, but Baines refused. It was up to Swinnerton to tell his boss. Baines said if no one called back from the *Truth,* we'd figure they agreed, like everyone else."

"Makes sense," Eliot said. "So neither of you guys got to anyone at the *Truth* office?"

"Swinnerton *might* have been in the office. I don't know where he called from." Hertmann was getting annoyed.

"I don't mean that. You didn't call any editors?"

"Why should we? He promised to call his desk. And he did. The proof is, this guy Hood called back twenty minutes later. See the entry?"

Sparling squinted at the sheet again: *4:30: Hood, LA Truth, called back.* "What'd Herbie say?"

"Who?"

"Herbie. Fat Herbie Hood. I used to work at the *Truth.* I know all the inmates. Did he want Rheinholdt also?"

"That's right. Baines asked the chief to talk to him, but the chief refused. We'd given them their chance, Rheinholdt said. Hood told us they'd print unless they had an assurance from the chief *personally* that everyone else was withholding."

"Hood said they'd *print?*" Eliot's hands shook slightly as he made notations in his pad: he was close to some enormous truth. "At 4:30?"

"Maybe a few minutes later. He told Baines the police would be to blame if the child was hurt."

Eliot rubbed his nose. "Lemme get this straight. Hood wanted Rheinholdt to give him a *personal* assurance everyone was laying off? He wouldn't take your word?"

"*Baines'* word. Unless it came from Rheinholdt, it was no go."

Eliot did some calculation. Hood had called at 4:30. He had spent at least five minutes on the phone. The *Truth's* edition was out at 5:07. Therefore, they must have been already printing, already preparing for circulation when Hood called. If Rheinholdt had talked to him, would they have really pulled back? Sparling could make little sense out of it. Why did Hood call? The old lizard would have pounced on every excuse in the book to get the edition out. Could he have had an incredible pang of conscience? A sense of disgust so overwhelming as to make him jeopardize the news beat of a lifetime?

"And this 6:04 call—that's one that you and the *Truth* agree on, right?"

"Yes," Hertmann said, getting out of the car. "Rheinholdt wanted to ream them out for what they'd done. It wasn't any request to lay off, like they said. We were way past that, and we knew it, and they knew it. The chief just wanted to blast them."

"They say it was the first *official* notification that they shouldn't print."

Hertmann shaded his face. "From the chief's own mouth, sure. But, I'm telling you, Swinnerton knew at 4:10. We were all set to call his paper when he called us for information; so we told *him*. What was wrong with that?"

"Hmm?" Eliot was staring at the yellow sheet. "Nothing, Clyde. You did the right thing."

"Besides, I don't see how that newspaper can talk the way they did," Hertmann went on. "This guy Hood—what's he?—the editor?"

"General manager."

"He called us *himself* at 4:30, and, by God, *he* knew. He told us they were printing it unless the chief talked to him personally. You ever hear anything so cheap?"

"It was pretty chicken."

The patrolman left him, then turned. "Just keep my name out of it. Last thing I want is to get hung if anything's happened to the kid." He crossed the parking lot, a slim man in a gray uniform—a cop with a good future if he kept his nose clean, made the right connections, offended no one.

Sparling studied his notes. Several things disturbed him. It seemed almost too fortuitous, too perfect for the police case that there had been not one but *two* calls from the *Truth's* people. Moreover, why had no one mentioned them the previous day? Why had Rheinholdt left them out of his statement that morning? The chief's generalities had been an open invitation to the *Truth*— and its confederates—to slaughter him. Eliot wondered: could Hertmann's willingness to meet with him—could the 4:10 call from Swinnerton and the 4:30 call from Hood—be fiction that the police had invented in the hope of shifting blame? The 6:04 call he knew to be verifiable: his girl friend Connie had taken it, and both the newspaper and the police agreed that it had occurred. Where they differed was in describing the *purpose* of the call—Hertmann contending that it was a bawling out, Hansel and Hood asserting that it was their first official notification. And, again, he was bothered by Hood's return call—if it had ever occurred. It did not mesh with his estimate of his former boss. Backing his Ford out of the Jumboburger lot, Sparling realized he had to get Swinnerton's version and, if possible, Hood's version. Perhaps he could pry something out of poor Harvey. But Hood! Fat Herbie would knee him in the groin before talking about the Andrus matter.

At 4:30 Laura left the house. In scuffed loafers, a gray pleated skirt, a sleeveless white blouse, she might have been off to the A&P. She carried the ransom package in a raffia shopping bag. McFeeley, looking at the remnants of the press corps, decided to attempt a ruse. He had her leave by the rear door. In the yard, in back of the swimming pool, he helped her over the four-foot rustic fence. Meanwhile, Milt Bannon drove the station wagon around the block. It was reasoned that she should drive her own car. The assumption was that the caller, if the actual kidnaper, knew her red station wagon. Her appearance in any other automobile might make him suspicious.

It was a good try on McFeeley's part. He had no way of knowing that Timmy Emerson was being paid a dollar an hour to watch the back of the Andrus house from his bedroom window. As soon as the teen-ager saw Mrs. Andrus being helped over the fence by two detectives, he ran from the house, crossed the street and informed the waiting group. Immediately, Duane Bosch, Dave Arnspeiger, and a photographer from the *Truth* took off in pursuit in Bosch's hot rod. McFeeley, accompanying Laura in her own car, which met her around the block, had no idea that pursuit was under way.

Laura drove slowly. The caller had stipulated *between 4:30 and 5:00*. It would take her about ten minutes to get to the intersection of Patio and New Toledo. McFeeley had reviewed the procedure with her a dozen times. She was to approach the Patio Road, do a full circle just beyond the overpass, then come back underneath it, traveling east. Thus, she could stop the car along the right-hand side, look for the folded newspaper, leave the package and depart quickly. Three blocks from the intersection, she was to halt, read the note and await McFeeley, who would accompany her home.

In accord with the whisperer's instructions, an additional two thousand dollars, these drawn by Fritzie from their own meager bank account, had been added to the ransom. *Sixty-two hundred dollars*. In the wasting heat, Laura shuddered. One spent that much —in the higher brackets in Fritzie's profession—for a sports car, a fur coat, on a boat, a down payment on a beach house, a vacation in Europe. It seemed a dreadfully small amount for her daughter. She wondered: does he know the agony he has caused us? Does he care? Can he imagine what we are suffering? The false assurances of the drugs had evanesced. Todd's soothing words of the previous day; the dumb insistence of the police that the child would be returned—neither of these had left any residue of courage in her. She was afraid now, sickeningly afraid. She had no more props—false, honest, contrived—for herself. That hard rationality that had stanched tears the previous day now served her poorly. It convinced her that the worst had happened, or would happen; that her miserable ritual of driving to the sunlit intersection, bright with mammoth automobiles, shops, gay browned people, was a fraud and a cheat. One went through the motions—turning a steering wheel, signaling for a right turn, depressing a brake—actions useless and doomed. She performed them in a trance, her mind frigid with terror. *How did he do it? Quickly? Painlessly? Telling her to look the other way? Distracting her with a toy?* A wail escaped her dry lips. *I will never fear death: I will never be mean or intolerant or impatient or cruel. . . .*

She felt as she did many years ago, when she was attending boarding school in Vermont. She had failed algebra. Her family—academicians and teachers all—was horrified. Laura Todd *had* to get good marks; it was expected of her; her *parents* had always gotten good marks. She could recall sitting in their stuffy, gloomy living room during the start of summer vacation, the insect hum outside, the heat penetrating the baking white boards, while a group of relatives pumped her eagerly about her work at school. *I'll bet you're the most popular girl there . . . and A's in everything . . . it's a Todd family tradition. . . .* And she and her parents had nodded, smiled, chatted about Laura's wonderful achievements at the Hosmer School, none of them mentioning the wrenching fact: *she had failed algebra.* She had sat through the hot ordeal as if sinking, dying: her answers, her smiles, her participation bore no relation to herself, the eviscerating fears within her. And now, guiding the car through traffic, past a blur of bright shops and sunny homes, she had that same sense of doomed, meaningless participation. In this narcotized state, she did not notice Duane Bosch's Model-A Ford trailing her.

She reached the intersection. A stretch of Patio had been converted into a thruway: grass islands, high concrete curbs, aluminum street lights. She drove to the point where this section ended, backed on to a side street, then approached the overpass from the opposite direction. As she turned right, off Patio, down the incline to New Toledo, she saw the old Ford car bounce by her. She remembered it as one of the cars that were parked across the street. She recognized the blond boy at the wheel. *They will follow me to the grave,* she thought, unable any longer to summon up anger, disgust, outrage. If her actions were pointless, what did it matter that they were witness to them? She did not slow down, nor look behind her to see Duane Bosch maneuver a frantic U turn on the highway, swerving from a truck at the last minute.

"What the hell's she doing?" Arnspeiger asked.

"Probably spotted us," Bosch piped. "I bet she's going back to squeal to McFeeley."

"His own fault," Arnspeiger grumbled. "Did he stop us? Did he say we couldn't follow her?"

"Ah, she was probably going to the beauty parlor, anyway," Bosch said. "We can't run after her every minute like this."

They followed her under the Patio overpass. As soon as they entered the brief tunnel, they saw that the station wagon had halted. The motor was still running. She had gotten out and was picking something up from the roadside. The thruway was four-lane; passing cars honked and drivers shouted at her as they whizzed by in the dim light. The reporter saw her set a package down. It was the same package she had left the night before—the fat manila envelope.

"Holy Jesus," Arnspeiger said. "Another drop."

"Should I move closer?" Bosch asked. His sneakered foot was light on the gas. With a light tap he could make the hot rod leap.

Laura got back into the car: she seemed to be carrying a newspaper. Her station wagon drove off. They could see it make a right turn and vanish from view.

"Another drop," Arnspeiger repeated.

"Well, heck, Dave, what should we do?" the boy asked. "I mean —someone might come. The guy——"

"Wait a minute," Arnspeiger said. "Hold your water. I got to think." The photographer hopped out of the car, ran half the length of the tunnel and took a photograph of the package lying against the side of the stone wall. As he did, the plain-clothes men, stationed in a dairy truck outside the overpass, saw him. They drove into the tunnel. The photographer hurried back to the waiting

Ford and the dairy truck pulled alongside him in the opposite lane. Arnspeiger recognized one of the men as a Sanlu detective, and, after a brief, sharp argument, the newsmen agreed to leave. Since the detectives made no threats of jailing, or other punishments, the model-A Ford and its three occupants merely retired to the access road outside the tunnel and waited.

Three blocks from the overpass, Laura stopped the car. McFeeley was waiting for her. He got into the station wagon, taking the wheel, and drove another two blocks. When they had reached a row of half-finished ranch houses, he stopped.

"You look at it yet?" he asked.

"No. You'd better do it." She handed him the newspaper. It was, as the whisperer had promised, a copy of the *Santa Luisa Register*— yesterday morning's edition, the one Timmy Emerson had been delivering when he saw Amy. McFeeley opened it. There was nothing on the front page. He began turning pages slowly, pausing at each one, searching for some code, some informative markings.

McFeeley kept turning pages, scanning the columns of news, sports, movie reviews, advertisements. CLEARANCE SELLING OUT ENTIRE STOCK greeted him. Then, as he turned two pages past the second section, they saw the obscenity—two words, the ultimate vulgar pronouncement. These had been scrawled—a four-letter word and a three-letter word—in giant black characters with a brush of some kind, and they filled the upper half of the page. Splotchy, vicious, they had size and smell and shape—a quality of inherent and insistent evil about them.

Laura covered her eyes. "It was a prank," she said sadly. "A joke."

Joe studied the obscene message and folded the paper carefully. He could think of no consolation. Yesterday, he had promised her the return of her child. That had been easy. What could he say in the face of the depraved affront?

"Some damn crank," he said. "We've got to expect it, Mrs. Andrus. You're fair game now." He swung the car around, heading back to the tunnel. "I'll pick the package up. Whoever it is, they'll never show." Then, as if to offer her some marginal comfort, he said: "We'll catch *this* one. Those psychos always try again. He should know what the penalty for extortion is. Twenty years—and he'll get all of it."

As he spoke, a wrenched, almost tearful note crept into his

emotional voice. He imagined she had not noticed; her eyes were shut and she was breathing heavily, as if recovering from an asthmatic attack, an attempted asphyxiation.

A garland of telegrams littered Theodore T. Hansel's desk. He had them so arranged that he could read them without picking them up, without shifting in the seat of authority. One was from the board chairman of the Organization. It read:

CONGRATULATIONS KIDNAP BEAT THIS OLD-FASH-IONED ENTERPRISE THAT BUILDS READERSHIP AND ADVERTISING REGARDS

Hansel's feverish face threw off a warmth as he reread the messages. He was still young enough to be moved by praise. When the executives had chosen him for the high post, he had been given a mandate: revive the *Truth*. For several years he had labored manfully: puzzle contests, an expanded entertainment section, more comics, serialized fiction, a TV-radio supplement—and all had failed. Now, he felt, he was on the right track. He believed in himself and in his mission. Unlike the Herbert Hoods, lesser men with lesser goals, he had never been depressed by the shoddiness, the inconsequentiality of his journal. Since this eluded him, he entered his assignment with a full heart and an energy that never flagged. He was dictating a memorandum to his general manager about the Andrus coverage when Mona Mears burst into the room, Hood trailing her. The latter never entered Hansel's office without a polite knock. Mona observed no such protocol. She could quit any day she wanted.

"How's my best girl?" Hansel asked. He rose and kissed the woman's scented cheek.

"I've got a hot one for tomorrow," Mears said. She sat beneath Hansel's Olympic Elk, crossing her marvelous legs. Hood remained standing. A cigarette's glowing stub was set at mid-point in his lips, and he appeared oblivious to its approaching fire, the smoke that drifted into his eyes.

"How could you top this morning's performance, sweetie?" Hansel asked. The Editor & Publisher held up the front page of the bulldog edition. Above the logo ran the red-lettered words:

MONA MEARS MAKES LONELY WALK WITH LAURA

"I'm having it framed for you," T.T. said. "The best, the absolutely best front page this paper has ever had. Don't you think so, Herbert?"

Hood had wandered to the window. One cheek of his fat butt rested on the sill. "You bet, Ted. It's a pee-whistler."

"You're both angels," the columnist said. "But like my daddy used to say—put it in money and save the compliments for Christmas."

Hansel threw his ruddy head back and laughed heartily. *What the hell was so funny about that?* Hood mused. *I've said funnier things, and you never laugh at me.*

"Have you gotten a police contact yet?" Hansel asked.

"Not yet. That idiot Rheinholdt won't say a word, and his flunkies are no help. That boy running things out there—McFeeley—there's a beauty. A donkey if ever I saw one. I can't abide shanty Irish, being part cut-glass mick myself."

Again, Hansel guffawed. "Well, I'm counting on you to pry it loose from him!" he cried. "Even your honor, Mona!"

"Ted, that went in 1928, when I got Mancini's confession from the New York cops!" They joined in laughter.

Hood could stand it no longer. "The mother made another trip out of the house a few minutes ago. No one's sure what it is. That's the second today."

Hansel looked at him as if he had never known anyone named Herbert Hood in his life, then looked again at Mona.

"It can't mean anything," Mears said. "She went to look at mug shots this morning. My Irish friend probably has her looking at a line-up of tramps."

"Ah—it might be more important," Hood stammered. "She tried to sneak out the back, but some of the boys saw her and followed. The reporters at the house have set up another pool."

Neither of them was listening. There was a bond between T. T. Hansel and Mona Mears, a gossamer net that united them and excluded the likes of Herb Hood. It was difficult to analyze this fragile web, but it had to do with friends in high seats of government, black-tie dinners at the right club, first-night openings, a half-dozen restaurants in the country—21, the Pump Room, Perino's, Ernie's—and, above all, a freewheeling right of way in the celebrity world. These were credentials Herbert Hood lacked; he was an all-night drinker who took his booze anywhere. He liked Chicago better than New York.

"Tell me what you've got for tomorrow," Hansel said, ignoring the general manager. "If you can top today's, I may marry you."

"Not a chance, Ted. I love you professionally, but you ain't my type."

Mona told of her visit with the Andrus family. The woman had been rude, abrupt, suspicious. The man, reeking of bourbon, had been worse and had thrown her out of the house with insulting language. She had promised to get Laura in touch with her underworld contacts—she mentioned the name of a famous Los Angeles hoodlum—but the Andrus woman would have none of it.

"There was something fishy about her," the columnist said. "I can't put my finger on it, but she's all wrong. Maybe a little nuts. Very eastern. Ivy League. Sculpture and a flat behind and all that jazz. But there's a wheel missing, or a gear slipped, or a few parts left out."

"That won't do for a column," Hood said hastily. Hansel quieted him with a wave of his hand. "Go on, Mona."

"I tried the neighbors. I had already been after the Emerson woman, that weepy slob next door, but she wouldn't say boo. Then there's a family of Greek fruit importers across the street. They looked me over like I was a Turk and wouldn't talk. Then I struck pay dirt."

"Pay dirt or just dirt?" Hood asked.

Hansel spun in his chair. "Herbert, you don't help with these comments. Can't you realize what Mona's done? Good God, she's making this story for us."

"Sorry, Ted. Sorry, Mona."

"*Niente,* Herb. The family on the other side is named Kahler, an older couple—the man's a retired naturotherapist. I had to loosen their tongues a little, but did I get a columnful when they opened up!"

The woman placed an odd, flat cigarette in the corner of her purple mouth. Hansel got up and lit it for her.

"Thanks, Teddy," she said. "Well, I won't bore you with the grisly details, but the message I got is this—*that woman hated the kid's guts, couldn't stand her.*"

Hansel folded his arms and listened. Hood got up from the window seat and turned his back.

"Both the Kahlers—old Yankee types—heard her say a dozen times she couldn't handle the child, that with the new baby she was going out of her mind taking care of the two."

T.T. frowned. "I'd be careful with that sort of stuff. I mean—they weren't poor people. The husband a television director, that big house. She could have had all the servants she wanted."

"She had a cleaning woman four times a week," Mears said quickly. "She's the kind who would deliberately make extra work so she could be martyred. She *likes* being in trouble. You ask me, she's wallowing in what's hit her now."

Hood could no longer keep silent. "I don't believe that," he said. "Mona, you have to go easy. Remember what happened when you wrote that that actress was on the booze?"

"She *was*," Mona said. "I proved it."

"Yeah, but we were in the courts for a year, and she ended up in a laughing academy. Her doctors said we helped."

"We won the case, didn't we?" the columnist said sharply. "Herb, if you'll stop interrupting, I'll make my point."

"Yes, yes. Herbert—stop talking nonsense." Hansel was annoyed.

"Well, Mrs. Kahler remembered the Andrus woman saying she didn't know how she could manage the girl, now that the baby took all her time."

"Go on," Hansel said.

"Evidently that little girl was something of a problem child. She was always in other people's houses, wandering around, getting lost, getting into trouble—mainly because her mother wouldn't bother to keep an eye on her. I'm a lousy psychologist, and I've never had kids, but it seems to me she *wanted* that kid to get lost. You know—like the guy who keeps misplacing the raincoat he can't stand because his mother gave it to him and he hates her."

"I know what you're getting at," Hood said thickly. "And I think you're nuts."

The two ignored him. Mears dragged on her cigarette. "Another thing—I know the girl was supposed to be bright as hell, precocious. But I learned she was kicked out of two nursery schools. She had a crazy habit of talking about a fictitious friend she invented—to anybody."

Hansel strode back to his desk. He sat on the edge, pensive. "Do I understand you correctly, Mona?" the Editor & Publisher asked. "Are you saying Mrs. Andrus is *glad* the child was kidnaped?"

The woman's face halted in mid-grimace. It was a shame, Hood thought, that she could not have her long corsets made eight inches higher to cover that mug. "I'm not sure, Ted," she said slowly. "That's the *minimum* charge I can make against her. God knows she's a cold one. Hasn't wept, broken down, made a scene. But I have something else in mind."

"Like what?" asked Hood.

"Like maybe it isn't a kidnaping at all."

"Oh, for Christ's sake," Herbert Hood said. "Let's not go off on that. There's a ransom note. There was a rendezvous with a kidnaper last night. A package of money. Every cop in Sanlu is out looking for a kidnaper. Jesus, Mona, you astound me sometimes."

She ignored him, addressing herself to T.T.: "Ted, do you know how rare actual kidnapings are? I called Washington this morning and checked the FBI. They're so rare the bureau doesn't even include them in their Uniform Crime Reports. But, beyond that, most of the cases classified as kidnapings aren't the real thing— you know, ransom asked, person seized and threatened. They're usually associated with theft and rape cases, someone getting carted across a state line, but there's no question of ransom payment involved. Hell, there were only thirty-seven convictions for *any* kind of kidnaping last year, twenty-three the year before. But there couldn't have been more than one or two that were true ransom kidnapings."

"What are you trying to prove?" Hood muttered.

Hansel said nothing: he was lost in admiration for her.

"I quote the federal law on kidnapings," Mears said, studying her memo pad. "The U. S. Code says its a kidnaping if you knowingly transport in interstate commerce any person unlawfully seized, confined, inveigled, decoyed, kidnaped, abducted or carried away and held for ransom or reward or otherwise. Get the *otherwise*. That would include a deputy sheriff carted off by escaping cons as a shield—no question of ransom. What I'm driving at, Ted, is that an actual kidnaping for ransom is the rarest crime in the world. Those convictions in the last two years—practically every one is like that deputy sheriff. You've got to scratch real hard to find a Lindbergh case—person seized, money asked. And that's why you've got to be suspicious when you confront a crime that's *supposed* to be a ransom kidnaping. They hardly ever happen. That's why I think this Andrus deal may be something else."

Hansel cocked his head. "What *do* you think?"

"Well, don't hang me. All I've got to go on is that woman's personality, that drunken jerk of a husband, and a kid that was a problem child. A happy home, if you know what I mean."

"And?" asked T.T.

"I think—I can't prove it yet—but I think she may have done the kid in herself."

Neither man spoke. Mona blew a cloud of smoke into the hollow, frozen silence. Perhaps she sensed she was going too far, perhaps not. The elegant legs uncrossed themselves, crossed again. Hansel walked to his chair but did not sit.

"That's a unique theory," he said. "We'd have to have more than that to go on."

"It stinks," Hood said. "I wouldn't touch it."

"May I remind you both," the columnist said, "that this thing has happened before? I can remember at least two suspected kidnapings that turned out to be infanticides. One was in Milwaukee—about 1934. The other was down south somewhere, Georgia or Alabama. The mother claimed it was a kidnaping. The kid, it turned out, was backward. I think they found the one in Milwaukee. They're still searching culverts for the other. Look—it's horrible. But these things happen."

"It's a *little* rough, Mona," Hansel said. "I don't see how we can tackle that angle. Now, if we learned that the *police* were pursuing this line of questioning, we might."

The columnist got up. "I give it to you for what it's worth. Can I try to hand out a 'More to This Than Meets the Eye' piece? Where I wouldn't make any charges, but just raise a lot of questions? The unhappy home, the separated couple, the frustrated mother? I'd like to set it up for the future. I have a feeling I'm going to be proven right."

"I hope not," Hood said.

"Yes, Mona. It would be horrible if that *were* the truth."

"Well, aren't you a couple of sweethearts! Gents, I got a bulletin for you. There's mean people in the world who do mean things. And we write it, and you print it, and they buy it."

Hansel blew her a kiss. "Herbert and I were just thinking about the little girl."

"Who isn't? I'd give six months' salary if we could bring her back. I have nothing against kids."

"Let me see your copy as soon as you have it," Hansel said. "We've got to play it by ear. You won't be mad at me if I use the blue pencil?"

"Not me, Ted. I've been censored by the best."

She left. Hood watched the indecent movements of her ironclad form and had a desire to throw a tomato at her. She was the only person in the shop to whom T. T. Hansel deferred.

"Swinnerton called a little while ago," Hood said. "You remember that kid Sparling I had on the overnight? The one we canned?"

Hansel looked blank.

"The one who got jailed yesterday for hanging around." Still there was no response. "The one who blabbed about Schlossmann's suicide."

"What about him?"

"He's with UBC now and he's poking around about our printing the story. He's been questioning people and trying to find out who's telling the truth—us or the cops. He got hold of Swinnerton and tried to pump him, but Harvey wouldn't talk."

"Why in the world should he do that?" asked Hansel.

"I don't know. UBC's always been friends of ours. We've done 'em favors on local stuff. Tom Ballstead knows me. It sounds like they're going to do a run-down on what happened yesterday and try to hang someone for it."

"Hang someone? What are you talking about, Herbert? Just make sure Swinnerton keeps his mouth shut. Besides, what can he say?"

"I don't know." Hood paced the office, his hands jammed in his rear pants pockets. "He wasn't in on what went on here."

T.T. would not be frightened. "It's idiotic. Herbert, Matthew Hinrichsen is one of my closest friends. He and his wife were over for dinner the other night. He even talked about some promotional tie-in between UBC advertisers and the *Truth*. If Ballstead and this moron Sparling get any wild ideas, I'll simply call Hinrichsen and straighten them out."

Hood sighed. "O.K. Who's Hinrichsen?"

"He's the West Coast vice-president." He lowered his head to some memoranda, then looked up. "What are you waiting for?"

"What about Swinnerton?"

"What about him?"

Hood loosened his tie. "We ought to do something about him."

"You're worried, aren't you, Herbert?"

"Nobody expects to see that child alive again. I don't believe Mona's pipe dreams about the mother being responsible. Could we get Swinnerton another job—in Chicago? Or Pittsburgh? Get him out of town?"

Hansel buzzed his intercom. "Nonsense, Herbert. This ridiculous affair will be forgotten in a few days. Our job is to stay on the story."

A voracious thirst roiled Hood's stomach, sucked his throat and mouth dry. He looked forward to another long night in the city room, followed by an evening's drinking at his favorite saloon, a few hours of sleep on his private cot.

After taking Laura home, Joe McFeeley stayed at the house long enough to check Bannon and Case on the log. There had been more calls: newspapers, magazines, radio stations, cranks, tipsters, the honestly helpful. Nothing worth-while had turned up. It was agreed that anyone wanting to talk with the parents would have to supply sentences from the ransom note. Laura would not be subjected to any more vain missions, any more degenerate pranks, any extortion plots. Bannon had interrogated Selena again; the colored maid had been surly but co-operative. She offered nothing that seemed of value. Two men were in Sanlu tracking down delivery boys, messengers, the Andrus gardener. The reports were being gathered in Rheinholdt's office. None of them showed anything in the way of a lead.

McFeeley spoke briefly to the parents before leaving. They were both quiet, numbed. The mother busied herself with the baby. The man drifted about the house—pitiful, lost, embarrassed by his helplessness. Joe told them a little about the lab work—the search for the ransom paper—and left.

At headquarters he ran up to the lab and gave Raffalovitch the copy of the *Santa Luisa Register* with its message. "Present for you," Joe said. "Turn to page twenty-three." The lab chief did so cautiously. His beaked face puckered when he saw the foul words. "You kiddin'?" he asked McFeeley. Joe explained how they had gotten the newspaper. He doubted that it had anything to do with the kidnaper. "Latent prints, ink analysis," Joe said. "I guess you can't do much beyond that."

"It'll have to wait its turn," Raffalovitch said. "Why don't you put in a good word for me when the budget comes up again?"

McFeeley asked him about the hunt for the office form.

"No go so far," Raffalovitch said. "There's two guys been phoning printers all afternoon. They've found forms with red on 'em, but not where we want it." He showed Joe two sheets of white bond paper, both 8½ by 11. On one, he had drawn a line with a red crayon along one long side, beginning about a half inch from the margin and extending to the opposite margin. The second had a red crayon line across the *width*, seven inches from the top. "I go for the first one," Raffalovitch said. "Some kind of red line or lettering, a quarter inch in, not quite seven inches down on the long side."

Frowning at it, he told Joe it was a tedious business. Raffalovitch pointed to the wall clock. "Almost 6:00. Most of these places are closing. We'll start 'em on it again tomorrow. Who knows? It might be a New York outfit printed the form."

"Or maybe it isn't a form," Joe added.

The lab chief shook his head. "Printer's ink doesn't get on by accident. It doesn't just lay around the house, like writing ink or paint."

Joe kneaded the back of his neck; he was agonizingly tired. "Raff—aren't there outfits like printers' associations? You know—a trade magazine or something? People who could circularize every printing firm in the United States for us?"

"Must be. I'll find out."

"Anything from the FBI documents file? New York?"

"Jesus, not so loud. I should know tomorrow."

He left Raffalovitch and hurried downstairs to catch the chief before he left. Rheinholdt sounded reasonably coherent. He discussed the lines of investigation sensibly and listened with much interest to Joe's account of the hunt he had started for the ransom note. All the interrogation reports were being gathered in a file on Rheinholdt's desk. To this would be added typescripts of the logs kept at the house, McFeeley's notes of the previous day, and any other data. The chief wanted Joe in his office in the morning for a full review of the material. Then he held up a second folder and his troglodyte's eyes glinted. "And this is my private file," he said. "Everything those newspapers write about me. You see the *Argus* this morning? That editorial? Doesn't that prove they're after me? I didn't attack *them*. It was just that other rag. But I'll get back at 'em when we've solved it. Not the FBI, not the LA cops. But us, McFeeley."

By the time Joe reached his home, his neck and back felt as if they had been worked over with bicycle chains—the kind teen-age galoots used in their rumbles. He tore off his jacket and tie, kicked off his shoes and collapsed on the bed. Roz sat beside him.

"Here. You want something to eat?"

"Wait a minute. I'm beat. You look fine. How am I?"

His wife studied his lean, slanted face. There was a smear of newsprint on his forehead, lines of weariness around his crooked mouth.

"You look awful, McFeeley, if you must know. I bet you hardly slept."

Joe yawned. "A few hours. It's not the lack of sleep. It's the work." He told her about the vain errand of the afternoon; the obscene message; the pointless cruelty.

"I think I hate that guy more than the kidnaper," he said. "I could stick my heel in his mouth and turn it a few times. How lousy can people be? Woman's eating herself up with misery and some nut has to add his miserable joke. I bet if we got him, he'd get off anyway—psycho!"

She shook her head. "All your problem, isn't it?"

"Why not? That's my job."

"Yeah. All forty-two hundred bucks a year's worth. Joe, you should get out. As soon as you finish night school, you should start looking. You had a chance—that sales job that Midge's brother-in-law wanted for you. Anything pays better than what you have."

"I can't help it. I'm a born cop. I like to be in charge." He sat up. "I better call Mr. Shapiro. I've missed two nights this week already. I'll have to have him give me a make-up exam in chemistry."

"Relax. I called him. He's so proud of his prize adult education student—working on the Andrus case."

Joey and Mary Grace trooped in. "Milton Berle's on tonight, Pop. You wanna watch with us?" Joey asked.

"C'n I stay up?" Mary Grace piped.

"No and no," Joe said. "That all you people can talk about? Television? No hello for your old man?"

"Hiya, Pop," Joey said. "You catch that guy yet?"

"He's in the trunk rack of the Dodge," Roz said. "Joey, what kind of question is that?"

"The kids at school were all talkin' about it today," Joey said.

Mary Grace nudged her brother. "Tell Pop what you heard them singin'."

"Aw, it was crazy. The big kids. They were chasin' each other and yellin', 'Who put the snatch on the Andrus baby—was it you, was it you, was it you?' " He sang in a high, sweet voice.

Roz winced. "That isn't so funny. Don't go around saying it."

"No, it's not funny at all, Joey," McFeeley said. He raised himself on one arm. "You shouldn't make jokes about it."

"Is she dead?" asked Mary Grace.

"Shut up!" Roz cried. "She isn't! Don't talk about it. The two of you downstairs."

"Don't forget, Pop," Joey said. "Milton Berle."

The children walked out. "Everyone's a comedian today," Roz said. "It's not how much you know, it's how funny you are."

"Yeah. I guess that's my trouble." He leaned back on the chenille bedspread, staring at the plasterboard ceiling, joined so poorly to the plasterboard wall. There was hardly room to turn around in the master bedroom (*Santa Luisa Garden Acres: Ranch Homes —$12,990: 6½ huge rooms*) now that they had moved a small desk into it, where he could do his homework. Homework. A thirty-four year-old cop doing homework.

"Chow?" Roz asked. "The kids finished the chicken. Want some bacon and eggs? A tuna fish salad?"

"No, baby." He squeezed her hand—red, the nails well chewed. "Some iced tea is all. I'm too tired to eat."

When she came back with it, fifteen minutes later—after breaking up a fight between Joey and Mary Grace and catching Jeanie in the act of climbing into the baby's crib—her husband was asleep, the harsh lights investing his face with the look of an exhausted boy.

Mayor Palmer Speed flicked on the radio on his desk to catch the 8:00 o'clock evening news on the local station, WSLR. The door of his office was opened and he could, by rising, peer over the brass railing around the second floor of City Hall and see the auditorium below. He stoked his pipe and listened to the announcer's mellow California tones.

"Here in Santa Luisa, another day of frustration for the parents of Amy Andrus. This afternoon, the kidnaped girl's mother was seen making a trip to the overpass at Patio and New Toledo in the outskirts of Sanlu. Mrs. Andrus left a package identical with the one spurned by the kidnaper last night and was seen picking up a newspaper. However, something evidently went wrong in the apparent move to contact the kidnaper, for, a few minutes later, detectives retrieved the package and Mrs. Andrus returned to her house on 4217 Nespoli Drive. . . ."

Mayor Speed had on his desk all of the day's newspapers but he had no stomach for them any longer. He had read the attacks on Rheinholdt's police administration too many times. In his good-natured view of the world he found it painful to listen to the sounds of anger. As he often advised his fellow Council members when the in-fighting got rough, *keep it clean, boys, keep it clean.* And he had kept it clean in Santa Luisa. The best local government for a city under 100,000 population in the state! He sighed noisily. Why did this thing have to happen in his beloved Santa Luisa? The radio droned on, and he listened, peeking over the railing every now and then at the meeting room below.

". . . criticism of Chief Rheinholdt's handling of the case continues to mount. A petition was circulated in Sanlu today demanding that Mayor Palmer Speed, who appointed Rheinholdt in 1943, dismiss him. Those spearheading the move to force Rheinholdt's resignation include officials of the Good Government League, the local opposition party. Emery Kalisher, chairman of the Good Government League, told station WSLR that he intends to bring up the matter of Rheinholdt's mishandling of the Andrus case at tonight's meeting. He says he hopes to get a majority of City Council members to vote with him. . . ."

They didn't give a hoot about Rheinholdt, Mayor Speed told himself. *They are after me. They will crucify me for this terrible thing because I appointed Caspar and I protected him.* Did they ever have a more honest police administration? A finer traffic and parking plan? How could they possibly blame Rheinholdt—in all the confusion of the previous day, with all those reporters hanging around? He, Speed, had been the essence of politeness to the press. True, Rheinholdt and Joe McFeeley had been a little hasty, but Palmer Speed understood and liked reporters. He had freed that fellow Sparling, and then he had intervened to allow the others to cover the ransom drop, when Joe was getting ready to arrest the mob! Not a line about Mayor Speed's considerate action—just denunciations, accusations, dark hints.

He walked stiffly out of his office, a handsome, white-maned man of sixty, a believer in the good in people (if we can talk things over, there's nothing we can't lick), and he gazed down at the crowd. It would be a full house. He could see the Good Government gang—the new tract housing people—with eastern accents and foreign names—filling the front rows, where they could put the pressure on him. And there was Emery Kalisher, the attorney, running around, petition in his hand, soliciting signatures, talking very fast and very loud. Emery Kalisher always sat in the first row and communicated with his cousin, Ingram Kalisher, the accountant, who was on the Council. Ingram was the dumb one and waited for Emery to cue him. Once, Palmer Speed had thrown a meeting into an uproar by asking Emery, in the front row: "Counselor Kalisher, would it be easier for you if I let you bring a railroad semaphore to the next meeting? Or a set of yachting flags?"

Speed removed his rimless eyeglasses and polished them on his tie. It was 8:30—thirty-six hours since Amy Andrus had been kidnaped, and time for Palmer Speed to confront his own private crisis arising from the crime. He reviewed quickly in his mind all the delaying tactics, all the circumventions, all the tricks of parliamentary procedure he could remember. He would need them all.

Laura, rummaging through Fritzie's desk for Scotch tape—the detectives needed it to tack the Santa Luisa map to the nursery wall—found a letter that she had long forgotten about.

> Dear Mrs. Andrus,
> I have discussed with the Board of the Sunny Sky Nursery School the matter of a refund on Amy's tuition fee. I regret that the Board has refused to honor your request. Amy's inability to adapt to nursery school, we feel, was not the fault of the school. Her tantrums and withdrawals, and, finally, the two occasions on which she ran away were, we feel, a result of your own failure to discipline her and impress upon her the need for a co-operative attitude. The school feels no responsibility for her failure to finish out the term.
> She is unquestionably a bright, inventive child, far advanced for her years. But these qualities are not sufficient in today's world. Her failure to realize her group responsibilities is a serious failure, and one that . . .

Laura placed the rumpled sheet on the desk. It seemed an eternity ago—yet it was only last May, just after they had moved to California.

Fritzie walked into the den and sat on the reclining chair. The house was silent. A desk lamp supplied the only illumination. The two detectives in the nursery had closed the door. They seemed to be phoning perpetually. Selena Masters, the last of the dinner dishes wedged into the washing machine, stopped by to say good night. "Want me tomorrow?" she asked. "I can come. Mrs. Kaplan won't mind losin' me the rest of the week."

"That'd be fine, Selena," Fritzie said. "Y'all come by." It did not seem illogical to them that his accent was more in the comic Negro tradition than hers. Fritzie liked colored people. They, in turn, accepted his corn-pone manner graciously, gauging him to be genuinely friendly.

"Sure hope there'll be good news tomorrow," the maid said. "I got a hunch there will. Good night." She left them, striding vigorously, an independent soul who understood *Ex-dividend* and *Comb. average.*

"I got to thank Selena for sparin' us the prayer bit," Fritzie said. "One more character prayin' for us, and I'll declare for the local atheist society."

Laura turned from the desk to face him. She still held the nursery school letter in her hand. "I guess Mona Mears used up all the prayer time. Fritzie, you were marvelous with her."

"She'll have my head. You know, she does a TV piece every now and then. Good-by career." He held his head. "Ah, hell, what right do I have to think about myself? My own miserable self and my career. I can't change, that's my trouble. I should be doin' something for Amy—if I knew what, if I knew how."

Laura wrapped her hands on her shoulders; her crossed arms made a white diagonal on her chest. "It's like getting ready to die," she said. Her voice was thin—transmitted from some distant star.

"Laura, don't talk that way."

"But it is. Why should we deceive ourselves? Do you think about death, Fritzie? No—don't have to answer me. I know you don't. You live so wonderfully in the present. You don't have time for it."

He appeared hurt, as if her analysis of his character indicated some shortcoming. She had meant it as a compliment. "Laura, I know I'm ridiculous and weak and all that——"

"I think about dying all the time," Laura said. "I'm horrified by it. I'm offended by it. It's one of the reasons I try to limit my pleasures—not to be too emotional—or too much in love, with you, with my children. I don't want a lot of money and I'm afraid of enjoying anything too much. Do you know why? Because I'm aware every second of my life that I must die, and I don't want to feel too bad about going. I want to feel—well, it wasn't so good, so I might as well give it up."

Andrus got up, embarrassed, and walked to the window. He kept his back to her. "I don't think about it because I guess I'm so wrapped up in myself I haven't time. I s'pose I'm still young enough to think I'll live forever."

"I wish you could teach me," she said wanly. "Do you know the worst of it? My careful defenses haven't done a bit of good. I've gone through thirty-five years limiting myself, putting myself on short rations, and what's happened? I'm more afraid than ever of the pit and the silence. I find myself feeling sorry for everyone I've known who's dead—as if my stupid sorrow can help—instead of grasping every minute I'm alive and using it, exploiting it, tasting it."

"I'm sorry, honey," Andrus said plaintively. "I didn't know you felt like that."

"No, no, Fritzie—there's nothing you could have done," she whispered.

He came to her side and put a hand on her shoulder.

"Today—when that monster called—the man who whispered—his voice sounded like a summons from death. Because I sensed he'd *kill*—whether he was the one who had Amy or not. He'd end life. And when I'd hung up, I realized how I'd cheated myself with my rotten game—refusing to love enough, refusing to find pleasure in everything, refusing to *enter*, to *partake*."

"You gotta stop analyzin' yourself. Don't do you no good."

"And the worst of it—what right have I to fear anything? To indulge myself? When Amy is gone. And then I understood. I didn't care about whether I lived or died any more—because I knew *she* was dead."

Andrus dropped to his knees and rested his head on her lap.

"Don't say that," he whispered. "You know it doesn't have to be true."

"It is. It is."

"Hell, you say. I can understand your being scared—I'm an authority on that. Ain't no one more scared of anything than me. I'm scared of everything—my work, my job, my health—they frighten me silly, so I go around struttin' and actin'. O.K., you can be scared, too. But not about Amy. People don't kill kids like that."

She lowered her head, resting her face on his thick blond mop. "My clear vision, Fritzie. I've never enjoyed anything—really. I've never believed in the triumph of good or the defeat of evil. I've expected the worst all my life, because I know I have to die some day."

"No! No, dammit!" he cried. "That is not so! You got no right to think like that! Y'all gonna be gloomy and miserable and think the worst's happened to Amy, do it on your own time! Not mine!"

She kissed his hair. It smelled of expensive toilet water, a Beverly Hills decoction that costs as much as an actress' cologne. The previous night she had sensed that grotesque strength in him—a strength that grew out of his weaknesses, his capacity to fictionalize, to build hope on illusion. That same cunning facet of his mind that could transmute a television critic's *praise* of a rival director's drama into an *attack* now enabled him to see only a happy end to their ordeal. Now, a day and a half after her daughter's disappearance, she was jealous of Fritzie's armor—and grateful for it. How odd that they should find their roles reversed! Yesterday, his weeping performance was disgusting in the face of her rigid calm. Tonight, it was his talent for fashioning a world on his own terms that was sustaining them. Death was an immanence to her—a hovering ghost, a snooper who didn't let you alone for a minute—and would surely claim their missing child. Not so for Francis M. Andrus. Secure in his castle of scripts and station breaks, he had no time for death. It simply wasn't good programing. And suppose he was deceiving them? Laura understood that the deception was valid. They had no control over the future. They were under the harsh dictates of the criminal, the faceless clipper of words from the *Los Angeles Argus*.

She stroked Fritzie's head, as if rewarding him for the sustenance he was providing. She saw him no differently now than she had through their years of courtship and marriage and separation. It was merely that his traits, once a source of amusement to her, later a source of aggravation, now seemed applicable and operative. In their misery, their confrontation with a terror so ravaging as to stun the will, his colored view of life appeared better suited than her own rationalism. She was like the logician, the social scientist who proves with graphs and lab work that bad sanitation causes infant mortality, and Fritzie was the flamboyant missionary priest who forces the natives to accept cleanliness with his *mystique*—a more effective tool than dry fact.

He looked up. "Y'all think I'm bein' an optimistic boob, don't you? That I act the way I do 'cause I'm too scared to do otherwise?"

"No, I don't. I'm glad you are the way you are."

"Like fun. I am scared. I'm fightin' the slow horrors every minute I'm awake. I know what might happen to Amy." He swallowed noisily, lowering his head. "Maybe it's happened already. But I just refuse to believe in the worst. I won't. I can't. You know why? 'cause I hate unhappy endings. It's bad for the audience."

"I wish I could be like you—now."

"It ain't much help except when the bottom falls out of your life." He hugged her—not with a passion, but for warmth, assurance, as one infantryman might hug another under bombardment. "I got a feeling we'll be O.K. tomorrow. That's the day. She'll be with us tomorrow."

He noticed the letter in her hand. "What's that?"

"An old letter from the nursery school. I was looking for something else in your desk." They had talked for months about buying a filing cabinet—for household accounts, tax papers, Fritzie's mounds of scripts and correspondence. It was on the list of things undone, plans unfulfilled.

Andrus took the letter from his wife's hand and began to read it, bending low to catch the light from the desk lamp. His handsome face, each generous feature weighted with sorrow, lost the bravado he had hoarded through the agonizing day. The words pricked him, summoning up a hundred memories of the child.

. . . *unquestionably a bright, inventive child, far advanced for her years.* . . . He remained stooped, transfixed by the message, then tossed it on the desk and walked to the window, as if by gazing out at the desert night he might see his daughter walking toward him across the parched grass, beneath the palms. Across the street the reporters' automobiles were still parked. He could see one man lounging against the fender of a station wagon, his cigar a blinking red ember. Laura came beside him and put a hand on his shoulder. Neither spoke. Neither had the strength to reflect on the fragmentation of their lives. The shock of the previous night's publicized rituals—the newspaper's publication, the unruly mob, the insane processional, the intrusion of the Mears woman—all these had been events unrelated to them—noxious events that they had read about somewhere.

Andrus pressed his forehead against the metal window frame. "Oh, dear God, save her," he moaned. "Save her."

And then Laura realized that the agony devouring him was no less intense, no less intractable than the pain she had been stifling for two days. His optimism was his defense; and she felt a rush of love for him because of it—that magnificent illusory world he created and was willing to share.

After leaving Patrolman Hertmann, Eliot was at liberty. He was not quite sure where next to go. In spite of his brashness, he did not have the courage to go directly to the office of the *Truth* and there attempt to draw information out of Herbert Hood, or Trigg, or Kalaidjian. He would be lucky if he got past the receptionist. Swinnerton had refused to tell him anything, but there was now the possibility that, faced with Clyde Hertmann's testimony, he might be induced to defend himself.

Eliot lifted one foot after another as if walking through tapioca. The fatigue that enveloped him was a gelatinous, colorless mass—impeding, tripping, draining the last droplets of strength from him. He found himself speaking slowly, walking with painful deliberation, driving his Ford with the movements of a man in a plaster cast. Once in the car, he now found himself without destination, driving aimlessly, like Tom Ballstead's father on his excursions to Ohio on Sunday afternoon. To return to his midget furnished room and attempt to sleep through the eye-scarring smog and the wicked heat did not appeal to him. So he drove instead to Nespoli Drive, arriving a few minutes after Laura Andrus' return with Joe McFeeley.

Eliot stood with George Brack and Steve Billik and the UBC crew and listened while Dave Arnspeiger briefed everyone from notes.

"There was this dairy truck on the side of the tunnel," Arnspeiger was saying, "and two detectives got out and picked up the package—not less than five minutes after Andrus left it."

Eliot winced at Arnspeiger's reference to the mother as *Andrus*. He knew Dave bore her no ill will, but the impersonal surname bothered Sparling. It reminded him of the way certain Communists he had known as a young man at CCNY used to call women by their patronyms. Women, in Eliot's book of rules, were Miss or Mrs. or had a first name.

"Wonder why?" Swinnerton asked. His mustache had a costume quality, a yellow thatch pasted on with gum arabic.

"I sure don't know," Arnspeiger said. "I've given up figuring out what the cops are up to. I used to like McFeeley, but I think he's flipped. Rheinholdt shouldn't leave him here alone any more."

George Brack appeared perturbed. His inviolate face, beneath its golden crown, was sorrowful. "Maybe we had something to do with it," Brack said.

They all looked at him strangely—Arnspeiger, Swinnerton, Bosch, a few others. Eliot, shading his tormented skull, a few paces behind Brack, blinked and swayed. He was having trouble standing erect.

"I mean," George Brack continued, "our trailing her. It was almost like last night. Are we doing the right thing?"

"So long as you don't get arrested, it's right," Arnspeiger said. He trudged off to the Skopas house to use the phone. Swinnerton followed him. Eliot shouted: "Harve! I wanna talk to you!" Swinnerton shook his head and kept walking.

After Brack had phoned in his account of the second ransom

drop, Eliot told the commentator about his efforts to establish the facts of the previous day. He told Brack about Walter Todd's disclosures and showed him Hertmann's list of telephone calls.

"Am I nuts?" Eliot asked. "Am I the only one in the world who cares about this?"

Brack's sunny features were grave. "I care, Eliot. Nobody should cover up something so serious."

"You gonna stick up for me, Georgie, when I go to Ballstead and ask him to give us time for my great investigatory report on who blew it?"

"I'd certainly want to know everything you learned," George said. "I'd think it was terrible if people would distort the truth. That child—what better reason could someone have to withhold a story?"

"I don't know." He yawned endlessly. "Maybe I'll know by tomorrow. If I could only get Swinnerton to tell me something. Or fat Herbie."

Steve Billik unloaded his camera and came up to Eliot and George. "Hey, kid," he said. "You goin' by the office? Give this to the lab. Two hundred feet, all silent. Exteriors. Nobody talked today. No statements, nothin'."

Sparling took the film and nodded.

"And tell somebody down there it's nuts wastin' overtime keeping a full crew here," Billik whined.

Overtime, two hundred feet of silent, full crews—these were the substantive matters that kept the world in motion, that propelled people through fifteen hours of wakefulness. He could not be wroth with Steve Billik. Arnspeiger, Bosch, Swinnerton, they were all men earning a living, terribly busy, most of them underpaid. He had no right to expect them to brim with moral indignation, with hot outrage.

Eliot left the film at the UBC newsroom, then drove to his furnished room. He suddenly remembered he had asked Connie to have dinner with him, to meet him at the Andrus house. Half asleep, he called her from the telephone in the lobby of his rooming house and advised her that he was exhausted; however, after a few hours' sleep and a shower, he would be fine. They agreed to meet at Rocco's, a bar and steak house near the *Truth* office, at 8:30. She would finish some letters for Mr. Hood and then write some of her own while she awaited him.

Eliot collapsed on his bed. He nudged off his space shoes, and each mammoth foot oozed into a relaxed dream. Taking off his shoes, Eliot thought, was one of the few things in life that gave him positive pleasure. In spite of his total enervation, he had trouble sleeping. The room was oppressively hot. It was narrow, furnished in cheap modern—a day bed, armchair, two occasional chairs, a tiny desk, some ceramic lamps. There was one bookcase, overladen with magazines, books, unpublished manuscripts, notes and trivia. It had a southern exposure, one casement window looking out on a blinding vista of cheap new apartments on one of those narrow streets between Sunset and Hollywood boulevards, a few blocks west of LaBrea. It was impossible to keep the room cool, and since Eliot was forced to live on a budget (the apartment alone was too expensive for his $102 a week), he had to forgo air conditioning. Thus, surrounded by the fading day's light and lingering heat, he remained wakeful during the two hours' grace he had allotted himself. At 8:00, the alarm sounded and he dragged himself from bed, showering and shaving, but earning no increment of energy from these acts. Overnight work had destroyed any capacity in him to relax, to establish rhythms of labor and rest. His life was a perpetual search for enough sleep, enough strength, enough momentum to propel him through one more night of work, one more stuffy day of entrapment in his depressing room. Withal, he maintained a rather buoyant front to the world and did his job exceedingly well. If he had failed as a reporter, he still was the fastest newscast writer in the West Coast office. Sparling owned no apologies for the salary United Broadcasting paid him. UBC! The thought of their genial castle thrilled him as he sloshed Aqua Velva on his pitted cheeks. He had very little to show for his 28 years, he felt, aside from his glorious membership in United.

Rocco's was a shabby approximation of a New York steak house. Its exterior—yellow-brick façade, tiny window with gold curtain, minute neon sign—was supposed to suggest such talkers' havens as the Pen & Pencil or the Press Box. However, the interior was a good deal shabbier and the meats were inferior. One generally ordered broiled chicken at Rocco's, after trying a steak. There was a good deal of lip-smacking and eye-rolling over the broiled chicken, and in the past few months some of the Hollywood crowd—the younger, blue-jeaned set—had been patronizing the restaurant. Eliot never understood the magic. To him, a broiled chicken was a broiled chicken, even if Rocco's wife cooked it herself in the dirty kitchen. The restaurant had yet another eminent trait. It was Herbert Hood's special place of retreat for a night's drinking. The general manager, on the average of once a week, would drink through the night at Rocco's, after which Rocco and his wife would lead him to a cot in the storage room, where Hood would spend the night. There was a small sink in the back, and Hood eventually stored an electric razor there. Rocco had known Mr. Hood in Chicago, back in the twenties. He considered him a high-class gent, a real old-timer, and he felt honored to be able to put him up now and then.

Eliot found Connie Potenza in a booth at the rear. She looked extremely pretty: each coffee-colored eye had a bright white glint—a reflection from the table lamp. She was wearing a prim blue shirtwaist dress, a schoolmarmish thing that worked to much advantage with her rounded figure, her dark face.

"Hiya. Who said you could order a drink?" Sparling asked.

"You're late. And, besides, it's only Seven-Up."

He eased into the booth opposite her. (Where did one sit in a booth with a woman? Two together? Facing? Eliot never answered the question to his own satisfaction. He had tried sitting on the same side as Connie but had given that up. His uncontrollable figure needed all the space it could get.)

"Tell me all," he said. "What'd you learn?"

"It was jumping all day. First the Rheinholdt thing, and then Mr. Hansel's answer. Most of the day they were in conference in Hansel's office. And the telegrams! Everybody's congratulating Mr. Hansel—even Mr. Hood got a few. From some of his Chicago friends."

A waitress—one of Rocco's daughters—tried to push the steak, but they opted for broiled chicken.

"Anybody worried about what Rheinholdt said?" Eliot asked.

"Well, from what I could hear, Trigg and Kalaidjian were kind of fidgety this morning. But after Hansel wrote his answer, everyone's convinced the paper is telling the truth. That dumb cop never called anyone there."

"Except he did."

Eliot went on to describe his internews—his talks with Todd and Patrolman Hertmann, the indications that the newpaper was aware of the police request.

"That policeman could be lying" Connie said.

"Why do you stick up for those burglars?"

"I'm not. But he could be lying. It might be a cover-up."

"That's what I have to find out." He picked listlessly at his chicken. It was superb: charred on the outside, snowy-white, tender and sweet within. Yet somehow Sparling had the feeling he should be eating breakfast. Some Wheaties and strawberries would have been good at the moment. That was one of the troubles with over-night labors—you lost track of mealtimes.

Connie studied him as if eager to help, utterly at a loss how to proceed. He had stopped toying with the chicken and appeared to be dozing off. "Eliot, why you have to exhaust yourself on this wild-goose chase, I don't know. Even Mr. Ballstead doesn't care. Why are you racing around like a maniac for nothing?"

"I got nothing else to do. I can't sleep."

"But you're always getting involved in things that can't help you professionally."

Sparling sulked. "Don't be so solicitous."

"You worried yourself sick over Schlossmann and got fired for it, and before that you kept trying to sell Mr. Hood on a series on the *braceros* and how they were being cheated by the farmers. Before that you had a great idea to do something on Indians. Why Indians? Now you're off again."

"It's my department," he said fuzzily. "I'm awaiting the primacy of the intellect."

"I don't know what *that* means. I just wish you'd do something to improve *yourself*. You're brilliant. They still talk about you at the paper—the amount of work you did by yourself. They have two men doing what you did."

"Yeah. And I was so cheap. Fifty-eight bucks a week and all the stationery I could steal."

"I can't talk to you. Why don't you get some public relations work on the side? Lot of fellows do that. Bill Trigg has a deal with an oil company. It pays him as much as the salary he gets at the *Truth*."

Eliot moaned. "Enough. Since we're discussing my uplift, what about you? Why don't you contribute?"

"*Me?* I contribute enough cheering you up."

"Yeah. It sure helps." He looked at her with what passed for admiration, affection on his long, morose face. She had an enviable capacity for enjoying life, the trivia of daily existence—a new shade of lipstick, a pretty child in the street, a flowering shrub on a lawn, the first cigarette after her morning coffee in the office—that would escape him all his life. If Connie could not teach him this gift for reacting, for using life properly, at least he could sit back and admire her talent for it. For Eliot, there were few joyful moments: he was a relentless pessimist, seeing the worst, expecting the worst, eternally suspicious.

"What are you staring at me for?" Connie asked. "Eat your chicken."

"Why don't you let me go to bed with you?"

"Be still. We've discussed it at length and the answer is no."

"You could at least try it. How do you know you won't like it unless you try it?"

"No. Eliot, I don't want to discuss it."

"Hah! Why should you be any different than the others? Am I really so horrible? So repulsive? I'm tall. I'm losing weight. That counts for something. I'm brilliant. How can a woman repeatedly refuse the advances of such a thoroughly brilliant man?"

"I know. I know. You wrote the whole overnight report yourself."

"And, what's more, I was a hero yesterday! I got beaten by the fascist police and lived to tell my story on TV. I have earned the right to go to bed with you."

As he attempted, with clumsy jests, to break down her resistance, he wondered what would happen if she agreed. The joy would be too intense, too exquisite to bear. He would die of anticipation. In his innermost heart, he was almost glad that she resisted him.

"You've earned nothing. Eliot, can't we keep our friendship on a simple basis? If I say yes, we'll mess it up with all kinds of sloppy and silly things." She sighed. "Maybe I'm being an old maid—scared to live a little. But I can't help it."

"How do you know it's sloppy and silly? Where'd you learn so much? Who'd you play around with?" He was invariably suspicious of her. Her spurning of him implied that she had had a long, sordid history of affairs with everyone from Herbert Hood to Vinnie, the overnight copy boy.

"Oh, stop. Eliot, for someone who thinks he's so intelligent, you make less sense than my brother Sal. He can't even pour concrete properly."

Eliot wedged himself into one corner of the booth and maneuvered his legs on to the seat. The brief rest in his hot apartment had done him no good; he felt collapse imminent. In his disintegrating state, he was in no mood to apologize. He was not actually suspicious of Connie's morality—it was just that he had been done in so thoroughly in the past. He had always, it seemed to him, dated girls who appeared the essence of primness, propriety, girls who exercised a fierce guardianship over their persons—not even permitting a kiss, a tweak, a squeeze, a few marginal movements of his hands. Then, at some point in their limited relationship, Eliot would learn that these towers of virginity were carrying on wild liaisons with other men: classmates, fellow staff members on the *Daily Bruin,* buddies in the Army Ordnance, associates at the *Truth.* It distressed him terribly. In time, his vain pursuit of sexual fulfillment became of a piece with his dazed search for sleep. No sleep? O.K., no sleep. No sex? O.K., no sex.

These ruminations were abruptly terminated. Into Rocco's walked two of his quarries: Herbert Hood and Harvey Swinnerton. Fat Herbie, sweating, had already taken a few belts from his secret bottle in the linen closet. Hood waddled. His froggish face was a lurid red. Swinnerton followed him sorrowfully. They sat on bar stools, out of Eliot's earshot, but still in his field of vision. Rocco himself came behind the bar to serve the general manager. Hood was not required to order and Rocco did not ask. Four Roses bloomed in front of the general manager and he poured himself the first of many. Swinnerton ordered a soft drink.

"My boys," Eliot said to Connie. "My two fellahs. If only they'd both get loaded and *talk.*"

Connie peered out of the booth. "It's an all-nighter. He made me buy some sheets and a blanket for the cot the other day."

"He should stay drunk the rest of his lousy life for what he did," Eliot whispered.

Whisky was beginning to invigorate Hood. The booze made him stronger, tougher, healthier. He took it as other men down vitamin pills, as blood donors eat red liver. It did not necessarily make him mean or pugnacious or vindictive. It simply added spring to his step, clarity to his voice, life to his tired musculature. "Now, Harvey," he was telling the reporter, "the important thing is what I mentioned upstairs. Keep your mouth shut. You're under no obligation to talk to a soul."

"You can depend on me, Mr. Hood."

"I know I can. Mr. Hansel doesn't seem upset. He feels nobody's interested, and besides, he's convinced we're in the clear. But I'm not so sure."

"That we're in the clear?" Swinnerton's voice was ghostly.

"No, no, no. Don't even hint at that. Of course we're clear. We did nothing wrong. I'm not sure that people aren't interested. Didn't you say Sparling's been nosing around?"

"He was at Dr. Todd's today and someone saw him talking to Rheinholdt's secretary. He tried to get me also."

Hood drank his liquor as lovingly as a desert prospector taking a hefty slug from a canteen. Another oddity of his alcoholism was that whisky assuaged his thirst, acting as a cold, refreshing quencher. In most drinkers, it had the reverse affect, causing dryness. Not so with Herb Hood; he could have written endorsements for the world's worst rotgut. *Deeee-licious and refreshing! Sooooo good on a hot day!*

"I was talking to T.T.," Hood said, "about our problem. I suggested the Organization might get you a transfer, perhaps a little boost in salary. After all, we've got twelve newspapers."

"I'm happy in Sanlu, Mr. Hood."

"I'm sure you are, Harvey, but this problem of ours—and it concerns us both—is serious, in spite of T.T.'s attitude. I tell you, it hasn't been off my mind since yesterday afternoon."

"Nor mine," said Swinnerton.

"I can understand Hansel's feelings. The pressure's on him—a lot more than on us. He's the one who's got to answer to New York about circulation and linage going down. Jesus, don't they ever do anything but go down? Television gets the dollar today, and where does that leave us?"

"I know. I know what a hard time Mr. Hansel must have."

"Now this matter of transferring you. There'd be a problem, of course. I needn't tell you nobody's getting hired these days."

"Yes, I'm sure it would be difficult." Swinnerton managed a weak smile; it barely peeked through his yellow mustache. "But really—Mr. Hood, I wouldn't want you or Mr. Hansel to trouble yourself on my account. I'll be quiet."

"Helluva thing," Hood muttered.

"What is?"

"Fifty-five years in the newspaper business, and in my old age people will suspect I helped murder a four-year-old girl."

"Don't say that, Mr. Hood. That isn't true. You said it wasn't."

"We're protected, Harvey. It's just people will suspect us. Those radio and TV people will see to that. The bastards stole our advertising revenue and now they'll crucify us on this."

"I don't see how they can."

"Neither does Hansel. I'm the Gloomy Gus. He says they wouldn't dare, and besides, he knows some mucky-muck over there."

He threw down his third double, cradling the booze for a moment in his mouth, then swallowing it in one sweet gulp. "Hansel's too sure of himself. I got a report from New York tonight that a couple of magazines are going to ream us out on this Andrus thing. It won't be as easy as he thinks. Sure, he whipped the LA papers into line—you know—the old manure—united front against censorship—public's right to know—and they came around." There was an odd ambivalence in his manner: he seemed almost happy that there would be attacks on the *Truth*.

"Is that why the *Argus* ran that editorial?"

"You betcha, Harvey. Wait'll you see the morning papers. Even that shopping throwaway in Sanlu. T.T. touched every base."

"About my getting out of town, Mr. Hood," Swinnerton said. "I'll do whatever you think is right." He laughed dryly. "I suppose you have me ticked off as a weakling, a bad sort, who'll talk. I'm not, really. But if you and Mr. Hansel want it that way . . ."

Eliot Sparling's graceless figure, sneaking up on rubbery feet, was beside them. Both men turned on the bar stools and studied him with distaste.

"Mr. Hood? Remember me? Hiya, Harve, old boy."

"Hello, Sparling," whispered Swinnerton.

"You." Hood uttered the single flat word as if it were an obscenity.

"We haven't seen each other since you canned me, sir. Best favor you ever did for me, turning me loose from that bat's nest."

"I can see you haven't learned much since then. Still shooting your big mouth off and talking too loud. I never could stand hearing you bellow for a copy boy." Hood turned his broad blue back on the young man.

"That's neither here nor there," Eliot said. "Look, Mr. Hood. I'm doing a little piece for UBC, an organization you may have heard of, about yesterday's occurrences. Notably how come your paper broke the story and thereby endangered a child's life. You want to tell me your side? You and Harve both?"

Hood turned around again. His bald pate reflected the subdued rose lighting. In the gloom, Rocco busied himself with polishing glasses. "Son, you're sticking that big nose of yours in where it doesn't belong. You tried it with Schlossmann and you lost a job. I didn't like firing you." Then he added cryptically: "You were at the top of the list."

What list? Eliot wondered. "That's a different geological era,

Mr. Hood. Everyone's forgotten about Werner Schlossmann, just the way they'll forget about Amy Andrus and her mother. I just think we need a clearing of the air."

"We stand on what we said before," Hood said bluntly; "6:04 was when we were officially notified."

"How about unofficially?"

"You're talking through your hat, boy," Hood said testily. "Don't get tricky with us. We're old friends of UBC's."

"Harve—you can talk—you *know*," Eliot pleaded.

"I have nothing to say to you, Sparling. Mr. Hood and Mr. Hansel are the only ones who can talk for the *Truth*."

Eliot's arms flapped upwards, suggesting a pelican's first efforts at flight. Then he clumped back to the booth, where Connie was hiding in the shadows, fearful that Hood would see her fraterniz ing with the enemy. "He say anything?" she asked.

"Nope. The freeze is on."

"It's just as well. Maybe now you'll forget the whole thing."

Five minutes later, Swinnerton, patting his mustache, his head downcast, searching the floor for some lost object, departed. Hood remained at the bar, his enormous butt welded to the stool. It would be an all-night souse for him, and then a few hours in his private cell.

When Swinnerton had vanished through the revolving door, into the steaming, impure street, Eliot asked her: "Can you get Swinnerton's address?"

"Why?"

"I wanna go see him tonight. I have a feeling he might open up. If he stews in his own guilt a couple of hours, he might want to talk."

"I'll get it," Connie said. She walked across the restaurant to the phone booth near the door and returned a few minutes later. "Here," she said. "It's Santa Luisa—3516 Guava Road."

"We're off in a cloud of sprocket holes," Eliot said. As they left, Hood turned mechanically in his seat. Was that his secretary consorting with Sparling? It looked like her. Yet the notion seemed idiotic. He conceived of her as *you* or *that girl* or *come here*. That she could be a functioning human being and seek the company of men was beyond his perception. He poured himself another double. Soon, his strength would be as the strength of ten, his mind splendidly free of Hansel and the *Truth* and the missing child.

The television failed to distract Rheinholdt. He sat lumpily in his chintz-bright living room, his mate at his side, watching a succession of Westerns and detective stories, wishing there was wrestling that night. The chief and his wife, both large, old and formless, confronted the speaking furniture like cave dwellers. They sat before its gray-green glow, silent, indestructible, saturnine— two primitives comforting themselves with a slow, smoldering night fire. A domesticated wolf should have been baying alongside them, but the only animal life in the room was Mrs. Rheinholdt's guppies.

They were remarkably homely people, yet they loved one another. She was enormous—one of those amorphous elderly women whose size increases geometrically from the neck down. Her gray hair, a mop of Brillo that had never known beauty parlor, stood atop her great pyramid of hard flesh, a steely pompon. They rarely spoke to one another; they never entertained; they never were entertained. Goodly and great, they lived only to honor Caspar's high rank, an eminence neither of them had ever gotten over. This night, Mrs. Rheinholdt understood his misery. She, too, had read the afternoon papers. She knew of the attacks on him; at the supermarket she had seen the petition being circulated demanding his ouster. At this very minute, she knew, the City Council was arguing about him—her good, her courageous husband.

The 11:00 P.M. television news began with a report on the Andrus case. The announcer displayed newspapers from around the country, all with big headlines—New York, Chicago, Miami, Omaha. Then there were several minutes of film—women bolting doors in Santa Luisa, locking windows, a woman buying a Doberman. Then there were pictures of the Andrus woman leaving the house, and then returning, and a few shots of Milt Bannon coming back with the envelope under his arm. Rheinholdt cursed to himself softly, so that his wife might not hear. They were everywhere, those lice—not giving the cops a chance. Mayor Speed said hands off, and hands off it was. It never occurred to the chief that in their tardy plan to keep the papers away, he had never mentioned anything about calling off the newsmen. He was too simple a man to understand that reporters will do anything they are permitted to do. Rheinholdt got up and walked to the hall closet for his jacket and his panama hat.

"Don't you want to see any more of the newsreels?" his wife asked.

"Nope. I need a little fresh air."

He walked a few blocks, greeting two of his men in a parked prowl car, wondering what they thought of him now that the world was screaming for his scalp. His sensitivity, extreme under normal conditions, was now like an intractably painful neural disease. He turned a corner and entered a shopping district. At the end of the street was an all-night pharmacy, one of those bloated California emporia dealing in vintage champagne, woven neckties, encyclopedias, and erector sets. At the newsstand, Rheinholdt bought a copy of the morning *Register*. He ignored the clerk's greeting—"Sure hope you catch that guy, Chief"—and walked out. Under the glare of the drugstore's street sign, he opened the newspaper. His head jerked back as if he had been slapped across the mouth. There was a main story on the case— the failure of the second ransom meeting—and, alongside it, under a four-column head, the words:

HOW RHEINHOLDT WRECKED THE ANDRUS CASE

Register Survey of Cal Police Chiefs
Reveals Errors, Oversights; His
Bungling Endangers Amy

He began to read the article. Some reporter had spent the day calling police chiefs from Sacramento to San Diego. All of them, it appeared, had harshly criticized Rheinholdt's handling of the case. One man said the FBI should have been called in at once; another that roadblocks were obligatory; a third that the presence of the chief's car at the house was a disastrous mistake. There was nothing in the long, detailed article about the mob of reporters at the house, the harassment of the police and the Andrus family, no comment about the *Truth's* role, nothing about the lunatic parade to Buena Terra Park, not a word about the pursuit of Mrs. Andrus that afternoon on her trip to Patio Road. All these were deemed inconsequential, unrelated to the crime.

The anger that boiled up in the old man's chest had no outlet: he had no desk to pound, no one to shout at, no reporter to call in for a good chewing out. He felt tears seeping into his tortured eyes, and he was ashamed of himself. With the newspaper under his arm, he walked back to his house, never to learn that the *Register* (somewhat better than a shopper's throwaway) had received the survey of police opinions from T. T. Hansel—a gift from above.

Nor did the chief know that when Bill Trigg, its author, gathered his material from police officials, he did not mention it would be used as a club to destroy Rheinholdt, who, after all, was their colleague. Trigg had, like any good reporter, merely asked questions. Then he had matched the answers with Rheinholdt's derelictions—and a half dozen of the chief's professional peers had denounced him as a bumbler, a fool—and possibly the mechanic of a child's death.

When he got home, his wife was in bed. "Caspar? You all right?" she called from upstairs.

"Yeah, honey. I'm fine. Be right up." Then he went into the kitchen, found a piece of official stationery, and sat at the table. He took his fountain pen from his pocket. Three times he opened it, poised it over the paper, and then returned it. The fourth time, he began writing, wincing and fighting back fresh tears as he saw the blue heading:

CITY OF SANTA LUISA
OFFICE OF THE CHIEF OF POLICE
CASPAR RHEINHOLDT

In a childish, slanting script, he wrote:

> Dear Mr. Mayor,
>   I hereby give you my resignation, effective immediately. I feel I have done nothing wrong in my handling of the Andrus case. However, the newspaper attacks on me have destroyed my value to the community you and I like so much. I will be glad to consult with the man you name to succeed me.
>
>   Very truly yours,
>   Caspar Rheinholdt
>   Chief of Police

Then he placed the letter in an official envelope, got up from the table and picked up the telephone on the wall. He dialed his headquarters.

"This is Chief Rheinholdt," he said hoarsely. "Get me the FBI in Los Angeles."

"Moreover," Ingram Kalisher was intoning from his seat on Mayor Speed's right, "the record is clear that Santa Luisa's police operation had been inefficient for years. As any student of police affairs knows—and I cite Shavelson and Mittler's *Problems of Urban Police Forces,* published by the Laurel Press, New York— the movement in police organization is toward greater centralization—a central detective bureau, a central traffic division. The precinct system is expensive, outmoded and inefficient. Why, then, did this City Council of Santa Luisa sit back three years ago and give Caspar Rheinholdt a free hand in *decentralizing* it?"

Mayor Speed passed a hand over his eyes. He would have to do something about the lighting. Too harsh. He tried thinking of other jobs around the City Hall—anything to get his mind off Ingram Kalisher's attack on him, on his police, making it sound as if Amy Andrus' kidnaping was his fault. In a sense, he couldn't blame the Good Government League. They'd waited years for something to hang him with, and maybe they'd found it. The meeting room was jammed with Good Government people—most of them younger than his faithful, better dressed, with eastern accents, the women in tight pants, the men wearing thick, dark-rimmed glasses and smoking pipes. It was about time, he thought, for Ingram to run out of steam and look helplessly at Emery, his brother, in the front row.

"In view of the tragic happenings in this Andrus case," Ingram Kalisher piped, "I have a motion to present to the City Council. But first let me recommend that all of you read tomorrow's *Santa Luisa Register*—it's on the stands tonight. That fine little newspaper tells better than I could what is rotten in our police operation. I hereby move—ah—hereby—move—ah——"

The councilman had run out of steam. His long, bald head bobbed around and his eyes found his brother—erect in the front row. *"Ad hoc,"* whispered Emery Kalisher to Ingram, *"ad hoc."*

"Ah, yes," said Ingram, "I hereby move that an *ad hoc* committee be set up to investigate the Santa Luisa police force and draw up recommendations for its total overhaul!"

There was a burst of applause from the assembly. Palmer Speed gaveled them into silence. "The motion is out of order," he said, smiling cheerily, in his best Hoosier manner.

"Mr. Mayor!" Ingram cried.

Emery Kalisher was on his feet. "This is a disgrace! You're protecting Rheinholdt for reasons of your own! I demand——"

Mayor Speed kept banging away. "You will all be silent!" he shouted, still smiling. "Under terms of the City Charter, ever since the abolition of the post of police commissioner, all police affairs are directly under the supervision of the mayor and the mayor alone. Other Council members can act only in an advisory capacity, and then only at the request of the mayor. I've made no requests, so the motion is out of order. Sit down, Mr. Kalisher. Both Mr. Kalishers."

Emery Kalisher was still on his feet. "Fascism!" he cried. "Dictatorship! This isn't Russia, Mr. Mayor! I propose the Good Government League boycott the rest of this meeting!" And he gathered up his petitions, his brief case, and his copy of *Problems of Urban Police Forces* and stalked out, followed by his supporters. Ingram looked shaken; he hated to be left alone, without Emery to cue him.

"Next order of business, Charlie," said Mayor Speed, crisply turning to the city clerk.

"Petition for erection of a neon restaurant sign on the corner of Charimoya Avenue and Eleventh Street. Petitioner is Luis Olmedo."

That was more like it, Mayor Speed thought. He grinned favorably at Luis Olmedo, who rose to state his request.

After taking Connie home, Eliot drove to Swinnerton's apartment. The reporter lived in a whitewashed four-story building—a relic of the twenties, set in a dingy plot of cacti and drooping palms. A small spotlight played halfheartedly on the sign: FURNISHED ROOMS 1½, 2, 2½. The lobby smelled unwashed, and Eliot, squinting at the mailboxes for Swinnerton's apartment number, felt sorry for the *Truth's* district man. He found the number—4C—and took the elevator to the top floor.

Swinnerton did not open the door on hearing the buzzer. His gentlemanly voice asked: "Who is it?"

"Eliot Sparling, Harve. I gotta talk to you."

Swinnerton opened the door. "For goodness' sake, Sparling, can't you let me alone?"

"No. Gimme a break, Harve. At least let's talk it over."

Reluctantly, Swinnerton unhooked the latch chain and let Eliot in.

The barrenness of the single narrow room was emphasized by its disarray. It did not mesh with Swinnerton's impeccable person. Then Eliot realized he was packing his meager possessions. A portable record player had been disconnected, the wire bound around its scuffed case. There were three sagging cardboard crates of books. All of Swinnerton's clothes—the striped ties and foulards, the button-down shirts, the tweedy suits and thick-soled shoes—had been laid out on the bed, ready for two ancient valises.

"You pulling out?" Eliot asked.

"Yes, not that it's your business." He started laying shirts and underwear into a valise.

"You leaving town?"

"You're a pokenose, Sparling. Yes, I am leaving."

"Where are you going?"

"As far as I can. Wherever I can land a job."

Eliot looked at him with sorrow. The man was forty-five years old, a Wandering Gentile of Journalism, a collector of odd jobs. He was not a stupid man, and surely not a bad one, and it seemed appalling to Eliot that he should be reduced to such an existence. Sparling recalled the stories of past greatness and wealth—Harvard, Nob Hill, the lost fortune in mines and oil.

"I'll give you a hand," Eliot said. He started placing some un-packed books in an empty carton: a dog-eared copy of *Pierre* by Melville; a coverless *Swann's Way;* the American Novels of Henry James. He thought miserably: in sixteen years will I be re-duced to this? Will I be the Harvey Swinnerton of LA when I am forty-five? "I guess Hood gave you the bum's rush tonight, is that it, Harve?" Eliot asked. "Getting you out of the way?"

"Nothing of the sort. I'm leaving on my own. I can't stand being blamed for anything. I hate fights. I have no desire to get further involved in this sticky affair. I admit it. I'm a coward."

"Who isn't?" shouted Eliot. He was delighted to find a fellow member of the great nonsectarian brotherhood. "Look at me! I was born yellow! Harve, if you're in the clear, why run?"

"I'm not quite *that* clear. I had something to do with it." He straightened up from the bed, where he had been folding a leather-elbowed jacket into a valise. "That child. That child." His re-fined voice was ghostly. "How did he do it? A rock when she wasn't looking?"

"Harve, Harve, no one knows for sure she's dead. Heck, she still might be O.K."

"I doubt it very much."

"Well, my personal opinion, for what it's worth, is you should tell me so I can have your side of it." An inspiration came to him. "Tom Ballstead would appreciate it. He's backing me one hundred per cent on this."

The invocation of Ballstead's name had a distinct effect on the reporter. He licked his mustache, then shook his head. "Sorry, Sparling. Good try." He walked to a writing table and began collecting blank paper, odd notes, a desk calendar, a mug full of neatly sharpened pencils.

"I just wanna know a few things," Eliot pleaded. "Like the first time you called Hood—then why you called the cops at 4:10——"

"No! Stop, blast you!" he cried. "You've no right to torment me like this! Am I a criminal! Am I a murderer? Look at me—Sparling—I haven't got the guts to go out with a woman—or a man. I'm nothing! I'm a contemptible cipher."

"No! You're a helluva guy!" Eliot bellowed. "You can be a hero if you level with me!"

"Stop ragging me," Swinnerton said miserably. "Just leave me alone, Sparling. I appreciate what you're trying to do, but it's not my dish of tea." He started strapping one of the valises. It was scuffed, misshapen, but still bearing evidences of former glory. Many years ago, Eliot fancied, Swinnerton's patrician mother, a fine-boned San Francisco beauty, had bought it in Mark Cross or Gucci's.

Eliot helped him by pressing his heft against the valise. Conjoined in manual labor, Sparling pursued his goal. "Now listen to me, Harve. If you don't tell me what you did, and what Hood did, you'll live with this curse on you the rest of your life. If you do— you'll be *loved*. That's the whole pitch in America today. *Confess*. It doesn't matter what—just *confess*. Do all kinds of horrible things, but just stand up and admit you're horrible and say you owe a debt to your fellow man and your eyes are now opened— and *whammo!* You're a hero. You can't miss, Harve. Just confirm a few facts, and you can go off to Omaha and never worry. People won't say, there goes Harvey Swinnerton, the guy who helped murder the Andrus child. No! They'll say, look at poor Harvey Swinnerton—a gallant, misunderstood man—he came clean when others lied—he admitted he was wrong! He is to be pitied, understood, *loved*. Yes, sir! It's love we need, Harve! Don't you read the books or go to movies or plays? *Love, love, love!*"

Swinnerton fastened the strap, then moved backward and collapsed in a chair. "Oh, be still. Just be still for a minute or two." He closed his eyes and rested his head on one hand.

"Well?" Eliot asked. "You gonna take my advice?" A Bronx street rhyme flitted across his mind: *Ladies and Gentlemen, take my advice, pull down your bloomers and fall on the ice.*

Swinnerton looked at him—badgered beyond resistance, immersed in guilt. "Tell you what, Sparling. I'll talk. But not just to you. I'll tell you whatever you want to know—provided Tom Ballstead is here to listen."

"Why?"

"Because that's the way I want it."

Sparling hesitated before going to the phone. Ballstead had never given him the network's approval in pursuing the story. Tom had advised him he was on his own. Now that he had lied to Swinnerton about Ballstead's hearty backing, he was in a trap. Still resourceful, he dialed Ballstead's home number, summoning up new deceits.

The news director was awake; he slept very little. Eliot explained the purpose of the call—Swinnerton would talk, but only in front of him.

Some wretched coughing preceded Ballstead's response. "Didn't I tell you we didn't care?" he asked. "What makes you think I'd go racing out to Sanlu in the middle of the night?"

"Because it's the right thing to do," Eliot persisted. "We can nail the *Truth*."

"Doesn't interest me that much."

"Ah—well—Swinnerton needs help, Tom. The poor guy's leaving town right now because Hood put the squeeze on him. He's broke and he has no job, and a few good words from you, a tip on some places to look for work would help him. Do a lot for his confidence."

Strapping his other valise, Swinnerton flushed with shame. "Good heavens, Sparling, you're compromising me," he muttered. "I didn't want you to ask Tom that."

"All right," Ballstead said. Eliot all but danced on the bare floor. He had located the exposed nerve—Ballstead's sense of responsibility for every underpaid newspaperman in the world—and Tom had responded. "Give me the address."

While they awaited Ballstead's arrival, Eliot helped Swinnerton carry his belongings down to the street. Swinnerton scrawled a note for his landlady—he explained he had paid a month's rent and she could use the balance for pending bills—and then he and Eliot began stacking luggage, cartons, clothes into the battered Austin. When they had finished, they sat inside. Swinnerton puffed a cigarette, lapsing into an almost comatose silence.

"Harve," Eliot said gently, "if I'm being too nosy, belt me in the mouth. But there's something I'd like to know—nothing to do with the Andrus deal."

"Hmm?" Swinnerton was befogged.

"I mean that bit about your family. You know—the old San Francisco oil money—Harvard—Europe. Am I being nosy?"

Swinnerton blew twin streams of smoke from his nose into the night air. "My father was a letter carrier in Oakland." He said it with a hard finality, as if he wanted, once and for all, to kill the myth.

"Oh, I'm sorry."

"Why are you sorry? I never invented those stories. God knows how they got started."

Ballstead arrived about ten minutes before midnight. Eliot and his quarry climbed out of the Austin to greet him. The news director had kept his pajama top on and had turned up the collar of his coat against the night air. More than ever, he seemed a consumptive shuffler through some hospital ward.

"Maybe you can use these," Ballstead said. He gave Swinnerton an unsealed white envelope. "Go on, look at 'em."

Swinnerton opened the envelope. Under the street lamp, he scanned the two sheets. One was a letter of recommendation. *The undersigned, Thomas Ballstead, had known Harvey Swinnerton for many years and would vouch, etc., etc.* . . . The second was a list of cities, newspapers and editors.

"Freese in Albuquerque is the best bet," Tom coughed. "I went as far east as Fort Wayne. You have any trouble, write to me."

Swinnerton inhaled deeply. "You're much too good, Tom. You're most generous."

"He lives for that," Eliot said. Then he went to his Ford and came back with the tape recorder. "Harve—you mind if we put it on tape?"

"No. Not at all." He was beyond resistance. In his debt to Ballstead, he would do anything. Besides, he would never see Santa Luisa again, never see Herbert Hood or T. T. Hansel again, never have to look Laura Andrus in the face again.

Swinnerton sat at the wheel of his car. Eliot squeezed into the rear seat with the recorder and Ballstead remained outside, scowling and coughing.

"Want me to quiz you—or do you just want to talk?" Eliot asked.

"I'll just talk, if you don't mind."

Eliot nodded, turned on the machine and spoke into the microphone. "Eliot Sparling recording a statement by Harvey Swinnerton, *Los Angeles Truth* reporter. Present: Tom Ballstead of UBC. Time: 11:52 P.M., Tuesday, September 18. Go ahead, Harve."

Swinnerton began with a detailed account of his interrogation of Walter Todd, outside the bank. He admitted freely that he had promised the dentist not to transmit the information to his editors —that it was "off the record."

"But you called Hood anyway, right?" Sparling interrupted.

"Of course," Swinnerton said, glancing at Tom Ballstead for approval.

Ballstead shivered in the thin air. "Don't look so holy, Sparling. He did what any reporter would do."

"Thank you, Tom," Swinnerton said. "Sparling has a terrible way of making me feel I'm—I'm—on trial."

"No, not just *you*, Harvey, baby," Eliot said—with genuine compassion. "Go on. So you called Hood—what time?"

"Oh, about ten minutes to four, I guess. Mr. Hood got very excited and made it a conference call. Mr. Hansel got on. I think Bill Trigg was transcribing what I said. I gave them all the details, assured them that as far as I knew, I was the only reporter and they were the only newspaper who had the story; and then I warned them that Todd had given it to me off the record, not for publication—and that, besides, the Santa Luisa police were about to call everyone and request secrecy."

"Then what?" asked Eliot.

"Ah—it's all rather mixed up." Swinnerton pressed both palms against his temples; he shuddered. "Mr. Hansel did most of the talking. I can't be too clear on it. He said something about that dentist being a private citizen who had no right to set conditions, that if he talked to a newspaperman, he had to be prepared for the consequences."

Sparling covered the mike. "He say anything about the child being prepared for the consequences?"

"Jesus, get on with it," Ballstead coughed. Eliot took his paw from the microphone and nodded at Swinnerton.

"Let me see," the latter continued. "Hansel didn't say definitely he intended to publish—I'm sure of that. He kept getting mad. At Todd, at the police, and mostly at me. There was some discussion about bringing Mona Mears down from San Francisco to replace me on the story. Then—and this I remember distinctly—Mr. Hood interrupted Mr. Hansel and said, 'Ted, I think we should go easy on this one.' "

Again, Eliot halted him. "Hood said *that?* Fat Herbie said *that* to Hansel?"

"I'm positive," Swinnerton replied. "Mr. Hansel was furious. He told Trigg to go ahead and write the story for an extra—to dig anything out of the morgue they had on the family, on past kidnapings—and to alert the composing room and the circulation department. But he did *not* definitely say they were going ahead with the story."

"What about Hood?"

"He suggested that we telephone Rheinholdt and try to pry something out of him—to get him to release the story. Mr. Hansel forbade him to do it. Then Mr. Hansel hung up, saying he was on his way down to the city room. Mr. Hood was still on the phone. He waited until Trigg was off, then he told *me* to call Rheinholdt— you know the old fable of the monkey making the cat pull the chestnuts out of the fire. He asked me to 'see what the status was, to feel them out.' But I wasn't to disclose that Mr. Hansel was considering printing the story. I suppose I was a little frightened, and then Mr. Hood said, 'Don't worry, Harvey, I'll take the rap.' "

Sparling turned the tape off for a moment; he looked challengingly at Ballstead. "Makin' you sick, Tom?"

"So far they haven't done anything I wouldn't have done," the news director said hoarsely. "Don't you understand what the hell it means to have a clear beat on a kidnaping? Could you ever understand that?"

"Sure, sure," Eliot said. He consulted the list he had copied from Patrolman Hertmann that afternoon. "And you then called the Santa Luisa cops at 4:10, right, Harvey?"

"That's correct. I spoke to Sergeant Baines and asked for Rheinholdt. He refused to let me talk to the chief, said he was in conference. However, Baines made me stay on and take the chief's message to the newspapers—not to print the story. I jotted it down as best I could. Then I told him we had all that information already and a lot more and pleaded again to be allowed to speak to Rheinholdt. Baines refused. He just kept saying"—Swinnerton gulped and shivered—"a child's life depended on our not printing."

"And what did you say, Harve?" asked Eliot kindly.

"I explained I had no authority to withhold a story. I was just a reporter, but that I'd convey the request to my superiors at once.

Baines then said if he didn't hear from us again, they'd assume we were not printing. He said everyone else they had called had agreed."

"And you called the *Truth*—right away?"

"Immediately."

"What time—closest you can come to it?"

Swinnerton paused. "It couldn't have been later than 4:20."

"And who'd you talk to?"

"Mr. Hood. I told him exactly what Baines had told me—there had been a kidnaping, that I had gotten a request from Rheinholdt to withhold, and that I was to transmit the request to my paper. I also told him all the other newspapers, according to Baines, had agreed to suppress the story."

"At 4:20?" Sparling bellowed. *"That* early?"

"I'm sure of it. I called the police at 4:10, and I couldn't have been on the phone ten minutes with Baines."

Eliot turned his elongated head angrily at Ballstead. "Hah! So they weren't notified until 6:04, hey, Tom? Oh, boy, do we have 'em by the lapels! No official notification from the police until 6:04! I got their 6:04!"

Ballstead scowled, raising the upturned collar of his jacket. "What'd Hood say then?" he asked.

"He told me not to call the police again, just to go to the Andrus house and wait for Mona Mears. I asked him point-blank— where I got the courage, I'll never know—if we were printing the story, and he told me not to concern myself with it. That was all I knew about it—until we learned that the story was out, from the radio."

"Anything else, Harve?" Eliot asked.

Swinnerton sighed. "Yes. If you use this on the air, I'd like to add a personal apology to Mr. and Mrs. Andrus. I'm sorry for what I've done. I should not have relayed Dr. Todd's disclosures to my desk. I know that's standard newspaper practice. But something should have deterred me. I hope they will forgive me, and I hope their daughter is well and will be returned to them soon." He paused, shaking his small, well-bred head. "I don't know. Everything seemed to go wrong. All those reporters at the house. The heat. The mystery. It's as if—as if—everyone was intent on being as rotten as they could, as mean and as stupid as they could. Everyone wanted to be part of the horror." He handed the microphone to Sparling. "Here. Have I done my part?"

"You bet, Harve," Eliot said. He turned off the recorder and wound up the cable. Then he and Ballstead shook hands with Swinnerton and wished him a good trip.

"Need some dough?" Ballstead asked.

"No thanks, Tom. I've saved a bit for emergencies."

"Take it easy on the road," Eliot said. "You get sleepy, stop and drink coffee."

Swinnerton managed a lost smile. "You're both good chaps," he said. Then he turned on the midget engine. The Austin, overloaded, hobbled off, *putt-putting* into the desert night.

"Whew," Eliot said. "He sure talked. Thanks to you, Tom. He wouldn't tell me—just you. The old father image."

Ballstead's raddled face worked itself into a fretwork. "Go on home," he said. "This is your day off." He started walking toward his car.

"How about it, Tom?" Eliot cried. "Are you with me? Can you deny the moral issue involved?"

"Oh, Jesus," Ballstead groaned. "At midnight on a street corner in Santa Luisa." He called from his car. "Talk to me tomorrow morning."

Ballstead drove off. Alone, exhausted, Eliot rested his chilled form against a palm trunk. Then he staggered to his Ford, placed the tape recorder on the rear seat and drove toward Hollywood. He had slept roughly ten hours of the past two and a half days and he was, in an obstinate, perverse way, almost as proud of his defiance of biology as he was of his imminent journalistic triumph.

WEDNESDAY

By WEDNESDAY morning, forty-eight hours after the kidnaping of Amy Andrus, remarkably few places on earth were ignorant of the crime. The word was relentless, incessant, repetitious—and it was wonderfully adapted to meet the special needs of different governments, different nationalities, different mores. In the "people's democracies," the crime was viewed as new evidence of capitalist depravity. A newspaper in Sofia, Bulgaria, called it *hooliganism*, a derivative word based on a vanished cartoon character once beloved in the very "imperialist" nation they were chastising. In the United Kingdom, an editorialist pointed out that kidnapings had been eliminated in the British Isles and in Canada by a simple act of legislation: the paying of ransom had been deemed a crime, too. If a note of smug pride crept into the voice of certain BBC announcers in reporting the Andrus case, the pride was perhaps pardonable. In the Latin press, notably in Italy, a preoccupation with blood and mutilation seemed uppermost in the minds of journalists. *Che fato orribile per la bambina Amy Andrus?* asked a Roman daily—and proceeded to list the manner in which a half-dozen prior kidnap victims had been murdered. (Was there much of a gap, an American newspaperman wondered, reading the account, between those fourteenth-century paintings of Saint Peter Martyr with the ax embedded in his skull and contemporary Italian journalism?) In France, a full page of murky photographs of the child, the house, the parents—muddied with cheap ink and poor newsprint—reduced the events to sordid fiction.

And so the word was spread: across oceans and deserts, on leased wires and by wireless; aired, printed, read, illustrated. By the time the sun had risen over southern California, parching throats and burning eyes, Amy Andrus' dark face was as well known as the price of bread.

In the house, Laura and Fritzie glanced at the morning news-papers, listened to the radio. Andrus was intrigued by the attack on Rheinholdt in the *Register*. "Seems like everyone's gonna get burned on this," he said thickly. "That dumb chief. It's almost like what's happened is so awful, it's gonna ruin us all."

"I can't find any sympathy for Rheinholdt," Laura said, "even though I know why the newspapers are doing it—to cover up their own rottenness. And we're in the middle." She cleared the break-fast dishes from the bar and went to the sink; Selena had not yet arrived. "I can't bear hearing my name again. Over and over and over. I couldn't even stand up in class to recite when I was in elementary school. I can't stand anyone staring at me. And now— I'm exhibit A."

"Can't be helped, honey," Andrus said.

"And does it matter any more? You and me, Fritzie—we should bottle up our own selfish lives—we're not important."

"No chance of that. *They* won't let us." He indicated the morn-ing papers.

"I suppose they won't," Laura said.

"And who can blame 'em?" Andrus cried. "We're *it,* Laura. We keep the wheels goin', the machinery greased. We're *celebrities.* We are just about the only things left anyone cares about, or cheers about, or worries about. Except the bomb—and there's no point fussin' over *that,* because one big *blam* and nothing matters. No, there's nothin' *left* for people any more, now that most of 'em are eatin' enough, and got houses, and can breed all they want, and shoot drugs into themselves so they won't die young. So the news-papers invented *us.* Anyone'll do. Any number can play. That chimpanzee on the TV. Rocket expert making speeches all the time. Quiz contest winner. Any broken-down actor or actress. Fag authors. Anyone who's *in* on it, who's *with* it. Now it's you and me, Laura. Whether we approve or not, we're victims of twentieth-century blandness. We're supplyin' the big emotional gap. Used to be religion, I guess, industrial progress, or some such thing— but that's all gone. No commitment, no emotions. No more saints; no more leaders; no more secessionists or populists. Just us. Con-test winners. Criminals. Experts. Funny people. Hell, they don't have to be people at all—like that monkey. A kind of mixed grill of nobodies."

"I'm not consoled," she said.

"I don't aim at consolin' you. I just wanted to be realistic, the way you always are, Laura."

The radio, humming through his colloquy, went a few decibels higher when he ended his oration.

". . . local police admit they're up against a stone wall. As for Police Chief Caspar Rheinholdt, he faces a barrage of new criticism for alleged bungling of the case. Last night's meeting of the Santa Luisa City Council was thrown into an uproar when Councilman Ingram Kalisher, a critic of Mayor Palmer Speed—who has supported Rheinholdt—proposed a probe of the Sanlu police force. Although Speed succeeded in tabling the motion, the Good Government League, Kalisher's party, said they were not finished. They claim to have collected nine thousand signatures in support of their move. Meanwhile, no new word from the police on the progress of the investigation. One source close to the police indicated that unless contact is made with the kidnaper in the next forty-eight hours, or, at least, before the weekend, hopes for Amy's safety will be considerably lessened. The source pointed out that the usual pattern in kidnapings is for . . ."

Fritzie turned off the noise. "They all got opinions, damn them. Nothin' to help us, but opinions." He rose from the stool and looked out the window. The reporters were still there —a half-dozen cars, a knot of men lounging alongside a station wagon. "Might've been all over except for them," he said. "Funny. Nobody seems to think that way. They all coverin' up for each other. Not just that paper that broke the story—but all of 'em—howlin' around here like savages and refusin' to move on."

He walked to the sink, where his wife was stacking dishes. "Why doesn't he call?" Andrus whispered. "He wants his money—we'll give it to him."

"Maybe today," Laura said. "Maybe today. And maybe tomorrow. I wonder how long we can go on saying that? How much courage do we have, Fritzie? Or does it take any courage at all? We'll live. We'll see light and dark—the sky, the seasons. But not Amy."

"No. Stop that. We went through this last night, Laura. Stop that hysterical talk."

She seemed distracted. "I've read about these parents who refuse to believe their sons have been killed—you know—missing in action, presumed dead. And years after the war, they go on insisting their boy is alive. They show up at veterans' conventions handing out leaflets, wearing sandwich boards with pictures of their son. He's rotting under some lagoon—and there they are, advertising their misery, parading their disbelief, as if their insolent refusal to accept death has some grandeur, bathing their egos in illusion and self-pity. Is that what we're destined for? Never to know? To spend our lives handing out photographs of Amy at conventions of police chiefs? Fritzie, it would be easier the other way—to *know* she were dead."

"Don't, don't," he cried softly. "Don't talk about it. Don't think about it. It won't be that way. You said you envied me my talent for illusion. Now come on, Laura, try some of it. It's easy. It's easier than thinkin'."

He left her. In the nursery he found Milt Bannon and Ed Case awaiting their relief. They had little to tell Andrus. Bannon commented that Rheinholdt was not yet at his desk. It was almost 9:00, and for as long as they had known the chief, he was always at work by 8:30. "Maybe it's good news," Case offered. "Only something big would keep the chief from getting in on time." Bannon nodded his agreement: "You can set your watch with him, Mr. Andrus." Fritzie smiled weakly at the two men: rather stupid, well-meaning louts—the kind who gravitated into police work. Their flimsy optimism hardly affected him; he had lost faith in the Santa Luisa police. He kept envisioning some infrahuman miracle, some massive shaking and moving of people and events, as the only salvation for his daughter.

McFeeley, arriving at headquarters just before nine, stopped at communications. Two uniformed men were resuming the telephone calls to printers and paper jobbers. The list seemed longer, more hopeless than the previous evening. McFeeley reminded them that any connection with the red-inked paper was to get top priority—he and Raffalovitch were to be notified at once.

When he hurried upstairs to Rheinholdt's office, he caught Clyde Hertmann's cautionary hand, admonishing him to stay in the corridor.

Puzzled, Joe complied, watching Hertmann peer innocently into the chief's office, then join him in the hallway. Farmer Baines got up and followed Hertmann. The two retainers guided Joe a few paces down the corridor.

"The FBI's here," Hertmann whispered. "A guy named Wagley."

McFeeley frowned. "Rheinholdt must have called them. Or the mayor. I guess last night's Council meeting tore it."

Hertmann shrugged. "I don't know what happened, Joe. Rheinholdt isn't in. He hasn't called."

"What did the agent say?" Joe asked.

"Wagley? Not a word. You know them. They wouldn't give the time of day to their grandmother." Hertmann peered covertly at the opened door.

Baines' wrinkled face was almost pathetic. "The chief would never do that. He'd never call the Bureau unless they forced him. That guy in the office—I bet he's got no right to be there."

"I better talk to him," McFeeley said. "He's just another cop who went to college, maybe law school."

"I guess you better," Hertmann said. "But don't commit the chief. Look, Joe, don't get sore—but you know how he carries on about the FBI. If he didn't ask them, you better not show him anything until Rheinholdt confirms."

"Don't worry," the detective said. "All he gets are the skull charts—the ones the Russian left." McFeeley walked into Rheinholdt's office, the two uniformed men trailing him sadly. Joe was a little annoyed with himself for again falling so naturally into the role of comforter. *What is it with me?* McFeeley wondered. *What qualities do I have that enforce people to lean on me? My crooked nose? Because I can shoot fouls? Who did I ever beat? And if I'm so smart, why ain't I rich?*

Wagley was a stocky man in his late thirties. He had the chest and shoulders of a football guard, but his legs and hips were lean —almost unequal to holding up the muscled torso. His thinning black hair had been combed across his tan pate with much care— each fine, dark strand preserving its own identity. The FBI man had a large-featured, friendly face, and he pumped Joe's hand warmly.

"You must be new," Joe said. "I knew a few of the LA men. Is Harley Betts still with you?"

"Yes. I just got out here. Reassigned from the east."

The east. The closemouthedness delighted Joe. They told you nothing, absolutely nothing—and they were marvels at getting things out of you. You had to hand it to them; they were professionals.

"I'm a little weary from the last few days," Joe said apologetically. "Maybe I missed a beat. Did Rheinholdt request your help?" He attempted to sound politely curious; yet a surliness crept into his voice.

"Last night."

Joe nodded. "That's funny. He didn't tell me about it."

"I don't know the details," Wagley said. "Apparently our office got a call. Frankly, we were expecting one. A lot sooner, in fact."

"You don't know Rheinholdt. He isn't very chummy with federal cops."

"I've heard that. It's just that this was a pretty rough deal for a local force. Even he should have realized that."

McFeeley started to get up. "Well, I guess you'll have to wait for him. He's usually in by now."

Wagley smiled. "You could give me a head start. You have a file I could look at?"

"Well—I'd like to—but only the chief is authorized to show files, and besides, I don't even know if you have a right to be here."

"You're a book cop," Wagley said.

"That's me. Look, I don't mean to be difficult, but I'm not very bright. I go to night school, so maybe I can be an FBI man someday."

"No offense, Joe. We'll see the files sooner or later. The sooner the better for the child. I don't mean to knock you people, but we're equipped for this. You're not."

McFeeley got up. "You think we booted it?"

"Maybe yes, maybe no. It's too much to ask a local police force to handle a ransom kidnaping. Like the way you let the newspapers get in your way."

Joe seemed to slump a little. "You tell me. What do you do with a hundred reporters who won't move? And a mayor who says they have to stay? And a pool agreement to cover—that everyone breaks? How would the Bureau handle that? You guys get along fine with the newspapers."

"Simple," Wagley said. "If we said go, they'd go. It's a matter of *respect*."

"And they didn't have any for us, right? For me in particular?"

"It looks that way."

"Yes, it does." The admission, forced from him by the FBI man, a professional, uninvolved cop, a man who had no reason to be critical of him, drenched McFeeley with self-disgust. The agent had put his finger on it. They had not *respected* him. He was Joe Mc-Feeley, a third-rate detective on a fourth-rate police force, an underpaid, uneducated mick. The self-knowledge galled McFeeley, hurtful because it was true. The reporters, lingering, bargaining, cheating, conniving, had been emboldened to behave as they did because they neither feared nor respected him. The FBI could have forced them to move—not Joe McFeeley.

All along, McFeeley had insisted that the events of Monday

night were beyond his control. He had done everything in his power. He had threatened to pack off the mob to the pokey; he had been firm, fair, cognizant of the child's safety. And now his inadequacy had been made apparent to him by the federal man. *They did not respect him.* There would have been no question of reporters' and photographers' talking back to an FBI agent, of presenting him with a prearranged "pool," of daring him to arrest them. They would have cleared out—without conditions, without cheating, without breaking their own arbitrary rules. As this awareness of his failings gnawed at him, McFeeley, after a few uneasy moments of self-analysis, reached one stubborn conclusion. Having failed once, he would now succeed. It sounded childish, a boy scout's view of life, but the young detective was something of a boy scout. Just as he would grimly fight his way through textbooks he partially understood, through chemistry formulae and equations that confused him, so now (he told himself) he would vindicate himself in the Andrus matter. He did not dislike Wagley (as Rheinholdt surely would), but he would have to conceive of him as the man he was assigned to guard in a basketball game. They would shake hands before the center jump, then try to outscramble each other for forty minutes.

McFeeley picked up the manila folder on Rheinholdt's desk that contained their limited file—photostats, photographs, reports from the crime search, the lab work, the logs, notes on interviews—and tucked it under one arm.

"That's it, Joe?" the FBI man asked.

"That's it."

"Don't trust me?" Wagley smiled. "Isn't it kind of silly to fool around with something so serious? You take my word for it. Rheinholdt called us last night. By this afternoon we'll have men from Frisco, Seattle and Phoenix moving into LA. Sure—you fellows'll be expected to help. But it'll be the Bureau's responsibility."

"You can have it. But I have to get orders from Rheinholdt. He should be in any minute. He says O.K.—it's yours."

Wagley did not seem overly annoyed. He shook his head slowly, as if unable to comprehend the pettiness of small-town police. "Listen, McFeeley," he said easily, "why don't *you* try to locate Rheinholdt? Ask your mayor. He must know. I did a little checking on your administrative setup. There isn't any police commissioner in Sanlu. Rheinholdt and the mayor abolished the job—so the mayor's the only answerable official. Why don't you buzz him?"

Admiring the man's thoroughness, Joe obliged him. He found Mayor Speed perplexed, unable to explain the FBI's entry in the case. He had not seen Rheinholdt that morning, had heard nothing from him. "It's only a little after nine, Joe," Palmer Speed said. "The chief should be in any minute. Just sit tight awhile. If the Bureau says he asked for them, I'm sure he did, and as soon as he confirms it, we'll have to give them every co-operation. I'll depend on you for that, Joe."

"Well, I guess we'd just better sit tight, as the mayor said," Joe advised Wagley.

"That's what I'll do," the FBI man said pleasantly. "We've got men at the house already talking to the family—witnesses—anyone. Crazy, isn't it? Everyone co-operates except you people."

"It's crazy," McFeeley agreed. He took the file with him as he left the chief's office, leaving it with Baines, with orders to lock it in his desk.

Rheinholdt had left his house at 8:15 that morning—his usual departure time. He carried with him the envelope containing his resignation. It had been his intention to deliver it personally to Mayor Speed at the latter's sporting goods store. It occurred to him that the mayor, in all likelihood, would not be in until after 9:00, and he did not like the idea of parking on the main street awaiting him: Rheinholdt had grown increasingly apprehensive of public stares and comments. As for going into the office, that, too, appalled him. There was the matter of cleaning out his desk and his locker, but he would have Hertmann do that for him. There remained one alternative—an automobile ride, his face hidden behind dark glasses, his tortured person anonymous. Thus, like some great wounded whale, he began to drive pointlessly in wide circles, out of Sanlu, across the Valley, on and off freeways, past the residential sections, the tract homes, a half-dozen shopping centers, a dozen towns—Encino, Van Nuys, Tarzana, Dorchester, Granada, Droitwich. . . . After a while, the driving lulled and calmed him. No one recognized him. No one pointed a finger at him. He was secure, protected in the shell of his black Dodge, an elderly southland gent, an avocado rancher or an insurance salesman, out on a morning's business. The notion of masquerade, of escape, pleased him and by 10:30 he was still driving about, observing traffic rules sedulously, signaling both with blinkers and his thick left arm, happily cocooned in midmorning's gritty heat.

Soon he forgot about the letter on the seat, the missing child, his leaderless department. He would settle for this the rest of his life—just driving around, unrecognized, away from the whole mess.

T. T. Hansel concluded his dictation, pleased with the manner in which he had subtly introduced the *Truth's* role in the Andrus affair in his speech for the graduate seminar in journalism at the University of California in Los Angeles. The Editor & Publisher was much in demand as a guest speaker in the academic world. He sought these forums as part of his campaign to give the *Truth* a higher tone. Playing back his recorded speech, he nodded approvingly.

. . . *We are faced with an ever-growing conspiracy of silence. We of the press, guardians of the public trust, of the people's right to know, are most aware of this conspiracy. Only in the past few days, we witnessed, here in Los Angeles, a crude and misguided attempt to suppress information to which the people were entitled . . .*

His secretary entered with a proof of the front page. Hansel interrupted his monitoring of his own voice to scan it. First he read Mona's piece swiftly. It was a little gamy, a little sneaky, but free of anything actionable. He had to admire Mears: she made her own news. It was a talk piece, something people would gossip about, from which they would draw chilling inferences.

Then it occurred to him that something was amiss. The eight-column banner for Mona's piece sounded different.

EXCLUSIVE: MONA MEARS INTERVIEWS AMY'S PARENTS!

After a few seconds of study, Hansel realized what had happened. The words had been intended for use as a streamer in smaller letters, *above* the actual seventy-two-point headline. What had it been? He remembered something about *tragedy—a troubled house.* But this had been deleted, and the simple announcement of Mona's interview had been used as the headline proper. The alteration angered Hansel. Immediately he called the city room. Mr. Hood was not in yet. Hansel summoned the managing editor, Ed Kalaidjian. That fearful man, engaged in checking thefts of stamps and pencils, only heightened Hansel's fury with his mumbling.

"We sure look great today, Ted," Kalaidjian said. "Mona is murdering the opposition."

"There are going to be some more murders around here. Who changed the head on the story?"

"Ch-changed?" Kalaidjian stuttered. "Not me. Not Trigg. We went home after you O.K.'d it."

"Where was Herbert last night?"

"Ah—he was talking to Swinnerton till about 9:00 or so."

"Did he change it?"

"I don't know, Ted. I don't know at all."

"Well, for God's sake, if it wasn't you or Trigg, it must have been Herbert. Mona and I had agreed on it. Who else would change it?"

Hansel hung up, disgusted. The trouble with former rivals was that they persisted; Hood had no business hanging around the shop after he had been bypassed. Now, he was a vestigial organ, a reminder to Hansel of a triumph that had been too easy. Hood was a dinosaur, a hang-over from a kind of newspapering that had died with orange editions and Sunday-supplement gorillas. What was worse, in his dotage, he was developing retroactive guilt, a latter-day conscience that served only to muddle the *Truth's* operation.

Hansel's secretary located Hood at Rocco's. His whereabouts were revealed to her by Connie Potenza, with an appeal to keep the old man's hideaway a secret. When Hansel's call reached him, Hood was squinting into a cracked mirror, working a recalcitrant electric razor over his rubbery cheeks. He had no hang-over; he was not tired; he had already downed a few eye openers. As ever, the booze had not failed him. The only reason for his dalliance in Rocco's storeroom—surrounded by crates of soda and ginger ale, cartons of fifths and assorted brooms, mops and furniture—was a growing sense of repugnance with his superior.

"Herbert? Where the devil are you?" Hansel shouted.

"Ah—just leaving my apartment, Ted. I took a sleeping pill last night and I'm still woozy." He felt idiotic, his fat, undershirted body crammed into the phone booth. Outside, downtown Los Angeles suffocated under a miasma of hot dust. Who ever heard of a man spending the night in the back of a saloon? An executive, at that! A member of Sigma Delta Chi and the Old-Timers' Press Club of Chicago! Once they had talked of Herbert Hood as the next board chairman of the Organization; now he was reduced to lying to T. T. Hansel.

"Herbert, did you change the headline on Mona's story?"

"Yes, I did, Ted. I came back to the shop about 11:30 to check the overnight and I didn't like the——"

"Do you know what you're doing? You don't know what you're doing."

Hansel's cutting voice nauseated him; the Editor & Publisher was using the tone he reserved for the likes of Kalaidjian.

"Just a minute, Ted. You have no right to talk to me like that. You worked for me once."

"I have every right in the world to. What do you mean countermanding my orders? Didn't the overnight tell you I had O.K.'d that head? That Mona and I had agreed on it?"

"They did, and I felt it stank."

"Really?" Hansel's voice was low and soft.

Was it possible, wondered Hood, that the man was a coward? A conniving yellowbelly?

"I did. Ted, what are you trying to do? Torture those parents till they die of shame? Good Christ, isn't what's happened to them enough without all that crap about the unhappy home, and the kid nobody loved, and the drunken husband?"

"Mona did not say that."

"She hinted at it—all that stuff about the bourbon bottle. And then that headline—*More Tragedy in a Tragic House*. Who said Mears is a judge of what's tragic? I tell you something, Ted, I wish I was braver than I am. I wouldn't have knocked that head off. I'd have thrown that whole column into the hellbox."

"You would?" T.T. asked. "What kept you from doing that?"

"I'm almost as rotten as you," Hood said swiftly. An erratic fluttering agitated his viscera; he had a sudden fear that he would die of coronary thrombosis—that instant.

"I think you're drunk, Herbert. I'll disregard what you just said."

"I mean it. I'm probably worse than you *and* Mears. You two—you just don't *see*, you don't *hear* anything else. You're too far gone. I still see and hear what's going on, but I haven't got the courage to do anything about it." He halted—but Hansel, not hanging up, was silent as death. "Like that dirty paragraph at the end of Mears' piece," Hood continued, "about a police source telling her that ransom kidnapings were the rarest of crimes and that you always had to suspect something else. Brother, what a tie-in with the stuff she had just written—about the tragic house and the child nobody loved."

For a bleak, revealing moment, Hansel found himself on the defensive. He cursed himself, cursed Hood, for having deftly maneuvered him to this unfamiliar attitude. "Herbert, don't you cast any aspersions on Mona's sources. Her informed source on this was——"

Gruffly, Hood cut him off. "Yeah, I know. Her imagination. A handout. Someone at the Press Club bar. I've spent a lifetime quoting informed sources, and most of them were my own inventions."

"I can't waste time arguing with you. I'm furious about the highhanded manner in which you changed that headline. I don't like it. I don't care about your senile guilt feelings, your emergence as a crusader for ethics in journalism. But I won't stand for tampering with my orders. I've never tolerated insubordination, from copy boys or general managers. You and I shall have a meeting this afternoon. And Herbert—don't try any of your little phone calls to New York. I know you have friends in the Organization, but I suspect their patience is wearing as thin as mine."

Hansel hung up. It was odd, odd beyond analysis the way their enmity had sparked, flared up, and now raged uncontrollably—over the matter of that four-year-old girl. It was even odder how the central issue—her survival—no longer concerned either of them. In the harsh words passed between himself and Hansel, not once had Amy Andrus' safety been mentioned.

Hood remained glued to the seat in the phone booth, his flanks overflowing it. A rapping on the glass street door roused him, and he looked up to see the shapeless figure of Eliot Sparling. The young man was grinning and waving one hand. His mouth kept forming unheard appeals; behind him a noisome green bus discharged passengers. Hood waddled to the door and opened it. The morning heat rushed into Rocco's air-conditioned restaurant; the hot effusion seemed a product of Sparling's intrusive presence.

"Whew. What a scorcher," Eliot said stupidly. He slammed the door, rattling its slatted blind. Inside the gloomy saloon—faintly aromatic of stale beer and ammonia—the two confronted each other.

"You back again?" Hood asked. His shaving had been interrupted, and he walked to the rear, where he resumed his labors with the electric shaver. Eliot rested his body in the doorway of the rear room, watching the general manager—as a male child will observe his father's morning shave—with slightly jealous fascination.

"Mr. Hood, I had a long talk with Swinnerton last night."

"You did?"

"Yep. Harve told me the works. Then he took off—for points

west. The *Truth* doesn't have any district man in Sanlu any more. Don't look at me—I got a job."

Hood administered a few halfhearted strokes to his neck. The white hairs refused to budge, and he succeeded only in raising red welts on his skin. He yanked the razor from the wall plug and started buttoning on a clean shirt.

"What am I supposed to say to that?" Hood asked.

"Doesn't it bother you? You can't let Swinnerton go uncontradicted. He told all, as they say. You knew about the cops' request for secrecy a little after 4:00. Swinnerton backed the cops' story."

"Not interested," Hood said. He returned to the mirror and began knotting a red tie. "Boy, you keep sticking that big nose of yours in where it doesn't belong, you'll get it lopped off."

"Oh, come on, Mr. Hood. Yesterday it was my big mouth. Today my big nose. Flattery gets you nowhere. I'd like to advise you that UBC is backing me on this deal. You know Tom Ballstead?"

"Yes, I do. He's an old friend and he wouldn't be party to any screwy scheme such as comparing the times phone calls were made."

"Hah-hah, the joke's on you," Sparling cawed—taunting a school-yard menace in the Bronx. "The joke's on you, because Mr. Ballstead was present when Swinnerton confessed last night, just before he left town because he couldn't face the music in case that child is dead. Mr. Ballstead's given his O.K. to whatever I do."

"Out of my way, son," Hood said. He hustled his torso into his dark-blue jacket, fiddling with a soiled pocket handkerchief, patting the inner pocket to remind himself that he had his wallet, his fountain pen.

"You'll regret it, Mr. Hood," Eliot said. "The onus is on you. Swinnerton called *you* before 4:00 o'clock. You knew the story was to be kept out. You yourself called the cops at 4:30, and Sergeant Baines asked you *again* not to use it. But the *Truth* printed it anyway and then excused itself by saying Rheinholdt refused to talk. I got it all."

"We'll deny it."

"I got it on tape. Swinnerton's voice—me and Ballstead as witnesses. The policeman you spoke to will willingly appear on our TV show exposing you." This last was Sparling's invention—but it was a good notion, and he would suggest it to Ballstead later, which almost made it a fact.

"We'll say they all lied to cover themselves."

"Will you say it, Mr. Hood? Or will Hansel *make* you say it?"

How old is he? Hood wondered. Twenty-eight? Twenty-nine? How could anyone so young, so loud, and so ugly stand there and have the nerve to threaten him, to dare him? Eliot Sparling was a smudge, a noisy, ill-mannered lout. Hood had fired him three months ago without a twinge of remorse, a flutter of sorrow. And now this oaf stood in front of him, demanding his concurrence in a betrayal of the Organization. And most dreadful of all—Sparling was right and Hood was wrong. Vaguely, the old man recalled Hansel's mentioning some big shot at UBC, a man who would suppress any attempt to besmirch the newspaper's role in the Andrus affair. Thus recalling, he succumbed. The thought of Hansel's pulling strings, forcing actions, evading responsibility infuriated Hood. It concentrated all his latent hatred of Hansel, it summoned up that final shred of lost honor that had served him so destructively ever since they had gotten the beat on the kidnaping.

"I don't want my name used," Hood said hoarsely.

"No. You have to be quoted."

"Impossible. Call me an *informed source*. Take it or leave it." Hood walked into the restaurant and sank into a booth. Eliot sat opposite him.

"Can I tape it?" Sparling asked.

"No, dammit. I said you couldn't use my name. Or my voice. *Informed source* is good enough for every newspaper in the country; it should be good enough for you."

Eliot nodded. "O.K., an informed source close to the *Truth?*"

"Yes, yes, goddam you. What do you want to know?"

Sparling reached into the pocket of his toxic green sports shirt and extracted a sheaf of yellow papers. In addition to Hertmann's schedule of telephone calls, he had with him a transcription of Harvey Swinnerton's taped testimony. He squinted at his notations. "The first you and Hansel knew about the kidnaping, Mr. Hood, was around 3:50 P.M.—when Swinnerton called you, right?"

Hood hesitated. His froggish head drooped, as if the weight of the revelations he was about to make was dragging it down. For a moment Eliot thought he was going to renege; then the old man spoke.

"Swinnerton called much earlier. When he saw you getting arrested, when you shouted at him. He didn't know it was a kidnaping then, but I was suspicious right off."

"I mean when he had it confirmed—from Dr. Todd. Around ten to four, right?"

"I guess so," Hood said.

"What happened at the paper? Did Mr. Hansel give the go-ahead?"

As if they were paining him, Hood removed his eyeglasses, folded them and stuffed them into his pocket. His eyes thus disarmed, he looked old and sickly. In Sparling's estimate of him, the general manager had always had a kind of indestructible alcoholic insensitivity: a man well adapted to pre-Christmas firings, denials of merit raises, all the harsh edicts that were peculiar to the *Truth*. Now he appeared quite as helpless as any of his victims.

"And it was you who asked Swinnerton to phone the cops at around 4:10?" Eliot asked softly, almost sweetly. "I mean—knowing they were getting ready to call you with the secrecy request? You had him call anyway?" Hood nodded, said nothing. "May I say, sir, I admire you for that?" Eliot asked rhetorically.

Herbert Hood shut his eyes. "You ever try to stop a team of runaway horses? I did once in Cicero when I was younger than you are now. Wagon belonged to the Pforzheim Brewery. The driver had a heart attack. Those goddam Percherons dragged me three blocks before I stopped them. I tell you, boy, it was a hell of a lot easier than trying to stop Ted Hansel when he knew we had an exclusive, a clear beat on that kidnaping."

"But—but—how could Hansel justify what he did?" asked Eliot. "O.K., you were the only ones who had it. O.K., the cops hadn't called you—yet. But after Swinnerton called *them* and was asked to tell you to lay off——"

Hood looked up suddenly. "What the hell do you know? What the hell do any of you know about the pressure on Ted Hansel? And the pressure he puts on us? Sure, Ted's a tough bastard, but he's got a paper to save."

"Ah, come on, Mr. Hood. Is the whole Organization worth the life of a four-year-old girl?"

"That hasn't got a goddam thing to do with it!" Hood said. He pounded the table top. "Not a goddam thing!"

Eliot waited for additional explanation; none was offered.

With utter weariness, Hood said to him: "Go on, get me the bottle of Four Roses and a double-shot glass."

Sparling slid out of the booth and walked behind the bar. The medicinal-beery odor of the saloon disturbed the young man; it was indecent, vaguely corrupt—particularly at 9:00 in the morning. He returned, poured his former boss a glassful, and watched him drain it as if it were cool, clear spring water.

How much do I have to tell him? Hood wondered. *How we all stood around in the composing room under those lights that make you look purple and green; and how we all shivered a little when we saw the wet, glistening page proof of the extra, with the big, big black type . . .*

TV DIRECTOR'S CHILD
KIDNAPED IN SANLU!

. . . and how we all felt the old thrill, the blood rising; and how not a one of us had time to think about what this would mean to the child and the parents; and how the circulation manager had the trucks and a few taxicabs standing by to get it on the street; and how when there was still time to hold it back, Swinnerton called, relaying the word from the cops. . . .

"I went to the mat with Hansel," Hood said thinly. "I told him we had no damn right to print that story. We were told. We knew. The word got to us at 4:20, and the paper wouldn't hit the street for another forty minutes."

"How—how could he possibly excuse what he did?" Eliot asked plaintively.

"He said we hadn't been called directly by the police, by the chief. He said every other paper had been telephoned—some responsible editor had received the request. On something so big, Hansel kept saying, we had the right to insist on the same treatment—a direct call from Rheinholdt."

"Rheinholdt didn't call *anyone* himself. Baines did."

"Ted didn't know that at the time. I told him the call could have come from a washerwoman at headquarters to the sports department copy boy and we'd have to honor it—but he wouldn't buy it."

The recollection disturbed Hood. He poured another glass of whisky and drank it slowly this time, thinking of the two of them—himself and Hansel—jammed into the chief compositor's tiny fly-specked office, arguing it out; they had had to shout at each other—in the pressroom they were rolling with the new front page for the extra.

"The goddamnedest thing happened," the general manager said, draining the last of the booze. "He met me halfway. I never believed he would, but he did."

Sweating, his hand trembling, Eliot shuffled the papers, located his copy of Patrolman Hertmann's schedule. "Am I right, Mr.

Hood? He let you call the cops back—to ask for Rheinholdt's personal assurance? At around 4:30? When there was still time to pull the paper back?"

"That's right. That idiot chief wouldn't come to the phone, and that was that. Hansel had an excuse now. Not much of an excuse, but an excuse. Good enough for him."

Eliot smiled grimly. "And good enough for everyone else in the business, right, Mr. Hood?"

"Looks that way, doesn't it?"

Sparling shook his head. "How could he possibly say no one was called until 6:04? How could he?"

Hood, grunting, grimacing, pushed his well-larded hulk across the booth and stood up. "He didn't lie. We weren't called until then. No official notification until 6:04."

"That was no notification," Eliot said. "Rheinholdt just called to bawl you out."

"And didn't he do a job," Hood said. He paused at the door. "Funny thing. I've been putting the blast on people all my life. I don't have to tell you, Sparling; you got it from me once. Now I was on the receiving end, and I got to hand it to that old bastard of a traffic cop. He laid me out. And you know what? I deserved it."

His behind waddled as he tugged at the door. The smoggy heat rushed in; Hood left.

In full throat Eliot yelled after him: "I don't think so, Mr. Hood! I don't think so at all!"

As Wagley had informed Joe McFeeley, the FBI would take the case over—at the invitation of Chief Rheinholdt himself. Unfortunately, no evidence existed of the invitation, aside from a phone conversation Rheinholdt had held with the agent on duty the previous night. And no one in official capacity in Santa Luisa knew of it. The one man who might have cleared up the confusion, Rheinholdt himself, was cruising southern California, finding in his meanderings blessed surcease from misery.

Consequently, when a second FBI agent appeared at the Andrus home that morning—a lean, blond man named Fewsmith—nobody was quite prepared for him. Irvin Moll greeted the federal man cordially and with a little awe, then telephoned headquarters. He spoke to McFeeley, who relayed the mayor's muddled advice: sit tight until the chief shows up, then give the Bureau every cooperation.

Agent Fewsmith accepted the ruling with an indifferent shrug. His manner indicated that, sooner or later, the local police would surrender jurisdiction, and the sooner the better. Like Fred Wagley, he was polite, efficient and detached. He made no effort to enforce his mandate on Moll, accepting the sergeant's relayed orders from McFeeley. "You've kept us waiting two days," Fewsmith said, smiling; "a few hours' delay won't hurt."

Fritzie Andrus was less amenable. The obstructionist tactics of the Santa Luisa police infuriated him and he let Moll know it. "Hell's fire!" he shouted. "Who ever heard of such an operation? Keystone Kops, that's all you are! Keystone Kops! You heard the agent, didn't you? If he *says* the FBI got a call from Rheinholdt, they *got* it! Fine time for your chief to disappear! Sweet Jesus, what a mess!"

As he paced the living room, pausing every now and then to shout at Moll (who kept darting back to the nursery to answer calls), Laura tried to pacify him. It did no good. His fury intensified; she realized it was a harmless outlet for all that churned within him. Fewsmith, taking advantage of one of Moll's absences, suggested Fritzie talk to him.

"You're not obliged to," the FBI man said, "until such time as somebody in authority here O.K.'s us—or Rheinholdt shows up. But we'll be in it soon enough, and no one can stop you from discussing it with me. Same for you, Mrs. Andrus."

"Fine!" Fritzie cried. "What do you want to know? Let's go! Let's get some action!"

"You mind coming with me?" the agent asked.

"Why not heah?"

"It might be better if we did it in my car. We'll drive somewhere, park and talk. No aspersions intended on anyone's police work, but we like to get a fresh start. With no one else around."

The notion of a secret conclave with the agent pleased Andrus. He left with Fewsmith, the latter advising Laura that he would be happy to discuss the case with her—under the same conditions, privately, with no listeners—as soon as they returned.

Some twenty minutes later, Joe McFeeley arrived with little new information. They had resumed calling printers and paper jobbers; as of ten minutes ago, they had had no luck. He told Laura that, in all likelihood, Rheinholdt had called the FBI: they were too efficient an organization not to have double-checked his invitation. Still, the mayor, as civilian head of the Sanlu police, had given instructions to await Rheinholdt's confirmation. It disturbed McFeeley when he learned that Andrus had gone off for a talk with the agent.

"Did it when my back was turned," Moll said sorrowfully.

"I guess we can't blame him," Joe said. "We don't look too hot so far. The way the newspapers have been laying us out. You saw the *Register* this morning."

The telephone rang—they had arranged for it to ring during the day but be silenced at night in favor of the blinker—and Moll lumbered back to the nursery. Joe tried to engage Laura in small talk: she was polite, but he sensed her numbness, her unwillingness to waste words or energy on anything but her lost child.

"Joe!" Moll stage-whispered from the nursery. "Joe! Guy says he has Amy! You got those questions?"

They had drawn up, after the fruitless trip to the overpass, a list of questions that any caller claiming to have the child, or information about the child, would be required to answer.

Laura followed McFeeley into the nursery. Moll had an ear nailed to the phone. He was breathing heavily; his stupid eyes were appealing to Joe. McFeeley opened the steno pad they had been using to log calls, turned to a page marked off with two paper clips, and extracted a sheet of white paper with a set of typewritten questions on it. Then he took the telephone from Moll.

"Hello," he said. "Who is this?"

The answering voice was muffled. "Who's this?" it repeated. "Who are you?"

"A friend of the family," McFeeley said.

"Oh, I want to talk to Mrs. Andrus."

"She's busy."

"I have to. I have her child."

Laura, hearing the filtered voice from the averted mouthpiece, staggered. Moll went to her side; both moved closer to McFeeley.

"Well, you see, we have a problem. A lot of cranks have been calling her," McFeeley said earnestly, "and we can't let her talk to anyone unless we're sure he has the child. She's not feeling so good, Mrs. Andrus, and the doctor says she can't speak to everyone. Tell me what you want. I'm authorized to talk."

He nodded toward the other telephone. Moll picked it up, turned his back and dialed headquarters. When he got the operator, he whispered instructions that a trace be placed on the incoming call. Then he hung up softly.

"I see," the caller said. "Well, I won't talk to anyone but her.

How do I know you aren't a cop?" The voice was getting more indistinct, more strangled.

"You don't know," Joe said. "I'll make a deal with you. If you can tell me something about the note, to prove you left it, I'll put Mrs. Andrus on."

The caller paused. Involuntarily, Laura's trembling hand reached out for the phone. McFeeley shook his head negatively, cautioned her with a finger to his lips.

"O.K. But you better play ball with me. I'll tell you what's in the note." He was now spacing his words, as well as muffling them—as if to disguise his cadence of speech.

"How much ransom did you ask?" Joe asked.

"Forty-two hundred dollars. In fifties."

"What are the first two words of the note?"

"Child safe."

"The last two?"

"Ah—otherwise trouble."

"What's the note made of?"

"What?"

"Made of. What kind of paper? What kind of lettering?"

"It's plain white paper. The words are cut out of a newspaper."

"What signature is on it?"

"There ain't—there isn't any."

Joe sucked his breath in. He steadied himself against the folding table. Moll had slipped a photostat of the note in front of him when he had begun the conversation, but Joe did not need it. The caller knew the note: he was either the criminal or a confederate.

"All right. What can we do about getting the child back?"

"You said you'd let me speak to Mrs. Andrus if I knew what was in the note. You must be a cop. I'll hang up, I'm warning you."

McFeeley gave the phone to Laura. With his lips he formed the words: "Keep him on. Keep talking."

"Hello," Laura said. "Is Amy all right? Can I speak to her?"

"She's O.K."

"Can I speak to her?"

"No. She isn't with me."

"Is she eating well? Does she sleep at night? What have you told her?"

"She's all right. She's safe."

"Please, please, let me hear her voice. You knew what was in the note—you must have her."

"No. She's staying at a friend's house. I'm calling somewhere else."

There was a deliberate quality about the voice that terrified her. He kept spacing the words, as if separating them with trios of periods, and he kept speaking in hoarse, hidden tones—possibly muffling his breath in a handkerchief.

"Please listen to me," Laura pleaded—a wash of tears distorting her voice. "Please. We have the money. It's right here. You can have it now. Whenever you say. When do you want to meet me? Where? I promise you, I promise you—no police. I don't care who you are. I don't want you to get caught. I just want—I just want——" She could not jail herself in fraudulent control any longer. She cried. "I—just—want—my child——"

"O.K.," the caller said. "O.K., you can have her. But what about yesterday? I read it in the papers. When you left the dough on that phony call—there were cops all over the place. How about that?"

"It won't happen today," Laura wept. "Let me have her, please, please."

"I can't talk any more. I know how they trace calls. I'll call you back at 7:00 tonight. Only you are to answer the phone. No police. The kid is safe—but I won't say for how long. You got till 7:00 to think it over. No cops. Not a cop anywhere. I'll arrange another meeting. You believe me?"

"Yes. Yes. Tell Amy I love her. Tell her I'll see her soon. Does she need anything? Does she have clean clothes? Is she eating? Tell me about her."

He had hung up. The phone was locked in her hand. McFeeley took it from her gently and guided her to a chair.

"That was him," the detective said. "Did I hear right? He said he'd call back at 7:00?"

Laura nodded; the tears kept rolling down her cheeks.

"How long was he on?" Joe asked Moll.

"Less than five minutes."

"Never trace him. I wonder if we'd recognize that voice again. He disguised it pretty good—and that crazy spacing."

"I'll play it back," Moll said. He flicked off the spinning plastic discs, and, as he did so, he noticed that the take-up reel was full, the other reel empty. An embarrassed flush rouged his ears, his neck. "Oh, my God," Moll said. "I think we ran out of tape. While he was on."

McFeeley stared at the discs. "Dammit. Didn't you watch the tape? Irv, for Pete's sake—"

"I'm sorry," Moll said faintly. "I'm sorry. It's my fault, my fault. Oh, what an idiot. Maybe we got most of it." He ran the tape backwards, and they listened to the squawky babble for a few seconds. Moll halted it and started the reel moving forward again. First, they listened to the end of a conversation with an AP reporter; then a conversation between Bannon and a volunteer fire department in the Valley, offering to round up searchers. When the caller's voice came on—first with his words to Moll, *I have Amy Andrus,* then his suffocated *who's this?*—they could see at once how little tape was left. Moll ran his hand nervously through his hair.

They heard McFeeley's first responses, then the caller's *I have her child*—and then the tape ended.

"I goofed it," Moll muttered. "I should have checked. I didn't figure it was running out. What I forgot was all the stuff we wasted testing it yesterday when it was on the blink."

"Irv, don't you know you can erase that stuff?" McFeeley asked sorrowfully. "Anybody knows that."

Moll blinked his pale eyes. "Yeah. I guess I did."

Joe looked miserably at Laura. She was patting her face with a handkerchief, unconcerned with this new evidence of their incompetence. "I'm doing what he said, Lieutenant," she said. "I'll talk to him myself tonight. I'll take the call myself. And none of you will be there. He said Amy's safe. I have to believe him. I can't believe anything else."

McFeeley could no longer argue with her, or caution her, or dare to hint that the man was lying, or insane, or capable of the vilest treachery. His own ineptitude; Moll's bungling; Rheinholdt's absence—all these disarmed him. He felt weak and thickskulled—a smalltime City Hall Irishman, in too deep. When the woman had left, he had Moll play back the bit they had recorded.

"Think you might recognize that if you heard it again?" Moll asked.

Joe shrugged. "I doubt it. I was hoping we could ask that speech teacher at UCLA, the guy who specializes in accents, to listen to it and give us a clue. Every little bit helps. But with this little bit— and the way he mumbled through his whiskers——"

"It's rough," Moll said, shaking his head.

"Ring headquarters again," Joe said. "Maybe Rheinholdt's in by now." He had not the faintest idea what help the chief could be to him, what recommendations he would have. While Moll was dialing, it dawned on him that he probably wanted nothing more than Rheinholdt's deferral to the FBI, once and for all. The newspapers were probably right—the likes of Caspar Rheinholdt and Joe McFeeley had no right trying to solve kidnapings.

Shortly before 10:00 that morning Eliot Sparling burst into the UBC newsroom flourishing a sheaf of yellow papers and bellowing to Jim Farrell, three news writers and two copy boys that he had "the goods on the LA *Truth!*" His alarming tones almost silenced the clattering teleprinters.

"Eliot, hold it down, will you?" Farrell asked politely. "Tom's got a bad stomach and a headache."

"I got to see him," Eliot said.

"You're not due in till 1:00 A.M.—tomorrow."

"Who can sleep? If I was a rich deskman like you, with twenty years' seniority and top minimum salary, I could afford air conditioning."

Farrell ignored him. "Did you see Mona Mears this morning?" he asked.

"Nope. What's she got today?"

"Exclusive interview with the family." Farrell rummaged through a copy spike on his desk and located WNA's teleprinter transmission of the Mears piece. "It's a little rough—even for her. It moved during the night. Some WNA clients refused to use it."

Sparling squinted at the capital letters, the rough yellow paper.

(FOR RELEASE IN AFTERNOON PAPERS OF WEDNESDAY, SEPT. 19)
EXCLUSIVE
BY MONA MEARS
(WORLD COPYWRIGHT, 1951, BY WORLD NEWS ASSOCIATION)
SANTA LUISA, CALIFORNIA, SEPT. 18—(WNA)—I SPOKE TO THE PARENTS OF LITTLE AMY ANDRUS TODAY.
I SAT IN THEIR LAVISH $60,000 HOUSE, WAS INVITED INTO THE MOTHER'S SCULPTURE STUDIO, SHARED A BOURBON BOTTLE WITH THE FATHER.
IT IS A TRAGIC HOUSE. AN UNHAPPY HOUSE. THE KIDNAPING OF THEIR DAUGHTER TWO DAYS AGO CAN ONLY BE REGARDED AS A MALIGN TRICK OF FATE—THE LAST FLICK OF A TYRANT'S WHIP. FOR

THERE HAS BEEN VERY LITTLE JOY AT 4217 NESPOLI DRIVE—EVEN BEFORE AMY'S DISAPPEARANCE. THE SPRAWLING RANCH HOME, THE LUXURIOUS GARDENS, THE HUGE SWIMMING POOL—THESE ARE STAGE PROPERTIES.

FRITZIE ANDRUS' SUCCESS AS A TV DIRECTOR; LAURA ANDRUS' ARTISTIC TALENTS; LITTLE AMY'S PRECOCITY—NONE OF THESE HAS BROUGHT HAPPINESS. I KNOW. I SPOKE TO THE PARENTS FOR SEVERAL HOURS TODAY. I SPOKE TO NEIGHBORS. WHAT EMERGES IS A PICTURE OF TWO TALENTED, TENSE PEOPLE—GIFTED IN THEIR CHOSEN FIELDS, UTTERLY LACKING IN THE SIMPLE EVERYDAY NEEDS OF FAMILY LIFE. A FIREMAN IN EL CENTRO, A BANK CLERK IN VAN NUYS, A PARKING LOT ATTENDANT IN ARCADIA —ANY SAMPLE OF CALIFORNIANS CHOSEN AT RANDOM—IS BETTER FITTED TO THE RESPONSIBILITIES OF HOME AND FAMILY. THIS IS NOT TO BLAME FRITZIE AND LAURA ANDRUS. IT IS SIMPLY THE OLD TRUTH THAT ARTISTIC TALENT AND FAMILY RESPONSIBILITY OFTEN ARE NOT COMPATIBLE.

Eliot held the column at arm's length. "Oh, it's nasty and dirty; take it away. Open up that window and let that foul air out."

"I'm a little disgusted by it." Farrell answered a phone, checked off some items on the AP budget.

"But shrewd?" Eliot asked. "She gets the slobs on her side. The fireman in El Centro. I got her fireman in El Centro." He scanned the rest of the piece—some direct quotes from Laura and Fritzie, some quotes from an unidentified neighbor about Amy's wanderings, and finally the enigmatic paragraph about the rarity of ransom kidnapings.

AND THE IRONY! THE IRONY! A HIGHLY PLACED POLICE SOURCE ADVISED ME TODAY THAT A TRUE KIDNAPING FOR RANSOM IS THE RAREST, THE MOST FREAKISH OF CRIMES. WHAT ARE CLASSIFIED AS KIDNAPINGS ARE USUALLY ENTIRELY DIFFERENT AFFAIRS—ABDUCTIONS ACROSS STATE LINES, CRIMES ALLIED WITH CAR THEFT, SEX OFFENSES AND THE LIKE. INDEED, I'M TOLD, WHAT OFTEN APPEARS TO BE A

KIDNAPING AT FIRST OFTEN PROVES TO BE AN EN-
TIRELY DIFFERENT SORT OF CRIME.
    IN ANY CASE, AMY ANDRUS NEEDS OUR PRAYERS.
AND IF PRAYERS ALONE COULD BRING HER BACK, THIS
REPORTER'S WOULD HAVE DONE SO LONG AGO.

"It's to vomit," Eliot said. "Listen—why can't I go see Tom?"
"He's exhausted. Said he couldn't sleep last night."
"My fault," Sparling conceded. "I had him out at Swinnerton's.
We got Swinnerton to talk."
Ballstead's door opened and the news director looked sourly at
the busy newsroom. There was a greenish cast to his face. One
starved hand, frozen in arthritic attitude, was pressed against his
diaphragm.
"Anything happen?" Ballstead asked Farrell.
"I just spoke to Brack. A guy showed up this morning, and
DeGroot, the AP man, said he was an FBI agent. Maybe we'll get
some action."
Ballstead nodded. "That idiot of a chief say anything?"
"No. The reporters are so mad they're getting up a petition to
the mayor. Nobody at Sanlu police will talk; this dentist Todd is
holed up; and you can bet the parents won't say anything. It's like
covering a Cominform meeting."
"Hah!" Eliot shouted. "The *reporters* are gonna petition! How
about Mr. and Mrs. Andrus petitioning? To send the reporters to
jail?"
Ballstead moaned. "Christ, that voice."
"I'm sorry," Eliot said. "Tom, I got the whole thing. I have
to tell you about it. Herbert Hood admitted everything. We can't
use his name, but he gave me the story. The *Truth* knew at about
4:15. The cops told Swinnerton, and he told Hood. Everything
after that was a hedge."
Uninvited, he followed Ballstead into the office. The fried egg
sandwich was still in its wax paper; the lid was on the
coffee container. Ballstead fell into his chair. He spent a few seconds
battling a flight of spasmodic coughs. Then, his eyes tearing, he
addressed Eliot. "Now what were you shouting about out there?"
"You're not mad at me, Tom?"
"No. I just can't stand you. You say Hood admitted they knew
about the embargo at 4:15?"
"That's right. But he's still blaming it on Rheinholdt. Rhein-

holdt wouldn't come to the phone at 4:30 to *personally* talk to Hood."

He spread his notes on Ballstead's desk. The news director had the attitude of a man listening to a dentist—he hated the message, but knew it was good for him. "Start here," Eliot said; "this is a copy of Patrolman Clyde Hertmann's record of telephone calls Monday afternoon. Then go on to this—a transcript of Swinnerton's statement last night—then, for dessert, what fat Herbie gave me a half hour ago in Rocco's."

Ballstead squinted at the papers. As jaded as he was, he still respected good reporting. The loudmouth deserved a hearing. "How'd you get so ambitious, Sparling?" he asked. "And so smart? On Monday you blew everything."

"That's just it," Eliot said. "It didn't take any brains. *Anybody* could have found out. Anybody could have got it out of them. DeGroot, Ringel, Arnspeiger—any reporter covering the Andrus case, any newspaperman who could speak and write English. That's exactly what intrigues me—maybe even more than the *Truth* printing it."

"What intrigues you?" asked Ballstead.

"Tom, it took me *one* afternoon, *one* night, and *one* morning of asking questions to find out what happened. I ask you again—why didn't any editor in this whole city bother assigning someone to it? Why did they assume the *Truth* was right—or that, if they were wrong, *it didn't matter?*"

Ballstead pressed a soiled handkerchief to his mouth and stifled a gasp. "Maybe it doesn't matter," he said thickly.

"The kid's life? The whole issue? It's like people forgetting about gas chambers."

"Sit down, shut up and watch television for ten minutes," the news director said. "Let me go through this stuff."

Beaming, Eliot left the cubicle.

McFeeley tried to locate the teacher at UCLA—the one who could pinpoint people's origins through speech patterns and accents. His reward was a half hour of wasted phone calls. The man had taught at USC, not UCLA. He had transferred six months ago to a midwestern college. Indeed, the head of his department at Southern Cal—through faint laughter and a few loaded comments—hinted he was something of a charlatan. He offered to have his secretary look up the teacher's forwarding address, but by then Joe realized the pointlessness of further search.

A half hour later, Agent Fewsmith returned with Fritzie. The FBI man and McFeeley exchanged friendly greetings. Joe made no mention of the phone call, indicating to Moll to observe silence on the matter also. The mother, giving Karen her bottle—concentrating on coaxing the murmuring child to take the nipple, burping the infant—was too unnerved to discuss the call. A few more hours of keeping them ignorant would not hurt, McFeeley thought stubbornly. Perhaps the break would come; perhaps he and Rheinholdt and the whole fumbling Santa Luisa police force might be able to make amends, to pay its debts to the parents, to establish that they were worthy of *respect,* as Wagley had so candidly phrased it.

Fewsmith asked Laura if she would like to talk to him—no more than half an hour of interrogation—in his car, privately. She pleaded with the baby to suck a few more drops of milk, then ported the child on her shoulder, patting its pink back. She was rewarded with a gross belch, and she smiled appreciatively. McFeeley, standing in the corridor watching her, sensed a growing disgust with himself, with his narrow selfishness. He felt he had no right to impede her with his own craving for self-justification. And yet, the detective wondered, was he any different from Dr. Walter Todd? From the mob of reporters? From Rheinholdt and Palmer Speed, worried about what people would *think* and *say* about them?

"Is that all right, Lieutenant?" Laura asked him.

"Is what?" McFeeley asked—lost in his ruminations.

"Mr. Fewsmith wants to interview me."

"I guess so. I mean, we're just waiting to get word from the chief. You're on your own, Mrs. Andrus. You go ahead if you want to."

Laura gave the baby to Selena. Then she left with the FBI man. The latter spoke to Joe before departing. "It's 10:30. I don't want to sound difficult, but isn't this getting ridiculous? Why don't you try raising your chief again?"

Joe complied. When Baines said, mournfully, that there was still no word from Rheinholdt, Joe called Mayor Speed at his sporting goods store. He, too, had no knowledge of the chief's whereabouts, and by now he was beginning to worry. "I'll be darned if I know what's happened to Caspar," Speed said. "I spoke to his wife fifteen minutes ago and she said he left the house at the usual time. I'd hate to start a search for him. I can see the newspapers hopping on us—in the midst of trying to find that little girl, our police are out looking for their own chief. What should we do, Joe?"

"I suppose we better throw the whole deal to the FBI. I hate to do it without Rheinholdt's O.K."

"Yes. It wouldn't look good."

Look good! Look good! The mayor's words galled him. Everybody in the world was concerned with looking good.

"On the other hand," McFeeley said, "it might be worse if we keep playing cute with them. The man out here is interrogating people. I can't keep the parents from talking to him."

"I guess it's my decision to make." He halted. "What can Caspar be up to? Have any reporters found out about the chief's disappearance?"

"I doubt it. They've given up trying to see him, so I guess they'd assume he's locked in his office."

"Many of them out at the house today?"

"Oh—eight or nine."

"Joe, I guess you'd better release the file. I'll authorize it."

"All right, Mr. Speed."

"Any good news? Anything at all?"

McFeeley told him about the phone call. But he did not mention that they were fairly certain, on the basis of the caller's familiarity with the note, that they suspected it to be the kidnaper. He was cautious, warning the mayor that it might well be another hoax.

"Have you told the agent about it?"

"Not yet."

"I guess you'd better. We might as well go all the way and take them into our confidence."

McFeeley phoned Rheinholdt's office and told Baines to give Wagley the folder that he had locked in his drawer. Unprotesting, but embittered, Baines agreed, informing Joe that a second FBI man had arrived to join Wagley.

When they had concluded their conversation, the police operator broke in. "Lieutenant McFeeley? Can you hang on a minute? Mr. Raffalovitch wants you."

Raffalovitch's whine pleased him. At least Raff was uncommitted —he had no time worrying how he *looked*, what the reporters thought of him, whether people respected him. He was self-sufficient in his world of spectroscopes and ballistic tests.

"McFeeley?" he asked. "I think we may have a lead on that hunk of paper."

Moll, across the aluminum table from Joe, seemed to awaken from the guilty lethargy that had drowned him since the tape had run out. He held up two crossed fingers, then clasped his hands in an attitude of prayer.

"Someone says they know it?" Joe asked.

"I'm not sure. I got on the phone myself and talked to the guy. It's hard to describe that paper, especially since the red mark could run on either side. The guy was suspicious—a cautious character. He wants to see us in person."

"Nobody mentioned it was in connection with Andrus, did they?"

"You think I'm dumb? Of course not. I just said we were trying to locate a printed form."

"Where's the place?"

"Way out on Olympic—Kay-Bee Printers. Mr. Feldman."

"Call him back and tell him we'll be there in half an hour. I'll pick you up."

"I did already. I'll be in front of headquarters."

Moll was grinning. "You think it's it, Joe? What should I tell that agent when he comes back? You want one of them to go with you?"

McFeeley, leaving, stopped. "No. They have a lot to catch up on. They have people to interview, the file. It's probably nothing anyway."

Speeding away from Nespoli, he tried to suppress a disconcerting bubbling of hope, a resurgence of optimism. Raffalovitch was a cautious man; he would not be so swift to ask Joe to make the call. And as for going out on a call himself—McFeeley could not remember the last time the lab chief had issued forth from his retorts and crucibles.

Tom Ballstead concluded his reading of Eliot's notes. He placed a brass paperweight on them (an award for radio reporting in the form of a microphone) and then stared unhappily at the young man. "So you proved it. Now what?"

"We ought to do a program on it."

"Why?" Ballstead asked.

"To prove they were wrong. Why should they be allowed to get away with it?"

"Because no one cares. If you want a better answer, they still could make out a case. They haven't told any lies. Read what Hansel said yesterday. The first *official* notification came at 6:04. In their book, a call from Rheinholdt was official."

"Oh, boy. Oh, boy, Tom. That's some reasoning."

"It'll be good enough for them."

"Is it good enough for you?"

Ballstead's sallow face went a shade darker. "My feelings are irrelevant. I think they did a lousy thing. But they *had* it. They *had* the story. They hedged, because that's their God-given right to do as a newspaper."

"You're on their side."

"I'm on nobody's side, you fool. What do you want me to do? Get the whole network in trouble?"

Sparling waved away these objections. "It could be done—diplomatically. I figured we could do it on 'Southland' tonight. George Brack would be a natural. Everyone loves George. I might even appear myself. I could get Patrolman Hertmann to go on, and we have Swinnerton's tape. Make a neat fifteen-minute show, Tom."

"Southland" was a triweekly fifteen-minute show that followed the 10:00 P.M. television news. It was bland and inoffensive, a chore performed by George Brack, who would interview dog trainers, stunt men, and various charitable and clerical people.

"And when it was all over, what would we have proved?" Ballstead asked. "That the *Truth* was smarter than the rest of us?"

"You can be cynical if you want, Tom. But if newspapers aren't honorable—what's left?"

"Listen, you idiot, a newspaper's only function is its own survival, on whatever terms it can dictate. They're no better or no worse than any institution. What do you think journalism is?"

"They have a duty to be better," Eliot persisted lamely. "And all they do is get worse. More junk. More entertainment. More evasions. It saddens me, because it's my chosen field of endeavor."

"You better choose something else." Ballstead spun about in his chair. Completing the circuit, he bent over the yellow sheets.

"You're hooked," Sparling said triumphantly. "I know you, Tom. You're too decent to let them get away with it."

"I'm in need of my job also. I've had my last fight with management. That's why I like television news, Los Angeles variety. Just get the weather and the ball scores right."

Eliot sensed he was doomed. He assembled his unco-ordinated hulk and got up. "I can't get it out of my thick head," the young man said sadly. "All those people hanging around that house, after they were *asked* time and time again to go. Not just the *Truth,* but all of us. Me, too. Ringel in the tree. Mona Mears. All of us so intent on beating the other guy's brains out, so scared our editors would ream us out if we missed something, so eager to tell the whole world about it, that we forgot about the child. Were we or were we not asked to move?"

"Nobody *asks* reporters. They have to be *told.*"

"Why? Why?" Eliot cried.

"Because that's the way it's always been, and that's the way it's going to be. I'm sorry about that kid. So's every man who was out there. I'll tell you something about news people, Sparling. I like them. By and large they're more generous and more honest than the rest of the world. If they weren't, they'd get out of the lousy underpaid business and open liquor stores. Why do you think I spend my spare time running an employment agency for broken-down newspapermen? Because I'm bighearted? Hell, no. It's because I respect them for hanging onto jobs where they're unappreciated, underpaid and under some publisher's half-assed authority. So don't go condemning Vic DeGroot and Dave Arnspeiger and any of the mob at the Andrus place. It's the system, the hard facts of the business."

"Good luck to 'em," Sparling said bitterly. "No wonder newspapers get worse every day. No wonder they're all folding up, losing money, being merged, running less real news. They deserve what they're getting."

Ballstead scowled. "You're bright, Sparling, but not that bright."

He levelled a skeletal finger at the muted television set to the right of his desk. "That's what's killing newspapers. The talking eye. It's eating up the advertising revenue. Fun. Laughs. Broads. Amusement. Why shouldn't people prefer fun to the United Nations? Or the Senate Agricultural Committee? And when the advertising buck goes, newspapers die. It's that simple. So the papers change. They go in for show biz, puzzles, jokes—trying to compete with the monster over there."

"A losing game," Eliot said. "They can't do it."

"What else can they do? And when you get an Andrus case— the nastiest kind of crime—what do you expect? They should be gentlemen? Especially when cannibals like you and Ringel and three dozen cameramen are running around the house—stealing the bread from their mouths? Newspapers have always been aggressive, persistent. Well, television's made 'em *desperate* also. It's a shame that Andrus family got caught in the middle, but——"

"But. But. No buts, Tom." At the door, Eliot paused. "I ever tell you why I got canned?" he asked.

"If you did, I can't remember."

"Got a minute?"

"Sure. You've used up half my morning already. Take the rest."

"Sorry. Anyhow, you remember Schlossmann? Werner Schlossmann? Who worked at WNA?"

"The guy who killed himself?"

"That's right. Werner was the World News overnight man in LA. He ran the whole operation between midnight and 8:00 A.M.— same hours I had for the *Truth*. You know what a WNA bureau is like. A hole with two teleprinters and one typewriter. I guess Werner was about fifty. You couldn't really tell. He was one of those round-shouldered intellectual-type European Jews with kind of darting eyes and the hair growing up in two frizzy bushes. You'd look at him and wonder how he survived. His whole family got it at Dachau. Wife, mother, two kids, all kinds of relatives. He always wore a black ribbon on his lapel. Warner used to be a big shot in Munich. He was a columnist for some socialist paper. More anti-Communist than you and me, because he understood it early. He also battled the Nazis right down to the wire, until he and his family were packed off. Oh, well, some Jews more or less, you might say."

"Why would I say that?" Ballstead asked, annoyed.

"Not you in particular, Tom. Just the whole world. Anyway, Werner had done some reporting for WNA on a space-rate basis, and the Organization used its pull with Goebbels to get him sprung and shipped to England. It was too late to get his family out. They got the treatment. You tired of these kind of stories by now, Tom?"

"Tell it, tell it."

"I got to hand it to the Organization. They do a lot of lousy things, but they were all right to Werner. They got him the LA spot because he thought the climate would help him—hah!— since he had picked up some bone disease in the camp. That's where I met him, the poor bastard, squinting at copy all night, sipping tea he used to bring in a thermos, punching up tape and running the mimeograph. He didn't complain. It was work. We used to talk a lot at night. I guess he liked me because I was loud and fresh and didn't go around apologizing to the world. We had some interesting discussions on literature's debt to Freud."

"I bet you did."

"Yes. He was quite a man," Eliot said reflectively. "Well, last spring, this German general came out here on a tour of the defense plants. Helmet Holtnagel. He was supposed to be de-Nazified, and

on our side, and so forth. But he wasn't. Werner told me so. In
it up to his Iron Cross. Oh, maybe he never personally crammed
some old lady into the furnace, but he was one of them. WNA
figured he'd be great for a signed series on "Europe Looks Ahead."
So what did WNA in New York tell the bureau here? Werner was
to be taken off the overnight for three days to work with the
general and translate his articles into English!"

"Didn't Schlossmann object?"

"Only to me. Only on the overnight when there was no one else
in the office. I can see him now, in that baggy black suit—the only
one he had—with the black ribbon on the lapel, and his eyes
kind of trying to leap out from behind his glasses, asking me, 'Vat
can I do, Eliot? Vat can I say to them?' And me, genius, I told
him he *had* to refuse to work with that Kraut. So Werner screws up
his courage and asks the bureau chief to get someone else, and the
bureau chief asks New York, and New York hollers that Schlossmann is an ingrate and should be glad to help Holtnagel, because
he's a good German, and if Schlossmann is so independent, let him
find another job. That was the crusher. The poor guy folded. He
did the translation, and WNA ran 'em—pretty dull stuff—but
Werner wasn't the same. He'd sit at his desk way in the back of the
office, muttering about betrayals, and one morning I heard the copy
boy let out a shriek. I looked up in time to see Schlossmann kind of
step off into space—from the fourteenth story."

"And you got canned for blabbing about it?"

"Sure. I knew why he killed himself. He was disgusted with himself for being yellow, after all he went through. That little job,
that little cubicle where he was boss from midnight to 8:00 A.M.
was all he had left. So he worked with the general, and then
couldn't bear to look at himself. WNA and the *Truth* ran a great
obit. About the poor man being hounded by memories of his family,
and how he was threatened for doing the series with Holtnagel.
The general went to his funeral and wore a *yarmulka*."

"But you—what about you? How'd they land on you?"

"I shot my mouth off in the greasy spoon. Some company fink
ratted to Herbie Hood and Herbie hit me with the iron ball. I
guess I deserved it. For being yellow. At least if I could have told
the world about Schlossmann—why he died—the way they destroyed him. But I didn't even get that satisfaction. It doesn't
figure."

"What doesn't?"

"Being yellow all your life. It's worth it to sound off."

"You were out of work how long, Sparling?" Ballstead asked.

"Three months. I know, I know. I was ready to call it quits till you saved me. Tom Ballstead, his network and his employment agency for troubled newsmen."

"And now you're off again?" The acerbity had left Ballstead's voice. It almost seemed that he was addressing the young man with warmth.

"I'm doomed. Well, I've wasted your morning. I'll just pick up my notes and stick 'em in my scrapbook." He walked to Ballstead's desk and reached for the sheaf of papers; the older man put one hand over them.

"Let me call the brass," Ballstead said. "I won't take the rap for this. I'm older than you, and the want ads specify no one over thirty-five. Maybe we can get a hearing with the In-law."

"Hinrichsen?" Eliot asked. "Mr. Upstairs? Never, Tom, he'd never O.K. it."

"He's in charge. Let *him* say no to you." Ballstead dialed the vice-president's office; an appointment was set for 2:30.

"You sure you want me along?" Eliot asked.

"Sure. You're moving up, Sparling. You sold me—almost. Now sell him."

"I want some help. George Brack should be there."

"Goldilocks? What can he offer?"

" 'Southland's' his show. He might have an opinion."

Ballstead agreed to bring Brack in from the Andrus house for the meeting. Outside, Eliot brayed his victory. Jim Farrell looked perturbed.

"Tom said he'd take you right to Hinrichsen with this?" the deskman asked.

"Right to the top," Eliot boomed.

"You must have backed him to the wall. He hates to go up there. Every time he sees Hinrichsen, he walks the other way." Farrell was whispering. "I don't know, Eliot, maybe you should have left him alone. That's all Tom wants—to be left alone. Hinrichsen'll probably get on his back about the film budget."

Compassion for Ballstead blunted Eliot's victory. It was thus with all his triumphs—forever undone by his talent for looking beyond.

Kay-Bee Printers occupied the ground floor of a dirty building on Olympic Boulevard, several blocks east of Central Avenue. It was a corner building with a grim institutional look—barred windows, heavy cornices, a loading platform, worn and layered with grease. A tractor-trailer was backed against the platform, and two Negroes, moving lazily in the heat, were wrestling cardboard crates into the van.

McFeeley and Raffalovitch entered the front door—the glass panes were reinforced with chicken wire—and were directed to Mr. A. M. Feldman, the cautious owner who wanted to see them personally.

He was a short, plump man in his sixties, sweating violently under the sashaying hum of a mammoth electric fan. He seemed to work from no office of his own, but rather used a corner of the print shop set aside for a half-dozen desks. Several girls were in evidence—typists and stenographers—and, a few steps below, in the shop, Joe could see at least three presses, tables for typesetting and other technical work, and, beyond, a storage area where giant rolls of papers were stacked. There were a half-dozen men in stained dungarees in the shop—none of them working terribly hard. None of the presses was running.

Joe showed Mr. Feldman his badge and introduced Raffalovitch. He had decided to tell the printer as little as possible—not to mention the Andrus case, but merely to indicate they were attempting to track down an office form.

"I couldn't make any sense out of that cop on the phone," Feldman said. "I tried to describe the form I had in mind, but he kept confusing me." McFeeley had expected an accent—New York, at least—but the owner of Kay-Bee Printers had none, other than a well-rolled California R.

He picked up a sheaf of white papers from his desk. Raffalovitch, leaning toward them, saw they were ordinary 8½-by-11 white bond. "Come closer, both you fellows," Feldman said, "and see if this is what you're after."

He riffled a stubby finger against the edge of the papers; there were about a dozen in the stack. "This is a composite shipping ticket. It comes in sets—a dozen sheets to a set. The first five are straight bills of lading. You don't understand me, or I'm going too fast, interrupt. The bill of lading is printed in black—all the information in the lower left-hand corner. See?" He began to read. "Straight bill of lading—short form—original—not negotiable—and so forth. The first one is called Original. Figures, it's the Original." Feldman turned it over. "Next, Short Form-Shipping Order. Next, Short Form-Memorandum Copy; next, Short Form-File Copy; and then, Short Form-Extra Copy. That's the first five pages." He looked at McFeeley and Raffalovitch, making sure they were getting it all.

"Those aren't what we're looking for," Raffalovitch said impatiently. "You said on the phone you had a form with *red* lettering—red marking in the lower left-hand corner on the long side. Or did you?"

"Be patient, be patient. I want to be thorough. Right, Lieutenant?"

"Go ahead, Mr. Feldman," Joe said.

Feldman turned the first five sheets face down. "Here's the rest of the set," he said. The next sheets had a single line of bright red printing in the lower left corner. In block letters, about a half inch high, set about a half inch from the bottom of the paper appeared the words:

6—BEYOND CARRIER'S COPY

Raffalovitch snatched it off the printer's desk. From his coat pocket he took out a plastic envelope containing the original note. With a tweezers, he extracted it and placed it over the form. Feldman nodded his round head. "I thought so. That kidnaping. But I kept quiet." He looked at McFeeley. "I recognized you from your picture on the television."

Both men ignored him. They were squinting at the ransom note, now set on top of the shipping form.

"It's not it," Raffalovitch said.

"Doesn't look that way," McFeeley said. "Ours is too short. Or this is too long."

The rough lower margin of the ransom note—the edge ripped by a steel-edged ruler, according to Raffalovitch—was about three-fourths of an inch above the top of the red lettering. Had the kidnaper made the note from Feldman's document, as they had suspected, the red traces would have been missing *altogether*. And since the upper and left-hand margins of the note were unquestionably machine-cut, it followed that the red markings had come from some other source.

McFeeley's slanted face betrayed his misery. Raffalovitch pointed to the papers. "What about the rest of them?"

"You wouldn't give me a chance," Feldman said. "Such impulsive young men." He resumed turning the sheets. All bore the large red lettering in the same position as the first red copy—at least three-fourths of an inch too low to have left any trace on the kidnap message.

They read the designations, angry with the sterile red letters that had held such hope—and had disappointed them.

7—DRAYMAN'S MEMO

8—DESTINATION OFFICE COPY

9—TRANSFER COPY

10—DOCK RECORD

11—TALLY-OUT

Feldman paused. "And the last one is what is referred to as a general copy." He turned 11—TALLY-OUT and, at the sight of the final page in the set of shipping tickets, McFeeley and Raffalovitch rose from their chairs. The legend, 12—GENERAL COPY, was in the same style of lettering as on the previous sheets. But, instead of being printed in red on the white background, the words appeared in *white,* surrounded by a long, bright-red rectangle. The rectangle began a quarter of an inch from the left margin and was about six inches long. It was over an inch and a half high—framing the enclosed white lettering.

"On the last sheet, the general copy is always printed in *reverse,*" Feldman explained. "Makes it easy for the multigraph operator. He knows it's the end of the set."

Neither of them was listening. Again Raffalovitch placed the ransom note over the shipping form. This time, there was no gap between the ragged bottom of the note and the upper border of red ink. The lab chief made certain that the left and top margins of the two sheets were flush; then he peered at the bottom of the note, his eyes popping. "A tiny, tiny bit of overhang," he said softly. "Just enough so a little bit of the red would rip off when he tore it. See?"

McFeeley saw. The rough lower edge of the ransom note infringed faintly on the upper red margin of the rectangle—enough so that it destroyed the evenly printed border.

"What kind of stock is this?" Raffalovitch asked.

"Sixteen-pound white bond. We use tons of it."

"What about the ink?" the lab man asked.

Feldman eased his round figure from the desk and waddled to a high steel closet at the rear of the office area. He came back with a small can. "Very Bright Red," he said.

Raffalovitch took the can. "Can I have this?"

"Sure. Need anything else?"

"Couple of sheets like these." He indicated the last page of the shipping set—the one marked 12—GENERAL COPY, with the elongated red rectangle.

"Help yourself," Feldman said. "You fellows act like you found something. I can't believe that fellow wrote the note on some of my paper. Who? Ridiculous."

Joe was frowning, leaning back in his chair. If the child were yet to be saved, thoroughness would have to be sacrificed to a pursuit of the percentages. He would have to decide where the most logical places were to look for someone who would use Feldman's shipping form; then they would be required to weed out *most likely candidates*—people with criminal records, people living in or near Sanlu, people who had the remotest connections with the Andrus family. Interrogation would have to concentrate on them; if the results were negative, they would have to start all over—questioning everyone who could have possibly had access to the document.

"Who uses these forms?" Joe asked. "Are they fairly common in LA?"

"Common? No. We make them up for only one firm. Look—read the bills of lading. See what it says? 'Received, subject to the classifications and tariffs in effect on the date of the issue of this shipping order from FOURSTATE. Then, on the bottom—in small print—it gives the full name—*Fourstate Shippers and Consigners, Inc.*"

Joe paused: he had to organize his thinking, plan his pursuit. Minutes counted; he could waste neither time nor motion. "Mr. Feldman, how long has this company been using these forms?"

Feldman rubbed his nose. "I could check it exactly. But I'd say three or four months, the most. They used the standard bill of lading shipping ticket, with all the stuff printed on it, but then Culligan decided this simplified form was better."

"Who's Culligan?" Joe asked.

"He's the boss at Four State. Want me to call him for you?"

"In a minute or so," McFeeley said.

Raffalovitch studied the sheet—white except for the bright-red rectangle in the lower left corner. "That's why we didn't find it in any of the document files. One outfit—new form." He got up. "I better beat it. I want to get to the LA lab and run the ink through the spectroscope. Also check out the paper stock. I'm sure this is what the guy made the note from, but let's be positive. O.K.?"

"Right. Thanks, Raff."

When the lab man had gone, Joe asked Feldman if he could take some more of his time. The other members of Kay-Bee Printers were leaving for lunch; the print shop was all but deserted. A Negro workman was opening a lunch box at the distant end of the shop; two girls came out of the ladies' room and left by a rear door.

"Mr. Feldman, suppose I told you I had to find the man who used this paper for the ransom note as soon as possible. To save that child's life. You've read about it, I guess."

"Go on." Feldman leaned forward.

"Well, you know what playing the percentage is?"

"Sure. You go with the possibility that figures. In baseball, you use the hit-and-run with a fast man on first and a fellah who can hit through second base at bat. Right?" McFeeley smiled, and the printer added: "I don't look it, but I played a lot of ball, once." Joe could believe him—his hands and feet had a quick vigor.

"That's the idea," the detective said. "So, right off, you'd assume that anyone who had access to those forms could be the one. You— or Mr. Culligan—or anybody who worked for either of you."

"True."

"Now, assuming I haven't got time to check every single person right now, how would I play the percentage? How would I con- centrate on certain people—right off—people who'd take office paper home with them? Am I making sense?"

"I think so." Feldman rested his sweating face against the back of his chair; the breeze from the fan did him no good.

"Of course, I can use my cop's instincts. Anyone with a criminal record—anyone in Santa Luisa—anyone who acts guilty. But right off, is there any way I could work the percentage? By the way—how many people do you employ?"

"It's slow now. Nineteen."

"And Mr. Culligan?"

"I'm not sure. He doesn't have a big operation either. He handles stuff from small manufacturers—people who can't be bothered running their own shipping department." He clasped his hands on the desk top. "What you said about percentages, I'd figure this way. Consider first that the theft of office supplies—stationery, pencils, stamps—is perpetual. Everybody steals. You know a billion dollars' worth of office supplies, machine tools, and so on were taken home last year? Almost impossible to prove it—dribs and drabs. And, boy, try to deduct it. Try to tell the government you took a $50,000 loss on supplies stolen by employees!"

"You mean anyone—here or at the shipper—could have taken it?"

"*Anybody*. What's more, he could have *given* it to someone—relative, friend. Your Mr. Kidnaper could be a neighbor of the guy who decided to take some free paper home. So where are you? Now between whether someone here took it—like me—or Harmon Bates, eating his lunch over there—and someone at Culligan's—I'd say *not* here—purely on your percentages."

McFeeley smiled. "I'm listening."

"The point is, anyone's gonna steal white paper to write letters on, for his kids to use in school, why should he steal stuff with *printing* on it when I got tons of plain white paper laying around? And, believe me, it gets stolen. I had a kid working as a pressman last year; he wanted to be a television writer. That little *goniff* walked home with a ream of superwhite bond with a kokle finish every week! So, offhand, I'd say it would be more likely the paper was taken by someone at Culligan's."

"But isn't there a lot of white paper laying around a shipper's office? Stuff that a guy who filched office supplies would be more likely to take?"

"Sure. But you asked percentages. There's a lot less of it *handy* than here. And a secretary probably keeps it locked up or is near it. Here—any *shnook* can grab it off a shelf and sneak it out. I've caught them."

Joe tapped the surface of Mr. Feldman's desk. "I don't know. Maybe I'm kidding myself." Feldman seemed the kind of man in front of whom one could indulge one's weaknesses and get a hearing.

Feldman picked up the forms and spread them, fanlike, in his pudgy hands, so that the printed matter showed. "Another thing I just thought of," he said. "You know, if one of these sheets gets botched in the multigraph—ink stains, or wrinkled, or the stencil is no good—then the rest are useless. They're just *scrap* paper—stuff to write notes on. They're good only in *sets*. So let's assume not everyone is a crook; but when office forms are scrap—useless sheets—a man might be more justified taking them home. After all, it isn't such a crime to take home useless papers. So someone in Four State's shipping department notices these sheets going to waste and takes them home. Again, this is on the percentage."

Was there substance to Feldman's theorizing? Did something about the notion of a man who would take home *only* scrap paper—disdaining virginal white sheets—tie in with McFeeley's vague image of the man? Joe recalled the immaculate note—the neatly clipped words, perfectly spaced; the meticulous manner in which the paper had been cropped. And there was his recollection of the voice—disguised, muffled to be sure, but precise, deliberate, the words as exactly spaced in speech as they were on the message.

"So you'd bet on someone at Culligan's place—probably someone with access to the department where they did the mimeographing——"

"Percentages," Feldman said. "I could be all wrong. Maybe I did it. Maybe a stranger from the street walked in and took the forms from my shelves. Who knows?"

Interrogation would have to start at once. McFeeley asked Feldman for the use of his telephone. He called headquarters and spoke to Bannon, ordering him, and any other detective available, to come out to the print shop at once. *Sotto voce*, Bannon advised him that there were now three FBI agents checking the files. Moll, calling from the Andrus house, had informed him that three more agents had joined Fewsmith and were conducting a crime search, a lab check, and were interviewing neighbors. The Bureau, it appeared, was taking over—now that Mayor Speed had given the green light. As for Rheinholdt, he was still among the missing.

Before hanging up, McFeeley told Milt Bannon what line of questioning to follow—nodding at Feldman to secure the printer's approval. "Nothing about the kidnaping. Just try to get a reading on the people. I'll have Mr. Feldman pull his records. Look for anyone with a police record. You can say we're investigating shipping frauds, trying to trace them through phony forms—make it a Santa Luisa company, so they won't wonder why Sanlu cops are on the case."

Feldman nodded his approval. "I'll eat lunch in," he said. "What's your friend's name? Bannon?" He jotted it down, then walked to a filing cabinet and pulled a tan folder labeled *personnel*.

"Milt?" Joe asked. "I'll be at Four State Shippers and Consigners—it's near the station; should be in the phone book. I'll be with a Mr. Culligan. We're almost positive the note came from a shipping form that was printed here and was used by them. O.K.?"

McFeeley got up—his feet felt light, eager—as if awaiting the opening tap of a basketball game.

"Anything else I can do for you?" Feldman asked.

"You might call Mr. Culligan. Tell him Lieutenant McFeeley is coming to see him, and if he hasn't gone to lunch, to wait for me. Just say it's a police matter. Don't mention the Andrus case."

By 12:30, four FBI agents were working the area near the Andrus house. Fewsmith, who seemed to be in a senior capacity, had returned with Laura. He spent some time with Moll, going through the logs of phone calls and visitors, and supervised a crime search of the house, the grounds, the garage. A photographer and a laboratory man spent several hours at the site, and two agents immediately began a house-to-house canvass of the entire block. The men were uniformly polite, competent, closemouthed. They exuded a hard professionalism that Laura and Fritzie could not help but admire. "That's how it shoulda been done," Fritzie said bitterly. "First thing Monday mornin', Laura—y'all shoulda called them in. Instead of those hicks—that fool Rheinholdt and that boy."

What particularly impressed Laura and Fritzie was the ease with which the agent handled the reporters. It was quite true that Fewsmith was not confronted with the madness that Joe McFeeley had had to contend with. The spirit of the chase had worn thin, and the ranks of the press had diminished. Nevertheless, the agent's command presence gave them heart; it seemed that, at long last, somebody was able to enforce discipline.

A little before noon, following Mayor Speed's instructions that the FBI was to be given charge of the case, Fewsmith walked out of the house and crossed the street. There were a half-dozen cars strung out. Breakfast leavings littered the gutter—wax wrappings, cardboard boxes, coffee containers. Two 16-millimeter cameras were set up, and on the tail gate of UBC's station wagon, Steve Billik, a *Truth* photographer, and three of their colleagues were playing poker. On Fewsmith's approach, the reporters roused themselves and surrounded him. Victor DeGroot recognized the FBI man and offered a greeting, which the agent politely returned. Martin Ringel, his tape recorder at the ready, young Duane Bosch, Arnspeiger, George Brack, and a few others began to throw queries at him.

"I'll have to ask you to move to the next block," the agent said. "It's not conducive to good investigative work to have you here."

No one acknowledged his request; they had questions to ask.

"How about the piece in the *Truth?*" Martin Ringel asked. "You read it? Is the FBI gonna work on the assumption that the mother —or the father—or both—may have something to do with the kid's disappearance?"

"How many have been assigned, Mr. Fewsmith?" DeGroot asked.

George Brack smiled helpfully. "I suppose you fellows will crack it pretty soon. Have you contacted the kidnaper?"

"I'm sorry," the agent said. "But for the time being there will be no statements issued here. You're all free to call the Bureau in Los Angeles. They'll be the only ones giving out information."

Ringel groaned. "Those closemouthed Charlies. They end up asking you more questions than you ask them. They wouldn't admit it's Wednesday."

"Could you start moving your cars now? Park on the next block. And, please, no loitering or parading up and down after you've moved."

His appeal was magical; perhaps by now the awareness of collective guilt was at work; perhaps the men felt that little would happen at the yellow ranch house. In five minutes the street was cleared.

When he returned to the house, Fritzie expressed his admiration. "Y'all shoulda been here Monday," he said. "You could have cleared that mob quick. 'Stead of those local cops." He laughed bitterly. "That McFeeley. They walked all over him."

Fewsmith took no credit for what he had done. "You can't blame him. It was too much for a small police organization."

The agent reviewed with Moll the kidnaper's call that morning, the arrangements for the 7:00 P.M. call, then went out to talk to the men conducting the crime search. During his tour of the house, Walter L. Todd's shiny black Buick bounced into the driveway. The dentist introduced himself to the agents, advised them of his role in the case, offered his full co-operation, and then hopped into the house to talk to the parents.

Laura found it difficult to be civil to him, but she had herself to blame for inviting the dentist, and this tempered her sense of disgust when he announced the purpose of his visit.

"Naturally," Todd said, "I'm available for any errands, missions, whatever you and Francis want of me. Now that the Federal Bureau of Investigation is on the job, I'm more prepared than ever to offer my services." His eyes glittered. "Ah—has anything new happened? Any word from that fellow?"

"No," Laura said—looking pointedly at Fritzie. Fewsmith had warned them not to discuss the case with anyone but the agents.

He had indicated that the wall of silence was to include the local police—even McFeeley.

"Nothin' at all, Walter," Fritzie said. "No press conferences, no more dirty words on newspapers. Shoot—this thing goes on, those reporters might even let us alone."

"Yes. One would imagine they'd let up by now." He opened a shiny black zipper case and took out several typewritten sheets. "That's one of the reasons I'm here. It's no secret to you, I'm sure, that I've been criticized for what some people regard as—ah—indiscretions on my part."

"Walter, we know you meant no harm," Laura said. The insincerity in her voice was apparent to Fritzie; it was lost on the dentist —just as Eliot Sparling's rudeness had been lost on him. Laura, studying his healthy face, envied him: how marvelous to be so free of doubt! Now, gripped by the minute-by-minute agony that left her debilitated, frightened, incapable of rousing herself to face another meaningless day of meals, baby diapering, answering doorbells, she found herself despising him—not for his feeding of information to a reporter, but simply for what he was, for that divinely endowed certitude that shone like a fourteenth-century gold halo around his head.

"How pleased I am to hear you say that, Laura," Todd said. "And you, Fritzie? Are you angry with me?"

"Ah, it's all done and gone. I reckon we'd have had no luck Monday night, with or without what the papers did, what you did."

In the heavy heat of the den, the three sat, momentarily immobilized, ill-shaded from the relentless sun, awaiting the same miracle, the same sign that McFeeley sought. Andrus, blinking his reddened eyes, his vivacious features weighted, could find only despair in Todd's indifference, the manner in which he reduced problems to dramatizations of his own self. Then it struck Fritzie that this characteristic had often been his own undoing. Two days ago he had hurled himself into the tragedy concerned only with his own fears, his own hatreds, his own rivalry with Laura.

"I've drawn up an account of my activities on Monday, from the time I got up, to the time I went to bed, in the hope that I might clear the air once and for all." Thoughtfully, he had made carbons. He gave a set to each parent. Laura glanced at the first page. It was titled:

REMARKS BY WALTER L. TODD, D.D.S.,
CONCERNING HIS ROLE IN THE KIDNAPING OF AMY ANDRUS

"I would not dream of releasing this to the papers until you, Laura, and you, Francis, have read it and pronounced it accurate. I also thought you might issue a small addendum to it, something on the order of—'We have read this statement by Dr. Todd and find it accurate. We do not hold him responsible for any of the unfortunate events of last Monday.' How does that strike you?"

Andrus flushed. His fist tightened around the sheaf of papers and he appeared ready to lose his temper. Laura saw the anger rising in him and cautioned him.

"It's all right, Walter. We really aren't up to reading it," she said weakly. "I'm sure it's in order. But if it's all the same to you, we won't put anything in writing. The FBI men have asked us to say no more, to give no more interviews."

Todd chuckled, fiddling with his pince-nez. "That poses a little problem, Laura dear. You see—I already wrote your statement—and appended it—to save time, naturally. All I had hoped for was your verbal agreement that I might send it to press along with my own, as it were, odyssey."

"Oh, Christ," Andrus groaned. "Laura, let him be. Let him do what he wants." He got up and walked out of the den.

"I appreciate Francis' sensitivity," Todd said solemnly. "It's a source of inspiration to me the way you two have stood up under this. I take it I have your concurrence?"

"Yes. Yes. You do what you think is best, Walter."

"Good." He bounced up. "I'll avail myself of the phone if I may. I have a messenger standing by with mimeographed copies to send out. Nothing like being prepared."

And he made his call, wished the agents well in their investigation, and was gone. When he had left, Laura, as if to cleanse herself of his presence, walked into Amy's room. One of the FBI men had just completed a survey of it—taking photographs, dusting again (vainly, Fewsmith admitted) for prints. "Is it all right if I sit here?" she asked. He said she could, and she rested on a green canvas folding chair—not Amy's, but an old patio piece the child had used for dolls, tossing them in a heap and rarely playing with them. She was not a child to fuss over dolls. Amy liked colored papers, crayons, paste, scissors, and Scotch tape. A big tube of Duco cement was one of her prized possessions. She liked to snip pictures from magazines, collect stamps (Fritzie had bought her an album), and glue scraps of colored paper to bottles, cardboard boxes, old lamp shades. Laura, sitting on the deck chair, looked at the cluttered table—the paste jars and glue dispensers, the beer mug laden with scissors and pencils, the ash tray acrawl with rubber bands, the mound of ragged coloring books and magazines. An involuntary moan escaped her lips; a bleaching sorrow robbed her of her last shred of strength. It was not just the child's disappearance, the awful potentialities, the shivering waiting; it was the fact of Amy's innocence, her nakedness. Around the vanished child, illuminating her martyrdom, hovered a host of adults—all, like Todd, concerned with how they *looked*, what was *written* about them, how they might aggrandize themselves, excuse their conduct, be a part of the agony.

She could bear the sight of the room no longer. The child should have been there, her dark form kneeling in the wooden chair, the frowning face riveted to a coloring book, the skillful fingers manipulating a scissors.

Matthew M. Hinrichsen, the man to whom Ballstead had agreed to carry Eliot's appeal, was poignantly aware of his sobriquet among the working stiffs of the network—*the In-law*. The nickname was embarrassing to him, a reminder that he had not quite made it on his own. As West Coast vice-president for UBC, his duties were largely administrative. New York made the major decisions. Yet he was a conscientious and sensitive man—despite a façade of clerical coldness.

Hinrichsen, secure, successful, guaranteed never to be jobless, never lacking for prestige, love or money, nonetheless suffered a pernicious hunger—the hunger for artistic fulfillment, for participation in the search for truth and excellence. As an undergraduate at Amherst, for example, Hinrichsen had spent a summer in Italy. While his companions pursued earthier goals, he had wandered about in search of della Francescas and had sedulously catalogued the master's works—where and when he had communed with each. Later, he had written one-act plays. While serving as a lieutenant (sg) in the Coast Guard, he had done wonders in assembling a ship's library and had instituted adult education courses for his enlisted men. He was not altogether the child of Mammon and good breeding that the news writers fancied him to be.

That morning, Ballstead's request for an audience concerning some exclusive information the news department had dredged up on the Andrus affair had come as a pleasant change for Hinrichsen. In the midst of an abrasive, ill-tempered meeting with a used car dealer, an uncouth ignoramus who demanded the right to censor scripts, Hinrichsen had suddenly found himself troubled by a lost vision of peeling churches and damp museums, where Beato Angelicos and Pinturicchios glowed in unearthly splendor. There were, the In-law kept telling himself, areas of the human condition more exalted than the shoddy commerce, the contemptible cheap amusements in which he dealt. It occurred to him, as his secretary ushered in Tom Ballstead and a strange young man, that perhaps the news director (an unlikely savior!) might present him with a problem, a proposal capable of mitigating his malaise.

Ballstead's companion, Hinrichsen noted, was distressingly ungainly and ill clad—the kind of vagrant upon whom the news director would look with compassion. The vice-president knew his reputation for saving souls: the newsroom was cluttered with deadwood, he was sure. The young man was introduced as Eliot Sparling, and he offered Hinrichsen a large, wet hand.

Ballstead, his bony limbs ensconced in a deep leather chair, rubbed a hand over his face a few times.

"Matt, I hate to bother you with this, but I promised Eliot I'd take it upstairs. I'll be damned if I know what to do. He's done some good digging and he's got some interesting stuff. Whether we want to use it or not—from a policy standpoint—well, that's not my department."

At once, Hinrichsen looked interested. "You said it concerned the Andrus kidnaping? Do we have a lead of any kind?"

"No," Ballstead said. "The cops are not talking. Now the FBI's in the act and you know how closemouthed they are. Incidentally, George Brack is on his way in for this meeting. He was supposed to be here at 2:30, but there was a latrine rumor that the woman was going to give another interview. Nothing happened."

"I see. Well—I'm listening. What's the problem?" Hinrichsen leaned back. He was feeling better; just brushing elbows with the newsroom people invigorated him. They were, after all, more concerned with the pursuit of truth, of facts, of the real world and its problems than he could ever be, with his ratings, his across-the-board sales.

"Go on, Eliot—tell Matt what you found out."

But Sparling, that splendid boob, was staring at three portraits hanging behind the vice-president's desk. They were determinedly modern—a blonde, long-necked woman, two slender young girls— and the style—cubes, angles, squares, each with an odd, grainy texture—hinted at some unrecognized genius in a Via Margutta attic.

"Excuse me. I was admiring those paintings," Sparling said.

"Do you really like them?" asked Hinrichsen. "My wife and two daughters. A chap in Seattle did them for me—a technique he developed himself."

"Ah—yes, they're quite original." Sparling had not the faintest idea whether he liked the portraits. But he could not help feeling a nudge of admiration for the In-Law. It took some daring to have one's family immortalized in stippled squares and cubes, predominantly chartreuse and olive drab.

"Well, what Mr. Ballstead is talking about," Eliot said, the course in art appreciation having ended, "is the question of newspaper mishandling of this case."

Sparling proceeded to enlighten the vice-president. He spoke rapidly and with much ease, delivering the facts of the case chronologically, not de-emphasizing his own role on Monday, then reading from his notes to build up the evidence. To his credit, he even managed to keep his booming voice down—an effort that required far more concentration than the relating of the involved circumstances of the *Truth's* publication of the story. When he had concluded his testimony, Hinrichsen closed his eyes and leaned back in his chair, resting his neck against clasped hands. "Tom, will you give me about thirty seconds to digest this?" he asked. "Your man has really thrown a mess at me."

A wondrous envy for the executive bloomed in Sparling. *Will I ever be like Matthew M. Hinrichsen?* he mused. *Will I ever have that ease of manner, that perfection of costume, that calm view of the world? Will I know a chap in Seattle who will paint geometric portraits of my wife and children?*

"As I see it," Hinrichsen said, "we will expose this newspaper's dereliction—its failure to agree to a police request—which, for all we know, may have cost this child's life—and then we will claim they did not tell the truth about their role. I'll accept this evidence, if you do, Tom."

"That's the idea, Matt," Ballstead said. "I figure we'd let George Brack do it tonight on 'Southland.' "

"I see a few red flags," Hinrichsen said. Eliot's lips turned downward; he seemed ready to cry.

"The point is, have we the right to attack this newspaper, when our *own* role was so dubious? I'm sorry you had to go to jail, Eliot, but the police had problems of their own. I'm sure you'd trade that little girl's life for a day in jail for you—a month in jail."

"Granted, Mr. Hinrichsen," Sparling said. "But I——"

Hinrichsen held up a hand. "A moment, if you will. That's only part of my objection—a minor one. I suppose a little *mea culpa* on our part is all right. What does disturb me is that this incident is isolated. It's true the paper acted wretchedly. But isn't it a unique thing? Tom, you stated that the police gave them every provocation to publish, that it was a miracle others didn't. And they still have a shred of justice—that police chief flatly refused to talk to anyone at the *Truth*."

"It doesn't change the moral issue!" shouted Eliot.

Hinrichsen had not yet suffered Sparling's full vocal strength; he looked mildly shocked, then went on. "No, it doesn't. But what I fear is that our attack on them will be interpreted as a general attack on the press. That's not what I want. That isn't in order. They all obeyed the secrecy request. If we discovered one crooked physician in Los Angeles, running a compensation racket, it would hardly call for a program charging that all Los Angeles physicians are thieves, would it?"

"No," Sparling conceded. "But what the *Truth* did is only one-third the story. You see, Mr. Hinrichsen, the whole press stands guilty on two other counts. O.K., only the *Truth* broke it. O.K., the rest of us *didn't*—mostly because we didn't have it confirmed. *But*"—and here the young news writer rose from his chair and addressed his betters like a daft preacher—"but—why didn't anybody leave the house? All of the reporters—that whole mob—a hundred people hanging around, sniffing for blood, making monkeys out of those cops and those parents, inventing excuses, hiding in trees, following the woman down the street when she's going to meet the kidnaper! *Why? Why did they stay?* That's number one. Number two—how come none of them bothered to find out what I found out? Why was it assumed the *Truth* was right? That's the way I see it, Mr. Hinrichsen."

"Tom, what do you think?" asked the executive.

Ballstead smeared both hands over his face, starting at his scrawny hairline, ending with finger tips on his narrow chin. "Jesus, I don't know what to think. Sparling's got a point. But does the public care? I doubt it. Is it fair to criticize newspapers for going after a story? That's their bread and butter. It's too bad somebody got burned, but somebody has to, I guess."

"A child!" shouted Eliot. "Yours, Tom! Yours, Mr. Hinrichsen!"

"Not so loud," Hinrichsen said indulgently. "You'll scare my secretary. Go on, Tom."

"I have to dump it in your lap, Matt." Ballstead sighed. "You don't criticize newspapers. Everyone else gets it—writers, politicians, television, industry, labor unions. But nobody ever blows the whistle on a newspaper. It's a tradition."

"Yes. I agree." Hinrichsen rubbed his soft palms together. "I know Ted Hansel quite well. It wouldn't sit well with him. I can't imagine a man like that *knowingly* harming a little girl. Why do you look so glum, Eliot?"

"Because you're slamming the door on the truth, Mr. Hinrichsen. I read your speech to the Press Club, sir, and I agree with you. If television can't upgrade people, if it can't enhance our lives, if it can't pursue truth and excellence, it has no *raison d'être*. I agree with those sentiments. Why can't we do all those things right now? All we need is fifteen minutes of 'Southland' tonight."

The outlandish young man's unexpected—and rather cunning— tribute to Hinrichsen's high seriousness gave the vice-president pause. That was one of the difficulties with inspirational words: they could be turned against one so easily. Hinrichsen glanced at Ballstead for succor, but the news director's shrunken face appeared gripped in gastric agony. The man's weary negativism disturbed Hinrichsen. There was something in Ballstead's cold reasoning— his contention that the inviolate essence of newspapers made it wrong for them to be criticized for their behavior in the Andrus matter—that unsettled the executive. He was young enough and innocent enough to feel that *exactly the opposite was the case:* that this very freedom enjoyed by the press made it all the more urgent that they now be made to answer for their conduct. And yet Hinrichsen was not notably courageous. He understood the practicalities of the situation, and he understood that he was entering an area in which he had little experience.

These ruminations were interrupted by the arrival of George Brack. The commentator, breathless and apologetic, burst his sunny presence into the office with a late bulletin from Nespoli Drive. Mrs. Andrus had said nothing, nor had the FBI. But Dr. Todd had enlivened things by distributing a long statement on his behavior on Monday. "It isn't much," George conceded, "but maybe it's a night lead. Evidently there's been no word from the kidnaper—but all kinds of rumors. Marty Ringel says the FBI is going to work on the maid."

Hinrichsen absorbed the report attentively. Then he explained to Brack the purpose of the meeting, finding occasion to praise Eliot's excellent "digging"—a word he had just heard Ballstead use. "We thought you should be party to this," the vice-president said, "because you've been close to the case, George. And if we decide to use Eliot's material, it would be on 'Southland' tonight."

Brack nodded. "What's the consensus?"

There was an air-conditioned pause. "This is a difficult decision Tom's asked me to make," Hinrichsen said. "But I guess I have to vote against it." Eliot's features drooped. "Discretion is not only the better part of valor—it's good policy. I agree with Tom. What would we accomplish? What good would we do? Moreover—assuming all of Eliot's facts are accurate—I don't want us to sound as if we're making a blanket indictment. This incident was a freak. One in a million. Add this to certain practical considerations—good will with newspapers, long-range thinking."

Ballstead got up. "O.K. Let's go, Sparling."

Eliot did not move. His eyes lurched from the executive, to Ballstead's rickety figure, to Brack's sunlit countenance.

"Ah, excuse me, Tom," Brack said politely. "But am I supposed to offer an opinion? I mean—I was asked here——"

Ballstead scratched his head. "Oh, Jesus, I'm sorry, George." But he was not really sorry: one simply did not invite George Brack— a voice, a trained parrot—to meetings. He earned his $70,000 a year reading beer commercials and sentences that news writers like Sparling constructed from AP copy. It was inconceivable that the likes of George Brack should be entitled to an audience for his opinions. Opinions, Ballstead believed, did not mix with commercials for beer and used cars. One thought of Brack in terms of cabin cruisers, barbecued steaks and pedigreed Irish setters; he was the man in the institutional advertisement titled, "What Makes America Strong"; he belonged.

"Why certainly, George," Hinrichsen said. "You wouldn't have been invited here if we didn't value your opinion."

"That's very generous of you, Matt," said Brack with no trace of sarcasm. "You see, I've worried a good deal about this Andrus matter. I have to credit El with arousing me. He got me thinking— what right had we to act like a bunch of wolves? To sass the police? To torture that woman? Yes, to disregard that little girl's safety, her chance to survive, just so we could have higher TV ratings or sell more newspapers? Is that all that matters in the world? After all, it wasn't only the *Truth* that misbehaved. It was each and every one of us—hounding those people, refusing to go away. It was a frightening example of irresponsibility, based, I'm afraid, on greed. It troubled me terribly. So last night, after we'd locked up the 11:00 P.M. news, I went to see my minister."

Brack halted his narration. There was a moment of surrealist revelation, as if each of his listeners had sighted a neon vision on an asphalt road to Damascus, California. They stared at Brack's manly face with insincere smiles—the smiles one affords a religious nut quoting apocrypha.

"You say you called on your minister?" asked the vice-president.

"Yes. I often drop by to chat with Dr. Otis whenever I have a problem. I find him most reliable for moral guidance."

A fit of coughing convulsed Ballstead; the commentator's purity was noxious to his breathing.

"You see," Brack continued, after Ballstead regained composure, "I've always been rather close to Dr. Otis and the Unified Church in general. I'm in charge of the Youth Program and I speak from the pulpit twice a year."

"What'd the doc say?" intruded Eliot.

"Well, we discussed the pros and cons far into the night. I knew about Eliot's desire to publicize his findings. But apart from that, I was having terrible misgivings myself about *our* behavior. I was quite objective. I made clear to Dr. Otis the pressures on each man, the highly competitive nature of the business, the fierce interest the public has in kidnapings. Then I asked him point-blank—should we, a broadcasting network, just as guilty as the others in destroying privacy, in ignoring the *Truth's* lapse, should we take it upon ourselves to criticize?"

Oh, how unfair! Hinrichsen thought. *Oh, what a rotten trick!* He knew what the minister's judgment would be—it was easy for ministers to make such judgments—not having sponsors, or corporate interests, or the revenge of aroused newspaper chains to contend with.

"His answer was unequivocal," Brack said. "Truth—small T— must be brought to light. *And the truth shall make ye free.* If we know, Dr. Otis said, that a lie has been fostered, we must point that out. Moreover, if we are cognizant of immoral behavior—even though we ourselves were party to it—and we have the power to expose this behavior, it is our duty to do so. So you see—that's where I stand. I sort of felt that before seeing Dr. Otis, but he confirmed my views."

"Attaboy, Georgie," Eliot said.

"Let's go, Sparling," Ballstead muttered. "George—thanks for joining us. You got a point, but you heard what Matt said."

Hinrichsen spun about in his chair. Manicured hands clasped behind his trim head, he was gazing out across a formless pastel vista of ugly apartments and office buildings, a few starved palms. *The purpose of art is to enhance life.* Where had he read that? How long ago? Memories of a young manhood dedicated to Simone Martini and Duccio shivered his slender body. He turned around.

"Can we do this thing, Tom—this sort of program—without *hurting* anyone? That's not quite what I mean—I mean—can we make sure that we're absolutely as objective as possible and that we give any offended parties a chance to respond?"

"They'll respond all right," Ballstead snarled. "We'll be on their list forever."

"We can!" shouted Eliot. "I know just how to do it! Besides, who'd get mad at George?"

Brack beamed. "I agree, Matt. It should be done, and it can be done tastefully. Just a factual narration of what happened on Monday."

"Let's try it," Hinrichsen said, almost gaily. "Of course, Tom and I will check the script very carefully."

Ballstead nodded. "You're in charge, Matt. You want publicity to get out an advance? So we can get coverage? You know—UBC about to put a big blast on the Andrus case?"

"Ah—yes, I suppose we should. No. Let's wait until we've checked the script." Courage, Hinrichsen knew, came in minute infusions—rather like a drip treatment.

In the corridor, outside the vice-president's office, Sparling grabbed Brack in a bear hug and lifted him off the marble floor. "Oh, my baby! My little Georgie!"

"For goodness' sake, El, cut it out. You're embarrassing me." Sparling set him down gently.

"Goddam dopes," Ballstead mumbled. "We'll all be looking for work by midnight."

Joe McFeeley ran into bad luck at Four State Shippers and Consigners. Mr. Feldman's call, a receptionist advised him, had come too late to catch Mr. Culligan, the boss. Mr. Culligan had left early to check on some shipments in Arcadia and would probably not be back until 2:00 P.M. The girl, aware that he was a detective, invited him into the office, which was new, large, and testified to Mr. Culligan's efficiency. The floor was black asphalt tile, the partitions were aluminum and frosted glass, the desks were immaculate—steel with rubberized tops. The exterior of the Four State building—

flanked by a loading platform and a rail siding—was old and dirt-crusted; but, within, Mr. Culligan had refurbished everything with care. Even the lighting was in modern fluorescent style—chandeliers resembling inverted ice-cube trays, giving off a gentle glow.

The receptionist advised Joe there was a lunchroom below, or he could use the vending machines in the supply area at the rear of the office. McFeeley thanked her, walked through the swinging doors and found several girls giggling around a bank of dispensers. Mr. Culligan went first class: there was a coffee machine, a milk and ice cream machine, a fruit juice machine, and others selling sandwiches, pies, cakes, candy, cigarettes and frosty red apples. He bought a cheese sandwich, a container of milk and an apple and ate his lunch standing up, next to a supply closet. Peering inside, he could see a shelf laden with Mr. Feldman's sets of combined shipping tickets. He picked up a sheaf of papers and riffled through them, exposing the final sheet with its challenging rectangle. *Very Bright Red.* Soon, he hoped, Raffalovitch would have the spectrograph reports on both ink and paper—confirmation that the ransom note had been fashioned from the peculiar office form. As he stared at the white sheet, at its red oblong with the legend 12—GENERAL COPY, he found it hard to believe that anyone employed by Culligan or Feldman—any of these lower middle-class people (so much like himself)—could have been responsible for the crime—a crime that ran the risk of death in the gas chamber. Two men in worn denims walked by, discussing a fight they had seen on television: one was slender, hipless and very blond, the other, a thickset Mexican with a boxer's nose. *One of them?* he wondered. Or the clerkish man pounding at the cigarette machine? Or the gray-haired man calling a bet into the wall telephone at the distant end of the corridor? Perhaps Feldman was right: the sheet of paper had simply found its way to the criminal, and nobody at either Kay-Bee Printers or Four State Shippers had the remotest connection with Amy Andrus. Yet, there remained the percentages: the strategy of following most likely candidates as quickly as possible. He took a final bite of his apple, tossed it into a trash bin and walked through the swinging doors into Culligan's office—to be greeted by Fred Wagley's burly figure.

"Hi, Joe," the agent said. "Nice of you to ask us down. Moll told me you were out on some chase of your own."

Joe smiled crookedly. "I guess whatever we got is yours from now on. Not that I'm being selfish or anything."

"Look, kid—we're after one thing. Let's work together."

"Right. You been briefed on the note?"

Wagley nodded. "Only what I read in your lab man's report."

The receptionist came into the office to advise them that Mr. Culligan had just telephoned. He was on his way back to talk to them, and would they please use his private office until he arrived? They walked into the shipping executive's glass-enclosed office. Like everything else, it was gleaming, clean, efficient. There was an electric typewriter, two dictaphones, giant framed maps of the southwest and of the Los Angeles area. The officers sat on an uncreased couch and looked at each other warily.

"Joe, take my word for it. Secrecy doesn't become you." Wagley's broad face was sympathetic. "It's not unusual for local cops to resent us. Rheinholdt's been sore at the FBI for years. But it doesn't sit with you."

"O.K., Wagley, I'm on the team. I'm sorry if I forgot to call you on this. You know—everything happening so fast. Rheinholdt disappearing. Has he shown up?"

"Nope."

McFeeley whistled. The old man had blown his lid. Someone should have seen it coming, gotten Mayor Speed's ear and done something about it. *I should have,* Joe thought. *I saw him going squirrelly Monday morning in the Andrus place.* He made no comment to the federal man.

"I tracked the ransom note down to this place—or the printer who makes them." He showed Wagley the sheaf of shipping tickets, pulling out the final copy with its red rectangle. "It matches the note perfectly. Raffalovitch is checking it out on the spectrograph to make sure." Then he disclosed his conversation with Feldman—how the two of them had evolved a theory of the theft of office paper. "It's a stab," McFeeley said apologetically, "but I thought we'd see if something turned up quickly—here or at the printer's—anyone with a record, anyone in debt, anyone who acts fishy when we interrogate.

"Sounds reasonable," Wagley said. "We'll have to get alibis from everyone and start checking them. You going to ask right out about the kidnaping?"

"What do *you* think? I mean—you're in charge."

"Cut it out, will you, Joe? You make me feel like a heel. Since you ask—I 'd prefer to hide it. We could be looking for a shipping theft."

"That's what I figured. I told Bannon already."

Wagley smiled. "You'd make a good agent, Joe. Ever think of a federal career?"

"I never went to college. I'm studying nights now."

"Oh. Well, that isn't all that counts." He paced Culligan's office. "That's good. We'll say we're after a larceny case—addresses changed on the cartons. Express loading racket. That would mean somebody in the firm, or at least with access to these forms."

Joe yawned mightily. "Your men turn anything up at the crime search?" he asked.

"Not yet. I suppose anything worth-while's been disturbed by now."

McFeeley nodded in agreement. They sat in the neat office awaiting Mr. Culligan, two wary, intense men—mutually respectful, yet not wholly trusting one another.

Chief Caspar Rheinholdt's aimless tour of southern California (a psychologist analyzing the Andrus case months later called it a temporary loss of sanity) ended a little after 1:00 P.M. Weary, finely coated with desert dust, he double-parked in front of Mayor Speed's sporting goods store and got out. He yanked the panama down over his head, looked neither right nor left, and strode into the store, finding the mayor in the process of selling a 12-gauge Winchester to a customer.

"Caspar," the mayor said. "Good heavens—Caspar." He summoned a clerk to help the customer and ushered the chief into his office.

"Caspar, you've had me worried stiff. Where have you been?" Speed spoke gently. "Have you been investigating on your own? You really should have left word. The FBI's in the case, you know."

"I know. I called 'em last night."

"You did? I'm glad to hear you took the initiative. I'm just perturbed you didn't tell me. Everything was at sixes and sevens this morning."

Rheinholdt reached in his breast pocket and handed Speed a rumpled envelope. The mayor opened it and took out the letter of resignation.

"Oh no. Oh no, indeed, Caspar. I won't accept this."

"You got to, Mr. Mayor. Did you read what the *Register* said about me? What those reporters did—calling the chiefs and trying to blame me for the mess on Monday? I can't fight all them liars. I can't do my job and fight them."

"That's no reason to quit," Mayor Speed said firmly. "I didn't think you were a quitter. Listen to me, Caspar. I'm on the griddle, too. They tried to blame me at the Council meeting last night. I won't have my nine terms as mayor—as the best mayor Santa Luisa's ever had—besmirched by this Andrus case. I'll fight it out. I'll wait it out. I'll beat them at their own game."

Rheinholdt's Aesopian head waggled sideways. "Then you better accept this. I ain't helping you by hanging on."

"That's where you're wrong, Caspar. I'm wiser in the ways of politics. If you quit now, while the investigation is in progress— we're both dead. I suppose you don't care; you can retire. And I shouldn't care either, because I don't need the money. The store is what supports me and what sends my daughters to Scripps and my boy to Stanford. It's my good name that concerns me. If you quit, it's an admission I've failed. If you stick it out and, by some chance —and there still is a chance—that child is found, the criminal caught—we're all home free."

"What if she ain't found? Suppose she's dead? Suppose that son-of-a-bitch never turns up?"

"We're no worse than if you quit now. At least if you stay on, we're taking a calculated risk. Who knows—with the FBI in, this may be solved in a few days." Deliberately, he ripped up Rhein-holdt's resignation and tossed the pieces into a wastebasket. "You get back to your office, Caspar, and take over. We're not licked yet."

"No," the chief said. "It can't come to no good."

"Caspar, I beg you to do as I say. Go back to your office. You can say you were out doing some investigating."

"Oh, it ain't that. It's like something I was proud of all my life was destroyed. I been a cop all my life. I never took a dishonest buck. I never disobeyed an order. And now everything is ruined." Swallowing, he fixed his tortured eyes on his superior. "Because I know that little girl is dead. That fellow was psycho. One of them Los Angeles nuts. I said that the first day. And now they'll be blaming me for it, for as long as I live." He got up, his flesh sagging on the mammoth bones. "I'll go back to the office, if you want me to, Mr. Mayor."

"Good man, Caspar," said Speed. "We'll ride this one out—wait and see."

Immediately upon receiving Hinrichsen's permission to proceed with the program, Eliot went into conference with George Brack. Ballstead gave them a grudging blessing and a schedule. They would go on the air at 10:15, after the 10:00 o'clock news. He wanted a full script by 6:00, in time to catch the vice-president before the latter left the office, to secure his approval. Tom was taking no raps for this, he made clear, somewhat to Eliot's sorrow.

"Here's the way I see it," Eliot told Brack. "We open cold with film of the mob outside the house—silent. Dissolve to you, recapping the story. Then you switch emphasis to the nature of the press coverage, and *Truth* coverage in particular. Then you cue me, and I'm sitting next to you, in a two shot. We discuss how I—let's make it you and I—decided to get the facts. Then we do it chronologically."

Brack gazed at him with unstinting admiration. "El, you're fantastic. How can you think so fast and so clearly? Goodness, the producers and writers I've worked with! They'd make what you just said the subject of a two-hour meeting!"

"That's why I'm a failure," Sparling muttered. "I move too quick. I got to learn to pause, reflect, puff a pipe. O.K., enough mutual love, Georgie. We show the *Truth* front pages—the story out. Then we run footage of Rheinholdt's conference—the part about the charge against the *Truth*. Next, the *Truth* response yesterday— you know—the manure about the people's right to know and the 6:04 gimmick. Then we start with Walter L. Todd—we can read a hunk out of that maniac's statement—the part where he spills his guts to Swinnerton. Next, we bring in Patrolman Hertmann *in person—in uniform*—to give us his version—his time checks. You interview him, Georgie; you're the star. Next, Swinnerton's tape; next, selected quotes from Herbie Hood, unattributed. All this we can do in like eight minutes. Then you ask me for a small summary of my reportage. Then you oughta take it for the moral crusher— who did what to who, who failed, what went wrong."

Brack, furiously writing notes, was enchanted. Like Hinrichsen, he felt some need to *relate*, to *improve*. Beer commercials were fine, ensuring the yearly trade-in of his cruiser for a more powerful model. But what availed the newest Chris-Craft if that inner urge, what his minister called the undying search for eternities, did not enhance a man's life? He wanted to convey his gratitude to his ungainly confederate, but Sparling was shouting into the phone, browbeating Patrolman Clyde Hertmann into a personal appearance. To Brack's amazement, Hertmann gave his consent.

"Rheinholdt said O.K.?" Eliot bellowed. "Thank him for me! Tell him no hard feelings—he can belt me around any time he wants!"

Clyde Hertmann promised to be at the studio at 9:00—in uniform, with his own list of telephone calls.

Sparling rubbed his hands. "We'll lay 'em out. Now—Georgie—go screen Rheinholdt's press conference and have the editors clip off what we need. Then we can go through Swinnerton's tape. Only let's not work too fast—we'll be finished in an hour, and Ballstead doesn't want the script till 6:00."

"You are a card," George said lovingly. Then, his unclouded face appeared thoughtful. "El—this pointing of the moral at the end of the program. Don't you think *you* should do it? After all, it was your investigative work. I'm just the voice."

Sparling gathered up his notes. "No. No, never, Georgie. You. Only you. *Only yooooo can be mah destineeeee . . .*"

"Cut it out, the whole newsroom is staring at you. Now, be serious, El."

"I'm serious, Georgie-Porgie. Only you. Why? If you blow the whistle, the world will pay attention. You are George Brack, *Amurrican*. Boat lover, father, scoutmaster, lay preacher—unstained, unblemished Protestant civil pillar. You realize what we're doing? Taking on the whole Army of Talkers? I wouldn't last five minutes —I'm all wrong. But, Georgie, you can hit 'em where it hurts, because, like Thomas E. Dewey in 1948, you come before the public with *clean hands*."

"Yes. And look what happened to him," Brack said—not certain whether his colleague was complimenting him or not.

Mr. Culligan—Francis M. Culligan—was a tall, prematurely gray man, with the good looks of a retired actor. He had the high color of a drinker, his features were hard and sharp, his eyes pale blue—and surprisingly innocent. He listened attentively as Joe McFeeley and Fred Wagley took turns explaining their problem. Wagley let Joe do most of the talking.

"You think someone in my place may have kidnaped that kid?" Culligan asked. He walked to a file cabinet and removed a manila folder.

"There's no way of telling," Joe said. "But one thing we do know. That ransom note originated here or at Kay-Bee Printers. How it got to the guy who wrote it is something else. But at least this is a start."

"And you want to interrogate everyone here?" he asked.

"That's the idea," Wagley said. "It would help if you had personnel files—we could check them out before talking to people."

Culligan tapped the folders. "All yours. I guess we have about twenty-eight people on payroll now. How about some we've canned? Or any who quit—in the past few months?"

"We'll have to track them down also," Wagley said. "Anything you have on them—addresses, phone numbers."

"When did you start using this form?" Joe asked.

The shipping executive shaded his eyes. "Let's see. Start of the fiscal year, I guess. June 1. Less than four months ago. Don't ask me why we started on that date—my bookkeeper said it would be easier." He unloosened his tie. "Listen. I'm a frustrated cop myself. I was an M.P. officer. Why don't you tell me what kind of a guy you're looking for? Maybe I'll have a bright idea."

"That's the trouble," McFeeley said. "This guy came and went like a spook—no prints, no marks, no handwriting. I guess we can tell you a little." He looked at Wagley for approval; the federal man nodded.

"Well—maybe he owned a tan or a light-brown Ford, '49 or '50. That's a reach—some kid thought he saw one cruising."

Culligan began to jot notes down.

McFeeley continued. "Well—he either worked here, or at Kay-Bee, or knew someone who did, or in some way had access to your shipping tickets."

"Could have borrowed a hunk of scrap paper from a neighbor," Culligan said.

"Right. Still, if we found the neighbor——"

"I'm with you."

"Ah—we heard his voice—we're pretty sure it was his—this morning—but it was muffled, and he was spacing words. We'd guess he was a white male, between twenty-five and forty-five, moderate amount of education—high school, maybe."

Culligan nodded. "I don't know how much I can help. I make it a practice not to be too friendly with employees. How do you want to do this?"

The FBI man explained the mode of questioning—it would concern stolen shipments, apparently through the theft of some of Mr. Culligan's shipping forms. They would save for last the matter of the alibi—the subject's whereabouts between 8:00 and 9:00 Monday morning.

"Good enough," Culligan said. "Why don't we go alphabetically?

I think everyone's back from lunch by now. If they're not, there'll be a few more ex-employees for you guys to work on." He buzzed for the receptionist and asked her to summon the man whose name appeared on the first personnel record. He gave the wide IBM form to Wagley. McFeeley peered over the FBI man's shoulder and read:

ANDREWS, CHARLES (NMI)—LOADER

Andrews, Charles, was a beige Negro in immaculate denims. He had the uncluttered face of a UCLA graduate student and he appeared not at all flustered by the questioning.

Culligan explained that the two gentlemen were police officers. They were trying to track down some missing shipments. Nobody at Four State was under suspicion, but everyone—including Mr. Culligan himself—would have to answer routine questions. Andrews nodded.

"Mr. Andrews," McFeeley said in his best City Hall manner, "you ever take any of Mr. Culligan's forms home with you—don't worry, he won't can you. Like shipping tickets, maybe scrap paper?"

"Nope."

Culligan waved his hand. "It's O.K., Charlie. Everyone robs office supplies. If you did, say so."

"Never did. I don't do much writin'."

"What kind of a car do you drive?" Joe asked.

"Chevy—'48."

"What color is it?"

"Blue, I guess you'd call it."

McFeeley glanced at the personnel sheet. "You still live at 8100 East Bentham?"

"I moved a few weeks back. The neighborhood's deteriatin'. I got a upper floor of a private house on East Williston, 9000 block."

McFeeley made a note of his new address. "Can you tell us what you were doing last Monday morning—between 8:00 and 9:00?"

"Huh?" asked the Negro, frowning. He appealed to his employer. "I thought no one here was under suspicion. He sounds like he's talkin' to a criminal."

Culligan rubbed his jaw. "No one's suspected yet, Charlie. It's a routine question."

"You want to know where I was Monday morning?" he asked McFeeley.

"That's right," Wagley added.

"Man, look at my timecard. The boss makes us punch 'em every morning. I got here a little before 8:30, just like every morning. Before that, I got dressed, washed, had breakfast and drove in."

When the Negro had left, Culligan smiled at the two investigators. "That should simplify a lot. Just check off the names on the time sheet. They all get to work around 8:30, some earlier. Pretty hard to have kidnaped that kid out in Sanlu, hidden her somewhere and then be here to do a day's work."

The FBI man was not insulted. "I thought of that. We're more interested in *who* they are, not what they did. Relatives, friends, anything in their background that might lead us somewhere. Now Charlie Andrews, for example—I don't think he'd lead us anywhere on this kind of crime."

Joe tapped his pencil against his steno pad. "I didn't ask him if he had a record. I couldn't imagine him getting up that note, pulling off a snatch."

"Just as well," Wagley said. "Besides—we're not through with any of them—for a long time. I'm going to detail a couple of dozen men to check everyone here, everyone at the printer's, anyone who's worked at either place since those forms went into use." He indicated the personnel records. "O.K. if I take these, Mr. Culligan?"

"Whatever you want," Culligan said. "I'll have the girl dig up the names of anybody who was canned or quit after June 1. Anything else?"

"Nope," Wagley said. "Next customer." He nodded at Joe. "You're doing fine, kid. Continue."

By 5:45 that afternoon, McFeeley and Wagley, with Culligan's assistance, had concluded their preliminary interrogations of personnel at Four State. There were two drivers unavailable, both out on calls, as well as six people who had been fired or had left the firm voluntarily after June 1—the date on which they had begun using the new shipping tickets printed by Kay-Bee. They had talked to twenty-six persons, and each one had an alibi for his whereabouts on Monday morning—the evidence of the time cards. This, of course, did not eliminate any of them from suspicion, or, at least, it did not eliminate them as links—no matter how remote, no matter how innocent—to the unknown who had used the form for his ransom note. These tenuous relationships, if they existed, would be further explored by Wagley. Joe realized that only the Bureau had the man power, the perfection of organization, to start probing the lives and backgrounds of all the employees at Culligan's place and at the printer's. It was a job, Joe knew, that would consume weeks—and each passing day lessened Amy Andrus' chance of survival.

A little before 6:oo, Milt Bannon called from Kay-Bee Printers. He, too, had concluded a fruitless afternoon's interrogation. At his side had been one of Wagley's colleagues, and they had run into the same pattern: to a man, the persons questioned had been on the way to work, or arriving, during that hour of the morning; none had appeared nervous or guilty during interrogation; none had appeared to be anything more than average lower middle-class Americans, incapable of committing so monstrous a crime. "There's one guy who admitted he was court-martialed twice in the Army," Bannon said sadly, "for belting a noncom once, and for A.W.O.L. the second time, but I couldn't hardly consider this a criminal record."

McFeeley told him to thank Mr. Feldman and lock up for the time being. Wagley then instructed his counterpart at the printer's to impound Feldman's personnel file. The agents would start working on them that night, cross-checking them against dozens of other existing records—prison files, parole documents, motor vehicle bureau records.

Just before they prepared to leave Four State Shippers and Consigners, Raffalovitch called McFeeley with a late report from the LA police lab. The spectrochemical analysis of Mr. Feldman's ink—Very Bright Red—had revealed it to be identical with the traces on the note. "I laid the two spectrograms on top of each other," Raffalovitch told Joe, "and they're the same, all right. Could have been out of the same bottle. I also got the documents man at LA to check the paper stocks. They're the same, too—six teen-pound white bond—same texture. It couldn't be a coincidence any more. That note was made from one of those orders."

The irrefutable evidence of the laboratory tantalized McFeeley more than ever (and elicited from Wagley a compliment on some damned good investigatory work). What person, who at some time had access to the shipping forms, either at Four State or at Kay-Bee Printers, had—either willfully or unwittingly—led the way to the preparation of the note? It seemed incredible to Joe that any of those bland, average Americans he had interrogated that afternoon could have ever entertained the remotest notion of kidnaping a child, threatening its life, causing agony to its parents. Charlie Andrews? Who worried that the old neighborhood was "deteri-atin'?" Mrs. Shanley (or a nephew or a neighbor?) with her motherly crown of white hair? Sobieski, Culligan's dispatcher—a Marine veteran of four invasions, with six children of his own? Not one of them, none of the twenty-six he and Wagley had interviewed, appeared capable of the crime. Nor, did he imagine, were any of Mr. Feldman's employees any more suspect. Yet, somehow, there had to be a connection between one of these wage-earning, TV-watching, installment-buying people and the bargainer who had stolen the child.

When McFeeley returned to headquarters, he went to see Rhein-holdt and report on the day's work. Fred Wagley went with him, cradling under one arm the personnel records from Four State Shippers and Consigners and from Kay-Bee Printers. Two other agents joined them in Rheinholdt's office and, in a few minutes, Mayor Speed himself showed up. The meeting was brief and to the point. "This is no reflection on you, Chief, or on Joe, or on any of the Sanlu police department—Mr. Wagley will bear me out, I'm sure—but I've made the decision, as ranking official in this city, of turning the investigation over to the Bureau. Joe, I've already discussed it with Chief Rheinholdt and he concurs."

"You mean—just like that?" McFeeley asked. There was little protest in his voice.

"I'm afraid so," Speed said. "Let's admit it, the Bureau is better equipped for this sort of thing. Naturally, you, Joe, and your men, all of us, will be on call to *assist* the FBI in its work. But we're giv-ing them the ball."

"That's right," Rheinholdt said. "Just what the mayor said." Joe could not help wonder at what inner torments were eating the old man: the attacks of the newspapers, and now, the worst insult of all—surrendering the case to the federal men.

"I don't mind being an errand boy," McFeeley said. "It's just that—well, I feel the department made a good comeback. Maybe I did some things wrong Monday, but still, if it hadn't been for the papers, we might have gotten the child."

"No one's denying that, Joe," Fred Wagley said. He lifted up the stack of manila folders. "But this is Big Casino. It's true you and your lab man ran down the note. But the next step is the hard one—who made it? This is going to take a couple of dozen men a week—maybe more—maybe less, if we're lucky."

"No one's taking a thing from you, Joe," Speed said.

"You'll get credit—you and Chief Rheinholdt here—and everyone in Sanlu," Wagley said soothingly, "if we get a break. I'll see to it that the papers get it right."

Mayor Speed shivered. "Don't mention papers, Mr. Wagley. Just you fellows get this thing over with."

McFeeley stopped at the lab to talk to Raffalovitch and to look at the new reports on the shipping form. "You better shoot this downstairs to Wagley," he told the lab man. "It's their show from now on. We can go back to rounding up vandals."

Then the detective called his wife, advising her that he would be home for dinner. "Regular hours from now on, Roz," he said miserably. "The whole thing's going to the Bureau. They might let me go out for coffee if I'm a good boy."

"What do you care?" Roz cried. "Joe—what do you care? You did your best. It wasn't your fault the newspapers ruined everything. What are you supposed to do—be responsible for the whole Sanlu department? One underpaid cop—Joseph Vincent McFeeley?"

"O.K., honey, don't get sore." He laughed. "I guess you're mad about the same thing. The old Irish temper—sticking up for the father of your children."

"Well, it is a rotten shame, them not letting you stay on the case after all the sweat you put in, all the abuse you took. I bet that woman had something to do with it."

"Who? Mona Mears?"

"No, no. The Andrus woman. I don't trust her."

Joe sighed. "Honey, she has nothing to do with it. I guess some pressure was put on Speed. Who can blame him? I can't argue when he says the Bureau can handle this better than I can. Even though I hate being closed out of it."

She changed the subject, briefing him on the children. Joey had lost his brace again; Mary Grace had gotten the lead in the play— she was going to be Saint Catherine of Siena; Theresa had started a new club for six year old girls on the block; the baby, Dale, had a terrible rash, and Dr. Matzkin thought he was allergic to orange juice.

His wife's report seemed one more facet of his general inade-

quacy. *Some got it and some ain't,* he thought. He did not earn
enough money, he wasn't much of a cop, and he wasn't even a
very good father. He wondered idly about dropping his outside
studies, forgetting about his dream of a college degree. Where
would it lead? What good would it do?

Raffalovitch roused him from his meanderings.

"Phone for you, McFeeley."

Joe took it at the lab chief's desk: an anatomical chart of the
human body dangled over the desk. That's me, McFeeley imagined
—exposed and skinned.

"McFeeley? This is Culligan."

"Oh, hello, Mr. Culligan."

"You got that list of people who were fired or who quit my place?
I have an added starter for you."

Wagley had taken everything—folders from both companies,
incidental data, notes from their interrogations. Joe had, however,
kept a copy of the six people who were no longer at Four State and
who, conceivably, might have had access to the paper.

"Read 'em off for me will you, McFeeley?" the shipper asked.

Joe flicked on Raffalovitch's desk lamp and studied the yellow
note paper. "Perkins, Arthur. Rosa, Jimmy. Burmeister, Fred.
LaPlace, J. C., Corriden, Mary. Stephenson, K."

"He's not on it," Culligan said. "After you and Wagley left, I
started racking my brain to see if there was anyone else around
here in the past few months. You asked me about people with
records, and this guy didn't have one—but I had to can him because he was behaving strangely. His name didn't show in my personnel files because he wasn't here long enough to fill out the form.
He was hired as temporary help in July, when we had some government contract work."

"Why'd you let him go?" Joe asked.

"He got too friendly with some outside truckers who were working for us," Culligan said.

"He was trying to pull something?"

"I don't know. I was too busy to find out, so I booted him. He
was hired as an assistant in the shipping department—paper work,
documentation. Then, the first day on the job, he started buddying
up to a couple of contract drivers. You know what happens—they
make some deal on dropping shipments, or losing some, or sending
out less than the tickets call for—and we have to pay. I shouldn't
have to explain express loading rackets to a cop. That was your
dodge this afternoon."

"You have his name? His address?" Joe asked.

"Just his name. He was temporary, and he hadn't filled out any papers in the rush over this government work. All I have is a memo from my foreman. Guy's name was Krebs. Maurice Krebs. K, r, e, b, s."

"No address?"

"Nope. We never bothered pushing anything against him."

Joe sighed. "Anything else you think of, Mr. Culligan, about this Krebs—call me. I'll start looking."

As soon as he had hung up, he reached for a Santa Luisa telephone directory and turned to the K's. There was only one Krebs listed:

Krebs, G.   3114 Amethyst   PI 5-1446-J

He jotted down the information, recalling that Amethyst was on the city's eastern fringes—new tract houses much like his own. Then he quickly went through the five regional Los Angeles phone books and listed all the Krebses he could find—sixteen all told, none of them with a first name of Maurice or an initial of M.

Raffalovitch changed from his white coat to his suit jacket and bade him good night, leaving him alone in the small laboratory. "Whyncha go home, McFeeley?" the lab man asked. "There's nothing left for us anyway. You found the note. Let *them* find the child."

Alone in the lab, McFeeley studied the list of people named Krebs. Culligan had called him, not knowing that the investigation was now out of his hands. He was obliged to take the new information downstairs to Wagley. He knew that the first thing in the morning, the federal man would set in motion a massive check-out on all people associated with the printer and the shipper. They would check birth and hospital records, drivers' licenses, social security files, service discharge papers, prison records, medical histories—until each and every employee of the two companies, current and past, would be without a secret. And somehow, out of this sea of facts, they would hope to find the kidnaper. They probably would, McFeeley reasoned, not bitterly. They were the best—professionals, unbeatable. He would do well to accept his role of errand boy. But, instead of hurrying downstairs to Wagley, he looked up the home telephone number of the assistant manager of the State Motor Vehicle Bureau office in Santa Luisa. The man, one Merlin Tripp, was an old friend of the detective's, and he presumed on this friendship to ask Tripp to open the office and look for something in the files.

"Gee, Joe, I got the barbecue going," Tripp complained. "And, besides, it's against regulations. I can't open the bureau after hours. There'd be hell to pay if the boss found out. Can't it wait till tomorrow morning?"

"It can't, Merlin," McFeeley said. "It's on the Andrus kidnaping. I have to know right away." He looked at the wall clock: 6:32.

"O.K., O.K. I'll run down there and raise the watchman. But you better back me up if I get in trouble. What do you want?"

"Anything on someone named Krebs. Make of car, year, address, any offenses. Particularly a Maurice Krebs, but any others with that second name."

"Right. K, r, e, b, s. Maurice. I'll call you in fifteen minutes."

Waiting, McFeeley ordered some coffee from the Jumboburger. Milt Bannon and Ed Case dropped by to commiserate with him. They, too, felt badly about the way they were being pulled off the case. There was a rumor around, Bannon said, that Rheinholdt had resigned and that Mayor Speed had refused it. Still unexplained was the old man's absence that morning—although some of the uniformed patrol claimed they had seen him driving around town, looking lost. "Don't quote me," Bannon whispered, "but I think Rheinholdt isn't long for the job. Not the way the City Council jumped on Speed last night. Crazy the way this Andrus deal loused so many people up."

Tripp called back sooner than Joe expected. "Joe? Merlin Tripp. Listen—there's only one car registered in Santa Luisa by a party named Krebs. Must be the same as you gave me. Gerhard Krebs, 3114 Amethyst."

"See if I can guess, Merlin. Is it a tan or brown Ford?"

"No. It's a black Buick tudor, 1947. License plate 3-C-1668. Want anything else?"

"What about Maurice Krebs? Or M. Krebs? Nothing?"

"No car registered. But he's got a driver's license."

McFeeley lowered his voice. Bannon and Case could still hear him, and they exchanged querying glances. "Maurice Krebs? A driver's license?"

"Yup. Number 52367788. No offenses. He's got the same address as Gerhard Krebs, Amethyst, so they must be in the same family."

"What are the birth dates for the two?"

"Ah—let's see—Gerhard is 8-4-92—April 8, 1884—that would

make him sixty-seven. Maurice is 27-11-10—November 27, 1910—which would make him forty-one. Probably a father and son."

McFeeley kept scribbling. "Address the same on both, right? And the only car registered for anyone named Krebs is the black Buick?"

"That's it. Joe—not a word about this. I just broke three state laws opening this place up for you without permission from the commissioner."

"It's just between us. I hope I didn't ruin your barbecue, Merlin. Much obliged."

Bannon and Case were waiting for him to say something.

"A late lead," Joe said. "The guy at Four State Shippers sent me a flash—somebody they fired last July."

Case gestured at the sheet of information he had just jotted down. "I guess you better give it to Wagley. He says they're going to start on those names tonight."

McFeeley's face appeared more out of whack than normal. "They've got names they haven't used yet. I'll keep this one—just for laughs." He got up, folding the paper, placing it in the breast pocket of his shirt. "You guys want to do me a favor? Start calling the auto rentals in Sanlu and ask if a tan or a brown Ford was rented Monday morning early, or maybe Sunday night, to someone named Maurice Krebs. Or Gerhard Krebs." He jotted the Krebs telephone number on a pad. "I'll be at this number for a while. Call me if you learn anything."

"Want any help?" Case asked. "Maybe it's the guy."

"I doubt it," McFeeley said. At the door, he added, "One of you guys buzz my wife, please? Tell her I can't make dinner tonight."

Shortly before 6:00 P.M., Bill Trigg, the acting city editor of the LA *Truth*, learned that United Broadcasting Corporation intended to devote fifteen minutes that night to an exposé of newspaper interference in the Andrus case. A resourceful young man, he had many friends in newsrooms around town, and one of his contacts at UBC phoned him the information. Trigg immediately informed Kalaidjian, and Kalaidjian informed Herbert Hood. The latter left word with T. T. Hansel's secretary. The Editor & Publisher was not yet back from his appearance at the UCLA School of Journalism, where he had lectured on "Why Censorship?" On his return, Hansel summoned all three underlings to his office, directing his first queries at Trigg.

"That kid Sparling is in back of it," Trigg said. "George Brack's going to voice it. Evidently they've got the permission of the brass at UBC to do it."

"But just what do they hope to do by attacking us?" Hansel asked. "What have we ever done to United?"

"The way I get it, Mr. Hansel," Trigg said, "they're going to say we lied. That we knew before 4:30 that the story was to be withheld, but we settled on that 6:04 time because nobody could check it."

"Check it?" Hansel asked, incredulous. "What was there to check? We received no official request until 6:04. Anyone who says otherwise is lying."

He really believes it, Hood marveled. *It is not guile, it is not self-deception, it is belief. He is what he is and where he is because he believes; he is untouchable; his grandeur will not perish.*

Hansel burst from his executive seat and was striding about his carpeted precincts. The handsome head had turned a splotchy claret, the jaw was outthrust, and if he were not deeply troubled, he was at least aroused. "Who the devil is Sparling? Why don't I know who he is?"

"I've told you already," Hood said. "That boy I fired on the Schlossmann business."

"Oh yes, Schlossmann." Hansel interrupted his pacing. Perhaps a disturbing memory of Werner Schlossmann's corpse athwart the *Truth's* truck siding gave him pause. "But why? Is United going to vilify us on the basis of what this—this—malcontent claims?"

"Hell, Ted," Hood said, "it was a disappointed office seeker shot James A. Garfield."

They ignored him. Young Bill Trigg scratched his red fuzz. "The way I get it, Mr. Hansel, Sparling has statements from a lot of people. The cops played ball with him. I'm told, but I don't know for sure, that Swinnerton talked to him."

"Swinnerton?" Hansel exploded. "Swinnerton?" He glared at Hood. "You told me he left town."

"He did. Either that or he committed suicide. We can't find him, and his landlady said he moved—no forwarding address. Maybe he talked to Sparling before he pulled out."

"Why didn't you stop him?" asked Hansel.

"Ted, I can't keep our reporters locked up, or under surveillance, or even give 'em orders about who they talk to or drink with—considering what we pay 'em. I asked you yesterday to do something about Swinnerton, but you refused. You said you weren't worried."

"I said nothing of the sort," T.T. said quickly.

"Tell him what else you heard," Ed Kalaidjian muttered to Trigg. His drooping face appeared the common depository for their unhappiness.

"Well, my buddy at UBC says that they're going to claim that an informed source, here at the *Truth,* backed up everything Sparling found out. You know—that Swinnerton relayed the police request to us before 4:30, and that we asked for assurances from Rheinholdt, and then printed before he called back."

Hansel sank into his chair. "An informed source? Here on the *Truth?* Someone in this organization *fed* material to this television person?"

Trigg nodded. "I gather that's their clincher."

The Editor & Publisher slapped a palm against his desk top. "Well, by God, I'll find out who it is. All of you here—Trigg, Ed, Herb—you're in on this little detective chore." He halted. "But who? We were the only ones in on it."

His choice of language, Hood felt, betrayed much. *In on it—* a conspiracy, a connivance, a scheme dreamed up by a few of the boys in the poolroom.

"Mr. Hansel," Trigg said hesitantly, "I have a theory, for what it's worth."

Herbert Hood darted a querulous glance at him. Was he, in his old age, to become the target of brash boys? Were the Sparlings and Triggs of the world to destroy him?

"What's that, Trigg?" Hansel asked.

"Well—maybe I shouldn't say this in front of Mr. Hood— but I'm just saying it because I have the Organization's interests at heart."

"What are you mumbling about, Trigg?" asked Hood angrily. "You saying I would spill the beans? With my loyalty to the Organization?"

"Oh no. Oh no, Mr. Hood," the redheaded young man said quickly. "Not that at all. But your secretary might."

"My *secretary?* What has she got to do with it?" Hood barely knew her name. She was a girl. She. You. Get me the overnight file. Call Mr. Hansel. Take a letter to Sacramento.

Trigg looked at Ed Kalaidjian for some marginal support, found none in that melting brown face, and continued. "She goes out with Sparling," he said. "She dates him all the time. I'll bet she talked. None of *us* would. Nobody in their right mind would tell him anything, knowing the unreliable type he is, and what he was up to. But his girl friend—and being Mr. Hood's secretary, where she could overhear things."

"What's her name?" Hansel asked. "That dark girl?"

"Potenza," Hood said. "I think that's it." He had used it so rarely that he honestly had trouble remembering it.

"Connie," Trigg added. "Constance Potenza. I have nothing against her personally, but I think she should be questioned about this."

Hansel got up. His squared-off, navy-blue figure, crowned with that florid face, advertised that he was no longer worried, no longer apprehensive about the television critique. A culprit had been found; a lance could be hurled. "What do you say to that, Herbert?"

"Ah—well—it's entirely possible. I don't keep tabs on that girl. But if Trigg says she's Sparling's friend, I suppose she is. Maybe she blabbed to him."

Hansel nodded at the two minor members. "You two can go. Trigg—see what else you can learn about UBC. I have some contacts there myself." When they had left, Hansel looked gravely at the general manager. "Didn't you warn that girl? Weren't you aware that she might talk to Sparling?"

"Never occurred to me, Ted. Swinnerton was the only one who worried me, and I was right. We have no proof my secretary said anything."

"But it points that way. Would *you* talk to that boy? Would *I*? Would Trigg or Kalaidjian?"

"No, no, not a chance." The old man did not move.

"Well—what are you waiting for? Go downstairs and fire her."

"Ah—fire her?"

"Of course. She's not in any union. She has no recourse. Tell her it's without prejudice, but try to get her to admit she was the one who gave information out. We'll need something for our rebuttal tomorrow."

"Righto, Ted. She's as good as fired."

All in all, both men agreed it was a splendid solution. From Hood's standpoint, it took the onus off him; and, moreover, he knew that secretaries can always find work. A girl who was willing to take dictation and type, to file and answer phones—and do all these well—was a rarity, a discovery, and would always work, especially if she were pretty. The pretty girls all wanted to be production assistants or copy writers or research associates. There was none left to type letters. As for Hansel, he had merely followed an honored tradition of his calling. In times of emergencies, this tradition decreed, minor personnel is fired. Receptionists, copy boys, secretaries, mail clerks—all these were the wreckage of the newspaper *en crise*.

At 7:00 P.M., the hour at which the kidnaper had promised to call again, Laura went into the nursery to await the muffled voice. The men from the FBI had taken over—totally, efficiently. Their own tape recorder—an awe-inspiring instrument—had replaced the Sanlu mechanism, the one that had run out of tape that morning. A technician from the phone company stood by; two agents were primed to monitor extensions; the telephone company in Santa Luisa had been alerted to start tracing calls immediately. Agent Fewsmith checked his watch and spoke to Laura. "You don't have to wait in here, Mrs. Andrus, if you don't want to. It can ring once or twice before you pick it up."

"That's all right," she said. "I don't mind—for a few minutes anyway."

Outside the nursery, she could hear Selena stacking the supper dishes, Fritzie talking in muted tones to Moll about the weather, the occasional throb of a car rushing by on Nespoli. All these casual noises picked at her, reminders of the trivial acts and words that compose the fabric of life, the bits and pieces that are the prize of the living. They filled her now with a damp sadness—for her child, for what the child might miss, for all she might never know.

"7:05," Fewsmith said. "You'd be more at ease outside, Mrs. Andrus—maybe with your husband."

She walked into the den. Moll excused himself; his clumsy figure was more inutile than ever. She sat at Fritzie's desk. The electric desk clock (a gift from some grateful sponsor) goaded her. She turned its face to the wall.

"Hell of a thing," Fritzie said. "Why doesn't he call? Like he said he would."

Laura said nothing. They sat quietly in the den, hearing the murmur of the officers' voices. Soon it was 7:10, then 7:15. The phone had rung once—Laura running in to answer it and hearing only Eliot Sparling's brash voice advising her that they were going to "expose" the *Truth* and the press in general that night at 10:15

on UBC, and did she have any statement. She told the young man that she did not, thanked him for his solicitude, and returned to the den.

"Fine time to call," Fewsmith said to his aides. "After tonight, I think we'd better discontinue both numbers and start all over."

By now it appeared unlikely that the call would come through. The parents looked helplessly at each other, each entertaining the same atrocious thought: *we shall spend the rest of our lives waiting for a telephone call, a sign, a hint, a word of hope; we shall die with that hope, waiting for that call that never comes. . . .*

"I s'pose this is what we're going to have to live with," Andrus said huskily. "All the rest of our lives . . . waitin' . . . hopin' . . ."

"He said 7:00, I'm sure. Of course, I could have been wrong."

"See? You know he said 7:00, and now it's almost 7:20, so you're hopin' also. Tellin' yourself things that ain't so. It pains me, Laura, because that's an effort for you. You suffer from an imbalance of truth. Clear vision. You've got the power of analysis in you. You need a good dose of unreason in your blood—like me. More instinct and less intellect. Didn't you once tell me that's what was wrong with my directin'?"

"I'm sure I did. Does it matter any more? All the trivial arguments we've indulged in? All the sniping and carping and backbiting? Pretending our meanness and our jealousies were justified because we were—creative?"

"Yeah," Andrus said, sighing. "Me more than you." He smiled at her weakly. "Creative. What a damn joke. Funny thing is, I always had a hunch you had more on the ball than I did. If you'd have had a chance, some encouragement, and didn't have to be soothing my ego all the time, you might have made it with those ole statues."

"I don't care any more. I don't think I ever did."

They sat in silence. Laura had no desire to pursue the conversation. Their self-analyses seemed the ultimate in selfishness; courage and hope were demanded of them, not the whining post-mortems toward which Fritzie had been directing her. Yet, in his last words, she had sensed a halting apology, a glimmer of understanding on his part that was both new and surprising. Throughout their marriage she had willingly—too willingly—subdued her own artistic impulses, her own undeniable talents with clay and bronze and wood, to his world of wind. She had done a disservice to her own skills in appeasing his vanity. She had never complained about the arrangement; and he, up to this moment, had never acknowledged her sacrifice. "It doesn't mean a damn to me to have a show or to keep going to classes," Laura used to say. "I've got my hands full with the children and the house." And, she might have added, with a husband who had to be center stage at all times, a star performer who would tolerate no distracting supporting actors. Often, working in pleasant solitude in her studio, watching forms and shapes rise under the workings of her skilled, strong hands, she experienced a sense of loss, of unfulfillment, indeed, of cowardice. She simply lacked the national urge for self-aggrandizement, for quick entry into the celebrity complex. Unlike Fritzie and his brave company of players, she was afraid to dare exposure before the cruel public eye. She was a bad competitor, an artist who preferred to keep her art a private, partially realized hobby.

Yet, like all such people, she knew that was only half the story. Whatever impulses she had to subdue her talents had been happily encouraged by her husband. No words of praise for her vigorous moldings and castings and carvings ever escaped his fleshy lips; no bold attempts to advance her career were ever volunteered by him; no hints for the advertisement and merchandising of her statues ever came from him. Perhaps she would have rejected them; perhaps not. She wondered if she had not been playing a cruel joke on herself. Maybe she would have had fewer migraine headaches if she had worked harder at publicizing her product, if she had entered Fritzie's gassy empire, gotten her picture in the magazines, shown, sold, discussed, been acclaimed.

She concluded dismally. *there is nothing honorable or admirable in what I have done or not done with my skills.* Her self-negation—rooted in a stubborn insistence on privacy, nurtured by Fritzie's hoggish demands—seemed to her just another failing, another half-hearted enterprise.

His voice, choked, wavering, surprised her. "Laura, I want to move back in."

She said nothing, turning the clock to face her. It was 7:22.

"Why?" she asked. "Because you're sorry for me? That's not a good enough reason."

"It is. It counts for somethin'. I got a duty here. There's another child, maybe one to come someday. I'm kin. Don't turn your head away from me. I can't help sounding like a fool, but that's how I feel. I'm askin' you to let me move back in now, while we're both expectin' the worst. Maybe if Amy were back here, I wouldn't. I'd just be enough of a heel to pick up where I left off."

"What makes you think we can do any better with our lives than we did before? Every day another contest, another battle of words and wits, waiting for the other to move."

Andrus moved his blond head forward. "We can do better."

She closed her eyes. "I don't know what to say. You make it hard for me to say no."

"Listen. Listen to me. I know it's a calculated risk. I know what you're thinking. Just like me to make the *beau geste* in the middle of our misery. Why didn't I ask you last week? Or the day after I moved out? Why now? I tell you why. Because, some time or other, I got to lick this damned insufferable ego, that inability to love anyone, except if they're facets of *me*. I did it to you, and I know damn well you rebelled against it, from the start. I did it to the children."

"You didn't, you didn't."

"Hell, I didn't. They were O.K. to tell funny stories about at the studio, and for items in the columns, but they weren't O.K. when they infringed on my glorious self. You accepted 'em, and loved 'em, and let 'em erode you and dilute you. And, dammit, how I hated you for bein' able to do that—that gift for immolatin' yourself on their altar. I got to learn. I'm only thirty-four, and I reckon I got time to grow up."

She touched his hand. "It might hurt you," she said.

"What have I got to get hurt? My fraudulent talent? My ability to teach actors to mimic real life? Anybody can do what I do if he's got enough nerve."

"Are you sure you want to come back?" she asked. "Is it just because you're sorry for me now?"

"What if it is?" he asked. "That's a better reason than what I been yappin' about—helpin' myself grow up. That's like me, selfish to the end. Laura, if I have a generous impulse now and then, you do me a disservice discouraging it." His words were blurred, indistinct. "I want to be near you at night, when I get scared. I want to feel your body in the bed next to me, knowin' there's someone I can hold and talk to, and caress when the holy terrors come on."

"Do we love each other any longer?"

"I don't know," Andrus said innocently. "But I sure would like to find out. I can't let you be here alone, waitin', like you are now."

"All right," she said. "Whatever you want."

"That ain't enough. You have to want it this way also."

"I do."

Andrus rubbed his sleeve across his moist eyes. "I'll run back to the hotel tomorrow and get my stuff. You reckon it's all right if I run by the studio? I mean—we got to start our lives over again, no matter what."

"I don't see why not."

He pulled himself out of the chair and moved toward the living room. "Stay here a little while," she said. Then, glancing at the clock, she added: "I don't imagine he'll call." It was 7:30.

Joe McFeeley arrived at the Amethyst Place address shortly before 7:00 P.M. It was already dark. The desert air was edged with a hard chill. The house was a member of an enormous tract—perhaps two hundred homes—all of them quite new. Many of the houses were empty, the plots barren of grass, the windows dark and smeared with whitewashed X's. At the entrance to the development, a large welcoming sign greeted him.

DROITWICH HILLS

7½-ROOM CALIFORNIA RANCHERS

DELUXE BATHS—MODERN ELECTRIC KITCHENS

LANDSCAPING—DRY WELLS

$13,500 AND UP

The houses were gingerbready—roofs shingled with irregular chunks, picture windows sectioned off by diagonally intersecting dividers, colors running to fairy-tale pastels. Lawn statuary was much favored by the residents of Droitwich Hills (as flat and as barren as the rhubarb farm it had once been). The detective counted three fawns, two Negro grooms and six ducks on his ride to the Krebs house at 3114 Amethyst.

The streets were laid out with an attempt to simulate rolling terrain—dead ends, cul-de-sacs, looping curves that doubled back on themselves. The house he sought was at the bottom of one such loop, and, after finding it, he rode beyond it and parked several houses away to afford himself a few moments of observation. 3114 seemed no different than its neighbors—a one-story, undersized ranch with a peaked roof. Disneyland had clearly influenced the architect: it evoked memories of Hansel and Gretel, Grimm's fairy tales. There were four major colors available—beige, light green, turquoise blue, rose. The Krebs house was of light green shingling, irregularly hewn to accentuate the *Schwarzwald* motif. As McFeeley approached, he could see light in the living room, the gray-green glow of a television screen.

In the driveway, which led to a carport, a black Buick was parked, and under the harsh illumination of an exterior light, a man was washing the automobile. He was applying a soapy mixture from a bucket, using a long-handled brush. After he had gently laved a section, he would hose it down, study his work, then proceed to another section, working his way backwards from engine to right-hand door, and so on. To McFeeley, the car's unwashed parts appeared spotless, but the man kept at his work with ritual diligence, stirring the bubbly mixture, adjusting the hose pressure, whistling tunelessly.

The detective smiled and, in his best political manner, asked: "Excuse me, can you tell me where I can find a Mr. Maurice Krebs?"

"That's me," the man said. He directed the hose at a blob of lather on the front right door and watched it vanish in the clear stream.

"I'm sorry to bother you, Mr. Krebs," Joe said. "I'm Lieutenant McFeeley from the Santa Luisa police—"

"Police?" He laughed. "I do something?"

"I don't think so. You don't look the type. It's about some shipments."

"Shipments? What would I know about that?"

"Well—it has to do with Four State Shippers and Consigners. You worked there last July, didn't you?"

Krebs turned the hose off and sloshed the brush around inside the pail. He lifted it out, sopping with suds, and began to soap down the rear right door. It was a special brush, the kind advertised in the back of *Popular Mechanics,* the kind one could buy only by writing to a man in Coessee, Indiana.

"I was with them three days. That guy Culligan didn't treat me very fairly. Did you talk to him?"

"Yes." Joe said nothing else.

"I suppose he told you I was trying to work something with the truckers. He accused me of trying to work a loading racket. I knew better than that. I was a shipping clerk fifteen years and never had a rap against me."

"You think Culligan was unfair? Why didn't you tell the union?"

"I wouldn't rat to any union." He looked at McFeeley with a candor that disarmed the officer. Krebs had a round, unlined face.

His skin was fair and freckled at the hairline, and his hair, a red-dish-brown, was parted in the middle. His features, moderate in size, evenly spaced, were forgettable and bland; rimless spectacles dominated the mild countenance. In the pocket of his white shirt were three automatic writing tools; his shirt and his gray slacks were unstained with water, despite his labors.

He replaced the brush in the bucket and picked up the hose.

"Would you mind chatting a little about—things in general—at Four State—and what you've been doing since?" asked the detective.

"Do I have to?" He directed the stream at the car.

"You don't have to tell me a thing. This is a routine police call. We're interrogating about fifty people on this. I doubt you have anything to do with it. You haven't been at Four State since July— over two months. You don't *have* to co-operate, but we can make you."

"You can?"

"Yes. But you seem to be a fellow with above-average intelligence. It would be cleaner all around if you just co-operated."

Krebs nodded. "That sounds O.K. What I can tell you?"

McFeeley lit a cigarette. He was about to drop the match on Krebs' manicured lawn when the man cautioned him. "There's a butt can in the carport, if you don't mind."

"Righto." McFeeley complied.

"Here's the thing, Maurice," Joe said with painful earnestness. "This racket was worked with a batch of shipping tickets that were stolen from Four State." He watched Krebs; there was no reaction. Hosing and soaping appeared all that would ever interest him; these, and the care of his lawn.

"Shipping tickets?"

"Yes. Those forms Four State uses." He took a sheaf from his coat pocket and opened them, fanlike, in front of Krebs. "You remem-ber the five top sheets in black, then seven with the red lettering, and the last with the red box at the bottom?"

"Oh yeah." Krebs barely glanced at them. "Culligan's idea. Per-sonally, I think they're a rotten form. I've had experience in this line of work, and there are easier forms."

"Well, evidently someone stole a bunch of them and is working some angle with the drivers. Somewhere between Four State and the destination, they've been switching shipping tickets and alter-ing amounts. Then the consignee hollers he's been shortchanged and Culligan has to make good. Of course, they're insured against this, but the insurance company won't make good until we give them a report."

Krebs turned his hose off. "May I ask—how come a Santa Luisa detective is involved in this? Four State is an LA firm. You mind my asking?"

Joe waved his cigarette in the night air. "We're only working on one shipment. It was destined for a machine tool outfit in Sanlu—Harmon Precision Extruders—and it never got there. We have a feeling the stuff was relabeled and sent out of state. We're in this only from Harmon's angle."

"I got nothing to tell you," Krebs said. "They fired me, without cause, two months ago. I've never been back there, and I don't have any friends there."

"Ever take any of these home with you—as scrap paper or writing paper?" He held the shipping forms out.

"No. If Culligan says I did, he's lying. He didn't like me from the start. Him and his foreman—the two."

Joe blew a cloud of smoke skyward, watching it dissipate against the purple-blue desert night. He had no right to be questioning the likes of Maurice Krebs, a car-washing shipping clerk. The notion that this self-pitying man could have had the audacity to seize Amy Andrus, demand money for her safety, possibly murder her . . . Besides, it was the FBI's job now, not his. He had saved Maurice Krebs for himself like a boy who is forced to surrender a hoard of stolen candy and hides one last lollipop in his shirt front. And now the lollipop was tasteless, unworthy of the effort he had made to cache it.

"You know what else?" Krebs asked. "I think Four State marked me bad with the other outfits around here. I haven't worked since then. A good thing I get unemployment insurance."

"I'm sorry to hear that," Joe said. "That isn't fair."

"You bet it isn't."

"I mean, a nice house like this, and I guess you have a family to support. I can see it would be rough."

Krebs concluded his hosing. He directed a few squirts at the rear window, then started to coil the hose. "That '47 Buick is still the best they ever made," he said. "You can have all the new ones with the fancy chrome. This is my baby."

"You sure keep it neat, Maurice." McFeeley looked approvingly at the chassis—not a scratch, not a mark. Inside, the pale-gray seat covers were luminous. The dashboard glittered.

"Be with you in a second," Krebs said. He drove the Buick into the carport, got out, dried his hands on a piece of toweling and joined the detective. "Anything else?"

Joe smiled politely. "I hate to keep bothering you," McFeeley said, "but there are a few other things I have to ask. Would it upset your wife if we talked in the house?"

"I have no wife. I live with my folks."

"I see. Well—would your folks mind?"

Krebs frowned and rubbed his nose. "I guess not. Come on in."

McFeeley followed him through an elaborate screen door. In a living room, at the right, two elderly people were watching a television quiz program. He got a glimpse of a bald, short man, puffing a pipe with that total satisfaction one finds only in elderly Middle Europeans. He saw, too, a white-haired, stout woman.

"Bubi?" the man asked. "Is that you? That fellah you like is coming on. Who makes all the wisecracks."

Krebs did not introduce McFeeley, but gestured to him to follow him up the stairs. "No, thanks, Pop. I have a guest."

In the attic, a dormer window had been inserted in the roof to make a small bedroom. "I use this as a study," Krebs said. "I finished it off myself."

Krebs turned on a bed lamp and motioned Joe to sit on a sofa. The room was furnished with secondhand things, but it was neat and orderly. There was a small writing table, and alongside it a half-filled bookcase.

"You're more ambitious than I am," McFeeley said, smiling. "I have one of these expandable ranch jobs, but I paid to have the attic done. I can't drive a nail straight."

"You have enough patience, it isn't hard. Besides, how could I afford to pay for the work—being out of a job so long?"

"You say you haven't worked since July?" the detective asked.

"That's right. I did some odd work here and there—salesclerking, helping out at the supermarket. I just can't seem to latch on."

"Well, it's none of my business, Maurice," the detective said gently, "but how do you make out? I mean—I have an idea what mortgage payments run on a house like this."

"We don't. My father—you saw him downstairs—has a government pension. He was with the U. S. Department of Agriculture back in Illinois. We're from Batavia, Illinois, until we moved here for Pop's asthma. Then I get unemployment insurance. And we live modest. We aren't fancy people."

"How long have you had this place?"

"Oh—we moved in in June. I was counting on that job at Four

State to keep us in good shape. I put quite a bit in this place—air conditioning, a patio, a good lawn. That stuff doesn't come free, you know. I financed the air conditioning. Murder."

"Don't I know. The prices those guys get."

"Yes, and you know *who* gets those prices," Krebs said enigmatically. "*They* make out all right—but let an ordinary citizen try to get a break." He sat down at the opposite end of the sofa. In the dull light, beneath the canted ceiling, he seemed the ultimate in inconsequentiality. "You say your name was McFeeley?" Joe nodded. "I can level with you. You know what I'm referring to."

"I don't follow you, Maurice," said the detective.

Krebs' eyes were invisible under the light-choked lenses, his neat mouth smiling with some inner knowledge. "That's why I was fired, I'm sure. *They* had it in for me."

"Who had it in for you?" McFeeley asked.

Krebs locked his hands—they were lightly fuzzed with red hairs, delicately freckled—around one knee and leaned back. "I'm not sure I should tell you."

"Do what you want. I came here to try and get a lead on those shipments. You aren't a suspect. There isn't a bad mark against you. In fact, I kind of feel Culligan did the wrong thing canning you. If you want to tell me something—shoot. I think you and I understand each other." He ventured a crafty wink.

"Yes, I have a feeling I can discuss this with you." Krebs paused. "Back in Illinois, before the war—World War II, that is—I was active in certain patriotic groups. Militant nationalists, you might say. I wasn't too active—I just went to meetings. Then we broke up, or rather the government broke us up, when the war began. I wasn't even a member for more than a month. But I'm pretty sure that thing has followed me. *They* knew about it. That's the reason Culligan canned me. Before that, I lost my job with Anderson-Weston Shippers. Now I haven't worked for two months. It's part of a scheme."

McFeeley shrugged. "That certainly is no reason to hold a grudge against a good man. We all make mistakes when we're young." Joe leaned forward. "You know, Maurice, if you feel so strongly, you could get some help. There are committees to help people like you, to see that you get a fair shake."

"No, it won't help. I'm sort of cursed. But I know who they are and what they're up to."

There was a polite knocking at the door, and the elder Krebs entered. "You Mr. McFeeley who's in here with Bubi?" he asked. "Fellah wants you on the telephone downstairs."

"Oh, thank you," Joe said. "Maurice—you've been very helpful. I enjoy talking to someone who has something intelligent to say. You know—in my line of work—the people I meet."

"My pleasure," Krebs said. "I'll walk down with you."

The telephone was in a narrow corridor alongside the stairs. The elder Krebs, puffing happily on his pipe, returned to the television; his son lingered in the hallway, watching the detective.

"Joe?" the caller asked. "Bannon. Listen—are you clear-voyant or something?"

"Why?"

"Your man Krebs. Maurice Krebs. He sure rented a brown Ford on Monday morning."

McFeeley labored to betray nothing—not by a change in posture, a gesture, an inflection of voice. "No kidding? That's a break."

"He rented it at 7:30 A.M. from Arnold's Auto Rental System on North Juniper and he returned it at 10:15 A.M. The license number he gave checks with the one you gave me."

"I tell you what," McFeeley said—hearing the fierce pounding of his heart, glancing down the corridor to Krebs' neat figure—the figure of a car-washer, a lawn lover, a hater of people who were out to get him—"I think you better impound it and bring Raffalovitch in to look it over. He'll get sore, but he'll do it for me." He glanced at his watch. It was a few minutes before eight. "Then you hang around and wait for me. I'll be in in a few minutes."

"Alone? With someone?"

"I don't know yet." He hung up and walked down the hallway.

"You fellows keep hopping all hours of the day and night," Krebs said. "It's an interesting career, police work."

"It's a living," Joe said. "Maurice, would you mind coming down to Sanlu headquarters for a few minutes? I have a few more things to ask you, and it's a little difficult here, what with your folks, and so on."

"Why? I told you everything. I don't know a thing about any shipments."

"Our men just came up with some additional information you might be helpful on."

"Like what? I don't have to go if I don't want to." For the first time, a hardness crept into his middling voice. "You have no right to drag me into a police station over nothing."

"I'm asking you to co-operate. I don't think you've done anything. I'd just like you to look at some stuff we have. Some photostats, papers."

Krebs glanced at the living room, where his parents sat, tranquilized, before the silvery images. "Well, only because of them. I don't want Mom and Pop to get worried, with you hanging around like this. It won't be long, will it?"

"It won't be long."

Krebs walked into the living room. Joe heard him telling his mother and father that Mr. McFeeley wanted to discuss a business deal and they were going out for a beer. "Don't come back too late, Bubi," he heard the woman say.

"Let's go," Krebs said. "But I'm warning you, it's just because I'm good-natured. I really don't have to go."

Outside, walking toward Joe's Dodge, the detective patted him on the shoulder. "Don't think I don't appreciate it. If most people were co-operative like you, our job would be a lot easier."

Mona Mears had another smasher: she had spent the day interviewing Fritzie Andrus' professional associates, and she had evolved an intriguing picture of the kidnaped child's father. "Oh, what a boy is our Fritzie!" she told T. T. Hansel jubilantly. "I talked to some of his colleagues over at the network—girls and boys. That guy was perpetual sex motion. No wonder that fishy wife and he split up. Fritzie never hired an actress unless she passed the couch test."

Hansel nodded. "I don't know quite how far we want to go with this sort of thing, Mona."

"This is all for future reference. I still have my suspicions about this affair. I won't go with the mob about it's being an open-and-shut kidnaping. The more I think about it, the more I *hae me doots.*"

T. T. seemed preoccupied, distracted. He was not favoring the columnist with his usual flattery, his boyish admiration for her skills. She sensed it, and she guessed that he was upset about the television program that, reportedly, would reveal the newspaper's role in the Andrus affair.

"I latched on to a lawyer named Salter, some shyster on Wilshire," the woman continued. "Ba-rother! Did he give me an earful. The morning the kid was *alleged* to be kidnaped, Andrus was with Salter trying to get visiting privileges to see the brats. Salter tells me he carried on in the office like a madman—burst into hysterics, insulted him, and flew out of the office screaming! Picture getting clearer? Are there loose screws in that family or not?"

"I continue to be in awe of your thoroughness, Mona," Hansel said. "Have you done tomorrow's piece?"

"I wanted to chew it over with you a little. I want to use some of this material—like the visit with the lawyer. God knows there's no news coming out of the house. I don't think anything's going to happen. That child is long gone. She's under some culvert or in an arroyo."

An invisible shudder traveled the length of Hansel's spine. He was a little afraid of Mears, he realized. She had a power that disturbed him; his fear was rather like a dictator's misgivings about his secret police chief.

"Well, it isn't a very pleasant affair—for anybody," Hansel said reflectively. "It's too bad the criminal didn't avail himself of our offer to surrender. That would have given us the hat trick."

"You kidding?" she asked. "I'm betting on the old lady. Catch that one handing herself in." She uncrossed her young legs and left. "You look gloomy, Ted," she said at the door. "You shouldn't be. I hear the circulation figures for the past two days have been great."

Hansel smiled appreciatively. He buzzed his secretary and asked her to get Mr. Hinrichsen at United Broadcasting.

The vice-president came to the phone with a disarming laugh. "Hi, Ted," Hinrichsen said. "I expected I'd hear from you before the day was over."

T.T. could laugh also—bellow, chortle, chuckle, snicker—he had a fine repertory of laughs. The occasion called for a warm, confiding chuckle.

"I hear you fellows are going to do us harm tonight," Hansel said. "My spies say you're going to accuse the *Truth* of everything from incest to Populism."

"Not quite," laughed Hinrichsen. "We *are* doing a study in depth of press handling of the Andrus case, and, naturally, the *Truth* figures in it."

"The way I got it, it was primarily an *attack* on us. If that's the case, Matt——"

"But it isn't the case, Ted." It was very hard arguing with the publisher. Hinrichsen was a child of advertising and television; these newer arenas of the *word* were, in their outward manifestations at least, polite, friendly, courteous. Hansel was of an older, tougher breed of talker; circulation wars, libel suits and the destruction of careers and characters were bred in his bone.

"I hope not, Matt. Let me warn you about one thing. I understand a young man named Sparling is behind this—one of your reporters. He's a troublemaker and a malcontent. He was fired for spreading lies about the *Truth*. You realize, Matt, this matter of press coverage—who said what, what time certain things were said —is loaded with pitfalls. You're taking a calculated risk listening to Sparling, considering the grudge he has against us."

The young man so virulently under attack was at that moment standing in front of Hinrichsen's desk, flanked by Brack and Ballstead. He did not appear singularly malevolent, much of a threat to anyone. Hinrichsen was devoid of curiosity about his employees, particularly the people in the newsroom who swore fealty to Tom Ballstead. And Sparling, swaying on free-form shoes, hardly seemed worthy of Hansel's denunciation. Yet the attack called for a rejoinder. "I've just read Sparling's script, Ted," the vice-president said warmly, "and while it does criticize the *Truth*, I'm afraid they are fair criticisms. He appears to have his case documented and backed up with facts, including a statement from someone in your own organization."

"Who?" cried Hansel. "Who? I have a right to know!"

Hinrichsen looked helplessly at Tom Ballstead. "He wants to know who at the *Truth* gave us our information. Shall I tell him?"

In Sparling's marbled mind was summoned up a childhood memory of a radio comedian, a dialectician (Parkyakarkus? Mr. Kitzel?), who evoked laughter with this refrain delivered in a Russo-Jewish accent: *Shall I tell him?* Yes, Eliot decided, that was what was needed: Hinrichsen should have a vaudeville Yiddish accent, and all would be well with the world.

"Hell, no," Ballstead snarled. "Let him run his own Gestapo."

"I'm sorry, Ted," Hinrichsen said, "but Tom Ballstead says we can't tell you. It's a privileged source, I gather. Incidentally, to allay your fears about Sparling being the wicked genius behind this, it just isn't so. Tom Ballstead and George Brack—I think you met George at my place in Palm Springs last March—are behind it one hundred per cent." He paused, then added: "And so am I."

"Very well, Matt," Hansel said briskly. "I can't dissuade you. You have a right to get into this, I suppose. Personally, I don't think this is television's place. You fellows are all right for musical shows and Westerns, but the area of *ideas* is all wrong for you. It's a shame you and I have to be at odds like this. We've always had good relations with United, and I wonder how the UBC people in New York will feel about this."

"I've cleared it with them," Hinrichsen said. "Ted, you've got to take my word that this program is more in the nature of a general critique than a scolding of your paper. Moreover, we blame ourselves for a lot of the things that took place on Monday."

"I'll be watching," Hansel said firmly. "And I'd better warn you —as an old friend—we'll hit back. We'll not only defend ourselves, we'll make it rough for you." The warm, secretive chuckle returned. "You chaps have gone after that advertising dollar with a vengeance, and I say more power to you. But look out for us when we get sore. Fair enough?"

"Fair enough, Ted."

Ballstead's sour face, rejecting all that was pleasant and effortless in the world, disturbed Hinrichsen. "Hansel screaming?" Tom asked.

"Not really," the vice-president said. "He says we have a right to do what we're doing." Hinrichsen waved the script at the three men. "This looks fine. I'd tone down those comments about Mona Mears, because they *are* sort of personal, Tom, but, otherwise, I think it's a nice little show."

"Give El the credit," George Brack said, beaming. "He did it."

Hinrichsen wondered whether this disclosure might not be cause for alarm. Unquestionably, there was something bothersome about the bulking young man who had pressed the case for the special program. The vice-president could not truthfully proclaim, as did Conrad's narrator about Lord Jim, that Sparling "was one of us."

Arriving at headquarters, McFeeley took Maurice Krebs to the garage, below street level, where he rang for the elevator, and then ascended to the second floor, where the interrogation room was located. A few uniformed men passed them in the hallway and said nothing beyond casual greetings. There were no handcuffs on the detective's companion; he did not appear to be resisting McFeeley; and, moreover, Krebs was the kind of man who never attracted attention. He was of the army of the faceless—an electrician's assistant whom no householder can ever recall; a man in the seventh row of a creaky grandstand at a high school baseball game; a passenger standing at the rear of a crowded bus, cradling a paper-wrapped bundle.

Joe opened the door of the interrogation room, turned on the discreet lighting and motioned Krebs to take a seat. "Make yourself comfortable, Maurice," he said. "I'll be back in a minute." Outside, he signaled a uniformed man to join him. With his lips he formed the words: "Wait here till I get back." The patrolman planted himself at the door.

At the end of the corridor, McFeeley entered the detective division. Bannon and Case were waiting for him. They had summoned Irvin Moll from his home.

"I have Krebs in interrogation," McFeeley said.

"Holy Jesus," Bannon said. "Just like that? He say anything?"

"No," McFeeley said. "I haven't started to ask him about Andrus. I've been needling him about lost shipments from Four State, the place where he worked. If he *is* the guy, I'd say he's the least likely candidate in California."

Moll rubbed his chin. "We know he had a brown Ford for three hours on Monday, right? And he could have gotten one of those shipping forms for the note, right?"

"And that's all," Joe said. "I think he's in debt. He hasn't worked since he was fired." McFeeley paced the room—the green lockers surrounded him like a jury of mechanical monsters. He paused, then turned to face his colleagues. "I can't see him doing it. I can't. He's a gabber, one of these jerks who spends his life feeling sorry for himself."

"Let me work him over, Joe," Moll said. "A few slaps and he'll talk."

"No, no," McFeeley said. "He's the kind who'd love it. It would prove he's right—the world's against him." He sank into a chair. "Are the agents still around? He really belongs to them. I stole him."

"Wagley's downstairs," Bannon said. "The rest of them went back to LA with the files. Shall I call him?"

Joe waited a moment. "Let's try to be heroes ourselves. We've looked so lousy on this; maybe we can get lucky." He got up. "Set up the tape recorder. I'm going to chat with Maurice. When I buzz you in here, it means I want the photostat of the note. One of you guys call the state attorney's office and have them send someone in an hour." He looked at his watch. It was 8:20. "Also, at 9:30 call Rheinholdt and ask him to come down."

He started to leave, a round-shouldered, weary man, trying to control an agitated pumping in his chest, trying to hide his fear of failure.

"You want me in there?" Moll asked. "We could play Mutt and Jeff. I'd be the heavy—slap him around and threaten him, and then you could come in and buddy up."

"I don't think so," Joe said. "I'll play it by ear. I'll give myself until 10:00. If I can't do any good, he's Wagley's."

The interrogation room was Rheinholdt's pride, patterned after the latest concepts in police practice, decorated and equipped to give every advantage to the officer, to put the suspect at ease. It did not look like a police station room. It was almost square and was painted a pleasant pale green. The floor was carpeted with nubby gray wool, and the one large window (heavily barred on the outside) was covered with a matching gray drape. There were two large floor lamps, a glass-topped walnut desk, behind which the interrogator sat, and a single dark-green upholstered leather chair for the subject. There were no paintings, no photographs, no bulletin boards, no telephone on the desk top, which did hold two large copper ash trays and a calendar pad. The latter concealed a microphone connected to a tape recorder outside the wall: the interviewer did not have to take notes.

Krebs blended marvelously with the room. It seemed to McFeeley, studying his subject, now comfortably seated in the chair, that the room had been waiting since its creation three years ago for such an inhabitant. The air conditioning was silent, cooling; the lights were just right, not too dim, not too bright.

Joe offered him a cigarette. Krebs declined.

"Like some coffee?" the detective asked.

Krebs folded his hands on the rise of his small paunch. "I don't think so, thanks. You sound as if this is going to take all night."

"I hope not," McFeeley laughed. "My wife expected me home for dinner."

"You shouldn't be so conscientious. I did bend your ear a lot—gabbing about my own problems."

"Not at all, Maurice. That's part of our job. If you're a good cop, you're ready to listen." McFeeley flicked ashes into one of the trays and squinted at the rising smoke. He was groping for the right approach.

"I told you all I know about that Culligan deal. I don't see what I can add," Krebs said.

"Well, I tell you, Maurice. We were running a general check on you—don't look upset: it happens to thousands of innocent people, and they have nothing to worry about if they are innocent. As I was saying, we ran this check and something turned up that got me started in another direction. You follow me?"

"I'm afraid not, Joe." This was the first good sign: when they started to call you by your first name, they wanted love, affection, understanding.

"Maurice, did you rent an automobile on Monday morning?"

"Automobile?"

"Yes. A brown Ford from Arnold's Auto Rental System on North Juniper."

"Yes, I did. What about it?"

"You rented it—around 7:30—and returned it at 10:15 A.M.?"

"I'm not sure of the exact times, but I guess that was about it, yes."

"You have your own car, don't you? Why'd you rent one?"

Krebs patted the little peak of sandy hair on his freckled pate. "That's no mystery. Mother and Dad needed the car that morning to go out to West Covina. I always spend Monday morning looking for work. I check off jobs in the Sunday papers, and then on Monday morning I travel around applying. That's what I did Monday."

"And you were out only two and a half hours?"

Krebs looked hurt. "Joe, I'm no millionaire. I'm not the type who can afford a rented car all day. I looked at a few places, and then I went back to Arnold's with the car and went home."

"Can you remember the places you called on to see about jobs?"

"Let's see. There was an outfit in San Fernando. And one other job. A shipping-room job. In Westwood."

"You have the names of the places?" McFeeley leaned across the desk. "Maurice, this is serious stuff. Between you and me, I think you're telling the truth, because I don't think you're the sort of fellow who'd lie. But you know what an *alibi* is. I need proof you really went to these places. Do you have their names? You recall who you talked to?"

"I have the names at home," Krebs said. "I didn't get to see any specific person at either place. I just spoke to secretaries, and they said the jobs were filled."

"Can't recall the names? Could you phone home and ask your folks to look them up?"

"No. I just checked them off in the Sunday paper and I didn't save it. I'll think of them."

McFeeley took out his steno pad and laid it on the desk. He

tapped at it with his pen. Then he printed in large characters: *San Fernando, Westwood.*

"You taking notes?" asked Krebs.

"Hmm?" McFeeley asked. He had been doodling on the pad, feigning inattention.

"Those places I went to. I'll get you the names."

"Right, Maurice. Can you hang around for a minute or so?" The detective pressed his knee against a buzzer below the desk. In a few seconds Moll entered. He did not look at Krebs and handed McFeeley a photostat of the ransom note.

"Thanks, Irv," McFeeley said. "Anything on the car?"

"Raffalovitch is going over it—dusting for prints, traces. I don't think he'll find much. It's been out three times since Monday, and the rental outfit said they cleaned it yesterday."

Krebs evinced no concern; his face was vacant. When Moll had left, he asked easily: "That the car I rented? All that fuss over it?"

"It's routine."

"You fellows are too mysterious for me. Some shipments get lost or stolen and you bother a poor guy like me, who has plenty of problems of his own, tracing down a car I rented just to look for a job."

McFeeley shoved the photostat across the desk. "That ring a bell with you, Maurice?"

Krebs picked up the glossy print and read the message, the neatly spaced, cannibalized newsprint, beginning, CHILD SAFE UNLESS. His hands did not shake, his manner did not change, his color remained the same. He frowned at the detective. "I don't get it."

"You don't? Doesn't mean anything to you?"

"Nope." Suddenly his mouth opened and he pointed a finger at McFeeley. "Oh! Now I get it. That kidnaping! That little girl!" He took his eyeglasses off and rubbed them against his shirt front rapidly, put them on again and reread the note. "This is the ransom note, right?"

"That's right. A copy of it."

Krebs settled back in the chair. A kind of amused awareness, a revelation that he was now wise to McFeeley's tricks, appeared on his face.

"So that's it. All this time you were asking about the shipments, you were really asking me about that little girl. Andrus—that's the name. Oh boy, Joe. That's all I can say."

"That's all?"

"What do you expect? Am I a kidnaper? I can't even bluff my way out of a traffic ticket. I get scared when I see a cop stare at me. Me, a criminal. That's a hot one."

"I guess it is," McFeeley agreed. "I just want you to understand my position. We can't let a thing go by. If you're innocent of any connection with this, and personally I think you are, there's nothing to be concerned about."

"Innocent! That gets me. What makes you think I could be anything else? I don't appreciate these accusations."

"I haven't made any."

"No, but you're hinting." Krebs laughed sardonically. "What a joke on me. Out of work two months, and now this. I want to make a certain thing clear, Joe. My parents are not to know of anything that transpired between us."

"They won't, Maurice, don't worry. This is strictly between us." McFeeley set the pad in front of him and adopted a crisper tone. "Now Maurice, tell me this. You returned to your house about 10:20 on Monday morning, after returning that Ford to Arnold's, right? Can you give me an account of what you did the rest of the day?"

Krebs folded his arms. "I wonder if I should."

McFeeley showed him the photostat. "See this, Maurice? Well, you can't see it on this photostat, but we traced the paper back to a printer who makes them up specially for Four State. There were some red spots at the bottom and it checked with the design and the ink of Four State's shipping forms. So——" He studied the bespectacled face opposite him and found it untroubled. "So—we are—as a matter of routine—interviewing every single employee, past and present, of both that printer and the shipper. There's over fifty different people involved, and we're interrogating them all, and checking their whereabouts on Monday."

"I get it. I'm just one of many?"

"Right. I know it's a pain in the neck to you, but, after all, that little girl's life is at stake. We can't worry about hurting someone's feelings. I'm sure you'll understand."

"I certainly do. You should have got right to the point instead of all that stuff about a lost shipment."

"We thought they might be tied in."

"How can you compare those two things?" Krebs asked.

"It's farfetched. Well, anyway, how about what we were discussing—what you did Monday when you got home."

"I went to my room and read."

"For the rest of the morning?"

"Oh, till about noon. I went through the newspapers, *Popular Mechanics*. Sort of browsed in my books. I read a lot."

"You were alone in the house?"

"Yes. Mother and Dad went to West Covina in the car and I was by myself."

"No one to back this up? I mean—no one who could confirm you were upstairs reading all this time?"

"Why should I need anyone to confirm it? If I tell you I was, I was. I'm no liar."

"Don't get sore. Then, after that, what?"

"I fixed myself some lunch around noon. A hard-boiled egg sandwich with mayo on white bread and iced tea. And then I took a nap, around 1:00, and slept till 3:00. In the afternoon I went to the movies."

"Where?"

"The Valley Theatre."

"What did you see?"

"A double feature. One was a Western—I can't recall the title. The other was about the Navy. *Pacific Guns*, I think. They both stank."

"Then?"

"I got home around 6:30 and worked on the lawn. That's the best time of day for a lawn—dusk or dawn. I weeded and put some 4-2-2——"

"Pardon?"

"It's a fertilizer. You own a house and you don't know what 4-2-2 is?"

McFeeley smiled. "I'm a lousy gardener. I let my wife do it. We have a nice crop of weeds."

"It's easy. Takes a little time, that's all. Oh, you want to know what else I did. Well, my folks were back by then, so I just took it easy around the house—I guess I worked on some wiring I was replacing in the dining room, and then we ate. Anything else?"

"No, that's fine, Maurice. And the only people who can vouch for all this would be—let's see—the cashier at the movie and your parents?"

"I'd say so, yes."

"But between 7:35 A.M., when you left Arnold's, and 3:00 P.M., when you went to the theater, you were sort of lost to the world, right?"

Krebs looked pained. "Hey, what kind of memory do you have? I looked for work at two places."

"Right you are. In San Fernando and Westwood. And you'll get me those names."

"First thing tomorrow. I suppose I could tonight, but I'm about ready to poop out. It don't—it doesn't matter—tonight or tomorrow—does it, seeing how this is all what you call routine anyway?"

A faint quivering agitated McFeeley's stomach. The man's quick correction of the ungrammatical *it don't* jabbed at some remembrance. At once he knew: the caller that morning had thus corrected himself. The recording was lost to them, but the detective knew his memory to be infallible. *There ain't—there isn't any.*

"We might as well do it now. I'll send downstairs for Sunday's papers, and you can find me those two places you called at, and we can check 'em in the morning—and you'll be off the hook. O.K.?"

Krebs shrugged. "If you want to, it's all right with me."

McFeeley nudged the buzzer beneath the desk. Moll stuck his head in the door. "Want something, Joe?"

"Irv," he said, "could you dig up last Sunday's papers? All the LA papers and the Sanlu *Register.*"

"You bet. Anything else?"

Joe smiled at Krebs. "Like some coffee, Maurice? A nice cold Coke?"

"Coffee would go swell," Krebs said. "Milk, no sugar."

"Black," McFeeley added. As Moll closed the door, he called after him: "You might buzz Rheinholdt and ask him to come down."

"Rheinholdt?" Krebs asked. "He's the chief here, isn't he? The one who's in so much trouble over this kidnaping?"

McFeeley held a cautionary finger to his lips. "Shhh. Somebody might be listening."

Krebs winked. "I bet somebody is."

At 10:10 that evening, while McFeeley was interrogating Maurice Krebs, Studio 4-C at United Broadcasting was the scene of some last-minute changes in the script for "Southland." These were not changes of an editorial nature, but merely excisions, necessitated by Eliot Sparling's overflowing pen. In the run-through, which had been held from 9:45 to 10:00, it was discovered that the script was four minutes over. To aid in these secretarial chores, Eliot's friend, Connie Potenza, now jobless, had joined the young news writer and George Brack in the broadcasting studio.

Connie was not terribly upset over her loss of job. She explained to an outraged Eliot that it was the unfairness of it all that bothered her, not the prospect of unemployment. She knew she could get a job tomorrow—one paying a better salary—in any law office in Los Angeles. She was a whiz at shorthand, a tireless typist —and she was pretty. All the pretty girls wanted to be production assistants, she said. That left the secretarial field wide open to her. "But the nerve of him!" she said, enlarging her espresso-colored eyes. "The nerve of that dope! Saying I gave you information about the Andrus case—*when he did it himself!*"

"I gotta right to expose him, too," muttered Sparling darkly. "Herbie Hood, informer."

"Oh, but you can't," Connie said. "You promised you wouldn't. I feel a little sorry for him. The things Mr. Hansel must have told him! When they all came down from his office—Trigg and Kalaidjian and Mr. Hood—they looked like they'd been *whipped.*"

One accepted the perverseness of the *Truth* as a matter of course; its employees—the Connie Potenzas, the Sparlings, the Werner Schlossmanns—learned to expect the worst, to view meanness and pettiness as the norms of human conduct. Sparling would spend his life forever in blissful admiration of United Broadcasting—or any other company which treated its minions with a modicum of decency. After the *Truth,* the rest of the world glowed.

With crisp, deft moves, Connie finished her typing, collated the scripts, and gave George Brack a fresh first copy. Eliot took the first carbon. It was now 10:10. Brack sat in one of three chairs behind a wide desk. Eliot sat at his right. At Eliot's right, Patrolman Clyde Hertmann was seated. At Brack's left elbow was a tape recorder, and directly in front of him, a stack of newspapers.

"Nervous, Georgie?" asked Eliot, grinning.

"Me?" George asked. He ran his ubiquitous comb through his lustrous coiffure. "You're the one should be nervous, El."

"Hah! Brack, baby, if I didn't have that dentalized T and if I wasn't so ugly, I'd be in this racket. I'd be cleaning up pushing used cars. Like a certain party I know. You'd be outa work."

"You heard him, officer," Brack said, smiling. "He threatened my livelihood."

Patrolman Hertmann tugged at his tight collar, adjusted his

black tie. His narrow face had lost its patina of calm; he was tense. "Be glad when this is over," he said.

The floor manager signaled *one minute.* Connie excused herself and walked to the control room. The solitary cameraman—"Southland" was a sustaining program and could afford but one camera —watched her perky stride, rear view, and whispered, as was his workingman's privilege: "More bounce to the ounce!"

A finger was pointed at George Brack. The camera framed his manly face, and the commentator invoked his sincerest tones.

"Good evening and welcome to 'Southland,'" he began; "George Brack reporting. 'Southland'—dedicated to our great and growing Los Angeles area—its people, its places, its problems. Tonight 'Southland' presents a special report on the kidnaping of Amy Andrus, a story that has captured the interest of the entire world. It is our plan to examine one aspect of the case alone and, we hope, shed some light on it. That aspect is the question of press coverage and press responsibility in the kidnaping of Amy Andrus."

Brack drew in his breath, turned a sheet of blue paper and resumed, fixing his manly eyes on the lens. "It is the contention of 'Southland' that the American press did not have one of its finest hours in the Andrus case. It is our further contention that the press —newspapers, radio, television, all of us in what is collectively known as journalism—through interference, through callousness, through a competitive ferocity that overrode any considerations of charity, possibly prevented the safe return of Amy Andrus. It is also our contention that, having acted meanly, we then ignored our own wickedness, assumed our behavior was ethical, closed ranks against criticism, and compounded our original sins. I speak for United Broadcasting Company, and for myself, in stating that we at UBC accept fully our share of the guilt in the Andrus affair."

Brack's magnificent tones never wavered. He read as convincingly as he did when praising the thirst-quenching virtues of Oak Barrel Lager.

"Let us proceed chronologically," Brack said. "Amy Andrus was kidnaped some time between 8:00 and 9:00 o'clock on Monday morning, September 17. She was last seen, it is believed, by a newsboy . . ."

The Andruses had asked Harry and Babe Emerson to join them in watching "Southland." Both Fritzie and Laura felt the need for companionship; their burden might be eased—however slightly— through a resumption of the normal rhythms of daily life. The

Emersons were the only neighborhood friends they had; Babe and Harry leaped to the invitation. "Ole Harry's O.K.," Fritzie said, "and if that Babe'll keep her mouth shut, I'll be obliged to them for a little break in the misery." Laura had told him nothing about Babe's tearful confession of the previous day. Nothing would be gained by it, and Laura had come to the sad conclusion that whether or not her neighbor had telephoned Sparling, the news would have leaked out—perhaps an hour or two later, but with the same lacerating results.

The Emersons sat with Laura and Fritzie in the den, watching George Brack's innocent good looks, hearing his reasonable, rich voice delivering Eliot's indictment.

"I love this guy," Harry Emerson said. "No matter what he says, he sounds like he's peddling a 1948 Nash."

Brack's handsome features dissolved. There followed a film sequence: the crush of reporters and photographers outside the house on Monday morning, McFeeley pleading with them, the comings and goings of assorted detectives, lab men, telephone company technicians. Walter L. Todd figured in one sequence, and, finally, there was a sound-on-film clip of Laura's appeal to the reporters to leave.

"I don't get it," Fritzie said. "I know that UBC operation pretty good. I know Hinrichsen. Can't understand him stickin' that Ivy League neck of his out like this. Why, the newspapers will pounce on him like a cottonmouth on a frog."

"You can't tell about these guys," Harry said, yawning. "Every now and then they get religion."

Laura said nothing. The expectation of seeing a wrong righted— of setting the record straight—had given her a momentary optimism earlier that evening. But now, watching and hearing the painful recital of past errors, blunders and deviousness, she found no balm in what seemed nothing more than a quixotic arraignment of people who couldn't care less. The nagging arguments over who said what, who dissembled, who made excuses, who was lax, who was greedy—all these seemed determinedly ex post facto. They were of a recent past without relation to her agonized, eroding present. Her child was missing. Her child was quite possibly dead. Her capacity for involvement, for relating to the outside world, began and ended with that one fact. All the circumlocutions surrounding it, all the charges and alibis and accusations, the collective and individual guilts now appeared hopelessly irrelevant to her. She imagined she owed something to Sparling, to Brack, to whoever had authorized the program. Yet what did any of it mean—if Amy did not come home?

Brack had introduced Eliot, and the young man began his narration of his own role in the Andrus affair. He began by describing, with heavy-handed humor, his encounter with Rheinholdt, his manhandling, his imprisonment, his eventual release. "At the time," Eliot said to his audience—with an occasional nod at Brack—"at the time, I was deeply resentful. But I realize now that Chief Rheinholdt, for all the criticism leveled at him, was right. I was wrong. All of us were wrong for hanging around 4217 Nespoli Drive. If that child's safety meant jailing—yes, slapping—one hundred reporters, that's what should have been done. Is there a man—or a woman—who took part in the madness outside the Andrus house on Monday who would not have willingly taken a few hard smacks in the face, a few hours in jail, if it would have insured Amy's return?"

Sparling went on to relate his role in the procession down Nespoli Drive on Monday evening—the effort by Laura to leave the ransom money, the escort party of journalists—the pool men, Mears, himself, the arboreal Ringer. "I couldn't help thinking, George," Eliot said grandly, "about my own role in this story——"

"Confess, confess," Emerson said, "that's the ticket today!"

"Ssssh!" Babe cried—somewhat resentful of his bitterness. She, like Sparling, had known guilt and confession. She could have told her husband a few things about both—notably the feebleness of the latter.

"——and it seemed to me, George, that the problem warranted further examination. Since I was no longer concerned with the coverage of the Andrus kidnaping per se, I decided to ask questions and try to find out what had gone wrong—what had impelled us to behave so inhumanly, to disregard a police request for co-operation, a mother's plea for her child's security. I started with Dr. Walter L. Todd, a Santa Luisa dentist, who is a distant cousin of Mrs. Andrus and who had evidently given the story to a reporter——"

Alone in his office, Walter L. Todd listened attentively to Sparling's recital of the dentist's role. Eliot read from Todd's own statement. The facts presented therein, refulgent in the man's rich prose, told the story fully, honestly. Todd had not dissembled. He did not have to, since he was convinced of his own blamelessness. As he listened, Todd nodded approvingly. He felt vindicated. He made a note to contact someone at UBC for a kinescoped recording of the program. It would provide fruity material for his autobiography, the title for which he had now found. He would call it *Teeth, Truth and Time.*

". . . my next stop," Eliot continued, "was the Santa Luisa police. It took me about fifteen minutes to establish that the *Los Angeles Truth's* claim that it had not been notified until 6:04 was not in agreement with the police version of the events. But I'd best let Patrolman Clyde Hertmann, who is Chief Caspar Rheinholdt's secretary and who is here in our UBC newsroom tonight, relate those events. Officer?"

Young Hertmann tugged at his collar, his black tie, one ear. In a strained voice, he began to read his schedule of telephone calls. When he concluded, Eliot resumed.

"The question may be fairly asked—and I asked it myself—if the police *had* notified the newspaper at 4:10 P.M., in the person of Harvey Swinnerton, an employee of the *Truth,* and if the general manager himself, Mr. Herbert Hood, *had* been in contact with the police at 4:30, well in advance of the newspaper's publication at 5:07, why had Chief Rheinholdt neglected to reveal this information at his press conference this morning?" Eliot turned a page in his script and boomed on. "This oversight can only be attributed to the confusion inherent in any kidnaping and to the long history of ill feeling between Mr. Rheinholdt and the press. I needed more evidence, more testimony. So I sought out the reporter himself, Harvey Swinnerton, to check Patrolman Hertmann's schedule. I found Mr. Swinnerton ready to disclose his part willingly . . ."

Rheinholdt never saw the program. He had learned about it when Hertmann had asked permission to appear, but he had little interest in it. Young Sparling's efforts in his behalf were no balm to him. Squinting at the conclusion of a private eye show (they always got their man; they never had to resign), he made up his mind to call it quits by the end of the week. A dead child, a child still missing, a case unsolved—Palmer Speed would have to find a new chief.

It was not quite 10:00 when the telephone rang.

Rheinholdt yawned, drained the last of his beer from a pint can, and got up from his chair. He was a considerate husband and did not want to disturb the Missus, who had gone to sleep—worn out by the misery of the house.

The caller was Sergeant Moll, advising the chief that Joe Mc-
Feeley was questioning a suspect. "A guy named Krebs," Moll said.
"He hasn't told us anything yet, but Joe thinks he may have some
connection with it."

"Who else knows about it?" Rheinholdt asked.

"Just us—you and me and Joe, and maybe three or four others."

"How about the Bureau?" Rheinholdt asked.

"Well, Wagley is still here, but he's working in your office. Joe
brought the guy in through the basement, right to interrogation.
Chief, maybe you better come upstairs and not go to your office.
Joe asked that no one should break into interrogation. He's trying
to make Krebs trust him like a brother."

The chief paused. Would they all be saved? Was this nightmare
of accusations, of guilt, of lost honor coming to an end? He told
Moll he would leave at once.

"There was still one gap in my investigation, George," Sparling
said. Brack nodded his head. "What was that, Eliot?"

"There was the chance that both Swinnerton and the police
were covering up, trying to remove the blame from their shoulders.
The fact that Swinnerton left town right after he made this tape
gave me second thoughts. What I needed was confirmation from a
person present at the *Los Angeles Truth* when the decision was
made to publish the Andrus story—someone who would verify
both Swinnerton's and the police's account of the phone calls, particularly someone who would back up the last two calls in question
—the one made by Mr. Herbert Hood, the general manager, at
roughly 4:30, at which time an executive of the newspaper, not
merely a reporter, received the request for secrecy, and finally the
6:04 call, which the newspaper contends was their first *official* notification . . ."

"And did you succeed?" Brack asked.

"This morning, a man who works at the LA *Truth* confirmed
everything both Patrolman Clyde Hertmann and Harvey Swinnerton said. I cannot disclose his name. I cannot reveal his position on
the paper. He himself suggested I simply call him an informed
source . . ."

T. T. Hansel, watching the program in the television room of
a Pasadena friend, heard these words and had his moment of vision.
Informed source. Herbert Hood had taunted him with those very

words that afternoon, while making some slurring references to Mona's column. There was no question in Hansel's mind. He should have guessed that Hood had been the one to blab. The eagerness with which the old frog had jumped on Trigg's suggestion that his secretary—that faceless girl—had been the sinner should have tipped him. Hansel felt annoyed with his lapse of cunning; long service to the Organization had endowed him with a sensitive nose for conspiracy. It had been Hood. There was no doubt it had been Hood.

The young man on the TV screen boomed on, citing times, names, quotes, laboriously building his case against the *Truth*. Hansel, alone in the leathery room—the host's other dinner guests, including Mrs. Hansel, were playing canasta—stifled a tremor. Could this conceivably hurt them? Would his rocketing career sputter out because of this ludicrous incident—this numbskull's probing—that had resulted in his journal's being placed in the unheard-of position of having to defend sound news practices? The scarlet intensified in his square face: he tried to remain calm, but the pumping of his heart quickened. How little anyone knew about the pressures on him! How little they understood! He had taken the *Truth* over with a harsh mandate from New York: *make it pay in a year or get out*. The year was almost over and still the *Truth* lagged—circulation static, advertising revenue down. It had improved under his leadership, but there were limits to what he could do.

Now had come the Andrus affair: the *Truth* had owned the story, had dominated it, controlled it, manipulated it. They had sold out on Monday and Tuesday. They were on the road back. Would all his efforts crumble because of Sparling's accusations—falsehoods though they were? He shifted his legs and reached for the phone on his host's desk. Then he thought he had best wait for the program to end. Herbert Hood could be fired fifteen minutes later, and he did not want to miss any of the lies.

"And that's pretty much the wrap-up on what I found out about the *Truth* and the Santa Luisa police. What amazed me, and what still does, George, is that it wasn't particularly brilliant reporting on my part. Anyone could have put a little pressure on the people involved and gotten the story. But no one bothered. No one cared. Harvey Swinnerton said something last night to me, and I think, in a way, it sums up a lot that happened in the Andrus case. He said everyone was determined to be as rotten as they could, as mean and stupid as they could—everyone wanted to be *part of the horror*. George—I'm no sociologist or psychologist, so I can't possibly give reasons for the behavior of the press in the Andrus case. I just know that Swinnerton summed it up pretty well. I don't exclude my own role or that of UBC. And no amount of palaver about press freedom and the public's right to know can make amends for what we did."

Brack nodded sagely. "Thanks, Eliot. Now, if I may, I'd like to add a few words of my own. . . ."

In the control room, surrounded by knob-turners and pony-tailed young women (who paid them all? where did they all come from?) Tom Ballstead found himself granting Sparling's perform-ance a grudging admiration. He had to hand it to the ugly bastard. He had the goods on them. Withal, Ballstead could not overcome a conviction that the program was essentially inutile, nonfunctional. It got down to these essentials: the *Truth* had a beat; the *Truth* had used every excusable trick in the book to get it into print. If the excuses were somewhat transparent, they were still excuses. They would cling to *6:04*—O magical incantation!—the way others had shouted *54-40 or fight* and *Golden Gate in '48*.

With a shrewdness born of long hours in city rooms, he knew already what their last defense would be. They would maintain that no *official* notification had come until 6:04, choosing to regard Sergeant Baines as *unofficial*. They would bolster this defense by pointing to their twice-repeated appeal to Rheinholdt to speak to them personally. And, in a way, they would be right. The fact that other papers—the radio and TV people—had accepted Baines as authoritative, they would dust away. *They* had the story; *they* merited special treatment.

Ballstead sighed. Brack was concluding the program with his holy tones; the news director found the liquid syllables abrasive rather than soothing. The words Sparling had written for him were rather strong words. Neither the *Truth* nor the other papers would appreciate them. With the struggle for the advertising dollar getting bloodier each year, they could expect plenty of return fire. Ball-stead would let Hinrichsen worry about that. Hinrichsen had made the decision to go with the exposé; let Hinrichsen explain things to New York when the Organization turned its hatchet men loose.

"How's it going?" Connie Potenza whispered to him.

Ballstead managed a cracked smile. He wondered how the girl—

attractive, vivacious, cheerful—put up with Sparling. Ballstead had taken a liking to her that evening, and he felt he could find her a job at the network—or with another Los Angeles newspaper.

"Pretty good," Ballstead coughed. "Your fellah got all the facts. Too many, maybe. I think we lost the audience after the fourth time check."

"Really?" she asked. "You think so?"

"I don't know," Ballstead said. "Don't worry about it. The main thing is he spoke loud and clear. The television audience never understands anything anyway. He might get an offer to be talent after tonight."

"Eliot? Oh, come on, Mr. Ballstead. Eliot could never be talent— he loves news too much."

Her naïveté did not displease him. It was nice to listen to her enthusiasm, to contemplate young people who "loved" news. The simple chore of dispensing facts had become appallingly involved. The smallest truths had to be yelled and screamed to be heard above the mad din of entertainment, fun, the cacophony of mass communications. Somebody had to find out how high the church steeple was; who got paid for the sewer contract; where the body was buried.

The body buried. His musings ended as the phrase came to his mind. That was where all speculation on the Andrus case eventually settled. He shuddered; the control room was frigid. He heard one of the knob-turners inform another: "Wind Brack up—we're a minute over."

Maurice Krebs finished his coffee and got up. "That hit the spot," he said.

"Want to stretch a little?" McFeeley asked.

"I'd like to beat it."

"Could you spare me a few more minutes—fifteen or so, Maurice?"

"Why? I already showed you those ads in the newspapers—the places I called on Monday. They'll never remember me. You can't expect some receptionist who sees dozens of applicants to recall a single face." He laughed. "Especially one like mine."

"You've got me there," McFeeley conceded. He toyed with the steno pad—searching, probing, trying to find an approach to the bland, dead-center man on the opposite side of the desk.

"Maurice, are you sure you didn't ride around Nespoli Drive on Monday morning?" Joe asked. "I mean, forget about any suspicion on my part that you had anything to do with this. The fact remains we have witnesses who saw a car just like the one you rented on Nespoli." He paused, warming to the small lie, a lie he knew would not render any confession inadmissable, and continued: "We also have a good description of the man who was driving that tan Ford. It's very likely you may have driven by there— innocently—and been spotted by someone. What I'm saying is, if you're not guilty of anything, tell me. Tell me if you were in the neighborhood that morning."

McFeeley watched Krebs' right hand rise to scratch his nose. He had given him a grand temptation: almost an alibi. Now he could claim, yes, he was on Nespoli Drive, but had no connection with the crime. This would take care of any witnesses who saw him. On the other hand—an admission that he *was* there would move him that much closer to apprehension, were he guilty.

"No," Krebs finally said.

"No what?"

"No, I won't answer any more of your questions. I know what my rights are. I don't have to talk."

"Do you mean you're quitting on me, Maurice?" McFeeley asked.

"That's right. I won't answer another thing. I want a lawyer."

"You said before you don't even have one."

"I'll get one tomorrow." Krebs got up. "I want to go home."

The detective pushed his chair from the desk. He leaned backward, his shirt-sleeved elbows touching the pale-green wall. "Maurice, do I read you right? You don't want to answer any more questions?"

"That's the general idea."

"Well, I guess I should inform you of a court ruling here in California. The courts of this state have held that an accusation of crime against a person under arrest—or merely in the custody of an officer—calls for a reply, provided the circumstances surrounding him indicate he's completely *free* to reply if he chooses to."

"What does that mean in plain English?" Krebs asked.

"It means if I question you, you have to answer. If you don't— and it's your privilege not to—your silence may be assumed to show an admission of the truth of my charges."

"Are you accusing me of kidnaping that child? You're nuts, Joe."

McFeeley got up from the swivel chair and walked slowly, his long figure slouching, his off-center face bathed in fraudulent tolerance for sufferers. He put a hand on Krebs' shoulder and fixed him with an understanding eye.

"I wouldn't throw you a curve. You know why? If I'm after a confession—and if you do confess—I have to be very careful how I get it."

McFeeley directed him, with gentle nudges of his hand, toward the easy chair. Krebs sat down again. "If I lie to you," Joe went on, "or threaten you, or sock you, or promise you you'll get off the hook, or that it'll go easier with you—anything like that—the court may toss the confession out. It's as simple as that. I *have* to be truthful." He placed his hand on Krebs' shoulder again. "And, Maurice, I'd like you to be as honest with me as I am with you."

Krebs did not respond. He drew up one knee and laced his fingers on it. His uncommitted face, the light-blue eyes diffusing behind the rimless spectacles told the detective nothing. Joe returned to his swivel chair.

"Maurice, suppose I told you a telephone call was made to Mrs. Andrus this morning at 10:00. Suppose I told you we have a tape recording of that conversation. We are convinced the man who called is the kidnaper, or is in some way party to the crime, because of his familiarity with the note. Suppose I also told you we called a fellow who was a speech expert, a professor over at UCLA, and he listened to that tape. The man who called disguised his voice. He whispered, and he spaced his words in a funny way. But that professor from UCLA, who has made a lifetime study of accents, told us there were certain quirks in the man's way of talking that made it possible to identify him. Of course, such an identification is never foolproof evidence, and I don't think a court would accept it. It's circumstantial. However, if it was tied in with other things— like identification of a car, recollections of someone's face, a note made on certain paper, and so forth——"

He paused. He had told several lies now. No one had furnished a description of the driver of the Ford. The tan car had not been seen by "several" witnesses, but only by Timmy Emerson. They had no complete recording of the call—just a few words. And the professor who knew regional accents was in Indiana or Michigan. Such chicanery was a calculated risk. Shrewd subjects often sensed they were being lied to; their resistance hardened.

"I didn't make any phone call to anyone," Krebs said warily. "I don't care how many professors listen to your tape."

"How badly are you in debt?" McFeeley asked.

"What?"

"How much money do you owe? You told me how rough it's

been. Like for storm windows, gardening stuff, finishing that attic, and so forth. Six thousand? Five thousand? Less?"

"You don't make much sense, Joe. You must be getting tired. I have a little money owed here and there, but I manage. What's that got to do with anything?"

"It's got a lot to do. The person who wrote this note wanted forty-two hundred dollars. You could pay for a lot of screens and storm windows and finish a lot of attics with that. Might even have something left over for the air-conditioning payments."

"That's *some* reason to kidnap somebody," Krebs said.

McFeeley rested his head on one hand, elbow on the desk top, and looked sorrowfully at Krebs. Krebs smiled at him. They were two of the boys—pals in the bowling club, members of the group that rented the fishing boat every Sunday and went after yellowtail and barracuda, neighbors who traded lawn mowers and electric drills, who confided to each other the secrets of a green lawn and a cool attic. *Krebs was so close to him!* They should have been heisting a few brews on the patio, watching Friday night fights on the portable TV set, discussing baseball. It occurred to McFeeley that perhaps this was an asset rather than a debit in his struggle to break the man down. He would keep it on a level as long as he could—two of the boys, two pals, two lower middle-class, frustrated, incomplete, dissatisfied men, with common prejudices and common needs.

"You said something before that interested me," McFeeley said. "You know—about some people who get the breaks, who stick together——"

Krebs shifted in his seat. "Did I?"

"Back at your place. I can sympathize. In my job as a cop, I'm not supposed to have these feelings. But believe me, Maurice, I know what it's like—the way *they* stick together and look out for one another. And where does it leave ordinary citizens like us? Oh, things will change."

"I don't know if they will. *They* control everything. Newspapers, business, the government."

"It isn't that bad. I mean—people who think alike—you and me, for example—who have common problems. We're entitled to a say. You think I don't know what it is to be in debt? To owe the finance company? I can understand a guy like you getting so mad being in debt that he might do something rash—something he'd be sorry for."

Krebs sensed the changing wind of the conversation. Every move of the detective toward the sensitive area of the crime turned him alert, cautious, careful with words. He sat in silence.

"It's never too late to admit you've done something wrong, Maurice," McFeeley said. "When a person does something wrong, something he should have known better than to do, when that person is not really a criminal, not really bad in his heart—it's always best to come clean. I tell you this, Maurice, because I haven't for one minute suspected you're a criminal. Maybe you did something wrong. You thought up a crazy scheme so you could pay off your debts. But now you're sorry. So what do you do? Keep denying everything until you're caught by evidence? Or do you tell us truthfully what you did Monday morning and *help* us?"

"Joe, I've told you ten times, I don't know anything about that girl, or this note, or Nespoli Drive. That's the truth."

"Let me hear again just what you did from the time you got up on Monday," McFeeley said impersonally.

Rheinholdt, shoveling from his benumbed mind Moll's warnings, stormed into his office and found Fred Wagley studying typewritten lists of names. The chief stopped at the threshold when he saw the FBI man.

"Hello, Chief," Wagley said. "You don't mind my camping here for a while, do you?"

"No," Rheinholdt muttered. "You got the case now."

"I'm sorry we had to do it this way," Wagley said. "You fellows should have called us the first day. It would have made everything easier." He glanced at the log. "Has anyone questioned the gardener? What's his name? Valdez?"

"Which gardener?" asked Rheinholdt.

"The Andrus family's," Wagley said patiently. He decided to ask him nothing else. The old man seemed beyond help.

Rheinholdt, viewing the agent's broad, pleasant face, the face of a competent man, sensed the old challenge again. He had given his word to Mayor Speed that the case would be turned over *in toto* to the FBI, that all clues, all suspects, all evidence, all leads would be theirs. Yet these promises he now interred. The information from Moll—that McFeeley was interrogating someone—restored his proprietary pugnacity.

"Wouldn't you guys be sore if we cracked it," the chief said enigmatically.

"Sore? We'd be delighted. It's no question of *us* or *you*. You're supposed to be working with us." Wagley cocked his large, tanned head. "You wouldn't be concealing something? Off on some adventure of your own?"

"Never mind," Rheinholdt said archly. He left the office.

Wagley followed him into the corridor. "I wouldn't advise you to start playing secrets, Chief. Joe McFeeley tried it this afternoon, but I think Joe's gotten the message."

Rheinholdt said nothing. His seamed face did not even honor the agent with recognition. He plodded upstairs, Wagley at his side.

"The request that you turn the case over to us," the FBI man said reasonably, "was made by Mayor Speed—your boss. We can't shoot our way into it, and we don't work that way. Besides, in a week's time—four days to be exact—it's our case anyway."

Rheinholdt turned the corridor and headed toward the interrogation room. If Wagley had exercised suspicions, he now felt them confirmed: Moll was stationed outside the door of the room like a mastiff.

At the door, Rheinholdt confronted Moll. He ignored Wagley. "McFeeley in there?" he asked.

"Yeah, Chief."

"Who is it?" Wagley asked. "Anyone we mentioned today? Someone from the shipping outfit? The printer?"

The sergeant stammered, looked helplessly at Rheinholdt, then said: "A guy who used to work for the printer. Krebs, his name is."

Frowning, Wagley shook his head. The overhead fluorescent lights illuminated each carefully plastered hair on his speckled crown. "We agreed on that. *We* were supposed to track those people down. I'm sorry, Chief, I don't like the way this is going. I've never encountered anything like this in my life." He started to leave. "I'm calling your mayor, and I'm calling my boss. We've got to come to an understanding on this."

McFeeley opened the door and came into the hall.

With admirable patience, Wagley spoke to him. "This isn't fair, Joe. And it isn't very smart."

"No excuses," McFeeley said. "This guy's name came up late. Culligan remembered him and called me. I suppose I should have given it to you, with the rest."

"Why didn't you?" pleaded the agent.

"I'm stubborn. I had to save something."

"What do you have on him?" Wagley asked. All four men moved

a few steps down the hall. McFeeley, his voice weakened by his sustained efforts with Krebs, spoke slowly, thinly. "He was fired at Four State in July. In debt. No criminal record. He rented a——" McFeeley stopped. "Look, Wagley. Give me till midnight with him, alone. I think he may lead us somewhere."

"We can't make deals," the FBI man said.

"Ah, come on, Mr. Wagley," Moll pleaded. "If you knew how much it meant to me and Joe. Sure, we booted a lot of things. Sure, maybe we didn't handle the reporters. The breaks were against us. Didn't Joe find the note—where it came from?"

"Don't beg him!" Rheinholdt snapped. "I don't care what the mayor said. We found this guy. You take the others."

"Oh, good God," Wagley said. "Am I dreaming this? Joe, let me take him down to our office in LA. He must be more than a routine suspect the way you're acting, the way you shut up before."

McFeeley hesitated. He found himself resting his pained back against the cool wall of the corridor; he had an abrupt desire to be at home, drinking beer, watching television—just what Maurice Krebs would be doing if he were not being questioned.

"Give me till 11:00 tonight," McFeeley said. He looked at the hall clock: 10:14.

"This is the most asinine thing I've ever had to contend with," Wagley said angrily. "I should walk in and grab him. You sneak in here without telling me; you interrogate him without my knowing about it."

McFeeley rubbed his eyes. "Give me till 10:30, Wagley. I'll quit after that. If it's O.K. with the chief, he's yours."

"Out of the question," the FBI man said.

"Come on, Wagley," Joe almost whined. "Give me a break. I'm just a poor Irish boy trying to get ahead."

"Oh, for God's sake," Wagley said. "What makes you think you can get anything out of him in another fifteen minutes?"

"He's beginning to respect me," McFeeley said.

Wagley studied the detective's weary face. He had liked McFeeley from the start—an honest, well-meaning young cop, suffering in a job too big for him, a responsibility he never should have been given. The FBI man had never agreed to such a scheme in his career, and he knew he never would again; but he felt constrained to grant McFeeley's request. He laughed dryly. "O.K., Joe. I'll be waiting out here to change places with you."

Rheinholdt nodded his approval of the arrangement. The detective walked back into the interrogation room.

"What is truth? asked jesting Pilate," George Brack intoned, while Eliot winced off camera (the line was George's and had drawn raucous criticism from Sparling, who maintained that Will Rogers had been a "jesting pilot"). Tom Ballstead, in the enshadowed control room, stifled a coughing fit.

"We may well ask that question today, when the facts concerning the behavior of the press in the Andrus kidnaping are being conveniently forgotten. Let us review. It is our contention that a newspaper ignored a request for secrecy and thereby hindered the police investigation and endangered the child's safety. It is also our contention that the defense published by the newspaper was not in accord with the facts. No repeated shoutings of the magic number 6:04 can alter the fact that a reporter *and* an executive of the newspaper received this appeal for secrecy between 4:10 and 4:30 Monday afternoon—well in advance of the newspaper's appearance on the street at 5:07. In journalism a clear beat is always tempting; when it is a clear beat on a kidnaping, the most intriguing of crimes, it is irresistible. One can ask the question: Is a child's safety worth a headline, a rise in circulation? Decency dictates one answer. We weigh our words carefully, blaming not a single newspaper, but a *state of mind,* a professional code, if you will, which declares that nothing is private, nothing privileged, nothing exempt from the heartless light of the press. Forget about the *Truth's* lapse; they were tempted; they fell. Perhaps there is some justice in their use of the words 'official notification'; perhaps there is justice in their appeal to the chief of police to make the secrecy request *personally.* But where were the rest of us when the lights went out? Who protested the *Truth's* action? Who, except a UBC reporter—by his own admission, party to the shameful events of Monday night—bothered to investigate the 6:04-5:07 incantation? And please note the target selected by the press—Chief Rheinholdt and his force. We have no desire to defend the chief. It is obvious that he and his men were guilty of too many errors, too many oversights. But the press remains silent on one overwhelming failure of the police—and that is their failure to arrest the mob that camped outside the Andrus house on Monday, ignored a mother's appeal, dictated terms of cooperation, then broke their own agreements. Of course, the press has made no mention of police laxity. This would be like a child, caught stealing cookies, blaming his mother for not hiding the jar."

Brack inhaled and fixed his unclouded eyes on the camera. To his right, Eliot, unseen by the audience, pinched Brack's enflanneled thigh. Ballstead, in the dark room, shook off a moment's distress: had he allowed that stuff to go through? He thought of Hinrichsen—a man who would never have to worry about his children's education, the next insurance payment, the pain of joblessness and the ignominy of getting fired. What in God's name had brought Matt Hinrichsen, the In-law, to sanction this outrage? Ballstead remembered George Brack's minister; the project assumed an idiocy that titillated him. It had to be viewed as a grand joke; otherwise the truth might sicken him.

"You will recall that when Laura Andrus made her pilgrimage on Monday night, accompanied by reporters and cameramen, there was a man hiding in a tree, making a recording of the event. Perhaps the man in the tree is symbolic. Is it possible that man, having climbed down from the branches a million years ago, in the Cenozoic era, will now *revert* to them—thanks to our mass media? We hope not. If ever our nation stood in need of a rallying of moral vigor, a reassessment of values, of honest leadership, it is now. And God preserve us if the custodians of the printed and spoken word are not ready to assume that leadership."

Brack turned his last page. "In concluding this edition of 'Southland,' I want to add a personal note. I want to convey my own apologies to Mrs. Andrus. Mrs. Andrus, the burden you are now bearing is tragedy enough. What you have been subjected to by the press has made your ordeal all the more painful. Your desire for secrecy, for privacy—two conditions of life that apparently have vanished forever in our society—was ignored. And so you suffered. Indeed, I have heard talk among my colleagues that 'you brought this on yourself,' that 'had you played ball with them, everything would have been all right,' that 'you lied to reporters and have to pay the penalty.' These are direct quotes from some of the people covering the story. *What a mockery!* As if anything could have concerned you beyond your daughter's safety! As if you were expected to worry about the commercial health of newspapers, radio and television stations! As if these bloodless institutions were worthy of equation with the life of a child! I submit, Mrs. Andrus, we, all of us, owe you apologies. No amount of after-the-fact wellwishing can atone for the behavior of our fraternity. To ask your forgiveness would be too much; we can only plead for understanding. This is George Brack reporting on 'Southland.' Good night."

The screen went black. A station-break commercial, an animated cartoon advertising cat food, appeared. Eliot shook hands with the commentator. "You read it like an Old Testament prophet, Georgie. Now all we got to do is find new jobs."

There was very little other handshaking, congratulating—and no words of praise from the crew: they were too busy arguing a company regulation concerning meals.

Outside the control room, Ballstead, scowling, nodded at Brack and Sparling. "It proved you could read," he said.

"You looked marvelous, Eliot!" Connie said. "Gee, Mr. Brack—you almost had me in tears at the end."

"Wait till tomorrow," Ballstead growled. "We'll all be weeping." He gestured with a shoulder. "Come on. I'll buy coffee."

Theodore T. Hansel waited until the cat food commercial had ended, then switched the set off. He crossed his legs and allowed indignation, righteous anger, outrage to boil and bubble within him. *The impertinence! The insolence! How any member of that bastard art, television—how any of its soiled practitioners—could dare point a finger at his newspaper!* They—who pandered to the lowest tastes, who allowed their programs to be dictated by advertisers, who had defiled the public air, rent the general ear with inanities and obscenities—they dared to accuse the *Truth,* the press in general!

Some long-range assault was in order, something that would redress the balance, turn public anger against that flickering screen that had snatched away so much of the advertiser's dollar. For the time being, an answer was needed for the morning newspaper. Yet Hansel's fertile mind, at that moment, seemed curiously planless. And the reason was, he simply could not honor any of the network's contentions. All their pinpointing about times, places and persons was unworthy of an answer. He, Hansel, had said there had been no official notification until 6:04; that was an end of it.

He picked up the telephone and dialed the office. A nightside man answered and Hansel advised him he wanted to dictate an editorial for the next day. It was to appear in all editions—not a front-page piece, but a short, simple statement at the bottom of the editorial page.

"Call it 'The *Truth* Stands Firm,' " he advised the deskman.

The Editor & Publisher paused. He heard his wife's throaty cackle; it unnerved him. She was old, rich and strong, more welcome in these grand places than he had ever been. Only five years ago he had been a starveling night editor for a newspaper in the chain; now he was consulted on foreign policy and won awards from journalism schools. A shiver of doubt made composition difficult;

he wondered if his grandeur might some day crumble, if he would be discarded as an *arriviste*.

"Begin it this way," Hansel said. "A certain television station last night made reckless charges concerning the role of this newspaper in the Andrus case. The *Truth* stands firm on its original statement, the one issued Tuesday in response to Chief Rheinholdt's charges—charges already proven baseless. What motivated this TV station to act as it did is unclear, but the *Truth* hopes to advise its readers on this curious development in the future. For the time being, we content ourselves with denying anything stated last night on the United Broadcasting Corporation's program. We are proud as members of the journalistic profession to match our honor, our words and our deeds, against those of a business based on dishonesty and fraud. We submit that John Peter Zenger and Elijah Lovejoy are better sources of inspiration than half-witted comedians."

"That all, Mr. Hansel?" the deskman asked.

"Yes. I want it in all editions." He paused. "Has Mr. Hood been around tonight?"

The man hesitated. "I think he was in Rocco's earlier. He may have gone home by now."

"Have the operator get him for me, and then have her tell Mr. Hood to call me back at Sycamore 4-5679."

In a few minutes Herbert Hood was on the phone. His voice was thick with the booze, but he was by no means depressed or abject.

"Herbert," Hansel said, "Did you see that program?"

"Loved every minute of it," Hood gargled. "They really put the blocks to us, didn't they, Ted?"

"You seem strangely happy about it," Hansel said.

"You asked for it. I warned you not to print it."

"Herbert, I'm in no mood for your I-told-you-so's. I couldn't be less concerned with those fools on television. If you think it will cost us one reader, or a line of advertising, you're more stupid than I thought. Besides, we did nothing wrong."

Hood exhaled his whiskery breath so violently that the gassy noise came to Hansel's ear like steam issuant from a lidded pot. "By Jesus, you are all alone, aren't you, Ted? You're by yourself somewhere, not hearing anyone's voice, not listening. Don't you know there's a difference between 4:30 and 6:04?"

"That's not the point of this conversation, Herbert. I don't need any spies to tell me who at the *Truth* spoke to Sparling. As soon as he used the words *informed source,* it was apparent to me. All that nonsense about your secretary!"

"It wasn't my idea about her. It was Trigg's." Hood sounded gleeful.

"You're through, Herbert. You've been a millstone around my neck too long. Tomorrow morning I'm discussing this matter with New York, and I'll put it to them on a you-or-me basis. I believe they'll be happy to accept your resignation. I hardly think they'll find a sinecure for you. Those jobs are reserved for loyal retainers. The word loyal doesn't obtain in your instance."

Hood sighed. "Just see to it I get my full severance pay." He hung up. Waddling back to the bar and his booze, he blocked out a happy future: a one-room apartment near Lake Michigan, a poker game once a week, a season ticket for the White Sox games. The rest of the time he would devote to writing his memoirs.

"I suppose we should be grateful to them," Laura said when the program was over.

"Yeah," Fritzie agreed. "Truth comes in li'l bits and pieces. They did a fine job—not that it matters. We just had the bad luck to get caught in the meat grinder."

The television blabbed on, its hum reminding them of the lulling rhythms of daily life, days of small duties and obligations, nights of small diversions. The beauty of these acts, the mosaic they formed to give life size and texture, never seemed more precious to them. Seated in the darkened room with Babe and Harry Emerson, the Andruses might have been any of the well-adapted, unworried families on Nespoli Drive. The wound in their lives seemed to have been sewn up, hidden. Back in the postures of normal living, they struggled to ignore the darkness that engulfed them on Monday morning. It seemed to Laura, watching Fritzie's flushed head, observing the Emersons' generous attempts to assist them in this fraud, that the tragedy should have left a palpable, visible mark on them—commensurate with the ravaging of their souls and minds—perhaps a bleeding gap on Fritzie's cheek, a suppurating sore on her arm.

"I don't know," Harry Emerson said, igniting his cigar, so that it flamed torchlike and endowed the room with a campfire glow, "I worked on newspapers, magazines, for TV and now on my own. I never saw newspapermen carry on the way they did here. I think it's because they're desperate. Papers are in trouble. Every day one of 'em folds. More one-paper towns. They can't seem to make it any more. TV, movies, barbecues, boats. Who wants to read about the UN or disarmament? So they run entertainment and less news. But when it comes to entertainment, they can't compete with television. So they go under. Those bastards at the *Truth* die a little every day, waitin' for the paper to fold, for someone to buy them out. So along comes a big story. They got it all alone. *Wham!* They print, no matter what. I ain't excusing what they did, Laura—it was horrible. But that's the way I see it."

"I suppose you're right, Harry," Laura said. "I'm not in a forgiving mood."

"Oh, you and your theories," Babe said. She looked up brightly. "Scrabble, anyone? We haven't played in ages!"

Fritzie seemed pleased by the idea. "How 'bout it, Laura?"

"I guess so. We could play one game before going to bed." She went to the bedroom for the set, nodding at the two men on duty in the nursery. They smiled at her, advising her there had been no important calls, nothing worth her attention.

When she returned, Fritzie was on his feet, his eyes transfixed on the television set. Evidently, he had risen to turn it off, now, its message had him hypnotized. On the screen was a rude drawing of a gorilla clutching a young woman. . . . *tonight and every night this week on your midnight movie, see* Mighty Joe Young, *an all-time movie classic, about a giant gorilla's love for a young woman . . .*

Fritzie turned the knob. Then he staggered back from the set, as if absorbing a blow in his paunch. "Her favorite picture," he said poignantly. "Her favorite picture. Laura? You remember how she sat through it every night? And made me imitate the gorilla with the piano on his head? I sure could stop her cryin'—just had to make believe I was Mighty Joe Young. Funny thing—she never could figure out if he was good or bad. 'Is he good, Daddy? Is Mighty Joe Young good, Daddy?' An' one night she woke up hollerin'— 'He's a good gorilla, *he's a good gorilla!*' "

Krebs yawned, patted his mouth and apologized. "What was all that fuss out there? Was I under discussion?"

McFeeley did not answer. He knew he had made a mistake running out of the room on hearing Rheinholdt's blustering voice. He had had the sensation he was reaching some understanding with Krebs. And it was a rule of interrogation not to break off a good line of questioning. The hiatus often gave a wary subject a chance to re-examine what had been said, to backtrack and then grow silent again. The detective feigned an answering yawn. "You've got me doing it, Maurice."

"We both need a snooze," said Krebs. "Why can't we knock off and start again tomorrow? That is, if you're still convinced I'm such a terrible person."

McFeeley stared mournfully down his crooked nose at the shipping clerk.

"Maurice, if you know anything about this, you better tell me. You'll get caught sooner or later. We have too much to work with. The car you rented—which the lab is going over right now. Suppose we find one of your hairs in it? Or one of the child's? A trace of blood? We have the recording of the telephone call this morning. We've taped our conversations *here,* and that speech fellow, that professor, is coming over tonight to compare them. Then there's the ransom note—made from a shipping form from the firm at which *you* worked. And, finally, you were in debt—enough in debt to make a decent citizen like yourself upset enough to do something he really didn't want to do, something he's sorry he did. There's just too much, Maurice. We'll get to you, somehow. It might as well be now, since you and I seem to talk the same language. You know the FBI's in this case—and I don't think they'll be as sympathetic to you."

He could tell very little from Krebs' face. Sometimes a gesture would suggest weakening—an ear tugged, a nose rubbed, the lips pursed. But when the suspect would resume speaking, his voice would be calm and clear. Not a word would be slurred, no tremor would intrude.

"It would be a big thing for a small-town cop to crack a kidnaping, wouldn't it, Joe?" Krebs asked.

"I suppose it would."

"And what would I get out of it?"

"What are you getting at, Maurice?" Joe asked.

"One hand washes the other," Krebs said, laughing. He might have been asking a mechanic to put in a new set of spark plugs—free, unknown to the boss—in exchange for a pass to a movie.

"Let me get you straight," McFeeley said. He got up and sat on the edge of the desk, making sure he did not block the desk pad and its clandestine microphone. "Are you saying you're ready to tell me something?"

"Could be," Krebs said. He was smiling—one eyebrow arched, his small mouth twisting to one corner. "But you've got to help *me*. After all that talk about understanding me and us being the same kind of fellows. I want to know what's in it for me. I'm not saying I did this; I'm hinting I might know a little about it."

He was speaking pridefully and McFeeley noticed the change in him. He was the low man on the bowling team, the little guy at the end of the bar, nursing his beer, to whom no one ever paid any attention: all that had changed. He had inside dope; he knew something; he would divulge it only at a price.

"Why don't you tell me, Maurice? You'd feel better if you did."

"Joe, you didn't listen to me. I want something in return. Like special consideration, if we ever got into court. That's done all the time."

McFeeley nodded. "I have to point out to you, Maurice, that I'm in no position to promise you anything. I'm just a cop. If I say you won't be prosecuted, or things will go easy with you, and then you confess—well, the court may toss your confession out. I'm not allowed to hold any inducements out to you. Even the state's attorney can't do that. The courts in California are strict on this."

Krebs drew back in the seat. "Well, then I say nuts to them. Why should I tell what I know if I don't get anything in return?"

"I'll tell you why, Maurice. It's got to do with the kidnaping law in this state."

The detective was at point of no return: the man was impossible. The habitual criminal's power to resist was lacking in him. In its place, he possessed something infinitely more difficult to break down: an unwavering belief in his own innocence, the conviction that he was a suffering, put-upon little fellow—incapable of any wrong act.

"I haven't kidnaped anyone," Krebs said.

"Maybe you have and maybe you haven't. But you should know what the law is. In the State of California, kidnaping is a capital offense when the person who commits it seizes anyone for ransom, reward, or to commit extortion or robbery, and if the victim suffers *bodily harm*."

"What exactly is a capital offense?"

"Punishable by death in the gas chamber, or life imprisonment with no chance of parole—*ever*."

Krebs inclined his head. He might have been advised that it would rain tomorrow and he could turn off his lawn sprinklers.

McFeeley glanced at his watch: 10:21. In nine minutes he would surrender Krebs to Wagley. Nine minutes to make up for his mistakes, his stupidity, his failure to make people respect him. He had taken a considerable risk in explaining the law to Krebs. If he had harmed the child, it would serve to close his mouth even tighter: he would understand the gravity of his act. On the other hand, if Amy Andrus were still unhurt, the knowledge furnished Krebs might well be the lever that would make him talk.

"Bodily harm," Krebs said slowly. "What exactly does that mean?"

"If the person isn't actually hurt, it would not constitute bodily harm; but, again, that would be something for the courts to rule on. If the child is alive and well——" He shrugged, offering Krebs another opening.

The shipping clerk locked his fingers and thrust his arms between his thighs. Thus constricted, his shoulders drawn downward, his face lowered, he was more insignificant than ever.

"I guess that's my way of life," Krebs said. "I never really finish anything or do anything well."

"You did it, didn't you, Maurice?"

"You might say I did. I was forced into it. By circumstances. By not getting a break. If I had only kept that job——"

"You shouldn't have gone so heavy on the storm windows and the air conditioning. You can go broke buying that stuff."

"I know, I know. You've been a sport to me, Joe. You're all right." He was without remorse, without any awareness of what he had done.

"Where's the girl—right now?" McFeeley asked.

"Berman has her."

Joe walked behind the chair and patted his shoulder. "Come on, Maurice. You know where she is. I can tell you do. Who's Berman?"

"He put me up to it. He was the brains behind it. He took her, after I picked her up on Monday morning. He was waiting at my house, and he drove off in his own car. That's the last I saw of him. And of her."

"You're lying, Maurice. I know you are. I want you to know I feel badly about that, after the way you and I hit it off. You answered too fast about Berman. You know where Amy is. Now tell me."

"I would if I could. Joe, I'm telling the truth. Berman has her. He's a fellow I met at the Green Lantern Bar last week. It was his idea. I just went and got the kid. He had clippings from the newspapers and he made the note himself——"

"Out of paper you gave him? From Four State?"

"Well, we made it together."

"I see. But only you went to Nespoli Drive that morning? Why didn't he go along?"

"We figured one man in a car wouldn't be remembered as easy as two. Also, he had to be ready with his own car to take her away to wherever he took her. The idea was, he was to bring her back that night, like we planned. I was to pick up the money, and he was to drive the little girl a block away from her house, and she'd walk home."

"And you never saw him again? Never saw the child?"

"Nope. I know what happened. He was scared off when the story was printed in the newspapers that night and on the radio. He knew there'd be cops all over, and so did I. If the papers and police had stayed out, everything would have gone fine. The girl would be home, we'd have the money, and we'd be even up."

"Even up," McFeeley said sadly. "You want to start from the top and tell us everything, Maurice? I have to ask some other people to witness it. You won't get scared and not talk when the others come in?"

"Heck, no. I'm not ashamed of what I did. I was forced into it."

"How about Berman? You want to stick with him? Or do you want to withdraw that—and admit you did it yourself?"

"He's got the child. I never had any intent to hurt her. He thought it up, but I took her—and I handed her over to him that morning. That's the last I seen—I saw—of her."

There was a rapping at the door. Joe cursed quietly and looked at his watch. Wagley was holding him to it. It was exactly 10:30. McFeeley walked outside. In the corridor, besides the FBI man, Rheinholdt and Moll, was a fourth man. McFeeley recognized him as Roy Brand, the state's attorney. He was a natty little man with a beach-boy's tan, his eyebrows and mustache bleached yellow by sun and salt water.

"You know Roy Brand, Joe," Wagley said. He pointed at the recording room next door. "We listened. Congratulations."

"It's not on paper yet," said McFeeley. "And he's lying about the child." He looked wearily at Rheinholdt. "I think he's killed her. He gives me the creeps. All that stuff about Berman taking her. He invented that."

Roy Brand took McFeeley's hand and squeezed it. "A helluva job, Joe. God, we're proud of you. I suggest we go in and get whatever he'll give in writing. I brought our stenographer."

McFeeley nodded; exhaustion was coating him like heavy oil.

The state's attorney looked at Wagley. "Shall we do it?"

Wagley nodded. He, in turn, looked placatingly at Rheinholdt. What passed for a smile was wrinkling the chief's square face: Aesop triumphant.

McFeeley excused himself and went into the adjoining sound-proofed room, where two uniformed men were manning the recorder. He made sure they had gotten everything, had them put on a new reel, then returned to the corridor.

Rheinholdt grunted his readiness and McFeeley opened the door. Moll came hustling down the corridor with three more chairs. They filed in: McFeeley, Rheinholdt, Wagley, Roy Brand, Brand's stenographer, and finally Moll.

Krebs smiled as if welcoming them. The interrogation room had become his castle. "All these people just for me?" he asked pleasantly. "It's a regular convention."

Brand took the swivel chair. The others sat, except for Rheinholdt, who remained standing at the door.

"Maurice," McFeeley said, "these gentlemen are here to take down your formal statement. This is Mr. Wagley from the FBI; Mr. Brand, the state's attorney; Chief Rheinholdt; and that's Mr. Hemsley, the stenographer. You ready, Maurice?"

"Some turnout," Krebs said. "I'm ready."

Brand spoke to the stenographer, a gray, middle-aged man who pecked at his machine fastidiously.

"Maurice Krebs, statement of, taken at the Santa Luisa police headquarters, California, on September 19, 1951, at 10:44 P.M., Pacific Daylight Saving Time. Present: Mr. Roy M. Brand, assistant state's attorney; Lieutenant Joseph McFeeley, chief of detectives, Precinct A; Sergeant Irvin Moll, Precinct A; Police Chief Caspar Rheinholdt; Frederic Wagley, Federal Bureau of Investigation, Los Angeles office; and George Hemsley, stenotypist."

"An all-star team," Krebs said.

"What is your name?" asked Brand.

"Maurice Krebs."

"Where do you live, Mr. Krebs?"

"I live at 3114 Amethyst, Droitwich Hills, Santa Luisa."

"Mr. Krebs, I am Roy M. Brand, assistant state's attorney, working under the direction of the attorney general of the State of California. I am now going to ask you some questions concerning a child named Amy Andrus, who lives in Santa Luisa. I am told by Lieutenant McFeeley that you know something about her disappearance last Monday, September 17. Are you ready to answer my questions?"

"Shoot."

"Mr. Krebs, could you just answer yes?"

"Yes. Sure."

Brand nodded. "Has anyone threatened you to make you answer?"

"No."

"Has anyone made any promises of leniency to you?"

"Ah—no."

"You're positive?"

"Positive. Joe explained that to me. He isn't allowed to."

"And whatever answers you now give me, and these other gentlemen, will be of your own free will?"

"Yes, sir."

"Will they be the truth?"

"Yes." Krebs took off his glasses and polished them. He changed position in his chair, settling back, as if in charge of the interrogation.

Brand turned to McFeeley. "Lieutenant, since you are familiar with the details of this matter, would you please assume the questioning now?"

Joe cleared his throat. It was an effort to get the words out, more of an effort to maintain his intimate manner with the kidnaper. "You know who I am, Maurice?"

"Right. You're Lieutenant McFeeley. Joe."

"Now, Maurice, tell us exactly what you did from the time you woke up on Monday, September 17. I will interrupt you to clarify things now and then, but you keep talking and try to remember everything you did that relates to the disappearance of Amy Andrus. All set?"

"I am," Krebs said.

"All right. Now what did you do after getting up on Monday?"

"I showered and shaved. My electric razor wasn't working so hot, so I made a note to have it repaired. I ate a light breakfast—some sweet rolls and coffee—and then I told Mother and Dad I'd be gone for the day, that I was answering some want ads. They said O.K., was I taking the car, and I said no, and I suggested they take it to West Covina to see Dad's cousin, Harry Stempf. Then I left the house at around 7:20, I guess."

McFeeley halted him with a raised hand. "What did you take with you, Maurice? I mean—any papers, or whatnot?"

"Well, I had a copy of the want-ad section from the *Times.*"

"Did you take a note with you?"

"What?"

McFeeley picked up the ransom note, still in its plastic folder. "Did you take the original of this sheet of white paper with the words on it that are cut from newspapers?"

"Yes," he said, "as a matter of fact I did."

"Tell us something about the note. When did you make it?"

"I'd been clipping words out of the paper over the weekend."

"Several papers? Just one?"

"The *Argus.* They have big print."

"And where did you get the paper to paste the words on?"

Krebs laughed. "Heck, you know that, Joe. You can answer it yourself. That's how you found me."

"I think these other gentlemen would like to know."

"O.K. I trimmed a shipping form that I had from when I worked at Four State Shippers. A piece of scrap paper."

"How did you trim it, Maurice?"

"A steel-edged ruler."

McFeeley would have to do something grand for Raffalovitch: perhaps burn the film of him being goosed and not being goosed.

"So you had that note and you set out from your house at what time?"

"Early. About 7:20 or so. I like to get an early start."

"You have anything else with you—like a toy or candy?"

"A toy? No."

"Something that might attract a child."

"I wouldn't exactly call it that. It wasn't my idea to take it along. It was Berman's idea." He was speaking faster, his colorless voice rising. "I met him at the Green Lantern Bar on Friday, the Friday before, and he showed me these clippings about this family breaking up, and he said he had cased the neighborhood and seen this little girl walking around the house by herself in the morning, and would I be interested. He said we'd share what we got and wouldn't hurt the kid. He said I'd pick her up, and then he'd take her and worry about hiding her all day, and he'd give her back at night. He told me what to put in the note, what to say, and how to make it up so no one could trace it."

"You mean you never saw this man before, Maurice? He just came up to you at a bar and told you this, and you went for it?"

Maurice Krebs sighed. "I guess I did wrong. He put the idea in my head. If I could get my hands on him——"

"What's his first name?" Roy Brand asked suddenly.

"Who? Oh. Berman. I never found out. Big. A big fellow, kind of fat. Curly hair. He had a New York accent."

Brand pointed a finger at Krebs. "Now, Mr. Krebs, remember, you are going to swear that everything you tell us is the truth. You have already so stated. Are you sticking with this story about a man named Berman who gave you the idea to kidnap Amy Andrus?"

"It's no story. It happened."

Brand's sunburned face was impassive. He told McFeeley to continue.

"You were saying, Maurice, that you took something with you that morning when you left the house. You took the want ads, this note here, and another thing. What was it?"

"A thermos bottle. It was Berman's idea. I made it up the night before."

"What was in it?"

"Chocolate milk. It was a pint bottle, one I used to use when I was working. I filled it about half full on Sunday night with milk and then I mixed in chocolate syrup."

"And you took this with you?"

"Yes. Here's where his idea comes in. I put some stuff in it."

"What kind of stuff?" asked McFeeley.

"Oh, ordinary sleeping pills."

"How many?"

"Only four. They were those little red ones in capsules. I had a bottle in the house, but I hardly use them. I opened the capsules and emptied the powder into the chocolate milk and shook it up. It tasted bitter, so I added more syrup."

Brand leaned over the desk. "What was the name of the tablets, Maurice?"

"Gee, I don't recall, Mr. Brand."

"Seconal? Nembutal?" Brand asked.

"I don't recall."

Joe turned to Brand. "Want me to continue, Mr. Brand?"

"Yes, Joe."

"O.K., Maurice," McFeeley said, "you left the house and where did you go?"

"Well, as you found out, Joe, I went to Arnold's Auto Rental System on North Juniper and rented a Ford car. I registered it in my own name, put the thermos bottle in the glove compartment, made sure the note was in my pocket and drove off."

"What time was this?" Joe asked.

"Around 7:40."

"And you went right to Nespoli Drive?"

"Yes. But I took a roundabout route. You see, I knew—that is, Berman told me—the little girl often came out of the house around 8:00, and I wanted to time it just right."

"You remember when you got to the Andrus house?"

"I can't be too sure. I was a little nervous. Anyway, I rode around the block twice. Once I saw a kid delivering papers, and once a guy in a white Cadillac passed me, but it was real quiet. The second time around—maybe it was 8:15, I can't be sure—I saw the girl. She was standing near a closed-in patio at one end of the house."

"What did you do?"

"I stopped the car, but I kept the engine going. Then I called to her and asked her did she want to ride in my car. She said she wasn't allowed to; but knowing, as I did, her father wasn't living there, I said I'd take her to see him. She said someone had told her he was coming home, but I convinced her I knew where he worked, and then I said I'd leave a note for her mother. I stuck it under a rock on the path. She came in and off we went. I got on the freeway and headed for Los Angeles. The kid started to talk a lot. She kept asking where was her father, and I kept saying it would take a little while to find him, there being so much traffic. Then I asked her was she thirsty, she said yes, and I poured a cupful of the chocolate milk. She drank most of it down, and pretty soon she was drowsy."

"Where did you do this? What time?"

"Well, I pulled off the freeway outside of Burbank. It was around 9:15, I guess."

"Then?"

"She fell asleep. I made her comfortable on the seat and kept driving."

"How long?" asked McFeeley.

"Not too long. Another fifteen minutes. The arrangement was for me to meet Berman at 9:30 at the old service road that leads to the airport. It's an old dirt road—no one uses it—at the far end of the field. He was waiting for me. The kid was out cold by now. She looked O.K., just sweating a little, but comfortable, and I took her from my car to his, and he drove off. He said he'd call me later about the pickup that night. That's the last I saw of him and of her."

"What kind of car did he have?" asked Brand quickly.

"Ah—a Ford, like the one I rented. Black, I think. Dark gray." McFeeley blinked his eyes. "Did he call you again?"

"As a matter of fact, he did. He called around 6:30 that night to tell me it was impossible to pick up the ransom and bring the child back. He said now that the newspapers and radio had it, and there were cops all over the place, it was impossible. He said if the papers hadn't printed anything, we'd have returned her. This way he just said we had to lay low a few days."

"Did he say where he was with the child?" Joe asked.

"Nope. That was our understanding. He said he had a good hideaway. He said it was impossible to hide a kid where I lived—all them neighbors and my folks and all."

McFeeley asked: "Did he say if the child was all right? He hadn't harmed her?"

Krebs paused. "Gee, I don't recollect. I didn't ask. And he didn't say. I assumed she was O.K. Those few pills couldn't kill her."

"You haven't seen or heard from him since?" asked Brand.

"Not a word."

"Maurice, you did call Mrs. Andrus this morning at 10:00, didn't you?" McFeeley asked.

"Yes, as a matter of fact, I did."

"And you offered to call her back at 7:00? You said the child was not hurt, and you would return her, but they had to co-operate and call off the cops?"

He laughed appreciatively. "Did I say all that?"

"We've got it recorded."

He looked around the room at the unsmiling men. "I guess I did, then."

"What I'd like to know, Maurice," McFeeley pursued, "is if the last you saw of Amy Andrus was when this Berman took her at 9:30 Monday morning, how come you could make a promise like that to Mrs. Andrus? Are you sure you didn't know exactly where she was all the time—and that right this second you know where she is?"

"I was bluffing," Krebs said. "I was desperate. I wanted the money. I figured if that woman would play ball, I could then call Berman and set a new time and place."

"Then you had a phone number for him? You knew where to reach him?" McFeeley asked.

"Not exactly. But he was supposed to keep in touch with me. I figured he'd call."

"But the last call he made was 6:30 P.M. Monday—not a word all day Tuesday—nothing this morning——"

"I suppose he got scared. As scared as I did, after the papers printed it."

Roy Brand stood up. He spoke to Moll. "Irv, will you stay here a few minutes? I want to talk to the others outside."

Rheinholdt, Wagley and McFeeley followed the state's attorney outside. They walked down the corridor.

"He's not only a bad crook, he's a bad liar," Wagley said gloomily.

McFeeley shook his head. "The way he sticks with that story—this way he'll claim he didn't harm her, and he thinks he might beat the gas chamber. It may also mean we have to look for a corpse."

"We'll get the story out of him," Rheinholdt muttered. "Give me fifteen minutes alone with the bastard."

Brand patted his golden mustache. "I wish I could let you, Caspar. I'd like to wring his neck myself. Of course, there's a chance he's telling *some* truth—maybe he did have a partner—maybe the child is alive—and maybe he's holding out for a deal."

"I told him he can't get any," Joe said. "He knows if we promise leniency, his confession can be tossed out."

"I don't know what to do," Brand said. "Should we book him right now? Should we keep trying? I'm willing to try it all night, if we can break him, if he'll tell us where the child is."

McFeeley appealed to the state's attorney and to Wagley. "O.K. with you if I try him alone a few minutes? We were having a love affair before. Maybe he's still carrying the torch."

"Go ahead," said Wagley. "You're doing great."

McFeeley walked back to the room and knocked. Moll let him in. "Irv, I'd like to be alone with Maurice a few minutes." Moll left.

Joe did not sit. He circled the floor. "Maurice, you've let me down."

"How come?" asked Krebs.

"You just have, and I feel badly about it. I don't think you're telling the truth. I don't think there is a Berman. I don't think you gave him Amy. I think you know where she is. I want you to tell me truthfully just what you did with her."

"I've told you the truth, Joe."

McFeeley stopped pacing behind the desk. He leaned over the back of the swivel chair and fixed his Irish-blue eyes on the shipping clerk. A random phrase from a textbook on interrogation technique flitted through his mind. *References to God, the hereafter, patriotism and suspect's mother, used in inducing a confession, have been held perfectly proper.*

"Maurice," the detective said, "I want you to think about some things that are important to all of us. O.K., you did something wrong. O.K., you're sorry. You want to make it up. But you must make it up totally. You must tell *all* the truth. You know why? Because of the Man Upstairs. I don't care what a man's religion is —he must have one. Maurice—the Good Lord up there expects better of you. I saw your Mother and Dad tonight—two swell people. They'll be hurt by this, Maurice; but if you tell the truth, you'll hurt them less, because the world will respect you for confessing. And, finally, there is your country. You once worried about your country's safety. You stood up and were counted. Will you let them down now? Maurice, it's as simple as that—the Man Upstairs, your Mom, and your flag. They want you to tell me everything. Where is the little girl?"

Krebs' face had grown solemn during the detective's peroration. It had the look of a stupid college freshman learning from a physics professor that his last examination paper was disappointing. "Can I get up and stretch?" he asked.

"Sure, Maurice."

Krebs got up and walked to the drawn green drapes on the window, then back to his chair. The detective realized he was a rather small man—neatly proportioned and immaculate, but small. Again Krebs walked to the drapes and, this time, somewhat wistfully, pulled them aside. He was greeted, not with a vista of the brightly lit street, but a fretwork of thick steel bars and a heavily wired frosted glass. He studied them a moment, shook his head once—as if to acknowledge the thoroughness of his captors—then released the drapes. It was a sad, lost gesture; McFeeley understood that Krebs had gone to the window to contemplate a freedom that would never be his again. The world was closing off, the waters were rising; now, for the first time, he was frightened by the cold future.

"O.K., I lied to you about Berman."

"Then you know where Amy is?"

"Well, yes. That is, I think I do."

"Tell me."

Krebs drew his breath in. He was still standing near the window. "I'll make a deal with you," he said.

"No more deals, Maurice. We want the girl."

"I'll tell everything. But I want that newspaper reporter here when I do." He smiled again—as if having played a trump card.

"Who? What reporter?"

"That woman, Mona Mears. Who's been writing all those articles about the case in the *Truth*. I'll tell it to her."

"The hell you will," McFeeley said angrily. "You'll tell me! You're through making bargains!"

"No," Krebs said firmly. "Her or no one." Then he added generously: "You can be in the room also."

"Maurice, you're in no position to dictate terms. Why do you want that woman here? She'll make it worse for you."

"Oh no," Krebs said with a cunning tilt of his head, "I know how these things work. I need someone to stick up for me. If I tell her where the girl is, she'll help me." His voice quivered. "You know, I'm not all bad. You said so yourself. I have a side to this story."

McFeeley said no more to Krebs, but walked out of the room.

In the recording room next door, the others had listened on headsets to Krebs' proposal. None was prepared to accede to it. Rheinholdt was almost violent: his popping eyes bulged the rimless glasses from his face, his bristling hair appeared charged with electricity. He cleared his throat with a few mighty rattles and advised his colleagues: "No! No lousy reporters again! The bastards can't even come here when we announce the arrest!"

Roy Brand looked at Wagley. "Fred," he said, "we're still in the investigatory stage. You're in charge. I'm just here to prepare the state's case. You make the decision and we'll go with it. I don't like following a suspect's orders. When they start, they never stop. He's told us a pack of lies already. What's to keep him from lying to Mears? And lying again—just to keep us in circles? Good God, maybe he lied about everything—maybe he isn't even the man we want."

"We'd know for sure if he led us to the child," McFeeley said.

Moll came lumbering down the corridor. "I just talked to Doc Edwards," he said. "He figures from the way Krebs described those capsules, they were probably three-quarter-grain. That means there were three grains of the stuff in the chocolate milk. If she drank it all, it would sure put her to sleep for a long time—twelve, fifteen hours."

"Would it put her to sleep for good?" McFeeley asked.

"Doc didn't think so," Moll said. "That is, if she has a normal heart, nothing wrong with her."

"He said she drank *most* of it," Brand said.

"And they might have been bigger than three-quarter-grain pills," added Wagley. "And how do we know all he gave her was four? Suppose it was six?"

Conversation halted. They had arrived at the ultimate imponderable: was she alive?

"Look—if it means saving the kid," McFeeley said, "I vote for Mears."

"No, dammit!" Rheinholdt shouted. "We'll find her ourselves!"

All except Rheinholdt turned toward Wagley. The FBI man craned his neck, stroked his Adam's apple. "I hate getting involved with her," he said, "Once she starts——"

"Hell, let's ask the parents," McFeeley said quickly. "She's their child. We might get it out of Krebs and we might not. Maybe he'll tell the truth to Mears."

Wagley glanced at his wrist watch. It was 11:05. "I don't like bringing in the family, either." No one spoke for several seconds. Then the FBI man nodded at McFeeley. "O.K. Call them."

The Scrabble game had been a failure. No one had been able to concentrate; the game was abandoned halfway through The Emersons left; Fritzie and Laura decided to go to bed.

In the bedroom, Fritzie began making notations in a small leather memo book. It was a gift from a sponsor; his signature, cast in gold, was mounted on the black calfskin jacket. Like many disorderly men, he was constantly writing memoranda to himself, reminding himself of duties, obligations, tasks, functions. When he would be very rich someday, he told Laura, he would hire someone—perhaps an older woman, efficient as a vacuum cleaner—to keep track of his life. Laura had noted in him a kind of stubborn incompetence in mundane matters which she would forever associate with show-business people—directors, actors, designers. They spent their early years eating cold beans from the can, shopping in Sunday delicatessens, buying clothes once a year, paying rent in driblets of precious cash, visiting doctors only *in extremis,* so that the routine acts of life loomed awesomely complex. Even when they became rich and successful, they were incapable of arranging school transportation for their children, confounded by a supermarket, paralyzed by the prospect of filling in an auto license application, terrified of having the house repainted. They splurged on domestics: maids, cooks, gardeners, secretaries, governesses—even those whose income was modest, even in families where the wife had long ceased performing and had become a suburban housewife. On Sundays they took a dexedrine pill and a tranquilizer to get them through the terrors, the unforeseen problems (buying a rake) of the helpless day. Fritzie was a charter member of their company. It took him a day's telephoning to arrange a dinner party for three couples: a week's debate to decide what kind of folding bridge table to buy. A dental appointment was beyond him. For all his impulsiveness in his work, his soaring flights of nonsense, he was a thickskulled fumbler in the arts of daily existence. The notes he now laboriously wrote to himself, sitting on the edge of their bed, squinting in the glow of the goosenecked lamp, were, it seemed to Laura, pitiful efforts to enter a world he could never make—the world of real people doing real things.

"Lemme see," he was mumbling. "I better call ole Bates and see what he wants me to do next. Maybe I oughta have lunch with Arnie and talk about that movie deal. Damn cordovan loafers need soles." He looked up. "Funny how everything piles up. You stop livin' three days, and it takes three weeks to get caught up."

She smiled at his innocent selfishness. His cordovan loafers were of great moment to him—one had to apply much thought to the problem of having them resoled. Andrus saw her smile. She was undressing, her slender figure semi-nude. He knew what had amused her, and he started to apologize.

"I know, I know, I sound like a damn fool," Andrus said.

"I didn't say anything, Fritzie."

"You don't have to. I saw your face. You're right. Any man spends his life writin' notes about getting his shoes fixed ain't much of a man. I can't he'p it. I don't expect I'll change. Maybe you'll throw me out again in a few weeks."

"I won't."

Andrus got up from the bed and stretched. "I can't *act*, that's my problem. I can talk, but I can't act."

"Fritzie, you couldn't have prevented what's happened to us. You couldn't have stopped the newspapers from printing it or doing all those other things."

"I guess not. Maybe we ain't alone. Maybe we are all victims of them big rolling, grumbling institutions. They oughta make a rumbling kind of growly noise the way they eat people up."

Laura tried not to look at him; his agony was the saddest in the world—the sorrow of someone crying against the impersonal façade of man's own structures. His particular wailing wall was made of words, phrases, ideas—and it was deafer than death.

Ed Case was rapping politely at the door, his pleasant California voice a whisper. "Mrs. Andrus? Mr. Andrus? You awake?"

Fritzie went to the door. Laura put on a bathrobe and followed him. Case's face was rippled with excitation. Behind him, a new FBI man, assigned that day, waited.

"I hate to bother you, but Lieutenant McFeeley just called. He'd like both of you to come to headquarters right away."

Fritzie ran his hand through his hair. "He say why?"

"No. Just that it's very important. I'll escort you."

"Dammit, why didn't he say why? What's he hidin'?" Fritzie cried. "Why doesn't he tell us? If it's bad news—let's have it!"

"I'm sorry, Mr. Andrus," Case muttered. "He didn't even tell me. Maybe it's good news."

"No. It never is," Fritzie said. "Good news they tell—the bad they keep secret."

He shut the door and rested his back against it. Laura began to dress quickly.

"I ain't sure I can go," he said. "I ain't got the guts to go."

"Come on, Fritzie," she said thinly. "I don't have any guts either —but we'll keep trying. It's all we can do."

McFeeley met them in the lobby and hurried them up to Rheinholdt's office. Brand, Wagley and the chief were waiting for them. Wagley explained the situation: they had a confession from a man named Maurice Krebs, but up to now he had refused to divulge where their daughter was. He had told one story, then admitted it was a lie. The FBI man said nothing about the doped chocolate milk; but he hid nothing else. Krebs, Wagley continued, had offered to tell where the child was to Mona Mears, evidently in the hope that the woman would give him a favorable press in exchange for the information.

"It's a terrible thing," Wagley said slowly. "The worst scum in the world think they're entitled to public relations. They worry about how they'll look to the rest of the world, about getting their story across." He looked at Fritzie. "We called you and your wife in, Mr. Andrus, to let you decide. It's irregular. It's bad police work. I'm against it. I'd rather sweat it out all night with Krebs. He may lie to Mears. But I'm forgetting my job and my good judgment as a law officer for the moment and thinking about Amy. We'll abide by what you say. Do you want her called in?"

Fritzie looked at his wife. "That old biddy," he said softly. "Murderin' us in print—and now she's gonna save us. Wouldn't that grow scales on a chipmunk."

"You decide, Fritzie," Laura said.

Andrus covered his eyes. "Might as well," he said. "We got to make agreements with the devil, I suppose."

Hansel assumed personal command. Notified of the police request for Mona, he located her at a private screening in a producer's castle and dispatched her to Santa Luisa. All dark and brooding thoughts about the malicious broadcast vanished from the executive mind. He was convinced something of enormous import was about to break. Perhaps an arrest had been made. Perhaps the child had been found. Perhaps the child had been found *dead*—under circumstances that might well support Mona's hypothesis that the disappearance was *not* a kidnaping. Yes, Hansel speculated, that was probably it. They wanted to interrogate her about what she knew when she wrote the column hinting at *other* explanations for Amy Andrus' vanishing. Wishing Mona Godspeed, he felt the blood of competition pumping healthily through his veins. What would New York say to this! Let them shout now about their deadlines and declining circulation!

Mona Mears accepted the call to Sanlu with less than trembling apprehension. She was an old cat, a wise cat. She took the breaks that came her way like a fat gray tabby with prior rights to the best mousehole in the world. Too practical to waste energies in guesswork, she blasted over the perfumed mountains, whizzing by the yellow night lights of realtors, television executives and dairy owners, on to the neon and stucco flatlands of the valley, to the black highway that led to Santa Luisa.

It was agreed that the Andruses would not have to meet with the columnist. Waiting for her in Rheinholdt's office, McFeeley and Wagley told them more about Krebs: how he had been caught, his confession, his lies, his retractions. The parents had difficulty envisioning him. The colossal violation of decency in which he had indulged, the atrocious personal affront to them, made him as incomprehensible as if he were a form of life from Betelgeuse or some galaxy millions of light years' distant.

"We'd let you look at him," Wagley said gently, "but right now it wouldn't serve any purpose. He's teetering on the brink of telling us something. If he sees you, he might change."

"I suppose I'm supposed to have feelings of murder in my heart," Fritzie said. "I guess I'm expected to steal your gun, Mr. Wagley, and race in and blast his head off."

"I don't think so," the agent said. "People who have been victimized don't usually react that way. The criminal—what he stands for, what he's done—is so far from their experience, they can't connect with him in any way. Emotionally, morally, it's impossible. Maybe you'll feel differently later."

McFeeley rolled up his sleeves; the gesture seemed to indicate he was prepared to beat the daylights out of Krebs before the night was over, but he was merely doing it to cool off. "He's the damnedest I've ever seen," Joe said. "It's the world against him. A normal, hard-working citizen of a Los Angeles suburb, watering his lawn and changing the electrical circuits in his house. You should see the grillwork on his screen door. All that worries him is where he's going to get money for the payments on the air conditioning."

Andrus was staring at the detective with puzzled respect. "Lieutenant," Fritzie said, "I reckon I owe you an apology. You and Mr. Wagley here—all of you people—you performed some kind of miracle. I guess I should choke on some of them mean things I said about you. My wife'll tell you—I can't he'p blowin' off. But when I say I'm sorry, I mean it."

"No hard feelings," Joe said. "You couldn't be expected to have any patience with us. You had other worries."

"Still got 'em, I guess," Fritzie said.

"Let's hope not," said the detective.

Laura studied McFeeley's slender, canted face. What could they pay him? Five thousand dollars a year? Less? What could induce an ambitious and intelligent man to make such work his career—risk his life, live under the perpetual scorn of his fellow citizens, be forever exposed to the worst and meanest in men? She remembered her harsh sentiments about him—only two days ago. Now she felt the need of giving voice to her gratitude. Something was owed this political, soft-soaping, plodding young man who had viewed their tragedy as a personal insult and who, for all his mistakes and misgivings, had apparently succeeded in solving the crime. But Laura hoarded her emotions; she tried to find words, tried to add something to what Fritzie (unblushing, unashamed) had blurted out, and found herself unequal to it. McFeeley saw her staring at him— pained, grateful, trying to communicate—and, shrewd cop that he was, he knew. In that exchanged glance, Laura, too, realized that he had acknowledged her mute apology, her silent gratitude. Later, she told herself, she would write to him—it would be easier than attempting to verbalize her sentiments. Perhaps, she told herself, it would embarrass McFeeley also if she spoke.

A uniformed patrolman had been sent to meet Mona Mears and escort her directly to the recording room next to the chamber where Krebs was being detained.

McFeeley and Wagley went to meet her; Rheinholdt and Roy Brand were already there. The FBI man explained the crisis and the role that had fallen to her. Her eyes popped a little from the withered face; the neck strained under its load of semi-precious stones.

"Let me do a little arithmetic, gents, and make one phone call," she said.

"Mona, I'd like you to move on this," Wagley said firmly.

"Freddie, sweetie," she crooned. "I'm a reporter first and a policeman's buff second."

McFeeley escorted her down the corridor to communications. She called Hansel, still in Pasadena (he had advised her he would stand by at his friend's house), and spoke to him briefly. The Editor & Publisher controlled himself: he was a lion who knew how to suppress roars when approaching live game. Immediately, he summoned a full staff to the *Truth* offices—Trigg, Kalaidjian, linotype operators, compositors, rewrite men. Nothing less than an extra was called for. They would stand by, awaiting Mona's call. As an afternoon paper, they would not normally be on the street until 10:30 the next morning; but Hansel could not run the risk of being beaten by a morning newspaper once the story was released.

Back in the recording room, the columnist winked. "We're all ready, boys," she said. "Only one condition. As soon as I do my chore, I want a one-hour delay before our competition gets notified that there's a confession—and whatever else he tells me. One hour, so we can be out while the others are slobbering."

"You *what?*" shouted Rheinholdt. *"You?* You people who broke your word? You're asking us now to do you special favors?"

Mears looked at him as if he were a species of garden slug— brutally ugly, harmless. "Yes, Caspar. You've been watching too many television shows. You'll start believing what those morons say about us, and you'll be in trouble. What's one hour? Hell—make it more. Don't tell the others at all! Let 'em steal it from us."

Wagley agreed. "All right, Mona. One hour, no more. We've gone this far with you."

"Been fun, ain't it?" she said.

McFeeley opened the interrogation room for her and followed her in. Krebs stood up and bowed slightly.

"How do, Miss Mears," Krebs said. "I'm a great admirer of your column. Never miss it."

She studied him with the eye of a middle-class housewife encountering her first mink stole: it was hers, every precious hair of it.

"Maurice Krebs, is that the name?" she asked, readying her pad and her pen.

"Esquire," he said.

"You are a beaut," Mona said admiringly. "You are really it. McFeeley, did he *really* do it? *Him?*"

"He's confessed," Joe said.

"Can I see it?" she asked.

"I'm afraid not. It's evidence. You can ask Mr. Brand, but I'm sure you won't be able to." He addressed Krebs. "O.K., Maurice. I filled Miss Mears in on what you've told us. Now you promised you'd tell her, in my presence, just where Amy is, where we can find her."

"Ah, yes, so I did." He patted his forehead—it was sweatless.

"I'm waiting. A promise is a promise, Maurice."

The kidnaper looked at the columnist. "I'd like to ask Miss Mears beforehand if she's inclined to give me a break in her paper. I'm doing her a big favor with this scoop, and I want fair treatment in return. After all, I'm no criminal. I made a mistake. I'm sorry. I need a little understanding."

She walked to him and touched her wrinkled, lavender-scented hand to his bare forearm, stroking the blonde hairs. "Maurice, baby, you're mine. Stick with Mona and you'll make it. Just never say a word to those other reporters. Not a word to them—just Mona. I'll see you get a fair shake. Between us, you might even beat the rap. I mean it. You and me, Maurice, we're with it."

McFeeley rapped the desk with his knuckles. "Let's go, Maurice. You took Amy in the car about 8:20. Sometime around 8:30 or 8:40 you gave her that doped chocolate milk, and a few minutes later she fell asleep. Right?"

Mears was scribbling furiously. Her nose twitched at the hint of blood and death.

"Yes, that's correct," Krebs said.

"Then what?" McFeeley asked.

"I rode around for maybe an hour. Probably less. I was terribly scared, you see—the seriousness of what I done—what I did—dawned on me. I was too scared to bring her back now she was asleep. I knew the drug couldn't hurt her permanently, just make her doze. So I sort of rode around and around, on and off the freeway, with her sleeping on the floor in the back."

"Nobody noticed her?"

"Nope." He shut his eyes and leaned back. His mouth opened once—as if trying to get words out, failing, and then settling for an intake of air.

"Go on, Maurice," Joe urged.

"Yes," Krebs said. "I drove into the mountains and took the state road to Cloud Canyon. Then I went up Cloud Canyon Highway. It was pretty deserted, not many cars around. I found a dirt road that looked like one of those old logging roads. I pulled the car in there. I just sat there, maybe an hour or so, thinking. I was sorry for what I had done. But I had no idea what to do next. I panicked. That's it. I panicked." He looked for approval at the detective, then at the woman.

"We understand, Maurice," said Mona. "What did you do then?"

"I thought maybe I should go back to town and drop her off. But I didn't."

"Why didn't you?" Joe asked.

"What? And get caught?"

Even Mears started a little at this. But she never broke stride with her pen.

"So?" Joe pursued. "What then?"

"I picked her up and started walking into the brush. Boy, it was hot. I must have sweated gallons. She was really asleep. I don't know how far I walked. The road twisted and turned, and wasn't really graded or anything, and couldn't have been a roadbed. I walked—I don't know how far, or how long—kind of going up. The brush got pretty thick after a while, and it was rough going. So I found a comfortable spot about fifty feet off the path and left her there."

"Just left her?" asked McFeeley.

"I made her comfortable, put her head a little higher than her body. It was a sandy place, yuccas and wild grass all around. You could never see it from the highway."

"You do anything else to her?" the detective asked sharply.

"No!" cried Krebs. "Not a thing! I had no intent to hurt her, not at all! It was my hope she would be found, alive and well, in a little while!"

"In a place you couldn't see from the highway?" Joe pursued. "Nothing nearby? No houses? No shacks? Just wilderness?"

"I panicked!" shouted Krebs. "I had no idea what I was doing!"

"You never thought about going back for her?" Joe asked.

"I wanted to!" cried Krebs. "I certainly wanted to! But how could I? When I heard the newspapers knew about it, and there were cops all over the place, how could I possibly get her? I'd get caught!"

"But you got caught anyway," McFeeley said. "And you kept lying to us about Amy. Why?"

Krebs looked wistfully at the curtained window. "I wanted to make sure my position was understood. I had no intention of harming that little girl. None at all."

McFeeley opened the door. "Let's go, Miss Mears."

"Hey!" cried the columnist. "I got forty-eight questions to ask blue-eyes here! Not so quick, Irish!"

"Shanty Irish," McFeeley said. "The worst kind. Come on, Mona, you got the beat and you got one hour's grace."

She got up, patting Krebs' head. "Stick with Mama, Maurice. Remember—no spikka da English to the other slobs!"

Trailing lavender, she flew down the hall to communications.

Wagley and Moll started immediate arrangements for a mass search of the area. Rheinholdt had the medical examiner and an ambulance with full equipment alerted. The FBI man ordered out a dozen of his own men; state policemen were called in; local cops available were summoned. It was decided to assemble at a forest ranger's station several miles from the junction of the two highways.

No one ventured to speculate if Krebs had lied again: all of them refused to entertain the possibility. Yet it persisted—another lie to cover up what had really happened. A convenient story—carrying the child into the woods, leaving her there—the body vanishing. In Krebs' self-righteous mind, perhaps the high underbrush, searingly hot by day, freezing at night, was a shifty substitute for the non-existent Berman. He would keep ringing in other people, other circumstances, anything to slide past the justice that awaited him. Withal, the story seemed more credible than the account of the mysterious Berman. There was no speculation about Amy's fate in the event Krebs had *not* lied again: they all understood what three days of exposure on the parched mountain could mean.

It devolved upon McFeeley to talk to the parents, who were still waiting in Rheinholdt's office.

"Go on, tell us the truth, Lieutenant," Fritzie said. "What do you think her chances are?"

"Pretty good, if he didn't lie. Of course—three days by herself. I don't think she'd starve in that time."

Laura was weeping softly: she wept without facial distortion, her eyes clear, her chin firm, the tears streaming gently and apologetically.

"Kids are tough," McFeeley said. "We're organizing the search parties right now. With a break, we'll find her tonight. The guy was pretty definite about where she was."

"I'll go along," Fritzie said. "Lemme go."

"Maybe you better not," McFeeley said. "It might be better if you stay here with Mrs. Andrus."

"Yeah," Andrus choked out. "I know. O.K. We'll wait."

When the detective had left, he fell to his knees and put his head in Laura's lap. "Don't you go weepin', now. That's my act. Don't you go hysterical. Maybe we'll know the good news soon."

Their lives had reached some chasm: a soundless and airless period of waiting. Both had known these before—*was the biopsy to prove malignant or nonmalignant? Had the answers to the final examination in chemistry been right or wrong? Was the coveted job still open—or had some unknown rival been hired?* In the confines of Rheinholdt's office, surrounded by green walls and brown furniture, the books that the old chief never read, under the harsh institutional lights, they waited. Soon McFeeley, that neutral Irishman, would have more to tell them—and, like the awaited word from the pathologist, the chemistry professor, the personnel manager, it would bend and shape their lives forever.

Mona Mears, her honed mind cutting its way through the bits and pieces of information she had gotten from McFeeley, from Krebs, from Wagley, got in touch with T. T. Hansel. A conference call was set up, and the *Truth*, in its creaky fashion, began its pursuit of the story. Hansel, hearing her nasal voice, was in awe of her. He had ordained that his newspaper would own the Andrus case; he had been fulfilled. Through dumb luck (Swinnerton's), through boldness (his own), and through the fruits of fame (Krebs' affection for Mears), he had swept the field. He took their triumph calmly, listening to the columnist's feverish babble, adding a word of direction, of emphasis. Bill Trigg, taking down her frantic report, was shouting orders on another phone to reporters and photographers being rushed to the search.

"I'm too old to go hiking around Cloud Canyon," Mona said. "I'll hang around the station house. I think Andrus and his wife are there. Let me see if I can break in on them." She dictated some final information to Trigg: "Who cracked the case? The FBI, I guess. Who else? I can't believe these rube cops could have found the guy."

"What do they think about the child?" Hansel interrupted. "Alive?"

"Nobody knows. The kid might survive those sleeping pills he gave her, but what about three nights of cold in the mountains? Nobody's too optimistic."

"One thing, Mona," said T.T., "and this is terribly important. Did I understand you to say this man Krebs claims he abandoned the girl *immediately* after he picked her up?"

"An hour later—something like that. Why is that so important?"

Hansel laughed. "Don't you see? It clears us! The police and those morons at UBC, our friends in television, have been claiming the child was *not* returned Monday night because our publication of the story scared the kidnaper off and he presumably did away with the child. But now it develops we didn't have a blessed thing to do with it! *The child was drugged and tossed in the woods long before we ever printed a word!*"

"Was that *really* worrying you, Teddy? What those jerks had to say?" To Mona Mears, United Broadcasting's attack on them was a mountain of inconsequence. She had been singularly unmoved by the fuss.

"Not worrying me, but annoying me a little. And imagine! We solve the case—that fellow Krebs confessing to you! I want to hit that hard. Trigg?"

"Yes, Mr. Hansel."

"Scratch that editorial I dictated earlier in answer to those TV idiots. Do you have it?"

"Yes, sir, right here."

"I'm going to give you three editorials—front-page pieces. One in case the child is still being sought; one in the event she's found alive; one in the event she's dead. Ready?"

Trigg was always ready. Hansel proceeded to dictate his trio of editorials. The essentials of them were the same: the *Truth,* acting in the finest traditions of the free press, guarding the people's right to know, *had solved the Andrus case.* He used but one sentence to demolish UBC, Sparling, Brack and Rheinholdt—all those who had dared insinuate that the paper had behaved in any manner other than honorable. Finally, he dictated three alternate final paragraphs to cover the three eventualities—a search still in progress, a living child, a dead child.

In his moment of victory, he thought not at all of Herbert Hood. It would be several days before he got around to the business of having him retired.

Wagley, McFeeley and Rheinholdt sped out to the highway intersection in the chief's car. Krebs, handcuffed, sat between the detective and the FBI man in the rear seat. Farmer Baines drove; Rheinholdt, smug and silent, sat beside him. All of them wore pile-lined jackets, borrowed from the traffic division. An escort of four motorcycle cops, sirens screaming, preceded them along the freeways and into the cold hills.

Wagley and McFeeley estimated that they would have at least fifty men on hand to start the search. If they had no luck during the night, they would treble the number of searchers in the morning, calling in volunteer fire departments, hiking clubs, boy scouts.

They roared through the dark desert, lulled into silence by the ululating moan of the sirens. Nothing more remained to be said. Their work as law officers had ended—except for the child. As they rushed past dazzling neon roadhouses, gasoline stations longer and wider than football fields, groves of citrus trees pungent in the chilling night, McFeeley could not help an occasional sidelong glance at the kidnaper, huddled next to him, sunken into his jacket like a weekend hunter returning from a good day in the fields—two rabbits, a half-dozen quail.

Rheinholdt's car reached the rendezvous point shortly after midnight. Three other police cars from Santa Luisa followed, bringing portable radio gear, ten uniformed men and six detectives. Wagley was met by his colleague Fewsmith and a dozen other agents who had raced out from Los Angeles. A captain of the state police, a burly man named Adamic, whom McFeeley had met before, was on hand with about fifteen troopers, equipped with heavy clothing, walkie-talkies, portable floodlights, a first-aid truck, and a loudspeaker system.

The trucks and cars were pulled up on a shoulder of the winding blacktop. Around them rose Pacific pines and cypresses, and above these the dusty red hills of the Sierras, the blue-black cold sky, thick with impersonal stars. Wagley had put in a call for the chief forest ranger for the area, and the latter had been among the first to arrive, bringing with him a detailed topographical map of the mountains. He had tacked the map to the side of a panel truck and was directing a yellow cone of light at it when the group from Santa Luisa arrived. Wagley introduced himself, McFeeley, Rheinholdt. Krebs, head erect, his eyes alert to everything said, taking in the assembled agents of the law, the trucks of radio gear, the ambulance, the file of official cars, appeared to be exercising some kind of mute approval. He was gratified that all these fine men had been called out on his account. Now that he had squared everything by confessing, it was proper that such a mighty army be gathered to find Amy Andrus—for whom he bore no ill will.

"That him?" asked the forest ranger. He was a bespectacled man, wearing a wide-brimmed, olive-drab hat and an olive-drab pea jacket. His name was Temple; McFeeley recalled an article about him in a Los Angeles newspaper—a fellow with a Ph.D. in botany who lectured at high schools.

"That's him," Wagley said. "Maurice Krebs."

"How do," Krebs said, smiling.

"Can you read a map, Krebs?" Wagley asked. "Show the ranger where you think it was you took Amy."

The group pressed around the side of the truck; the play of flashlights and lanterns formed a pool of light on the map. By now it was quite cold. The search party's combined breaths rose in a filmy cloud and there was much foot-stamping and arm-swinging (many of the hastily summoned officers were still in summer-weight suits).

"Now let me see," Krebs said thoughtfully. "Would you fellows mind turning off a few of those lights? They hurt my eyes."

"We're right here," Ranger Temple said. "The intersection of Cloud Canyon Highway and Highway 68. Just this side of it. You say you drove north on the highway from here?"

"I believe I did."

"Then you turned off—where?"

"A dirt road. Oh, just a few miles up. I'm not sure, but I think it was the first one on my left."

"Probably this," the ranger said. He indicated a dotted blue line winding into the hills. The men around the truck edged closer to catch a glimpse of it. The ranger untacked the map and rolled it up. Then he addressed Wagley, McFeeley and the state police captain. "It's an old access road. They dug it out in '43 when they built the firebreak, so they could move in trucks. It doesn't go very far in—not more than fifty yards."

"It leads to the firebreak?" Wagley asked.

"Right to it. Then the break winds up and down the mountain either way. We'd better do it on foot—at least till daylight."

The signal was given and the cars rumbled off toward the dirt road. They proceeded slowly on the twisting blacktop, headlights painting yellow smears on the desolate hills, the rocks, the coarse trees and shrubs. The occupants strained their eyes, squinting into the roadsides; somewhere a small child in a red play suit and red sneakers might appear. The ranger halted them after less than two miles.

Again, the men assembled at the intersection of roads.

"Is this it?" Wagley asked Krebs.

"I think so."

"What do you mean you think so?" the FBI man asked. "Is it or isn't it?"

"Well, it's so dark now, and all these places look alike."

Wagley spoke to Joe and the state police captain. "Let's four or five of us go in at first. We might find her on the first try. If there's no trace of her, we'll organize a crime search as best we can. In the morning we'll get some more men, bloodhounds. If he's telling the truth, I don't see why we shouldn't be able to find her before long." Wagley shuddered. "That kid was wearing a summer play suit and sneakers, and this would be her third night here. I got a lined jacket on and I'm shivering after fifteen minutes." He looked sorrowfully at Krebs. "You proud of yourself?"

"No, I'm not," Krebs said. "I've made that clear, Mr. Wagley. I know I did a rotten thing."

The ranger walked first, swinging his huge lantern. Behind him came Krebs and Wagley, and behind them the state policeman, McFeeley and Rheinholdt.

"This look familiar?" the ranger asked.

"It's hard to say," Krebs said. "Offhand, I'd say yes, but I couldn't be sure. If it was daylight——"

"Walk gently," Ranger Temple said. "You step on something that wiggles, just be nonchalant."

"Rattlers?" the FBI man asked.

"Place is full of them," the ranger said. "Don't worry, they're more afraid of you than you of them. That's characteristic of *Crotalus*—they run away. Also, it's not a rattle. It's more like a buzzing sound. So if you step on something and it buzzes, just kind of waltz away."

"Cheerful guy," McFeeley said.

"I hate snakes," Krebs added. "They give me the creeps."

He had included himself in the group: he was one of the boys off on a nature hike, looking for a nice spot for the picnic. The man was adaptable as a nail; he was an interchangeable spare part.

The ranger's light swung around them in a wide saffron arc, illuminating yuccas, stunted pines, the stubborn shrubbery of high altitudes. "You call out when you think we're at the place," Wagley said to Krebs.

After a short walk, the dirt road ended. At its termination, they could see the beginnings of the firebreak, a swath of sandy soil, about ten feet wide, twisting upwards and downwards, a bald tawny scar on the dark-green hills, like a streak of alopecia on a man's head.

"Here's where the break starts," the ranger said. "You say you walked upwards and away from it with her?"

"I guess so. I believe I did." Krebs peered into the dark shrubs.

"Let's have a look," Wagley said. "Go ahead, Ranger."

They followed the man in the broad-brimmed hat into the thickets. "You stop us when you think you've reached the place," Temple said.

They kept walking, turning their lights on the irregular, rising ground—cold red sand and gray rocks, tangled cruel thickets and cacti—each man looking for some indication of the child. The ranger stopped at a point where several giant yucca plants formed a green wall. The hill climbed more severely above them, and it seemed a logical place for Krebs to have stopped.

"How about here?" he asked Krebs.

"This might be it. Could I look around a little?" the shipping clerk asked.

He circled the gray-green forest of spikes, inspecting the earth at their base. "This sure looks like the place," Krebs said. "Right here, I laid her down, in the shade, so she wouldn't be too hot in the sun."

"And what'd you do about her being too cold at night?" asked McFeeley.

"I had no intention of harming her," Krebs said. "It was my hope she'd awaken in a few hours and walk back to the highway and be found, which is probably what happened."

Wagley, not looking at him, on his knees with the ranger, scratching at the earth, said: "Sure. A four-year-old girl would have no trouble at all getting out of this wilderness. Especially with no food, no warm clothes, thirsty."

"I panicked," Krebs said. "I admitted that."

The men circled the clump of yuccas, getting on their knees, fingering the ground, playing their lights on the earth. There was no sign to indicate that the ground had been disturbed in any way, no remnants of clothing, nothing.

"Kid that size wouldn't make much of an impression anyway," Wagley said. He looked up at the state police captain. "We better call everyone in and start working our way up and down the mountain. My guess is she woke up and wandered off. She couldn't have gone too far."

The captain nodded. He and Rheinholdt walked back to the highway. The FBI man addressed the ranger. "Mr. Temple, are there any houses around here—occupied or empty? Any old road-houses or farms? Someplace the child could have gotten to for shelter?"

"No. It's mostly state land here. If she wandered into anything like a filling station or a roadhouse, they'd sure know who she was and have called us. The child's picture's been everywhere; the story's been all over the papers."

"Nothing at all?" Wagley persisted. "How about something like an old prospector's cabin? I know they have them all over the canyons up north."

"Well, there's the retreat—about seven miles further up. I don't see how she could have made it there. And they'd have called somebody if a strange little girl walked in."

"Retreat?" asked McFeeley. "What is it—a monastery?"

"Not exactly," said the ranger. "One of those California religious outfits. Bunch of guys in braided beards and shaved heads. They weave their own clothes, don't use money. I forget what the religion is exactly, but they call the place the *Sanctuary of the New Era.*"

Wagley straightened up, dusting earth from his pants. He looked at McFeeley. "Let's take a ride over there. You want to show us, Temple?"

The ranger nodded. They could hear the other members of the

search party coming down the access road. Lanterns and flashlights painted huge swaths of light in the black-green wasteland. One man was carrying an electric megaphone and calling out: *Amy! Amy! Amy—holler if you're here!* It sounded like a child's sidewalk game.

Krebs was left in Rheinholdt's custody. McFeeley and Wagley got into the ranger's station wagon. Red light flashing on its roof, siren screaming, the car lurched off, climbing higher on the blacktop. In a few minutes, they approached another dirt road. It was no more than a wide path into the hills, but it was barred by a wooden gate. On either side, barbed-wire fences stretched, bordered by rows of trimmed pine trees. The ranger pulled up to the gate and got out. There was a bronze cowbell attached to a leather thong, and he rang it several times. He turned to the two men in the car. "Last time I was here, it was to warn them about chopping trees down on state property."

Waiting, he directed his lantern to a hand-painted sign on one of the gateposts.

SANCTUARY OF THE NEW ERA

PRIVATE   NO TRESPASSING

Beyond, in a thicket of trees, they could see a flaking white-stucco mansion, a sprawling house with a high portico. No one responded to the ranger's ringing, so he shouted several times. "Anyone home? This is the police! Open up!"

After a few seconds, lights burned in the vaulted windows in the lower story of the house. A door opened and a ghostly figure carrying a candle came down the path toward the gate. The candle bearer had an egg-bald head; his beard, on the other hand, had been braided into twin strands. The effect was that of a little girl's head turned upside down, the features rearranged, the child's hairless chin serving as pate, her braids as his beard. He wore a white robe of coarse cloth.

"Excuse me for bothering you," Temple said, "but I'm the forest ranger. I'm here with police officers. We're looking for a lost child we think was wandering around the mountains. Have you seen a little girl around here?"

The bald one raised his candle. "It is improper to interrupt the hours of revivification," he said. He spaced his words with mystic dignity; but his accent was bland Californian and might have belonged to a carhop or a lifeguard.

"We don't want to interrupt anyone getting revivified," McFeeley said. "But you can help us. Have you seen a little girl about four years old? Dark-brown hair, dark-brown eyes, wearing a red play suit and red sneakers?"

The bald-headed man's eyes gleamed. "You have come to take her," he said sadly. "She had been sent to us."

"You mean she's here?" Wagley shouted. "For Chrissake——" He stopped. "Excusing your presence, Mr.——"

"Brother Vespasian." He unlocked the gate and they followed the candlelight down the path to the peeling old house.

"Say a few Irish prayers, Joe," Wagley said.

"He could be crazy, too," McFeeley said. "I mean—with the whiskers."

They entered a drafty, high foyer, almost devoid of furnishings. What chairs and tables there were, were of stark simplicity—possibly the products of the brotherhood's handicrafts program.

"Wait," said Brother Vespasian. He walked down a corridor, vanishing in the murk. A second man, older and fatter, similarly shaven, his beard identically plaited, came down a flight of stairs. He seemed friendlier. Smiling, he fingered a medallion on his chest. It was neither cross nor star of David, but a seven-pronged device with a human ear in the middle.

"Welcome to the Sanctuary of the New Era," he said. "Our gate is always open for the weary. I'm Brother Trajan."

"Thanks," said McFeeley.

Brother Vespasian came back down the corridor. He carried a child, wrapped in a coarse brown blanket, asleep, in his arms. He was not halfway back when McFeeley knew that it was Amy. He had seen enough photographs of her to be certain, even in the candlelit gloom of the foyer. Her pinched, dark face was restful in sleep. She breathed regularly and appeared unharmed except for a few ruby-headed mosquito bites on her forehead.

"How long have you had her?" McFeeley asked. He was like a man at the end of a forty-mile forced march, removing his field gear, his pack, his rifle, slowly, very slowly, to savor each delicious second of relief, of deliverance.

"Brother Vespasian found her on Monday at eventide. The child was wandering in the wilderness like the great Gautama Buddha." Brother Trajan, the fat, cheerful devotee of the New

Era, continued, "Yea, like the children of Israel. Or John the Baptist. Wandering and friendless."

"Well for Chris——" Wagley stopped again. "I mean—you found her out here in the woods and you never told anyone?"

"No," Brother Vespasian said peevishly. "She was ours."

"I'm afraid not, brothers," McFeeley said. "This little girl is Amy Andrus. She was kidnaped on Monday morning and abandoned seven miles from here. Her parents live in Santa Luisa and are waiting for her right now. We have to take her back."

"A shame," Brother Trajan said. "We thought a miracle had been wrought. But whatever you say, officer——"

"Why didn't you get in touch with the police?" McFeeley asked. "This child's name has been on every radio broadcast, all the newspapers, television. There's been a nationwide search for her. She's the best-known four-year-old girl in the world. You fellows should have tried to find out about her."

"Oh, we could not do that," Brother Trajan said. He fiddled with his twin braids

"Why?" asked Wagley.

"We are allowed no communications with the Old Era. Our brotherhood forbids the reading of the contaminated newspapers of the Old Era, listening to their impure radio or television, or using their unsanctified telephones. We live our lives in full isolation from the Old Era, for otherwise we would be infected. We are the Sanctuary of the New Era."

The FBI man, the detective, Ranger Temple spent a few dazed moments exchanging disbelieving glances: Amy Andrus had been in the arms of the brotherhood for three days.

"But the child," McFeeley appealed. "Didn't she tell you who she was? Didn't she cry?"

"She seemed subdued, drugged, just up until this morning. She asked about her mother, but could tell us nothing else. She was happy here. We let her play with the sheep."

"Yes," McFeeley said. "That sounds logical enough." He looked again at Wagley. The FBI man was shaking his head. He had trailed Russian spies and Nazi agents; apprehended smugglers and bank robbers; but the Sanctuary of the New Era and its bald-headed brothers were beyond his experience.

Amy stretched and mumbled in Brother Vespasian's arms. Joe held his arms out. "O.K., men, we'll take her back." The three men started walking to the opened door. McFeeley turned. "You fellows will be needed to make depositions tomorrow. Are we allowed to send you a telegram when you're wanted? Or is that too contaminating?"

Brother Trajan grinned and fingered his medallion. (What was the ear for? wondered McFeeley.) "We will make an exception," he said. "Advise the parents we meant no harm."

Wagley nodded as they left. "We will. And you make sure you don't keep any more lost children. Next time you find one wandering in the canyon, go right to the nearest policeman, you hear?"

"Eternal love from the New Era," said Brother Trajan. It was not much of an answer, McFeeley felt, but under the circumstances it would do.

At the encampment of police cars and trucks, a state police physician examined Amy. She awakened while he was probing for fractures and wailed mightily. Her voice was harsh, loud, and had the cutting edge characteristic of small girls whose tonsils have been removed. "She seems O.K.," the doctor said. "There's a few scratches and bruises on her knees and calves, but I suppose it's from wandering around the woods. Her lungs and heart sound good. No fractures—no contusions or lacerations."

The doctor was a young man with an actor's mustache. McFeeley envisioned him graduating to a Beverly Hills trade in a few years. "Seems fine," he said, poking and probing the child's meager frame. "I was worried about exposure. She could have come down with some respiratory infections out here in the cold with almost no clothes on."

Amy's eyes were bright, alert, opened wide. She looked mistrustfully at the strange faces around her. The doctor covered her again with the ambulance blanket. Suddenly she yelled: "I want my *Maaaaaaaamy!*" The voice was alarming; it crashed and slammed around the white-enameled interior of the ambulance, a welcome, vigorous noise.

"Does she have to be hospitalized or anything, Doc?" asked McFeeley.

"I don't think so. Not now anyway. She should have a complete physical tomorrow, but let's get her back to her parents first and let her spend the night with them."

Again Amy freed the demon in her larynx. "*Maaaaaaaamy! Where's Maaaaaaaamy!*" No tears stained her dark face. She was an unwhimpering child, absurdly self-sufficient, possessed of a hard, one-directional mind. "I'm cold," she said with a nasal flatness. "I'm cold and I want to eat. All those men in the nightgowns gave me was oatmeal. I want a hamburber."

"With onions?" McFeeley asked. "And mustard and ketchup?"

"I hate mustard. It's spicy."

"Hold the mustard," Joe said. "We'll let your mommy and daddy cook hamburgers for you." McFeeley looked at Wagley. "Can we move off, Fred?" he asked.

"I don't see why not," the agent said. "I'll have my people take pictures in the morning and interrogate the New Era."

"Good luck," McFeeley laughed.

Joe said he would ride in the ambulance with Amy and the physician. Wagley and Rheinholdt walked back to the latter's car through the crowd of law officers. The chief ignored the FBI man when the latter held the rear door open for him. Instead, he hoisted his bulk into the front seat, next to Baines. Wagley sat alone in the rear.

"We showed *you*," Rheinholdt said. He would never admit, not for the rest of his life, that he had been incredibly lucky.

When "Southland's" critique of journalism had ended, at 10:30, those responsible for the program lingered for a while in the UBC newsroom to await some reaction to the program. There had been very little. Matthew Hinrichsen had called and had spoken briefly to Ballstead. *A nice job*, the In-law had said, *very nice. Keep everyone on their toes. Be prepared for those people to hit back. They won't take it lying down.* . . . There was a handful of additional calls. By and large, the callers had not understood the program. One man protested that it was an attempt to smear the FBI and the Justice Department; a shrill woman called to say the Andrus kidnaping was a fraud, that the child was living in Burbank under an assumed name; some teen-age boys phoned, giggling obscenities, to claim they were the kidnapers. It was a sordid and sickening response to Elliot Sparling's crusade, and the young newsman, fresh from his debut before the cameras, slipped into a viscous gloom. His girl friend Connie, in need of a job and a night's sleep, had left.

Sparling sat with George Brack and Tom Ballstead in the news director's office, listening to the rhythmic clacking of the teleprinters outside, the voices of the nightside writers, the punctuating rings of the news-department telephones. All three men liked the newsroom at night. It had a pleasant atmosphere of practicality about it, a continuum of facts and information, of an endless process that might, conceivably, be instrumental in some marginal improvement of human conduct. Eliot Sparling believed so implicitly. Ballstead, eroded beyond repair, would never *admit* he believed it. And George Brack, struggling manfully to cross over from his world of pale ale and used cars to the kingdom of fact, was coming to believe in it. Yet the belief, like most worth-while beliefs, was annoyingly abstract, as diaphanous as angel's breath, as obscured as a fly drowning in spilled ink. They had attempted that night to set the record straight, to light up a millimeter of truth—and now, an hour and a half after their brave effort, nobody cared.

"I guess we went up like a cement balloon, hey, Tom?" Sparling yelled. "Well, we had a few laughs anyway."

"I'll settle for that," Ballstead said. He coughed for a few seconds—his close-to-the-grave cough. "Less people notice us, the better."

"I think we'll make quite an imprint on the national conscience," Brack said thoughtfully. "I wouldn't be surprised if the wire services pick us up. Maybe a news magazine."

The nightside deskman poked his head into the door. He was a new man, young, and much in awe of Tom Ballstead. "Sir?" he asked. "Mr. Ballstead? I just got a call from someone I know at the *Argus*. About the Andrus case."

The three men looked at him curiously. Eliot smothered a yawn; Ballstead rubbed his skeletal hands together. "Yeah?" Tom asked.

"Well, this friend of mine says they have a tip the *Truth* is getting an extra ready. They got another beat on the case—he didn't know what, but the *Argus* is sending a man to Sanlu police headquarters."

Eliot leaped from the couch. "Georgie! Let's go! Something happened! O.K. if I go, Tom?"

"Christ, yes. Get lost," Ballstead said.

When Eliot and George reached the Sanlu station house, it was apparent that a major announcement was imminent. About forty reporters and photographers had assembled in the waiting room on the ground level of the station. They were all there: DeGroot, dignified as ever; Bosch, the boy from the *Register;* Arnspeiger, looking weary and showing his sixty-odd years; Ringel, scurrying around with his portable tape machine and trying to sneak past the uniformed cops guarding the staircase.

Sparling was treated with cool contempt. Most of them had seen the program and were disgusted by it. Ringel particularly was upset. "At least I kept my mouth shut, up in the tree," he said to

Eliot. "Not like some blabbermouths I know." Ringel was a head
shorter than Sparling, but he felt no fear in insulting him freely.
Dave Arnspeiger showed his contempt for Sparling by haranguing
him with caustic insults before the amused grins of his peers. Even
the desk sergeant—theoretically a partisan of Sparling, who had
tilted a lance for the beleaguered cops—joined in the general fun.

"Jerk," Arnspeiger cried. "Big jerk! You did yourself proud,
didn't you? You know how the cops cracked the case? They got
this guy only after he confessed to Mona Mears! A newspaperwoman! The *Los Angeles Truth!* You and your speeches—you
showed 'em—6:04—5:07!"

"Why are you defending her—them?" bleated Eliot. "They're
your competition."

Arnspeiger shouted: "Because I respect good reporting even
though I hate their guts for beating me! You'll look great tomorrow, Sparling—you and your company denounce the newspapers
and the *Truth*—and *they* crack the case!"

Eliot felt his ears and his neck warming to a lush scarlet. He tried
to shout back at Arnspeiger, but he was too exhausted. George
Brack, diplomatically, contented himself with trying to question
the desk sergeant: he was told nothing. There was, by now, a good
deal of speculation in the waiting room. Everyone knew that Mona
Mears was upstairs. It was also suspected that the Andrus parents
were hiding somewhere in the building. The *Truth* had a beat, and
the extra was expected on the street any minute. Leaks from the
Truth office indicated that the police had a confession; that Mears
had helped in getting the confession; but that the child was still
missing, the subject of a search.

Desperate, humiliated, Sparling looked about for an ally. He
found none. Victor DeGroot, at least, seemed neutral. He was
sitting, legs crossed, on a mahogany bench, reading a morning
newspaper. "How about it, Mr. DeGroot? Did I tell the truth or
not? Wasn't everything I said absolutely the truth? About
Swinnerton and Todd and the rest? Don't I get any credit for that?"

"You're young," DeGroot said quietly. "You're young and loud
and ambitious."

"*The kid may be dead because of us!*" shouted Sparling.

"Yes, but from what I gather, Mears helped get the confession.
I'll bet this bird, whoever he is, asked for *her* because he read
Hansel's editorial on Monday afternoon."

"No!" cried Eliot. "Never! We're wrong—we're all wrong! We
cover up for each other! We——"

His last words, delivered in an impassioned crescendo to the dignified ears of the AP man, were lost in a rising shout, a wild rush toward the main stairway. Caspar Rheinholdt, ruddy of countenance, a smug smile broadening Aesop's chipped face, was descending. Behind him came Lieutenant Joe McFeeley and Fred Wagley.

"The *Truth* says you got a confession!" shouted Duane Bosch. "That true?"

"Who is he?" cried Arnspeiger.

"Where's the girl?" boomed Eliot.

Rheinholdt let them mill and mutter below him a few seconds. Then he held up a traffic cop's hand. "The child has been found safe. She's with her mommy and daddy. We got a full confession. You will shut up and wait your turn."

Sparling, his head bobbling atop his big body, looked at his adversary of Monday past with frank admiration. There had been a dumb rightness about Rheinholdt's attitude from the start. Perhaps he was thick, and incompetent, and unfit for any investigation more complicated than car theft: the fact remained he had wanted to jail every reporter at the house (beginning with Eliot) and he had been wiser than anyone in his rude judgment. Only Mayor Palmer Speed's fears about how he would look in the papers had stopped the chief. And yet, Sparling mused, listening to Rheinholdt's uneducated drawl as he gave the frantic journalists driblets of information—*his name is Maurice Krebs . . . K, r, e, b, s . . . he lives in Santa Luisa . . . the child was found unharmed*—would any precautions whatever have helped? Had not the luck of the draw been more crucial than any sedulous plans?

How Rheinholdt savored victory! He glanced now and then at Fred Wagley, as if asking approval. And the latter, a kindhearted man, and, by rights, the only official purveyor of information to the press, let the old rock-head continue. By now the chief was getting names and places wrong and McFeeley found himself answering questions to clarify Rheinholdt's garbled account.

Pencils and pens raced across copy paper and steno pads; plates were slammed in and out of cameras; several of the radio correspondents raced for the telephones. In the midst of Rheinholdt's confused revelations, the boy from the UP, the eastern type with dazzling teeth, came in waving the *Truth's* special edition. Tribute was paid to Mona Mears by the group; at the same time, they gleaned minor solace because she had not been able to publish the happy ending. The *Truth* had hit the street unaware that Amy Andrus had been found.

"Can we see Amy?" George Brack shouted.

"Can we talk to the parents?" asked DeGroot.

"Nothing at all wrong with the kid—no sexual assault—anything like that?" cried Martin Ringel.

"No," McFeeley said. "The doctor says she's all right. Just a few scratches from wandering around. She was found by some—some——" He looked at Wagley. "What would you call those guys?"

The FBI man laughed. "A monastic order, I guess. They call themselves the Sanctuary of the New Era."

"They found her on Monday?" Eliot blasted as people around him cringed. "And never called the cops?"

"They didn't know who she was," McFeeley said, "and they don't believe in telephones, radio, television or newspapers."

"Who can blame 'em?" Eliot yelled—thrusting the pencil mike closer to McFeeley as George Brack advanced to get in range of UBC's 16-millimeter camera.

But, like all of Eliot's sallies, it was unheard and ignored; his feeble protests had long since dissolved in the great sea of victory.

At 12:06 A.M. the state police captain radioed Santa Luisa police headquarters and conveyed a message for Mr. and Mrs. Andrus. Irvin Moll, grinning and babbling, sprinted from the communications center to the chief's office. He burst in on Fritzie and Laura, bouncing up and down like a boy under a Christmas tree.

"She's safe! She's safe! They found her! They found her!" He grabbed Laura from the chair and hugged her, kissed her, lifted her off the ground. "She ain't hurt!" Moll yelled. "Safe! Safe!"

Andrus, slumped in Rheinholdt's swivel chair, blinked his eyes a few times. Then he began to laugh and cry, mingling the two with marvelous theatricality—great wet tears sliding down his ruddy face, his eyes and mouth not downturned, but stretching his skin in clownish distortions of joy. The laughter burst from his fleshy mouth, and he raced around the desk, joining his wife and Moll in a three-handed dance. They embraced and squeezed one another impartially, traded wet kisses, laughed chaotically, the bearish body of the detective, that dumb well-meaning man, mingling with those of husband and wife—as if to bestow on them the general blessing of the public in their good fortune.

McFeeley, carrying Amy in a gray blanket from the ambulance through the subterranean garage and up the elevator, came to them like a delivering angel. The child was distressingly awake, evincing little confusion, less fear. Fritzie and Laura ran to her, the mother taking her from Joe's arms, pressing her against her breast, kissing her dark, pointed face.

"Don't kiss me so much, Mommy. I can't breeve." She squinted under the glare of the fluorescent lights—the child needed eyeglasses, Laura thought.

"You feel O.K., baby?" Fritzie cried. The tears and the silly giggling would not stop.

"I'm hungry. My stomach hurts. I want a hamburber."

"You don't have a cold? Nothing?" Laura pleaded—almost hoping the child suffered from some small ailment that she might minister to, some bruise that needed a scotch-plaid band-aid, a headache that called for orange-flavored aspirin. Amy was healthy, unmoved. "A man gave me chocolate milk and I got sleepy," she said. "And another man with braids found me, and I hated that house where they ate oatmeal. But I didn't cry."

Laura pressed her face against the child's cheek—a mother's daughter who did not cry, who took the world on, no privileges asked.

"The doctor says you can take her home," McFeeley said. "O.K., Mr. Brand?" Roy Brand, the state's attorney, nodded. "I'm afraid we'll be bothering you a lot, Mrs. Andrus," he said. "We're arraigning Krebs in a few minutes. Tomorrow, I'll have to start getting some statements from you."

"No sweat," Fritzie said generously.

"And try not to talk to reporters," Brand said. "Remember, we're preparing a case now, and anything you or Mr. Andrus say can have a bearing on our prosecution."

"That ain't gonna be hard," Fritzie mumbled. "If I never see them bastards—excuse me, Laura—I forget the little one's here—it'll be fine with me."

"Bastards," Amy said.

"They're waiting right now," McFeeley said. "Maybe if you showed your faces just once and answered a few questions, they'd leave you alone tonight."

"Yeah," Andrus said. "An' if we cut off our phones, sell our car, build a fifteen-foot stone fence 'round the house, and then move to Iceland, that'll keep 'em away."

Joe shrugged. "It's up to you. I have to go downstairs with the chief and keep them happy." He looked at Moll. "While we have them on the hook, why don't you try sneaking out the back with Mr. and Mrs. Andrus and Amy?"

The subterfuge was doomed. Spies had been posted at the rear entrance, and when the family, following Moll, was spotted by a man from the *Argus*, the fifty-odd people assembled in the foyer rushed down the station house steps, trampled Rheinholdt's lawns and flower beds, and surrounded the escape party. Under the glare of the Jumboburger sign, they shouted questions, made demands, called people by first names, popped flash bulbs. Ringel, Eliot and three other TV-radio people battled their way to the mother, the father, the child. Moll, in high good humor, could not resist them. The mob surged and swayed, the bodies backing and filling on the asphalt; again they assumed one fused, hot identity—a multi-headed, many legged organism. Somewhere Eliot Sparling had read about a primordial seaworm that assembles in agglutinized groups to form what approximates a more complex form of underwater life. So were they—a congress of sea worms swarming into a new mutation, a sport created by man's perverse institutions.

Through the frenzy, the child blinked and squinted, unafraid, curious. "Why they making them big lights, Mommy?" Amy cried. "Ask them to make those lights again!"

A photographer obliged her, bursting a flashbulb; everyone laughed with the child.

"Hey, Laura!" Dave Arnspeiger called out, "you could do us a big favor—tell us you're not mad at us anymore!"

"Why should I?" she asked.

"Come on, Laura," drawling Duane Bosch (eighteen years old, a mover and shaker), "we aren't as bad as everyone says—are we?"

"The thing is this, Mrs. Andrus," Victor DeGroot said gently, "we've taken a lot of abuse in the past few days, and it would help clear the air if you indicated you're not holding a grudge against the press. After all, you have Amy back—and I speak for all of us in saying how delighted we are—and, besides, Chief Rheinholdt just confirmed what a lot of us suspected. Krebs abandoned her about an hour after he took her."

"Why should that be so important?" Laura asked.

"It takes the onus off the *Truth*—and, believe me, Mrs. Andrus, my job isn't to defend them or make a case for them." DeGroot's eyeglasses were two puddles of yellow light under the drive-in sign.

"Hell, let's go," Fritzie said, "we ain't got time for seminars on the ethics of journalism."

"This is important," DeGroot persisted. "You see, the *Truth's* publication of the story had *nothing* to do with what Krebs did. We assumed, and he claimed at first, that it was the paper's printing everything that made him decide not to come back for the money and return Amy. But he had *already* left her in the hills."

There was a murmur of assent; DeGroot had stated the case quite well. In asking Laura "to clear the air," he had done a first-rate job of air-clearing himself.

"That ain't the point!" boomed Sparling. "They lied! they covered it up! They jeopardized the kid's life! And then you—all of you—accepted it and covered up for them! It don't answer anything if Krebs left her right away! Maybe he would have gone *back* for her if they hadn't printed—suppose those gooks in the braids hadn't found her?"

They studied him as if he had gone insane—an ungainly, wobbling young man in a green sports shirt. "And what about the way none of us left the house, hah? Or followed Mrs. Andrus down the street? How about that, hey, DeGroot? You're just reaching for excuses—don't excuse us, Mrs. Andrus, don't excuse any of us! You stay mad all you want! Give us hell!"

"Will you stop bellowing in my ear?" DeGroot asked with marked annoyance. More bulbs flashed; the hum of a half-dozen newsreel cameras suggested a swarm of wasps buzzing through the night air.

"Don't say you forgive us!" cried Sparling. "Don't give an inch! We deserve your contempt!"

"El, you're being a little ridiculous," George Brack whispered to his colleague. But Sparling, groggy, his sour triumph on television reduced to a pitiful excursion into unimportant causes and effects, heard him not.

"Tell us, Mrs. Andrus!" he howled. "We almost ruined you! It's just lucky Amy got back! We all lied! We tortured you——"

"What about Mona Mears?" asked a reporter from the *Truth*—a nightside man hastily ordered out to Sanlu. "She's the one who got the confession out of Krebs. You have any good words for her?"

Andrus beheld the dedicated purveyors of the word. They were kin to him, and this relationship endowed him with generosity, forbearance. "Considerin' she all but accused me and Miz Andrus of doin' in our own child, I find it hard to make a speech in praise of her. Let's just say we got no hard feelings."

Laura brushed back her hair. The lights flashed again; the metallic ring of microphones edged nearer.

"Shut up, shut up!" Martin Ringel screamed. "She's saying something—she's saying something!"

Laura wondered: does it ever end? She said: "I won't be a hypocrite and say everything is forgiven. We're grateful Amy is with us. That's all. If you want, I'll say I'm not mad at any of you, but I'd be lying. I have too good a memory of the last three days. Now will you please leave us alone? Leave the child alone? Don't hang around our house and don't call us."

"Make the lights go!" cried Amy. "Make them go *pop!*"

Encouraged by the child, the reporters pushed forward en masse. Sparling, as lightheaded as Puck, as weary as Ahab, tripped on his own feet. These pedestals collapsed and the young man hit the asphalt just as the front ranks of reporters made their ultimate assault. Immediately Moll guided the family into the waiting police sedan. The detective braced himself against the side of the car to hold back the mob, but they came anyway, thrusting microphones through the window, flashing bulbs, poking the snouts of newsfilm cameras into the automobile, shouting, crying, pleading, cajoling— and still, insanely enough—threatening. (*Duane Bosch, eighteen: You gotta say more, Laura, you gotta! We'll hang around all day!*)

At the bottom of this wailing, throbbing group, prone on the blacktop, sprawled Eliot Sparling. Feet stomped over him, cable cords slapped at him, but he rested inert. Fully conscious, rather relaxed, he envisioned his act as symbolic defiance, a form of Ghandi- esque passive resistance, a protest against his colleagues. Through his fuzzed brain ran the memory of a World Series some years past— Ernie Lombardi, the oversized catcher for the Cincinnati Reds, prostrate at home plate, conscious, awake, semiparalyzed— as the New York Yankees trampled over him with the winning runs. Through a forest of churning limbs and convulsed torsos he saw the yellow-and-green Jumboburger sign winking at him. He winked back, thinking, for some reason, of the late Werner Schlossmann.

With considerable difficulty, the station house was cleared of reporters. They were allowed to be present at Krebs' arraignment, which took place in the police court and for which a judge had been summoned. They were allowed to question Roy Brand, the state's attorney, for a few minutes, and to take photographs of Krebs—Krebs surrounded by Wagley, McFeeley, Rheinholdt and

Brand—one rabbit, it appeared, trapped by four mighty huntsmen. No details of the ransom note, the tracking down of the criminal, the nature of his confession were released. Brand regarded all these as privileged materials, and although he was an ambitious and vain man, with an eye on posts higher than an assistant state's attorney's job, he wanted a quick, clean trial, unencumbered by newspaper interference. Mona Mears, prowling the upper regions of the police station, vaporizing lavender in the green rooms, had, of course, a word-for-word account of Krebs' final interrogation. This would be printed fully, copyrighted, in the first regular edition of the *Truth* on Thursday. Moreover, she had locked Krebs up. He would give her his life story, make his parents available to her, and generally assign his future to the Organization, so his "story might be told." *Truth* reporters were already in the Krebs' house in Droitwich Hills, comforting and advising the two old people, who were at a loss to comprehend the trouble that "Bubi" had gotten into.

Eventually, Mears, too, was ushered out of the station house—by Rheinholdt himself, who caught her going through his desk in search of the original ransom note and other pertinent papers. Tireless, she sped to the *Truth* office to share with T. T. Hansel one more famous victory. Only Herbert Hood, preparing to accept his discharge, was not on hand.

Joe McFeeley called his wife after one o'clock. Midge Callahan had awakened her with the news that the Andrus case was solved; they had interrupted the late movie to announce it. Roz had turned on the television and the radio, waiting for more details— specifically a mention of her husband's name. She had waited in vain. "All they said was that the FBI with the help of local police solved it," she whined. "I bet you did it—or did most of it."

"I guess I did," McFeeley said. "But I'm so tired, I'm not sure."

"I sure hope it means money in the bank for us. Let 'em save the medals and raise your salary."

"They can't. I'm Civil Service."

"Then tell 'em you'll quit. Honest, Joe, I can't see you plodding along all your life chasing teen-age kids in stolen cars. You're better than that. And think of your children—they deserve better—don't they? Sister Agnes said Joey is a very gifted child in science, that we should start planning now about his education. I felt like asking her—how do you do that on a detective's salary?"

McFeeley had no answer for her. He had reached that point of physical and mental exhaustion where little mattered except falling into bed and sleeping for twelve hours. He could not contest the justice of Roz's griping; he was underpaid, without much future, too ambitious to remain a cop. And now even the triumph would turn sour; he was, after all, a small-town cop who had bungled the early investigation of the Andrus case and whom people would have a hard time believing had actually caught Krebs. It would be inevitable to assume the federal people had done it; and, in truth, had not Culligan phoned him with the name of the added starter, and had he not elected to hide the late entry from Wagley, the FBI surely would have caught Krebs in a matter of days.

He realized, talking to his wife, listening to her complaints, her indignation over who would get credit for solving the case, that she was right. He would never be known as the *Man Who Solved The Andrus Case*. Somehow, in the mass of information that would be printed and broadcast, his role would be diminished. McFeeley, at that moment of eroding fatigue, could not find it in himself to be resentful. Rather, like the good City Hall Irishman he was, he recognized the absurd justice of the matter. *FBI Cracks Andrus Case*—and assuredly they would have. His dumb luck was beside the point. Moreover, as Rheinholdt's chief lieutenant, he would be spared any heroic acclaim. It would be emphasized that the press, in the person of Mona Mears, had elicited the confession from Krebs, that the information the criminal gave her was what resulted in Amy's recovery from the wilderness.

"So I won't be a hero," McFeeley said. "I'm not the type. Why should we kid ourselves? I got lucky. I deserved to, I guess, after the way we fouled everything up Monday."

"Boy, you are a beauty," Roz said. "If we could afford it, we should hire a press agent. Haven't any of those reporters asked you for your personal story about how you did it? They pay big dough for those. Midge Callahan said you could——"

"Oh, honey," Joe sighed, "don't listen to Midge. I'm satisfied. I proved to myself I'm smart. Rheinholdt would skewer me if I started giving interviews to the papers. You know something? He's right. We have no business doing it. He isn't right about much, but he's right about that."

She yawned prodigiously. "I suppose so. Coming home?"

"Don't wait up," he said. "And don't invite the neighbors over for a victory dinner and dance."

"How can I sleep now? I want to hear all about it." She laughed without humor. "How did you do it, Joe?"

"He fell in love with me. He was so much like me, he couldn't resist telling everything."

"You're nutty."

As his wife hung up, he realized that he had told her the truth. He and Maurice Krebs were remarkably alike—self-improving, ambitious, small-timers, minor men. With that similarity as key, the detective had opened the shipping clerk's mouth. He drove home, not especially proud of himself, but with a good cynic's sense of having evened a score, of having put himself ahead for a little while.

Amy flew around the house as if she had been gone for a month —running, jumping, sliding, slamming doors and closets and toy chests until Karen awakened, howling. She inspected toys, pulled clothes from hangers, turned the television on. "Mommy! Did you give my Lucille doll to Karen? Mommy—I want railroad trains, just like Jeffrey Emerson! Daddy—I need a new bike, a big red one!" She refused to stop to let Laura put her in her pajamas; she still wore the soiled red playsuit and sneakers. She demanded hamburger. Laura put some in the electric broiler.

"Amy, please!" Laura called. "You can look at your toys tomorrow!"

"Hell, Laura, let her be," Andrus laughed. "Wish I had some of that enthusiasm."

"Hell! Hell!" cried Amy. She dragged a ragged cardboard box from her room into the living room and dumped its contents on the carpeting. Then she begin drawing, coloring, snipping, pasting, with the dexterity and vigor of a ten-year-old.

"What you makin', honey?" Andrus asked.

"A whole school. A whole nursery school, like Sunny Sky. And all the teachers can't come."

Fewsmith, the FBI man, walked into the living room from the nursery. "You want to take any calls? Dr. Todd called before to congratulate everyone, but I said you weren't back yet."

"Good," Laura laughed. "I'm sure he'll be here tomorrow. He can wait." Karen, wailing grievously, was irreparably awake. Laura was porting her from kitchen to living room to den, trying to arrest the noise. The infant, normally as placid as a spayed cat, sensed that something had gone wrong in her schedule: there was too much light and too much noise in the house.

"There's a Mr. Mailman on the phone, a friend of Mr. Andrus'. Said he'd like to talk to you." Fewsmith waited. "Shall I tell him to call back tomorrow?"

Fritzie looked at Laura—as if for approval. "Nothin' wrong in gettin' back into the old routine, is there?"

"No," she said. "We're in it already."

Fritzie went to the nursery. Laura, forcing a warmed bottle between Karen's lips, could hear his voice—growing louder, more excited, edged again with comical self-confidence. "Cy baby? Yeah —we got lucky. We won the whole game! Oh, she's fine, fat and sassy like a possum. Yeah—it's that ridge-runner blood, I guess. The kid was no more afraid of bein' lost in the woods than my gran'pappy woulda been in a pine barren. Hey—what's new at the store? Copley doin' my show Sunday? He'll wreck it. How come they always get the fags to do the love stories? Shoot—he ain't had a good show on the TV since he was jugglin' puppets in Cincinnati! Well, ole Fritzie got some surprises for 'em. You tell that gal who reads scripts for Applebaum to look out—Andrus is ridin' the range again. . . ."

He was off on one of his flights—borne, engineless, through the wide, wide spaces of talkerdom by his own high wind. It was the kind of performance that, as much as anything, had led to their separation. But Laura understood that she was constrained to tolerate it, to give him every possible chance.

She found herself almost enjoying his buoyant monologue with Cy Mallman. She settled in the den with Karen; Amy bustled among her crayons, her scissors, her cutouts, looking up once to yell: "There's no *glitter!* I can't do this without *glitter!*"

Andrus walked back into the living room; his older daughter fixed him with an imperious eye. "I need glitter, Daddy!"

"Well, honey, we'll get some for you."

"Right now."

"Amy, baby, it's after one o'clock in the mornin'."

"There's a drugstore open. I know it. Mommy, make Daddy get me glitter right now."

"Oh, Jesus," Andrus moaned. "Here we go." He swept Amy into his arms and tossed her in the air. She was a weightless child.

"Higher!" she shouted, slicing the air with the sharp blade of her voice. "Higher and higher! Don't do it to Karen!"

"You know something?" Andrus asked. "Cy said we're all over the television right now! They breakin' into their movies for us! Let's go look!"

He tossed Amy on the chair next to Laura. The set's eternal light was on, but it had not been tuned. Andrus flicked the selector knob a few times. An enormous gorilla bloomed in front of them —a mechanical monster rolling awesome eyes, threatening two drunks who stood outside his cage offering him whisky.

"Mighty Joe Young!" screamed Amy. "Mighty Joe Young! Oh, Daddy, leave it! Leave it! I got to see it!"

The drunks were tormenting Mighty Joe Young with a cigarette lighter, burning his papier-mâché fingers.

"Is he good?" Amy asked. "Is he a good gorilla?"

"Why sure, honey. He's the greatest." Andrus patted her hair— it was gritty, uncombed.

"How come he's a good gorilla? Gorillas are bad."

"They's good and bad," Andrus said.

Mighty Joe Young started bending the bars of his cage. The men screamed and ran upstairs to the night club. Amy's eyes froze, her chin trembled; she hugged her father, wallowing in the shadowy horror of the silver rectangle. She held a fat hamburger, drippy with ketchup, in her hands, too excited to eat it. Karen's eyeballs moved sideways in her placid face to stare at the uncomprehended movements, the raucous noise.

It seemed to Laura a plausible ending to their ordeal. At 1:30 of a weekday morning, they were united again, sharing some concocted, outrageous terror—four people existing rather precariously in a converted desert, observing the spurious depredations of a mechanical ape.

Karen slept; Amy remained hypnotized by Mighty Joe Young. Now he was tossing lions around as if they were kittens, hurling them at night-club patrons, smashing glass windows. "She'll be up all night," Laura said. "Those sleeping pills. They've reversed her whole cycle."

"Let her stay up," Fritzie said. "It's her night."

EPILOGUE

MAURICE KREBS, some months later, was found guilty under the California Penal Code, Section 209. The statute is a complicated one and covers "any person who seizes, confines, inveigles, entices, decoys, abducts, conceals, kidnaps or carries away any individual by any means whatsoever . . ." As far as Krebs was concerned, the important part of the legislation was its reference to the victim's suffering "bodily harm." In such cases, the statute decrees that if the defendant is found guilty, he must suffer death in the gas chamber or life imprisonment *without possibility of parole*. On the other hand, "in cases where persons do not suffer bodily harm," the punishment, as set down in Section 209, shall be imprisonment for life *with possibility of parole*.

Krebs' lawyers argued successfully that the minor scratches suffered by Amy Andrus, the half day she spent sleeping and wandering in the canyon did not constitute "bodily harm." Krebs' *intent* —which State's Attorney Roy Brand maintained was nothing less than the slow, painful death of the child through exposure and starvation—was ruled immaterial by the presiding judge. The law said nothing about the *intent* of kidnapers.

Moreover, Krebs testified that his original intent had been to spend the day driving around with the drugged child and to return her that evening, unhurt. He admitted losing his head, but, under questioning by his attorney, stated he *might* have returned for Amy if the newspapers had not printed the story.

During and after the trial, he remained a self-righteous, self-pitying figure. True to his agreement with Mona Mears, he favored her with special stories, leaked information to the *Truth,* and, after his sentencing, began a seven-part story of his life for the newspapers. The series proved a dud. Even T. T. Hansel was forced to admit this. There was something so determinedly drab about Maurice Krebs as to defeat any attempts to render him a celebrity.

He remained a smudge, a blob, the kind of man one never remem
bers. To Mona's credit, she was the first to concede this. Halfway
through the *Truth's* exploration of the Life and Times of Maurice
Krebs, she advised Hansel to chuck the mess. "If only the little
jerk was a fairy or a sex fiend," the columnist told the Editor &
Publisher, "I could do something with him. But how can I ghost-
write the life story of a guy who's sad because he didn't make the
bowling team?"

Thus immortalized in newsprint, Krebs is now serving his life
term. Since he was sentenced *with* possibility of parole, it is considered likely that in anywhere from five to ten years he will appeal
for his freedom. He may very well receive it.

Mona Mears' disappointment in the Krebs "exclusive" had its
counterpart in a deeper frustration suffered by Theodore T. Hansel. That vigorous man reaped nothing but bitterness after the
Andrus case. The *Truth's* circulation rose encouragingly during the
kidnaping, through the trial, and for a few weeks following. Then
readership began slipping back to its pre-Andrus levels. The crime
concluded, people returned to other newspapers or watched television. Even more disheartening, advertising linage refused to perk
up—and it was this failing that most plagued the newspaper. Hansel discovered that despite his brilliant performance in the Andrus
kidnaping, he was still very much *in precarium* with New York.
After the initial congratulatory letters and telegrams had been forgotten, old questions were raised by the titans: *Why are we still
running sixth in a city with six daily newspapers? Why haven't we
cracked the department stores?* One morning, a few days prior to
Christmas, smog burning his eyes and searing his lungs, Hansel
answered a call from New York and found himself being screamed
at by a man in position to demand his resignation. Hansel screamed
back. The New York hierarch demanded results, not excuses. T. T.
shouted back: *I am doing my utmost in a thankless job! What
about the way we cleaned up in the Andrus case?* Abruptly, Hansel
realized the man had hung up. A half hour later, the Editor & Publisher suffered a mild coronary occlusion. His rich, red coloring
had been a bad omen: his hot blood pumped too fast. The Organization put him on an extended leave of absence. A job would
be found for him on his return, New York said. Hansel and his
wife embarked on a seventy-five-day cruise, which included stops
in the Fiji Islands, Nauru and the Maldives. From his Chicago
hideaway (the Organization had put him to pasture with the man-

aging editorship of *American Plumbing*), Herbert Hood toyed with the notion of applying for the top job in Los Angeles, then dismissed it from his mind. He had a season ticket to the White Sox games, an apartment on the lake, and had renewed friendships with three hospitable bars, one of which agreed to furnish him with a cot in its storeroom.

The decline of the *Truth* and the fall of Theodore T. Hansel, Eliot Sparling is eager to point out, should not be taken as inevitable punishments delivered by the Great Unseen. The *Truth* is at best a vestige, an old freak. Hansel probably deserved a better organ for his talents; perhaps a respectable newspaper would have made him more compassionate, less of a tinhorn tyrant. Moreover, Sparling states, newspapers more honorable than the old *Truth* have withered away in the new age of talk; others more indecent grow fat and sleek.

A sense of precious escape often cheers and warms Harvey Swinnerton through the long, cold prairie nights. He is now an overnight man for a newspaper in western Oklahoma. He remains polite, obscure, respected. The stories about his patrician background are already being circulated. Although he has never shown it to anyone, he is proud of a letter he received from Laura Andrus, in answer to his own written apology, forgiving him for his role in the publication of the story.

Of all the people involved in the Andrus kidnaping, none has woven it more firmly into the fabric of his life than Dr. Walter L. Todd. The dentist has just concluded a chapter on his participation in the crime. It will loom large in his autobiography. "When disaster strikes," Dr. Todd writes, "I have always stood ready to lend a helping hand. And disaster takes strange and terrifying forms. All of us remember, with a shudder, I am sure, the tragic kidnaping of little Amy Andrus. It pleased the fates that I should be chosen by the stricken family to . . ." In the course of the chapter, Todd avers that his revelations to Harvey Swinnerton were instrumental in the solution of the crime. He reasons, ingeniously, that with the full, fearless light of the press shining on the event, the police were forced to act more vigorously.

Few members of the Santa Luisa police would agree with him. In any event, they are under firm orders from Chief Rheinholdt not to discuss the case with anyone. The files marked *Andrus* remain locked. Dozens of enterprising reporters, looking for Sunday features, have tried to gain access to them, but the chief and his loyal aides, Sergeant Baines and Patrolman Hertmann, will not even discuss the case with them, let alone open the dossiers. Rheinholdt, at Mayor Speed's urging, has remained in his job, to the horror of the Good Government League. But their protests are unavailing. Amy Andrus is alive and Maurice Krebs is in jail, and the Sanlu police department—as badly administered, as badly organized, as decentralized as ever—keeps bumbling along.

Irvin Moll is now chief of Precinct A. He won his lieutenant's rating when Joe McFeeley resigned to accept a job with Francis Culligan, the head of Four State Shippers. Shortly after the trial of Krebs, Culligan offered Joe a job as personnel manager. McFeeley said, truthfully, that he had no experience in that line, that he was poor at paper work and loved being a cop. But the combined pressures of Roz (Culligan would almost double his salary, starting him at eight thousand dollars a year) and the shipper himself changed the detective's mind. McFeeley still studies at night and hopes to get his A.B. degree in two years. He will be thirty-six then, and he is not certain whether he should go on to law school. He and Roz still live in the crowded ranch house. They have decided to save as much as they can for the children's education. McFeeley's resignation—*the hero cop of the Andrus case!*—stirred another violent scene at the Santa Luisa City Council, at which the Good Government League demanded an immediate increase in police salaries. Nothing came of it.

McFeeley rather likes his new job and is delighted to see Roz happier, less burdened. However, he misses police work terribly and every now and then will drop in on a Saturday to talk things over with Moll and James Raffalovitch. The latter has covered his bulletin board with clippings about his work in the Andrus case, notably the ingenious manner in which he and Joe tracked down the ransom note through a trace of red printer's ink. Occasionally, McFeeley has lunch with Fred Wagley. There are no hard feelings between the two men, but the FBI man does not try to hide his disapproval of Joe's departure from law enforcement.

The terror of those three parched days in September is slow in leaving the Andrus home. Laura gives her husband much credit for helping dissipate the horrid memory. Fritzie's capacity to dramatize has helped immeasurably. Just as his wild exercises proved intolerable on that hot hateful Monday, so, now that their lives are reaching an equilibrium, does his gift of the tongue act as a balm. At times, Laura grows impatient with his surrealist perorations, but she has learned to indulge him, to spare him any criticisms of his professional vanities.

Recently, Laura resumed attending art classes at the studio of a well-known sculptor. She remains her own harshest critic, but she is convinced her work is improving, that her talent is real and viable. Indeed, she plans to have a show in the near future. Fritzie has entered this project wholeheartedly—almost too wholeheartedly. He plans a cocktail party, invitations to all of his show-business friends, and will even arrange a small "fix." Cy Mailman has promised to buy two of Laura's exhibits, sight unseen, and thus stimulate interest among art-loving television folk. Laura regards it as a sign of her maturity that she has not objected too vehemently to the conspiracy. She sees the humor of the situation; her teacher has approved of the scheme, since he is convinced of her ability and is a realist.

That their marriage is an enviably and completely happy one is far from the case. Fritzie still favors leggy girls with eastern-campus accents. Laura suspects him and, from time to time, is irritable and taciturn with him. Nevertheless, they are both making honest efforts to preserve their marriage, and there are increasing moments—hours and days, for that matter—when they are convinced that these efforts are valid and precious, particularly in regard to their children.

Amy is certainly not the easiest child in the world to serve in this capacity—the cement to unite two fractious, brittle people. But she does rather well at it. She is a delightful oddball. She still refuses to attend nursery school. Some weeks after her rescue, she started her own nursery school in the garage. She and Cally Horner are the only students. She will not go back to Sunny Sky School, arguing that the lunches are messy and everyone shouts in the station wagon. She is right on both counts.

And what of Eliot Sparling? That loudmouthed, self-appointed crusader for Fair Play is still with his beloved United Broadcasting. He is a regular on the overnight, where he turns out flowing copy for the morning newscasters, including George Brack. Sparling writes his newscasts so quickly that he has much time left over for indulging his malformed imagination. Recently he started a list of "People We've Heard Enough From," which he posted on the newsroom bulletin board and occasionally augments. The charter members are Wernher von Braun, Bernard Baruch, Nehru, Lady Astor and Casey Stengel. Sparling's booming voice still gives Tom Ballstead the willies, and the poor news executive, ravaged by insecurity and ulcers, needs all the quiet he can find. He wants no more crusades, and although Matthew Hinrichsen has not quite made up his vice-presidential mind about either the wisdom of the "Southland" program or Ballstead's general competence, he has observed a hands-off policy regarding the newsroom ever since the Andrus affair ruffled his calm.

George Brack has bought a new, cruiser-sized boat, one of the biggest anchored at Balboa. He brings "El" fresh coffee and a doughnut every morning. After reading the brilliant copy Sparling has prepared, he advises Eliot to marry Connie Potenza. Eliot refuses to do so until he gets off the overnight. He cannot envision trying to be a good husband when he must work from 1:00 A.M. to 9:00 A.M., and struggle for sleep the rest of the day.

His life drags on, but he is only twenty-eight and he is ambitious. He adores UBC—everything from the clean lavatories to the generous paycheck. Concerning the Andrus kidnaping, he has become something of a crank. He collects any scrap of information he can find on the crime and has filled three large notebooks with his evidence, building a case which he knows will never get to court—any court. Diligently, Sparling corresponds with journalism schools, officers of journalistic societies, and orders (fraternities, associations of editors, congeries of publishers, etc.) and solicits their opinions on press behavior in the events at Nespoli Drive. Many of these groups are not even aware that the press was charged with offenses in the Andrus case; none has initiated investigations of its own. The general feeling, Eliot has concluded sorrowfully, is that since the child was unhurt, the criminal apprehended and convicted, there is very little left to argue about. The dispute over ethics, these journalistic high priests argue, has become academic.

But Sparling persists: the *talker world,* he asserts in his letters, behaved greedily and wantonly, without regard for minimal decency—indeed, without regard for a human life. More and more, the people to whom he addresses his complaints tend to regard his letters as those of a screwball. Most of his correspondents have stopped answering them.